PRAISE FOR THESE
TOP-SELLING AUTHORS

TESS GERRITSEN

"Tess Gerritsen brings us action, adventure
and compelling romance."
—*Romantic Times*

Gerritsen delivers "thrillers from beginning to
end...she can rev up the action in a hurry."
—*Portland Press Herald*

STELLA CAMERON

"Her narrative is rich, her style is distinct,
and her characters are wonderfully wicked."
—*Publishers Weekly*

"No one does suspense and sensuality
like Stella Cameron."
—*New York Times* bestselling author
Linda Lael Miller

AMANDA STEVENS

"Amanda Stevens always delivers what I want most
in a book—excitement, romance, adventure—but
she adds something special to the mix. Her stories
are filled with tenderness that keeps the reader
emotionally involved to the very end."
—bestselling author Susan Wiggs

Tess Gerritsen is an accomplished woman with an interesting history. Once a practicing physician, she has chosen instead to write full-time. A woman of many talents, she even plays the fiddle in a band! Tess has cowritten *Adrift*, a CBS screenplay, and has several other screenplays optioned for HBO. Having lived in Hawaii, she now resides in Camden, Maine, with her physician husband and two sons.

Stella Cameron is the bestselling author of more than forty books, and possesses the unique talent of being able to switch effortlessly from historical to contemporary fiction. In a one-year period, her titles appeared more than eight times on the *USA TODAY* bestseller list. This British-born author was working as an editor in London when she met her husband, an officer in the American air force, at a party. He asked her to dance, and they've been together ever since. They now make their home in Seattle, are the parents of three grown children and recently became grandparents.

Born and raised in a small Southern town, **Amanda Stevens** frequently draws on memories of her birthplace to create atmospheric settings and casts of eccentric characters. She is the author of over twenty-five novels, the recipient of a *Romantic Times* Career Achievement Award for Romantic Mystery and a 1999 RITA® Award finalist in the Gothic/Romantic Suspense category. She now resides in Texas with her husband, teenage twins and her cat, Jesse, who also makes frequent appearances in her books.

Unveiled

TESS GERRITSEN

STELLA CAMERON

AMANDA STEVENS

HARLEQUIN®

TORONTO • NEW YORK • LONDON
AMSTERDAM • PARIS • SYDNEY • HAMBURG
STOCKHOLM • ATHENS • TOKYO • MILAN • MADRID
PRAGUE • WARSAW • BUDAPEST • AUCKLAND

ISBN 0-373-83538-8

UNVEILED

CONTENTS

WHISTLEBLOWER
Tess Gerritsen

PROLOGUE

Branches whipped his face, and his heart was pounding so hard he thought his chest would explode, but he couldn't stop running. Already, he could hear the man gaining on him, could almost imagine the bullet slicing through the night and slamming into his back. Maybe it already had. Maybe he was trailing a river of blood; he was too numb with terror to feel anything now, except the desperate hunger to live. The rain was pouring down his face, icy, blinding sheets of it, rattling on the dead leaves of winter. He stumbled through a pool of darkness and found himself sprawled flat on his belly in the mud. The sound of his fall was deafening. His pursuer, alerted by the sharp crack of branches, altered course and was now headed straight for him. The thud of a silencer, the zing of a bullet past his cheek, told him he'd been spotted. He forced himself to his feet and made a sharp right, zigzagging back toward the highway. Here in the woods, he was a dead man. But if he could flag down a car, if he could draw someone's attention, he might have a chance.

A crash of branches, a coarse oath, told him his pursuer had stumbled. He'd gained a few precious seconds. He kept running, moving only by an instinctive sense of direction. There was no light to guide his way, nothing except the dim glow of the clouds in the night sky. The road had to be just ahead. Any second now, his feet would hit pavement.

And then what? What if there's no car to flag down, no one to help me?

Then, through the trees ahead, he saw a faint flickering, two watery beams of light.

With a desperate burst of speed, he sprinted toward the car. His lungs were on fire, his eyes blinded by the lash of branches and rain. Another bullet whipped past him and thudded into a tree trunk, but the gunman behind him had suddenly lost all importance. All that mattered was those lights, beckoning him through the darkness, taunting him with the promise of salvation.

When his feet suddenly hit the pavement, he was shocked. The lights were still ahead, bobbing somewhere beyond the trees. Had he missed the car? Was it already moving away, around a curve? No, there it was, brighter now. It was coming this way. He ran to meet it, following the bend of the road and knowing all the time that here in the open, he was an easy target. The sound of his shoes slapping the wet road filled his ears. The lights twisted toward him. At that instant, he heard the gun fire a third time. The force of the impact made him stumble to his knees, and he was vaguely aware of the bullet tearing through his shoulder, of the warmth of his own blood dribbling down his arm, but he was oblivious to pain. He could focus only on staying alive. He struggled back to his feet, took a stumbling step forward...

And was blinded by the onrush of headlights. There was no time to throw himself out of the way, no time even to register panic. Tires screamed across the pavement, throwing up a spray of water.

He didn't feel the impact. All he knew was that he was suddenly lying on the ground and the rain was pouring into his mouth and he was very, very cold.

And that he had something to do, something important.

Feebly, he reached into the pocket of his windbreaker, and his fingers curled around the small plastic cylinder. He couldn't quite remember why it mattered so much, but it was still there and he was relieved. He clutched it tightly in his palm.

Someone was calling to him. A woman. He couldn't see her face through the rain, but he could hear her voice, hoarse with panic, floating through the buzz in his head. He tried to speak, tried to warn her that they had to get away, that death was waiting in the woods. But all that came out was a groan.

CHAPTER ONE

Three miles out of Redwood Valley, a tree had fallen across the road, and with the heavy rains and backed-up cars, it took Catherine Weaver nearly three hours to get past the town of Willits. By then it was already ten o'clock and she knew she wouldn't reach Garberville till midnight. She hoped Sarah wouldn't sit up all night waiting for her. But knowing Sarah, there'd be a supper still warm in the oven and a fire blazing in the hearth. She wondered how pregnancy suited her friend. Wonderfully, of course. Sarah had talked about this baby for years, had chosen its name—Sam or Emma—long before it was conceived. The fact she no longer had a husband was a minor point. "You can only wait around so long for the right father," Sarah had said. "Then you have to take matters into your own hands."

And she had. With her biological clock furiously ticking its last years away, Sarah had driven down to visit Cathy in San Francisco and had calmly selected a fertility clinic from the yellow pages. A liberal-minded one, of course. One that would understand the desperate longings of a thirty-nine-year old single woman. The insemination itself had been a coolly clinical affair, she'd said later. Hop on the table, slip your feet into the stirrups, and five minutes later, you were pregnant. Well, almost. But it was a simple procedure, the donors were certifiably healthy, and best of all, a woman could fulfill her maternal instincts without all that foolishness about marriage.

Yes, the old marriage game. They'd both suffered through it. And after their divorces, they'd both carried on, albeit with battle scars.

Brave Sarah, thought Cathy. *At least she has the courage to go through with this on her own.*

The old anger washed through her, still potent enough to make her mouth tighten. She could forgive her ex-husband Jack for a lot of things. For his selfishness. His demands. His infidelity. But she could never forgive him for denying her the chance to have a child. Oh, she could have gone against his wishes and had a baby anyway, but she'd wanted him to want one as well. So she'd waited for the time to be right. But during their ten years of marriage, he'd never been "ready," never felt it was the "right time."

What he should have told her was the truth: that he was too self-centered to be bothered with a baby.

I'm thirty-seven years old, she thought. *I no longer have a husband. I don't even have a steady boyfriend. But I could be content, if only I could hold my own child in my arms.*

At least Sarah would soon be blessed.

Four months to go and then the baby was due. Sarah's baby. Cathy had to smile at that thought, despite the rain now pouring over her windshield. It was coming down harder now; even with the wipers thrashing at full speed, she could barely make out the road. She glanced at her watch and saw it was already eleven-thirty; there were no other cars in sight. If she had engine trouble out here, she'd probably have to spend the night huddled in the backseat, waiting for help to arrive.

Peering ahead, she tried to make out the road's dividing line and saw nothing but a solid wall of rain. This was ridiculous. She really should have stopped at that motel in Willits, but she hated the thought of being only fifty miles from her goal, especially when she'd already driven so far.

She spotted a sign ahead: Garberville, 10 Miles. So she was closer than she'd thought. Twenty-five miles more, then there'd be a turn-off and a five-mile drive through dense woods to Sarah's cedar house. The thought of being so close fueled her impatience. She fed the old Datsun some gas and sped up to forty-five miles an hour. It was a reckless thing to do, especially in these conditions, but the thought of a warm house and hot chocolate was just too tempting.

The road curved unexpectedly; startled, she jerked the wheel to the right and the car slid sideways, tobogganing wildly across the rain-slicked pavement. She knew enough not to slam on the brakes. Instead, she clutched the wheel, fighting to regain control. The tires skidded a few feet, a heart-stopping ride that took her to the very edge of the road. Just as she thought she'd clip the trees, the tires gripped the pavement. The car was still moving twenty miles an hour, but at least it was headed in a straight line. With clammy hands, she managed to negotiate the rest of the curve.

What happened next caught her completely by surprise. One instant she was congratulating herself for averting disaster, the next, she was staring ahead in disbelief.

The man had appeared out of nowhere. He was crouched in the road, captured like a wild animal in the glare of her headlights. Reflexes took over. She slammed on the brakes, but it was already too late. The screech of her tires was punctuated by the thud of the man's body against the hood of her car.

For what seemed like eternity, she sat frozen and unable to do anything but clutch the steering wheel and stare at the windshield wipers skating back and forth. Then, as the reality of what she'd just done sank in, she shoved the door open and dashed out into the rain.

At first she could see nothing through the downpour, only a glistening strip of blacktop lit by the dim glow of her taillights. *Where is he?* she thought frantically. With water streaming past her eyes, she traced the road backward, struggling to see in the darkness. Then, through the pounding rain, she heard a low moan. It came from somewhere off to the side, near the trees.

Shifting direction, she plunged into the shadows and sank ankle-deep in mud and pine needles. Again she heard the moan, closer now, almost within reach.

"Where are you?" she screamed. "Help me find you!"

"Here..." The answer was so weak she barely heard it, but it was all she needed. Turning, she took a few steps and practically stumbled over his crumpled body in the darkness. At first, he seemed to be only a confusing jumble of soaked clothes, then she managed to locate his hand and feel for his pulse. It was fast but steady, probably steadier than her own pulse, which was skipping wildly. His fingers suddenly closed over hers in a desperate grip. He rolled against her and struggled to sit up.

"Please! Don't move!" she said.

"Can't—can't stay here—"

"Where are you hurt?"

"No time. Help me. Hurry—"

"Not till you tell me where you're hurt!"

He reached out and grabbed her shoulder in a clumsy attempt to rise to his feet. To her amazement, he managed to pull himself halfway up. For an instant they wobbled against each other, then his strength seemed to collapse and they both slid to their knees in the mud. His breathing had turned harsh and irregular and she wondered about his injuries. If he was bleeding internally he could die within minutes. She had to get him to a hospital now, even if it meant dragging him back to the car.

"Okay. Let's try again," she said, grabbing his left arm and draping it around her neck. She was startled by his gasp of agony. Immediately she released him. His arm left a sticky trail of warmth around her neck. *Blood.*

"My other side's okay," he grunted. "Try again."

She shifted to his right side and pulled his arm over her neck. If she weren't so frantic, it would have struck her as a comical scene, the two of them struggling like drunkards to stand up. When at last he was on his feet and they stood swaying together in the mud, she wondered if he even had the strength to put one foot in front of the other. She certainly couldn't move them both. Though he was slender, he was also a great deal taller than she'd expected, and much more than her five-foot-five frame could support.

But something seemed to compel him forward, a kindling of some hidden reserves. Even through their soaked clothes, she could feel the heat of his body and could sense the urgency driving him onward. A dozen questions formed in her head, but she was breathing too hard to voice them. Her every effort had to be concentrated on getting him to the car, and then to a hospital.

Gripping him around the waist, she latched her fingers through his belt. Painfully they made their way to the road, struggling step by step. His arm felt taut as wire over her neck. It seemed everything about him was wound up tight. There was something desperate about the way his muscles strained to move forward. His urgency penetrated right through to her skin. It was a panic as palpable as the warmth of his body, and she was suddenly infected with his need to flee, a need made more desperate by the fact they could move no faster than they already were. Every few feet she had to stop and shove back her dripping hair just to see where she was going. And all around them, the rain and darkness closed off all view of whatever danger pursued.

The taillights of her car glowed ahead like ruby eyes winking in the night. With every step the man grew heavier and her legs felt so rubbery she thought they'd both topple in the road. If they did, she wouldn't have the strength to haul him back up again. Already, his head was sagging against her cheek and water trickled from his rain-matted hair down her neck. The simple act of putting one foot in front of the other was so automatic that she never even considered dropping him on the road and backing the car to him instead. And the taillights were already so close, just beyond the next veil of rain.

By the time she'd guided him to the passenger side, her arm felt ready to fall off. With the man on the verge of sliding from her grasp, she barely managed to wrench the door open. She had no strength left to be gentle; she simply shoved him inside.

He flopped onto the front seat with his legs still hanging out. She bent down, grabbed his ankles, and heaved them one by one into the car, noting with a sense of detachment that no man with feet this big could possibly be graceful.

As she slid into the driver's seat, he made a feeble attempt to raise his head, then let it sink back again. "Hurry," he whispered.

At the first turn of the key in the ignition, the engine sputtered and died. Dear God, she pleaded. Start. *Start!* She switched the key off, counted slowly to three, and tried again. This time the engine caught. Almost shouting with relief, she jammed it into gear and made a tire-screeching takeoff toward Garberville. Even a town that small must have a hospital or, at the very least, an emergency clinic. The question was: could she find it in this downpour? And what if she was wrong? What if the nearest medical help was in Willits, the other direction? She might be wasting precious minutes on the road while the man bled to death.

Suddenly panicked by that thought, she glanced at her passenger. By the glow of the dashboard, she saw that his head was still flopped back against the seat. He wasn't moving.

"Hey! Are you all right?" she cried.

The answer came back in a whisper. "I'm still here."

"Dear God. For a minute I thought..." She looked back at the road, her heart pounding. "There's got to be a clinic somewhere—"

"Near Garberville—there's a hospital—"

"Do you know how to find it?"

"I drove past it—fifteen miles…"

If he drove here, where's his car? she thought. "What happened?" she asked. "Did you have an accident?"

He started to speak but his answer was cut off by a sudden flicker of light. Struggling to sit up, he turned and stared at the headlights of another car far behind them. His whispered oath made her look sideways in alarm.

"What is it?"

"That car."

She glanced in the rearview mirror. "What about it?"

"How long's it been following us?"

"I don't know. A few miles. Why?"

The effort of keeping his head up suddenly seemed too much for him, and he let it sink back down with a groan. "Can't think," he whispered. "Christ, I can't think…"

He's lost too much blood, she thought. In a panic, she shoved hard on the gas pedal. The car seemed to leap through the rain, the steering wheel vibrating wildly as sheets of spray flew up from the tires. Darkness flew at dizzying speed against their windshield. *Slow down, slow down! Or I'll get us both killed.*

Easing back on the gas, she let the speedometer fall to a more manageable forty-five miles per hour. The man was struggling to sit up again.

"Please, keep your head down!" she pleaded.

"That car—"

"It's not there anymore."

"Are you sure?"

She looked at the rearview mirror. Through the rain, she saw only a faint twinkling of light, but nothing as definite as headlights. "I'm sure," she lied and was relieved to see him slowly settle back again. *How much farther?* she thought. *Five miles? Ten?* And then the next thought forced its way into her mind: *He might die before we get there.*

His silence terrified her. She needed to hear his voice, needed to be reassured that he hadn't slipped into oblivion. "Talk to me," she urged. "Please."

"I'm tired...."

"Don't stop. Keep talking. What—what's your name?"

The answer was a mere whisper: "Victor."

"Victor. That's a great name. I like that name. What do you do, Victor?"

His silence told her he was too weak to carry on any conversation. She couldn't let him lose consciousness! For some reason it suddenly seemed crucial to keep him awake, to keep him in touch with a living voice. If that fragile connection was broken, she feared he might slip away entirely.

"All right," she said, forcing her voice to remain low and steady. "Then *I'll* talk. You don't have to say a thing. Just listen. Keep listening. My name is Catherine. Cathy Weaver. I live in San Francisco, the Richmond district. Do you know the city?" There was no answer, but she sensed some movement in his head, a silent acknowledgement of her words. "Okay," she went on, mindlessly filling the silence. "Maybe you don't know the city. It really doesn't matter. I work with an independent film company. Actually, it's Jack's company. My ex-husband. We make horror films. Grade B, really, but they turn a profit. Our last one was *Reptilian*. I did the special-effects makeup. Really gruesome stuff. Lots of green scales and slime..." She laughed—it was a strange, panicked sound. It had an unmistakable note of hysteria.

She had to fight to regain control.

A wink of light made her glance up sharply at the rearview mirror. A pair of headlights was barely discernible through the rain. For a few seconds she watched them, debating whether to say anything to Victor. Then, like phantoms, the lights flickered off and vanished.

"Victor?" she called softly. He responded with an unintelligible grunt, but it was all she needed to be reassured that he was still alive. That he was listening. *I've got to keep him awake,* she thought, her mind scrambling for some new topic of conversation. She'd never been good at the glib sort of chitchat so highly valued at filmmakers' cocktail parties. What she needed was a joke, however stupid, as long as it was vaguely funny. *Laughter heals.* Hadn't she read it somewhere? That a steady barrage of comedy could shrink tumors? *Oh sure,* she chided herself. *Just make him laugh and the bleeding will miraculously stop....*

But she couldn't think of a joke, anyway, not a single damn one. So she returned to the topic that had first come to mind: her work.

"Our next project's slated for January. *Ghouls.* We'll be filming in Mexico, which I hate, because the damn heat always melts the makeup...."

She looked at Victor but saw no response, not even a flicker of movement. Terrified that she was losing him, she reached out to feel for his pulse and discovered that his hand was buried deep in the pocket of his windbreaker. She tried to tug it free, and to her amazement he reacted to her invasion with immediate and savage resistance. Lurching awake, he blindly lashed at her, trying to force her away.

"Victor, it's all right!" she cried, fighting to steer the car and protect herself at the same time. "It's all right! It's me, Cathy. I'm only trying to help!"

At the sound of her voice, his struggles weakened. As the tension eased from his body, she felt his head settle slowly against her shoulder. "Cathy," he whispered. It was a sound of wonder, of relief. "Cathy..."

"That's right. It's only me." Gently, she reached up and brushed back the tendrils of his wet hair. She wondered what color it was, a concern that struck her as totally irrelevant but nonetheless compelling. He reached for her hand. His fingers closed around hers in a grip that was surprisingly strong and steadying. *I'm still here,* it said. *I'm warm and alive and breathing.* He pressed her palm to his lips. So tender was the gesture, she was startled by the roughness of his unshaven jaw against her skin. It was a caress between strangers, and it left her shaken and trembling.

She returned her grip to the steering wheel and shifted her full attention back to the road. He had fallen silent again, but she couldn't ignore the weight of his head on her shoulder or the heat of his breath in her hair.

The torrent eased to a slow but steady rain, and she coaxed the car to fifty. The Sunnyside Up cafe whipped past, a drab little box beneath a single streetlight, and she caught a glimpse of Victor's face in the brief glow of light. She saw him only in profile: a high

forehead, sharp nose, a jutting chin, and then the light was gone
and he was only a shadow breathing softly against her. But she'd
seen enough to know she'd never forget that face. Even as she
peered through the darkness, his profile floated before her like an
image burned into her memory.

"We have to be getting close," she said, as much to reassure
herself as him. "Where a cafe appears, a town is sure to follow."
There was no response. "Victor?" Still no response. Swallowing
her panic, she sped up to fifty-five.

Though they'd passed the Sunnyside Up over a mile ago, she
could still make out the streetlight winking on and off in her mirror.
It took her a few seconds to realize it wasn't just one light she was
watching but two, and that they were moving—a pair of headlights,
winding along the highway. Was it the same car she'd spotted earlier?

Mesmerized, she watched the lights dance like twin wraiths
among the trees, then, suddenly, they vanished and she saw only
darkness. A ghost? she wondered irrationally. Any instant she expected the lights to rematerialize, to resume their phantom twinkling
in the woods. She was watching the mirror so intently that she
almost missed the road sign:

Garberville, Pop, 5,750
Gas—Food—Lodging

A half mile later streetlights appeared, glowing a hazy yellow in
the drizzle; a flatbed truck splashed by, headed in the other direction. Though the speed limit had dropped to thirty-five, she kept her
foot firmly on the gas pedal and for once in her life prayed for a
police car to give chase.

The *Hospital* road sign seemed to leap out at her from nowhere.
She braked and swerved onto the turnoff. A quarter mile away, a
red *Emergency* sign directed her up a driveway to a side entrance.
Leaving Victor in the front seat, she ran inside, through a deserted
waiting room, and cried to a nurse sitting at her desk: "Please, help
me! I've got a man in my car...."

The nurse responded instantly. She followed Cathy outside, took one look at the man slumped in the front seat, and yelled for assistance.

Even with the help of a burly ER physician, they had difficulty pulling Victor out of the car. He had slid sideways, and his arm was wedged under the emergency hand brake.

"Hey, Miss!" the doctor barked at Cathy. "Climb in the other side and free up his arm!"

Cathy scrambled to the driver's seat. There she hesitated. She would have to manipulate his injured arm. She took his elbow and tried to unhook it from around the brake, but discovered his wristwatch was snagged in the pocket of his windbreaker. After unsnapping the watchband, she took hold of his arm and lifted it over the brake. He responded with a groan of pure agony. The arm slid limply toward the floor.

"Okay!" said the doctor. "Arm's free! Now, just ease him toward me and we'll take it from there."

Gingerly, she guided Victor's head and shoulders safely past the emergency brake. Then she scrambled back outside to help load him onto the wheeled stretcher. Three straps were buckled into place. Everything became a blur of noise and motion as the stretcher was wheeled through the open double doors into the building.

"What happened?" the doctor barked over his shoulder at Cathy.

"I hit him—on the road—"

"When?"

"Fifteen—twenty minutes ago."

"How fast were you driving?"

"About thirty-five."

"Was he conscious when you found him?"

"For about ten minutes—then he sort of faded—"

A nurse said: "Shirt's soaked with blood. He's got broken glass in his shoulder."

In that mad dash beneath harsh fluorescent lights, Cathy had her first clear look at Victor, and she saw a lean, mud-streaked face, a jaw tightly squared in pain, a broad forehead matted damply with light brown hair. He reached out to her, grasping for her hand.

"Cathy—"

"I'm here, Victor."

He held on tightly, refusing to break contact. The pressure of his fingers in her flesh was almost painful. Squinting through the pain, he focused on her face. "I have to—have to tell you—"

"Later!" snapped the doctor.

"No, wait!" Victor was fighting to keep her in view, to hold her beside him. He struggled to speak, agony etching lines on his face.

Cathy bent close, drawn by the desperation of his gaze. "Yes, Victor," she whispered, stroking his hair, longing to ease his pain. This link between their hands, their gazes, felt forged in timeless steel. "Tell me."

"We can't delay!" barked the doctor. "Get him in the room."

All at once, Victor's hand was wrenched away from her as they whisked him into the trauma suite, a nightmarish room of stainless steel and blindingly bright lights. He was lifted onto the surgical table.

"Pulse 110," said a nurse. "Blood pressure eight-five over fifty!"

The doctor ordered, "Let's get two IVs in. Type and cross six units of blood. And get hold of a surgeon. We're going to need help...."

The machine-gun fire of voices, the metallic clang of cabinets and IV poles and instruments was deafening. No one seemed to notice Cathy standing in the doorway, watching in horrified fascination as a nurse pulled out a knife and began to tear off Victor's bloody clothing. With each rip, more and more flesh was exposed, until the shirt and windbreaker were shredded off, revealing a broad chest thickly matted with tawny hair. To the doctors and nurses, this was just another body to labor over, another patient to be saved. To Cathy, this was a living, breathing man, a man she cared about, if only because they had shared those last harrowing moments. The nurse shifted her attention to his belt, which she quickly unbuckled. With a few firm tugs, she peeled off his trousers and shorts and threw them into a pile with the other soiled clothing. Cathy scarcely noticed the man's nakedness, or the nurses and technicians shoving past her into the room. Her shocked gaze had focused on Victor's left shoulder, which was oozing fresh blood onto the table. She remembered how his whole body had resonated with pain when she'd grabbed that shoulder; only now did she understand how much he must have suffered.

A sour taste flooded her throat. She was going to be sick.

Struggling against the nausea, she somehow managed to stumble away and sink into a nearby chair. There she sat for a few minutes, oblivious to the chaos whirling around her. Looking down, she noted with instinctive horror the blood on her hands.

"There you are," someone said. A nurse had just emerged from the trauma room, carrying a bundle of the patient's belongings. She motioned Cathy over to a desk. "We'll need your name and address in case the doctors have any more questions. And the police will have to be notified. Have you called them?"

Cathy shook her head numbly. "I—I guess I should..."

"You can use this phone."

"Thank you."

It rang eight times before anyone answered. The voice that greeted her was raspy with sleep. Obviously, Garberville provided little late-night stimulation, even for the local police. The desk officer took down Cathy's report and told her he'd be in touch with her later, after they'd checked the accident scene.

The nurse had opened Victor's wallet and was flipping through the various ID cards for information. Cathy watched her fill in the blanks on a patient admission form: *Name: Victor Holland. Age: 41. Occupation: Biochemist. Next of kin: Unknown.*

So that was his full name. Victor Holland. Cathy stared down at the stack of ID cards and focused on what appeared to be a security pass for some company called Viratek. A color photograph showed Victor's quietly sober face, its green eyes gazing straight into the camera. Even if she had never seen his face, this was exactly how she would have pictured him, his expression unyielding, his gaze unflinchingly direct. She touched her palm, where he had kissed her. She could still recall how his beard had stung her flesh.

Softly, she asked, "Is he going to be all right?"

The nurse continued writing. "He's lost a lot of blood. But he looks like a pretty tough guy...."

Cathy nodded, remembering how, even in his agony, Victor had somehow dredged up the strength to keep moving through the rain. Yes, she knew just how tough a man he was.

The nurse handed her a pen and the information sheet. "If you could write your name and address at the bottom. In case the doctor has any more questions.''

Cathy fished out Sarah's address and phone number from her purse and copied them onto the form. ''My name's Cathy Weaver. You can get hold of me at this number.''

''You're staying in Garberville?''

''For three weeks. I'm just visiting.''

''Oh. Terrific way to start a vacation, huh?''

Cathy sighed as she rose to leave. ''Yeah. Terrific.''

She paused outside the trauma room, wondering what was happening inside, knowing that Victor was fighting for his life. She wondered if he was still conscious, if he would remember her. It seemed important that he *did* remember her.

Cathy turned to the nurse. ''You will call me, won't you? I mean, you'll let me know if he...''

The nurse nodded. ''We'll keep you informed.''

Outside, the rain had finally stopped and a belt of stars twinkled through a parting in the clouds. To Cathy's weary eyes, it was an exhilarating sight, that first glimpse of the storm's end. As she drove out of the hospital parking lot, she was shaking from fatigue. She never noticed the car parked across the street or the brief glow of the cigarette before it was snuffed out.

CHAPTER TWO

Barely a minute after Cathy left the hospital, a man walked into the emergency room, sweeping the smells of a stormy night in with him through the double doors. The nurse on duty was busy with the new patient's admission papers. At the sudden rush of cold air, she looked up to see a man approach her desk. He was about thirty-five, gaunt-faced, silent, his dark hair lightly feathered by gray. Droplets of water sparkled on his tan Burberry raincoat.

"Can I help you, sir?" she asked, focusing on his eyes, which were as black and polished as pebbles in a pond.

Nodding, he said quietly, "Was there a man brought in a short time ago? Victor Holland?"

The nurse glanced down at the papers on her desk. That was the name. Victor Holland. "Yes," she said. "Are you a relative?"

"I'm his brother. How is he?"

"He just arrived, sir. They're working on him now. If you'll wait, I can check on how he's doing—" She stopped to answer the ringing telephone. It was a technician calling with the new patient's laboratory results. As she jotted down the numbers, she noticed out of the corner of her eye that the man had turned and was gazing at the closed door to the trauma room. It suddenly swung open as an orderly emerged carrying a bulging plastic bag streaked with blood. The clamor of voices spilled from the room:

"Pressure up to 110 over 70!"

"OR says they're ready to go."

"Where's that surgeon?"

"On his way. He had car trouble."

"Ready for X rays! Everyone back!"

Slowly the door closed, muffling the voices. The nurse hung up just as the orderly deposited the plastic bag on her desk. "What's this?" she asked.

"Patient's clothes. They're a mess. Should I just toss 'em?"

"I'll take them home," the man in the raincoat cut in. "Is everything here?"

The orderly flashed the nurse an uncomfortable glance. "I'm not sure he'd want to...I mean, they're kind of...uh, dirty...."

The nurse said quickly, "Mr. Holland, why don't you let us dispose of the clothes for you? There's nothing worth keeping in there. I've already collected his valuables." She unlocked a drawer and pulled out a sealed manila envelope labeled: Holland, Victor. Contents: Wallet, Wristwatch. "You can take these home. Just sign this receipt."

The man nodded and signed his name: David Holland. "Tell me," he said, sliding the envelope in his pocket. "Is Victor awake? Has he said anything?"

"I'm afraid not. He was semiconscious when he arrived."

The man took this information in silence, a silence that the nurse found suddenly and profoundly disturbing. "Excuse me, Mr. Holland?" she asked. "How did you hear your brother was hurt? I didn't get a chance to contact any relatives...."

"The police called me. Victor was driving my car. They found it smashed up at the side of the road."

"Oh. What an awful way to be notified."

"Yes. The stuff of nightmares."

"At least someone was able to get in touch with you." She sifted through the sheaf of papers on her desk. "Can we get your address and phone number? In case we need to reach you?"

"Of course." The man took the ER papers, which he quickly scanned before scrawling his name and phone number on the blank marked Next of Kin. "Who's this Catherine Weaver?" he asked, pointing to the name and address at the bottom of the page.

"She's the woman who brought him in."

"I'll have to thank her." He handed back the papers.

"Nurse?"

She looked around and saw that the doctor was calling to her from the trauma room doorway. "Yes?"

"I want you to call the police. Tell them to get in here as soon as possible."

"They've been called, Doctor. They know about the accident—"

"Call them again. This is no accident."

"What?"

"We just got the X rays. The man's got a bullet in his shoulder."

"A *bullet?*" A chill went through the nurse's body, like a cold wind sweeping in from the night. Slowly, she turned toward the man in the raincoat, the man who'd claimed to be Victor Holland's brother. To her amazement, no one was there. She felt only a cold puff of night air, and then she saw the double doors quietly slide shut.

"Where the hell did he go?" the orderly whispered.

For a few seconds she could only stare at the closed doors. Then her gaze dropped and she focused on the empty spot on her desk. The bag containing Victor Holland's clothes had vanished.

"Why did the police call again?"

Cathy slowly replaced the telephone receiver. Even though she was bundled in a warm terry-cloth robe, she was shivering. She turned and stared across the kitchen at Sarah. "That man on the road—they found a bullet in his shoulder."

In the midst of pouring tea, Sarah glanced up in surprise. "You mean—someone *shot* him?"

Cathy sank down at the kitchen table and gazed numbly at the cup of cinnamon tea that Sarah had just slid in front of her. A hot bath and a soothing hour of sitting by the fireplace had made the night's events seem like nothing more than a bad dream. Here in Sarah's kitchen, with its chintz curtains and its cinnamon and spice smells, the violence of the real world seemed a million miles away.

Sarah leaned toward her. "Do they know what happened? Has he said anything?"

"He just got out of surgery." She turned and glanced at the telephone. "I should call the hospital again—"

"No. You shouldn't. You've done everything you possibly can." Sarah gently touched her arm. "And your tea's getting cold."

With a shaking hand, Cathy brushed back a strand of damp hair and settled uneasily in her chair. A bullet in his shoulder, she thought. Why? Had it been a random attack, a highway gunslinger blasting out the car window at a total stranger? She'd read about it in the newspapers, the stories of freeway arguments settled by the pulling of a trigger.

Or had it been a deliberate attack? Had Victor Holland been targeted for death?

Outside, something rattled and clanged against the house. Cathy sat up sharply. "What was that?"

"Believe me, it's not the bogeyman," said Sarah, laughing. She went to the kitchen door and reached for the bolt.

"Sarah!" Cathy called in panic as the bold slid open. "Wait!"

"Take a look for yourself." Sarah opened the door. The kitchen light swung across a cluster of trash cans sitting in the carport. A shadow slid to the ground and scurried away, trailing food wrappers across the driveway. "Raccoons," said Sarah. "If I don't tie the lids down, those pests'll scatter trash all over the yard." Another shadow popped its head out of a can and stared at her, its eyes glowing in the darkness. Sarah clapped her hands and yelled, "Go on, get lost!" The raccoon didn't budge. "Don't you have a home to go to?" At last, the raccoon dropped to the ground and ambled off into the trees. "They get bolder every year," Sarah sighed, closing the door. She turned and winked at Cathy. "So take it easy. This isn't the big city."

"Keep reminding me." Cathy took a slice of banana bread and began to spread it with sweet butter. "You know, Sarah, I think it'll be a lot nicer spending Christmas with you than it ever was with old Jack."

"Uh-oh. Since we're now speaking of ex-husbands—" Sarah shuffled over to a cabinet "—we might as well get in the right frame of mind. And tea just won't cut it." She grinned and waved a bottle of brandy.

"Sarah, you're not drinking alcohol, are you?"

"It's not for *me*." Sarah set the bottle and a single wine glass in front of Cathy. "But I think *you* could use a nip. After all, it's been a cold, traumatic night. And here we are, talking about turkeys of the male variety."

"Well, since you put it that way..." Cathy poured out a generous shot of brandy. "To the turkeys of the world," she declared and took a sip. It felt just right going down.

"So how *is* old Jack?" asked Sarah.

"Same as always."

"Blondes?"

"He's moved on to brunettes."

"It took him only a year to go through the world's supply of blondes?"

Cathy shrugged. "He might have missed a few."

They both laughed then, light and easy laughter that told them their wounds were well on the way to healing, that men were now creatures to be discussed without pain, without sorrow.

Cathy regarded her glass of brandy. "Do you suppose there *are* any good men left in the world? I mean, shouldn't there be *one* floating around somewhere? Maybe a mutation or something? One measly decent guy?"

"Sure. Somewhere in Siberia. But he's a hundred-and-twenty years old."

"I've always liked older men."

They laughed again, but this time the sound wasn't as light-hearted. So many years had passed since their college days together, the days when they had *known,* had never doubted, that Prince Charmings abounded in the world.

Cathy drained her glass of brandy and set it down. "What a lousy friend I am. Keeping a pregnant lady up all night! What time is it, anyway?"

"Only two-thirty in the morning."

"Oh, Sarah! Go to bed!" Cathy went to the sink and began wetting a handful of paper towels.

"And what are you going to do?" Sarah asked.

"I just want to clean up the car. I didn't get all the blood off the seat."

"I already did it."

"What? When?"

"While you were taking a bath."

"Sarah, you idiot."

"Hey, I didn't have a miscarriage or anything. Oh, I almost forgot." Sarah pointed to a tiny film canister on the counter. "I found that on the floor of your car."

Cathy shook her head and sighed. "It's Hickey's."

"Hickey! Now *there's* a waste of a man."

'He's also a good friend of mine.''

"That's all Hickey will ever be to a woman. A *friend*. So what's on the roll of film? Naked women, as usual?''

"I don't even want to know. When I dropped him off at the airport, he handed me a half-dozen rolls and told me he'd pick them up when he got back. Guess he didn't want to lug 'em all the way to Nairobi.''

"Is that where he went? Nairobi?''

"He's shooting 'gorgeous ladies of Africa' or something.'' Cathy slipped the film canister into her bathrobe pocket. "This must've dropped out of the glove compartment. Gee. I hope it's not pornographic.''

"Knowing Hickey, it probably is.''

They both laughed at the irony of it all. Hickman Von Trapp, whose only job it was to photograph naked females in erotic poses, had absolutely no interest in the opposite sex, with the possible exception of his mother.

"A guy like Hickey only goes to prove my point,'' Sarah said over her shoulder as she headed up the hall to bed.

"What point is that?''

"There really *are* no good men left in the world!''

It was the light that dragged Victor up from the depths of unconsciousness, a light brighter than a dozen suns, beating against his closed eyelids. He didn't want to wake up; he knew, in some dim, scarcely functioning part of his brain, that if he continued to struggle against this blessed oblivion he would feel pain and nausea and something else, something much, much worse: terror. Of what, he couldn't remember. Of death? No, no, this was death, or as close as one could come to it, and it was warm and black and comfortable. But he had something important to do, something that he couldn't allow himself to forget. He tried to think, but all he could remember was a hand, gentle but somehow strong, brushing his forehead, and a voice, reaching to him softly in the darkness.

My name is Catherine....

As her touch, her voice, flooded his memory, so too did the fear. Not for himself (he was dead, wasn't he?) but for her. Strong, gentle Catherine. He'd seen her face only briefly, could scarcely remember it, but somehow he knew she was beautiful, the way a blind man knows, without benefit of vision, that a rainbow or the sky or his own dear child's face is beautiful. And now he was afraid for her.

Where are you? he wanted to cry out.

"He's coming around," said a female voice (not Catherine's, it was too hard, too crisp) followed by a confusing rush of other voices.

"Watch that IV!"

"Mr. Holland, hold still. Everything's going to be all right—"

"I said, watch the IV!"

"Hand me that second unit of blood—"

"Don't move, Mr. Holland—"

Where are you, Catherine? The shout exploded in his head. Fighting the temptation to sink back into unconsciousness, he struggled to lift his eyelids. At first, there was only a blur of light and color, so harsh he felt it stab through his sockets straight to his brain. Gradually the blur took the shape of faces, strangers in blue, frowning down at him. He tried to focus but the effort made his stomach rebel.

"Mr. Holland, take it easy," said a quietly gruff voice. "You're in the hospital—the recovery room. They've just operated on your shoulder. You just rest and go back to sleep...."

No. No, I can't, he tried to say.

"Five milligrams of morphine going in," someone said, and Victor felt a warm flush creep up his arm and spread across his chest.

"That should help," he heard. "Now, sleep. Everything went just fine...."

You don't understand, he wanted to scream. *I have to warn her—* It was the last conscious thought he had before the lights once again were swallowed by the gentle darkness.

Alone in her husbandless bed, Sarah lay smiling. No, laughing! Her whole body seemed filled with laughter tonight. She wanted to sing, to dance. To stand at the open window and shout out her joy! It was all hormonal, she'd been told, this chemical pandemonium of pregnancy, dragging her body on a roller coaster of emotions. She knew she should rest, she should work toward serenity, but tonight she wasn't tired at all. Poor exhausted Cathy had dragged herself up the attic steps to bed. But here was Sarah, still wide awake.

She closed her eyes and focused her thoughts on the child resting in her belly. *How are you, my love? Are you asleep? Or are you listening, hearing my thoughts even now?*

The baby wiggled in her belly, then fell silent. It was a reply, secret words shared only between them. Sarah was almost glad there was no husband to distract her from this silent conversation, to lie here in jealousy, an outsider. There was only mother and child, the ancient bond, the mystical link.

Poor Cathy, she thought, riding those roller coaster emotions from joy to sadness for her friend. She knew Cathy yearned just as deeply for a child, but eventually time would snatch the chance away from her. Cathy was too much of a romantic to realize that the man, the circumstances, might never be right. Hadn't it taken Cathy ten long years to finally acknowledge that her marriage was a miserable failure? Not that Cathy hadn't tried to make it work. She had tried to the point of developing a monumental blind spot to Jack's faults, primarily his selfishness. It was surprising how a woman so bright, so intuitive, could have let things drag on as long as she did. But that was Cathy. Even at thirty-seven she was open and trusting and loyal to the point of idiocy.

The clatter of gravel outside on the driveway pricked Sarah's awareness. Lying perfectly still, she listened and for a moment heard only the familiar creak of the trees, the rustle of branches against the shake roof. Then—there it was again. Stones skittering across the road, and then the faint squeal of metal. Those raccoons again. If she didn't shoo them off now, they'd litter garbage all over the driveway.

Sighing, she sat up and hunted in the darkness for her slippers. Shuffling quietly out of her bedroom, she navigated instinctively down the hallway and into the kitchen. Her eyes found the night too comfortable; she didn't want to assault them with light. Instead of flipping on the carport switch, she grabbed the flashlight from its usual spot on the kitchen shelf and unlocked the door.

Outside, moonlight glowed dimly through the clouds. She pointed the flashlight at the trash cans, but her beam caught no raccoon eyes, no telltale scattering of garbage, only the dull reflection of stainless steel. Puzzled, she crossed the carport and paused next to the Datsun that Cathy had parked in the driveway.

That was when she noticed the light glowing faintly inside the car. Glancing through the window, she saw that the glove compartment was open. Her first thought was that it had somehow fallen open by itself or that she or Cathy had forgotten to close it. Then she spotted the road maps strewn haphazardly across the front seat.

With fear suddenly hissing in her ear, she backed away, but terror made her legs slow and stiff. Only then did she sense that someone was nearby, waiting in the darkness; she could feel his presence, like a chill wind in the night.

She wheeled around for the house. As she turned, the beam of her flashlight swung around in a wild arc, only to freeze on the face of a man. The eyes that stared down at her were as slick and as black as pebbles. She scarcely focused on the rest of his face: the hawk nose, the thin, bloodless lips. It was only the eyes she saw. They were the eyes of a man without a soul.

"Hello, Catherine," he whispered, and she heard, in his voice, the greeting of death.

Please, she wanted to cry out as she felt him wrench her hair backward, exposing her neck. *Let me live!*

But no sound escaped. The words, like his blade, were buried in her throat.

Cathy woke up to the quarreling of blue jays outside her window, a sound that brought a smile to her lips for it struck her as somehow whimsical, this flap and flutter of wings across the panes, this maniacal crackling of feathered enemies. So unlike the morning roar of buses and cars she was accustomed to. The blue jays' quarrel moved to the rooftop, and she heard their claws scratching across the shakes in a dance of combat. She trailed their progress across the ceiling, up one side of the roof and down the other. Then, tired of the battle, she focused on the window.

Morning sunlight cascaded in, bathing the attic room in a soft haze. Such a perfect room for a nursery! She could see all the changes Sarah had already made here—the Jack-and-Jill curtains, the watercolor animal portraits. The very prospect of a baby sleeping in this room filled her with such joy that she sat up, grinning, and hugged the covers to her knees. Then she glanced at her watch on the nightstand and saw it was already nine-thirty—half the morning gone!

Reluctantly, she left the warmth of her bed and poked around in her suitcase for a sweater and jeans. She dressed to the thrashing of blue jays in the branches, the battle having moved from the roof to the treetops. From the window, she watched them dart from twig to twig until one finally hoisted up the feathered version of a white flag and took off, defeated. The victor, his authority no longer in question, gave one last screech and settled back to preen his feathers.

Only then did Cathy notice the silence of the house, a stillness that magnified her every heartbeat, her every breath.

Leaving the room, she descended the attic steps and confronted the empty living room. Ashes from last night's fire mounded the grate. A silver garland drooped from the Christmas tree. A cardboard angel with glittery wings winked on the mantelpiece. She followed the hallway to Sarah's room and frowned at the rumpled bed, the coverlet flung aside. ''Sarah?''

Her voice was swallowed up in the stillness. How could a cottage seem so immense? She wandered back through the living room and into the kitchen. Last night's teacups still sat in the sink. On the windowsill, an asparagus fern trembled, stirred by a breeze through the open door.

Cathy stepped out into the carport where Sarah's old Dodge was parked. ''Sarah?'' she called.

Something skittered across the roof. Startled, Cathy looked up and suddenly laughed as she heard the blue jay chattering in the tree above—a victory speech, no doubt. Even the animal kingdom had its conceits.

She started to head back into the house when her gaze swept past a stain on the gravel near the car's rear tire. For a few seconds she stared at the blot of rust-brown, unable to comprehend its meaning. Slowly, she moved alongside the car, her gaze tracing the stain backward along its meandering course.

As she rounded the rear of the car, the driveway came into full view. The dried rivulet of brown became a crimson lake in which a single swimmer lay open-eyed and still.

The blue jay's chatter abruptly ceased as another sound rose up and filled the trees. It was Cathy, screaming.

"Hey, mister. Hey, mister."

Victor tried to brush off the sound but it kept buzzing in his ear, like a fly that can't be shooed away.

"Hey, mister. You awake?"

Victor opened his eyes and focused painfully on a wry little face stubbled with gray whiskers. The apparition grinned, and darkness gaped where teeth should have been. Victor stared into that foul black hole of a mouth and thought: *I've died and gone to hell.*

"Hey, mister, you got a cigarette?"

Victor shook his head and barely managed to whisper: "I don't think so."

"Well, you got a dollar I could borrow?"

"Go away," groaned Victor, shutting his eyes against the daylight. He tried to think, tried to remember where he was, but his head ached and the little man's voice kept distracting him.

"Can't get no cigarettes in this place. Like a jail in here. Don't know why I don't just get up and walk out. But y'know, streets are cold this time of year. Been rainin' all night long. Least in here it's warm...."

Raining all night long... Suddenly Victor remembered. The rain. Running and running through the rain.

Victor's eyes shot open. "Where am I?"

"Three East. Land o' the bitches."

He struggled to sit up and almost gasped from the pain. Dizzily, he focused on the metal pole with its bag of fluid dripping slowly into the plastic intravenous tube, then stared at the bandages on his left shoulder. Through the window, he saw that the day was already drenched in sunshine. "What time is it?"

"Dunno. Nine o'clock, I guess. You missed breakfast."

"I've got to get out of here." Victor swung his legs out of bed and discovered that, except for a flimsy hospital gown, he was stark naked. "Where's my clothes? My wallet?"

The old man shrugged. "Nurse'd know. Ask her."

Victor found the call button buried among the bed sheets. He stabbed it a few times, then turned his attention to peeling off the tape affixing the IV tube to his arm.

The door hissed open and a woman's voice barked, *"Mr. Holland! What do you think you're doing?"*

"I'm getting out of here, that's what I'm doing," said Victor as he stripped off the last piece of tape. Before he could pull the IV out, the nurse rushed across the room as fast as her stout legs could carry her and slapped a piece of gauze over the catheter.

"Don't blame me, Miss Redfern!" screeched the little man.

"Lenny, go back to your own bed this instant! And as for you, Mr. Holland," she said, turning her steel-blue eyes on Victor, "you've lost too much blood." Trapping his arm against her massive biceps, she began to retape the catheter firmly in place.

"Just get me my clothes."

"Don't argue, Mr. Holland. You have to stay."

"Why?"

"Because you've got an IV, that's why!" she snapped, as if the plastic tube itself was some sort of irreversible condition.

"I want my clothes."

"I'd have to check with the ER. Nothing of yours came up to the floor."

"Then call the ER, damn you!" At Miss Redfern's disapproving scowl, he added with strained politeness, *"If* you don't mind."

It was another half hour before a woman showed up from the business office to explain what had happened to Victor's belongings.

"I'm afraid we—well, we seem to have…lost your clothes, Mr. Holland," she said, fidgeting under his astonished gaze.

"What do you mean, *lost?"*

"They were—" she cleared her throat "—er, stolen. From the emergency room. Believe me, this has never happened before. We're really very sorry about this, Mr. Holland, and I'm sure we'll be able to arrange a purchase of replacement clothing.…"

She was too busy trying to make excuses to notice that Victor's face had frozen in alarm. That his mind was racing as he tried to remember, through the blur of last night's events, just what had happened to the film canister. He knew he'd had it in his pocket during the endless drive to the hospital. He remembered clutching it there, remembered flailing senselessly at the woman when she'd tried to pull his hand from his pocket. After that, nothing was clear, nothing was certain. *Have I lost it?* he thought. *Have I lost my only evidence?*

"…While the money's missing, your credit cards seem to be all there, so I guess that's something to be thankful for."

He looked at her blankly. "What?"

"Your valuables, Mr. Holland." She pointed to the wallet and watch she'd just placed on the bedside table. "The security guard found them in the trash bin outside the hospital. Looks like the thief only wanted your cash."

"And my clothes. Right."

The instant the woman left, Victor pressed the button for Miss Redfern. She walked in carrying a breakfast tray. "Eat, Mr. Holland," she said. "Maybe your behavior's all due to hypoglycemia."

"A woman brought me to the ER," he said. "Her first name was Catherine. I have to get hold of her."

"Oh, look! Eggs and Rice Krispies! Here's your fork—"

"Miss Redfern, will you forget the damned Rice Krispies!"

Miss Redfern slapped down the cereal box. "There is no need for profanity!"

"I have to find that woman!"

Without a word, Miss Redfern spun around and marched out of the room. A few minutes later she returned and brusquely handed him a slip of paper. On it was written the name Catherine Weaver followed by a local address.

"You'd better eat fast," she said. "There's a policeman coming over to talk to you."

"Fine," he grunted, stuffing a forkful of cold, rubbery egg in his mouth.

"And some man from the FBI called. He's on his way, too."

Victor's head jerked up in alarm. "The FBI? What was his name?"

"Oh, for heaven's sake, how should I know? Something Polish, I think."

Staring at her, Victor slowly put down his fork. "Polowski," he said softly.

"That sounds like it. Polowski." She turned and headed out of the room. "The FBI indeed," she muttered. "Wonder what he did to get *their* attention...."

Before the door had even swung shut behind her, Victor was out of bed and tearing at his IV. He scarcely felt the sting of the tape wrenching the hair off his arm; he had to concentrate on getting the hell out of this hospital before Polowski showed up. He was certain the FBI agent had set him up for that ambush last night, and he wasn't about to wait around for another attack.

He turned and snapped at his roommate, "Lenny, where are your clothes?"

Lenny's gaze traveled reluctantly to a cabinet near the sink. "Don't got no other clothes. Besides, they wouldn't fit you, mister..."

Victor yanked open the cabinet door and pulled out a frayed cotton shirt and a pair of baggy polyester pants. The pants were too short and about six inches of Victor's hairy legs stuck out below the cuffs, but he had no trouble fastening the belt. The real trouble was going to be finding a pair of size twelve shoes. To his relief, he discovered that the cabinet also contained a pair of Lenny's thongs. His heels hung at least an inch over the back edge, but at least he wouldn't be barefoot.

"Those are mine!" protested Lenny.

"Here. You can have this." Victor tossed his wristwatch to the old man. "You should be able to hock that for a whole new outfit."

Suspicious, Lenny put the watch up against his ear. "Piece of junk. It's not ticking."

"It's quartz."

"Oh. Yeah. I knew that."

Victor pocketed his wallet and went to the door. Opening it just a crack, he peered down the hall toward the nurses' station. The coast was clear. He glanced back at Lenny. "So long, buddy. Give my regards to Miss Redfern."

Slipping out of the room, Victor headed quietly down the hall, away from the nurses' station. The emergency stairwell door was at the far end, marked by the warning painted in red: Alarm Will Sound If Opened. He walked steadily towards it, willing himself not to run, not to attract attention. But just as he neared the door, a familiar voice echoed in the hall.

"Mr. Holland! You come back here this instant!"

Victor lunged for the door, slammed against the closing bar, and dashed into the stairwell.

His footsteps echoed against the concrete as he pounded down the stairs. By the time he heard Miss Redfern scramble after him into the stairwell, he'd already reached the first floor and was pushing through the last door to freedom.

"Mr. Holland!" yelled Miss Redfern.

Even as he dashed across the parking lot, he could still hear Miss Redfern's outraged voice echoing in his ears.

Eight blocks away he turned into a K Mart, and within ten minutes had bought a shirt, blue jeans, underwear, socks and a pair of size-twelve tennis shoes, all of which he paid for with his credit card. He tossed Lenny's old clothes into a trash can.

Before emerging back outside, he peered through the store window at the street. It seemed like a perfectly normal mid-December morning in a small town, shoppers strolling beneath a tacky garland of Christmas decorations, a half-dozen cars waiting patiently at a red light. He was just about to step out the door when he spotted the police car creeping down the road. Immediately he ducked behind an undressed mannequin and watched through the nude plastic limbs as the police car made its way slowly past the K Mart and continued in the direction of the hospital. They were obviously searching for someone. Was he the one they wanted?

He couldn't afford to risk a stroll down Main Street. There was no way of knowing who else besides Polowski was involved in the double cross.

It took him at least an hour on foot to reach the outskirts of town, and by then he was so weak and wobbly he could barely stand. The surge of adrenaline that had sent him dashing from the hospital was at last petering out. Too tired to take another step, he sank onto a boulder at the side of the highway and halfheartedly held out his thumb. To his immense relief, the next vehicle to come along—a pickup truck loaded with firewood—pulled over. Victor climbed in and collapsed gratefully on the seat.

The driver spat out the window, then squinted at Victor from beneath an Agway Seeds cap. "Goin' far?"

"Just a few miles. Oak Hill Road."

"Yep. I go right past it." The driver pulled back onto the road. The truck spewed black exhaust as they roared down the highway, country music blaring from the radio.

Through the plucked strains of guitar music, Victor heard a sound that made him sit up sharply. A siren. Whipping his head around, he saw a patrol car zooming up fast behind them. *That's it,* thought Victor. *They've found me. They're going to stop this truck and arrest me....*

But for what? For walking away from the hospital? For insulting Miss Redfern? Or had Polowski fabricated some charge against him?

With a sense of impending doom, he waited for the patrol car to overtake them and start flashing its signal to pull over. In fact, he was so certain they *would* be pulled over that when the police car sped right past them and roared off down the highway, he could only stare ahead in amazement.

"Must be some kinda trouble," his companion said blandly, nodding at the rapidly vanishing police car.

Victor managed to clear his throat. "Trouble?"

"Yep. Don't get much of a chance to use that siren of theirs but when they do, boy oh boy, do they go to town with it."

With his heart hammering against his ribs, Victor sat back and forced himself to calm down. He had nothing to worry about. The police weren't after him, they were busy with some other concern. He wondered what sort of small-town catastrophe could warrant blaring sirens. Probably nothing more exciting than a few kids out on a joyride.

By the time they reached the turnoff to Oak Hill Road, Victor's pulse had settled back to normal. He thanked the driver, climbed out, and began the trek to Catherine Weaver's house. It was a long walk, and the road wound through a forest of pines. Every so often he'd pass a mailbox along the road and, peering through the trees, would spot a house. Catherine's address was coming up fast.

What on earth should he say to her? Up till now he'd concentrated only on reaching her house. Now that he was almost there, he had to come up with some reasonable explanation for why he'd dragged himself out of a hospital bed and trudged all this way to see her. A simple *thanks for saving my life* just wouldn't do it. He had to find out if she had the film canister. But she, of course, would want to know why the damn thing was so important.

You could tell her the truth.

No, forget that. He could imagine her reaction if he were to launch into his wild tale about viruses and dead scientists and double-crossing FBI agents. *The FBI is out to get you? I see. And who else is after you, Mr. Holland?* It was so absurdly paranoid he almost felt like laughing. No, he couldn't tell her any of it or he'd end up right back in a hospital, and this time in a ward that would make Miss Redfern's Three East look like paradise.

She didn't need to know any of it. In fact, she was better off ignorant. The woman had saved his life, and the last thing he wanted to do was put her in any danger. The film was all he wanted from her. After today, she'd never see him again.

He was so busy debating what to tell her that he didn't notice the police cars until well after he'd rounded the road's bend. Suddenly he froze, confronted by three squad cars—probably the entire police fleet of Garberville—parked in front of a rustic cedar house. A half-dozen neighbors lingered in the gravel driveway, shaking their heads in disbelief. Good God, had something happened to Catherine?

Swallowing the urge to turn and flee, Victor propelled himself forward, past the squad cars and through the loose gathering of onlookers, only to be stopped by a uniformed officer.

"I'm sorry, sir. No one's allowed past this point."

Dazed, Victor stared down and saw that the police had strung out a perimeter of red tape. Slowly, his gaze moved beyond the tape, to the old Datsun parked near the carport. Was that Catherine's car? He tried desperately to remember if she'd driven a Datsun, but last night it had been so dark and he'd been in so much pain that he hadn't bothered to pay attention. All he could remember was that it was a compact model, with scarcely enough room for his legs. Then he noticed the faded parking sticker on the rear bumper: Parking Permit, Studio Lot A.

I work for an independent film company, she'd told him last night.

It was Catherine's car.

Unwillingly, he focused on the stained gravel just beside the Datsun, and even though the rational part of him knew that that peculiar brick red could only be dried blood, he wanted to deny it. He wanted to believe there was some other explanation for that stain, for this ominous gathering of police.

He tried to speak, but his voice sounded like something dragged up through gravel.

"What did you say, sir?" the police officer asked.

"What—what happened?"

The officer shook his head sadly. "Woman was killed here last night. Our first murder in ten years."

"*Murder?*" Victor's gaze was still fixed in horror on the blood-stained gravel. "But—*why?*"

The officer shrugged. "Don't know yet. Maybe robbery, though I don't think he got much." He nodded at the Datsun. "Car was the only thing broken into."

If Victor said anything at that point, he never remembered what it was. He was vaguely aware of his legs carrying him back through the onlookers, past the three police cars, toward the road. The sunshine was so brilliant it hurt his eyes and he could barely see where he was going.

I killed her, he thought. *She saved my life and I killed her....*

Guilt slashed its way to his throat and he could scarcely breathe, could barely take another step for the pain. For a long time he stood there at the side of the road, his head bent in the sunshine, his ears filled with the sound of blue jays, and mourned a woman he'd never known.

When at last he was able to raise his head again, rage fueled the rest of his walk back to the highway, rage against Catherine's murderer. Rage at himself for having put her in such danger. It was the film the killer had been searching for, and he'd probably found it in the Datsun. If he hadn't, the house would have been ransacked, as well.

Now what? thought Victor. He dismissed the possibility that his briefcase—with most of the evidence—might still be in his wrecked car. That was the first place the killer would have searched. Without the film, Victor was left with no evidence at all. It would all come down to his word against Viratek's. The newspapers would dismiss him as nothing more than a disgruntled ex-employee. And after Polowski's double cross, he couldn't trust the FBI.

At that last thought, he quickened his pace. The sooner he got out of Garberville, the better. When he got back to the highway, he'd hitch another ride. Once safely out of town, he could take the time to plan his next move.

He decided to head south, to San Francisco.

CHAPTER THREE

From the window of his office at Viratek, Archibald Black watched the limousine glide up the tree-lined driveway and pull to a stop at the front entrance. Black snorted derisively. The cowboy was back in town, damn him. And after all the man's fussing about the importance of secrecy, about keeping his little visit discreet, the idiot had the gall to show up in a limousine—with a uniformed driver, no less.

Black turned from the window and paced over to his desk. Despite his contempt for the visitor, he had to acknowledge the man made him uneasy, the way all so-called men of action made him uneasy. Not enough brains behind all that muscle. Too much power in the hands of imbeciles, he thought. Is this an example of who we have running the country?

The intercom buzzed. "Mr. Black?" said his secretary. "A Mr. Tyrone is here to see you."

"Send him in, please," said Black, smoothing the scorn from his expression. He was wearing a look of polite deference when the door opened and Matthew Tyrone walked into the office.

They shook hands. Tyrone's grip was unreasonably firm, as though he was trying to remind Black of their relative positions of power. His bearing had all the spit and polish of an ex-marine, which Tyrone was. Only the thickening waist betrayed the fact that Tyrone's marine days had been left far behind.

"How was the flight from Washington?" inquired Black as they sat down.

"Terrible service. I tell you, commercial flights aren't what they used to be. To think the average American pays good money for the privilege."

"I imagine it can't compare with Air Force One."

Tyrone smiled. "Let's get down to business. Tell me where things stand with this little crisis of yours."

Black noted Tyrone's use of the word *yours*. *So now it's my problem,* he thought. Naturally. That's what they meant by deniability: When things go wrong, the other guy gets the blame. If any of this leaked out, Black's head would be the one to fall. But then, that's why this contract was so lucrative—because he—meaning Viratek—was willing to take that risk.

"We've recovered the documents," said Black. "And the film canisters. The negatives are being developed now."

"And your two employees?"

Black cleared his throat. "There's no need to take this any further."

"They're a risk to national security."

"You can't just kill them off!"

"Can't we?" Tyrone's eyes were a cold, gun-metal gray. An appropriate color for someone who called himself "the Cowboy." You didn't argue with anyone who had eyes like that. Not if you had an instinct for self-preservation.

Black dipped his head deferentially. "I'm not accustomed to this sort of…business. And I don't like dealing with your man Savitch."

"Mr. Savitch has performed well for us before."

"He killed one of my senior scientists!"

"I assume it was necessary."

Black looked down unhappily at his desk. Just the thought of that monster Savitch made him shudder.

"Why, exactly, did Martinique go bad?"

Because he had a conscience, thought Black. He looked at Tyrone. "There was no way to predict it. He'd worked in commercial R and D for ten years. He'd never presented a security problem before. We only found out last week that he'd taken classified documents. And then Victor Holland got involved…."

"How much does Holland know?"

"Holland wasn't involved with the project. But he's clever. If he looked over those papers, he might have pieced it together."

Now Tyrone was agitated, his fingers drumming the desktop. "Tell me about Holland. What do you know about him?"

"I've gone over his personnel file. He's forty-one years old, born and raised in San Diego. Entered the seminary but dropped out after a year. Went on to Stanford, then MIT. Doctorate in biochemistry. He was with Viratek for four years. One of our most promising researchers.''

''What about his personal life?''

''His wife died three years ago of leukemia. Keeps pretty much to himself these days. Quiet kind of guy, likes classical jazz. Plays the saxophone in some amateur group.''

Tyrone laughed. ''Your typical nerd scientist.'' It was just the sort of moronic comment an ex-marine like Tyrone would make. It was an insult that grated on Black. Years ago, before he created Viratek Industries, Black too had been a research biochemist.

''He should be a simple matter to dispose of,'' said Tyrone. ''Inexperienced. And probably scared.'' He reached for his briefcase. ''Mr. Savitch is an expert on these matters. I suggest you let him take care of the problem.''

''Of course.'' In truth, Black didn't think he had any choice. Nicholas Savitch was like some evil, frightening force that, once unleashed, could not be controlled.

The intercom buzzed. ''Mr. Gregorian's here from the photo lab,'' said the secretary.

''Send him in.'' Black glanced at Tyrone. ''The film's been developed. Let's see just what Martinique managed to photograph.''

Gregorian walked in carrying a bulky envelope. ''Here are those contact prints you requested,'' he said, handing the bundle across the desk to Black. Then he cupped his hand over his mouth, muffling a sound suspiciously like laughter.

''Yes, Mr. Gregorian?'' inquired Black.

''Nothing, sir.''

Tyrone cut in, ''Well, let's see them!''

Black removed the five contact sheets and lay them out on the desk for everyone to see. The men stared.

For a long time, no one spoke. Then Tyrone said, ''Is this some sort of joke?''

Gregorian burst out laughing.

Black said, ''What the hell is this?''

''Those are the negatives you gave me, sir,'' Gregorian insisted. ''I processed them myself.''

"These are the photos you got back from Victor Holland?" Tyrone's voice started soft and rose slowly to a roar. "Five rolls of *naked women?*"

"There's been a mistake," said Black. "It's the wrong film—"

Gregorian laughed harder.

"Shut up!" yelled Black. He looked at Tyrone. "I don't know how this happened."

"Then the roll we want is still out there?"

Black nodded wearily.

Tyrone reached for the phone. "We need to clean things up. Fast."

"Who are you calling?" asked Black.

"The man who can do the job," said Tyrone as he punched in the numbers. "Savitch."

In his motel room on Lombard Street, Victor paced the avocado-green carpet, wracking his brain for a plan. Any plan. His well-organized scientist's mind had already distilled the situation into the elements of a research project. Identify the problem: someone is out to kill me. State your hypothesis: Jerry Martinique uncovered something dangerous and he was killed for it. Now they think I have the information—and the evidence. Which I don't. Goal: Stay alive. Method: *Any damn way I can!*

For the last two days, his only strategy had consisted of holing up in various cheap motel rooms and pacing the carpets. He couldn't hide out forever. If the feds were involved, and he had reason to believe they were, they'd soon have his credit card charges traced, would know exactly where to find him.

I need a plan of attack.

Going to the FBI was definitely out. Sam Polowski was the agent Victor had contacted, the one who'd arranged to meet him in Garberville. No one else should have known about that meeting. Sam Polowski had never shown up.

But someone else had. Victor's aching shoulder was a constant reminder of that near-disastrous rendezvous.

I could go to the newspapers. But how would he convince some skeptical reporter? Who would believe his stories of a project so dangerous it could kill millions? They would think his tale was some fabrication of a paranoid mind.

And I am not paranoid.

He paced over to the TV and switched it on to the five o'clock news. A perfectly coiffed anchorwoman smiled from the screen as she read a piece of fluff about the last day of school, happy children, Christmas vacation. Then her expression sobered. Transition. Victor found himself staring at the TV as the next story came on.

"And in Garberville, California, there have been no new leads in the murder investigation of a woman found slain Wednesday morning. A houseguest found Sarah Boylan, 39, lying in the drive-way, dead of stab wounds to the neck. The victim was five months pregnant. Police say they are puzzled by the lack of motive in this terrible tragedy, and at the present time there are no suspects. Moving on to national news…"

No, no, no! Victor thought. She wasn't pregnant. Her name wasn't Sarah. It's a mistake.…

Or was it?

My name is Catherine, she had told him.

Catherine Weaver. Yes, he was sure of the name. He'd remember it till the day he died.

He sat on the bed, the facts spinning around in his brain. Sarah. Cathy. A murder in Garberville.

When at last he rose to his feet, it was with a swelling sense of urgency, even panic. He grabbed the hotel room phone book and flipped to the *W*s. He understood now. The killer had made a mistake. If Cathy Weaver was still alive, she might have that roll of film—or know where to find it. Victor had to reach her.

Before someone else did.

Nothing could have prepared Cathy for the indescribable sense of gloom she felt upon returning to her flat in San Francisco. She had thought she'd cried out all her tears that night in the Garberville motel, the night after Sarah's death. But here she was, still bursting into tears, then sinking into deep, dark meditations. The drive to the city had been temporarily numbing. But as soon as she'd climbed the steps to her door and confronted the deathly silence of her second-story flat, she felt overwhelmed once again by grief. And bewilderment. Of all the people in the world to die, why Sarah?

She made a feeble attempt at unpacking. Then, forcing herself to stay busy, she surveyed the refrigerator and saw that her shelves were practically empty. It was all the excuse she needed to flee her apartment. She pulled a sweater over her jeans and, with a sense of escape, walked the four blocks to the neighborhood grocery store. She bought only the essentials, bread and eggs and fruit. Enough to tide her over for a few days, until she was back on her feet and could think clearly about any sort of menu.

Carrying a sack of groceries in each arm, she walked through the gathering darkness back to her apartment building. The night was chilly, and she regretted not wearing a coat. Through an open window, a woman called, "Time for dinner!" and two children playing kickball in the street turned and scampered for home.

By the time Cathy reached her building, she was shivering and her arms were aching from the weight of the groceries. She trudged up the steps and, balancing one sack on her hip, managed to pull out her keys and unlock the security door. Just as she swung through, she heard footsteps, then glimpsed a blur of movement rushing toward her from the side. She was swept through the doorway, into the building. A grocery bag tumbled from her arms, spilling apples across the floor. She stumbled forward, catching herself on the wood banister. The door slammed shut behind her.

She spun around, ready to fight off her attacker.

It was Victor Holland.

"You!" she whispered in amazement.

He didn't seem so sure of *her* identity. He was frantically searching her face, as though trying to confirm he had the right woman. "Cathy Weaver?"

"What do you think you're—"

"Where's your apartment?" he cut in.

"What?"

"We can't stand around out here."

"It's—it's upstairs—"

"Let's go." He reached for her arm but she pulled away.

"My groceries," she said, glancing down at the scattered apples.

He quickly scooped up the fruit, tossed it in one of the bags, and nudged her toward the stairs. "We don't have a lot of time."

Cathy allowed herself to be herded up the stairs and halfway down the hall before she stopped dead in her tracks. "Wait a minute. You tell me what this is all about, Mr. Holland, and you tell me right now or I don't move another step!"

"Give me your keys."

"You can't just—"

"Give me your keys!"

She stared at him, shocked by the command. Suddenly she realized that what she saw in his eyes was panic. They were the eyes of a hunted man.

Automatically she handed him her keys.

"Wait here," he said. "Let me check the apartment first."

She watched in bewilderment as he unlocked her door and cautiously eased his way inside. For a few moments she heard nothing. She pictured him moving through the flat, tried to estimate how many seconds each room would require for inspection. It was a small flat, so why was he taking so long?

Slowly she moved toward the doorway. Just as she reached it, his head popped out. She let out a little squeak of surprise. He barely caught the bag of groceries as it slipped from her grasp.

"It's okay," he said. "Come on inside."

The instant she stepped over the threshold, he had the door locked and bolted behind her. Then he quickly circled the living room, closing the drapes, locking windows.

"Are you going to tell me what's going on?" she asked, following him around the room.

"We're in trouble."

"You mean *you're* in trouble."

"No. I mean *we.* Both of us." He turned to her, his gaze clear and steady. "Do you have the film?"

"What are you talking about?" she asked, utterly confused by the sudden shift of conversation.

"A roll of film. Thirty-five millimeter. In a black plastic container. Do you have it?"

She didn't answer. But an image from that last night with Sarah had already taken shape in her mind: a roll of film on the kitchen counter. Film she'd thought belonged to her friend Hickey. Film she'd slipped into her bathrobe pocket and later into her purse. But she wasn't about to reveal any of this, not until she found out why he wanted it. The gaze she returned to him was purposefully blank and unrevealing.

Frustrated, he forced himself to take a deep breath, and started over. "That night you found me—on the highway—I had it in my pocket. It wasn't with me when I woke up in the hospital. I might have dropped it in your car."

"Why do you want this roll of film?"

"I need it. As evidence—"

"For what?"

"It would take too long to explain."

She shrugged. "I've got nothing better to do at the moment—"

"*Damn it!*" He stalked over to her. Taking her by the shoulders, he forced her to look at him. "Don't you understand? That's why your friend was killed! The night they broke into your car, they were looking for that film!"

She stared at him, a look of sudden comprehension and horror. "Sarah..."

"Was in the wrong place at the wrong time. The killer must have thought she was *you.*"

Cathy felt trapped by his unrelenting gaze. And by the inescapable threat of his revelation. Her knees wobbled, gave way. She sank into the nearest chair and sat there in numb silence.

"You have to get out of here," he said. "Before they find you. Before they figure out you're the Cathy Weaver they're looking for."

She didn't move. She couldn't move.

"Come on, Cathy. There isn't much time!"

"What was on that roll of film?" she asked softly.

"I told you. Evidence. Against a company called Viratek."

She frowned. "Isn't—isn't that the company you work for?"

"Used to work for."

"What did they do?"

"They're involved in some sort of illegal research project. I can't tell you the particulars."

"Why not?"

"Because I don't know them. I'm not the one who gathered the evidence. A colleague—a friend—passed it to me, just before he was killed."

"What do you mean by killed?"

"The police called it an accident. I think otherwise."

"You're saying he was murdered over a research project?" She shook her head. "Must have been dangerous stuff he was working on."

"I know this much. It involves biological weapons. Which makes the research illegal. And incredibly dangerous."

"Weapons? For what government?"

"Ours."

"I don't understand. If this is a federal project, that makes it all legal, right?"

"Not by a long shot. People in high places have been known to break the rules."

"How high are we talking about?"

"I don't know. I can't be sure of anyone. Not the police, not the Justice Department. Not the FBI."

Her eyes narrowed. The words she was hearing sounded like paranoid ravings. But the voice—and the eyes—were perfectly sane. They were sea-green, those eyes. They held an honesty, a steadiness that should have been all the assurance she needed.

It wasn't. Not by a long shot.

Quietly she said, "So you're telling me the FBI is after you. Is that correct?"

Sudden anger flared in his eyes, then just as quickly, it was gone. Groaning, he sank onto the couch and ran his hands through his hair. "I don't blame you for thinking I'm nuts. Sometimes I wonder if I'm all there. I thought if I could trust anyone, it'd be you...."

"Why me?"

He looked at her. "Because you're the one who saved my life. You're the one they'll try to kill next."

She froze. No, no, this was insane. Now he was pulling her into his delusion, making her believe in his nightmare world of murder and conspiracy. She wouldn't let him! She stood up and started to walk away, but his voice made her stop again.

"Cathy, think about it. Why was your friend Sarah killed? Because they thought she was *you*. By now they've figured out they killed the wrong woman. They'll have to come back and do the job right. Just in case you know something. In case you have evidence—''

"This is crazy!" she cried, clapping her hands over her ears. "No one's going to—"

"They already have!" He whipped out a scrap of newspaper from his shirt pocket. "On my way over here, I happened to pass a newsstand. This was on the front page." He handed her the piece of paper.

She stared in bewilderment at the photograph of a middle-aged woman, a total stranger. "San Francisco woman shot to death on front doorstep," read the accompanying headline.

"This has nothing to do with me," she said.

"Look at her name."

Cathy's gaze slid to the third paragraph, which identified the victim.

Her name was Catherine Weaver.

The scrap of newsprint slipped from her grasp and fluttered to the floor.

"There are three Catherine Weavers in the San Francisco phone book," he said. "That one was shot to death at nine o'clock this morning. I don't know what's happened to the second. She might already be dead. Which makes you next on the list. They've had enough time to locate you."

"I've been out of town—I only got back an hour ago—"

"Which explains why you're still alive. Maybe they came here earlier. Maybe they decided to check out the other two women first."

She shot to her feet, suddenly frantic with the need to flee. "I have to pack my things—"

"No. Let's just get the hell out of here."

Yes, do what he says! an inner voice screamed at her.

She nodded. Turning, she headed blindly for the door. Halfway there, she halted. "My purse—"

"Where is it?"

She headed back, past a curtained window. "I think I left it by the—"

Her next words were cut off by an explosion of shattering glass. Only the closed curtains kept the shards from piercing her flesh. Pure reflex sent Cathy diving to the floor just as the second gun blast went off. An instant later she found Victor Holland sprawled on top of her, covering her body with his as the third bullet slammed into the far wall, splintering wood and plaster.

The curtains shuddered, then hung still.

For a few seconds Cathy was paralyzed by terror, by the weight of Victor's body on hers. Then panic took hold. She squirmed free, intent on fleeing the apartment.

"Stay down!" Victor snapped.

"They're trying to kill us!"

"Don't make it easy for them!" He dragged her back to the floor. "We're getting out. But not through the front door."

"How—"

"Where's your fire escape?"

"My bedroom window."

"Does it go to the roof?"

"I'm not sure—I think so—"

"Then let's move it."

On hands and knees they crawled down the hall, into Cathy's unlit bedroom. Beneath the window they paused, listening. Outside, in the darkness, there was no sound. Then, from downstairs in the lobby, came the tinkle of breaking glass.

"He's already in the building!" hissed Victor. He yanked open the window. "Out, out!"

Cathy didn't need to be prodded. Hands shaking, she scrambled out and lowered herself onto the fire escape. Victor was right behind her.

"Up," he whispered. "To the roof."

And then what? she wondered, climbing the ladder to the third floor, past Mrs. Chang's flat. Mrs. Chang was out of town this week, visiting her son in New Jersey. The apartment was dark, the windows locked tight. No way in there.

"Keep going," said Victor, nudging her forward.

Only a few more rungs to go.

At last, she pulled herself up and over the edge and onto the asphalt roof. A second later, Victor dropped down beside her. Potted plants shuddered in the darkness. It was Mrs. Chang's rooftop garden, a fragrant mélange of Chinese herbs and vegetables.

Together, Victor and Cathy weaved their way through the plants and crossed to the opposite edge of the roof, where the next building abutted theirs.

"All the way?" said Cathy.

"All the way."

They hopped onto the adjoining roof and ran across to the other side, where three feet of emptiness separated them from the next building. She didn't pause to think of the perils of that leap, she simply flung herself across the gap and kept running, aware that every step took her farther and farther from danger.

On the roof of the fourth building, Cathy finally halted and stared over the edge at the street below. End of the line. It suddenly occurred to her that it was a very long drop to the ground below. The fire escape looked as sturdy as a Tinkertoy.

She swallowed. "This probably isn't a good time to tell you this, but—"

"Tell me what?"

"I'm afraid of heights."

He clambered over the edge. "Then don't look down."

Right, she thought, slithering onto the fire escape. *Don't look down.* Her palms were so slick with sweat she could barely grip the rungs. Suddenly seized by an attack of vertigo, she froze there, clinging desperately to that flimsy steel skeleton.

"Don't stop now!" Victor whispered up to her. "Just keep moving!"

Still she didn't move. She pressed her face against the rung, so hard she felt the rough edge bite into her flesh.

"You're okay, Cathy!" he said. "Come on."

The pain became all-encompassing, blocking out the dizziness, even the fear. When she opened her eyes again, the world had steadied. On rubbery legs, she descended the ladder, pausing on the third floor landing to wipe her sweaty palms on her jeans. She continued downward, to the second-floor landing. It was still a good fifteen-foot drop to the ground. She unlatched the extension ladder and started to slide it down, but it let out such a screech that Victor immediately stopped her.

"Too noisy. We have to jump!"

"But—"

To her astonishment, he scrambled over the railing and dropped to the ground. "Come on!" he hissed from below. "It's not that far. I'll catch you."

Murmuring a prayer, she lowered herself over the side and let go.

To her surprise he did catch her—but held on only for a second. The bullet wound had left his injured shoulder too weak to hold on. They both tumbled to the ground. She landed smack on top of him, her legs astride his hips, their faces inches apart. They stared at each other, so stunned they could scarcely breathe.

Upstairs, a window slid open and someone yelled, "Hey, you bums! If you don't clear out this instant, I'm calling the cops!"

Instantly Cathy rolled off Victor, only to stagger into a trash can. The lid fell off and slammed like a cymbal against the sidewalk.

"That's it for rest stops," Victor grunted and scrambled to his feet. *"Move it."*

They took off at a wild dash down the street, turned up an alley, and kept running. It was a good five blocks before they finally stopped to catch their breath. They glanced back.

The street was deserted.

They were safe!

Nicholas Savitch stood beside the neatly made bed and surveyed the room. It was every inch a woman's room, from the closet hung with a half-dozen simple but elegant dresses, to the sweetly scented powders and lotions lined up on the vanity table. It took only a single circuit around the room to tell him about the woman whose bedroom this was. She was slim, a size seven dress, size six-and-a-half shoe. The hairs on the brush were brown and shoulder-length. She owned only a few pieces of jewelry, and she favored natural scents, rosewater and lavender. Her favorite color was green.

Back in the living room, he continued to gather information. The woman subscribed to the Hollywood trade journals. Her taste in music, like her taste in books, was eclectic. He noticed a scrap of newspaper lying on the floor. He picked it up and glanced at the article. Now this was interesting. The death of Catherine Weaver I had not gone unnoticed by Catherine Weaver III.

He pocketed the article. Then he saw the purse, lying on the floor near the shattered window.

Bingo.

He emptied the contents on the coffee table. Out tumbled a wallet, checkbook, pens, loose change, and…an address book. He opened it to the *B*s. There he found the name he was looking for: Sarah Boylan.

He now knew this was the Catherine Weaver he'd been seeking. What a shame he'd wasted his time hunting down the other two.

He flipped through the address book and spotted a half dozen or so San Francisco listings. The woman may have been clever enough to slip away from him this time. But staying out of sight was a more difficult matter. And this little book, with its names of friends and relatives and colleagues, could lead him straight to her.

Somewhere in the distance, a police siren was wailing.

It was time to leave.

Savitch took the address book and the woman's wallet and headed out the door. Outside, his breath misted in the cold air as he walked at a leisurely pace down the street,

He could afford to take his time.

But for Catherine Weaver and Victor Holland, time was running out.

CHAPTER FOUR

There was no time to rest. They jogged for the next six blocks, miles and miles, it seemed to Cathy. Victor moved tirelessly, leading her down side streets, avoiding busy intersections. She let him do the thinking and navigating. Her terror slowly gave way to numbness and a disorienting sense of unreality. The city itself seemed little more than a dreamscape, asphalt and streetlights and endless twists and turns of concrete. The only reality was the man striding close beside her, his gaze alert, his movements swift and sure. She knew he too must be afraid, but she couldn't see his fear.

He took her hand; the warmth of that grasp, the strength of those fingers, seemed to flow into her cold, exhausted limbs.

She quickened her pace. "I think there's a police substation down that street," she said. "If we go a block or two further—"

"We're not going to the police."

"What?" She stopped dead, staring at him.

"Not yet. Not until I've had a chance to think this through."

"Victor," she said slowly. "Someone is trying to kill us. Trying to kill *me*. What do you mean, you need time to *think this through?*"

"Look, we can't stand around talking about it. We have to get off the streets." He grabbed her hand again. "Come on."

"Where?"

"I have a room. It's only a few blocks away."

She let him drag her only a few yards before she mustered the will to pull free. "Wait a minute. Just *wait.*"

He turned, his face a mask of frustration, and confronted her. "Wait for what? For that maniac to catch up? For the bullets to start flying again?"

"For an explanation!"

"I'll explain it all. When we're safe."

She backed away. "Why are you afraid of the police?"

"I can't be sure of them."

"Do you have a reason to be afraid? What have you done?"

With two steps he closed the gap between them and grabbed her hard by the shoulders. "I just pulled you out of a death trap, remember? The bullets were going through your window, not mine!"

"Maybe they were aimed at you!"

"Okay!" He let her go, let her back away from him. "You want to try it on your own? Do it. Maybe the police'll be a help. Maybe not. But I can't risk it. Not until I know all the players behind this."

"You—you're letting me go?"

"You were never my prisoner."

"No." She took a breath—it misted in the cold air. She glanced down the street, toward the police substation. "It's…the reasonable thing to do," she muttered, almost to reassure herself. "That's what they're there for."

"Right."

She frowned, anticipating what lay ahead. "They'll ask a lot of questions."

"What are you going to tell them?"

She looked at him, her gaze unflinchingly meeting his. "The truth."

"Which'll be at best, incomplete. And at worst, unbelievable."

"I have broken glass all over my apartment to prove it."

"A drive-by shooting. Purely random."

"It's their job to protect me."

"What if they don't think you need protection?"

"I'll tell them about you! About Sarah."

"They may or may not take you seriously."

"They have to take me seriously! Someone's trying to kill me!" Her voice, shrill with desperation, seemed to echo endlessly through the maze of streets.

Quietly he said, "I know."

She glanced back toward the substation. "I'm going."

He said nothing.

"Where will you be?" she asked.

"On my own. For now."

She took two steps away, then stopped. "Victor?"

"I'm still here."

"You did save my life. Thank you."

He didn't respond. She heard his footsteps slowly walk away. She stood there thinking, wondering if she was doing the right thing. Of course she was. A man afraid of the police—with a story as paranoid as his was—had to be dangerous.

But he saved my life.

And once, on a rainy night in Garberville, she had saved his.

She replayed all the events of the last week. Sarah's murder, never explained. The other Catherine Weaver, shot to death on her front doorstep. The film canister that Sarah had retrieved from the car, the one Cathy had slipped into her bathrobe pocket...

Victor's footsteps had faded.

In that instant she realized she'd lost the only man who could help her find the answers to all those questions, the one man who'd stood by her in her darkest moment of terror. The one man she knew, by some strange intuition, she could trust. Facing that deserted street, she felt abandoned and utterly friendless. In sudden panic, she whirled around and called out: "Victor!"

At the far end of the block, a silhouette stopped and turned. He seemed an island of refuge in that crazy, dangerous world. She started toward him, her legs moving her faster and faster, until she was running, yearning for the safety of his arms, the arms of a man she scarcely knew. Yet it didn't feel like a stranger's arms gathering her to his chest, welcoming her into his protective embrace. She felt the pounding of his heart, the grip of his fingers against her back, and something told her that this was a man she could depend upon, a man who wouldn't fold when she needed him most.

"I'm right here," he murmured. "Right here." He stroked through her windblown hair, his fingers burying deep in the tangled strands. She felt the heat of his breath against her face, felt her own quick and shuddering response. And then, all at once, his mouth hungrily sought hers and he was kissing her. She responded with a kiss just as desperate, just as needy. Stranger though he was, he had been there for her and he was still here, his arms sheltering her from the terrors of the night.

She burrowed her face against his chest, longing to press ever deeper, ever closer. "I don't know what to do! I'm so afraid, Victor, and I don't know what to do...."

"We'll work this out together. Okay?" He cupped her face in his hands and tilted it up to his. "You and I, we'll beat this thing."

She nodded. Searching his eyes, connecting with that rock-solid gaze, she found all the assurance she needed.

A wind gusted down the street. She shivered in its wake. "What do we do first?" she whispered.

"First," he said, pulling off his windbreaker and draping it over her shoulders, "We get you warmed up. And inside." He took her hand. "Come on. A hot bath, a good supper, and you'll be operating on all cylinders again."

It was another five blocks to the Kon-Tiki Motel. Though not exactly a five-star establishment, the Kon-Tiki was comfortingly drab and anonymous, one of a dozen on motel row. They climbed the steps to Room 214, overlooking the half-empty parking lot. He unlocked the door and motioned her inside.

The rush of warmth against her cheeks was delicious. She stood in the center of that utterly charmless space and marveled at how good it felt to be safely surrounded by four walls. The furnishings were spare: a double bed, a dresser, two nightstands with lamps, and a single chair. On the wall was a framed print of some nameless South Pacific island. The only luggage she saw was a cheap nylon bag on the floor. The bedcovers were rumpled, recently napped in, the pillows punched up against the headboard.

"Not much," he said. "But it's warm. And it's paid for." He turned on the TV. "We'd better keep an eye on the news. Maybe they'll have something on the Weaver woman."

The Weaver woman, she thought. *It could have been me.* She was shivering again, but now it wasn't from the cold. Settling onto the bed she stared numbly at the TV, not really seeing what was on the screen. She was more aware of *him.* He was circling the room, checking the windows, fiddling with the lock on the door. He moved quietly, efficiently, his silence a testimony to the dangers of their situation. Most men she knew began to babble nonsense when they were scared; Victor Holland simply turned quiet. His mere presence was overwhelming. He seemed to fill the room.

He moved to her side. She flinched as he took her hands and

gently inspected them, palm side up. Looking down, she saw the bloodied scratches, the flakes of rust from the fire escape embedded in her skin.

"I guess I'm a mess," she murmured.

He smiled and stroked her face. "You could use some washing up. Go ahead. I'll get us something to eat."

She retreated into the bathroom. Through the door she could hear the drone of the TV, the sound of Victor's voice ordering a pizza over the phone. She ran hot water over her cold, numb hands. In the mirror over the sink she caught an unflattering glimpse of herself, her hair a tangled mess, her chin smudged with dirt. She washed her face, rubbing new life, new circulation into those frigid cheeks. Glancing down, she noticed Victor's razor on the counter. The sight of that blade cast her situation into a new focus—a frightening one. She picked up the razor, thinking how lethal that blade looked, how vulnerable she would be tonight. Victor was a large man, at least six foot two, with powerful arms. She was scarcely five foot five, a comparative weakling. There was only one bed in the next room. She had come here voluntarily. What would he assume about her? That she was a willing victim? She thought of all the ways a man could hurt her, kill her. It wouldn't take a razor to finish the job. Victor could use his bare hands. *What am I doing here?* she wondered. *Spending the night with a man I scarcely know?*

This was not the time to have doubts. She'd made the decision. She had to go by her instincts, and her instincts told her Victor Holland would never hurt her.

Deliberately she set down the razor. She would have to trust him. She was afraid not to.

In the other room, a door slammed shut. Had he left?

Opening the door a crack, she peered out. The TV was still on. There was no sign of Victor. Slowly she emerged, to find she was alone. She began to circle the room, searching for clues, anything that would tell her more about the man. The bureau drawers were empty, and so was the closet. Obviously he had not moved into this room for a long stay. He'd planned only one night, maybe two. She went to the nylon bag and glanced inside. She saw a clean pair of socks, an unopened package of underwear, and a day-old edition of the *San Francisco Chronicle.* All it told her was that the man kept himself informed and he traveled light.

Like a man on the run.

She dug deeper and came up with a receipt from an automatic teller machine. Yesterday he'd tried to withdraw cash. The machine had printed out the message: *Transaction cannot be completed. Please contact your bank.* Why had it refused him the cash? she wondered. Was he overdrawn? Had the machine been out of order?

The sound of a key grating in the lock caught her by surprise. She glanced up as the door swung open.

The look he gave her made her cheeks flush with guilt. Slowly she rose to her feet, unable to answer that look of accusation in his eyes.

The door swung shut behind him.

"I suppose it's a reasonable thing for you to do," he said. "Search my things."

"I'm sorry. I was just..." She swallowed. "I had to know more about you."

"And what terrible things have you dug up?"

"Nothing!"

"No deep dark secrets? Don't be afraid. Tell me, Cathy."

"Only...only that you had trouble getting cash out of your account."

He nodded. "A frustrating state of affairs. Since by my estimate I have a balance of six thousand dollars. And now I can't seem to touch it." He sat down in the chair, his gaze still on her face. "What else did you learn?"

"You—you read the newspaper."

"So do a lot of people. What else?"

She shrugged. "You wear boxer shorts."

Amusement flickered in his eyes. "Now we're getting personal."

"You..." She took a deep breath. "You're on the run."

He looked at her a long time without saying a word.

"That's why you won't go to the police," she said. "Isn't it?"

He turned away, gazing not at her but at the far wall. "There are reasons."

"Give me one, Victor. One good reason is all I need and then I'll shut up."

He sighed. "I doubt it."

"Try me. I have every reason to believe you."

"You have every reason to think I'm paranoid." Leaning forward, he ran his hands over his face. "Lord, sometimes *I* think I must be."

Quietly she went to him and knelt down beside his chair. "Victor, these people who are trying to kill me—who are they?"

"I don't know."

"You said it might involve people in high places."

"It's just a guess. It's a case of federal money going to illegal research. Deadly research."

"And federal money has to be doled out by someone in authority."

He nodded. "This is someone who's bent the rules. Someone who could be hurt by a political scandal. He just might try to protect himself by manipulating the Bureau. Or even your local police. That's why I won't go to them. That's why I left the room to make my call."

"When?"

"While you were in the bathroom. I went to a pay phone and called the police. I didn't want it traced."

"You just said you don't want them involved."

"This call I had to make. There's a third Catherine Weaver in that phone book. Remember?"

A third victim on the list. Suddenly weak, she sat down on the bed. "What did you say?" she asked softly.

"That I had reason to think she might be in danger. That she wasn't answering her phone."

"You tried it?"

"Twice."

"Did they listen to you?"

"Not only did they listen, they demanded to know my name. That's when I picked up the cue that something must already have happened to her. At that point I hung up and hightailed it out of the booth. A call can be traced in seconds. They could've had me surrounded."

"That makes three," she whispered. "Those two other women. And me."

"They have no way of finding you. Not as long as you stay away from your apartment. Stay out of—"

They both froze in panic.

Someone was knocking on the door.

They stared at each other, fear mirrored in their eyes. Then, after a moment's hesitation, Victor said: "Who is it?"

"Domino's," called a thin voice.

Cautiously, Victor eased open the door. A teenage boy stood outside, wielding a bag and a flat cardboard box.

"Hi!" chirped the boy. "A large combo with the works, two Cokes and extra napkins. Right?"

"Right." Victor handed the boy a few bills. "Keep the change," he said and closed the door. Turning, he gave Cathy a sheepish look. "Well," he admitted. "Just goes to show you. Sometimes a knock at the door really is just the pizza man."

They both laughed, a sound not of humor but of frayed nerves. The release of tension seemed to transform his face, melted his wariness to warmth. Erase those haggard lines, she thought, and he could almost be called a handsome man.

"I tell you what," he said. "Let's not think about this mess right now. Why don't we just get right down to the really important issue of the day. Food."

Nodding, she reached out for the box. "Better hand it over. Before I eat the damn bedspread."

While the ten o'clock news droned from the television set, they tore into the pizza like two ravenous animals. It was a greasy and utterly satisfying banquet on a motel bed. They scarcely bothered with conversation—their mouths were too busy devouring cheese and pepperoni. On the TV, a dapper anchorman announced a shakeup in the mayor's office, the resignation of the city manager, news that, given their current situation, seemed ridiculously trivial. Scarcely thirty seconds were devoted to that morning's killing of Catherine Weaver I; as yet, no suspects were in custody. No mention was made of any second victim by the same name.

Victor frowned. "Looks like the other woman didn't make it to the news."

"Or nothing's happened to her." She glanced at him questioningly. "What if the second Cathy Weaver is all right? When you called the police, they might've been asking you routine questions. When you're on edge, it's easy to—''

"Imagine things?" The look he gave her almost made her bite her tongue.

"No," she said quietly. "Misinterpret. The police can't respond to every anonymous call. It's natural they'd ask for your name."

"It was more than a request, Cathy. They were champing at the bit to interrogate me."

"I'm not doubting your word. I'm just playing devil's advocate. Trying to keep things level and sane in a crazy situation."

He looked at her long and hard. At last he nodded. "The voice of a rational woman," he sighed. "Exactly what I need right now. To keep me from jumping at my own shadow."

"And remind you to eat." She held out another slice of pizza. "You ordered this giant thing. You'd better help me finish it."

The tension between them instantly evaporated. He settled onto the bed and accepted the proferred slice. "That maternal look becomes you," he noted wryly. "So does the pizza sauce."

"What?" She swiped at her chin.

"You look like a two-year-old who's decided to fingerpaint her face."

"Good grief, can you hand me the napkins?"

"Let me do it." Leaning forward, he gently dabbed away the sauce. As he did, she studied his face, saw the laugh lines creasing the corners of his eyes, the strands of silver intertwined with the brown hair. She remembered the photo of that very face, pasted on a Viratek badge. How somber he'd looked, the unsmiling portrait of a scientist. Now he appeared young and alive and almost happy.

Suddenly aware that she was watching him, he looked up and met her gaze. Slowly his smile faded. They both went very still, as though seeing, in each other's eyes, something they had not noticed before. The voices on the television seemed to fade into a far-off dimension. She felt his fingers trace lightly down her cheek. It was only a touch, but it left her shivering.

She asked, softly, "What happens now, Victor? Where do we go from here?"

"We have several choices."

"Such as?"

"I have friends in Palo Alto. We could turn to them."

"Or?"

"Or we could stay right where we are. For a while."

Right where we are. In this room, on this bed. She wouldn't mind that. Not at all.

She felt herself leaning toward him, drawn by a force against which she could offer no resistance. Both his hands came up to cradle her face, such large hands, but so infinitely gentle. She closed her eyes, knowing that this kiss, too, would be a gentle one.

And it was. This wasn't a kiss driven by fear or desperation. This was a quiet melting together of warmth, of souls. She swayed against him, felt his arms circle behind her to pull her inescapably close. It was a dangerous moment. She could feel herself tottering on the edge of total surrender to this man she scarcely knew. Already, her arms had found their way around his neck and her hands were roaming through the silver-streaked thickness of his hair.

His kisses dropped to her neck, exploring all the tender rises and hollows of her throat. All the needs that had lain dormant these past few years, all the hungers and desires, seemed to stir inside her, awakening at his touch.

And then, in an instant, the magic slipped away. At first she didn't understand why he suddenly pulled back. He sat bolt upright. The expression on his face was one of frozen astonishment. Bewildered, she followed his gaze and saw that he was focused on the television set behind her. She turned to see what had captured his attention.

A disturbingly familiar face stared back from the screen. She recognized the Viratek logo at the top, the straight-ahead gaze of the man in the photo. Why on earth would they be broadcasting Victor Holland's ID badge?

"...Sought on charges of industrial espionage. Evidence now links Dr. Holland to the death of a fellow Viratek researcher, Dr. Gerald Martinique. Investigators fear the suspect has already sold extensive research data to a European competitor...."

Neither one of them seemed able to move from the bed. They could only stare in disbelief at the newscaster with the Ken doll haircut. The station switched to a commercial break, raisins dancing crazily on a field, proclaiming the wonders of California sunshine. The lilting music was unbearable.

Victor rose to his feet and flicked off the television.

Slowly he turned to look at her. The silence between them grew agonizing.

"It's not true," he said quietly. "None of it."

She tried to read those unfathomable green eyes, wanting desperately to believe him. The taste of his kisses were still warm on her lips. The kisses of a con artist? *Is this just another lie? Has everything you've told me been nothing but lies? Who and what are you, Victor Holland?*

She glanced sideways, at the telephone on the bedside stand. It was so close. One call to the police, that's all it would take to end this nightmare.

"It's a frame-up," he said. "Viratek's releasing false information."

"Why?"

"To corner me. What easier way to find me than to have the police help them?"

She edged toward the phone.

"Don't, Cathy."

She froze, startled by the threat in his voice.

He saw the instant fear in her eyes. Gently he said, "Please. Don't call. I won't hurt you. I promise you can walk right out that door if you want. But first listen to me. Let me tell you what happened. Give me a chance."

His gaze was steady and absolutely believable. And he was right beside her, ready to stop her from making a move. Or to break her arm, if need be. She had no other choice. Nodding, she settled back down on the bed.

He began to pace, his feet tracing a path in the dull green carpet.

"It's all some—some incredible lie," he said. "It's crazy to think I'd kill him. Jerry Martinique and I were the best of friends. We both worked at Viratek. I was in vaccine development, he was a microbiologist. His specialty was viral studies. Genome research."

"You mean—like chromosomes?"

"The viral equivalent. Anyway, Jerry and I, we helped each other through some bad times. He'd gone through a painful divorce and I…" He paused, his voice dropping. "I lost my wife three years ago. To leukemia."

So he'd been married. Somehow it surprised her. He seemed like the sort of man who was far too independent to have ever said, "I do."

"About two months ago," he continued, "Jerry was transferred to a new research department. Viratek had been awarded a grant for some defense project. It was top security—Jerry couldn't talk about it. But I could see he was bothered by something that was going on in that lab. All he'd say to me was, 'They don't understand the danger. They don't know what they're getting into.' Jerry's field was the alteration of viral genes. So I assume the project had something to do with viruses as weapons. Jerry was fully aware that those weapons are outlawed by international agreement."

"If he knew it was illegal, why did he take part in it?"

"Maybe he didn't realize at first what the project was aiming for. Maybe they sold it to him as purely defensive research. In any event, he got upset enough to resign from the project. He went right to the top—the founder of Viratek. Walked into Archibald Black's office and threatened to go public if the project wasn't terminated. Four days later he had an accident." Anger flashed in Victor's eyes. It wasn't directed at her, but the fury in that gaze was frightening all the same.

"What happened to him?" she asked.

"His wrecked car was found at the side of the road. Jerry was still inside. Dead, of course." Suddenly, the anger was gone, replaced by overwhelming weariness. He sank onto the bed. "I thought the accident investigation would blow everything into the open. It was a farce. The local cops did their best, but then some federal transportation "expert" showed up on the scene and took over. He said Jerry must've fallen asleep at the wheel. Case closed. That's when I realized just how deep this went. I didn't know who to go to, so I called the FBI in San Francisco. Told them I had evidence."

"You mean the film?" asked Cathy.

Victor nodded. "Just before he was killed, Jerry told me about some duplicate papers he'd stashed away in his garden shed. After the…accident, I went over to his house. Found the place ransacked. But they never bothered to search the shed. That's how I got hold of the evidence, a single file and a roll of film. I arranged a meeting with one of the San Francisco agents, a guy named Sam Polowski. I'd already talked to him a few times on the phone. He offered to meet me in Garberville. We wanted to keep it private, so we agreed to a spot just outside of town. I drove down, fully expecting him to show. Well, someone showed up, all right. Someone who ran me off the road.'' He paused and looked straight at her. ''That's the night you found me.''

The night my whole life changed, she thought.

''You have to believe me,'' he said.

She studied him, her instincts battling against logic. The story was just barely plausible, halfway between truth and fantasy. But the man looked solid as stone.

Wearily she nodded. ''I do believe you, Victor. Maybe I'm crazy. Or just gullible. But I do.''

The bed shifted as he sat down beside her. They didn't touch, yet she could almost feel the warmth radiating between them.

''That's all that matters to me right now,'' he said. ''That you know, in your heart, I'm telling the truth.''

''In my heart?'' She shook her head and laughed. ''My heart's always been a lousy judge of character. No, I'm guessing. I'm going by the fact you kept me alive. By the fact there's another Cathy Weaver who's now dead…''

Remembering the face of that other woman, the face in the newspaper, she suddenly began to shake. It all added up to the terrible truth. The gun blasts into her apartment, the other dead Cathy. And Sarah, poor Sarah.

She was gulping in shaky breaths, hovering on the verge of tears.

She let him take her in his arms, let him pull her down on the bed beside him. He murmured into her hair, gentle words of comfort and reassurance. He turned off the lamp. In darkness they held each other, two frightened souls joined against a terrifying world. She felt safe there, tucked away against his chest. This was a place where no one could hurt her. It was a stranger's arms, but from the smell of his shirt to the beat of his heart, it all seemed somehow familiar. She never wanted to leave that spot, ever.

She trembled as his lips brushed her forehead. He was stroking her face now, her neck, warming her with his touch. When his hand slipped beneath her blouse, she didn't protest. Somehow it seemed so natural, that that hand would come to lie at her breast. It wasn't the touch of a marauder, it was simply a gentle reminder that she was in safekeeping.

And yet, she found herself responding....

Her nipple tingled and grew taut beneath his cupping hand. The tingling spread, a warmth that crept to her face and flushed her cheeks. She reached for his shirt and began to unbutton it. In the darkness she was slow and clumsy. By the time she finally slid her hand under the fabric, they were both breathing hard and fast with anticipation.

She brushed through the coarse mat of hair, stroking her way across that broad chest. He took in a sharp breath as her fingers skimmed a delicate circle around his nipple.

If playing with fire had been her intention, then she had just struck the match.

His mouth was suddenly on hers, seeking, devouring. The force of his kiss pressed her onto her back, trapping her head against the pillows. For a dizzy eternity she was swimming in sensations, the scent of male heat, the unyielding grip of his hands imprisoning her face. Only when he at last drew away did they both come up for air.

He stared down at her, as though hovering on the edge of temptation.

"This is crazy," he whispered.

"Yes. Yes, it is—"

"I never meant to do this—"

"Neither did I."

"It's just that you're scared. We're both scared. And we don't know what the hell we're doing."

"No." She closed her eyes, felt the unexpected bite of tears. "We don't. But I *am* scared. And I just want to be held. Please, Victor. Hold me, that's all. Just hold me."

He pulled her close, murmuring her name. This time the embrace was gentle, without the fever of desire. His shirt was still unbuttoned, his chest bared. And that's where she lay her head, against that curling nest of hair. Yes, he was right, so wise. They were crazy to be making love when they both knew it was fear, nothing else, that had driven their desire. And now the fever had broken.

A sense of peace fell over her. She curled up against him. Exhaustion robbed them both of speech. Her muscles gradually fell limp as sleep tugged her into its shadow. Even if she tried to, she could not move her arms or legs. Instead she was drifting free, like a wraith in the darkness, floating somewhere in a warm and inky sea.

Vaguely she was aware of light sliding past her eyelids.

The warmth encircling her body seemed to melt away. No, she wanted it back, wanted *him* back! An instant later she felt him shaking her.

"Cathy. Come on, wake up!"

Through drowsy eyes she peered at him. "Victor?"

"Something's going on outside."

She tumbled out of bed and followed him to the window. Through a slit in the curtains she spotted what had alarmed him: a patrol car, its radio crackling faintly, parked by the motel registration door. At once she snapped wide awake, her mind going over the exits from their room. There was only one.

"Out, now!" he ordered. "Before we're trapped."

He eased open the door. They scrambled out onto the walkway. The frigid night air was like a slap in the face. She was already shivering, more from fear than from the cold. Running at a crouch, they moved along the walkway, away from the stairs, and ducked past the ice machine.

Below, they heard the lobby door open and the voice of the motel manager: "Yeah, that'll be right upstairs. Gee, he sure seemed like a nice-enough guy...."

Tires screeched as another patrol car pulled up, lights flashing.

Victor gave her a push. *"Go!"*

They slipped into a breezeway and scurried through, to the other side of the building. No stairways there! They climbed over the walkway railing and dropped into the parking lot.

Faintly they heard a banging, then the command: "Open up! This is the police."

At once they were sprinting instinctively for the shadows. No one spotted them, no one gave chase. Still they kept running, until they'd left the Kon-Tiki Motel blocks and blocks behind them, until they were so tired they were stumbling.

At last Cathy slowed to a halt and leaned back against a doorway, her breath coming out in clouds of cold mist. "How did they find you?" she said between gasps.

"It couldn't have been the call...." Suddenly he groaned. "My credit card! I had to use it to pay the bill."

"Where now? Should we try another motel?"

He shook his head. "I'm down to my last forty bucks. I can't risk a credit card again."

"And I left my purse at the apartment. I—I'm not sure I want to—"

"We're not going back for it. They'll be watching the place."

They. Meaning the killers.

"So we're broke," she said weakly.

He didn't answer. He stood with his hands in his pockets, his whole body a study in frustration. "You have friends you can go to?"

"I think so. Uh, no. She's out of town till Friday. And what would I tell her? How would I explain you?"

"You can't. And we can't handle any questions right now."

That leaves out most of my friends, she thought. Nowhere to go, no one to turn to. Unless...

No, she'd promised herself never to sink that low, never to beg for *that* particular source of help.

Victor glanced up the street. "There's a bus stop over there." He reached in his pocket and took out a handful of money. "Here," he said. "Take it and get out of the city. Go visit some friends on your own."

"What about you?"

"I'll be okay."

"Broke? With everyone after you?" She shook her head.

"I'll only make things more dangerous for you." He pressed the money into her hand.

She stared down at the wad of bills, thinking: *This is all he has. And he's giving it to me.* "I can't," she said.

"You have to."

"But—"

"*Don't argue with me.*" The look in his eyes left no alternative. Reluctantly she closed her fingers around the money.

"I'll wait till you get on the bus. It should take you right past the station."

"Victor?"

He silenced her with a single look. Placing both hands on her shoulders, he stood her before him. "You'll be fine," he said. Then he pressed a kiss to her forehead. For a moment his lips lingered, and the warmth of his breath in her hair left her trembling. "I wouldn't leave you if I thought otherwise."

The roar of a bus down the block made them both turn.

"There's your limousine," he whispered. "Go." He gave her a nudge. "Take care of yourself, Cathy."

She started toward the bus stop. Three steps, four. She slowed and came to a halt. Turning, she saw that he had already edged away into the shadows.

"Get on it!" he called.

She looked at the bus. *I won't do it,* she thought.

She turned back to Victor. "I know a place! A place we can both stay!"

"What?"

"I didn't want to use it but—"

Her words were drowned out as the bus wheezed to the stop, then roared away.

"It's a bit of a walk," she said. "But we'd have beds and a meal. And I can guarantee no one would call the police."

He came out of the shadows. "Why didn't you think of this earlier?"

"I did think of it. But up till now, things weren't, well...desperate enough."

"Not desperate enough," he repeated slowly. He moved toward her, his face taut with incredulity. "Not *desperate* enough? Hell, lady. I'd like to know exactly what kind of crisis would qualify!"

"You have to understand, this is a last resort. It's not an easy place for me to turn to."

His eyes narrowed in suspicion. "This place is beginning to sound worse and worse. What are we talking about? A flophouse?"

"No, it's in Pacific Heights. You could even call the place a mansion."

"Who lives there? A friend?"

"Quite the opposite."

His eyebrow shot up. "An enemy?"

"Close." She let out a sigh of resignation. "My ex-husband."

CHAPTER FIVE

"Jack, open up! Jack!" Cathy banged again and again on the door of the formidable Pacific Heights home. There was no answer. Through the windows they saw only darkness.

"Damn you, Jack!" She gave the door a slap of frustration. "Why aren't you *ever* home when I need you?"

Victor glanced around at the neighborhood of elegant homes and neatly trimmed shrubbery. "We can't stand around out here all night."

"We're not going to," she muttered. Crouching on her knees, she began to dig around in a red-brick planter.

"What are you doing?"

"Something I swore I'd never do." Her fingers raked the loamy soil, searching for the key Jack kept buried under the geraniums. Sure enough, there it was, right where it had always been. She rose to her feet, clapping the dirt off her hands. "But there are limits to my pride. Threat of death being one of them." She inserted the key and felt a momentary dart of panic when it didn't turn. But with a little jiggling, the lock at last gave way. The door swung open to the faint gleam of a polished wood floor, a massive bannister.

She motioned Victor inside. The solid thunk of the door closing behind them seemed to shut out all the dangers of the night. Cloaked in the darkness, they both let out a sigh of relief.

"Just what kind of terms are you on with your ex-husband?" Victor asked, following her blindly through the unlit foyer.

"Speaking. Barely."

"He doesn't mind you wandering around his house?"

"Why not?" She snorted. "Jack lets half the human race wander through his bedroom. The only prerequisite being XX chromosomes."

She felt her way into the pitch-dark living room and flipped on the light switch. There she froze in astonishment and stared at the two naked bodies intertwined on the polar bear rug.

"*Jack!*" she blurted out.

The larger of the two bodies extricated himself and sat up. "Hello, Cathy!" He raked his hand through his dark hair and grinned. "Seems like old times."

The woman lying next to him spat out a shocking obscenity, scrambled to her feet, and stormed off in a blur of wild red hair and bare bottom toward the bedroom.

"That's Lulu," yawned Jack, by way of introduction.

Cathy sighed. "I see your taste in women hasn't improved."

"No, sweetheart, my taste in women hit a high point when I married you." Unmindful of his state of nudity, Jack rose to his feet and regarded Victor. The contrast between the two men was instantly apparent. Though both were tall and lean, it was Jack who possessed the striking good looks, and he knew it. He'd always known it. Vanity wasn't a label one could ever pin on Victor Holland.

"I see you brought a fourth," said Jack, giving Victor the once-over. "So, what'll it be, folks? Bridge or poker?"

"Neither," said Cathy.

"That opens up all *sorts* of possibilities."

"Jack, I need your help."

He turned and looked at her with mock incredulity. *"No!"*

"You know damn well I wouldn't be here if I could avoid it!"

He winked at Victor. "Don't believe her. She's still madly in love with me."

"Can we get serious?"

"Darling, you never did have a sense of humor."

"*Damn you,* Jack!" Everyone had a breaking point and Cathy had reached hers. She couldn't help it; without warning she burst into tears. "For once in your life will you *listen* to me?"

That's when Victor's patience finally snapped. He didn't need a degree in psychology to know this Jack character was a first-class jerk. Couldn't he see that Cathy was exhausted and terrified? Up till this moment, Victor had admired her for her strength. Now he ached at the sight of her vulnerability.

It was only natural to pull her into his arms, to ease her tear-streaked face against his chest. Over her shoulder, he growled out an oath that impugned not only Jack's name but that of Jack's mother as well.

The other man didn't seem to take offense, probably because he'd been called far worse names, and on a regular basis. He simply crossed his arms and regarded Victor with a raised eyebrow. "Being protective, are we?"

"She needs protection."

"From what, pray tell?"

"Maybe you haven't heard. Three days ago, someone murdered her friend Sarah."

"Sarah...Boylan?"

Victor nodded. "Tonight, someone tried to kill Cathy."

Jack stared at him. He looked at his ex-wife. "Is this true? What he's saying?"

Cathy, wiping away tears, nodded.

"Why didn't you tell me this to begin with?"

"Because you were acting like an ass to begin with!" she shot back.

Down the hall came the *click-click* of high-heeled shoes. "She's absolutely right!" yelled a female voice from the foyer. "You *are* an ass, Jack Zuckerman!" The front door opened and slammed shut again. The thud seemed to echo endlessly through the mansion.

There was a long silence.

Suddenly, through her tears, Cathy laughed. "You know what, Jack? I *like* that woman."

Jack crossed his arms and gave his ex-wife the critical once-over. "Either I'm going senile or you forgot to tell me something. Why haven't you gone to the police? Why bother old Jack about this?"

Cathy and Victor glanced at each other.

"We can't go to the police," Cathy said.

"I assume this has to do with *him?*" He cocked a thumb at Victor.

Cathy let out a breath. "It's a complicated story...."

"It must be. If you're afraid to go to the police."

"I can explain it," said Victor.

"Mm-hm. Well." Jack reached for the bathrobe lying in a heap by the polar bear rug. "Well," he said again, calmly tying the sash. "I've always enjoyed watching creativity at work. So let's have it."

He sat down on the leather couch and smiled at Victor. "I'm waiting. It's showtime."

Special Agent Sam Polowski lay shivering in his bed, watching the eleven o'clock news. Every muscle in his body ached, his head pounded, and the thermometer at his bedside read an irrefutable 101 degrees. So much for changing flat tires in the pouring rain. He wished he could get his hands on the joker who'd punched that nail in his tire while he was grabbing a quick bite at that roadside cafe. Not only had the culprit managed to keep Sam from his appointment in Garberville, thereby shredding the Viratek case into confetti, Sam had also lost track of his only contact in the affair: Victor Holland. And now, the flu.

Sam reached over for the bottle of aspirin. To hell with the ulcer. His head hurt. And when it came to headaches, there was nothing like Mom's time-tested remedy.

He was in the midst of gulping down three tablets when the news about Victor Holland flashed on the screen.

"...New evidence links the suspect to the murder of fellow Viratek researcher, Dr. Gerald Martinique...."

Sam sat up straight in bed. "What the hell?" he growled at the TV.

Then he grabbed the telephone.

It took six rings for his supervisor to answer. "Dafoe?" Sam said. "This is Polowski."

"Do you know what time it is?"

"Have you seen the late-night news?"

"I happen to be in bed."

"There's a story on Viratek."

A pause. "Yeah, I know. I cleared it."

"What's with this crap about industrial espionage? They're making Holland out to be a—"

"Polowski, drop it."

"Since when did he become a murder suspect?"

"Look, just consider it a cover story. I want him brought in. For his own good."

"So you sic him with a bunch of trigger-happy cops?"

"I said drop it."

"But—"

"You're off the case." Dafoe hung up.

Sam stared in disbelief at the receiver, then at the television, then back at the receiver.

Pull me off the case? He slammed the receiver down so hard the bottle of aspirin tumbled off the nightstand.

That's what you think.

"I think I've heard about enough," said Jack, rising to his feet. "I want this man out of my house. And I want him out now."

"Jack, please!" said Cathy. "Give him a chance—"

"You're buying this ridiculous tale?"

"I believe him."

"Why?"

She looked at Victor and saw the clear fire of honesty burning in his eyes. "Because he saved my life."

"You're a fool, babycakes." Jack reached for the phone. "You yourself saw the TV. He's wanted for murder. If you don't call the police, I will."

But as Jack picked up the receiver, Victor grabbed his arm. "No," he said. Though his voice was quiet, it held the unmistakable note of authority.

The two men stared at each other, neither willing to back down.

"This is more than just a case of murder," said Victor. "This is deadly research. The manufacture of illegal weapons. This could reach all the way to Washington."

"Who in Washington?"

"Someone in control. Someone with the federal funds to authorize that research."

"I see. Some lofty public servant is out knocking off scientists. With the help of the FBI."

"Jerry wasn't just any scientist. He had a conscience. He was a whistleblower who would've taken this to the press to stop that research. The political fallout would've been disastrous, for the whole administration."

"Wait. Are we talking Pennsylvania Avenue?"

"Maybe."

Jack snorted. "Holland, I *make* Grade B horror films. I don't live them."

"This isn't a film. This is real. Real bullets, real bodies."

"Then that's all the more reason I want nothing to do with it." Jack turned to Cathy. "Sorry, sweetcakes. It's nothing personal, but I detest the company you keep."

"Jack," she said. "You have to help us!"

"You, I'll help. Him—no way. I draw the line at lunatics and felons."

"You heard what he said! It's a frame-up!"

"You are so gullible."

"Only about you."

"Cathy, it's all right," said Victor. He was standing very still, very calm. "I'll leave."

"No, you won't." Cathy shot to her feet and stalked over to her ex-husband. She stared him straight in the eye, a gaze so direct, so accusing, he seemed to wilt right down into a chair. "You owe it to me, Jack. You owe me for all the years we were married. All the years I put into *your* career, *your* company, *your* idiotic flicks. I haven't asked for anything. You have the house. The Jaguar. The bank account. I never asked because I didn't want to take a damn thing from this marriage except my own soul. But now I'm asking. This man saved my life tonight. If you ever cared about me, if you ever loved me, even a little, then you'll do me this favor."

"Harbor a criminal?"

"Only until we figure out what to do next."

"And how long might that take? Weeks? Months?"

"I don't know."

"Just the kind of definite answer I like."

Victor said, "I need time to find out what Jerry was trying to prove. What it is Viratek's working on—"

"You had one of his files," said Jack. "Why didn't you read the blasted thing?"

"I'm not a virologist. I couldn't interpret the data. It was some sort of RNA sequence, probably a viral genome. A lot of the data was coded. All I can be sure of is the name: Project Cerberus."

"Where is all this vital evidence now?"

"I lost the file. It was in my car the night I was shot. I'm sure they have it back."

"And the film?"

Victor sank into a chair, his face suddenly lined by weariness. "I don't have it. I was hoping that Cathy…" Sighing, he ran his hands through his hair. "I've lost that, too."

"Well," said Jack. "Give or take a few miracles, I'd say this puts your chances at just about zero. And I'm known as an optimist."

"I know where the film is," said Cathy.

There was a long silence. Victor raised his head and stared at her. "What?"

"I wasn't sure about you—not at first. I didn't want to tell you until I could be certain—"

Victor shot to his feet. *"Where is it?"*

She flinched at the sharpness of his voice. He must have noticed how startled she was—his next words were quiet but urgent. "I need that film, Cathy. Before they find it. Where is it?"

"Sarah found it in my car. I didn't know it was yours! I thought it was Hickey's."

"Who's Hickey?"

"A photographer—a friend of mine—"

Jack snorted. "Hickey. Now *there's* a ladies' man."

"He was in a rush to get to the airport," she continued. "At the last minute he left me with some rolls of film. Asked me to take care of them till he got back from Nairobi. But all his film was stolen from my car."

"And my roll?" asked Victor.

"It was in my bathrobe pocket the night Sarah—the night she—" She paused, swallowing at the mention of her friend. "When I got back here, to the city, I mailed it to Hickey's studio."

"Where's the studio?"

"Over on Union Street. I mailed it this afternoon—"

"So it should be there sometime tomorrow." He began to pace the room. "All we have to do is wait for the mail to arrive."

"I don't have a key."

"We'll find a way in."

"Terrific," sighed Jack. "Now he's turning my ex-wife into a burglar."

"We're only after the film!" said Cathy.

"It's still breaking and entering, sweetie."

"You don't have to get involved."

"But you're asking me to harbor the breakers and enterers."

"Just one night, Jack. That's all I'm asking."

"That sounds like one of *my* lines."

"And your lines always work, don't they?"

"Not this time."

"Then here's another line to chew on: 1988. Your federal tax return. Or lack of one."

Jack froze. He glowered at Victor, then at Cathy. "That's below the belt."

"Your most vulnerable spot."

"I'll get around to filing—"

"More words to chew on. Audit. IRS. Jail."

"Okay, okay!" Jack threw his arms up in surrender. "God, I *hate* that word."

"What, *jail?*"

"Don't laugh, babycakes. The word could soon apply to all of us." He turned and headed for the stairs.

"Where are you going?" Cathy demanded.

"To make up the spare beds. Seems I have houseguests for the night...."

"Can we trust him?" Victor asked after Jack had vanished upstairs.

Cathy sank back on the couch, all the energy suddenly drained from her body, and closed her eyes. "We have to. I can't think of anywhere else to go...."

She was suddenly aware of his approach, and then he was sitting beside her, so close she could feel the overwhelming strength of his presence. He didn't say a word, yet she knew he was watching her.

She opened her eyes and met his gaze. So steady, so intense, it seemed to infuse her with new strength.

"I know it wasn't easy for you," he said. "Asking Jack for favors."

She smiled. "I've always wanted to talk tough with Jack." Ruefully she added, "Until tonight, I've never quite been able to pull it off."

"My guess is, talking tough isn't in your repertoire."

"No, it isn't. When it comes to confrontation, I'm a gutless wonder."

"For a gutless wonder, you did pretty well. In fact, you were magnificent."

"That's because I wasn't fighting for me. I was fighting for you."

"You don't consider yourself worth fighting for?"

She shrugged. "It's the way I was raised. I was always told that sticking up for yourself was unladylike. Whereas sticking up for other people was okay."

He nodded gravely. "Self-sacrifice. A fine feminine tradition."

That made her laugh. "Spoken like a man who knows women well."

"Only two women. My mother and my wife."

At the mention of his dead wife, she fell silent. She wondered what the woman's name was, what she'd looked like, how much he'd loved her. He must have loved her a great deal—she'd heard the pain in his voice earlier that evening when he'd mentioned her death. She felt an unexpected stab of envy that this unnamed wife had been so loved. What Cathy would give to be as dearly loved by a man! Just as quickly she suppressed the thought, appalled that she could be jealous of a dead woman.

She turned away, her face tinged with guilt. "I think Jack will go along," she said. "Tonight, at least."

"That was blackmail, wasn't it? That stuff about the tax return?"

"He's a careless man. I just reminded him of his oversight."

Victor shook his head. "You are amazing. Jumping along rooftops one minute, blackmailing ex-husbands the next."

"You're so right," said Jack, who'd reappeared at the bottom of the stairs. "She is an amazing woman. I can't wait to see what she'll do next."

Cathy rose wearily to her feet. "At this point I'll do anything." She slipped past Jack and headed up the stairs. "Anything I have to to stay alive."

The two men listened to her footsteps recede along the hall. Then they regarded each other in silence.

"Well," said Jack with forced cheerfulness. "What's next on the agenda? Scrabble?"

"Try solitaire," said Victor, hauling himself off the couch. He was in no mood to share pleasantries with Jack Zuckerman. The man was slick and self-centered and he obviously went through women the way most men went through socks. Victor had a hard time imagining what Cathy had ever seen in the man. That is, aside from Jack's good looks and obvious wealth. There was no denying the fact he was a classic hunk, with the added attraction of money thrown in. Maybe it was that combination that had dazzled her.

A combination I'll certainly never possess, he thought.

He crossed the room, then stopped and turned. "Zuckerman?" he asked. "Do you still love your wife?"

Jack looked faintly startled by the question. "Do I still love her? Well, let me see. No, not exactly. But I suppose I have a sentimental attachment, based on ten years of marriage. And I respect her."

"Respect her? You?"

"Yes. Her talents. Her technical skill. After all, she's my number-one makeup artist."

That's what she meant to him. An asset he could use. *Thinking of himself, the jerk.* If there was anyone else Victor could turn to, he would. But the one man he would've trusted—Jerry—was dead. His other friends might already be under observation. Plus, they weren't in the sort of tax brackets that allowed private little hideaways in the woods. Jack, on the other hand, had the resources to spirit Cathy away to a safe place. Victor could only hope the man's sentimental attachment was strong enough to make him watch out for her.

"I have a proposition," said Victor.

Jack instantly looked suspicious. "What might that be?"

"I'm the one they're really after. Not Cathy. I don't want to make things any more dangerous for her than I already have."

"Big of you."

"It's better if I go off on my own. If I leave her with you, will you keep her safe?"

Jack shifted, looked down at his feet. "Well, sure. I guess so."

"Don't guess. Can you?"

"Look, we start shooting a film in Mexico next month. Jungle scenes, black lagoons, that sort of stuff. Should be a safe-enough place."

"That's next month. What about now?"

"I'll think of something. But first you get yourself out of the picture. Since you're the reason she's in danger in the first place."

Victor couldn't disagree with that last point. *Since the night I met her I've caused her nothing but trouble.*

He nodded. "I'm out of here tomorrow."

"Good."

"Take care of Cathy. Get her out of the city. Out of the country. Don't wait."

"Yeah. Sure."

Something about the way Jack said it, his hasty, whatever-you-say tone, made Victor wonder if the man gave a damn about anyone but himself. But at this point Victor had no choice. He had to trust Jack Zuckerman.

As he climbed the stairs to the guest rooms, it occurred to him that, come morning, it would be goodbye. A quiet little bond had formed between them. He owed his life to her and she to him. That was the sort of link one could never break.

Even if we never see each other again.

In the upstairs hall, he paused outside her closed door. He could hear her moving around the room, opening and closing drawers, squeaking bedsprings.

He knocked on the door. "Cathy?"

There was a pause. Then, "Come in."

One dim lamp lit the room. She was sitting on the bed, dressed in a ridiculously huge man's shirt. Her hair hung in damp waves to her shoulders. The scent of soap and shampoo permeated the shadows. It reminded him of his wife, of the shower smells and feminine sweetness. He stood there, pierced by a sense of longing he hadn't felt in over a year, longing for the warmth, the love, of a woman. Not just any woman. He wasn't like Jack, to whom a soft body with the right equipment would be sufficient. What Victor wanted was the heart and soul; the package they came wrapped in was only of minor importance.

His own wife Lily hadn't been beautiful; neither had she been unattractive. Even at the end, when the ravages of illness had left her shrunken and bruised, there had been a light in her eyes, a gentle spirit's glow.

The same glow he'd seen in Catherine Weaver's eyes the night she'd saved his life. The same glow he saw now.

She sat with her back propped up on pillows. Her gaze was silently expectant, maybe a little fearful. She was clutching a handful of tissues. *Why were you crying?* he wondered.

He didn't approach; he stood just inside the doorway. Their gazes locked together in the gloom. "I've just talked with Jack," he said.

She nodded but said nothing.

"We both agree. It's better that I leave as soon as possible. So I'll be taking off in the morning."

"What about the film?"

"I'll get it. All I need is Hickey's address."

"Yes. Of course." She looked down at the tissues in her fist.

He could tell she wanted to say something. He went to the bed and sat down. Those sweet woman smells grew intoxicating. The neckline of her oversized shirt sagged low enough to reveal a tempting glimpse of shadow. He forced himself to focus on her face.

"Cathy, you'll be fine. Jack said he'd watch out for you. Get you out of the city."

"Jack?" What sounded like a laugh escaped her throat.

"You'll be safer with him. I don't even know where I'll be going. I don't want to drag you into this—"

"But you already have. You've dragged me in over my head, Victor. What am I supposed to do now? I can't just—just sit around and wait for you to fix things. I owe it to Sarah—"

"And I owe it to you not to let you get hurt."

"You think you can hand me over to Jack and make everything be fine again? Well, it won't be fine. Sarah's dead. Her baby's dead. And somehow it's not just your fault. It's mine as well."

"No, it's not. Cathy—"

"It is my fault! Did you know she was lying there in the driveway all night? In the rain. In the cold. There she was, dying, and I slept through the whole damn thing...." She dropped her face in her hands. The guilt that had been tormenting her since Sarah's death at last burst through. She began to cry, silently, ashamedly, unable to hold back the tears any longer.

Victor's response was automatic and instinctively male. He pulled her against him and gave her a warm, safe place to cry. As soon as he felt her settle into his arms, he knew it was a mistake. It was too perfect a fit. She felt as if she belonged there, against his heart, felt that if she ever pulled away there would be left a hole so gaping it could never be filled. He pressed his lips to her damp hair and inhaled her heady scent of soap and warm skin. That gentle fragrance was enough to drown a man with need. So was the softness of her face, the silken luster of that shoulder peeking out from beneath the shirt. And all the time he was stroking her hair, murmuring inane words of comfort, he was thinking: *I have to leave her. For her sake I have to abandon this woman. Or I'll get us both killed.*

"Cathy," he said. It took all the willpower he could muster to pull away. He placed his hands on her shoulders, made her look at him. Her gaze was confused and brimming with tears. "We have to talk about tomorrow."

She nodded and swiped at the tears on her cheeks.

"I want you out of the city, first thing in the morning. Go to Mexico with Jack. Anywhere. Just keep out of sight."

"What will you do?"

"I'm going to take a look at that roll of film, see what kind of evidence it has."

"And then?"

"I don't know yet. Maybe I'll take it to the newspapers. The FBI is definitely out."

"How will I know you're all right? How do I reach you?"

He thought hard, fighting the distraction of her scent, her hair. He found himself stroking the bare skin of her shoulder, marveling at how smooth it felt beneath his fingers.

He focused on her face, on the look of worry in her eyes. "Every other Sunday I'll put an ad in the Personals. *Los Angeles Times.* It'll be addressed to, let's say, Cora. Anything I need to tell you will be there."

"Cora." She nodded. "I'll remember."

They looked at each other, a silent acknowledgment that this parting had to be. He cupped her face and pressed a kiss to her mouth. She barely responded; already, it seemed, she had said her goodbyes.

He rose from the bed and started for the door. There he couldn't resist asking, one more time: "You'll be all right?"

She nodded, but it was too automatic. The sort of nod one gave to dismiss an unimportant question. "I'll be fine. After all, I'll have Jack to watch over me."

He didn't miss the faint note of irony in her reply. Jack, it seemed, didn't inspire confidence in either of them. *What's my alternative? Drag her along with me as a moving target?*

He gripped the doorknob. No, it was better this way. He'd already ripped her life apart; he wasn't going to scatter the pieces as well.

As he was leaving, he took one last backward glance. She was still huddled on the bed, her knees drawn up to her chest. The oversized shirt had slid off one bare shoulder. For a moment he thought she was crying. Then she raised her head and met his gaze. What he saw in her eyes wasn't tears. It was something far more moving, something pure and bright and beautiful.

Courage.

In the pale light of dawn, Savitch stood outside Jack Zuckerman's house. Through the fingers of morning mist, Savitch studied the curtained windows, trying to picture the inhabitants within. He wondered who they were, in which room they slept, and whether Catherine Weaver was among them.

He'd find out soon.

He pocketed the black address book he'd taken from the woman's apartment. The name C. Zuckerman and this Pacific Heights address had been written on the inside front cover. Then the Zuckerman had been crossed out and replaced with Weaver. She was a divorcée, he concluded. Under Z, he'd found a prominent listing for a man named Jack, with various phone numbers and addresses, both foreign and domestic. Her ex-husband, he'd confirmed, after a brief chat with another name listed in the book. Pumping strangers for information was a simple matter. All it took was an air of authority and a cop's ID. The same ID he was planning to use now.

He gave the house one final perusal, taking in the manicured lawns and shrubbery, the trellis with its vines of winter-dormant wisteria. A successful man, this Jack Zuckerman. Savitch had always admired men of wealth. He gave his jacket a final tug to assure himself that the shoulder holster was concealed. Then he crossed the street to the front porch and rang the doorbell.

CHAPTER SIX

At first light, Cathy awakened. It wasn't a gentle return but a startling jerk back to consciousness. She was instantly aware that she was not in her own bed and that something was terribly wrong. It took her a few seconds to remember exactly what it was. And when she did remember, the sense of urgency was so compelling she rose at once from bed and began to dress in the semidarkness. *Have to be ready to run...*

The creak of floorboards in the next room told her that Victor was awake as well, probably planning his moves for the day. She rummaged through the closet, searching for things he might need in his flight. All she came up with was a zippered nylon bag and a raincoat. She searched the dresser next and found a few men's socks. She also found a collection of women's underwear. *Damn Jack and all his women,* she thought with sudden irritation and slammed the drawer shut. The thud was still resonating in the room when another sound echoed through the house.

The doorbell was ringing.

It was only seven o'clock, too early for visitors or deliverymen. Suddenly her door swung open. She turned to see Victor, his face etched with tension.

"What should we do?" she asked.

"Get ready to leave. Fast."

"There's a back door—"

"Let's go."

They hurried along the hall and had almost reached the top of the stairs when they heard Jack's sleepy voice below, grumbling: "I'm coming, dammit! Stop that racket, I'm coming!"

The doorbell rang again.

"Don't answer it!" hissed Cathy. "Not yet—"

Jack had already opened the door. Instantly Victor snatched Cathy back up the hall, out of sight. They froze with their backs against the wall, listening to the voices below.

"Yeah," they heard Jack say. "I'm Jack Zuckerman. And who are you?"

The visitor's voice was soft. They could tell only that it was a man.

"Is that so?" said Jack, his voice suddenly edged with panic. "You're with the *FBI*, you say? And what on earth would the *FBI* want with my *ex-wife?*"

Cathy's gaze flew to Victor. She read the frantic message in his eyes: *Which way out?*

She pointed toward the bedroom at the end of the hall. He nodded. Together they tiptoed along the carpet, all the time aware that one misstep, one loud creak, might be enough to alert the agent downstairs.

"Where's your warrant?" they heard Jack demand of the visitor. "Hey, wait a minute! You can't just barge in here without a court order or something!"

No time left! thought Cathy in panic as she slipped into the last room. They closed the door behind them.

"The window!" she whispered.

"You mean jump?"

"No." She hurried across the room and gingerly eased the window open. "There's a trellis!"

He glanced down dubiously at the tangled vines of wisteria. "Are you sure it'll hold us?"

"I know it will," she said, swinging her leg over the sill. "I caught one of Jack's blondes hanging off it one night. And believe me, she was a *big* girl." She glanced down at the ground far below and felt a sudden wave of nausea as the old fear of heights washed through her. "God," she muttered. "Why do we always seem to be hanging out of windows?"

From somewhere in the house came Jack's outraged shout: "You can't go up there! You haven't shown me your warrant!"

"Move!" snapped Victor.

Cathy lowered herself onto the trellis. Branches clawed her face as she scrambled down the vine. An instant after she landed on the dew-soaked grass, Victor dropped beside her.

At once they were on their feet and sprinting for the cover of shrubbery. Just as they rolled behind the azalea bushes, they heard a second-floor window slide open, and then Jack's voice complaining loudly: "I know my rights! This is an illegal search! I'm going to call my lawyer!"

Don't let him see us! prayed Cathy, burrowing frantically into the bush. She felt Victor's body curl around her back, his arms pulling her tightly to him, his breath hot and ragged against her neck. For an eternity they lay shivering in the grass as mist swirled around them.

"You see?" they heard Jack say. "There's no one here but me. Or would you like to check the garage?"

The window slid shut.

Victor gave Cathy a little push. "Go," he whispered. "The end of the hedge. We'll run from there."

On hands and knees she crawled along the row of azalea bushes. Her soaked jeans were icy and her palms scratched and bleeding, but she was too numbed by terror to feel any pain. All her attention was focused on moving forward. Victor was crawling close behind her. When she felt him bump up against her hip, it occurred to her what a ridiculous view he had, her rump swaying practically under his nose.

She reached the last bush and stopped to shove a handful of tangled hair off her face. "That house next?" she asked.

"Go for it!"

They both took off like scared rabbits, dashing across the twenty yards of lawn between houses. Once they reached the cover of the next house, they didn't stop. They kept running, past parked cars and early-morning pedestrians. Five blocks later, they ducked into a coffee shop. Through the front window, they glanced out at the street, watching for signs of pursuit. All they saw was the typical Monday morning bustle: the stop-and-go traffic, the passersby bundled up in scarves and overcoats.

From the grill behind them came the hiss and sizzle of bacon. The smell of freshly brewed coffee wafted from the counter burner. The aromas were almost painful; they reminded Cathy that she and Victor probably had a total of forty dollars between them. Damn it, why hadn't she begged, borrowed or stolen some cash from Jack?

"What now?" she asked, half hoping he'd suggest blowing the rest of their cash on breakfast.

He scanned the street. "Let's go on."

"Where?"

"Hickey's studio."

"Oh." She sighed. Another long walk, and all on an empty stomach.

Outside, a car passed by bearing the bumper sticker: Today is the First Day of the Rest of Your Life.

Lord, I hope it gets better than this, she thought. Then she followed Victor out the door and into the morning chill.

Field Supervisor Larry Dafoe was sitting at his desk, pumping away at his executive power chair. Upper body strength, he always said, was the key to success as a man. Bulk out those muscles *pull!*, fill out that size forty-four jacket *pull!*, and what you got was a pair of shoulders that'd impress any woman, intimidate any rival. And with this snazzy 700-buck model, you didn't even have to get out of your chair.

Sam Polowski watched his superior strain at the system of wires and pulleys and thought the device looked more like an exotic instrument of torture.

"What you gotta understand," gasped Dafoe, "is that there are other *pull!* issues at work here. Things you know nothing about."

"Like what?" asked Polowski.

Dafoe released the handles and looked up, his face sheened with a healthy sweat. "If I was at liberty to tell you, don't you think I already would've?"

Polowski looked at the gleaming black exercise handles, wondering whether he'd benefit from an executive power chair. Maybe a souped-up set of biceps was what he needed to get a little respect around this office.

"I still don't see what the point is," he said. "Putting Victor Holland in the hot seat."

"The point," said Dafoe, "is that you don't call the shots."

"I gave Holland my word he'd be left out of this mess."

"He's *part* of the mess! First he claims he has evidence, then he pulls a vanishing act."

"That's partly my fault. I never made it to the rendezvous."

"Why hasn't he tried to contact you?"

"I don't know." Polowski sighed and shook his head. "Maybe he's dead."

"Maybe we just need to find him." Dafoe reached for the exercise handles. "Maybe you need to get to work on the Lanzano file. Or maybe you should just go home. You look terrible."

"Yeah. Sure." Polowski turned. As he left the office, he could hear Dafoe once again huffing and puffing. He went to his desk, sat down and contemplated his collection of cold capsules, aspirin and cough syrup. He took a double dose of each. Then he reached in his briefcase and pulled out the Viratek file.

It was his own private collection of scrambled notes and phone numbers and news clippings. He sifted through them, stopping to ponder once again the link between Holland and the woman Catherine Weaver. He'd first seen her name on the hospital admission sheet, and had later been startled to hear of her connection to the murdered Garberville woman. Too many coincidences, too many twists and turns. Was there something obvious here he was missing? Might the woman have an answer or two?

He reached for the telephone and dialed the Garberville police department. They would know how to reach their witness. And maybe she would know how to find Victor Holland. It was a long shot but Sam Polowski was an inveterate horseplayer. He had a penchant for long shots.

The man ringing his doorbell looked like a tree stump dressed in a brown polyester suit. Jack opened the door and said, "Sorry, I'm not buying today."

"I'm not selling anything, Mr. Zuckerman," said the man. "I'm with the FBI."

Jack sighed. "Not again."

"I'm Special Agent Sam Polowski. I'm trying to locate a woman named Catherine Weaver, formerly Zuckerman. I believe she—"

"Don't you guys ever know when to quit?"

"Quit what?"

"One of your agents was here this morning. Talk to him!"

The man frowned. "One of *our* agents?"

"Yeah. And I just might register a complaint against him. Barged right in here without a warrant and started tramping all over my house."

"What did he look like?"

"Oh, I don't know! Dark hair, terrific build. But he could've used a course in charm school."

"Was he about my height?"

"Taller. Skinnier. Lots more hair."

"Did he give you his name? It wasn't Mac Braden, was it?"

"Naw, he didn't give me any name."

Polowski pulled out his badge. Jack squinted at the words: Federal Bureau of Investigation. "Did he show you one of these?" asked Polowski.

"No. He just asked about Cathy and some guy named Victor Holland. Whether I knew how to find them."

"Did you tell him?"

"That jerk?" Jack laughed. "I wouldn't bother to give him the time of day. I sure as hell wasn't going to tell him about—" Jack paused and cleared his throat. "I wasn't going to tell him anything. Even if I knew. Which I don't."

Polowski slipped his badge into his pocket, all the time gazing steadily at Jack. "I think we should talk, Mr. Zuckerman."

"What about?"

"About your ex-wife. About the fact she's in big trouble."

"That," sighed Jack, "I already know."

"She's going to get hurt. I can't fill you in on all the details because I'm still in the dark myself. But I do know one woman's already been hit. Your wife—"

"My ex-wife."

"Your ex-wife could be next."

Jack, unconvinced, merely looked at him.

"It's your duty as a citizen to tell me what you know," Polowski reminded him.

"My duty. Right."

"Look, cooperate, and you and me, we'll get along just fine. Give me grief, and I'll give *you* grief." Polowski smiled. Jack didn't. "Now, Mr. Zuckerman. Hey, can I call you Jack? Jack, why don't you tell me where she is? Before it's too late. For both of you."

Jack scowled at him. He drummed his fingers against the door frame. He debated. At last he stepped aside. "As a law-abiding citizen, I suppose it is my duty." Grudgingly, he waved the man in. "Oh, just come in, Polowski. I'll tell you what I know."

The window shattered, raining slivers into the gloomy space beyond.

Cathy winced at the sound. "Sorry, Hickey," she said under her breath.

"We'll make it up to him," said Victor, knocking off the remaining shards. "We'll send him a nice fat check. You see anyone?"

She glanced up and down the alley. Except for a crumpled newspaper tumbling past the trash cans, nothing moved. A few blocks away, car horns blared, the sounds of another Union Street traffic jam.

"All clear," she whispered.

"Okay." Victor draped his windbreaker over the sill. "Up you go."

He gave her a lift to the window. She clambered through and landed among the glass shards. Seconds later, Victor dropped down beside her.

They were standing in the studio dressing room. Against one wall hung a rack of women's lingerie; against the other were makeup tables and a long mirror.

Victor frowned at a cloud of peach silk flung over one of the chairs. "What kind of photos does your friend take, anyway?"

"Hickey specializes in what's politely known as 'boudoir portraits.'"

Victor's startled gaze turned to a black lace negligee hanging from a wall hook. "Does that mean what I think it means?"

"What do you think it means?"

"You know."

She headed into the next room. "Hickey insists it's not pornography. It's tasteful erotic art...." She stopped in her tracks as she came face-to-face with a photo blowup on the wall. Naked limbs— eight, maybe more—were entwined in a sort of human octopus. Nothing was left to the imagination. Nothing at all.

"Tasteful," Victor said dryly.

"That must be one of his, uh, commercial assignments."

"I wonder what product they were selling."

She turned and found herself staring at another photograph. This time it was two women, drop-dead gorgeous and wearing not a stitch.

"Another commercial assignment?" Victor inquired politely over her shoulder.

She shook her head. "Don't ask."

In the front room they found a week's worth of mail piled up beneath the door slot, darkroom catalogues and advertising flyers. The roll of film Cathy had mailed the day before was not yet in the mound.

"I guess we just sit around and wait for the postman," she said.

He nodded. "Seems like a safe-enough place. Any chance your friend keeps food around?"

"I seem to remember a refrigerator in the other room."

She led Victor into what Hickey had dubbed his "shooting gallery." Cathy flipped the wall switch and the vast room was instantly illuminated by a dazzling array of spotlights.

"So this is where he does it," said Victor, blinking in the sudden glare. He stepped over a jumble of electrical cords and slowly circled the room, regarding with humorous disbelief the various props. It was a strange collection of objects: a genuine English phone booth, a street bench, an exercise bicycle. In a place of honor sat a four-poster bed. The ruffled coverlet was Victorian; the handcuffs dangling from the bedposts were not.

Victor picked up one of the cuffs and let it fall again. "Just how good a friend *is* this Hickey guy, anyway?"

"None of this stuff was here when he shot me a month ago."

"He photographed *you?*" Victor turned and stared at her.

She flushed, imagining the images that must be flashing through his mind. She could feel his gaze undressing her, posing her in a sprawl across that ridiculous four-poster bed. With the handcuffs, no less.

"It wasn't like—like these other photos," she protested. "I mean, I just did it as a favor...."

"A favor?"

"It was a purely *commercial* shot!"

"Oh."

"I was fully dressed. In overalls, as a matter of fact. I was supposed to be a plumber."

"A lady plumber?"

"I was an emergency stand-in. One of his models didn't show up that day, and he needed someone with an ordinary face. I guess that's me. Ordinary. And it really was just my face."

"And your overalls."

"Right."

They looked at each other and burst out laughing.

"I can guess what you were thinking," she said.

"I don't even want to *tell* you what I was thinking." He turned and glanced around the room. "Didn't you say there was some food around here?"

She crossed the room to the refrigerator. Inside she found a shelf of film plus a jar of sweet pickles, some rubbery carrots and half a salami. In the freezer they discovered real treasures: ground Sumatran coffee and a loaf of sourdough bread.

Grinning, she turned to him. "A feast!"

They sat together on the four-poster bed and gnawed on salami and half-frozen sourdough, all washed down with cups of coffee. It was a bizarre little picnic, paper plates with pickles and carrots resting in their laps, the spotlights glaring down like a dozen hot suns from the ceiling.

"Why did you say that about yourself?" he asked, watching her munch a carrot.

"Say what?"

"That you're ordinary. So ordinary that you get cast as the lady plumber?"

"Because I am ordinary."

"I don't think so. And I happen to be a pretty good judge of character."

She looked up at a wall poster featuring one of Hickey's super models. The woman stared back with a look of glossy confidence. "Well, I certainly don't measure up to *that*."

"*That*," he said, "is pure fantasy. *That* isn't a real woman, but an amalgam of makeup, hairspray and fake eyelashes."

"Oh, I know that. That's my job, turning actors into some movie-goer's fantasy. Or nightmare, as the case may be." She reached into the jar and fished out the last pickle. "No, I really meant *underneath* it all. Deep inside, I *feel* ordinary."

"I think you're quite extraordinary. And after last night, I should know."

She gazed down, at the limp carrot stretched out like a little corpse across the paper plate. "There was a time—I suppose there's always that time, for everyone, when we're still young, when we feel special. When we feel the world's meant just for us. The last time I felt that way was when I married Jack." She sighed. "It didn't last long."

"Why did you marry him?"

"I don't know. Dazzle? I was only twenty-three, a mere apprentice on the set. He was the director." She paused. "He was *God*."

"He impressed you, did he?"

"Jack can be very impressive. He can turn on the power, the charisma, and just overwhelm a gal. Then there was the champagne, the suppers, the flowers. I think what attracted him to me was that I didn't immediately fall for him. That I wasn't swooning at his every look. He thought of me as a challenge, the one he finally conquered." She gave him a rueful look. "That accomplished, he moved onto bigger and better things. That's when I realized that I wasn't particularly special. That I'm really just a perfectly ordinary woman. It's not a bad feeling. It's not as if I go through life longing to be someone different, someone special."

"Then who do you consider special?"

"Well, my grandmother. But she's dead."

"Venerable grandmothers always make the list."

"Okay, then. Mother Teresa."

"She's on everyone's list."

"Kate Hepburn. Gloria Steinem. My friend Sarah…" Her voice faded. Looking down, she added softly: "But she's dead, too."

Gently he took her hand. With a strange sense of wonder she watched his long fingers close over hers and thought about how the strength she felt in that grasp reflected the strength of the man himself. Jack, for all his dazzle and polish, had never inspired a fraction of the confidence she now felt in Victor. No man ever had.

He was watching her with quiet sympathy. "Tell me about Sarah," he said.

Cathy swallowed, trying to stem the tears. "She was absolutely lovely. I don't mean in *that* way." She nodded at the photo of Hickey's picture-perfect model. "I mean, in an inner sort of way. It was this look in her eyes. A perfect calmness. As though she'd found exactly what she wanted while all the rest of us were still grubbing around for lost treasure. I don't think she was born like that. She came to it, all by herself. In college, we were both pretty unsure of ourselves. Marriage certainly didn't help either of us. My divorce—it was nothing short of devastating. But Sarah's divorce only seemed to make her stronger. Better able to take care of herself. When she finally got pregnant, it was exactly as she planned it. There wasn't a father, you see, just a test tube. An anonymous donor. Sarah used to say that the primeval family unit wasn't man, woman and child. It was just woman and child. I thought she was brave, to take that step. She was a lot braver than I could ever be...." She cleared her throat. "Anyway, Sarah *was* special. Some people simply are."

"Yes," he said. "Some people are."

She looked up at him. He was staring off at the far wall, his gaze infinitely sad. What had etched those lines of pain in his face? She wondered if lines so deep could ever be erased. There were some losses one never got over, never accepted.

Softly she asked, "What was your wife like?"

He didn't answer at first. She thought: *Why did I ask that? Why did I have to bring up such terrible memories?*

He said, "She was a kind woman. That's what I'll always remember about her. Her kindness." He looked at Cathy and she sensed it wasn't sadness she saw in those eyes, but acceptance.

"What was her name?"

"Lily. Lillian Dorinda Cassidy. A mouthful for such a tiny woman." He smiled. "She was about five foot one, maybe ninety pounds sopping wet. It used to scare me, how small she always seemed. Almost breakable. Especially toward the end, when she'd lost all that weight. It seemed as if she'd shrunk down to nothing but a pair of big brown eyes."

"She must have been young when she died."

"Only thirty-eight. It seemed so unfair. All her life, she'd done everything right. Never smoked, hardly ever touched a glass of wine. She even refused to eat meat. After she was diagnosed, we kept trying to figure out how it could've happened. Then it occurred to us what might have caused it. She grew up in a small town in Massachusetts. Directly downwind from a nuclear power plant."

"You think that was it?"

"One can never be sure. But we asked around. And we learned that, just in her neighborhood, at least twenty families had someone with leukemia. It took four years and a class-action suit to force an investigation. What they found was a history of safety violations going back all the way to the plant's opening."

Cathy shook her head in disbelief. "And all those years they allowed it to operate?"

"No one knew about it. The violations were hushed up so well even the federal regulators were kept in the dark."

"They shut it down, didn't they?"

He nodded. "I can't say I got much satisfaction, seeing the plant finally close. By that time Lily was gone. And all the families, well, we were exhausted by the fight. Even though it sometimes felt as though we were banging our heads against a wall, we knew it was something we had to do. *Somebody* had to do it, for all the Lilys of the world." He looked up, at the spotlights shining above. "And here I am again, still banging my head against walls. Only this time, it feels like the Great Wall of China. And the lives at stake are yours and mine."

Their gazes met. She sat absolutely still as he lightly stroked down the curve of her cheek. She took his hand, pressed it to her lips. His fingers closed over hers, refusing to release her hand. Gently he tugged her close. Their lips met, a tentative kiss that left her longing for more.

"I'm sorry you were pulled into this," he murmured. "You and Sarah and those other Cathy Weavers. None of you asked to be part of it. And somehow I've managed to hurt you all."

"Not you, Victor. You're not the one to blame. It's this windmill you're tilting at. This giant, dangerous windmill. Anyone else would have dropped his lance and fled. You're still going at it."

"I didn't have much of a choice."

"But you did. You could have walked away from your friend's death. Turned a blind eye to whatever's going on at Viratek. That's what Jack would have done."

"But I'm not Jack. There are things I can't walk away from. I'd always be thinking of the Lilys. All the thousands of people who might get hurt."

At the mention once again of his dead wife, Cathy felt some unbreachable barrier form between them—the shadow of Lily, the wife she'd never met. Cathy drew back, at once aching from the loss of his touch.

"You think that many people could die?" she asked.

"Jerry must have thought so. There's no way to predict the outcome. The world's never seen the effects of all-out biological warfare. I like to think it's because we're too smart to play with our own self-destruction. Then I think of all the crazy things people have done over the years and it scares me...."

"Are viral weapons that dangerous?"

"If you alter a few genes, make it just a little more contagious, raise the kill ratio, you'd end up with a devastating strain. The research alone is hazardous. A single slip-up in lab security and you could have millions of people accidentally infected. And no means of treatment. It's the kind of worldwide disaster a scientist doesn't want to think about."

"Armageddon."

He nodded, his gaze frighteningly sane. "If you believe in such a thing. That's exactly what it'd be."

She shook her head. "I don't understand why these things are allowed."

"They aren't. By international agreement, they're outlawed. But there's always some madman lurking in the shadows who wants that extra bit of leverage, that weapon no one else has."

A madman. That's what one would have to be, to even think of unleashing such a weapon on the world. She thought of a novel she'd read, about just such a plague, how the cities had lain dead and decaying, how the very air had turned poisonous. But those were only the nightmares of science fiction. This was real.

From somewhere in the building came the sound of whistling.

Cathy and Victor both sat up straight. The melody traveled along the hall, closer and closer, until it stopped right outside Hickey's door. They heard a rustling, then the slap of magazines hitting the floor.

"It's here!" said Cathy, leaping to her feet.

Victor was right behind her as she hurried into the front room. She spotted it immediately, sitting atop the pile: a padded envelope, addressed in her handwriting. She scooped it up and ripped the envelope open. Out slid the roll of film. The note she'd scribbled to Hickey fluttered to the floor. Grinning in triumph, she held up the canister. "Here's your evidence!"

"We hope. Let's see what we've got on the roll. Where's the darkroom?"

"Next to the dressing room." She handed him the film. "Do you know how to process it?"

"I've done some amateur photography. As long as I've got the chemicals I can—" He stopped and glanced over at the desk.

The phone was ringing.

Victor shook his head. "Ignore it," he said and turned for the darkroom.

As they left the reception room, they heard the answering machine click on. Hickey's voice, smooth as silk, spoke on the recording. "This is the studio of Hickman Von Trapp, specializing in tasteful and artistic images of the female form...."

Victor laughed. "Tasteful?"

"It depends on your taste," said Cathy as she followed him up the hall.

They had just reached the darkroom when the recording ended and was followed by the message beep. An agitated voice rattled from the speaker. "Hello? Hello, Cathy? If you're there, answer me, will you? There's an FBI agent looking for you—some guy named Polowski—"

Cathy stopped dead. "It's Jack!" she said, turning to retrace her steps toward the front room.

The voice on the speaker had taken on a note of panic. "I couldn't help it—he made me tell him about Hickey. Get out of there now!"

The message clicked off just as Cathy grabbed the receiver. "Hello? *Jack?*"

She heard only the dial tone. He'd already hung up. Hands shaking, she began to punch in Jack's phone number.

"There's no time!" said Victor.

"I have to talk to him—"

He grabbed the receiver and slammed it down. "Later! We have to get out of here!"

She nodded numbly and started for the door. There she halted. "Wait. We need money!" She turned back to the reception desk and searched the drawers until she found the petty cash box. Twenty-two dollars was all it contained. "Always keep just enough for decent coffee beans," Hickey used to say. She pocketed the money. Then she reached up and yanked one of Hickey's old raincoats from the door hook. He wouldn't miss it. And she might need it for concealment. "Okay," she said, slipping on the coat. "Let's go."

They paused only a second to check the corridor. From another suite came the faint echo of laughter. Somewhere above, high heels clicked across a wooden floor. With Victor in the lead, they darted down the hall and out the front door.

The midday sun seemed to glare down on them like an accusing eye. Quickly they fell into step with the rest of the lunch crowd, the businessmen and artists, the Union Street chic. No one glanced their way. But even with people all around her, Cathy felt conspicuous. As though, in this bright cityscape of crowds and concrete, she was the focus of the painter's eye.

She huddled deeper into the raincoat, wishing it were a mantle of invisibility. Victor had quickened his pace, and she had to run to keep up.

"Where do we go now?" she whispered.

"We've got the film. Now I say we head for the bus station."

"And then?"

"Anywhere." He kept his gaze straight ahead. "As long as it's out of this city."

CHAPTER SEVEN

That pesky FBI agent was ringing his doorbell again.

Sighing, Jack opened the front door. "Back already?"

"Damn right I'm back." Polowski stamped in and shoved the door closed behind him. "I want to know where to find 'em next."

"I told you, Mr. Polowski. Over on Union Street there's a studio owned by Mr. Hickman—"

"I've been to Von Whats-his-name's studio."

Jack swallowed. "You didn't find them?"

"You knew I wouldn't. You warned 'em, didn't you?"

"Really, I don't know why you're harrassing me. I've tried to be—"

"They left in a hurry. The door was wide open. Food was still lying around. They left the empty cash box just sitting on the desk."

Jack drew himself up in outrage. "Are you calling my ex-wife a petty thief?"

"I'm calling her a desperate woman. And I'm calling you an imbecile for screwing things up. Now where is she?"

"I don't know."

"Who would she turn to?"

"No one I know."

"Think harder."

Jack stared down at Polowski's turgid face and marveled that any human being could be so unattractive. Surely the process of natural selection would have dictated against such unacceptable genes?

Jack shook his head. "I honestly don't know."

It was the truth, and Polowski must have sensed it. After a moment of silent confrontation, he backed off. "Then maybe you can tell me this. Why did you warn them?"

"It—it was—" Jack shrugged helplessly. "Oh, I don't know!

After you left, I wasn't sure I'd done the right thing. I wasn't sure whether to trust you. *He* doesn't trust you.''

"Who?"

"Victor Holland. He thinks you're in on some conspiracy. Frankly, the man struck me as just the slightest bit paranoid.''

"He has a right to be. Considering what's happened to him so far.'' Polowski turned for the door.

"Now what happens?''

"I keep looking for them.''

"Where?''

"You think I'd tell *you?*'' He stalked out. "Don't leave town, Zuckerman,'' he snapped over his shoulder. "I'll be back to see you later.''

"I don't think so,'' Jack muttered softly as he watched the other man lumber back to his car. He looked up and saw there wasn't a cloud in the sky. Smiling to himself, he shut the door.

It would be sunny in Mexico, as well.

Someone had left in a hurry.

Savitch strolled through the rooms of the photo studio, which had been left unlocked. He noted the scraps of a meal on the four-poster bed: crumbs of sourdough bread, part of a salami, an empty pickle jar. He also took note of the coffee cups: there were two of them. Interesting, since Savitch had spotted only one person leaving the studio, a squat little man in a polyester suit. The man hadn't been there long. Savitch had observed him climb into a dark green Ford parked at a fifteen-minute meter. The meter still had three minutes remaining.

Savitch continued his tour of the studio, eyeing the tawdry photos, wondering if this wasn't another waste of his time. After all, every other address he'd pulled from the woman's black book had turned up no sign of her. Why should Hickman Von Trapp's address be any different?

Still, he couldn't shake the instinct that he was getting close. Clues were everywhere. He read them, put them together. Today, this studio had been visited by two hungry people. They'd entered through a broken window in the dressing room. They'd eaten scraps taken from the refrigerator. They (or the man in the polyester suit) had emptied the petty cash box.

Savitch completed his tour and returned to the front room. That's when he noticed the telephone message machine blinking on and off.

He pressed the play button. The string of messages seemed endless. The calls were for someone named Hickey—no doubt the Hickman Von Trapp of the address book. Savitch lazily circled the room, half listening to the succession of voices. Business calls for the most part, inquiring about appointments, asking when proofs would be ready and would he like to do the shoot for *Snoop* magazine? Near the door, Savitch halted and stooped down to sift through the pile of mail. It was boring stuff, all addressed to Von Trapp. Then he noticed, off to the side, a loose slip of paper. It was a note, addressed to Hickey.

"Feel awful about this, but someone stole all those rolls of film from my car. This was the only one left. Thought I'd get it to you before it's lost, as well. Hope it's enough to save your shoot from being a complete waste—"

It was signed "Cathy."

He stood up straight. Catherine Weaver? It had to be! The roll of film—where the hell was the roll of film?

He rifled through the mail, searching, searching. He turned up only a torn envelope with Cathy Weaver's return address. The film was gone. In frustration, he began to fling magazines across the room. Then, in mid-toss, he froze.

A new message was playing on the recorder.

"Hello? Hello, Cathy? If you're there, answer me, will you? There's an FBI agent looking for you—some guy named Polowski. I couldn't help it—he made me tell him about Hickey. Get out of there now!"

Savitch stalked over to the answering machine and stared down as the mechanism automatically whirred back to the beginning. He replayed it.

Get out of there now!

There was now no doubt. Catherine Weaver had been here, and Victor Holland was with her. But who was this agent Polowski and why was he searching for Holland? Savitch had been assured that the Bureau was off the case. He would have to check into the matter.

He crossed over to the window and stared out at the bright sunshine, the crowded sidewalks. So many faces, so many strangers. Where, in this city, would two terrified fugitives hide? Finding them would be difficult, but not impossible.

He left the suite and went outside to a pay phone. There he dialed a Washington, D.C., number. He wasn't fond of asking the Cowboy for help, but now he had no choice. Victor Holland had his hands on the evidence, and the stakes had shot sky-high.

It was time to step up the pursuit.

The clerk yelled, "Next window, please!" and closed the grate.

"Wait!" cried Cathy, tapping at the pane. "My bus is leaving right now!"

"Which one?"

"Number 23 to Palo Alto—"

"There's another at seven o'clock."

"But—"

"I'm on my dinner break."

Cathy stared helplessly as the clerk walked away. Over the PA system came the last call for the Palo Alto express. Cathy glanced around just in time to see the Number 23 roar away from the curb.

"Service just ain't what it used to be," an old man muttered behind her. "Get there faster usin' yer damn thumb."

Sighing, Cathy shifted to the next line, which was eight-deep and slow as molasses. The woman at the front was trying to convince the clerk that her social security card was an acceptable ID for a check.

Okay, Cathy thought. *So we leave at seven o'clock. That puts us in Palo Alto at eight. Then what? Camp in a park? Beg a few scraps from a restaurant? What does Victor have in mind...?*

She glanced around and spotted his broad back hunched inside one of the phone booths. Whom could he possibly be calling? She saw him hang up and run his hand wearily through his hair. Then he picked up the receiver and dialed another number.

"Next!" Someone tapped Cathy on the shoulder. "Go ahead, Miss."

Cathy turned and saw that the ticket clerk was waiting. She stepped to the window.

"Where to?" asked the clerk.

"I need two tickets to…" Cathy's voice suddenly faded.

"Where?"

Cathy didn't speak. Her gaze had frozen on a poster tacked right beside the ticket window. The words Have You seen This Man? appeared above an unsmiling photo of Victor Holland. And at the bottom were listed the charges: Industrial espionage and murder. If you have any information about this man, please contact your local police or the FBI.

"Lady, you wanna go somewhere or not?"

"What?" Cathy's gaze jerked back to the clerk, who was watching her with obvious annoyance. "Oh. Yes, I'm—I'd like two tickets. To Palo Alto." Numbly she handed over a fistful of cash. "One way."

"Two to Palo Alto. That bus will depart at 7:00, Gate 11."

"Yes. Thank you…" Cathy took the tickets and turned to leave the line. That's when she spotted the two policemen, standing just inside the front entrance. They seemed to be scanning the terminal, searching—for what?

In a panic, her gaze shot to the phone booth. It was empty. She stared at it with a sense of abandonment. *You left me! You left me with two tickets to Palo Alto and five bucks in my pocket!*

Where are you, Victor?

She couldn't stand here like an idiot. She had to do something, had to move. She pulled the raincoat tightly around her shoulders and forced herself to stroll across the terminal. *Don't let them notice me,* she prayed. *Please. I'm nobody. Nothing.* She paused at a chair and picked up a discarded *San Francisco Chronicle*. Then, thumbing through the Want Ads, she sauntered right past the two policemen. They didn't even glance at her as she went out the front entrance.

Now what? she wondered, pausing amidst the confusion of a busy sidewalk. Automatically she started to walk and had taken only half a dozen steps down the street when she was wrenched sideways, into an alley.

She reeled back against the trash cans and almost sobbed with relief. "Victor!"

"Did they see you?"

"No. I mean, yes, but they didn't seem to care—"

"Are you sure?" She nodded. He turned and slapped the wall in frustration. "What the hell do we do now?"

"I have the tickets."

"We can't use them."

"How are we going to get out of town? Hitchhike? Victor, we're down to our last five dollars!"

"They'll be watching every bus that leaves. And they've got my face plastered all over the damn terminal!" He slumped back against the wall and groaned. "*Have you seen this man?* God, I looked like some two-bit gangster."

"It wasn't the most flattering photo."

He managed to laugh. "Have you *ever* seen a flattering wanted poster?"

She leaned back beside him, against the wall. "We've got to get out of this city, Victor."

"Amend that. *You've* got to get out."

"What's that supposed to mean?"

"The police aren't looking for you. So *you* take that bus to Palo Alto. I'll put you in touch with some old friends. They'll see you make it somewhere safe."

"No."

"Cathy, they've probably got my mug posted in every airport and car rental agency in town! We've spent almost all our money for those bus tickets. I say you use them!"

"I'm not leaving you."

"You don't have a choice."

"Yes I do. I choose to stick to you like glue. Because you're the only one I feel safe with. The only one I can count on!"

"I can move faster on my own. Without you slowing me down." He looked off, toward the street. "Hell, I don't even *want* you around."

"I don't believe that."

"Why should I care what you believe?"

"Look at me! Look at me and say that!" She grabbed his arm, willing him to face her. "Say you don't want me around!"

He started to speak, to repeat the lie. She knew then that it *was* a lie; she could see it in his eyes. And she saw something else in that gaze, something that took her breath away.

He said, "I don't—I won't have you—"

She just stood there, looking up at him, waiting for the truth to come.

What she didn't expect was the kiss. She never remembered how it happened. She only knew that all at once his arms were around her and she was being swept up into some warm and safe and wonderful place. It started as an embrace more of desperation than passion, a coming together of two terrified people. But the instant their lips met, it became something much more. This went beyond fear, beyond need. This was a souls' joining, one that wouldn't be broken, even after this embrace was over, even if they never touched again.

When at last they drew apart and stared at each other, the taste of him was still fresh on her lips.

"You see?" she whispered. "I was right. You do want me around. You do."

He smiled and touched her cheek. "I'm not a very good liar."

"And I'm not leaving you. You need me. You can't show your face, but I can! I can buy bus tickets, run errands—"

"What I really need," he sighed, "is a new face." He glanced out at the street. "Since there's no plastic surgeon handy, I suggest we hoof it over to the BART station. It'll be crowded at this hour. We might make it to the East Bay—"

"God, I'm such an *idiot!*" she groaned. "A new face is exactly what you need!" She turned toward the street. "Come on. There isn't much time...."

"Cathy?" He followed her up the alley. They both paused, scanning the street for policemen. There were none in sight. "Where are we going?" he whispered.

"To find a phone booth."

"Oh. And who are we calling?"

She turned and the look she gave him was distinctly pained. "Someone we both know and love."

* * *

Jack was packing his suitcase when the phone rang. He considered not answering it, but something about the sound, an urgency that could only have been imagined, made him pick up the receiver. He was instantly sorry he had.

"Jack?"

He sighed. "Tell me I'm hearing things."

"Jack, I'm going to talk fast because your phone might be tapped—"

"You don't say."

"I need my kit. The whole shebang. And some cash. I swear I'll pay it all back. Get it for me right now. Then drop it off where we shot the last scene of *Cretinoid*. You know the spot."

"Cathy, you wait a minute! I'm in trouble enough as it is!"

"One hour. That's all I can wait."

"It's rush hour! I can't—"

"It's the last favor I'll ask of you." There was a pause. Then, softly, she added, "Please."

He let out a breath. "This is the absolute last time, right?"

"One hour, Jack. I'll be waiting."

Jack hung up and stared at his suitcase. It was only half packed, but it would have to do. He sure as hell wasn't coming back *here* tonight.

He closed the suitcase and carried it out to the Jaguar. As he drove away it suddenly occurred to him that he'd forgotten to cancel his date with Lulu tonight.

No time now, he thought. I've got more important things on my mind—like getting out of town.

Lulu would be mad as a hornet, but he'd make it up to her. Maybe a pair of diamond ear studs. Yeah, that would do the trick.

Good old Lulu, so easy to please. Now there was a woman he could understand.

The corner of Fifth and Mission was a hunker-down, chew-the-fat sort of gathering place for the street folk. At five forty-five it was even busier than usual. Rumor had it the soup kitchen down the block was fixing to serve beef Bourguignonne, which, as those who remembered better days and better meals could tell you, was made with red wine. No one passed up the chance for a taste of the grape, even if every drop of alcohol was simmered clean out of it. And so they stood around on the corner, talking of other meals they'd had, of the weather, of the long lines at the unemployment office.

No one noticed the two wretched souls huddled in the doorway of the pawnshop.

Lucky for us, thought Cathy, burying herself in the folds of the raincoat. The sad truth was, they were both beginning to fit right into this crowd. Just a moment earlier she'd caught sight of her own reflection in the pawnshop window and had almost failed to recognize the disheveled image staring back. *Has it been that long since I've combed my hair? That long since I've had a meal or a decent night's sleep?*

Victor looked no better. A torn shirt and two days' worth of stubble on his jaw only emphasized that unmistakable look of exhaustion. He could walk into that soup kitchen down the block and no one would look twice.

He's going to look a hell of a lot worse when I get through with him, she thought with a grim sense of humor.

If Jack ever showed up with the kit.

"It's 6:05," Victor muttered. "He's had an hour."

"Give him time."

"We're running out of time."

"We can still make the bus." She peered up the street, as though by force of will she could conjure up her ex-husband. But only a city bus barreled into view. *Come on, Jack, come on! Don't let me down this time....*

"Will ya lookit that!" came a low growl, followed by general murmurs of admiration from the crowd.

"Hey, pretty boy!" someone called as the group gathered on the corner to stare. "What'd you have to push to get yerself wheels like that?"

Through the gathering of men, Cathy spied the bright gleam of chrome and burgundy. "Get away from my car!" demanded a querulous voice. "I just had her waxed!"

"Looks like Pretty Boy got hisself lost. Turned down the wrong damn street, did ya?"

Cathy leaped to her feet. "He's here!"

She and Victor pushed through the crowd to find Jack standing guard over the Jaguar's gleaming finish.

"Don't—don't touch her!" he snapped as one man ran a grimy finger across the hood. "Why can't you people go find yourselves a job or something?"

"A job?" someone yelled. "What's that?"

"Jack!" called Cathy.

Jack let out a sigh of relief when he spotted her. "This is the last favor. The absolute *last* favor—"

"Where is it?" she asked.

Jack walked around to the trunk, where he slapped away another hand as it stroked the Jaguar's burgundy flank. "It's right here. The whole kit and kaboodle." He swung out the makeup case and handed it over. "Delivered as promised. Now I gotta run."

"Where are you going?" she called.

"I don't know." He climbed back into the car. "Somewhere. Anywhere!"

"Sounds like we're headed in the same direction."

"God, I hope not." He started the engine and revved it up a few times.

Someone yelled: "So long, Pretty Boy!"

Jack gazed out dryly at Cathy. "You know, you really should do something about the company you keep. Ciao, sweetcakes."

The Jaguar lurched away. With a screech of tires, it spun around the corner and vanished into traffic.

Cathy turned and saw that every eye was watching her. Automatically, Victor moved close beside her, one tired and hungry man facing a tired and hungry crowd.

Someone called out: "So who's the jerk in the Jag?"

"My ex-husband," said Cathy.

"Doin' a lot better than you are, honey."

"No kidding." She held up the makeup case and managed a careless laugh. "I ask the creep for my clothes, he throws me a change of underwear."

"Babe, now ain't that just the way it works?"

Already, the men were wandering away, regrouping in doorways, or over by the corner newsstands. The Jaguar was gone, and so was their interest.

Only one man stood before Cathy and Victor, and the look he gave them was distinctly sympathetic. "That's all he left you, huh? Him with that nice, fancy car?" He turned to leave, then glanced back at them. "Say, you two need a place to stay or somethin'? I got a lot of friends. And I hate to see a lady out in the cold."

"Thanks for the offer," said Victor, taking Cathy's hand. "But we've got a bus to catch."

The man nodded and shuffled away, a kind but unfortunate soul whom the streets had not robbed of decency.

"We have a half hour to get on that bus," said Victor, hurrying Cathy along. "Better get to work."

They were headed up the street, toward the cover of an alley, when Cathy suddenly halted. "Victor—"

"What's the matter?"

"Look." She pointed at the newsstand, her hand shaking.

Beneath the plastic cover was the afternoon edition of the *San Francisco Examiner*. The headline read: "Two Victims, Same Name. Police Probe Coincidence." Beside it was a photo of a young blond woman. The caption was hidden by the fold, but Cathy didn't need to read it. She could already guess the woman's name.

"Two of them," she whispered. "Victor, you were right...."

"All the more reason for us to get out of town." He pulled on her arm. "Hurry."

She let him lead her away. But even as they headed down the street, even as they left the newsstand behind them, she carried that image in her mind: the photograph of a blond woman, the second victim.

The second Catherine Weaver.

Patrolman O'Hanley was a helpful soul. Unlike too many of his colleagues, O'Hanley had joined the force out of a true desire to serve and protect. The "Boy Scout" was what the other men called him behind his back. The epithet both annoyed and pleased him. It told him he didn't fit in with the rough-and-tumble gang on the force. It also told him he was above it all, above the petty bribe-taking and backbiting and maneuverings for promotion. He wasn't out to glorify the badge on his chest. What he wanted was the chance to pat a kid on the head, rescue an old granny from a mugging.

That's why he found this particular assignment so frustrating. All this standing around in the bus depot, watching for a man some witness *might* have spotted a few hours ago. O'Hanley hadn't noticed any such character. He'd eyeballed every person who'd walked in the door. A sorry lot, most of them. Not surprising since, these days, anyone with the cash to spare took a plane. By the looks of these folks, none of 'em could spare much more than pennies. Take that pair over there, huddled together in the waiting area. A father and daughter, he figured, and both of 'em down on their luck. The daughter was bundled up in an old raincoat, the collar pulled up to reveal only a mop of windblown hair. The father was an even sorrier sight, gaunt-faced, white-whiskered, about as old as Methuselah. Still, there was a remnant of pride in the old codger— O'Hanley could see it in the way the man held himself, stiff and straight. Must've been an impressive fellow in his younger years since he was still well over six feet tall.

The public speaker announced final boarding for number fourteen to Palo Alto.

The old man and his daughter rose to their feet.

O'Hanley watched with concern as the pair shuffled across the terminal toward the departure gate. The woman was carrying only one small case, but it appeared to be a heavy one. And she already had her hands full, trying to guide the old man in the right direction. But they were making progress, and O'Hanley figured they'd make it to the bus okay.

That is, until the kid ran into them.

He was about six, the kind of kid no mother wants to admit she produced, the kind of kid who gives all six-year-olds a bad name. For the last half hour the boy had been tearing around the terminal, scattering ashtray sand, tipping over suitcases, banging locker doors. Now he was running. Only this kid was doing it *backward*.

O'Hanley saw it coming. The old man and his daughter were crossing slowly toward the departure gate. The kid was scuttling toward them. Intersecting paths, inevitable collision. The kid slammed into the woman's knees; the case flew out of her grasp.

She stumbled against her companion. O'Hanley, paralyzed, expected the codger to keel over. To his surprise, the old man simply caught the woman in his arms and handily set her back on her feet.

By now O'Hanley was hurrying to their aid. He got to the woman just as she'd regained her footing. "You folks okay?" he asked.

The woman reacted as though he'd slapped her. She stared up at him with the eyes of a terrified animal. "What?" she said.

"Are you okay? Looked to me like he hit you pretty hard."

She nodded.

"How 'bout you, Gramps?"

The woman glanced at her companion. It seemed to O'Hanley that there was a lot being said in that glance, a lot he wasn't privy to.

"We're both fine," the woman said quickly. "Come on, Pop. We'll miss our bus."

"Can I give you a hand with him?"

"That's mighty kind of you, officer, but we'll do fine." The woman smiled at O'Hanley. Something about that smile wasn't right. As he watched the pair shuffle off toward bus number fourteen, O'Hanley kept trying to figure it out. Kept trying to put his finger on what was wrong with that pair of travelers.

He turned away and almost tripped over the fallen case. The woman had forgotten it. He snatched it up and started to run for the bus. Too late; the number fourteen to Palo Alto was already pulling away. O'Hanley stood helplessly on the curb, watching the taillights vanish around the corner.

Oh, well.

He turned in the makeup case at Lost and Found. Then he stationed himself once again at the entrance. Seven o'clock already and still no sighting of the suspect Victor Holland.

O'Hanley sighed. What a waste of a policeman's time.

Five minutes out of San Francisco, aboard the number fourteen bus, the old man turned to the woman in the raincoat and said, "This beard is killing me."

Laughing, Cathy reached up and gave the fake whiskers a tug. "It did the trick, didn't it?"

"No kidding. We practically got a police escort to the getaway bus." He scratched furiously at his chin. "Geez, how do those actors stand this stuff, anyway? The itch is driving me up a wall."

"Want me to take it off?"

"Better not. Not till we get to Palo Alto."

Another hour, she thought. She sat back and gazed out at the highway gliding past the bus window. "Then what?" she asked softly.

"I'll knock on a few doors. See if I can dig up an old friend or two. It's been a long time, but I think there are still a few in town."

"You used to live there?"

"Years ago. Back when I was in college."

"Oh." She sat up straight. "A *Stanford* man."

"Why do you make it sound just a tad disreputable?"

"I rooted for the Bears, myself."

"I'm consorting with the arch enemy?"

Giggling, she burrowed against his chest and inhaled the warm, familiar scent of his body. "It seems like another lifetime. Berkeley and blue jeans."

"Football. Wild parties."

"Wild parties?" she asked. "You?"

"Well, *rumors* of wild parties."

"Frisbee. Classes on the lawn…"

"Innocence," he said softly.

They both fell silent.

"Victor?" she asked. "What if your friends aren't there any longer? Or what if they won't take us in?"

"One step at a time. That's how we have to take it. Otherwise it'll all seem too overwhelming."

"It already does."

He squeezed her tightly against him. "Hey, we're doing okay. We made it out of the city. In fact, we waltzed out right under the nose of a cop. I'd call that pretty damn impressive."

Cathy couldn't help grinning at the memory of the earnest young Patrolman O'Hanley. "All policemen should be so helpful."

"Or blind," Victor snorted. "I can't believe he called me *Gramps*."

"When I set out to change a face, I do it right."

"Apparently."

She looped her arm through his and pressed a kiss to one scowling, bewhiskered cheek. "Can I tell you a secret?"

"What's that?"

"I'm crazy about older men."

The scowl melted away, slowly reformed into a dubious smile. "How much older are we talking about?"

She kissed him again, this time full on the lips. "Much older."

"Hm. Maybe these whiskers aren't so bad, after all." He took her face in his hands. This time he was the one kissing her, long and deeply, with no thought of where they were or where they were going. Cathy felt herself sliding back against the seat, into a space that was inescapable and infinitely safe.

Someone behind them hooted: "Way to go, Gramps!"

Reluctantly, they pulled apart. Through the flickering shadows of the bus, Cathy could see the twinkle in Victor's eyes, the gleam of a wry smile.

She smiled back and whispered, "Way to go, Gramps."

The posters with Victor Holland's face were plastered all over the bus station.

Polowski couldn't help a snort of irritation as he gazed at that unflattering visage of what he knew in his gut was an innocent man. A damn witchhunt, that's what this'd turned into. If Holland wasn't already scared enough, this public stalking would surely send him diving for cover, beyond the reach of those who could help him. Polowski only hoped it'd also be beyond the reach of those with less benign intentions.

With all these posters staring him in the face, Holland would've been a fool to stroll through this bus depot. Still, Polowski had an instinct about these things, a sense of how people behaved when they were desperate. If he were in Holland's shoes, a killer on his trail and a woman companion to worry about, he knew what *he'd* do—get the hell out of San Francisco. A plane was unlikely. According to Jack Zuckerman, Holland was operating on a thin wallet. A credit card would've been out of the question. That also knocked out a rental car. What was left? It was either hitchhike or take the bus.

Polowski was betting on the bus.

His last piece of info supported that hunch. The tap on Zucker-man's phone had picked up a call from Cathy Weaver. She'd arranged some sort of drop-off at a site Polowski couldn't identify at first. He'd spent a frustrating hour asking around the office, trying to locate someone who'd not only seen Zuckerman's forgettable film, *Cretinoid,* but could also pinpoint where the last scene was filmed. The Mission District, some movie nut file clerk had finally told him. Yeah, she was sure of it. The monster came up through the manhole cover right at the corner of Fifth and Mission and slurped down a derelict or two just before the hero smashed him with a crated piano. Polowski hadn't stayed to hear the rest; he'd made a run for his car.

By that time, it was too late. Holland and the woman were gone, and Zuckerman had vanished. Polowski found himself cruising down Mission, his doors locked, his windows rolled up, wondering when the local police were going to clean up the damn streets.

That's when he remembered the bus depot was only a few blocks away.

Now, standing among the tired and slack-jawed travelers at the bus station, he was beginning to think he'd wasted his time. All those wanted posters staring him in the face. And there was a cop standing over by the coffee machine, taking furtive sips from a foam cup.

Polowski strolled over to the cop. "FBI," he said, flashing his badge.

The cop—he was scarcely more than a boy—instantly straightened. "Patrolman O'Hanley, sir."

"Seeing much action?"

"Uh—you mean today?"

"Yeah. Here."

"No, sir." O'Hanley sighed. "Pretty much a bust. I mean, I could be out on patrol. Instead they got me hanging around here eyeballing faces."

"Surveillance?"

"Yes, sir." He nodded at the poster of Holland. "That guy. Everyone's hot to find him. They say he's a spy."

"Do they, now?" Polowski took a lazy glance around the room. "Seen anyone around here who looks like him?"

"Not a one. I been watching every minute."

Polowski didn't doubt it. O'Hanley was the kind of kid who, if you asked him to, would scrub the Captain's boots with a toothbrush. He'd do a good job of it, too.

Obviously Holland hadn't come through here. Polowski turned to leave. Then another thought came to mind, and he turned back to O'Hanley. "The suspect may be traveling with a woman," he said. He pulled out a photo of Cathy Weaver, one Jack Zuckerman had been persuaded to donate to the FBI. "Have you seen her come through here?"

O'Hanley frowned. "Gee. She sure does look like... Naw. That can't be her."

"Who?"

"Well, there was this woman in here 'bout an hour ago. Kind of a down and outer. Some little brat ran smack into her. I sort've brushed her off and sent her on her way. She looked a lot like this gal, only in a lot worse shape."

"Was she traveling alone?"

"She had an old guy with her. Her pop, I think."

Suddenly Polowski was all ears. That instinct again—it was telling him something. "What did this old man look like?"

"Real old. Maybe seventy. Had this bushy beard, lot of white hair."

"How tall?"

"Pretty tall. Over six feet..." O'Hanley's voice trailed off as his gaze focused on the wanted poster. Victor Holland was six foot three. O'Hanley's face went white. "Oh, God..."

"Was it him?"

"I—I can't be sure—"

"Come on, come on!"

"I just don't know... Wait. The woman, she dropped a makeup case! I turned it in at that window there—"

It took only a flash of an FBI badge for the clerk in Lost and Found to hand over the case. The instant Polowski opened the thing, he knew he'd hit pay dirt. It was filled with theatrical makeup supplies. Stenciled inside the lid was: Property of Jack Zuckerman Productions.

He slammed the lid shut. "Where did they go?" he snapped at O'Hanley.

"They—uh, they boarded a bus right over there. That gate. Around seven o'clock."

Polowski glanced up at the departure schedule. At seven o'clock, the number fourteen had departed for Palo Alto.

It took him ten minutes to get hold of the Palo Alto depot manager, another five minutes to convince the man this wasn't just another Prince-Albert-in-the-can phone call.

"The number fourteen from San Francisco?" came the answer. "Arrived twenty minutes ago."

"What about the passengers?" pressed Polowski. "You see any of 'em still around?"

The manager only laughed. "Hey, man. If you had a choice, would *you* hang around a stinking bus station?"

Muttering an oath, Polowski hung up.

"Sir?" It was O'Hanley. He looked sick. "I messed up, didn't I? I let him walk right past me. I can't believe—"

"Forget it."

"But—"

Polowski headed for the exit. "You're just a rookie," he called over his shoulder. "Chalk it up to experience."

"Should I call this in?"

"I'll take care of it. I'm headed there, anyway."

"Where?"

Polowski shoved open the station door. "Palo Alto."

CHAPTER EIGHT

The front door was answered by an elderly oriental woman whose command of English was limited.

"Mrs. Lum? Remember me? Victor Holland. I used to know your son."

"Yes, yes!"

"Is he here?"

"Yes." Her gaze shifted to Cathy now, as though the woman didn't want her second visitor to feel left out of the conversation.

"I need to see him," said Victor. "Is Milo here?"

"Milo?" At last here was a word she seemed to know. She turned and called out loudly in Chinese.

Somewhere a door squealed open and footsteps stamped up the stairs. A fortyish oriental man in blue jeans and chambray shirt came to the front door. He was a dumpling of a fellow, and he brought with him the vague odor of chemicals, something sharp and acidic. He was wiping his hands on a rag.

"What can I do for you?" he asked.

Victor grinned. "Milo Lum! Are you still skulking around in your mother's basement?"

"Excuse me?" Milo inquired politely. "Am I supposed to know you, sir?"

"Don't recognize an old horn player from the Out of Tuners?"

Milo stared in disbelief. "Gershwin? That can't be *you?*"

"Yeah, I know," Victor said with a laugh. "The years haven't been kind."

"I didn't want to say anything, but…"

"I won't take it personally. Since—" Victor peeled off his false beard "—the face isn't all mine."

Milo gazed down at the lump of fake whispers, hanging like a dead animal in Victor's grasp. Then he stared up at Victor's jaw, still blotchy with spirit gum. "This is some kind of joke on old Milo, right?" He stuck his head out the door, glancing past Victor at the sidewalk. "And the other guys are hiding out there some-where, waiting to yell *surprise!* Aren't they? Some big practical joke."

"I wish it were a joke," said Victor.

Milo instantly caught the undertone of urgency in Victor's voice. He looked at Cathy, then back at Victor. Nodding, he stepped aside. "Come in, Gersh. Sounds like I have some catching up to do."

Over a late supper of duck noodle soup and jasmine tea, Milo heard the story. He said little; he seemed more intent on slurping down the last of his noodles. Only when the ever-smiling Mrs. Lum had bowed good-night and creaked off to bed did Milo offer his comment.

"When you get in trouble, man, you sure as hell do it right."

"Astute as always, Milo," sighed Victor.

"Too bad we can't say the same for the cops," Milo snorted. "If they'd just bothered to ask around, they would've learned you're harmless. Far as I know, you're guilty of only one serious crime."

Cathy looked up, startled. "What crime?"

"Assaulting the ears of victims unlucky enough to hear his sax-ophone."

"This from a piccolo player who practises with earplugs," ob-served Victor.

"That's to drown out extraneous noise."

"Yeah. Mainly your own."

Cathy grinned. "I'm beginning to understand why you called yourselves the Out of Tuners."

"Just some healthy self-deprecating humor," said Milo. "Some-thing we needed after we failed to make the Stanford band." Milo rose, shoving away from the kitchen table. "Well, come on. Let's see what's on that mysterious roll of film."

He led them along the hall and down a rickety set of steps to the basement. The chemical tang of the air, the row of trays lined up on a stainless-steel countertop and the slow drip, drip of water from the faucet told Cathy she was standing in an enormous darkroom. Tacked on the walls was a jumble of photos. Faces, mostly, appar-ently snapped around the world. Here and there she spotted a newsworthy shot: soldiers storming an airport, protestors unfurling a banner.

"Is this your job, Milo?" she asked.

"I wish," said Milo, agitating the developing canister. "No, I just work in the ol' family business."

"Which is?"

"Shoes. Italian, Brazilian, leather, alligator, you name it, we import it." He cocked his head at the photos. "That's how I get my exotic faces. Shoe-buying trips. I'm an expert on the female arch."

"For that," said Victor, "he spent four years at Stanford."

"Why not? Good a place as any to study the fine feet of the fair sex." A timer rang. Milo poured out the developer, removed the roll of film, and hung it up to dry. "Actually," he said, squinting at the negatives, "it was my dad's dying request. He wanted a son with a Stanford degree. I wanted four years of nonstop partying. We both got our wishes." He paused and gazed off wistfully at his photos. "Too bad I can't say the same of the years since then."

"What do you mean?" asked Cathy.

"I mean the partying's long since over. Gotta earn those profits, keep up those sales. Never thought life'd come down to the bottom line. Whatever happened to all that rabble-rousing potential, hey, Gersh? We sort of lost it along the way. All of us, Bach and Ollie and Roger. The Out of Tuners finally stepped into line. Now we're all marching to the beat of the same boring drummer." He sighed and glanced at Victor. "You make out anything on those negatives?"

Victor shook his head. "We need prints."

Milo flipped off the lights, leaving only the red glow of the darkroom lamp. "Coming up."

As Milo laid out the photographic paper, Victor asked, "What happened to the other guys? They still around?"

Milo flipped the exposure switch. "Roger's VP at some multinational bank in Tokyo. Into silk suits and ties, the whole nine yards. Bach's got an electronics firm in San José."

"And Ollie?"

"What can I say about Ollie?" Milo slipped the first print into the bath. "He's still lurking around in that lab over at Stanford Med. I doubt he ever sees the light of day. I figure he's got some secret chamber in the basement where he keeps his assistant Igor chained to the wall.''

"This guy I have to meet," said Cathy.

"Oh, he'd love you." Victor laughed and gave her arm a squeeze. "Seeing as he's probably forgotten what the female of the species looks like."

Milo slid the print into the next tray. "Yeah, Ollie's the one who never changed. Still the night owl. Still plays a mean clarinet." He glanced at Victor. "How's the sax, Gersh? You keeping it up?"

"Haven't played in months."

"Lucky neighbors."

"How did you ever get that name?" asked Cathy. "Gersh?"

"Because," said Milo, wielding tongs as he transferred another batch of prints between trays, "he's a firm believer in the power of George Gershwin to win a lady's heart. 'Someone to Watch Over Me,' wasn't that the tune that made Lily say..." Milo's voice suddenly faded. He looked at his friend with regret.

"You're right," said Victor quietly. "That was the tune. And Lily said yes."

Milo shook his head. "Sorry. Guess I still have a hard time remembering she's gone."

"Well, she is," said Victor, his voice matter-of-fact. Cathy knew there was pain buried in the undertones. But he hid it well. "And right now," Victor said, "we've got other things to think about."

"Yeah." Milo, chastened, turned his attention back to the prints he'd just developed. He fished them out and clipped the first few sheets on the line to dry. "Okay, Gersh. Tell us what's on this roll that's worth killing for."

Milo switched on the lights.

Victor stood in silence for a moment, frowning at the first five dripping prints. To Cathy, the data was meaningless, only a set of numbers and codes, recorded in an almost illegible hand.

"Well," grunted Milo. "That sure tells me a lot."

Victor's gaze shifted quickly from one page to the next. He paused at the fifth photo, where a column ran down the length of the page. It contained a series of twenty-seven entries, each one a date followed by the same three letters: EXP.

"Victor?" asked Cathy. "What does it mean?"

He turned to them. It was the look in his eyes that worried her. The stillness. Quietly he said, "We need to call Ollie."

"You mean tonight?" asked Milo. "Why?"

"This isn't just some experiment in test tubes and petri dishes. They've gone beyond that, to clinical trials." Victor pointed to the last page. "These are monkeys. Each one was infected with a new virus. A manmade virus. And in every case the results were the same."

"You mean this?" Milo pointed to the last column. "EXP?"

"It stands for expired," said Victor. "They all died."

Sam Polowski sat on a bench in the Palo Alto bus terminal and wondered: If I wanted to disappear, where would I go next? He watched a dozen or so passengers straggle off to board the 210 from San José, noting they were by and large the Birkenstock and backpack set. Probably Stanford students heading off for Christmas break. He wondered why it was that students who could afford such a pricey university couldn't seem to scrape up enough to buy a decent pair of jeans. Or even a decent haircut, for that matter.

At last Polowski rose and automatically dusted off his coat, a habit he'd picked up from his early years of hanging around the seamier side of town. Even if the grime wasn't actually visible, he'd always *felt* it was there, coating any surface he happened to brush against, ready to cling to him like wet paint.

He made one phone call—to Dafoe's answering machine, to tell him Victor Holland had moved on to Palo Alto. It was, after all, his responsibility to keep his supervisor informed. He was glad he only had to talk to a recording and not to the man himself.

He left the bus station and strolled down the street, heading Lord knew where, in search of a spark, a hunch. It was a nice-enough neighborhood, a nice-enough town. Palo Alto had its old professors' houses, its bookshops and coffee houses where university types, the ones with the beards and wire-rim glasses, liked to sit and argue the meaning of Proust and Brecht and Goethe. Polowski remembered his own university days, when, after being subjected to an hour of such crap from the students at the next table, he had finally stormed over to them and yelled, "Maybe Brecht meant it that way, maybe not. But can you guys answer this? *What the hell difference does it make?"*

This did not, needless to say, enhance his reputation as a serious scholar.

Now, as he paced along the street, no doubt in the footsteps of more serious philosophers, Polowski turned over in his head the question of Victor Holland. More specifically the question of where such a man, in his desperation, would hide. He stalked past the lit windows, the glow of TVs, the cars spilling from garages. Where in this warren of suburbia was the man hiding?

Holland was a scientist, a musician, a man of few but lasting friendships. He had a Ph.D. from MIT, a B.S. from Stanford. The university was right up the road. The man must know his way around here. Maybe he still had friends in the neighborhood, people who'd take him in, keep his secrets.

Polowski decided to take another look at Holland's file. Somewhere in the Viratek records, there had to be some employment reference, some recommendation from a Stanford contact. A friend Holland might turn to.

Sooner or later, he would have to turn to *someone.*

It was after midnight when Dafoe and his wife returned home. He was in an excellent mood, his head pleasantly abuzz with champagne, his ears still ringing with the heart-wrenching aria from *Samson and Delilah.* Opera was a passion for him, a brilliant staging of courage and conflict and *amore,* a vision of life so much grander than the petty little world in which he found himself. It launched him to a plane of such thrilling intensity that even his own wife took on exciting new aspects. He watched her peel off her coat and kick off her shoes. Forty pounds overweight, hair streaked with silver, yet she had her attractions. *It's been three weeks. Surely she'll let me tonight....*

But his wife ignored his amorous looks and wandered off to the kitchen. A moment later, the rumble of the automatic dishwasher announced another of her fits of housecleaning.

In frustration, Dafoe turned and stabbed the blinking button on his answering machine. The message from Polowski completely destroyed any amorous intentions he had left.

"...Reason to believe Holland is in, or has just left, the Palo Alto area. Following leads. Will keep you informed...."

Polowski, you half-wit. Is following orders so damn difficult?

It was 3:00 a.m. Washington time. An ungodly hour, but he made the phone call.

The voice that answered was raspy with sleep. "Tyrone here."

"Cowboy, this is Dafoe. Sorry to wake you."

The voice became instantly alert, all sleep shaken from it. "What's up?"

"New lead on Holland. I don't know the particulars, but he's headed south, to Palo Alto. May still be there."

"The university?"

"It is the Stanford area."

"That may be a very big help."

"Anything for an old buddy. I'll keep you posted."

"One thing, Dafoe."

"Yeah?"

"I can't have any interference. Pull all your people out. We'll take it from here."

Dafoe paused. "I might...have a problem."

"A problem?" The voice, though quiet, took on a razor's edge.

"It's, uh, one of my men. Sort of a wild card. Sam Polowski. He's got this Holland case under his skin, wants to go after him."

"There's such a thing as a direct order."

"At the moment, Polowski's unreachable. He's in Palo Alto, digging around in God knows what."

"Loose cannons. I don't like them."

"I'll pull him back as soon as I can."

"Do that. And keep it quiet. It's a matter of utmost security."

After Dafoe hung up, his gaze shifted automatically to the photo on the mantelpiece. It was a '68 snapshot of him and the Cowboy: two young marines, both of them grinning, their rifles slung over their shoulders as they stood ankle-deep in a rice paddy. It was a crazy time, when one's very life depended on the loyalty of buddies. When Semper Fi applied not only to the corps in general but to each other in particular. Matt Tyrone was a hero then, and he was a hero now. Dafoe stared at that smiling face in the photo, disturbed by the threads of envy that had woven into his admiration for the man. Though Dafoe had much to be proud of—a solid eighteen years in the FBI, maybe even a shot at assistant director somewhere in his stars, he couldn't match the heady climb of Matt Tyrone in the NSA. Though Dafoe wasn't clear as to exactly what position the Cowboy held in the NSA, he had heard that Tyrone regularly attended cabinet meetings, that he held the trust of the president, that he dealt in secrets and shadows and security. He was the sort of man the country needed, a man for whom patriotism was more than mere flag-waving and rhetoric; it was a way of life. Matt Tyrone would do more than die for his country; he'd live for it.

Dafoe couldn't let such a man, such a friend, down.

He dialed Sam Polowski's home phone and left a message on the recorder.

This is a direct order. You are to withdraw from the Holland case immediately. Until further notice you are on suspension.

He was tempted to add, *by special request from my friends in Washington,* but thought better of it. No room for vanity here. The Cowboy had said national security was at stake.

Dafoe had no doubt it truly was. He'd gotten the word from Matt Tyrone. And Matt Tyrone's authority came direct from the President himself.

"This does not look good. This does not look good at all."

Ollie Wozniak squinted through his wire-rim glasses at the twenty-four photographs strewn across Milo's dining table. He held one up for a closer look. Through the bottle-glass lens, one pale blue eye stared out, enormous. One only saw Ollie's eyes; everything else, hollow cheeks, pencil lips and baby-fine hair, seemed to recede into the background pallor. He shook his head and picked up another photo.

"You're right, of course," he said. "Some of these I can't interpret. I'd like to study 'em later. But these here are definitely raw mortality data. Rhesus monkeys, I suspect." He paused and added quietly, "I hope."

"Surely they wouldn't use people for this sort of thing," said Cathy.

"Not officially." Ollie put down the photo and looked at her. "But it's been done."

"Maybe in Nazi Germany."

"Here, too," said Victor.

"What?" Cathy looked at him in disbelief.

"Army studies in germ warfare. They released colonies of Serratia Marcescens over San Francisco and waited to see how far the organism spread. Infections popped up in a number of Bay Area hospitals. Some of the cases were fatal."

"I can't believe it," murmured Cathy.

"The damage was unintentional, of course. But people died just the same."

"Don't forget Tuskegee," said Ollie. "People died in those experiments, too. And then there was that case in New York. Mentally retarded kids in a state hospital who were deliberately exposed to hepatitis. No one died there, but the ethics were just as shaky. So it's been done. Sometimes in the name of humanity."

"Sometimes not," said Victor.

Ollie nodded. "As in this particular case."

"What exactly are we talking about here?" asked Cathy, nodding at the photos. "Is this medical research? Or weapons development?"

"Both." Ollie pointed to one of the photos on the table. "By all appearances, Viratek's engaged in biological weapons research. They've dubbed it Project Cerberus. From what I can tell, the organism they're working on is an RNA virus, extremely virulent, highly contagious, producing over eighty-percent mortality in its lab animal hosts. This photo here—" he tapped one of the pages "—shows the organism produces vesicular skin lesions on the infected subjects."

"Vesicular?"

"Blisterlike. That could be one route of transmission, the fluid in those lesions." He sifted through the pile and pulled out another page. "This shows the time course of the illness. The viral counts, periods of infectiousness. In almost every case the course is the same. The subject's exposed here." He pointed to Day One on the time graph. "Minor signs of illness here at Day Seven. Full-blown pox on Day Twelve. And here—" he tapped the graph at Day Fourteen "—the deaths begin. The time varies, but the result's the same. They all die."

"You used the word *pox*," said Cathy.

Ollie turned to her, his eyes like blue glass. "Because that's what it is."

"You mean like chickenpox?"

"I wish it was. Then it wouldn't be so deadly. Almost everyone gets exposed to chickenpox as a kid, so most of us are immune. But this one's a different story."

"Is it a new virus?" asked Milo.

"Yes and no." He reached for an electron micrograph. "When I saw this I thought there was something weirdly familiar about all this. The appearance of the organism, the skin lesions, the course of illness. The whole damn picture. It reminded me of something I haven't read about in decades. Something I never dreamed I'd see again."

"You're saying it's an old virus?" said Milo.

"Ancient. But they've made some modifications. Made it more infectious. And deadlier. Which turns this into a real humdinger of a weapon, considering the millions of folks it's already killed."

"*Millions?*" Cathy stared at him. "What are we talking about?"

"A killer we've known for centuries. Smallpox."

"That's impossible!" said Cathy. "From what I've read, we conquered smallpox. It's supposed to be extinct."

"It was," said Victor. "For all practical purposes. Worldwide vaccination wiped it out. Smallpox hasn't been reported in decades. I'm not even sure they still make the vaccine. Ollie?"

"Not available. No need for it since the virus has vanished."

"So where did *this* virus come from?" asked Cathy.

Ollie shrugged. "Probably someone's closet."

"Come on."

"I'm serious. After smallpox was eradicated, a few samples of virus were kept alive in government labs, just in case someone needed it for future research. It's the scientific skeleton in the closet, so to speak. I'd assume those labs are top security. Because if any of the virus got out, there could be a major epidemic." He looked at the stack of photos. "Looks like security's already been breached. Someone obviously got hold of the virus."

"Or had it handed to them," said Victor. "Courtesy of the U.S. government."

"I find that incredible, Gersh," said Ollie. "This is a powderkeg experiment you're talking about. No committee would approve this sort of project."

"Right. That's why I think this is a maverick operation. It's easy to come up with a scenario. Bunch of hardliners cooking this up over at NSA. Or joint chiefs of staff. Or even the Oval Office. Someone says: 'World politics have changed. We can't get away with nuking the enemy. We need a new weapons option, one that'll work well against a Third World army. Let's find one.' And some guy in that room, some red, white and blue robot, will take that as the go-ahead. International law be damned."

"And since it's unofficial," said Cathy, "it'd be completely deniable."

"Right. The administration could claim it knew nothing."

"Sounds like Iran-Contra all over again."

"With one big difference," said Ollie. "When Iran-Contra fell apart, all you had were a few ruined political careers. If Project Cerberus goes awry, what you'll have is a few million dead people."

"But Ollie," said Milo. "I got vaccinated for smallpox when I was a kid. Doesn't that mean I'm safe?"

"Probably. Assuming the virus hasn't been altered too much. In fact, everyone over 35 is probably okay. But remember, there's a whole generation after us that never got the vaccine. Young adults and kids. By the time you could manufacture enough vaccine for them all, we'd have a raging epidemic."

"I'm beginning to see the logic of this weapon," said Victor. "In any war, who makes up the bulk of combat soldiers? Young adults."

Ollie nodded. "They'd be hit bad. As would the kids."

"A whole generation," Cathy murmured. "And only the old would be spared." She glanced at Victor and saw, mirrored in his eyes, the horror she felt.

"They chose an appropriate name," said Milo.

Ollie frowned. "What?"

"Cerberus. The three-headed dog of Hades." Milo looked up, visibly shaken. "Guardian of the dead."

* * *

It wasn't until Cathy was fast asleep and Milo had retired upstairs that Victor finally broached the subject to Ollie. It had troubled him all evening, had shadowed his every moment since they'd arrived at Milo's house. He couldn't look at Cathy, couldn't listen to the sound of her voice or inhale the scent of her hair without thinking of the terrible possibilities. And in the deepest hours of night, when it seemed all the world was asleep except for him and Ollie, he made the decision.

"I need to ask you a favor," he said.

Ollie gazed at him across the dining table, steam wafting up from his fourth cup of coffee. "What sort of favor?"

"It has to do with Cathy."

Ollie's gaze shifted to the woman lying asleep on the living room floor. She looked very small, very defenseless, curled up beneath the comforter. Ollie said, "She's a nice woman, Gersh."

"I know."

"There hasn't really been anyone since Lily. Has there?"

Victor shook his head. "I guess I haven't felt ready for it. There were always other things to think about...."

Ollie smiled. "There are always excuses. I should know. People keep telling me there's a glut of unattached female baby boomers. I haven't noticed."

"And I never bothered to notice." Victor looked at Cathy. "Until now."

"What're you gonna do with her, Gersh?"

"That's what I need you for. I'm not the safest guy to hang around with these days. A woman could get hurt."

Ollie laughed. "Hell, a *guy* could get hurt."

"I feel responsible for her. And if something happened to her, I'm not sure I could ever..." He let out a long sigh and rubbed his bloodshot eyes. "Anyway, I think it's best if she leaves."

"For where?"

"She has an ex-husband. He'll be working down in Mexico for a few months. I think she'd be pretty safe."

"You're sending her to her ex-husband?"

"I've met him. He's a jerk, but at least she won't be alone down there."

"Does Cathy agree to this?"

"I didn't ask her."

"Maybe you should."

"I'm not giving her a choice."

"What if she wants the choice?"

"I'm not in the mood to take any crap, Okay? I'm doing this for her own good."

Ollie took off his glasses and cleaned them on the tablecloth. "Excuse me for saying this, Gersh, but if it was me, I'd want her nearby, where I could sort of keep an eye on her."

"You mean where I can watch her get killed?" Victor shook his head. "Lily was enough. I won't go through it with Cathy."

Ollie thought it over for a moment, then he nodded. "What do you want me to do?"

"Tomorrow I want you to take her to the airport. Buy her a ticket to Mexico. Let her use your name. Mrs. Wozniak. Make sure she gets safely off the ground. I'll pay you back when I can."

"What if she won't get on the plane? Do I just shove her aboard?"

"Do whatever it takes, Ollie. I'm counting on you."

Ollie sighed. "I guess I can do it. I'll call in sick tomorrow. That'll free up my day." He looked at Victor. "I just hope you know what you're doing."

So do I, thought Victor.

Ollie rose to his feet and tucked the envelope with the photos under his arm. "I'll get back to you in the morning. After I show these last two photos to Bach. Maybe he can identify what those grids are."

"If it's anything electronic, Bach'll figure it out."

Together they walked to the door. There they paused and regarded each other, two old friends who'd grown a little grayer and, Victor hoped, a little wiser.

"Somehow it'll all work out," said Ollie. "Remember. The system's there to be beaten."

"Sounds like the old Stanford radical again."

"It's been a long time." Grinning, Ollie gave Victor a clap on the back. "But we're still not too old to raise a little hell, hey, Gersh? See you in the morning."

Victor waved as Ollie walked away into the darkness. Then he closed the door and turned off all the lights.

In the living room he sat beside Cathy and watched her sleep. The glow of a streetlight spilled in through the window onto her tumbled hair. *Ordinary,* she had called herself. Perhaps, if she'd been a stranger he'd merely passed on the street, he might have thought so, too. A chance meeting on a rainy highway in Garberville had made it impossible for him to ever consider this woman ordinary. In her gentleness, her kindness, she was very much like Lily.

In other ways, she was very different.

Though he'd cared about his wife, though they'd never stopped being good friends, he'd found Lily strangely passionless, a pristine, spiritual being trapped by human flesh. Lily had never been comfortable with her own body. She'd undress in the dark, make love— the rare times they did—in the dark. And then, the illness had robbed her of what little desire she had left.

Gazing at Cathy, he couldn't help wondering what passions might lie harbored in her still form.

He cut short the speculation. What did it matter now? Tomorrow, he'd send her away. *Get rid of her,* he thought brutally. It was necessary. He couldn't think straight while she was around. He couldn't stay focused on the business at hand: exposing Viratek. Jerry Martinique had counted on him. Thousands of potential victims counted on him. He was a scientist, a man who prided himself on logic. His attraction to this particular woman was, in the grand scheme of things, clearly unimportant.

That was what the scientist in him said.

That problem finally settled, he decided to get some rest while he could. He kicked off his shoes and stretched out beside her to sleep. The comforter was large enough—they could share it. He climbed beneath it and lay for a moment, not touching her, almost afraid to share her warmth.

She whimpered in her sleep and turned toward him, her silky hair tumbling against his face.

This was more than he could resist. Sighing, he wrapped his arms around her and felt her curl up against his chest. It was their last night together. They might as well spend it keeping each other warm.

That was how he fell asleep, with Cathy in his arms.

Only once during the night did he awaken. He had been dreaming of Lily. They were walking together, in a garden of pure white flowers. She said absolutely nothing. She simply looked at him with profound sadness, as if to say, *Here I am, Victor. I've come back to you. Why doesn't that make you happy?* He couldn't answer her. So he simply took her in his arms and held her.

He'd awakened to find he was holding Cathy, instead.

Joy instantly flooded his heart, warmed the darkest corners of his soul. It took him by surprise, that burst of happiness; it also made him feel guilty. But there it was. And the joy was all too short-lived. He remembered that today she'd be going away.

Cathy, Cathy. What a complication you've become.

He turned on his side, away from her, mentally building a wall between them.

He concentrated on the dream, trying to remember what had happened. He and Lily had been walking. He tried to picture Lily's face, her brown eyes, her curly black hair. It was the face of the woman he'd been married to for ten years, a face he should know well.

But the only face he saw when he closed his eyes was that of Catherine Weaver.

It took Nicholas Savitch only two hours to pack his bags and drive down to Palo Alto. The word from Matt Tyrone was that Holland had slipped south to the Stanford area, perhaps to seek out old friends. Holland was, after all, a Stanford man. Maybe not the red-and-white rah-rah Cardinals type, but a Stanford man nonetheless. These old school ties could run deep. It was only a guess on Savitch's part; he'd never gone beyond high school. His education consisted of what a hungry and ambitious boy could pick up on Chicago's south side. Mainly a keen, almost uncanny knack for crawling into another man's head, for sensing what a particular man would think and do in a given situation. Call it advanced street psychology. Without spending a day in college, Savitch had earned his degree.

Now he was putting it to use.

The *finder,* they called him. He liked that name. He grinned as he drove, his leather-gloved hands expertly handling the wheel. Nicholas Savitch, diviner of human souls, the hunter who could ferret a man out of deepest hiding.

In most cases it was a simple matter of logic. Even while on the run, most people conformed to old patterns. It was the fear that did it. It made them seek out their old comforts, cling to their usual habits. In a strange town, the familiar was precious, even if it was only the sight of those ubiquitous golden arches.

Like every other fugitive, Victor Holland would seek the familiar.

Savitch turned his car onto Palm Drive and pulled up in front of the Stanford Arch. The campus was silent; it was 2:00 a.m. Savitch sat for a moment, regarding the silent buildings, Holland's alma mater. Here, in his former stomping grounds, Holland would turn to old friends, revisit old haunts. Savitch had already done his homework. He carried, in his briefcase, a list of names he'd culled from the man's file. In the morning he'd start in on those names, knock on neighbors' doors, flash his government ID, ask about new faces in the neighborhood.

The only possible complication was Sam Polowski. By last report, the FBI agent was also in town, also on Holland's trail. Polowski was a dogged operator. It'd be messy business, taking out a Bureau man. But then, Polowski was only a cog, the way the Weaver woman was only a cog, in a much bigger wheel.

Neither of them would be missed.

CHAPTER NINE

In the cold, clear hours before dawn, Cathy woke up shaking, still trapped in the threads of a nightmare. She had been walking in a world of concrete and shadow, where doorways gaped and silhouettes huddled on street corners. She drifted among them, one among the faceless, taking refuge in obscurity, instinctively avoiding the light. No one pursued her; no attacker lunged from the alleys. The real terror lay in the unending maze of concrete, the hard echoes of the streets, the frantic search for a safe place.

And the certainty that she would never find it.

For a moment she lay in the darkness, curled up beneath a down comforter on Milo's living room floor. She barely remembered having crawled under the covers; it must have been sometime after three when she'd fallen asleep. The last she remembered, Ollie and Victor were still huddled in the dining room, discussing the photographs. Now there was only silence. The dining room, like the rest of the house, lay in shadow.

She turned on her back, and her shoulder thumped against something warm and solid. Victor. He stirred, murmuring something she couldn't understand.

"Are you awake?" she whispered.

He turned toward her and in his drowsiness enfolded her in his arms. She knew it was only instinct that drew him to her, the yearning of one warm body for another. Or perhaps it was the memory of his wife sleeping beside him, in his mind always there, always waiting to be held. For the moment, she let him cling to the dream. *While he's still half asleep, let him believe I'm Lily,* she thought. *What harm can there be? He needs the memory. And I need the comfort.*

She burrowed into his arms, into the safe spot that once had belonged to another. She took it without regard for the consequences, willing to be swept up into the fantasy of being, for this moment, the one woman in the world he loved. How good it felt, how protected and cared for. From the soap-and-sweat smell of his chest to the coarse fabric of his shirt, it was sanctuary. He was breathing warmly into her hair now, whispering words she knew were for another, pressing kisses to the top of her head. Then he trapped her face in his hands and pressed his lips to hers in a kiss so undeniably needy it ignited within her a hunger of her own. Her response was instinctive and filled with all the yearning of a woman too long a stranger to love.

She met his kiss with one just as deep, just as needy.

At once she was lost, whirled away into some grand and glorious vortex. He stroked down her face, her neck. His hands moved to the buttons of her blouse. She arched against him, her breasts suddenly aching to be touched. It had been so long, so long.

She didn't know how the blouse fell open. She knew only that one moment his fingers were skimming the fabric, and the next moment, they were cupping her flesh. It was that unexpected contact of skin on forbidden skin, the magic torment of his fingers caressing her nipple, that made any last resistance fall away. How many chances were left to them? How many nights together? She longed for so many more, an eternity, but this might be all they had. She welcomed it, welcomed him, with all the passion of a woman granted one last taste of love.

With a knowing touch, she slid her hands down his shirt, undoing buttons, stroking her way through the dense hair of his chest, to the top of his trousers. There she paused, feeling his startled intake of breath, knowing that he too was past retreat.

Together they fumbled at buttons and zippers, both of them suddenly feverish to be free. It all fell away in a tumult of cotton and lace. And when the last scrap of clothing was shed, when nothing came between them but the velvet darkness, she reached up and pulled him to her, on her.

It was a joyful filling, as if, in that first deep thrust within her, he also reached some long-empty hollow in her soul.

"Please," she murmured, her voice breaking into a whimper.

He fell instantly still. "Cathy?" he asked, his hands anxiously cupping her face. "What—"

"Please. Don't stop...."

His soft laughter was all the reassurance she needed. "I have no intention of stopping," he whispered. "None whatsoever..."

And he didn't stop. Not until he had taken her with him all the way, higher and further than any man ever could, to a place beyond thought or reason. Only when release came, wave flooding upon wave, did she know how very high and far they had climbed.

A sweet exhaustion claimed them.

Outside, in the grayness of dawn, a bird sang. Inside, the silence was broken only by the sound of their breathing.

She sighed into the warmth of his shoulder. "Thank you."

He touched her face. "For what?"

"For making me feel...wanted again."

"Oh, Cathy."

"It's been such a long time. Jack and I, we—we stopped making love way before the divorce. It was me, actually. I couldn't bear having him..." She swallowed. "When you don't love someone anymore, when they don't love you, it's hard to let yourself be... touched."

He brushed his fingers down her cheek. "Is it still hard? Being touched?"

"Not by you. Being touched by you is like...being touched the very first time."

By the window's pale light she saw him smile. "I hope your very first time wasn't too awful."

Now she smiled. "I don't remember it very well. It was such a frantic, ridiculous thing on the floor of a college dorm room."

He reached out and patted the carpet. "I see you've come a long way."

"Haven't I?" she laughed. "But floors can be terribly romantic places."

"Goodness. A carpet connoisseur. How do dorm room and living room floors compare?"

"I couldn't tell you. It's been such a long time since I was eighteen." She paused, hovering on the edge of baring the truth. "In fact," she admitted, "it's been a long time since I've been with anyone."

Softly he said, "It's been a long time for both of us."

She let that revelation hang for a moment in the semi-darkness. "Not—not since Lily?" she finally asked.

"No." A single word, yet it revealed so much. The three years of loyalty to a dead woman. The grief, the loneliness. How she wanted to fill that womanless chasm for him! To be his savior, and he, hers. Could she make him forget? No, not forget; she couldn't expect him ever to forget Lily. But she wanted a space in his heart for herself, a very large space designed for a lifetime. A space to which no other woman, dead or alive, could ever lay claim.

"She must have been a very special woman," she said.

He ran a strand of her hair through his fingers. "She was very wise, very aware. And she was kind. That's something I don't always find in a person."

She's still part of you, isn't she? She's still the one you love.

"It's the same sort of kindness I find in you," he said.

His fingers had slid to her face and were now stroking her cheek. She closed her eyes, savoring his touch, his warmth. "You hardly know me," she whispered.

"But I do. That night, after the accident, I survived purely on the sound of your voice. And the touch of your hand. I'd know them both, anywhere."

She opened her eyes and gazed at him. "Would you really?"

He pressed his lips to her forehead. "Even in my sleep."

"But I'm not Lily. I could never be Lily."

"That's true. You can't be. No one can."

"I can't replace what you lost."

"What makes you think that's what I want? Some sort of replacement? She was my wife. And yes, I loved her." By the way he said it, his answer invited no exploration.

She didn't try.

From somewhere in the house came the jingle of a telephone. After two rings it stopped. Faintly they heard Milo's voice murmuring upstairs.

Cathy sat up and reached automatically for her clothes. She dressed in silence, her back turned to Victor. A new modesty had sprung up between them, the shyness of strangers.

"Cathy," he said. "People do move on."

"I know."

"You've gotten over Jack."

She laughed, a small, tired sound. "No woman ever really gets over Jack Zuckerman. Yes, I'm over the worst of it. But every time a woman falls in love, really falls in love, it takes something out of her. Something that can never be put back."

"It also gives her something."

"That depends on who you fall in love with, doesn't it?"

Footsteps thumped down the stairs, creaked across the dining room. A wide-awake Milo stood in the doorway, his uncombed hair standing out like a brush. "Hey, you two!" he hissed. "Get up! Hurry."

Cathy rose to her feet in alarm. "What is it?"

"That was Ollie on the phone. He called to say some guy's in the area, asking questions about you. He's already been down to Bach's neighborhood."

"What?" Now Victor was on his feet and hurriedly stuffing his legs into his trousers.

"Ollie figures the guy'll be knocking around here next. Guess they know who your friends are."

"Who was asking the questions?"

"Claimed he was FBI."

"Polowski," muttered Victor, pulling his shirt on. "Has to be."

"You know him?"

"The same guy who set me up. The guy who's been tailing us ever since."

"How did he know we're here?" said Cathy. "No one could've followed us—"

"No one had to. They have my profile. They know I have friends here." Victor glanced at Milo. "Sorry, buddy. Hope this doesn't get you into trouble."

Milo's laugh was distinctly tense. "Hey, I didn't do nothin' wrong. Just harbored a felon." The bravado suddenly melted away. He asked, "Exactly what kind of trouble should I expect?"

"Questions," said Victor, quickly buttoning his shirt. "Lots of 'em. Maybe they'll even take a look around. Just keep cool, tell 'em you haven't heard from me. Think you can do it?"

"Sure. But I don't know about Ma—"

"Your Ma's no problem. Just tell her to stick to Chinese." Victor grabbed the envelope of photos and glanced at Cathy. "Ready?"

"Let's get out of here. Please."

"Back door," Milo suggested.

They followed him through the kitchen. A glance told them the way was clear. As he opened the door, Milo added, "I almost forgot. Ollie wants to see you this afternoon. Something about those photos."

"Where?"

"The lake. Behind the boathouse. You know the place."

They stepped out into the chill dampness of morning. Fog-borne silence hung in the air. *Will we ever stop running?* thought Cathy. *Will we never stop listening for footsteps?*

Victor clapped his friend on the shoulder. "Thanks, Milo. I owe you a big one."

"And one of these days I plan to collect!" Milo hissed as they slipped away.

Victor held up his hand in farewell. "See you around."

"Yeah," Milo muttered into the mist. "Let's hope not in jail."

The Chinese man was lying. Though the man betrayed nothing in his voice, no hesitation, no guilty waver, still Savitch knew this Mr. Milo Lum was hiding something. His eyes betrayed him.

He was seated on the living room couch, across from Savitch. Off to the side sat Mrs. Lum in an easy chair, smiling uncomprehendingly. Savitch might be able to use the old biddy; for now, it was the son who held his interest.

"I can't see why you'd be after him," said Milo. "Victor's as clean as they come. At least, he was when I knew him. But that was a long time ago."

"How far back?" asked Savitch politely.

"Oh, years. Yeah. Haven't seen him since. No, sir."

Savitch raised an eyebrow. Milo shifted on the couch, shuffled his feet, glanced pointlessly around the room.

"You and your mother live here alone?" Savitch asked.

"Since my dad died."

"No tenants? No one else lives here?"

"No. Why?"

"There were reports of a man fitting Holland's description in the neighborhood."

"Believe me, if Victor was wanted by the police, he wouldn't hang around here. You think I'd let a murder suspect in the house? With just me and my old Ma?"

Savitch glanced at Mrs. Lum, who merely smiled. The old woman had sharp, all-seeing eyes. A survivor's eyes.

It was time for Savitch to confirm his hunch. "Excuse me," he said, rising to his feet. "I had a long drive from the city. May I use your restroom?"

"Uh, sure. Down that hall."

Savitch headed into the bathroom and closed the door. Within seconds he'd spotted the evidence he was looking for. It was lying on the tiled floor: a long strand of brown hair. Very silky, very fine.

Catherine Weaver's shade.

It was all the proof he needed to proceed. He reached under his jacket for the shoulder holster and pulled out the semiautomatic. Then he gave his crisp white shirt a regretful pat. Messy business, interrogation. He would have to watch the bloodstains.

He stepped out into the hall, casually holding his pistol at his side. He'd go for the old woman first. Hold the barrel to her head, threaten to pull the trigger. There was an uncommonly strong bond between this mother and son. They would protect each other at all costs.

Savitch was halfway down the hall when the doorbell rang. He halted. The front door was opened and a new voice said, "Mr. Milo Lum?"

"And who the hell are you?" came Milo's weary reply.

"The name's Sam Polowski. FBI."

Every muscle in Savitch's body snapped taut. No choice now; he had to take the man out.

He raised his pistol. Soundlessly, he made his way down the hall toward the living room.

"*Another* one?" came Milo's peevish voice. "Look, one of your guys is already here—"

"What?"

"Yeah, he's back in the—"

Savitch stepped out and was swinging his pistol toward the front doorway when Mrs. Lum shrieked.

Milo froze. Polowski didn't. He rolled sideways just as the bullet thudded into the door frame, splintering wood.

By the time Savitch got off a second shot, Polowski was crawling somewhere behind the couch and the bullet slammed uselessly into the stuffing. That was it for chances—Polowski was armed.

Savitch decided it was time to vanish.

He turned and darted back up the hall, into a far bedroom. It was the mother's room; it smelled of incense and old-lady perfume. The window slid open easily. Savitch kicked out the screen, scrambled over the sill and sank heel-deep into the muddy flower bed. Cursing, he slogged away, trailing clumps of mud across the lawn.

He heard, faintly, "Halt! FBI!" but continued running.

He nursed his rage all the way back to the car.

Milo stared in bewilderment at the trampled pansies. "What the hell was that all about?" he demanded. "Is this some sort of FBI practical joke?"

Sam Polowski didn't answer; he was too busy tracking the footprints across the grass. They led to the sidewalk, then faded into the road's pebbly asphalt.

"Hey!" yelled Milo. "What's going on?"

Polowski turned. "I didn't really see him. What did he look like?"

Milo shrugged. "I dunno. Efrem Zimbalist-type."

"Meaning?"

"Tall, clean-cut, great build. Typical FBI."

There was a silence as Milo regarded Polowski's sagging belly.

"Well," amended Milo, "maybe not *typical*..."

"What about his face?"

"Lemme think. Brown hair? Maybe brown eyes?"

"You're not sure."

"You know how it is. All you white guys look alike to me."

An eruption of rapid Chinese made them both turn. Mrs. Lum had followed them out onto the lawn and was jabbering and gesticulating.

"What's she saying?" asked Polowski.

"She says the man was about six foot one, had straight dark brown hair parted on the left, brown eyes, almost black, a high forehead, a narrow nose and thin lips, and a small tattoo on his inside left wrist."

"Uh—is that all?"

"The tattoo read PJX."

Polowski shook his head in amazement. "Is she always this observant?"

"She can't exactly converse in English. So she does a lot of watching."

"Obviously." Polowski took out a pen and began to jot the information in a notebook.

"So who was this guy?" prodded Milo.

"Not FBI."

"How do I know *you're* FBI."

"Do I look like it?"

"No."

"Only proves my point."

"What?"

"If I wanted to pretend I was an agent, wouldn't I at least try to *look* like one? Whereas, if I *am* one, I wouldn't bother to try and look like one."

"Oh."

"Now." Polowski slid the notebook in his pocket. "You're still going to insist you haven't seen, or heard from, Victor Holland?"

Milo straightened. "That's right."

"And you don't know how to get in touch with him?"

"I have no idea."

"That's too bad. Because I could be the one to save his life. I've already saved yours."

Milo said nothing.

"Just why the hell do you think that guy was here? To pay a social visit? No, he was after information." Polowski paused and added, ominously, "And believe me, he would've gotten it."

Milo shook his head. "I'm confused."

"So am I. That's why I need Holland. He has the answers. But I need him alive. That means I need to find him before the other guy does. Tell me where he is."

Polowski and Milo looked at each other long and hard.

"I don't know," said Milo. "I don't know what to do."

Mrs. Lum was chattering again. She pointed to Polowski and nodded.

"Now what's she saying?" asked Polowski.

"She says you have big ears."

"For that, I can look in the mirror."

"What she means is, the size of your ears indicates sagacity."

"Come again?"

"You're a smart dude. She thinks I should listen to you."

Polowski turned and grinned at Mrs. Lum. "Your mother is a great judge of character." He looked back at Milo. "I wouldn't want anything to happen to her. Or you. You both have to get out of town."

Milo nodded. "On that particular point, we both agree." He turned toward the house.

"What about Holland?" called Polowski. "Will you help me find him?"

Milo took his mother by the arm and guided her across the lawn. Without even a backward look he said, "I'm thinking about it."

"It was those two photos. I just couldn't figure them out," said Ollie.

They were standing on the boathouse pier, overlooking the bed of Lake Lagunita. The lake was dry now, as it was every winter, drained to a reedy marsh until spring. They were alone, the three of them, sharing the lake with only an occasional duck. In the spring, this would be an idyllic spot, the water lapping the banks, lovers drifting in rowboats, here and there a poet lolling under the trees. But today, under black clouds, with a cold mist rising from the reeds, it was a place of utter desolation.

"I knew they weren't biological data," said Ollie. "I kept thinking they looked like some sort of electrical grid. So this morning, right after I left Milo's, I took 'em over to Bach's, down in San José. Caught him at breakfast."

"Bach?" asked Cathy.

"Another member of the Out of Tuners. Great bassoon player. Started an electronics firm a few years back and now he's working with the big boys. Anyway, the first thing he says as I walk in the door is, 'Hey, did the FBI get to you yet?' And I said, 'What?' and he says, 'They just called. For some reason they're looking for Gershwin. They'll probably get around to you next.' And that's when I knew I had to get you two out of Milo's house, stat.''

''So what did he say about those photos?''

''Oh, yeah.'' Ollie reached into his briefcase and pulled out the photos. ''Okay. This one here, it's a circuit diagram. An electronic alarm system. Very sophisticated, very secure. Designed to be breached by use of a keypad code, punched in at this point here. Probably at an entryway. You seen anything like it at Viratek?''

Victor nodded. ''Building C-2. Where Jerry worked. The keypad's in the hall, right by the Special Projects door.''

''Ever been inside that door?''

''No. Only those with top clearance can get through. Like Jerry.''

''Then we'll have to visualize what comes next. Going by the diagram, there's another security point here, probably another keypad. Right inside the first door, they've stationed a camera system.''

''You mean like a bank camera?'' asked Cathy.

''Similar. Only I'd guess this one's being monitored twenty-four hours a day.''

''They went first class, didn't they?'' said Victor. ''Two secured doors, plus inspection by a guard. Not to mention the guard at the outside gate.''

''Don't forget the laser lattice.''

''What?''

''This inner room here.'' Ollie pointed to the diagram's core. ''Laser beams, directed at various angles. They'll detect movement of just about anything bigger than a rat.''

''How do the lasers get switched off?''

''Has to be done by the security guard. The controls are on his panel.''

''You can tell all this from the diagram?'' asked Cathy. ''I'm impressed.''

''No problem.'' Ollie grinned. ''Bach's firm designs security systems.''

Victor shook his head. ''This looks impossible. We can't get through all that.''

Cathy frowned at him. "Wait a minute. What are you talking about? You aren't considering going into that building, are you?"

"We discussed it last night," said Victor. "It may be the only way—"

"Are you crazy? Viratek's out to kill us and you want to break *in?*"

"It's the proof we need," said Ollie. "You try going to the newspapers or the Justice Department and they'll demand evidence. You can bet Viratek's going to deny everything. Even if someone does launch an investigation, all Viratek has to do is toss the virus and, *poof!* your evidence is gone. No one can prove a thing."

"You have photos—"

"Sure. A few pages of animal data. The virus is never identified. And all that evidence could've been fabricated by, say, some disgruntled ex-employee."

"So what *is* proof? What do you need, another dead body? Victor's, for instance?"

"What we need is the virus—a virus that's supposed to be extinct. Just a single vial and the case against them is nailed shut."

"Just a single vial. Right." Cathy shook her head. "I don't know what I'm worried about. No one can get through those doors. Not without the keypad codes."

"Ah, but those we have!" Ollie flipped to the second photo. "The mysterious numbers. See, they finally make sense. Two sets of seven digits. Not phone numbers at all! Jerry was pointing the way through Viratek's top security."

"What about the lasers?" she pointed out, her agitation growing. They couldn't be serious! Surely they could see the futility of this mission. She didn't care if her fear showed; she had to be their voice of reason. "And then there's the guards," she said. "Two of them. Do you have a way past them? Or did Jerry also leave you the formula for invisibility?"

Ollie glanced uneasily at Victor. "Uh, maybe I should let you two discuss this first. Before we make any other plans."

"I thought I was part of all this," said Cathy. "Part of every decision. I guess I was wrong."

Neither man said a thing. Their silence only fueled Cathy's anger.

She thought: *So you left me out of this. You didn't respect my opinion enough to ask me what I think, what I want.*

Without a word she turned and walked away.

Moments later, Victor caught up with her. She was standing on the dirt path, hugging herself against the cold. She heard his approach, sensed his uncertainty, his struggle to find the right words. For a moment he simply stood beside her, not speaking.

"I think we should run," she said. She gazed over the dry lake bed and shivered. The wind that swept across the reeds was raw and biting; it sliced right through her sweater. "I want to get away," she said. "I want to go somewhere warm. Some place where the sun's shining, where I can lie on a beach and not worry about who's watching me from the bushes...." Suddenly reminded of the terrible possibilities, she turned and glanced at the oaks hulking behind them. She saw only the fluttering of dead leaves.

"I agree with you," said Victor quietly.

"You do?" She turned to him, relieved. "Let's go, Victor! Let's leave now. Forget this crazy idea. We can catch the next bus south—"

"This very afternoon. You'll be on your way."

"*I* will?" She stared at him, at first not willing to accept what she'd heard. Then the meaning of his words sank in. "You're not coming."

Slowly he shook his head. "I can't."

"You mean you won't."

"Don't you see?" He took her by the shoulders, as though to shake some sense into her. "We're backed into a corner. Unless we do something—I do something—we'll always be running."

"Then let's *run!*" She reached for him, her fingers clutching at his windbreaker. She wanted to scream at him, to tear away his cool mask of reason and get to the raw emotions beneath. They had to be there, buried deep in that logical brain of his. "We could go to Mexico," she said. "I know a place on the coast—in Baja. A little hotel near the beach. We could stay there a few months, wait until things are safer—"

"It'll never be safer."

"Yes, it will! They'll forget about us—"

"You're not thinking straight."

"I am. I'm thinking I want to stay alive."

"And that's exactly why I have to do this." He took her face in his hands, trapping it so she could look nowhere but at him. No longer was he the lover, the friend—his voice now held the cold, steady note of authority and she hated the sound of it. "I'm trying to keep you alive," he said. "With a future ahead of you. And the only way I can do that is to blow this thing wide open so the world knows about it. I owe it to you. And I owe it to Jerry."

She wanted to argue with him, to plead with him to go with her, but she knew it was useless. What he said was true. Running would only be a temporary solution, one that would give them a few sweet months of safety, but a temporary one just the same.

"I'm sorry, Cathy," he said softly. "I can't think of any other way—"

"—But to get rid of me," she finished for him.

He released her. She stepped back, and the sudden gulf between them left her aching. She couldn't bear to look at him, knowing that the pain she felt wouldn't be reflected in his eyes. "So how does it work?" she said dully. "Do I leave tonight? Will it be plane, train or automobile?"

"Ollie will drive you to the airport. I've asked him to buy you the ticket under his name—Mrs. Wozniak. He'll have to be the one to see you off. We thought it'd be safer if I didn't come along to the airport."

"Of course."

"That'll get you to Mexico. Ollie'll give you enough cash to keep you going for a while. Enough to get you anywhere you want to go from there. Baja. Acapulco. Or just hang around with Jack if you think that's best."

"Jack." She turned away, unwilling to show her tears. "Right."

"Cathy." She felt his hand on her shoulder, as though he wanted to turn her toward him, to pull her back one last time into his arms. She refused to move.

Footsteps approached. They both glanced around to see Ollie, standing a few feet away. "Ready to go?" he asked.

There was a long silence. Then Victor nodded. "She's ready."

"Uh, look," Ollie mumbled, suddenly aware that he'd stepped

in at a bad time. "My car's over by the boathouse. If you want, I can, uh, wait for you there...."

Cathy furiously dashed away her tears. "No," she said with sudden determination. "I'm coming."

Victor stood watching her, his gaze veiled by some cool, impenetrable mist.

"Goodbye, Victor," she said.

He didn't answer. He just kept looking at her through that terrible mist.

"If I—if I don't see you again..." She stopped, struggling to be just as brave, just as invulnerable. "Take care of yourself," she finished. Then she turned and followed Ollie down the path.

Through the car window, she glimpsed Victor, still standing on the lake path, his hands jammed in his pockets, his shoulders hunched against the wind. He didn't wave goodbye; he merely watched them drive away.

It was an image she'd carry with her forever, that last, fading view of the man she loved. The man who'd sent her away.

As Ollie turned the car onto the road, she sat stiff and silent, her fists balled in her lap, the pain in her throat so terrible she could scarcely breathe. Now he was behind them. She couldn't see him, but she knew he was still standing there, as unmoving as the oaks that surrounded him. *I love you,* she thought. *And I will never see you again.*

She turned to look out. He was a distant figure now, almost lost among the trees. In a gesture of farewell, she reached up and gently touched the window.

The glass was cold.

"I have to stop off at the lab," said Ollie, turning into the hospital parking lot. "I just remembered I left the checkbook in my desk. Can't get you a plane ticket without it."

Cathy nodded dully. She was still in a state of shock, still trying to accept the fact that she was now on her own. That Victor had sent her away.

Ollie pulled into a stall marked Reserved, Wozniak. "This'll only take a sec."

"Shall I come in with you?"

"You'd better wait in the car. I work with a very nosy bunch. They see me with a woman and they want to know everything. Not that there's ever anything to know." He climbed out and shut the door. "Be right back."

Cathy watched him stride away and vanish into a side entrance. She had to smile at the thought of Ollie Wozniak squiring around a woman—any woman. Unless it was someone with a Ph.D. who could sit through his scientific monologues.

A minute passed.

Outside, a bird screeched. Cathy glanced out at the trees lining the hospital driveway and spotted the jay, perched among the lower branches. Nothing else moved, not even the leaves.

She leaned back and closed her eyes.

Too little sleep, too much running, had taken its toll. Exhaustion settled over her, so profound she thought she would never again be able to move her limbs. *A beach,* she thought. *Warm sand. Waves washing at my feet...*

The jay's cry cut off in mid-screech. Only vaguely did Cathy register the sudden silence. Then, even through her half sleep, she sensed the shadowing of the window, like a cloud passing before the sun.

She opened her eyes. A face was staring at her through the glass.

Panic sent her lunging for the lock button. Before she could jam it down, the door was wrenched open. A badge was thrust up to her face.

"FBI!" the man barked. "Out of the car, please."

Slowly Cathy emerged, to stand weak-kneed against the door. *Ollie,* she thought, her gaze darting toward the hospital entrance. *Where are you?* If he appeared, she had to be ready to bolt, to flee across the parking lot and into the woods. She doubted the man with the badge would be able to keep up; his stubby legs and thick waist didn't go along with a star athlete.

But he must have a gun. If I bolt, would he shoot me in the back?

"Don't even think about it, Miss Weaver," the man said. He took her arm and gave her a nudge toward the hospital entrance. "Go on. Inside."

"But—"

"Dr. Wozniak's waiting for us in the lab."

Waiting didn't exactly describe Ollie's predicament. Bound and trussed would have been a better description. She found Ollie bent over double in his office, handcuffed to the foot of his desk, while three of his lab colleagues stood by gaping in amazement.

"Back to work, folks," said the agent as he herded the onlookers out of the office. "Just a routine matter." He shut the door and locked it. Then he turned to Cathy and Ollie. "I have to find Victor Holland," he said. "And I have to find him fast."

"Man," Ollie muttered into his chest. "This guy sounds like a broken record."

"Who are you?" demanded Cathy.

"The name's Sam Polowski. I work out of the San Francisco office." He pulled out his badge and slapped it on the desk. "Take a closer look if you want. It's official."

"Uh, excuse me?" called Ollie. "Could I maybe, possibly, get into a more comfortable position?"

Polowski ignored him. His attention was focused on Cathy. "I don't think I need to spell it out for you, Miss Weaver. Holland's in trouble."

"And you're one of his biggest problems," she retorted.

"That's where you're wrong." Polowski moved closer, his gaze unflinching, his voice absolutely steady. "I'm one of his hopes. Maybe his only hope."

"You're trying to kill him."

"Not me. Someone else, someone who's going to succeed. Unless I can stop it."

She shook her head. "I'm not stupid! I know about you. What you've been trying to—"

"Not me. The other guy." He reached for the telephone on the desk. "Here," he said, holding the receiver out to her. "Call Milo Lum. Ask him what happened at his house this morning. Maybe he'll convince you I'm on your side."

Cathy stared at the man, wondering what sort of game he was playing. Wondering why she was falling for it. *Because I want so much to believe him.*

"He's alone out there," said Polowski. "One man trying to buck the U.S. government. He's new to the game. Sooner or later he's going to slip, do something stupid. And that'll be it." He dialed the phone for her and again held out the receiver. "Go on. Talk to Lum."

She heard the phone ring three times, followed by Milo's answer "Hello? Hello?"

Slowly she took the receiver. "Milo?"

"Is that you? Cathy? God, I was hoping you'd call—"

"Listen, Milo. I need to ask you something. It's about a man named Polowski."

"I've met him."

"You *have?*" She looked up and saw Polowski nodding.

"Lucky for me," said Milo. "The guy's got the charm of an old shoe but he saved my life. I don't know what Gersh was talking about. Is Gersh around? I have to—"

"Thanks, Milo," she murmured. "Thanks a lot." She hung up.

Polowski was still looking at her.

"Okay," she said. "I want your side of it. From the beginning."

"You gonna help me out?"

"I haven't decided." She crossed her arms. "Convince me."

Polowski nodded. "That's just what I plan to do."

CHAPTER TEN

For Victor it was a long and miserable afternoon. After leaving the lake, he wandered around the campus for a while, ending up at last in the main quad. There in the courtyard, standing among the buildings of sandstone and red tile, Victor struggled to keep his mind on the business at hand: exposing Viratek. But his thoughts kept shifting back to Cathy, to that look she'd given him, full of hurt abandonment.

As if I'd betrayed her.

If she could just see the good sense in his actions. He was a scientist, a man whose life and work was ruled by logic. Sending her away was the logical thing to do. The authorities were closing in, the noose was growing ever tighter. He could accept the danger to himself. After all, he'd chosen to take on Jerry's battle, to see this through to the end.

What he hadn't chosen was to put Cathy in danger. *Now she's out of the mess and on her way to a safe place. One less thing to worry about.Time to put her out of my mind.*

As if I could.

He stared up at one of the courtyard's Romanesque arches and reminded himself, once again, of the wisdom of his actions. Still, the uneasiness remained. Where was she? Was she safe? She'd been gone only an hour and he missed her already.

He gave a shrug, as though by that gesture, he could somehow cast off the fears. Still they remained, constant and gnawing. He found a place under the eaves and huddled on the steps to wait for Ollie's return.

At dusk he was still waiting. By the last feeble light of day, he paced the stone courtyard. He counted and recounted the number of hours it should've taken Ollie to drive to San José Airport and return. He added in traffic time, red lights, ticket-counter delays.

Surely three hours was enough. Cathy had to be on a plane by now, jetting for warmer climes.

Where was Ollie?

At the sound of the first footstep, he spun around. For a moment he couldn't believe what he was seeing, couldn't understand how she could be standing there, silhouetted beneath the sandstone archway. "Cathy?" he said in amazement.

She stepped out, into the courtyard. "Victor," she said softly. She started toward him, slowly at first, and then, in a jubilant burst of flight, ran toward his waiting arms. He swept her up, swung her around, kissed her hair, her face. He didn't understand why she was here but he rejoiced that she was.

"I don't know if I've done the right thing," she murmured. "I hope to God I have."

"Why did you come back?"

"I wasn't sure—I'm still not sure—"

"Cathy, what are you doing here?"

"You can't fight this alone! And he can help you—"

"Who can?"

From out of the twilight came another voice, gruff and startling. "*I* can."

At once Victor stiffened. His gaze shifted back to the arch behind Cathy. A man emerged and walked slowly toward him. Not a tall man, he had the sort of body that, in a weight-loss ad, would've been labeled Before. He came up to Victor and planted himself squarely on the courtyard stones.

"Hello, Holland," he said. "I'm glad we've finally met. The name is Sam Polowski."

Victor turned and looked in disbelief at Cathy. "Why?" he asked in quiet fury. "Just tell me that. *Why?*"

She reacted as though he'd delivered a physical blow. Tentatively she reached for his arm; he pulled away from her at once.

"He wants to help," she said, her voice wretched with pain. "*Listen* to him!"

"I'm not sure there's any point to listening. Not now." He felt his whole body go slack in defeat. He didn't understand it, would never understand it. It was over, the running, the scraping along on fear and hope. All because Cathy had betrayed him. He turned matter-of-factly to Polowski. "I take it I'm under arrest," he said.

"Hardly," said Polowski, nodding toward the archway. "Seeing as he's got my gun."

"What?"

"Hey, Gersh! Over here!" Ollie yelled. "See, I got him covered!"

Polowski winced. "Geez, do ya have to wave the damn thing?"

"Sorry," said Ollie.

"Now, does that convince you, Holland?" asked Polowski. "You think I'd hand my piece over to an idiot like him if I didn't want to talk to you?"

"He's telling the truth," insisted Cathy. "He gave the gun to Ollie. He was willing to take the risk, just to meet you face-to-face."

"Bad move, Polowski," said Victor bitterly. "I'm wanted for murder, remember? Industrial espionage? How do you know I won't just blow you away?"

"'Cause I know you're innocent."

"That makes a difference, does it?"

"It does to me."

"Why?"

"You're caught up in something big, Holland. Something that's going to eat you up alive. Something that's got my supervisor doing backflips to keep me off the case. I don't like being pulled off a case. It hurts my delicate ego."

The two men gazed at each other through the gathering darkness, each sizing up the other.

At last Victor nodded. He looked at Cathy, a quiet plea for forgiveness, for not believing in her. When at last she came into his arms, he felt the world had suddenly gone right again.

He heard a deliberate clearing of a throat. Turning, he saw Polowski hold out his hand. Victor took it in a handshake that could very well be his doom—or his salvation.

"You've led me on a long, hard chase," said Polowski. "I think it's time we worked together."

* * *

"Basically," said Ollie, "What we have here is just your simple, everyday mission impossible."

They were assembled in Polowski's hotel room, a five-member team that Milo had just dubbed the "Older, Crazier Out of Tuners," or Old COOTS for short. On the table in the center of the room lay potato chips, beer and the photos detailing Viratek's security system. There was also a map of the Viratek compound, forty acres of buildings and wooded grounds, all of it surrounded by an electrified fence. They had been studying the photos for an hour now, and the job that lay before them looked hopeless.

"No easy way in," said Ollie, shaking his head. "Even if those keypad codes are still valid, you're faced with the human element of recognition. Two guards, two positions. No way they're gonna let you pass."

"There has to be a way," said Polowski. "Come on, Holland. You're the egghead. Use that creative brain of yours."

Cathy looked at Victor. While the others had tossed ideas back and forth, he had said very little. *And he's the one with the most at stake—his life,* she thought. It took incredible courage —or foolhardiness—even to consider such a desperate move. Yet here he was, calmly scanning the map as though he were planning nothing more dangerous than a Sunday drive.

He must have felt her gaze, for he slung his arm around her and tugged her close. Now that they were reunited, she savored every moment they shared, committed to memory every look, every caress. Soon he could be wrenched away from her. Even now he was making plans to enter what looked like a death trap.

He pressed a kiss to the top of her head. Then, reluctantly, he turned his attention back to the map.

"The electronics I'm not worried about," he said. "It's the human element. The guards."

Milo cocked his head toward Polowski. "I still say ol' J. Edgar here should get a warrant and raid the place."

"Right," snorted Polowski. "By the time that order gets through the judge and Dafoe and your Aunt Minnie's cousin, Viratek'll have that lab turned into a baby-milk factory. No, we need to get in on our own. Without anyone getting word of it." He looked at Ollie. "And you're sure this is the only evidence we'll need?"

Ollie nodded. "One vial should do it. Then we take it to a reputable lab, have them confirm it's smallpox, and your case is airtight."

"They'll have no way around it?"

"None. The virus is officially extinct. Any company caught playing with a live sample is, ipso facto, dead meat."

"I like that," said Polowski. "That ipso facto stuff. No fancy Viratek attorney can argue that one away."

"But first you gotta get hold of a vial," said Ollie. "And from where I'm standing, it looks impossible. Unless we're willing to try armed robbery."

For one frightening moment, Polowski actually seemed to give that thought serious consideration. "Naw," he conceded. "Wouldn't go over well in court."

"Besides which," said Ollie, "I refuse to shoot another human being. It's against my principles."

"Mine, too," said Milo.

"But theft," said Ollie, "that's acceptable."

Polowski looked at Victor. "A group with high moral standards."

Victor grinned. "Holdovers from the sixties."

"Sounds like we're back to the first option," said Cathy. "We have to steal the virus." She focused on the map of the compound, noting the electrified fence that circled the entire complex. The main road led straight to the front gate. Except for an unpaved fire road, labeled *not maintained,* no other approaches were apparent.

"All right," she said. "Assume you do get through the front gate. You still have to get past two locked doors, two separate guards and a laser grid. Come on."

"The doors are no problem," said Victor. "It's the two guards."

"Maybe a diversion?" suggested Milo. "How about we set a fire?"

"And bring in the town fire department?" said Victor. "Not a good idea. Besides, I've dealt with this night guard at the front gate. I know him. And he goes strictly by the book. Never leaves the booth. At the first hint of anything suspicious, he'll hit the alarm button."

"Maybe Milo could whip up a fake security pass," said Ollie.

"You know, the way he used to fix us up with those fake drivers' licenses."

"He falsified IDs?" said Polowski.

"Hey, I just changed the age to twenty-one!" protested Milo.

"Made great passports, too," said Ollie. "I had one from the kingdom of Booga Booga. It got me right past the customs official in Athens."

"Yeah?" Polowski looked impressed. "So what about it, Holland? Would it work?"

"Not a chance. The guard has a master list of top-security employees. If he doesn't know the face, he'll do a double check."

"But he does let some people through automatically?"

"Sure. The bigwigs. The ones he recognizes on—" Victor suddenly paused and turned to stare at Cathy "—on sight. Lord. It just might work."

Cathy took one look at his face and immediately read his mind. "No," she said. "It's not that easy! I need to see the subject! I need molds of his face. Detailed photos from every angle—"

"But you *could* do it. You do it all the time."

"On film it works! But this is face-to-face!"

"It's at night, through a car window. Or through a video camera. If you could just make me pass for one of the exec's—"

"What are you talking about?" demanded Polowski.

"Cathy's a makeup artist. You know, horror films, special effects."

"This is different!" Cathy said. The difference being it was Victor's life on the line. No, he couldn't ask her to do this. If anything went wrong, she would be responsible. Having his death on her conscience would be more than she could live with.

She shook her head, praying he'd read the deadly earnestness in her gaze. "There's too much at stake," she insisted. "It's not as simple as—as filming *Slimelords*!"

"You did *Slimelords*?" asked Milo. "Terrific flick!"

"Besides," said Cathy, "it's not that easy, copying a face. I have to cast a mold, to get the features just right. For that I need a model."

"You mean the real guy?" asked Polowski.

"Right. The real guy. And I hardly think you're going to get some Viratek executive to sit down and let me slap plaster all over his face.''

There was a long silence.

''That does present a problem,'' said Milo.

''Not necessarily.''

They all turned and looked at Ollie.

''What are you thinking?'' asked Victor.

''About this guy who works with me once in a while. Down in the lab...'' Ollie looked up, and the grin on his face was distinctly smug. ''He's a veterinarian.''

The events of the past few weeks had weighed heavily on Archibald Black, so heavily, in fact, that he found it difficult to carry on with those everyday tasks of life. Just driving to and from his office at Viratek was an ordeal. And then, to sit down at his desk and face his secretary and pretend that nothing, absolutely nothing, was wrong—that was almost more than he could manage. He was a scientist, not an actor.

Not a criminal.

But that's what they would call him, if the experiments in C wing ever came to light. His instinct was to shut the lab down, to destroy the contents of those incubators. But Matthew Tyrone insisted the work continue. They were so close to completion. After all, Defense had underwritten the project, and Defense expected a product. This matter of Victor Holland was only a minor glitch, soon to be solved. The thing to do was carry on.

Easy for Tyrone to say, thought Black. *Tyrone had no conscience to bother him.*

These thoughts had plagued him all day. Now, as Black packed up his briefcase, he felt desperate to flee forever this teak-and-leather office, to take refuge in some safe and anonymous job. It was with a sigh of relief that he walked out the door.

It was dark when he pulled into his gravel driveway. The house, a saltbox of cedar and glass tucked among the trees, looked cold and empty and in need of a woman. Perhaps he should call his neighbor Muriel. She always seemed to appreciate an impromptu dinner together. Her snappy wit and green Jell-O salad almost made up for the fact she was 75. What a shame his generation didn't produce many Muriels.

He stepped out of his car and started up the path to the front door. Halfway there, he heard a soft *whht!* and almost simultaneously, a sharp pain stung his neck. Reflexively he slapped at it; something came away in his hands. In wonderment, he stared down at the dart, trying to understand where it had come from and how such a thing had managed to lodge in his neck. But he found he couldn't think straight. And then he found he was having trouble seeing, that the night had suddenly darkened to a dense blackness, that his legs were being sucked into some sort of quagmire. His briefcase slipped from his grasp and thudded to the ground.

I'm dying, he thought. And then, *Will anyone find me here?*

It was his last conscious thought before he collapsed onto the leaf-strewn path.

"Is he dead?"

Ollie bent forward and listened for Archibald Black's breathing. "He's definitely alive. But out cold." He looked up at Polowski and Victor. "Okay, let's move it. He'll be out for only an hour or so."

Victor grabbed the legs, Ollie and Polowski, the arms. Together they carried the unconscious man a few dozen yards through the woods, toward the clearing where the van was parked.

"You—you sure we got an hour?" gasped Polowski.

"Plus or minus," said Ollie. "The tranquilizer's designed for large animals, so the dose was only an estimate. And this guy's heavier than I expected." Ollie was panting now. "Hey, Polowski, he's slipping. Pull your weight, will ya?"

"I am! I think his right arm's heavier than his left."

The van's side door was already open for them. They rolled Black inside and slid the door closed. A bright light suddenly glared, but the unconscious man didn't even twitch.

Cathy knelt down at his side and critically examined the man's face.

"Can you do it?" asked Victor.

"Oh, I can do it," she said. "The question is, will you pass for him?" She glanced up and down the man's length, then back at

Victor. "Looks about your size and build. We'll have to darken your hair, give you a widow's peak. I think you'll pass." She turned and glanced at Milo, who was already poised with his camera. "Take your photos. A few shots from every angle. I need lots of hair detail."

As Milo's strobe flashed again and again, Cathy donned gloves and an apron. She pointed to a sheet. "Drape him for me," she directed. "Everything but his face. I don't want him to wake up with plaster all over his clothes."

"Assuming he wakes up at all," said Milo, frowning down at Black's inert form.

"Oh, he'll wake up," said Ollie. "Right where we found him. And if we do the job right, Mr. Archibald Black will never know what hit him."

It was the rain that awakened him. The cold droplets pelted his face and dribbled into his open mouth. Groaning, Black turned over and felt gravel bite into his shoulder. Even in his groggy state it occurred to him that this did not make sense. Slowly he took stock of all the things that were not as they should be: the rain falling from the ceiling, the gravel in his bed, the fact he was still wearing his shoes...

At last he managed to shake himself fully awake. He found to his puzzlement that he was sitting in his driveway, and that his briefcase was lying right beside him. By now the rain had swelled to a downpour—he had to get out of the storm. Half crawling, half walking, Black managed to make it up the porch steps and into the house.

An hour later, huddled in his kitchen, a cup of coffee in hand, he tried to piece together what had happened. He remembered parking his car. He'd taken out his briefcase and apparently had managed to make it halfway up the path. And then...what?

A vague ache worried its way into his awareness. He rubbed his neck. That's when he remembered something strange had happened, just before he blacked out. Something associated with that ache in his neck.

He went to a mirror and looked. There it was, a small puncture in the skin. An absurd thought popped into his head: *Vampires.*

Right. *Damn it, Archibald. You are a scientist. Come up with a rational explanation.*

He went to the laundry hamper and fished out his damp shirt. To his alarm he spotted a droplet of blood on the lapel. Then he saw what had caused it: a common, everyday tailor's pin. It was still lodged in the collar, no doubt left there by the dry cleaners. There was his rational explanation. He'd been pricked by a collar pin and the pain had sent him into a faint.

In disgust, he threw the shirt down. First thing in the morning, he was going to complain to the Tidy Girl cleaners and demand they do his suit for free.

Vampires, indeed.

"Even with bad lighting, you'll be lucky if you pass," said Cathy.

She stood back and gave Victor a long, critical look. Slowly she walked around him, eyeing the newly darkened hair, the resculpted face, the new eye color. It was as close as she could make it, but it wasn't good enough. It would never be good enough, not when Victor's life was at stake.

"I think he's the spitting image," said Polowski. "What's the problem now?"

"The problem is, I suddenly realize it's a crazy idea. I say we call it off."

"You've been working on him all afternoon. You got it right down to the damn freckles on his nose. What else can you improve on?"

"I don't know. I just don't feel *good* about this!"

There was a silence as she confronted the four men.

Ollie shook his head. "Women's intuition. That's a dangerous thing to disregard."

"Well, here's *my* intuition," said Polowski. "I think it'll work. And I think it's our best option. Our chance to nail the case."

Cathy turned to Victor. "You're the one who'll get hurt. It's your decision." What she really wanted to say was, *Please. Don't do it. Stay with me. Stay alive and safe and mine.* But she knew, looking into his eyes, that he'd already made his decision, and no matter how much she might wish for it, he would never really be hers.

"Cathy," he said. "It'll work. You have to believe that."

"The only thing I believe," she said, "is that you're going to get killed. And I don't want to be around to watch it."

Without another word, she turned and walked out the door.

Outside, in the parking lot of the Rockabye Motel, she stood in the darkness and hugged herself. She heard the door shut, and then his footsteps moved toward her across the blacktop.

"You don't have to stay," he said. "There's still that beach in Mexico. You could fly there tonight, be out of this mess."

"Do you want me to go?"

A pause, then, "Yes."

She shrugged, a poor attempt at nonchalance. "All right. I suppose it all makes perfect sense. I've done my part."

"You saved my life. At the very least, I owe you a measure of safety."

She turned to him. "Is that what weighs most on your mind, Victor? The fact that you *owe* me?"

"What weighs most on my mind is that you might get caught in the crossfire. I'm prepared to walk through those doors at Viratek. I'm prepared to do a lot of stupid things. But I'm not prepared to watch you get hurt. Does that make any sense?" He pulled her against him, into a place that felt infinitely warm and safe. "Cathy, Cathy. I'm not crazy. I don't want to die. But I don't see any way around this...."

She pressed her face against his chest, felt his heartbeat, so steady, so regular. She was afraid to think of that heart not beating, of those arms no longer alive to hold her. He was brave enough to go through with this crazy scheme; couldn't she somehow dredge up the same courage? She thought, *I've come this far with you. How could I dream of walking away? Now that I know I love you?*

The motel door opened, and light arced across the parking lot. "Gersh?" said Ollie. "It's getting late. If we want to go ahead, we'll have to leave now."

Victor was still looking at her. "Well?" he said. "Do you want Ollie to take you to the airport?"

"No." She squared her shoulders. "I'm coming with you."

"Are you sure that's what you want to do?"

"I'm never sure of anything these days. But on this I've decided.

I'll stick it out.'' She managed a smile. ''Besides, you might need me on the set. In case your face falls off.''

''I need you for a hell of a lot more than that.''

''Gersh?''

Victor reached out for Cathy's hand. She let him take it. ''We're coming,'' he said. ''Both of us.''

''I'm approaching the front gate. One guard in the booth. No one else around. Copy?''

''Loud and clear,'' said Polowski.

''Okay. Here I go. Wish me luck.''

''We'll be tuned in. Break a leg.'' Polowski clicked off the microphone and glanced at the others. ''Well, folks, he's on his way.''

To what? Cathy wondered. She glanced around at the other faces. There were four of them huddled in the van. They'd parked a half mile from Viratek's front gate. Close enough to hear Victor's transmissions, but too far away to do him much good. With the microphone link, they could mark his progress.

They could also mark his death.

In silence, they waited for the first hurdle.

''Evening,'' said Victor, pulling up at the gate.

The guard peered out through the booth window. He was in his twenties, cap on straight, collar button fastened. This was Pete Zahn, Mr. By-the-book Extraordinaire. If anyone was to cut the operation short, it would be this man. Victor made a brave attempt at a smile and prayed his mask wouldn't crack. It seemed an eternity, that exchange of looks. Then, to Victor's relief, the man smiled back.

''Working late, Dr. Black?''

''Forgot something at the lab.''

''Must be important, huh? To make a special trip at midnight.''

''These government contracts. Gotta be done on time.''

''Yeah.'' The guard waved him through. ''Have a nice night.''

Heart pounding, Victor pulled through the gate. Only when he'd rounded the curve into the empty parking lot did he manage a sigh of relief. ''First base,'' he said into the microphone. ''Come on, guys. Talk to me.''

''We're here,'' came the response. It was Polowski.

"I'm heading into the building—can't be sure the signal will get through those walls. So if you don't hear from me—"

"We'll be listening."

"I've got a message for Cathy. Put her on."

There was a pause, then he heard, "I'm here, Victor."

"I just wanted to tell you this. I'm coming back. I promise. Copy?"

He wasn't sure if it was just the signal's waiver, but he thought he heard the beginning of tears in her reply. "I copy."

"I'm going in now. Don't leave without me."

It took Pete Zahn only a minute to look up Archibald Black's license plate number. He kept a Rolodex in the booth, though he seldom referred to it as he had a good memory for numbers. He knew every executive's license by heart. It was his own little mind game, a test of his cleverness. And the plate on Dr. Black's car just didn't seem right.

He found the file card. The auto matched up okay: a gray 1991 Lincoln sedan. And he was fairly certain that *was* Dr. Black sitting in the driver's seat. But the license number was all wrong.

He sat back and thought about it for a while, trying to come up with all the possible explanations. That Black was simply driving a different auto. That Black was playing a joke on him, testing him.

That it hadn't been Archibald Black, at all.

Pete reached for the telephone. The way to find out was to call Black's home. It was after midnight, but it had to be done. If Black didn't answer the phone, then that must be him in the Lincoln. And if he *did* answer, then something was terribly wrong and Black would want to know about it.

Two rings. That's all it took before a groggy voice answered, "Hello?"

"This is Pete Zahn, night man at Viratek. Is this—is this Dr. Black?"

"Yes."

"Dr. *Archibald* Black?"

"Look, it's late! What is it?"

"I don't know how to tell you this, Dr. Black, but..." Pete cleared his throat. "Your double just drove through the gate...."

* * *

"I'm through the front door. Heading up the hall to the security wing. In case anyone's listening." Victor didn't expect a reply, and he heard none. The building was a concrete monstrosity, designed to last forever. He doubted a radio signal would make it through these walls. Though he'd been on his own from the moment he'd entered the front gate, at least he'd had the comfort of knowing his friends were listening in on the progress. Now he was truly alone.

He moved at a casual pace to the locked door marked Authorized Personnel Only. A camera hung from the ceiling, its lens pointed straight at him. He pointedly ignored it and turned his attention to the security keypad mounted on the wall. The numbers Jerry had given him had gotten him through the front door; would the second combination get him through this one? His hands were sweating as he punched in the seven digits. He felt a dart of panic as a beep sounded and a message flashed on the screen: *Incorrect security code. Access denied.*

He could feel the sweat building up beneath the mask. Were the numbers wrong? Had he simply transposed two digits? He knew someone was watching him through the camera, wondering why he was taking so long. He took a deep breath and tried again. This time, he entered the digits slowly, deliberately. He braced himself for the warning beep. To his relief, it didn't go off.

Instead, a new message appeared. *Security code accepted. Please enter.*

He stepped through, into the next room.

Third hurdle, he thought in relief as the door closed behind him. Now for the home run.

Another camera, mounted in a corner, was pointed at him. Acutely conscious of that lens, he made his way across the room to the inner lab door. He turned the knob and a warning bell sounded.

Now what? he thought. Only then did he notice the red light glowing over the door, and the warning *Laser grid activated.* He needed a key to shut it off. He saw no other way to deactivate it, no way to get past it, into the room beyond.

It was time for desperate measures, time for a little chutzpah. He patted his pockets, then turned and faced the camera. "Hello?" He waved.

A voice answered over an intercom. "Is there a problem, Dr. Black?"

"Yes. I can't seem to find my keys. I must have left them at home...."

"I can cut the lasers from here."

"Thanks. Gee, I don't know how this happened."

"No problem."

At once the red warning light shut off. Cautiously Victor tried the door; it swung open. He gave the camera a goodbye wave and entered the last room.

Inside, to his relief, there were no cameras anywhere—at least, none that he could spot. A bit of breathing space, he thought. He moved into the lab and took a quick survey of his surroundings. What he saw was a mind-numbing display of space-age equipment—not just the expected centrifuges and microscopes, but instruments he'd never seen before, all of them brand-new and gleaming. He headed through the decontamination chamber, past the laminar flow unit, and went straight to the incubators. He opened the door.

Glass vials tinkled in their compartments. He took one out. Pink fluid glistened within. The label read Lot #341. Active.

This must be it, he thought. This was what Ollie had told him to look for. Here was the stuff of nightmares, the grim reaper distilled to sub-microscopic elements.

He removed two vials, fitted them into a specially padded cigarette case, and slipped it into his pocket. *Mission accomplished,* he thought in triumph as he headed back through the lab. All that lay before him was a casual stroll back to his car. Then the champagne...

He was halfway across the room when the alarm bell went off.

He froze, the harsh ring echoing in his ears.

"Dr. Black?" said the guard's voice over some hidden intercom. "Please don't leave. Stay right where you are."

Victor spun around wildly, trying to locate the speaker. "What's going on?"

"I've just been asked to detain you. If you'll hold on, I'll find out what—"

Victor didn't wait to hear the reason—he bolted for the door. Even as he reached it, he heard the whine of the lasers powering on, felt something slash his arm. He shoved through the first door, dashed across the anteroom and out the security door, into the hallway.

Everywhere, alarms were going off. The whole damn building had turned into an echo chamber of ringing bells. His gaze shot right, to the front entrance. No, not that way—the guard was stationed there.

He sprinted left, toward what he hoped was a fire exit. Somewhere behind him a voice yelled, "Halt!" He ignored it and kept running. At the end of the hall he slammed against the opening bar and found himself in a stairwell. No exit, only steps leading up and down. He wasn't about to be trapped like a rat in the basement. He headed up the stairs.

One flight into his climb, he heard the stairwell door slam open on the first floor. Again a voice commanded, "Halt or I'll shoot!"

A bluff, he thought.

A pistol shot exploded, echoing up the concrete stairwell.

Not a bluff. With new desperation, he pushed through the landing door, into the second-floor hallway. A line of closed doors stretched before him. Which one, which one? There was no time to think. He ducked into the third room and softly shut the door behind him.

In the semidarkness, he spotted the gleam of stainless steel and glass beakers. Another lab. Only this one had a large window, now shimmering with moonlight, looming over the far countertop.

From down the hall came the slam of a door being kicked open and the guard's shouted command: "Freeze!"

He was down to one last escape route. Victor grabbed a chair, raised it over his head, and flung it at the window. The glass shattered, raining moonlight-silvered shards into the darkness below. He scarcely bothered to look before he leapt. Bracing himself for the impact, he jumped from the window and landed in a tangle of shrubbery.

"Halt!" came a shout from above.

That was enough to jar Victor back to his feet. He sprinted off

across a lawn, into the cover of trees. Glancing back, he saw no
pursuing shadow. The guard wasn't about to risk his neck leaping
out any window.

Got to make it out the gate...

Victor circled around the building, burrowing his way through
bushes and trees to a stand of oaks. From there he could view the
front gate, way off in the distance. What he saw made his heart
sink.

Floodlights illuminated the entrance, glaring down on the four
security cars blocking the driveway. Now a panel truck pulled up.
The driver went around to the back and opened the doors. At his
command two German shepherds leaped out and danced around,
barking at his feet.

Victor backed away, stumbling deeper into the grove of oaks. *No
way out,* he thought, glancing behind him at the fence, topped with
coils of barbed wire. Already, the dogs' barking was moving closer.
Unless I can sprout wings and fly, I'm a dead man....

CHAPTER ELEVEN

"Something's wrong!" Cathy cried as the first security car drove past.

Polowski touched her arm. "Easy. It could be just a routine patrol."

"No. Look!" Through the trees, they spotted three more cars, all roaring down the road at top speed toward Viratek.

Ollie muttered a surprisingly coarse oath and reached for the microphone.

"Wait!" Polowski grabbed his hand. "We can't risk a transmission. Let him contact us first."

"If he's in trouble—"

"Then he already knows it. Give him a chance to make it out on his own."

"What if he's trapped?" said Cathy. "Are we just going to sit here?"

"We don't have a choice. Not if they've blockaded the front gate—"

"We *do* have a choice!" said Cathy, scrambling forward into the driver's seat.

"What the hell are you doing?" demanded Polowski.

"Giving him a fighting chance. If we don't—"

They all fell instantly silent as a transmission suddenly hissed over the receiver. "Looks like I got myself in a bind, guys. Don't see a way out. You copy?"

Ollie snatched up the microphone. "Copy, Gersh. What's your situation?"

"Bad."

"Specify."

"Front gate's blocked and lit up like a football field. Big time alarms going off. They just brought in the dogs—"

"Can you get over the fence?"

"Negative. It's electrified. Low voltage, but more than I can handle. You guys better hit the road without me."

Polowski grabbed the microphone and barked, "Did you get the stuff?"

Cathy turned and snapped: "Forget that! Ask him where he is. *Ask him!*"

"Holland?" said Polowski. "Where are you?"

"At the northeast perimeter. Fence goes all the way around. Look, get moving. I'll manage—"

"Tell him to head for the east fence!" Cathy said. "Near the midpoint!"

"What?"

"Just tell him!"

"Go to the east fence," Polowski said into the microphone. "Midpoint."

"I copy."

Polowski looked up at Cathy in puzzlement. "What the hell are you thinking of?"

"This is a getaway car, right?" she muttered as she turned on the engine. "I say we put it to its intended use!" She threw the van into gear and spun it around, onto the road.

"Hey, you're going the wrong way!" yelled Milo.

"No, I'm not. There's a fire road, just off to the left somewhere. There it is." She made a sharp turn, onto what was little more than a dirt track. They bounced along, crashing through tree branches and shrubs, a ride so violently spine-shaking it was all they could do to hang on.

"How did you find this *wonderful* road?" Polowski managed to ask.

"It was on the map. I saw it when we were studying the plans for Viratek."

"Is this a scenic route? Or does it go somewhere?"

"The east fence. Used to be the construction entrance for the compound. I'm hoping it's still clear enough to get through...."

"And then what happens?"

Ollie sighed. "Don't ask."

Cathy steered around a bush that had sprung up in her path and ran head-on into a sapling. Her passengers tumbled to the floor. "Sorry," she muttered. Reversing gear, she spun them back on the road. "It should be just ahead...."

A barrier of chain link suddenly loomed before them. Instantly she cut the lights. Through the darkness, they could hear dogs barking, moving in. Where was he?

Then they saw him, flitting through the moonlight. He was running. Somewhere off to the side, a man shouted and gunfire spat the ground.

"Brace yourselves!" yelled Cathy. She snapped on her seatbelt and gripped the steering wheel. Then she stepped on the gas.

The van jerked forward like a bronco, barreled through the underbrush, and slammed into the fence. The chain link sagged; electrical sparks hissed in the night. Cathy threw the gears into reverse, backed up, and hit the gas again.

The fence toppled; barbed wire scraped across the windshield.

"We're through!" said Ollie. He yanked open the sliding door and yelled: "Come on, Gersh! Come on!"

The running figure zigzagged across the grass. All around him, gunfire exploded. He made a last flying leap across the coil of barbed wire and stumbled.

"Come on, Gersh!"

Gunfire spattered the van.

Victor struggled back to his feet. They heard the rip of clothing, then he was reaching up to them, being dragged inside, to safety.

The door slammed shut. Cathy backed up, wheeled the van around and slammed on the gas pedal.

They leaped forward, bouncing through the bushes and across ruts. Another round of bullets pinged the van. Cathy was oblivious to it. She focused only on getting them back to the main road. The sound of gunfire receded. At last the trees gave way to a familiar band of blacktop. She turned left and gunned the engine, anxious to put as many miles as possible between them and Viratek.

Off in the distance, a siren wailed.

"We got company!" said Polowski.

"Which way now?" Cathy cried. Viratek lay behind them; the sirens were approaching from ahead.

"I don't know! Just get the hell out of here!"

As yet her view of the police cars was blocked by trees, but she could hear the sirens moving rapidly closer. *Will they let us pass? Or will they pull us over?*

Almost too late she spotted a clearing, off to the side. On sudden impulse she veered off the pavement, and the van bounced onto a stubbly field.

"Don't tell me," groaned Polowski. "Another fire road?"

"Shut up!" she snapped and steered straight for a clump of bushes. With a quick turn of the wheel, she circled behind the shrubbery and cut her lights.

It was just in time. Seconds later, two patrol cars, lights flashing, sped right past the concealing bushes. She sat frozen, listening as the sirens faded in the distance. Then, in the darkness, she heard Milo say softly, "Her name is Bond. Jane Bond."

Half laughing, half crying, Cathy turned as Victor scrambled beside her, onto the front seat. At once she was in his arms, her tears wetting his shirt, her sobs muffled in the depths of his embrace. He kissed her damp cheeks, her mouth. The touch of his lips stilled her tremors.

From the back came the sound of a throat being cleared. "Uh, Gersh?" inquired Ollie politely. "Don't you think we ought to get moving?"

Victor's mouth was still pressed against Cathy's. Reluctantly he broke contact but his gaze never left her face. "Sure," he murmured, just before he pulled her back for another kiss. "But would somebody else mind driving...?"

"Here's where things get dangerous," said Polowski. He was at the wheel now, as they headed south toward San Francisco. Cathy and Victor sat in front with Polowski; in the back of the van, Milo and Ollie lay curled up asleep like two exhausted puppies. From the radio came the soft strains of a country western song. The dials glowed a vivid green in the darkness.

"We've finally got the evidence," said Polowski. "All we need to hang 'em. They'll be desperate. Ready to try anything. From here on out, folks, it's going to be a game of cat and mouse."

As if it wasn't already, thought Cathy as she huddled closer to Victor. She longed for a chance to be alone with him. There had been no time for tearful reunions, no time for any confessions of love. They'd spent the last two hours on a harrowing journey down backroads, always avoiding the police. By now the break-in at Viratek would have been reported to the authorities. The state police would be on the lookout for a van with frontal damage.

Polowski was right. Things were only getting more dangerous.

"Soon as we hit the city," said Polowski, "we'll get those vials off to separate labs. Independent confirmation. That should wipe any doubts away. You know names we can trust, Holland?"

"Fellow alum back in New Haven. Runs the hospital lab. I can trust him."

"Yale? Great. That'll have clout."

"Ollie has a pal at UCSF. They'll take care of the second vial."

"And when those reports get back, I know a certain journalist who loves to have a little birdie chirp in his ear." Polowski gave the steering wheel a satisfied slap. "Viratek, you are dead meat."

"You enjoy this, don't you?" said Cathy.

"Workin' the right side of the law? I say it's good for the soul. It keeps your mind sharp and your feet on their toes. It helps you stay young."

"Or die young," said Cathy.

Polowski laughed. "Women. They just never understand the game."

"I don't understand it, at all."

"I bet Holland here does. He just had the adrenaline high of his life. Didn't you?"

Victor didn't answer. He was gazing ahead at the blacktop stretching before their headlights.

"Well, wasn't it a high?" asked Polowski. "To claw your way to hell and back again? To know you made it through on nothing much more than your wits?"

"No," said Victor quietly. "Because it's not over yet."

Polowski's grin faded. He turned his attention back to the road. "Almost," he said. "It's almost over."

They passed a sign: San Francisco: 12 Miles.

Four in the morning. The stars were mere pinpricks in a sky washed out by streetlights. In a North Beach doughnut shop, five weary souls had gathered around steaming coffee and cheese Danish. Only one other table was occupied, by a man with bloodshot eyes and shaking hands. The girl behind the counter sat with her nose buried in a paperback. Behind her, the coffee machine hissed out a fresh brew.

"To the Old Coots," said Milo, raising his cup. "Still the best ensemble around."

They all raised their cups. "To the Old Coots!"

"And to our newest and fairest member," said Milo. "The beautiful—the intrepid—"

"Oh, *please,*" said Cathy.

Victor wrapped his arm around her shoulder. "Relax and be honored. Not everyone gets into this highly selective group."

"The only requirement," said Ollie, "is that you have to play a musical instrument badly."

"But I don't play anything."

"No problem." Ollie fished out a piece of waxed paper from the pile of Danishes and wrapped it around his pocket comb. "Kazoo."

"Fitting," said Milo. "Since that was Lily's instrument."

"Oh." She took the comb. Lily's instrument. It always came back to *her,* the ghost who would forever be there. Suddenly the air of celebration was gone, as though swept away by the cold wind of dawn. She glanced at Victor. He was looking out the window, at the garishly lit streets. *What are you thinking? Are you wishing she was here? That it wasn't me being presented this silly kazoo, but her?*

She put the comb to her lips and hummed an appropriately out-of-tune version of "Yankee Doodle." Everyone laughed and clapped, even Victor. But when the applause was over, she saw the sad and weary look in his eyes. Quietly she set the kazoo down on the table.

Outside, a delivery truck roared past. It was 5:00 a.m.; the city was stirring.

"Well, folks," said Polowski, slapping down a dollar tip. "We got a hotshot reporter to roust outta bed. And then you and I—" he looked at Victor "—have a few deliveries to make. When's United leave for New Haven?"

"At ten-fifteen," said Victor.

"Okay. I'll buy you the plane tickets. In the meantime, you see if you can't grow yourself a new mustache or something." Polowski glanced at Cathy. "You're going with him, right?"

"No," she said, looking at Victor.

She was hoping for a reaction, any reaction. What she saw was a look of relief. And, strangely, resignation.

He didn't try to change her mind. He simply asked, "Where will you be going?"

She shrugged. "Maybe I should stick to our original plan. You know, head south. Hang out with Jack for a while. What do you think?"

It was his chance to stop her. His chance to say, *No, I want you around. I won't let you leave, not now, not ever.* If he really loved her, that's exactly what he would say.

Her heart sank when he simply nodded and said, "I think it's a good idea."

She blinked back the tears before anyone could see them. With an indifferent smile she looked at Ollie. "So I guess I'll need a ride. When are you and Milo heading home?"

"Right now, I guess," said Ollie, looking bewildered. "Seeing as our job's pretty much done."

"Can I hitch along? I'll catch the bus at Palo Alto."

"No problem. In fact, you can sit in the honored front seat."

"Long as you don't let her behind the wheel," grumbled Milo. "I want a nice, quiet drive home if you don't mind."

Polowski rose to his feet. "Then we're all set. Everyone's got a place to go. Let's do it."

Outside, on a street rumbling with early-morning traffic, with their friends standing only a few yards away, Cathy and Victor said their goodbyes. It wasn't the place for sentimental farewells. Perhaps that was all for the best. At least she could leave with some trace of dignity. At least she could avoid hearing, from his lips, the brutal truth. She would simply walk away and hold on to the fantasy that he loved her. That in their brief time together she'd managed to work her way, just a little, into his heart.

"You'll be all right?" he asked.

"I'll be fine. And you?"

"I'll manage." He thrust his hands in his pockets and looked off at a bus idling near the corner. "I'll miss you," he said. "But I know it doesn't make sense for us to be together. Not under the circumstances."

I would stay with you, she thought. *Under any circumstances. If I only knew you wanted me.*

"Anyway," he said with a sigh, "I'll let you know when things are safe again. When you can come home."

"And then?"

"And then we'll take it from there," he said softly.

They kissed, a clumsy, polite kiss, all the more hurried because they knew their friends were watching. There was no passion here, only the cool, dry lips of a man saying goodbye. As they pulled apart, she saw his face blur away through the tears.

"Take care of yourself, Victor," she said. Then, shoulders squared, she turned and walked toward Ollie and Milo.

"Is that it?" asked Ollie.

"That's it." Brusquely she rubbed her hand across her eyes. "I'm ready to go."

"Tell me about Lily," she said.

The first light of dawn was already streaking the sky as they drove past the boxy row homes of Pacifica, past the cliffs where sea waves crashed and gulls swooped and dove.

Ollie, his gaze on the road, asked: "What do you want to know?"

"What kind of woman was she?"

"She was a nice person," said Ollie. "And brainy. Though she never went out of her way to impress people, she was probably the smartest one of all of us. Definitely brighter than Milo."

"And a lot better-looking than Ollie," piped a voice from the backseat.

"A real kind, real decent woman. When she and Gersh got married, I remember thinking, 'he's got himself a saint.'" He glanced at Cathy, suddenly noticing her silence. "Of course," he added quickly, "not every man *wants* a saint. I know I'd be happier with a lady who can be a little goofy." He flashed Cathy a grin. "Someone who might, say, crash a van through an electrified fence, just for kicks."

It was a sweet thing to say, a comment designed to lift her spirits. It couldn't take the edge off her pain.

She settled back and watched dawn lighten the sky. How she needed to get away! She thought about Mexico, about warm water and hot sand and the tang of fresh fish and lime. She would throw herself into working on that new film. Of course, Jack would be on the set, Jack with his latest sweetie pie in tow, but she could handle that now. Jack would never be able to hurt her again. She was beyond that now, beyond being hurt by any man.

The drive to Milo's house seemed endless.

When at last they pulled up in the driveway, the dawn had already blossomed into a bright, cold morning. Milo climbed out and stood blinking in the sunshine.

"So, guys," he said through the car window. "Guess here's where we go our separate ways." He looked at Cathy. "Mexico, right?"

She nodded. "Puerto Vallarta. What about you?"

"I'm gonna catch up with Ma in Florida. Maybe get a load of Disney World. Wanna come, Ollie?"

"Some other time. I'm going to go get some sleep."

"Don't know what you're missing. Well, it's been some adventure. I'm almost sorry it's over." Milo turned and headed up the walk to his house. On the front porch he waved and yelled, "See you around!" Then he vanished through the front door.

Ollie laughed. "Milo and his ma, together? Disney World'll never be the same." He reached for the ignition. "Next stop, the bus station. I've got just enough gas to get us there and—"

He didn't get a chance to turn the key.

A gun barrel was thrust in the open car window. It came to rest squarely against Ollie's temple.

"Get out, Dr. Wozniak," said a voice.

Ollie's reply came out in a bare croak. "What—what do you want?"

"Do it now." The click of the hammer being cocked was all the coaxing Ollie needed.

"Okay, okay! I'm getting out!" Ollie scrambled out and backed away, his hands raised in surrender.

Cathy, too, started to climb out, but the gunman snapped, "Not you! You stay inside."

"Look," said Ollie, "You can have the damn car! You don't need her—"

"But I do. Tell Mr. Holland I'll be in contact. Regarding Ms. Weaver's future." He went around and opened the passenger door. "You, into the driver's seat!" he commanded her.

"No. Please—"

The gun barrel dug into her neck. "Need I ask again?"

Trembling, she moved behind the wheel. Her knee brushed the car keys, still dangling from the ignition. The man slid in beside her. Though the gun barrel was still thrust against her neck, it was the man's eyes she focused on. They were black, fathomless. If any spark of humanity lurked in those depths, she couldn't see it.

"Start the engine," he said.

"Where—where are we going?"

"For a drive. Somewhere scenic."

Her thoughts were racing, seeking some means of escape, but she came up with nothing. That gun was insurmountable.

She turned on the ignition.

"Hey!" yelled Ollie, grabbing at the door. "You can't do this!"

Cathy screamed, "Ollie, no!"

The gunman had already shifted his aim out the window.

"Let her go!" yelled Ollie. "Let her—"

The gun went off.

Ollie staggered backward, his face a mask of astonishment.

Cathy lunged at the gunman. Pure animal rage, fueled by the instinct to survive, sent her clawing first for his eyes. At the last split second he flinched away. Her nails scraped down his cheek, drawing blood. Before he could shift his aim, she grabbed his wrist, wrenching desperately for control of the gun. He held fast. Not with all her strength could she keep the gun at bay, keep the barrel from turning toward her.

It was the last image she registered: that black hole, slowly turning until it was pointed straight at her face.

Something lashed at her from the side. Pain exploded in her head, shattering the world into a thousand slivers of light.

They faded, one by one, into darkness.

CHAPTER TWELVE

"Victor's here," said Milo.

It seemed to take Ollie forever to register their presence. Victor fought the urge to shake him to consciousness, to drag the words out of his friend's throat. He was forced to wait, the silence broken only by the hiss of oxygen, the gurgle of the suction tube. At last Ollie stirred and squinted through pain-glazed eyes at the three men standing beside his bed. "Gersh. I didn't—couldn't—" He stopped, exhausted by the effort just to talk.

"Easy, Ollie," said Milo. "Take it slow."

"Tried to stop him. Had a gun…" Ollie paused, gathering the strength to continue.

Victor listened fearfully for the next terrible words to come out. He was still in a state of disbelief, still hoping that what Milo had told him was one giant mistake, that Cathy was, at this very moment, on a bus somewhere to safety. Only two hours ago he'd been ready to board a plane for New Haven. Then he'd been handed a message at the United gate. It was addressed to passenger Sam Polowski, the name on his ticket. It had consisted of only three words: *Call Milo immediately.*

Passenger "Sam Polowski" never did board the plane.

Two hours, he thought in anguish. What have they done to her in those two long hours?

"This man—what did he look like?" asked Polowski.

"Didn't see him very well. Dark hair. Face sort of…thin."

"Tall? Short?"

"Tall."

"He drove off in your car?"

Ollie nodded.

"What about Cathy?" Victor blurted out, his control shattered. "He—didn't hurt her? She's all right?"

There was a pause that, to Victor, seemed like an eternity in hell. Ollie's gaze settled mournfully on Victor. "I don't know."

It was the best Victor could hope for. *I don't know.* It left open the possibility that she was still alive.

Suddenly agitated, he began to pace the floor. "I know what he wants," he said. "I know what I have to give him—"

"You can't be serious," said Polowski. "That's our evidence! You can't just hand it over—"

"That's exactly what I'm going to do."

"You don't even know how to contact him!"

"He'll contact *me.*" He spun around and looked at Milo. "He must've been watching your house all this time. Waiting for one of us to turn up. That's where he'll call."

"If he calls," said Polowski.

"He will." Victor touched his jacket pocket, where the two vials from Viratek still rested. "I have what he wants. He has what I want. I think we're both ready to make a trade."

The sun, glaring and relentless, was shining in her eyes. She tried to escape it, tried to close her lids tighter, to stop those rays from piercing through to her brain, but the light followed her.

"Wake up. *Wake up!*"

Icy water slapped her face. Cathy gasped awake, coughing, rivulets of water trickling from her hair. She struggled to make out the face hovering above her. At first all she saw was a dark oval against the blinding circle of light. Then the man moved away and she saw eyes like black agate, a slash of a mouth. A scream formed in her throat, to be instantly frozen by the cold barrel of a gun against her cheek.

"Not a sound," he said. "Got that?"

In silent terror she nodded.

"Good." The gun slid away from her cheek and was tucked under his jacket. "Sit up."

She obeyed. Instantly the room began to spin. She sat clutching her aching head, the fear temporarily overshadowed by waves of pain and nausea. The spell lasted for only a few moments. Then, as the nausea faded, she became aware of a second man in the room, a large, broad-shouldered man she'd never before seen. He sat off in a corner, saying nothing, but watching her every move. The room itself was small and windowless. She couldn't tell if it was day or night. The only furniture was a chair, a card table and the cot she was sitting on. The floor was a bare slab of concrete. *We're in a basement,* she thought. She heard no other sounds, either outside or in the building. Were they still in Palo Alto? Or were they a hundred miles away?

The man in the chair crossed his arms and smiled. Under different circumstances, she might have considered that smile a charming one. Now it struck her as frighteningly inhuman. "She seems awake enough," he said. "Why don't you proceed, Mr. Savitch?"

The man called Savitch loomed over her. "Where is he?"

"Who?" she said.

Her answer was met by a ringing slap to her cheek. She sprawled backwards on the cot.

"Try again," he said, dragging her back up to a sitting position. "Where is Victor Holland?"

"I don't know."

"You were with him."

"We—we split up."

"Why?"

She touched her mouth. The sight of blood on her fingers shocked her temporarily into silence.

"Why?"

"He—" She bowed her head. Softly she said, "He didn't want me around."

Savitch let out a snort. "Got tired of you pretty quick, did he?"

"Yes," she whispered. "I guess he did."

"I don't know why."

She shuddered as the man ran his finger down her cheek, her throat. He stopped at the top button of her blouse. *No,* she thought. *Not that.*

To her relief, the man in the chair suddenly cut in. "This is getting us nowhere."

Savitch turned to the other man. "You have another sug-gestion, Mr. Tyrone?"

"Yes. Let's try using her in a different way." Fearfully Cathy watched as Tyrone moved to the card table and opened a satchel.

"Since we can't go to him," he said, "we'll have Holland come to us." He turned and smiled at her. "With your help, of course."

She stared at the cellular telephone he was holding. "I told you. I don't know where he is."

"I'm sure one of his friends will track him down."

"He's not stupid. He wouldn't come for me—"

"You're right. He's not stupid." Tyrone began to punch in a phone number. "But he's a man of conscience. And that's a flaw that's every bit as fatal." He paused, then said into the telephone, "Hello? Mr. Milo Lum? I want you to pass this message to Victor Holland for me. Tell him I have something of his. Something that won't be around much longer…"

"It's him!" hissed Milo. "He wants to make a deal."

Victor shot to his feet. "Let me talk to him—"

"Wait!" Polowski grabbed his arm. "We have to take this slow. Think about what we're—"

Victor pulled his arm free and snatched the receiver from Milo. "This is Holland," he barked into the phone. "Where is she?"

The voice on the other end paused, a silence designed to emphasize just who held the upper hand. "She's with me. She's alive."

"How do I know that?"

"You'll have to take my word for it."

"Word, hell! I want proof!"

Again there was a silence. Then, through the crackle of the line, came another voice, so tremulous, so afraid, it almost broke his heart. "Victor, it's me."

"Cathy?" He almost shouted with relief. "Cathy, are you all right?"

"I'm…fine."

"Where are you?"

"I don't know—I think—" She stopped. The silence was agonizing. "I can't be sure."

"He hasn't hurt you?"

A pause. "No."

She's not telling me the truth, he thought. *He's done something to her…*

"Cathy, I promise. You'll be all right. I swear to you I'll—"

"Let's talk business." The man was back on the line.

Victor gripped the receiver in fury. "If you hurt her, if you just touch her, I swear I'll—"

"You're hardly in a position to bargain."

Victor felt a hand grasp his arm. He turned and met Polowski's gaze. *Keep your head* was the message he saw. *Go along with him. Make a bargain. It's the only way to buy time.*

Nodding, Victor fought to regain control. When he spoke again, his voice was calm. "Okay. You want the vials, they're yours."

"Not good enough."

"Then I'll throw myself into the bargain. A trade. Is that acceptable?"

"Acceptable. You and the vials in exchange for her life."

An anguished cry of *"No!"* pierced the dialogue. It was Cathy, somewhere in the background, shouting, "Don't, Victor! They're going to—"

Through the receiver, Victor heard the thud of a blow, followed by soft moans of pain. All his control shattered. He was screaming now, cursing, begging, anything to make the man stop hurting her. The words ran together, making no sense. He couldn't see straight, couldn't think straight.

Again, Polowski took his arm, gave it a shake. Victor, breathing hard, stared at him through a gaze blurred by tears. Polowski's eyes advised: *Make the deal. Go on.*

Victor swallowed and closed his eyes. *Give me strength,* he thought. He managed to ask, "When do we make the exchange?"

"Tonight. At 2:00 a.m."

"Where?"

"East Palo Alto. The old Saracen Theater."

"But it's closed. It's been closed for—"

"It'll be open. Just you, Holland. I spot anyone else and the first bullet has her name on it. Clear?"

"I want a guarantee! I want to know she'll be—"

He was answered by silence. And then, seconds later, he heard a dial tone.

Slowly he hung up.

"Well? What's the deal?" demanded Polowski.

"At 2:00 a.m. Saracen Theater."

"Half an hour. That barely gives us time to set up a—"

"I'm going alone."

Milo and Polowski stared at him. "Like hell," said Polowski.

Victor grabbed his jacket from out of the closet. He gave the pocket a quick pat; the cigarette case was right where he'd left it. He turned and reached for the door.

"But Gersh!" said Milo. "He's gonna kill you!"

Victor paused in the doorway. "Probably," he said softly. "But it's Cathy's only chance. And it's a chance I have to take."

"He won't come," said Cathy.

"Shut up," Matt Tyrone snapped and shoved her forward.

As they moved down the glass-strewn alley behind the Saracen Theater, Cathy frantically searched her mind for some way to sabotage this fatal meeting. It *would* be fatal, not just for Victor, but for her, as well. The two men now escorting her through the darkness had no intention of letting her live. The best she could hope for was that Victor would survive. She had to do what she could to better his chances.

"He's already got his evidence," she said. "You think he'd give that up just for me?"

Tyrone glanced at Savitch. "What if she's right?"

"Holland's coming," said Savitch. "I know how he thinks. He's not going to leave the little woman behind." Savitch gave Cathy's cheek a deceptively gentle caress. "Not when he knows exactly what we'll do to her."

Cathy flinched away, repelled by his touch. *What if he really doesn't come?* she thought. *What if he does the sensible thing and leaves me to die?*

She wouldn't blame him.

Tyrone gave her a push up the steps and into the building. "Inside. Move."

"I can't see," she protested, feeling her way along a pitch-black passage. She stumbled over boxes, brushed past what felt like heavy drapes. "It's too dark—"

"Then let there be light," said a new voice.

The lights suddenly sprang on, so bright she was temporarily blinded. She raised her hand to shield her eyes. Through the glare she could make out a third man, looming before her. Beyond him, the floor seemed to drop away into a vast blackness.

They were standing on a theater stage. It was obvious no performer had trod these boards in years. Ragged curtains hung like cobwebs from the rafters. Panels of an old set, the ivy-hung battlements of a medieval castle, still leaned at a crazy tilt against the back wall, framed by a pair of mops.

Tyrone said, "Any problems, Dafoe?"

"None," said the new man. "I've reconned the building. One door at the front, one backstage. The emergency side doors are padlocked. If we block both exits, he's trapped."

"I see the FBI deserves its fine reputation."

Dafoe grinned and dipped his head. "I knew the Cowboy would want the very best."

"Okay, Ms. Weaver." Tyrone shoved Cathy forward, toward a chair placed directly under the spotlight. "Let's put you right where he can see you. Center stage."

It was Savitch who tied her to the chair. He knew exactly what he was doing. She had no hope of working her hands free from such tight, professional knots.

He stepped back, satisfied with his job. "She's not going anywhere," he said. Then, as an afterthought, he ripped off a strip of cloth tape and slapped it over her mouth. "So we don't have any surprises," he said.

Tyrone glanced at his watch. "Zero minus fifteen. Positions, gentlemen."

The three men slipped away into the shadows, leaving Cathy alone on the empty stage. The spotlight beating down on her face was hot as the midday sun. Already she could feel beads of sweat forming on her forehead. Though she couldn't see them, by their voices she could guess the positions of the three men. Tyrone was close by. Savitch was at the back of the theater, near the building's front entrance. And the man named Dafoe had stationed himself somewhere above, in one of the box seats. Three different lines of fire. No route of escape.

Victor, don't be a fool, she thought. *Stay away...*

And if he doesn't come? She couldn't bear to consider that possibility, either, for it meant he was abandoning her. It meant he didn't care enough even to make the effort to save her.

She closed her eyes against the spotlight, against the tears. *I love you. I could take anything, even this, if I only knew you loved me.*

Her hands were numb from the ropes. She tried to wriggle the bonds looser, but only succeeded in rubbing her wrists raw. She fought to remain calm, but with every minute that passed, her heart seemed to pound harder. A drop of sweat trickled down her temple.

Somewhere in the shadows ahead, a door squealed open and closed. Footsteps approached, their pace slow and deliberate. She strained to see against the spotlight's glare, but could make out only the hint of shadow moving through shadow.

The stage floorboards creaked behind her as Tyrone strolled out from the wings. "Stop right where you are, Mr. Holland," he said.

CHAPTER THIRTEEN

Another spotlight suddenly sprang on, catching Victor in its glare. He stood halfway up the aisle, a lone figure trapped in a circle of brilliance.

You came for me! she thought. *I knew, somehow I knew, that you would....*

If only she could shout to him, warn him about the other two men. But the tape had been applied so tightly that the only sound she could produce was a whimper.

"Let her go," said Victor.

"You have something we want first."

"I said, *let her go!*"

"You're hardly in a position to bargain." Tyrone strolled out of the wings, onto the stage. Cathy flinched as the icy barrel of a gun pressed against her temple. "Let's see it, Holland," said Tyrone.

"Untie her first."

"I could shoot you both and be done with it."

"Is this what it's come to?" yelled Victor. "Federal dollars for the murder of civilians?"

"It's all a matter of cost and benefit. A few civilians may have to die now. But if this country goes to war, think of all the millions of Americans who'll be saved!"

"I'm thinking of the Americans you've already killed."

"Necessary deaths. But you don't understand that. You've never seen a fellow soldier die, have you, Holland? You don't know what a helpless feeling it is, to watch good boys from good American towns get cut to pieces. With this weapon, they won't have to. It'll be the enemy dying, not us."

"Who gave you the authority?"

"I gave myself the authority."

"And who the hell are *you?*"

"A patriot, Mr. Holland! I do the jobs no one else in the Administration'll touch. Someone says, 'Too bad our weapons don't have a higher kill ratio.' That's my cue to get one developed. They don't even have to ask me. They can claim total ignorance."

"So you're the fall guy."

Tyrone shrugged. "It's part of being a good soldier. The willingness to fall on one's sword. But I'm not ready to do that yet."

Cathy tensed as Tyrone clicked back the gun hammer. The barrel was still poised against her skull.

"As you can see," said Tyrone, "the cards aren't exactly stacked in her favor."

"On the other hand," Victor said calmly, "how do you know I've brought the vials? What if they're stashed somewhere, a publicity time bomb ticking away? Kill her now and you'll never find out."

Deadlock. Tyrone lowered the pistol. He and Victor faced each other for a moment. Then Tyrone reached into his pocket, and Cathy heard the click of a switchblade. "This round goes to you, Holland," he said as he cut the bindings. The sudden rush of circulation back into Cathy's hands was almost painful. Tyrone ripped the tape off her mouth and yanked her out of the chair. "She's all yours!"

Cathy scrambled off the stage. On unsteady legs, she moved up the aisle, toward the circle of the spotlight, toward Victor. He pulled her into his arms. Only by the thud of his racing heart did she know how close he was to panic.

"Your turn, Holland," called Tyrone.

"Go," Victor whispered to her. "Get out of here."

"Victor, he has two other men—"

"Let's have it!" yelled Tyrone.

Victor hesitated. Then he reached into his jacket and pulled out a cigarette case. "They'll be watching me," he whispered. "You move for the door. Go on. *Do it.*"

She stood paralyzed by indecision. She couldn't leave him to die. And she knew the other two gunmen were somewhere in the darkness, watching their every move.

"She stays where she is!" said Tyrone. "Come on, Holland. The vials!"

Victor took a step further, then another.

"No further!" commanded Tyrone.

Victor halted. "You want it, don't you?"

"Put it down on the floor."

Slowly Victor set the cigarette case down by his feet.

"Now slide it to me."

Victor gave the case a shove. It skimmed down the aisle and came to a rest in the orchestra pit.

Tyrone dropped from the stage.

Victor began to back away. Taking Cathy's hand, he edged her slowly up the aisle, toward the exit.

As if on cue, the click of pistol hammers being snapped back echoed through the theater. Reflexively, Victor spun around, trying to sight the other gunmen. It was impossible to see anything clearly against the glare of the spotlight.

"You're not leaving yet," said Tyrone, reaching down for the case. Gingerly he removed the lid. In silence he stared at the contents.

This is it, thought Cathy. *He has no reason to keep us alive, now that he has what he wants....*

Tyrone's head shot up. "Double cross," he said. Then, in a roar, *"Double cross! Kill them!"*

His voice was still reverberating through the far reaches of the theater when, all at once, the lights went out. Blackness fell, so impenetrable that Cathy had to reach out to get her bearings.

That's when Victor pulled her sideways, down a row of theater seats.

"Stop them!" screamed Tyrone in the darkness.

Gunfire seemed to erupt from everywhere at once. As Cathy and Victor scurried on hands and knees along the floor, they could hear bullets thudding into the velvet-backed seats. The gunfire quickly became random, a blind spraying of the theater.

"Hold your fire!" yelled Tyrone. "Listen for them!"

The gunfire stopped. Cathy and Victor froze in the darkness, afraid to give away their position. Except for the pounding of her own pulse, Cathy heard absolute silence. *We're trapped. We make a single move and they'll know where we are.*

Scarcely daring to breathe, she reached back and pulled off her shoe. With a mighty heave, she threw it blindly across the theater.

The clatter of the shoe's landing instantly drew a new round of gunfire. In the din of ricocheting bullets, Victor and Cathy scurried along the remainder of the row and emerged in the side aisle.

Again, the gunfire stopped.

"No way out, Holland!" yelled Tyrone. "Both doors are covered! It's just a matter of time...."

Somewhere above, in a theater balcony, a light suddenly flickered on. It was Dafoe, holding aloft a cigarette lighter. As the flame leapt brightly, casting its terrible light against the shadows, Victor shoved Cathy to the floor behind a seat.

"I know they're here!" shouted Tyrone. "See 'em, Dafoe?"

As Dafoe moved the flame, the shadows shifted, revealing new forms, new secrets. "I'll spot 'em any second. Wait. I think I see—"

Dafoe suddenly jerked sideways as a shot rang out. The flame's light danced crazily on his face as he wobbled for a moment on the edge of the balcony. He reached out for the railing, but the rotten wood gave way under his weight. He pitched forward, his body tumbling into a row of seats.

"Dafoe!" screamed Tyrone. "Who the hell—"

A tongue of flame suddenly slithered up from the floor. Dafoe's lighter had set fire to the drapes! The flames spread quickly, dancing their way along the heavy velvet fabric, toward the rafters. As the first flames touched wood, the fire whooshed into a roar.

By the light of the inferno, all was revealed: Victor and Cathy, cowering in the aisle. Savitch, standing near the entrance, semi-automatic at the ready. And onstage, Tyrone, his expression demonic in the fire's glow.

"They're yours, Savitch!" ordered Tyrone.

Savitch aimed. This time there was no place for them to hide, no shadows to scurry off to. Cathy felt Victor's arm encircle her in a last protective embrace.

The gun's explosion made them both flinch. Another shot; still she felt no pain. She glanced at Victor. He was staring at her, as though unable to believe they were both alive.

They looked up to see Savitch, his shirt stained in a spreading abstract of blood, drop to his knees.

"Now's your chance!" yelled a voice. *"Move, Holland!"*

They whirled around to see a familiar figure silhouetted against the flames. Somehow, Sam Polowski had magically appeared from behind the drapes. Now he pivoted, pistol clutched in both hands, and aimed at Tyrone.

He never got a chance to squeeze off the shot.

Tyrone fired first. The bullet knocked Polowski backward and sent him sprawling against the smoldering velvet seats.

"Get out of here!" barked Victor, giving Cathy a push toward the exit. "I'm going back for him—"

"Victor, you can't!"

But he was on his way. Through the swirling smoke she could see him moving at a half crouch between rows of seats. *He needs help. And time's running out....*

Already the air was so hot it seemed to sear its way into her throat. Coughing, she dropped to the floor and took in a few breaths of relatively smoke-free air. She still had time to escape. All she had to do was crawl up the aisle and out the theater door. Every instinct told her to flee now, while she had the chance.

Instead, she turned from the exit and followed Victor into the maelstrom.

She could just make out his figure, scrambling before a solid wall of fire. She raised her arm to shield her face against the heat. Squinting into the smoke, she crawled forward, moving ever closer to the flames. "Victor!" she screamed.

She was answered only by the fire's roar, and by a sound even more ominous: the creak of wood. She glanced up. To her horror she saw that the rafters were sagging and on the verge of collapse.

Panicked, she scurried blindly forward, toward where she'd last spotted Victor. He was no longer visible. In his place was a whirlwind of smoke and flame. Had he already escaped? Was she alone, trapped in this blazing tinderbox?

Something slapped against her cheek. She stared, at first uncomprehending, at the human hand dangling before her face. Slowly she followed it up, along the bloodied arm, to the lifeless eyes of Dafoe. Her cry of terror seemed to funnel into the fiery cyclone.

"*Cathy?*"

She turned at the sound of Victor's shout. That's when she saw him, crouching in the aisle just a few feet away. He had Polowski under the arms and was struggling to drag him toward the exit. But the heat and smoke had taken its toll; he was on the verge of collapse.

"The roof's about to fall!" she screamed.

"Get out!"

"Not without you!" She scrambled forward and grabbed Polowski's feet. Together they hauled their burden up the aisle, across carpet that was already alight with sparks. Step by step they neared the top of the aisle. Only a few yards to go!

"I've got him," gasped Victor. "Go—open the door—"

She rose to a half crouch and turned.

Matt Tyrone stood before her.

"Victor!" she sobbed.

Victor, his face a mask of soot and sweat, turned to meet Tyrone's gaze. Neither man said a word. They both knew the game had been played out. Now the time had come to finish it.

Tyrone raised his gun.

Just as he did, they heard the loud crack of splintering wood. Tyrone glanced up as one of the rafters sagged, spilling a shower of burning tinder.

That brief distraction was all the time Cathy needed. In an act of sheer desperation she lunged at Tyrone's legs, knocking him backward. The gun flew from his grasp and slid off beneath a row of seats.

At once Tyrone was back on his feet. He aimed a savage kick at her. The blow hit her in the ribs, an impact so agonizing she hadn't the breath to cry out. She simply sprawled in the aisle, stunned and utterly helpless to ward off any other blows.

Through the darkness gathering before her eyes, she saw two figures struggling. Victor and Tyrone. Framed against a sea of fire, they grappled for each other's throats. Tyrone threw a punch; Victor staggered back a few paces. Tyrone charged him like a bull. At the last instant Victor sidestepped him and Tyrone met only empty air. He stumbled and sprawled forward, onto the smoldering carpet. Enraged, he rose to his knees, ready to charge again.

The crack of collapsing timber made him glance skyward.

He was still staring up in astonishment as the beam crashed down on his head.

Cathy tried to cry out Victor's name but no sound escaped. The smoke had left her throat too parched and swollen. She struggled to her knees. Polowski was lying beside her, groaning. Flames were everywhere, shooting up from the floor, clambering up the last untouched drapes.

Then she saw him, stumbling toward her through that vision of hellfire. He grabbed her arm and shoved her toward the exit.

Somehow, they managed to tumble out the door, dragging Polowski behind them. Coughing, choking, they pulled him across the street to the far sidewalk. There they collapsed.

The night sky suddenly lit up as an explosion ripped through the theater. The roof collapsed, sending up a whoosh of flames so brilliant they seemed to reach to the very heavens. Victor threw his body over Cathy's as the windows in the building above shattered, raining splinters onto the sidewalk.

For a moment there was only the sound of the flames, crackling across the street. Then, somewhere in the distance, a siren wailed.

Polowski stirred and groaned.

"Sam!" Victor turned his attention to the wounded man. "How you doing, buddy?"

"Got...got one helluva stitch in my side...."

"You'll be fine." Victor flashed him a tense grin. "Listen! Hear those sirens? Help's on the way."

"Yeah." Polowski, eyes narrowed in pain, stared up at the flame-washed sky.

"Thanks, Sam," said Victor softly.

"Had to. You...too damn stupid to listen..."

"We got her back, didn't we?"

Polowski's gaze shifted to Cathy. "We—we did okay."

Victor rubbed a hand across his smudged and weary face. "But we're back to square one. I've lost the evidence—"

"Milo..."

"It's all in there." Victor stared across at the flames now engulfing the old theater.

"Milo has it," whispered Sam.

"What?"

"You weren't looking. Gave it to Milo."

Victor sat back in bewilderment. "You mean you *took* them? You took the vials?"

Polowski nodded.

"You—you stupid son of a—"

"Victor!" said Cathy.

"He stole my bargaining chip!"

"He saved our lives!"

Victor stared down at Polowski.

Polowski returned a pained grin. "Dame's got a head on her shoulders," he murmured. "Listen to her."

The sirens, which had risen to a scream, suddenly cut off. Men's shouts at once sliced through the hiss and roar of the flames. A burly fireman loped over from the truck and knelt beside Polowski.

"What've we got here?"

"Gunshot wound," said Victor. "And a wise-ass patient."

The fireman nodded. "No problem, sir. We can handle both."

By the time they'd loaded Polowski into an ambulance, the Saracen Theater had been reduced to little more than a dying bonfire. Victor and Cathy watched the taillights of the ambulance vanish, heard the fading wail of the siren, the hiss of water on the flames.

He turned to her. Without a word he pulled her into his arms and held her long and hard, two silent figures framed against a sea of smoldering flames and chaos. They were both so weary neither knew which was holding the other up. Yet even through her exhaustion, Cathy felt the magic of that moment. It was eerily beautiful, that last sputtering glow, the reflections dancing off the nearby buildings. Beautiful and frightening and final.

"You came for me," she murmured. "Oh, Victor, I was so afraid you wouldn't...."

"Cathy, you knew I would!"

"I *didn't* know. You had your evidence. You could have left me—"

"No, I couldn't." He buried a kiss in her singed hair. "Thank God I wasn't already on that plane. They'd have had you, and I'd have been two thousand miles away."

Footsteps crunched toward them across the glass-littered pavement. "Excuse me," a voice said. "Are you Victor Holland?"

They turned to see a man in a rumpled parka, a camera slung over his shoulder, watching them.

"Who are you?" asked Victor.

The man held out his hand. "Jay Wallace. *San Francisco Chronicle*. Sam Polowski called me, said there'd be some fireworks in case I wanted to check it out." He gazed at the last remains of the Saracen Theater and shook his head. "Looks like I got here a little too late."

"Wait. *Sam* called you? When?"

"Maybe two hours ago. If he wasn't my ex-brother-in-law, I'd a hung up on him. For days he's been dropping hints he had a story to spill. Never followed through, not once. I almost didn't come tonight. You know, it's a helluva long drive down here from the city."

"He told you about me?"

"He said you had a story to tell."

"Don't we all?"

"Some stories are better than others." The reporter glanced around, searching. "So where is Sam, anyway? Or didn't the Bozo show up?"

"That Bozo," said Victor, his voice tight with anger, "is a goddamn hero. Stick *that* in your article."

More footsteps approached. This time it was two police officers. Cathy felt Victor's muscles go taut as he turned to face them.

The senior officer spoke. "We've just been informed that a gunshot victim was taken to the ER. And that you were found on the scene."

Victor nodded. His look of tension suddenly gave way to one of overwhelming exhaustion. And resignation. He said, quietly, "I was present. And if you search that building, you'll find three more bodies."

"*Three?*" The two cops glanced at each other.

"Musta been some fireworks," muttered the reporter.

The senior officer said, "Maybe you'd better give us your name, sir."

"My name..." Victor looked at Cathy. She read the message in those weary eyes: *We've reached the end. I have to tell them. Now*

they'll take me away from you, and God knows when we'll see each
other again....

She felt his hand tighten around hers. She held on, knowing with
every second that passed that he would soon be wrenched from her
grasp.

His gaze still focused on her face, he said, "My name is Victor
Holland."

"Holland... Victor Holland?" said the officer. "Isn't that..."

And still Victor was looking at her. Until they'd clapped on the
handcuffs, until he'd been pulled away, toward a waiting squad car,
his gaze was locked on her.

She was left anchorless, shivering among the dying embers.

"Ma'am, you'll have to come with us."

She looked up, dazed, at the policeman. "What?"

"Hey, she doesn't have to!" cut in Jay Wallace. "You haven't
charged her with anything!"

"Shut up, Wallace."

"I've had the court beat. I know her rights!"

Quietly Cathy said, "It doesn't matter. I'll come with you, officer."

"Wait!" said Wallace. "I wanna talk to you first! I got just a
few questions—"

"She can talk to you later," snapped the policeman, taking Cathy
by the arm. "*After* she talks to us."

The policemen were polite, even kind. Perhaps it was her docile
acceptance of the situation, perhaps they could sense she was operating on her last meager reserves of strength. She answered all
their questions. She let them examine the rope burns on her wrists.
She told them about Ollie and Sarah and the other Catherine Weavers. And the whole time, as she sat in that room in the Palo Alto
police station, she kept hoping she'd catch a glimpse of Victor. She
knew he had to be close by. Were they, at that very moment, asking
him these same questions?

At dawn, they released her.

Jay Wallace was waiting outside near the front steps. "I have to
talk to you," he said as she walked out.

"Please. Not now. I'm tired...."

"Just a few questions."

"I can't. I need to—to—" She stopped. And there, standing on that cold and empty street, she burst into tears. "I don't know what to do," she sobbed. "I don't know how to help him. How to reach him."

"You mean Holland? They've already taken him to San Francisco."

"What?" She raised her startled gaze to Wallace.

"An hour ago. The big boys from the Justice Department came down as an escort. I hear tell they're flying him straight to Washington. First-class treatment all the way."

She shook her head in bewilderment. "Then he's all right—he's not under arrest—"

"Hell, lady," said Wallace, laughing. "The man is now a genuine hero."

A hero. But she didn't care what they called him, as long as he was safe.

She took a deep breath of bitingly chill air. "Do you have a car, Mr. Wallace?" she asked.

"It's parked right around the corner."

"Then you can give me a ride."

"Where to?"

"To..." She paused, wondering where to go, where Victor would look for her. Of course. Milo's. "To a friend's house," she said. "I want to be there when Victor calls."

Wallace pointed the way to the car. "I hope it's a long drive," he said. "I got a lot of gaps to fill in before this story goes to press."

Victor didn't call.

For four days she sat waiting near the phone, expecting to hear his voice. For four days, Milo and his mother brought her tea and cookies, smiles and sympathy. On the fifth day, when she still hadn't heard from him, those terrible doubts began to haunt her. She remembered that day by the lake bed, when he'd tried to send her away with Ollie. She thought of all the words he could have said, but never had. True, he'd come back for her. He'd knowingly walked straight into a trap at the Saracen Theater. But wouldn't he have done that for any of his friends? That was the kind of man he was. She'd saved his life once. He remembered his debts, and he paid them back. It had to do with honor.

It might have nothing to do with love.

She stopped waiting by the phone. She returned to her flat in San Francisco, cleaned up the glass, had the windows replaced, the walls replastered. She took long walks and paid frequent visits to Ollie and Polowski in the hospital. Anything to stay away from that silent telephone.

She got a call from Jack. "We're shooting next week," he whined. "And the monster's in terrible shape. All this humidity! Its face keeps melting into green goo. Get down here and do something about it, will you?"

She told him she'd think about it.

A week later she decided. Work was what she needed. Green goo and cranky actors—it was better than waiting for a call that would never come.

She reserved a one-way flight from San José to Puerto Vallarta. Then she packed, throwing in her entire wardrobe. A long stay, that's what she planned, a long vacation.

But before she left, she would drive down to Palo Alto. She had promised to pay Sam Polowski one last visit.

CHPATER FOURTEEN

(AP) Washington.

Administration spokesman Richard Jungkuntz repeated today that neither the President nor any of his staff had any knowledge of biological weapons research being conducted at Viratek Industries in California. Viratek's Project Cerberus, which involved development of genetically altered viruses, was clearly in violation of international law. Recent evidence, gathered by reporter Jay Wallace of the *San Francisco Chronicle,* has revealed that the project received funds directly authorized by the late Matthew Tyrone, a senior aide to the Secretary of Defense.

In today's Justice Department hearings, delayed four hours because of heavy snowstorms, Viratek president Archibald Black testified for the first time, promising to reveal, to the best of his knowledge, the direct links between the Administration and Project Cerberus. Yesterday's testimony, by former Viratek employee Dr. Victor Holland, has already outlined a disturbing tale of deception, cover-ups and possibly murder.

The Attorney General's office continues to resist demands by Congressman Leo D. Fanelli that a special prosecutor be appointed...

Cathy put down the newspaper and smiled across the hospital solarium at her three friends. "Well, guys. Aren't you lucky to be here in sunny California and not freezing your you-know-what's off in Washington."

"Are you kidding?" groused Polowski. "I'd give anything to be in on those hearings right now. Instead of hooked up to all these—

these *doohickeys.*'' He gave his intravenous line a tug, clanging a bottle against the pole.

"Patience, Sam," said Milo. "You'll get to Washington."

"Ha! Holland's already told 'em the good stuff. By the time they get around to hearing my testimony, it'll be back-page news."

"I don't think so," said Cathy. "I think it'll be front-page news for a long time to come." She turned and looked out the window at the sunshine glistening on the grass. *A long time to come.* That's how long it would be before she'd see Victor again. If ever. Three weeks had already passed since she'd last laid eyes on him. Via Jay Wallace in Washington, she'd heard that it was like a shark-feeding whenever Victor appeared in public, mobs of reporters and federal attorneys and Justice Department officials. No one could get near him.

Not even me, she thought.

It had been a comfort, having these three new friends to talk to. Ollie had bounced back quickly and was discharged—or kicked out, as Milo put it—a mere eight days after being shot. Polowski had had a rougher time of it. Post-operative infections, plus a bad case of smoke inhalation, had prolonged his stay to the point that every day was another trial of frustration for him. He wanted out. He wanted back on the beat.

He wanted a real, honest-to-God cheeseburger and a cigarette.

One more week, the doctors said.

At least there's an end to his waiting in sight, Cathy thought. *I don't know when I'll see or hear from Victor again.*

The silence was to be expected, Polowski had told her. Sequestration of witnesses. Protective custody. The Justice Department wanted an airtight case, and for that it would keep its star witness incommunicado. For the rest of them, depositions had been sufficient. Cathy had given her testimony two weeks before. Afterward, they'd told her she was free to leave town any time she wished.

Now she had a plane ticket to Mexico in her purse.

She was through with waiting for telephone calls, through with wondering whether he loved her or missed her. She'd been through this before with Jack, the doubts, the fears, the slow but inevitable realization that something was wrong. She knew enough not to be hurt again, not this way.

At least, out of all this pain, I've discovered three new friends. Ollie and Polowski and Milo, the most unlikely trio on the face of the earth.

"Look, Sam," said Milo, reaching into his backpack. "We brought ya something."

"No more hula-girl boxer shorts, okay? Caught hell from the nurses for that one."

"Naw. It's something for your lungs. To remind you to breathe deep."

"Cigarettes?" Polowski asked hopefully.

Milo grinned and held up his gift. "A kazoo!"

"I really needed one."

"You really do need it," said Ollie, opening up his clarinet case. "Seeing as we brought our instruments today and we weren't about to leave you out of this particular gig."

"You're not serious."

"What better place to perform?" said Milo, giving his piccolo a quick and loving rubdown. "All these sick, depressed patients lying around, in need of a bit of cheering up. Some good music."

"Some peace and quiet!" Polowski turned pleading eyes to Cathy. "They're not serious."

She looked him in the eye and took out her kazoo. "Dead serious."

"Okay, guys," said Ollie. "Hit it!"

Never before had the world heard such a rendering of "California, Here I Come!" And, if the world was lucky, never again. By the time they'd played the last note, nurses and patients had spilled into the solarium to check on the source of that terrible screeching.

"Mr. Polowski!" said the head nurse. "If your visitors can't behave—"

"You'll throw 'em out?" asked Polowski hopefully.

"No need," said Ollie. "We're packing up the pipes. By the way, folks, we're available for private parties, birthdays, cocktail hours. Just get in touch with our business manager—" at this, Milo smiled and waved "—to set up your own special performance."

Polowski groaned, "I want to go back to bed."

"Not yet," said the nurse. "You need the extra stimulation."

Then, with a sly wink at Ollie, she turned and whisked out of the room.

"Well," said Cathy. "I think I've done my part to cheer you up. Now it's time I hit the road."

Polowski looked at her in astonishment. "You're leaving me with these lunatics?"

"Have to. I have a plane to catch."

"Where you going?"

"Mexico. Jack called to say they're shooting already. So I thought I'd get on down there and whip up a few monsters."

"What about Victor?"

"What about him?"

"I thought—that is—" Polowski looked at Ollie and Milo. Both men merely shrugged. "He's going to miss you."

"I don't think so." She turned once again to gaze out the window. Below, in the walkway, an old woman sat in a wheelchair, her wan face turned gratefully to the sun. Soon Cathy would be enjoying that very sunshine, somewhere on a Mexican beach.

By their silence, she knew the three men didn't know what to say. After all, Victor was their friend, as well. They couldn't defend or condemn him. Neither could she. She simply loved him, in ways that made her decision to leave all the more right. She'd been in love before, she knew that the very worst thing a woman can sense in a man is indifference.

She didn't want to be around to see it in Victor's eyes.

Gathering up her purse, she said, "Guys, I guess this is it."

Ollie shook his head. "I really wish you'd hang around. He'll be back any day. Besides, you can't break up our great little quartet."

"Sam can take my place on the kazoo."

"No way," said Polowski.

She planted a kiss on his balding head. "Get better. The country needs you."

Polowski sighed. "I'm glad somebody does."

"I'll write you from Mexico!" She slung her purse over her shoulder and turned. One step was all she managed before she halted in astonishment.

Victor was standing in the doorway, a suitcase in hand. He cocked his head. "What's this about Mexico?"

She couldn't answer. She just kept staring at him, thinking how unfair it was that the man she was trying so hard to escape should look so heartbreakingly wonderful.

"You got back just in time," said Ollie. "She's leaving."

"What?" Victor dropped his suitcase and stared at her in dismay. Only then did she notice his wrinkled clothes, the day-old growth of beard shadowing his face. The toe of a sock poked out from a corner of the closed suitcase.

"You can't be leaving," he said.

She cleared her throat. "It was unexpected. Jack needs me."

"Did something happen? Is there some emergency?"

"No, it's just that they're filming and, oh, things are a royal mess on the set...." She glanced at her watch, a gesture designed to speed her escape. "Look, I'll miss my plane. I promise I'll give you a call when I get to—"

"You're not his only makeup artist."

"No, but—"

"He can do the movie without you."

"Yes, but—"

"Do you *want* to leave? Is that it?"

She didn't answer. She could only look at him mutely, the anguish showing plainly in her eyes.

Gently, firmly, he took her hand. "Excuse us, guys," he said to the others. "The lady and I are going for a walk."

Outside, leaves blew across the brown winter lawn. They walked beneath a row of oak trees, through patches of sun and shadow. Suddenly he stopped and pulled her around to face him.

"Tell me now," he said. "What gave you this crazy idea of leaving?"

She looked down. "I didn't think it made much difference to you."

"Wouldn't make a *difference?* Cathy, I was climbing the walls! Thinking of ways to get out of that hotel room and back to you! You have no idea how I worried. I wondered if you were safe—if this whole crazy mess was really over. The lawyers wouldn't let me call out, not until the hearings were finished. I did manage to sneak out and call Milo's house. No one answered."

"We were probably here, visiting Sam."

"And I was going crazy. They had me answering the same damn questions over and over again. And all I could think of was how much I missed you." He shook his head. "First chance I got, I flew the coop. And got snowed in for hours in Chicago. But I made it. I'm here. Just in time, it seems." Gently he took her by the shoulders. "Now. Tell me. Are you still flying off to Jack?"

"I'm not leaving for Jack. I'm leaving for *myself*. Because I know this won't work."

"Cathy, after what we've been through together, we can make *anything* work."

"Not—not this."

Slowly he let his hands drop, but his gaze remained on her face. "That night we made love," he said softly. "That didn't tell you something?"

"But it wasn't *me* you were making love to! You were thinking of Lily—"

"*Lily?*" He shook his head in bewilderment. "Where does she come in?"

"You loved her so much—"

"And you loved Jack once. Remember?"

"I fell out of love. You never did. No matter how much I try, I'll never measure up to her. I won't be smart enough or kind enough—"

"Cathy, stop."

"I won't be *her.*"

"I don't want you to be her! I want the woman who'll hang off fire escapes with me and—and drag me off the side of the road. I want the woman who saved my life. The woman who calls herself average. The woman who doesn't know just how extraordinary she really is." He took her face in his hands and tilted it up to his. "Yes, Lily was a wonderful woman. She was wise and kind and caring. But she wasn't you. And she and I—we weren't the perfect couple. I used to think it was my fault, that if I were just a better lover—"

"You're a wonderful lover, Victor."

"No. Don't you see, it's *you.* You bring it out in me. All the want and need." He pulled her face close to his and his voice dropped to a whisper. "When you and I made love that night, it

was like the very first time for me. No, it was even better. Because
I loved you."

"And I loved you," she whispered.

He pulled her into his arms and kissed her, his fingers burrowing
deep into her hair. "Cathy, Cathy," he murmured. "We've been
so busy trying to stay alive we haven't had time to say all the things
we should have...."

His arms suddenly stiffened as a startling round of applause
erupted above them. They looked up. Three grinning faces peered
down at them from a hospital balcony.

"Hit it, boys!" yelled Ollie.

A clarinet, piccolo and kazoo screeched into concert. The melody
was doubtful. Still, Cathy thought she recognized the familiar strains
of George Gershwin. "Someone to Watch Over Me."

Victor groaned. "I say we try this again, but with a different
band. And no audience."

She laughed. "Mexico?"

"Definitely." He grabbed her hand and pulled her toward a taxi
idling at the curb.

"But, Victor!" she protested. "What about our luggage? All my
clothes—"

He cut her off with another kiss, one that left her dizzy and
breathless and starved for more.

"Forget the luggage," she whispered. "Forget everything. "Let's
just go...."

They climbed into the taxi. That's when the band on the hospital
balcony abruptly switched to a new melody, one Cathy didn't at
first recognize. Then, out of the muddy strains, the kazoo screeched
out a solo that, for a few notes, was perfectly in tune. They were
playing *Tannhäuser*. Wedding music!

"What the hell's that terrible noise?" asked the taxi driver.

"Music," said Victor, grinning down at Cathy. "The most beautiful music in the world."

She fell into his arms, and he held her there.

The taxi pulled away from the curb. But even as they drove away,
even as they left the hospital far behind them, they thought they
could hear it in the distance: the sound of Sam Polowski's kazoo,
playing one last fading note of farewell.

MIRROR, MIRROR
Stella Cameron

CHAPTER ONE

Lauren Taylor was a good reason not to leave an otherwise deadly party. Looking at her had a strange effect on a man, oddly disturbing. The rapidly changing expressions on her arresting face held Jack captive; one instant he was quietly fascinated, the next aware of mounting excitement.

"Jack, you listening?"

He nodded, but he wasn't really hearing much of what Barney Middleton said. How long had it been since he'd seen Lauren, except from at a distance? A year, two…more? She was great to watch, even if he didn't particularly enjoy also having her ex-husband, to whom she was talking, in the frame.

Now he remembered their last face-to-face conversation. It was at an earlier version of this same party, Carlsbad's famed May Fling, when he'd awkwardly told her how sorry he was about her failed marriage. And that had been three years ago because he'd managed to avoid the two annual bashes previous to tonight's extravaganza. But he hadn't forgotten the disturbingly vivid impression the quietly controlled Lauren Taylor had made on him.

"You gotta get out more," Barney shouted over the din and elbowed him.

Jack steadied his Scotch and grimaced. He and Barney sat side by side on a white couch so low slung and soft that Jack's knees were at eye level.

"Time you had another woman in your life—the permanent variety. Someone to help look after young Andy."

This was the tape Jack listened to from Barney whenever they met, usually once or twice a week at Barney's restaurant.

"You hearin' me, Jacko?"

"I'm hearing you."

"Four years divorced is long enough and a nine-year-old boy needs a mother figure around. And there's lots of good women out there just dyin' for a chance at you." Barney's bald scalp glistened amid its luxuriant skirt of black hair. Sincerity shone in dark eyes set deep in a round and pudgy face.

Jack undid another button on his tuxedo shirt; the tie already hung loose. "Why doesn't that idea thrill me, I wonder? Damn, Barn, it's like an oven in here."

"Jack, I'm trying to make a point—"

"Yeah, Barney, okay. I get the message." How could Lauren still be civil to that creep Dan Taylor? There wasn't a soul in Carlsbad who didn't know the sordid little details of how Dan Taylor had ditched her. If Jack had the facts straight, the Taylors had been married sixteen years when Danny-boy decided to find grease for his libido with a twenty-three-year-old sales trainee in his real estate firm. Talk at the time was that Lauren was thirty-six, which meant she was now thirty-nine. A very good year on this lady.

The town's "in" people drifted in clumps through the Ocean Club. Elevator-style music rose and fell in insipid waves. The event was a fund-raiser for children's charities and Jack wondered why the organizers didn't save a lot of time and money by scratching the party and making a few arm-twisting personal calls instead. He stretched out his long legs. "How's business, Barn?"

"Stinks. That's why I can lounge around at parties on a Sunday night."

The standard response brought a smile to Jack's lips. Barney Middleton ran one of Carlsbad's most successful restaurants. Money was his middle name, but business always stank.

"How's the flower business?" Barney asked.

"Stinks," Jack said and laughed at Barney's malevolent stare. "No. Seriously, it's a great year so far. I guess the cut flowers interest me most." He considered. "Ah, well, maybe the poinsettia rush beats even that. Who knows? I like it all." He owned one of the leading poinsettia farm, bulb and cut-flower operations in the country and he'd never hankered to do anything else.

He sank into silence. Dan Taylor appeared to be irritated with

Lauren and, to Jack's annoyance, she seemed to be meekly accepting whatever he had to say.

She was pale-skinned with sleek, shoulder-length dark hair. Her eyes were almost black, her brows clearly arched, her nose uptilted and her mouth full. Stunning? Maybe compelling would be a better description. And lush was the word that came to mind for her tall, tastefully black-clad body. One classy woman. Jack drank deeply of his Scotch and swiveled his attention to Christie, Taylor's wife number two, who hovered near the soaring ice sculpture of a castle. Her eyes were narrowed in minute scrutiny of the other two. Not a happy camper tonight, this flouncy blond nymph whom Dan Taylor had needed to ease his ego through midlife. The pouting, cutesy type did nothing for Jack, particularly if the woman was…eleven years his junior? Christie had to be around twenty-six now, a stereotypical California girl. Evidently she didn't realise she was using a toothpick to systematically spear shrimp with what resembled murderous intent.

"Great pair, huh?"

Jack started. "What?"

"You've been staring at Lauren Taylor all night. And I said she's got a great pair."

"Yeah. Good legs." Jack didn't waste energy on the dirty look he was tempted to give Barney, who was famous for tasteless sexual innuendos and jokes.

"I wasn't looking at her—"

"How's Joannie?"

Barney snickered. "You've got a puritan heart, Jack Irving. My lovely wife is in her usual state of PMS. I can't remember whether that's pre or post at the moment. Doesn't make much difference."

The Middletons fought furiously. They also loved furiously, and Jack accepted the harmless comment for what it was—harmless. "Joannie is lovely," he said of the diminutive golden-haired woman who was Barney's wife. Tonight she was baby-sitting the first and still-new grandchild, or she would have been glued to her husband's side. "I never could figure out what she saw in an ugly, cantankerous guy like you."

Barney wiggled his bushy brows. "It's my body. She can't keep her hands off it. Do you know Lauren?"

The guy never gave up. "Sort of. I haven't seen her to talk to in years. When she and Dan were married they lived out by La Costa, not far from my place."

"Dan still lives there," Barney remarked tonelessly. "With the delectable new Mrs. Taylor."

"Right," Jack said, watching the blonde again. "And baby makes three, I hear."

"You hear right. Only the kid's gotta be two or three by now."

Jack grunted and studied his fingernails. "I think Christie hates her predecessor's guts. Take a look at her. Every time she stabs a shrimp she looks at it as if it's a voodoo doll with Lauren's name on it."

"She got what she thought she wanted. Only I don't think Dan's cut all of his ties to Lauren. Not that I blame him."

"No," Jack agreed slowly. Dan, handsome, as dark-haired as his ex-wife and evidently very fit, rested a hand on the wall behind Lauren while he talked intently. He looked like a possessive...husband? "I use her answering service," Jack added.

"So do we. Very efficient—growing, too, I should imagine."

"Mmm." He ought to change the subject.

"Lauren's some woman," Barney said and the serious note in his voice made Jack glance at him sharply. "One of these days some smart son of a gun's gonna realize what a prize she is and take her off the market."

Jack listened and brooded. He was here under protest and hadn't intended to stay. But two hours had passed since he'd walked through the doors and obviously Barney hadn't taken long to notice where his companion's attention was centered. He hadn't given Lauren Taylor a thought since the last time he'd seen her, so why change the pattern now? He wasn't sure why, but he was certainly thinking about her. The question was: Did he intend to do anything more than think about the lady?

"SO YOU WILL TAKE my advice?"

Lauren sighed. Some things never changed. Dan's overbearing

manner was one of them. So was his determination to get his own way. "No. Please drop the subject, Dan." Someone opened the French doors behind her and a blessedly cool breeze blew into the crowded room. She'd have liked to have escaped to the lanai.

"I don't understand you," Dan said. He bent over her so that she had to raise her chin to look into his serious blue eyes. "Have I ever steered you wrong? Have I ever insisted on anything I didn't think was for your own good?"

Lauren glanced away. She didn't love Dan anymore, thank God, but she still cared enough to stop herself from reminding him that he hadn't been considering her "own good" when he'd asked for a divorce because she "couldn't excite him the way Christie could."

"It's the little girl, isn't it?" he persisted. "You're pretending she's yours. Fantasizing about being a parent the same as you did with that boy you had in foster care. That was damn dangerous, too, and—"

"Leave it, Dan." To this day he hadn't figured out how much it hurt that she'd never been able to have a child of her own. Dan had a baby he adored now but he still couldn't relate to Lauren's disappointment. "Betty and Cara rent rooms from me, nothing more."

"You don't *need* to rent out rooms. You've got plenty of money—I saw to that."

He saw to that, in good part with money she'd helped amass. "I'm grateful to you," she said. "But the Floods stay. My town house is more than big enough for three and I enjoy them."

"You enjoy the girl," Dan continued stubbornly. "Why else would you live your life around her while her mother's free to come and go as she pleases?"

Lauren caught sight of Christie beyond Dan's shoulder and smiled. In return she received the frosted stare she'd come to expect. She sighed. "As I've explained many times during the past year, Betty's a night dispatcher for Coastal Ambulance. All I do is be there for Cara—she's only nine, Dan—and run her to school in the morning."

"She could catch the bus."

"The school's on my way to the office."

"Not exactly. They're taking advantage of you."

"How?" Her voice was too loud and she cleared her throat. "How are they taking advantage of me? They pay rent and what I choose to do, I choose to do." *And it's my business.*

"If that boy you took in hadn't gone back to his family you'd probably have had a break-in by now. You don't think things through."

Lauren brushed back her hair. "Joe needed a safe home for a while. For six months I was his anchor and I'm glad." And she'd missed the ten-year-old for months after he'd left. "Contrary to what you thought, his father was down-and-out, that's all, and not a criminal. As soon as he could bring his children together again, he did. Now drop the subject, please."

"Not till you agree to get rid of the Floods."

He was unbelievable. She turned her head and met the dark eyes of Jack Irving—again. He smiled. Funny, she'd never noticed the slow, crooked way his mouth curved up, or how his steady gaze remained serious. Lauren smiled back and he grinned broadly, showing very white teeth. She liked him. Once they'd been almost neighbors and he'd been the type of man who always had a pleasant word. Also, he'd been rejected by a spouse, just as she had, and that made her feel a bond with him.

"Lauren?"

"I told you, no," she said, furious. She avoided parties and wished she hadn't let a good customer browbeat her into attending this one. "I don't understand your preoccupation with this."

"You will when they take off in the middle of the night with your silver."

She didn't have any silver. That had been one of the many things Dan had felt he and Christie would have more use for than Lauren. And she'd agreed. "I'm not discussing the subject anymore. If Betty knew the kind of things you say she'd have cause to file suit against you. She's a very honest woman who had the misfortune to be left alone with a daughter to bring up. And she's doing a good job of that."

"With a lot of help from you. Lauren, I care about you. Whatever's happened between us, we've still got a lot of shared history and I can't forget that—I don't want to."

"I know." She wouldn't try, yet again, to explain that there was a difference between caring and smothering.

Jack Irving had rested his head against the back of the sofa where he sat with Barney Middleton. His curly, dark blond hair was unruly but he gave the impression of casual elegance, despite the dangling ends of his black tie and the open neck of his tuck-fronted shirt. She couldn't recall seeing him up close for ages, but he'd only become more handsome. The lines of his face were lean. That smile had produced deep dimples beside his mouth and the light picked out high cheekbones. His mouth held her attention. The upper lip was narrow, the lower full, a wide mouth, firm and sensual. And he was still staring at her. Lauren pursed her own mouth. Jack Irving, who probably didn't have any idea he was training his eyes in her direction, would find her assessment funny.

"Dan." Christie came to stand with them and Lauren felt the arctic front that arrived with the woman. "We should circulate."

He blinked and turned to her. "Why?"

Christie pouted and Lauren studied dark overhead beams. "Because it's good for business, you know that. And we shouldn't leave Wednesday with the sitter for too long. You know how she misses you."

The last was delivered with a satisfied stare at Lauren who tried to banish evil thoughts. "How is Thursday?" she asked and immediately felt ashamed.

"Wednesday," Dan said absently. "That's the day she was born, remember? She's fine."

"Good. I'd love to come and see her again," she said of the little girl and meant it. "It's been six months and I bet she's grown inches."

"She has, and she doesn't like strangers," Christie said pointedly, slipping her arm through her husband's. "Dan?"

"Lauren isn't a stranger, dear. Come anytime. We'd love to have you."

She didn't trust herself to meet Christie's eyes. A longing to get away made her feel almost faint. "Thanks."

"Remember what we've been talking about," Dan said. "I'll call you later in the week."

"Why?" Lauren said.

"What about?" Christie asked sharply.

"I'm trying to get Lauren to look out after her own interests," Dan said. "The same as I always have."

For an instant she almost felt sorry for him. He actually believed what he said. "I won't be making any changes along the lines you suggest," she told him. "So don't call if that's what you want to talk about."

"You know—" he sounded aggrieved "—sometimes I think you forget that I did much more than I had to do when we were divorced. You couldn't have bought your business and an oceanfront town house if I hadn't felt you had the money coming."

Money that she'd helped him earn. But she said, "I know that," because he was right. He could have got away with much less.

"Dan, may I talk to you?" A tall, silver-haired man Lauren recognized but didn't know, tapped Dan's shoulder and he turned away.

Christie, shielded from Dan by the newcomer, pinned Lauren with her pale blue glare. "You think I don't know what you're doing, don't you?"

"I—"

"Well I do know and it won't work. You can't get him back by pretending to need him, so give it up. You can't give him what he wants. I can. I'm young and I can have children."

JACK HEFTED HIMSELF UP from the elegantly uncomfortable couch.

"Where you goin'?" Barney asked.

"Around. See you next week." He pushed back his jacket and slid his hands into his pants pockets. Lauren Taylor looked like a woman who'd been punched in the solar plexus and Jack didn't have to be clairvoyant to figure out that she'd just received a verbal blow from the retreating, smug-faced Christie.

He approached Lauren with as much nonchalance as he could

muster. She appeared frozen in place, her face expressionless. The breeze blowing in across the lanai moved her sleek, shining hair.

"Hi. Long time—" He closed his mouth, totally disconcerted by her unfocused gaze.

"No see?" She'd heard him. The light returned to her almost opaque black eyes and she turned up the corners of her mouth. The comeback had been the right one, but delivered without spirit.

"You've got it," he said. Up close, she had flawless skin. Fine lines at the corners of her eyes and mouth stamped her as no stranger to laughter. Jack liked that. "I was trying to remember how long it's been since we actually talked."

She tilted her head and the dark hair swung away from her slender neck. "I'm not sure. Probably years. I don't go to parties usually—particularly on Sunday nights."

The fact that much had happened to change patterns in their private lives was unspoken between them.

"Neither do I," Jack murmured. Her black dress was of some soft stuff that draped. The bodice crisscrossed over her full breasts, plunging to a deep and alluring V. The skirt hugged gently curving hips and stopped just above the knee where black silk covered a long, long expanse of slender, shapely leg. Very high-heeled black pumps brought her to within a couple of inches of his own six-foot-two.

He was staring, but so was she. Jack smiled faintly. "You don't look as if you're enjoying yourself much."

"I'm not. I was just going home."

"I'm not enjoying it, either...or I wasn't."

She looked away immediately and he took a deep breath through his nose. Either his courting skills were hopelessly rusty, or he'd moved too fast or she couldn't stand the sight of him.

"Of course, we probably talk on the phone," he said quickly.

She frowned. "Really?"

"Irving Farms uses your service. We have for a couple of years."

"Oh, I see." Her smile lessened the tension around her eyes. "I don't usually answer phones at Contact. I hope you're satisfied with us."

"Very. Forgive me for the blunder. Of course you don't do the scut work."

"The phone work is the center of everything we do. It's essential."

Strike two. "Of course it is. I only meant that administrative work must keep you very busy."

"It does." She picked up a small black purse from a table. "It was nice to see you again."

"Yes." Not so fast, he thought. Rusty he might be, but he wasn't dead. "Have you seen the water from here at night?"

"My town house is on Ocean Street. I've got a great view. Please excuse—"

"I'd wager you don't spend much time gazing through the window at home." A waiter passed with a tray and Jack deftly removed two glasses of champagne, one of which he pressed into Lauren's unresisting hand. "Humor me. Brighten up a bored man's night for a while."

He stood back, inclining his head toward the lanai, and she walked out without a word.

They stood at the railing, separated by inches, looking at the night sky over the night sea. The breeze had dropped and the air was still. Palm trees rustled faintly and the sweetly exotic scent of shell ginger lingered. Jack glanced sideways. She didn't move. The hushed sound of unhurried surf on sand whispered in the distance. "I watched you in there," he said, never having planned to admit it.

"I thought you did."

"You look wonderful. The world of business agrees with you." The words came easily, but they still surprised him.

"Thank you," she said, sounding slightly breathless.

"The last time we talked was here, three years ago."

"You said you weren't sure how long ago it was."

"I lied," he said. "It was something to say."

She turned her face toward him. "Why?" Her eyes glittered in the silvered light.

Jack parted his lips, then paused. Yes, he was going to do something about Lauren Taylor. He still wasn't sure what it was, but the way he felt right now was too enticing not to be explored.

"I wanted to talk to you. You interest me."

"You don't know me." She laughed and the sound was soft, incredulous.

"Maybe we should do something about that."

"I don't think so."

"Why?"

She bowed her head and the smooth hair slipped forward. "I'm not at all interesting, Jack. I'm very dull, really."

"I doubt that. But why don't you let me find out?" If he stopped to think, he'd find his sudden approach bizarre, out of character and he'd retreat—and he'd regret it later. "Have dinner with me tomorrow night."

Lauren stirred. She tilted her head to sip champagne. The moon caught the glass, and the pale outline of her throat.

Jack swallowed. Every muscle in his body contracted as if he'd received a blow. "Lauren? How about it?"

"I don't have dinner dates anymore."

He narrowed his eyes. "Why?" Now he sounded like a record.

"Because my business uses all the energy I have and I like it that way." Her voice was low but clear. He'd like to hear it saying something personal, gentle to him.

"You know what they say about all work and no play." He moved closer and she held her ground, but she did stand a little straighter.

"I know what they say, and they're probably right. But I already told you I'm uninteresting, dull, if you like. How is your son?"

"Andy's great," Jack said, smiling despite his tension. "He's nine now. I enjoy every stage he goes through. We're into soccer at the moment."

He thought her shoulders rose a fraction. "Sounds wonderful. I probably wouldn't recognize him."

"Sure you would. He's taller is all. The face isn't so different from what it was three...three years ago."

"Don't feel awkward talking about my divorce. I don't. We have to get used to these things, don't we?"

"We sure do." And he had. And he wanted to spend time with Lauren. He wanted it more with every second. "Do you like Chinese food?"

"Yes."

"Good. How does seven sound?"

She handed him her glass. "Thanks, Jack, but I can't."

"Of course you can. Nobody works all the time. How about eight?"

"I can't."

"You mean you won't." Rather than defeat, he felt mounting excitement again. She'd barely seen the edges of his determination. "I'll have to find a way to change your mind."

Lauren moved around him toward the doors. "I'm known as a woman who doesn't change her mind. Good night."

He smiled. "I'm known as a man who can't resist a challenge. And I'm also known as a man who usually gets what he wants. Good night."

CHAPTER TWO

Lauren rolled down the car window and stuck out her hand to signal a left turn onto Christianson Way.

"Jimmy Sutter says you're eccentric."

Clearly pleased, both with her precocious vocabulary and with having secured complete attention, Cara Flood smiled impishly at Lauren.

"Jimmy Sutter doesn't know me," Lauren said.

"Yes, he does. I tell him about you."

"So you think I'm eccentric, too."

"Nope. I think it's fine that you don't use turn signals because you used to have a car that had broken ones and now you like sticking your arm out the window."

"Ah. I see. But Jimmy thinks that's weird."

"Jimmy's weird."

"I see." As they approached Washington and the center of town, red lights flashed ahead, warning of an approaching train. Lauren braked. "Jimmy's your best friend, isn't he?"

"Yes." Cara nodded solemnly, turning her small, pointed face up to Lauren. Wisps of light brown hair escaped long braids and sprang into curls. Thick glasses made the girl's bright blue eyes appear huge.

"Why would you have someone you think is weird, as a best friend?"

"'Cause we decided."

Lauren digested that.

"We both wear glasses and wear no-name stuff. So we decided to be friends."

Lauren thought some more. "Do other children make fun of both of you?" Her heart beat a little faster. "Is that why you and Jimmy are friends, because you both have to stand up against the others?"

"Nah. We don't care about that." But the jerky movement of the thin hands in the child's lap caught Lauren's attention. "When Billy Smith pushed Jimmy down, I stomped on Billy's foot and he cried. Jimmy and me don't worry about them."

Lauren swallowed hard and felt tears of frustration and anger prickle in her eyes. "It's time you had contact lenses."

After a moment's silence, Cara twisted in her seat. "I'd like that, I think." Pink suffused her pale cheeks. When she was happy she was almost pretty.

"I'll talk to your mom and we'll make an appointment." She wished she could do the same for Jimmy but had no idea how to go about it.

Cara was silent again. The sound of the train grew. Shops were opening on each side of the street and scurrying clusters of people moved into their Monday-morning routine.

"Don't say anything to Mom about contacts," Cara said quietly.

"Why not?" The train rushed past—a blur of green and black and rows of silver containers.

Cara sank low in her seat. "No reason. I don't want them."

Lauren wasn't fooled or put off. "You just said you'd like them."

"Changed my mind."

"What are you worried about?"

"Jimmy and Mom," Cara said, so softly Lauren had to strain to hear.

"You mom won't mind. She'd have done it herself, only she doesn't have a lot of spare time." By the time Betty Flood worked through the night and tried to catch up on some sleep during the mornings, her days were shot.

"She can't afford it," Cara said. "Anyway, if I had 'em, Jimmy and me wouldn't be the same anymore."

Lauren reached to squeeze a cold little hand. "You are a neat kid, Cara Flood. And I'll just bet you and Jimmy would still be friends." She'd leave the money angle alone until she could talk to Betty. They'd work that out between them.

"Maybe," Cara said. "We would still be no-names."

"You mean because you don't wear, what? Designer jeans and so on?"

"Yeah. Jimmy's folks don't have much money, either."

"I'll pick you up from school today and we'll go shopping." Even as she spoke she knew she was going too far, but she wanted to give this child everything.

"I don't want to," Cara said after some consideration. "Thank you, though," she added quickly.

"Do you want to explain that one to me?" The lights stopped flashing, the barriers rose and Lauren drove on.

"S'easy. Jimmy and me are different from the others. We like it that way. If we had designer jeans and stuff, we couldn't call ourselves the Out Group."

"The *out* group?" Lauren sputtered.

The school came into view. "Yeah. That's us. We put it on our book covers and everything. And when we grow up we're gonna show 'em all."

"I'm sure you will," Lauren said, a lump in her throat.

At the school gates, she drew to the curb and Cara unhitched her seat belt to throw open the door. "Bye. See you later."

"Have you got your lunch?"

"In my bag!"

Already Cara was in motion, running toward a skinny red-haired boy who waited near the fence. Jimmy Sutter, no doubt. Lauren had noticed him before but hadn't realized there was such a bond between him and Cara. The two children fell in step side by side, but Cara turned back to wave at Lauren.

The little girl was tiny for her age and Lauren doubted if she would ever be very big. All Cara's school reports showed her to be a bright student. In time she would go far, with or without help. Lauren felt strength in Cara. She wished the child were her own. Sighing, she made a U-turn and headed back the way she'd come.

Contact's offices were on Carlsbad Avenue, wedged between a florist and a bakery. The seven-day-a-week, twenty-four-hour-a-day operation kept Lauren and her staff of nine increasingly busy. And that was exactly the way Lauren liked it.

Once parked, Lauren pulled her briefcase from the back seat of her red Honda and hurried into the message center. Two of her employees, a man and a woman, sat with their backs to her, facing computer terminals while speaking into mouthpieces.

"Messages for me?" Lauren asked Susan Bailey, her office manager, who worked a third terminal and doubled as Lauren's secretary.

"On your desk," Susan responded, slipping off her headset and getting up. "Dan called. He sounded ticked you weren't here."

Lauren rolled her eyes. "Boy, he doesn't waste any time."

"What does that mean?" Susan followed Lauren into her cramped office.

"Nothing." A sheaf of pink memos was skewered to the cork globe that held an assortment of pens and pencils. Lauren retrieved the notes. "Well, you might as well know. It's the usual. Dan and I were at that charity bash at the Ocean Club last night."

"Was *she* there?" Susan, whom Lauren had inherited when she'd bought the answering service, was Lauren's self-appointed champion. She detested Christie Taylor.

"Yes," Lauren said, attempting to sound bored. "We didn't talk." Since last night she'd tried to forget Christie's cruel barbs—unsuccessfully—and she wasn't going to sharpen their impact by voicing them aloud now.

"So what was Dan's crusade this time? Or need I ask?"

"No. I'm sure you've already guessed. He still thinks Betty and Cara are out to divest me of my worldly wealth. How, he hasn't gotten around to explaining yet, but he won't leave the subject alone."

Susan shut the office door and sat on the edge of Lauren's desk. "Have you told the rat that he doesn't have a say in what you do anymore?"

"Yes. Many times."

"Have you reminded him that when he walked out, he blithely left you to rebuild your life from scratch and you've been doing that very satisfactorily ever since?"

"In those very words." She began to leaf through the memos.

"Then don't talk to him. If he comes to see you, walk away, or don't let him in, or whatever. And I won't put him through if he calls when you're here." Susan, thirty, glamorous and notoriously in control of her life, tossed back a riot of red curls. As invariably happened when she was outraged, a bright spot of color glowed on each cheek.

"Susan—" Lauren dropped into her chair "—I know I probably

ought to be tougher, but Dan really does want the best for me. We've known each other since we were kids. He thinks of us as friends and we still are, I suppose. He goes about things the wrong way, is all. He only knows how to proceed in bulldozer mode. I think I'd rather you weren't rude to him. Let me be the one to tell him what he can and can't do."

Susan grunted. "You should tell him he can't do anything where you're concerned."

"I have. More or less."

"Sure you have. But you haven't told him firmly enough. Betty and Cara are good for you. They filled a great big gap when Joe went back to his dad. You know it and so do I. That little girl is a sweetheart."

"Tell me about it," Lauren said softly.

Susan eyed her sharply. "You love the kid, don't you?"

"I... Not really." If she made eye contact, the lie would be obvious. "I've always had a weak spot for children, we both know that. No one would find it easy not to care for Cara."

Susan let out a loud sigh. "You're right. But I do worry about what will happen when—"

"*Don't.*" Lauren forced a laugh. "Don't worry about what will happen in the future. That can take care of itself. I knew when I took Betty and Cara in that it would be temporary. But they've been with me for a year and don't show any sign of leaving. Maybe it was fate that they made a mistake and thought I had rooms to rent. Maybe they will stay forever."

"Maybe."

Lauren didn't have to look at Susan to know there would be worry in those catlike green eyes. "Stop worrying about me. Any glitches around here I should know about?"

"Barnes, Cracknell Chiropractic wants a rate cut. Something about their high volume of calls being a good ad for Contact."

Lauren snorted. "Great. We work harder for less, huh? And we'll probably end up giving the jerks a break." She laughed. "Good pun, huh?"

Susan looked blank, then smiled disgustedly. "Jerks. Chiropractors. That's worse than your usual efforts. I thought you promised you wouldn't try to tell jokes."

"I didn't try. It happened. What's this?" She held up a memo for Susan to see.

"Irving Farms? Oh, yes. Mr. Irving himself called. They're delighted with our service." Susan wiggled her eyebrows. "Should have got that on tape for future replay. He's considering our switch-over service for whenever he's out of his office."

Lauren felt her color rise and kept her eyes down. "That's odd when he must have a secretary. We must have done some fantastic job on their after-hour calls."

"I guess so. He said something about wanting to give his secretary less to do. He also said he'd call back around one to talk to you in person about the idea."

So, Jack Irving was known as a man who couldn't resist a challenge and who usually got his own way. Evidently he'd set out to prove his words. "I won't be here at one."

Susan frowned. "Your sales call at that new medical/dental complex isn't until three."

"There's no reason you can't answer any questions he has," Lauren said, feeling both cowardly and defensive.

"I tried to tell him that, but no one except the head honcho around here will do for Mr. Irving." Susan smoothed an imaginary wrinkle from the thigh of her green slacks. "He has a sexy voice. Ever met him?"

Lauren kept her head bent. "Uh-huh."

"What's he like?"

"Okay." She shrugged. He was much more than okay, but so what? Romantic flings were a luxury—or, more accurately, a curse—she never ever intended to indulge in again.

What exactly *did* Jack Irving want from her? When she'd lived in the La Costa area they'd seen each other in passing as often as several times a week for years. They'd exchanged little more than pleasantries. He'd been divorced from that beautiful, but strangely silent wife of his before Dan dropped his little bombshell, and, by Jack's own admission, he'd known when Lauren was left on her own. He hadn't made any attempt to get to know her better then. Why now?

"Would you like me to try to get Mr. Irving on the phone now?"

"No!" Lauren cleared her throat and smiled sheepishly. "No

thanks, Susan. I want to get through a few things then attend to some personal business before making the sales call. I'm sure Mr. Irving won't mind calling back again." In the meantime, she'd have more time to decide how to deal with him.

Silence forced her to meet Susan's surprised gaze. "Is something wrong, Lauren?"

"Nothing." Except that she had the most extraordinarily clear picture of Jack Irving hovering in her mind and he didn't belong there. No man did anymore.

JACK HUNG UP the phone. He pushed his chair back from his desk, hoisted his feet onto the blotter and frowned into the distance. If he didn't know better, he'd think a certain dark-haired lady was avoiding him. But, no, that wasn't possible. What unattached, almost visibly passionate woman would avoid a virile, handsome male prize like Jack Irving? He grimaced. Lauren Taylor was avoiding him.

He glanced at the clock on his office wall. One-thirty. Ms. Taylor was out and wouldn't be back today, her secretary had told him. No, it probably wouldn't be possible to reach her elsewhere because she would be going to her aerobics class as soon as she'd finished making her business calls. But he could try again tomorrow morning.

What had happened when he'd seen Lauren last night—the sensation that he'd been hit between the eyes and liked it—hadn't happened before. Not ever. He and Mary had met and married in college. Then, what had felt so right had ended so wrong. He didn't want to think about it and rarely did, except when he needed to remind himself that the rejection Andy suffered at the age of five must never be repeated.

He'd known Lauren Taylor was single but somehow she'd seemed to remain bracketed to Dan...until last night. Who could explain attraction? Once a guy got past the physical reasons, the whole thing hinged on opportunity and mood, the stars in the right place, he guessed. Whatever. Yeah, and "whatever" hadn't all been motivated by testosterone where Lauren was concerned.

He locked his hands behind his neck. His "nerve center," as he sarcastically dubbed the partitioned-off areas at one end of a storage shed from which he conducted business, pleased him. Like his father before him, Jack preferred to feel close to the action. Beyond dusty windows, fields of spring-blooming flowers stretched in undulating waves. Irving's was a multifaceted outfit of cut flowers in season year-round, an extensive poinsettia business and an exclusive brand of seeds and bulbs. And Jack loved it all.

The intercom on his desk buzzed and he reached forward to flip a switch. "Yes, Joyce?"

"Len wants—"

Before Joyce could finish, the door slammed open and Len Gogh, Jack's right hand, marched in. Thickset, ruddy and dressed in ancient overalls, Len looked anything but what he was: an ex-professor of Floriculture with a doctorate from New York State College of Agriculture Cornell University.

"Hi, Len. Problems?"

"Yes, problems." Len went to stare through the windows. His wiry gray hair stood on end. "There's something going on here, Jack, something insidious."

Jack got slowly to his feet. "Such as?"

"It's happened again."

Len was famous for expecting too much of his listeners, which was probably one of the main reasons he'd chosen to quit the lecture hall. "I don't follow you," Jack said.

"We're ready to place the dianthus."

Len had always been a man of few words. "I know that."

"You'd better start saying your prayers."

"Meaning?"

"Meaning that some damn fool played with the thermostat again. Jeffries just told me—after he'd finished his lunch, of course—that when he checked this morning, the settings were at seventy."

"Seventy!" Jack sat down again with a thud. "That's not possible. They'll be ruined."

"It is possible. And they may be ruined." Len paced back and forth with measured steps. "As I said, say your prayers. But I also want you to remember that we had that little incident of lights-out with the antirrhinum back in January. We came through okay because it probably didn't happen on more than one night before it was noticed. But both incidents smell like something other than accidents to me.''

Jack chewed his lip. He ran the business as his father had, by being a hands-on part of the operation and only hiring the best. ''There isn't a worker on this farm who would deliberately try to harm the business.'' Now he even sounded like his dad. And at this moment, as so often happened, he wished Denton Irving hadn't chosen to retire the moment Jack's mother had died, virtually divorcing himself from the operation.

''Suit yourself,'' Len said. ''Think what you like. But I've done my duty by telling you I think something's wrong around here. And remember, Jack, Irving's is getting bigger every year. You've got one of the most thriving outfits of its kind on your hands. And that means things have changed. It isn't the cozy little family operation it was in your dad's time when everyone knew everyone.''

Jack studied his hands. It might not be the cozy little family operation it had been, but this was still the driving force in his life— next to Andy. And it was for Andy that he intended to make sure the legacy continued to grow. ''Point taken, Len. We'd better mount a more careful system for checking things out. Think about it, and I will too. Then we'll get together and put extra safeguards in operation. Do you feel comfortable with that?''

''I'm not comfortable with anything right now,'' Len said and his barrel chest expanded inside a frayed red plaid shirt. ''But that'll do for a start. We can't waste time, though, Jack. Matt agrees with me. He's almost camping out with the Pearl.'' Matt Carson was Jack's hotshot poinsettia man. The Pearl, Irving's Lava Pearl, was a new mutant plant destined to become the hit of the next season.

''We're not going to waste time. Make sure Matt knows I'm on top of things. This has the makings of a big year for us—maybe the biggest ever—and nothing's going to interfere with that. I won't let it.''

Len regarded him steadily. ''If my hunch is right, you may have your hands full making sure of that.''

He didn't wait for a response before leaving.

''LIFT THOSE KNEES, now! One and two, and one and two. And reach for the sky right, reach for the sky left. Everybody yell!''

Lauren yelled and laughed with the rest. The small aerobics studio bulged for the five-thirty session, the most popular of the day. The trick was not to miss a step unless you liked being elbowed or trampled.

"Come on. Let me feel that energy." The instructor, unruffled, makeup perfectly in place and not even shiny, threw herself into the routine, her smooth body gyrating in a silver spandex bodysuit. "Chicken walk forward, one and two and one and two and one and two. Flap those elbows. And back and two and back and two. Wow! Feel those little endorphins doing their thing?"

The thing Lauren felt was sweat coating every inch of her body, making her shiny pink-and-fuchsia striped leotard and matching tights stick to her skin. But she loved the feeling. Here she let the tension flow out and there was no time to think about anything else.

"Grapevine!" The instructor had one vocal pitch—high. Lauren smiled, exhilarated, and passed the back of a forearm over her forehead. For a thirty-nine-year-old lady, she was in pretty spectacular shape. Mirrors didn't lie. She knew the wrinkles were there, but they came with age and, as someone said, getting older was better than the alternative. Lauren grinned broadly and sashayed her grapevine with style. Life was mostly wonderful.

The music's heavy beat boomed, reverberating off the peeling white walls. The order came for the cool-down to begin. The group broke into a trot around the long room, past mirrored walls and the expanse of window that, as usual, afforded the laughing gallery on the sidewalk outside an unobstructed view. Lauren had learned to ignore the faces of people she characterized as jealous couch potatoes.

She jogged on, her eyes on the back of the man ahead. A great back and everything else. All men and women should take the time to make the best of themselves, she thought, even women like her who did so for purely personal reasons. Getting where she was hadn't been easy, but she was independent now, and liked it most of the time. She'd proven a woman didn't have to have a man to be complete. Never again would she be in a position where another human being could break her life into little pieces.

"March, kiddies. Slow it down, slow it down."

The customary chatter broke out. Lauren walked on, catching

sight of her reflection, wrinkling her nose and looking away again. Strands of wet hair clung to her temples below a soaked headband and her face, devoid of makeup, was flushed and shiny. She'd always considered her breasts too big and the damp leotard emphasized that fault.

"Keep going. Five more."

What did Jack Irving want from her? Last night he'd looked terrific. The tuxedo accentuated his tall, lean build, the nonchalant grace of a confident man. But Jack Irving didn't figure in her life one way or another. He probably wouldn't try to contact her again, and if he did, she'd give him the brush-off. He was younger than her, too—something she didn't like.

But he *was* interesting and nice. And sometimes she wished she had someone to do things with. Men didn't want women just as friends.

Telling him to get lost might be tougher than she'd like it to be. On the other hand...

A tap on the window startled her and she broke a rule: Lauren made eye contact with a "watcher." He tipped the brim of the black Stetson he wore tilted low over his eyes.

His eyes and his broad, slightly crooked smile, the dimples on each side of his mouth, stopped her.

Jack Irving.

CHAPTER THREE

The way out was through the front door or through the emergency exit into an alley behind the building.

Her car was parked in front.

Lauren backed away from the window.

And Jack walked toward the door, opened it and stuck his head inside. "Hi."

Hi. Just like that. As if they were comfortable old friends who "ran into one another" all the time. "Hello," she mumbled, aware of her ferocious frown, the damp pink-and-fuchsia leotard clinging to her body and her shiny face and mussed hair.

People filed past on their way to the showers and Jack smiled at her between the moving line. "Sorry I'm early." Taking off his hat, he stepped inside.

"I beg your pardon?" She had to raise her voice, but no way would she get an inch closer to anyone until she'd also had a shower.

"Early for dinner," Jack bellowed over the music and babble. "Sorry. I forgot to get your home address and had to track you down."

Passing faces glanced curiously from Jack to Lauren and heat flushed her cheeks.

Jack didn't appear to notice. "The woman I talked to at your office told me you'd be here now. I figured my only chance for a reprieve was to catch you before you left."

Lauren considered reminding him that they didn't have a dinner date, but he already knew as much and she wasn't enjoying her role as the afternoon's entertainment around here. Tomorrow, Susan would wish she hadn't been so free with details of her boss's personal agenda.

"I have to shower," she told him. And she wasn't fooled; her number and home address were in the phone book.

"Of course. I'll just wait here." Displaying another of his irresistible smiles, he sat on a chair by the windows, stretched out his legs and crossed his ankles. "Take your time."

Speechless, Lauren shifted her weight from foot to foot before turning and hurrying to the locker rooms. This was a calculated attempt to get his way by catching her off guard.

Marilyn Wood, owner of a copy shop close to Contact's offices, descended on Lauren as soon as she appeared. "Isn't that Jack Irving?" Marilyn knew everyone in town, and prided herself on being a reliable source of gossip.

Lauren opened her locker and took out a towel. "Yes," she said when it became obvious that Marilyn would wait as long as it took to get an answer.

"He's some hunk." Marilyn's blue eyes glittered avidly. "How long have you been dating him? He was seeing that Silky Harvey who models for some L.A. surfing equipment outfit. Guess that's over, huh?"

"I'm not dating him." She could almost feel listening ears all around. "And I don't know who he's involved with."

Marilyn smiled knowingly. "Defensive, aren't we?"

Lauren shook her head and stripped off her workout clothes.

"What do you call having dinner with a single, sexy and eligible male if it isn't a date?"

She wasn't having dinner with him, was she? "Excuse me," she said to Marilyn and hurried to the showers.

Within minutes she was deliciously clean, dry and dressed in the ancient faded jeans and sagging red cotton sweater she'd brought to relax in after her session. She combed her hair but left it wet and didn't apply makeup. One look at her—if he hadn't given up and left—should convince Jack that the only place she intended to go was home—on her own.

"Some people," Marilyn said, trailing back with a towel draped around her overly thin body.

"What does that mean?"

Marilyn wound her curly brown hair into a second towel and looked at Lauren in the mirror. "You," she said, turning the corners of her mouth down. "Old clothes, no makeup, wet hair and you look like a million dollars. Why don't sweaters look like that on me?" She held up her hand. "Don't answer that. I know why."

"You always look great," Lauren said honestly. Marilyn meant to be complimentary, but Lauren wasn't fooled. There was too much of her in the red sweater and her face might be described as striking by some, but she knew the lines were there. "See you Wednesday."

Jack sat where she'd left him, one ankle propped on his opposite thigh with the hat balanced on top. When she crossed the long room he made no attempt to move. Lauren felt his eyes on her and lengthened her stride. She wasn't a kid who could be embarrassed by a too-frank male stare.

"Ready?" he asked, standing as she reached him.

"I think we've got our wires crossed," Lauren said. A drop from her hair coursed down her face but she ignored it. "As you can see, I'm not dressed to go anywhere but home."

"Let's go outside." Jack eased the athletic bag from her hand and slung it over his shoulder before opening the door. "Come on. Live dangerously. Be led for once."

How did he know whether or not she ever allowed herself to be led? She went out onto the sidewalk and turned around, almost bumping into him.

Jack smiled. That darn smile. She stepped away, but he only followed, setting his hat in place and tilting it low over his eyes at the same time.

"Walk to the corner."

Short of making a fuss in front of people coming and going from the studio, she had no choice but to do as he asked.

"Look," she began when they stood under a striped awning a few businesses away, "this isn't going to—"

"I'd better quit playing games," he said. "I know you didn't agree to see me tonight, but I decided to try pushing my luck anyway. If you have time and you feel like it, I'd love to have dinner with you. If that isn't convenient, or you don't want to, say so and I'll get lost."

Lauren opened her mouth, closed it again and tried to think of a response. He stood, his weight balanced on one leg, a hopeful-boy look on his compelling face.

"Well—"

"I really will understand if it's no."

A man shouldn't look so good in well-worn jeans and a simple white cotton shirt. And a rough tweed sport jacket nonchalantly pushed back by the hand on his hip shouldn't make a woman want to stroke a wide shoulder, or feel her face there.

She was lonely.

"You want to say no, don't you?"

No, she didn't. "I'm a wreck."

"You look fantastic."

Before she could react, before she realized his intention, he stroked water from her cheek. Lauren lowered her eyes. This was a no-holds-barred attempt to sweep her off her feet and it had a chance of working.

"We could do something really simple if you'd feel more comfortable." He leaned closer and she looked up at him. "Fish-and-chips by the sea, maybe?"

His eyes were a tawny brown, warm and humorous. Maybe she could go for a quick meal. "Well..."

"Great. Let's go. We can walk, but let's stow your stuff first." He started toward a black pickup.

Lauren caught his arm. "My Honda's in front of the studio. It'll be easier to put my gear in there."

Without giving herself more time to think or to change her mind she walked ahead of Jack to her car, unlocked the trunk and let him put her bag inside.

A stiff wind had picked up, but the evening was warm. Strolling beside him along Elm Avenue, Lauren's senses were sharp to the scents of flowers, warm earth—and salt as they turned left on Carlsbad Boulevard and drew closer to the ocean, but she couldn't relax. With every step she was more aware that they were strangers with no reason to be together, and more aware that he, too, was silent, locked in with his secret thoughts.

What was he thinking?

"This is strange."

She glanced at him, taken aback.

Jack laughed. "You're going to think I'm nuts to say this, but you make me nervous."

Lauren looked at him again, her eyes narrowed in assessment. She made him nervous? "Really. Why?" She'd been out of circulation too long to know much about current rules of the man-stalks-woman game, but this sounded like quite a line.

"Not nervous exactly... Yeah, nervous. It's like we've known each other a long time without really knowing each other. And we've been part of another type of world where we never questioned being off-limits to one another, so this feels sort of...illicit?" He laughed and held her elbow. "Hell, what a lousy choice of terms. Forget I said anything."

"I know what you mean," she said, and she did. His honesty disarmed her. "We were both married and expected to stay that way. Or I did, anyway."

"Exactly. So did I. But my marriage is old history. Cross here."

The change in his tone suggested his openness about personal matters only went so far. And he'd reached his limit.

They crossed the boulevard at Pine and the ocean came into view. Lauren kept her eyes trained ahead but she could feel Jack, tall and solid beside her. A good feeling.

"Did you ever consider leaving Carlsbad?" Jack asked suddenly.

"No. Why would I?"

"You don't have family here, do you?"

"I don't have family anywhere. This is home now. Dan and I grew up in Laramie, but there's nothing there for me. My parents were older and I was their only child. They're both dead. I'm not aware of any other relatives." She let her eyes travel over the mix of European and Victorian buildings, interspersed with a heavy influence of romantic Spanish designs. Oddly, the architectural effect was charming rather than jarring. "I love this place."

"So do I. I guess I was wondering if you felt like getting away after your divorce."

"No. Did you?"

"My family has been here for three generations. Andy, my boy, had his routine here. And then there's my dad."

In other words, his situation couldn't be compared to hers? Lauren shrugged. He was only making statements.

Jack took her to a café near the beach and they both ordered fish-and-chips and beer. Sitting with him at a black wrought-iron table beside a frothy purple bougainvillea bush, Lauren ate and drank and found his silence more intriguing than disquieting.

"What else do you like to do?"

She started.

"Besides work and aerobics," Jack added.

"Grow flowers," Lauren said, caught off guard. How dull she sounded, but she had warned him.

"You have a garden?" Jack leaned forward. "What do you grow?"

"No garden. Just tubs in the courtyard and on the lanai." She felt foolish. "But I paint, too."

His gaze flickered and shifted away. "My son fills all my spare time. I like it that way."

Lauren frowned. His tone and face had hardened. What had she said? And if he preferred to be with his son, why had he deliberately tracked her down and virtually forced her to have dinner with him?

She looked at her watch. "Oh, no!" She hadn't realized how much time had passed.

"What is it?"

"I've got to be home by eight-thirty. That's ten minutes from now."

He got up immediately and dropped a bill on the table. "You should have said something. Am I keeping you from your painting?"

Lauren felt suddenly and unaccountably angry. This hadn't been her idea. "You're not keeping me from anything. I could have refused to come."

"But you did come, so why the hurry now?"

"I told you, I have to be..." She didn't owe him any explanations, but she believed in honesty. "Someone's expecting me."

He began to walk so fast that she had to jog to catch up to him.

"Who's expecting you?"

This was outrageous. "I've got a date," Lauren said. "I don't think I need to say more than that."

"How true." Jack inclined his head. "Forgive me for being rude."

They didn't speak until they reached her car and she let him take the keys to unlock the door. When she was inside, he dropped them into her outstretched palm and closed the door.

"Thank you," she said. "I enjoyed dinner." And she'd enjoyed him for a while.

"Thank *you*. And again, I'm sorry if I pushed. Have fun on your date."

He turned away and Lauren started the Honda's engine. Her throat ached. *Disappointment.* She'd turned him off and she wished she hadn't. Only it had been the right thing to do. Of course she'd have fun on her date. She always enjoyed being with Cara.

JACK GRINNED AND HELD his bottom lip between his teeth. "Mmm," he said into the phone, then, again, "mmm. I don't blame you, Charlotte. And I'm sorry Andy smuggled in his rat."

The phone had been ringing when Jack walked into the house. Charlotte Okita, mother of Andy's best friend, Rob, loved having Andy spend the night, but Jaws—as Rob and Andy knew—was not included in the invitation.

"Yes, Charlotte, I know you're afraid of rats." This wasn't the first Jaws emergency involving poor Charlotte. "I'll be right over to get Andy."

Jack listened while Charlotte insisted that Andy stay. The boys were asleep. She only wanted to be sure Jaws wouldn't "die of the cold" as the boys had insisted he would from being banished to a box in the Okitas' tool shed for the night.

"He'll be fine," Jack said. "Leave him out there. I'll pick him up in the morning." At home, Jaws spent most of his time entertaining himself in the elaborate play equipment Andy had devised for his pet.

Jack hung up, shrugged out of his sport jacket and tossed it across the back of the gray corduroy couch in his den. He picked up a photo of Andy from the desk. A face very much like a childhood version of his own smiled back, but the hair was dark, like Mary's.

She kept in touch sporadically, always tentatively signing off her calls from Paris with a request that Jack tell Andy she loved him. Mary usually avoided speaking to Andy in case she "upset him."

He replaced the photo and went to rest his forearms on the mantel. Love wasn't something you could switch on and off or put aside entirely to pursue a lackluster painting career halfway around the world, far from the responsibilities you had assumed and promised to honor. Not that he missed Mary. But Barney Middleton was right. A boy should have some feminine influence in his life on a regular basis. Dad was close to Andy. Jack sometimes felt he was competing with his father for his own son's time. But, with Mother gone, there wasn't a caring woman around Dad's place, either. Bernice, Jack's housekeeper, was kind but had a family of her own upon whom to lavish her attention. And the Silky Harveys of this world weren't interested in small boys who kept rats and anything else that crawled.

What about Lauren Taylor? And what about his unforgivable behavior tonight? She'd caught him off balance when she mentioned she liked to paint. Déjà vu. Was he wrong in assuming that because she'd never chosen to have kids, she didn't like them? He didn't think he was.

But he had been a boor, and he did want—more than he cared to examine too closely—to see her again.

He sat on the couch, then stretched out, his head on one arm. When he'd seen Lauren in that pink striped thing at the exercise studio his heart had almost left his body. She'd looked warm, and soft, and slightly mussed...and wonderful.

Jack closed his eyes. *What did he want?* She was dating.

He sat up. So she was dating. She wasn't married, or even significantly attached as far as he knew. A little competition had never stopped him from entering a race.

Before he could change his mind, he grabbed his jacket again and left the rambling single-story stucco house that sometimes felt too big, and pointed his pickup west, in the direction of the farm.

An hour later he nosed the Ford along Ocean Street. He'd taken Lauren's address from the phone book in his office. She lived in a town house, part of a two story Spanish-style complex with red tile roofs and an unobstructed view of the beach and sea. He remembered noticing and approving of the building.

When he parked, the dash clock showed eleven o'clock. The moon cast sharp white light and he was grateful the pickup was dark-colored.

Once out of the cab, he wrestled an oak tub of pink geraniums from the bed of the truck while he calculated which unit was Lauren's.

Staggering under its weight, he carried the planter across the street and puffed his relief at sighting the right number immediately. Intricate black iron gates stood open to a courtyard. On the far side a light shone through a glass panel covered by a metal grill in the center of the front door. Jack shouldered his way through the gates, making a mental note to find a way to tell Lauren they should be kept locked.

He placed the pot on her step, positioned an envelope among the blossoms and backed away. Was she back from her date yet? Probably not. She'd arrive and find his gift, and her "date," whoever he was, would get edgy. Great. Edginess could be a great advantage to an opponent.

Jack retreated. Tomorrow she'd call. Yes, surely she'd call.

The noise of the front door opening startled him. If he crossed the road his footsteps might be heard and the guy could decide to come after him. That would ruin everything. He pulled back behind a ginger bush near the gate.

"Yeah," a man's voice said. "Thanks, honey. Being with you always makes me feel good."

Jack stiffened and flattened himself against the wall. He should slip away like any decent human being would. He *was* a decent human being, but he had an interest here. Logic told him that was hogwash. But logic had very little to do with what he was feeling.

Lauren said something Jack couldn't hear.

"I'll remember that. But I'll call you about Thursday night. Hey, what's this?"

Jack leaned to see into the courtyard. A man bent over the tub of geraniums. He removed the card and started to open it. Jack opened his mouth to yell, but managed to close it firmly the instant before Lauren removed the envelope—from Dan Taylor's hands.

CHAPTER FOUR

"Lauren, I'm sorry!" Susan rushed through the front door, her red hair flying, her iridescent pink raincoat flapping open. "I overslept. Darned alarm. What can I tell you? I can't believe it."

Lauren held up a hand, continued speaking into her mouthpiece and watching the terminal screen. "Where can you be reached?" She typed in the number the caller gave. "Thank you, sir."

Susan took off her coat and pushed her fingers through her mass of hair. Lauren wished she wouldn't wear pink. "I'll take over now," Susan said, "unless you think I need forty lashes."

Twice in one week Susan had pleaded a faulty alarm as an excuse for her tardiness. Lauren glanced at the dark marks beneath her eyes and decided Susan must be enmeshed in a new heavy attachment that wasn't allowing much time for sleep.

Taking off the headset, Lauren stood. "It's all yours." Previous experience had taught her not to pry into Susan's love life. She was extremely private on the subject. "You might want to think about a new alarm."

"Yes, ma'am. I deserve at least that comment." Susan put her hands on her hips and narrowed her eyes. "You look... I do believe some would say you're glowing."

"It's a gorgeous day." Lauren laughed self-consciously and turned to catch the frankly curious stare of Jolene, one of five very good operators she'd inherited with the purchase of Contact.

Susan sat in front of the terminal. "Something tells me you've got more than sunshine and flowers on your mind."

"How did you—" A rush of heat to her face chagrined Lauren. "I've got a couple of calls to make. Try to make sure I'm not interrupted unless it's absolutely necessary."

The flower remark was a coincidence. But flowers were exactly what she had on her mind—beautiful double pink blooms, darker in the centers and with white rims.

Lauren shut herself into her office and sat on the edge of her desk. Pulling a scrap of paper from her pocket, she picked up the phone and punched in numbers.

A woman answered. "Irving Farms. Good morning."

In the second that followed, Lauren almost put the receiver down. Then she felt childish. "Good morning. This is Lauren Taylor. Is Mr. Irving in?"

"I'll see."

She waited. From her slacks pocket she removed the card Dan had almost read. The thought infuriated her. But Dan had his problems. He'd been an idiot, but, in some ways, he was paying a big price for that. Not that his frustration with a too young, too self-centered and rather foolish wife was her problem. And his apparent need to come to her for advice made her embarrassed for him.

"Are you still there, Ms. Taylor?"

"Yes."

"Do you want to keep holding?"

Lauren frowned. "Yes." He must be busy. She could have asked him to call her back.

She read the card.

Lauren.
If you need any instructions on caring for these, let me know.
If I was rude earlier, I'm sorry. Amend that. I was rude earlier.
Sorry.
Jack

She smiled. They'd both been awkward and he'd done all the reaching out. Now it was her turn. Her insides fluttered like a silly girl's, which she no longer was and hadn't been for a long time.

"This is Jack Irving."

"Jack, this is Lauren."

"Yes."

She opened her mouth and her mind blanked.

"Yes?" he repeated.

He sounded...ticked? "I found the beautiful geraniums." What was it with him?

"That's good." A muted tapping suggested he was using a computer keyboard while he talked.

"It was so nice of you." She should know what it was like to be interrupted at a bad time—and understood how difficult that could be.

The tapping continued and he said nothing.

"Anyway... Um, I'm very grateful." The bright bubbly sensation she'd felt on her way here this morning had definitely popped. "Um... I'll take really good care of them. I'm going to put them on my lanai."

"Good. You'd better get someone to move the tub for you."

Another furious blush rushed up her neck. "The gardener will be happy to do that." Why had she mentioned moving the thing? He undoubtedly thought she was hinting for him to come over.

"I'm glad you like the flowers."

Geez, he was prickly—and impossible to read. "I do." But he was kind and probably a little uncomfortable with her thanks. "Anyway, I won't keep you. I just wanted to tell you how touched I am, and surprised. It was a lovely surprise." She began to feel a gentling of the jumpiness in her stomach.

"It wasn't anything. Is that all you wanted?"

All she wanted? Lauren clenched her teeth. And he'd apologized for his rudeness of yesterday? "Yes, that's all. Except that I don't know why you bothered." He'd sought her out, not the reverse. None of this was her fault.

"I—"

"Goodbye," she said and cut off anything else he might have said with a smart smack of the receiver into its cradle.

"Temperamental ass," she muttered. "Men!"

Still muttering, cramming the card back into her pocket, she slid from the desk and yanked open a file drawer. She'd better figure out how much losing Irving's account would cost her if he was the type to bear grudges.

She located the folder and walked slowly to her desk. He'd been a customer for over two years. Minimal service agreement—after-hours switch-over only. But still she hated to lose the business.

A knock at the door was only a perfunctory courtesy before Susan came halfway into the room. "Finished with the phone?" she asked unnecessarily.

Lauren dropped into her chair. "Evidently." She couldn't summon a smile.

"Ooh, sudden mood change." Susan slipped all the way in, closed the door with a foot, and sidled closer, her hands behind her back. "What got to you? Or should I say who?"

Susan might be careful to keep her life outside the office mostly to herself, but she never hesitated to ask about Lauren's. "Nothing and no one," Lauren said. "Is there anything I should deal with before I get to my own work?"

"Ow. You're mad." Susan grimaced. "You are upset because I was late, aren't you?"

"No," Lauren said honestly. "You put in your time around here. I appreciate everything you do, Susan."

"Thanks." A smile softened anxious green eyes. "But something happened since you walked in. I know I shouldn't push, but maybe I could help."

"No—" Why not? Strong and silent wasn't anything she'd ever pretended or wanted to be. "Okay, yes. I am mad. I'm mad at the male of the species in general. Every time I try to treat one like a human being he turns around and stomps on my toes…"

Susan plunked into a chair and leaned forward. "Spill it. Dan again, I suppose."

"My toes are already pretty bloodied," Lauren said. Her lungs expanded hard. "I should call him back and give him some more home truths to think about."

"You should have done that a long time ago," Susan said. "And while you're at it, save a few for that sickening little airhead he's married to."

"He isn't married…not anymore."

"What! Dan got—"

"Not Dan." Lauren puffed and slumped. "Jack Irving. I'm talking about Jack Irving, alias Mr. Charm."

Susan raised delicately arched brows. For the first time in Lauren's memory, the ebullient Ms. Bailey seemed speechless.

"Anyway," Lauren said quickly, "enough of that."

"Jack Irving," Susan said, almost to herself. "I wondered why you behaved like a scalded cat when I tried to get you to speak to him on the phone. And then I wondered some more when he was so determined to track you down."

"I didn't behave any differently than I usually do when I've got a lot to do." Lauren felt defensive. She also wished she hadn't been indiscreet enough to mention Jack. "I had a lot to do yesterday, that's all. There wasn't time. And I meant to talk to you about not giving blow-by-blow descriptions of my itinerary to clients."

"I didn't talk about your private business. All I did was tell him why you couldn't return his call yesterday."

"And he tracked me down, Susan." Lauren bit her lip, remembering how frightful she must have looked. "There I was, leaping around in a leotard, sweating, thinking I was anonymous, when Irving's face appeared at the window. I didn't appreciate that." She wasn't being entirely fair but neither did she feel entirely rational.

"I'm sorry if I embarrassed you." Susan showed no sign of repentance.

"Forget it. In fact, forget it completely."

A determined set to Susan's features meant she had no intention of letting the subject go. "You just talked to him, didn't you?"

Lauren crossed her arms.

"Didn't you?"

"Yes, I talked to him. More's the pity." There, she was doing it again, letting her ire hang out.

"I knew it," Susan said triumphantly. "You can't fool me. Finally!" She got up and paced, grinning broadly.

"Finally?"

"Yes, finally. It's at least three years past the time for you to get involved with an interesting man."

"Do you know Jack Irving?"

"Never met him that I remember." The announcement didn't faze Susan's grin.

Lauren picked up a pencil and jabbed it into her desk calendar. "He isn't interesting."

"Yes he is. Dull men don't make women mad." She laughed. "Unless they're married to them."

Despite herself, Lauren smiled slightly. "Very funny."

"So?" Susan planted her hands on Lauren's desk. "What's it all about? Why are you angry with Jack Irving?"

The sooner she explained, the sooner they'd both get some work done. "I had dinner with him."

"Wow!" Susan tossed her hair back. "Wow! I can hardly believe it. That's terrific. Where did you go?"

"It was not terrific." As they'd sat above the beach, the breeze had ruffled Jack's hair, played with glinting traces of the sun's work. His eyes had taken on a curious, almost amber quality in the clear late-afternoon light. "Not terrific," she murmured. "We had fish-and-chips down on the boulevard. He's moody."

Susan breathed in, her eyes closed as if in ecstasy. "I *love* moody men. They're so sexy."

"Not to me." But she might as well get this subject over with. Susan wouldn't relax until she knew "all." Avoiding detail, Lauren filled in the picture of her encounter with Jack, finishing with finding the tub of geraniums on her doorstep late last night. Dan's visit was something she didn't mention. "So, I called this morning to thank him," she finished.

"And?"

"And he behaved like he'd just been kissed by a dog. He left me a gift with an apology for being rude, then turned right around and was even ruder. Now, let's get on with it."

"He's wild about you." Susan sat down again.

Lauren wrinkled her nose. "I don't follow you."

"I made some inquiries about him." Susan had the grace to appear uncomfortable. "Nothing direct. Just a word or two here and there. He hasn't had anyone serious in his life since he and his wife separated and divorced. There have been a few women, but apparently no one who held his interest for long."

Lauren regarded her coldly. "You're out of line—as usual. And, before you make any more brilliant observations, Jack Irving and I aren't even acquainted as far as I'm concerned, let alone 'serious' as you put it."

"Not yet, maybe." Smugness colored each word. "He's gun-shy is all. You mark my words. This is the start of something great."

"You sound like a mangled lyric. Go to work."

"I'm going. I'm going. But first I want you to promise me you'll go easy on him. Give him a chance to work his way through the shock he's feeling at having fallen in love at first sight."

Lauren rocked back and looked heavenward. "You're a nut. Jack Irving and I were a disaster from word one. The end. If he crawled through that door this minute and begged forgiveness, I'd stand on his fingers."

Susan laughed. "I knew it. You're crazy about him, too."

"I don't know the man," Lauren said, completely exasperated.

"But you want to. Give me that promise I asked for."

"What promise?"

Susan spread her hands and jutted her chin. "That you'll go easy on him. Give him a chance. Evidently he was badly hurt by his wife and he's been more or less in hiding ever since."

"In hiding? Most recently with Silky Harvey of the gorgeous bod?"

"Big deal. That was nothing. They went out a few times is all. Now he's seen someone worth getting involved with and he's scared. Men are like that."

"Sure." She knew what men were like. "Thanks for the benefit of your infinite wisdom on the subject. Not that I need it. I've made my peace with all of that."

"Meaning?" Susan asked.

"Meaning that women should learn at a very early age what their intended role is with the opposite sex."

"Really. Does that mean you've learned yours?"

"It sure does. The hard way." Lauren got up and walked to open the door for Susan. "As my marriage finally proved, the only thing I'm good at as far as the male's concerned is being a good buddy. With Jack Irving, there's never going to be a chance to get even that far."

WRONGLY PACKAGED SEEDS. Jack propped his elbows on his desk and scrubbed at his face. "Okay," he told Len Gogh. "I know how it looks right now, but we can't go to pieces on this."

"We could call in the police."

Jack snorted. "Like hell. A, they wouldn't do more than send a man out to take notes. Then they'd do nothing because there's nothing they can do. B, I don't want this getting out."

"It already is out," Len said, his hands tucked inside the bib of his overalls. "If it weren't, we wouldn't know about it."

"Damn," Jack said. "It had to have happened months ago. And it could have been an accident. Don't forget that."

"I'm not forgetting a thing. I just want to know what we're going to do."

Jack got up and went to stare through the window. "Nothing. That's what's so damned frustrating. All we can do right now is watch and wait and pray the whole thing goes away. Until something overt happens—and I hope to God it doesn't—but until it does, all we have are a bunch of isolated, potentially damaging incidents that could be explained away as accidents.

"I'll arrange for replacement stock to be sent to the locations where the mismarked product showed up and we'll send complimentary packages to any customers who are identified. This isn't widespread."

Len grunted. "Yeah. Not yet. I've got old hands in every area keeping an eye open for anything out of the norm."

"Great. Thanks, Len."

"Never mind the thanks. Keep up the prayers, and anything else you can think of."

Len left and Jack turned back to the room. If these incidents were deliberate, they were also clever. They left him with nothing to pin a real investigation on.

The phone kept pulling at his attention. He wished he could have a second chance at the conversation with Lauren. "Damn it all," he said through gritted teeth. What right did he have to censure what she did or who she saw? None. There could be a dozen explanations for Dan Taylor's presence at her town house last night.

Yeah, like he was married to a second wife and having an affair with his ex-wife. Jack rammed balled fists into his jeans pockets. Regardless of the fact that he had no right, he hated the thought of Dan and Lauren together. A flash of pale skin, dark hair, black eyes, passed through his mind. He must be losing it. Why else would he suddenly get a wild crush on a woman who'd been available for three years? Not that he'd had an opportunity to get close to her in those years.

He didn't have an opportunity now, unless he chose to make one. And for that to happen, he was going to have to do something he didn't like doing—grovel.

Damn. He picked up the phone, hit the button for a line out and dialed her office number.

"Contact. May we help you?"

They were prompt and efficient, but he'd expect that from anything she was involved in. "Is Lauren Taylor in, please?"

A breathy voice he recognized from the previous afternoon said "May I tell her who's calling?"

"Ah—" He thought a moment. "Look, this is an old friend and I'd like to surprise her. Do you suppose you could do me a favor and just put me through? It's okay, I promise."

What sounded suspiciously like a snicker came from the phone, then the clearing of the woman's throat. "It'll be my pleasure. One moment, please."

A moment passed, and another, before Lauren's voice came clearly to him. "Yes, Susan? Give me the figures."

Jack hunched his shoulders, hitched at the knee of his jeans and perched on his desk. "Please don't hang up, Lauren."

Silence greeted his request.

"This is mean Jack Irving, fastest mouth in the west—or south, I mean."

"Hello, Jack." And the frost was in that tone.

"We haven't exactly gotten off to a roaring start, have we?"

"I wasn't aware that we'd gotten off to a start of any kind."

The door opened and Joyce peered at him. Jack shook his head and she retreated. "Look, crass jerk isn't my preferred mode of approach. Again, I'm saying sorry and asking you to forgive me."

"Consider yourself forgiven."

And the ball was back in his court. She wasn't giving an inch. "Thanks. I don't deserve your kindness."

"Forget it."

Say thanks and hang up, Jack. "I can't forget it." He couldn't. It was as simple as that. For some reason it was becoming increasingly important to him to know this woman better.

The door opened again and this time his father put in one of his rare appearances in the office. "Just a minute, Lauren. Don't hang up, okay?" He covered the mouthpiece. "Great to see you, Dad. Take a pew. Unfortunately, this probably won't take long." To Lauren he said, "Are you still there?"

"Yes, but we will have to cut this short, I'm afraid." None of the cold front had left her voice.

"Look. I feel like a louse and I'd like to wave a white flag, okay?"

"That isn't necessary."

"It is to me. I—" he glanced at his father who was quietly regarding him "—I was a louse this morning. Unforgivable. When I see you I'll explain some of what's behind that. Things have been a bit tense around here. I'm sure you know how that can be."

"With business you mean?"

Jack relaxed at the slight softening he heard in her voice. "Exactly. But that doesn't excuse my taking it out on you and I want a chance to make up...clean the slate. Any chance of that?"

"Well..."

"That sounds hopeful. How about Saturday? At my place? Andy will be there to chaperon you and I'm told my cooking isn't so bad, especially if the pizza's delivered."

She laughed and he felt his shoulders drop. "Is that a yes?"

"You don't have to feed me. I really do understand getting up-tight about the job, Let's forget the whole thing."

"I won't if you don't come and eat. In fact, if you don't come, I'll probably go on a fast until you do." He avoided his father's eyes. "You wouldn't want a thing like that on your conscience."

"Mmm." She was bending, bending.

"Is that a yes?"

"Oh, I guess so. Okay, yes. What time?"

"I'll pick you up at, oh, six-thirty." The damndest feeling of exhilaration flooded him, like a sophomoric kid.

"That'll be fine. See you then."

"See you then, Lauren."

She'd hung up before he finished speaking and he was left look-ing at the receiver. He put it down slowly, softly.

"Who is she?"

He jumped at the sound of his father's voice. "Just a friend, Dad."

Denton Irving had taken up his favorite position near the win-dows overlooking the fields. "You sounded...determined. Like you weren't taking no for an answer."

"Did I?" The thought made Jack strangely pleased. "I was afraid I sounded uncertain."

"Well, since you obviously aren't volunteering, I'll have to ask again. Who is she?"

"Lauren Taylor."

His father, tall and rangy with thick white hair and beetling brows that were still dark, fixed him with a piercing brown stare. "Dan Taylor's wife? The real-estate people?"

"His ex-wife. They've been divorced three years. She's a nice woman, Dad. Not that this is anything major. Just someone I like."

"Sounded like more than that to me."

Had it? He guessed it probably had. Was it? Couldn't be. "I've reached a point where I'd like some intelligent female company. Someone to take to dinner, or to a show, who can manage more than a one-word answer from time to time."

"Like that Silky whatever her name was?" His dad dislodged

himself from the windowsill and prowled the room, looking at framed show prize certificates.

"Exactly. Silky's a nice kid. But that isn't exactly what I need."

Denton stopped prowling. "But you've decided you need something, huh?"

Jack felt irritated at his own careless comment. "No, I haven't. Don't make anything out of this."

"Okay. Forget I pried. I was hoping you'd let me take a look at the new mutant. This is still going to be the rollout year, huh?"

"Lava Pearl is as much yours as mine," Jack said of the mutant, orange-red and white poinsettia they'd been cultivating. "The same as everything else around here."

"Not anymore. Too many bosses spoil things. And I don't want the responsibility anymore. But we won't flog that subject again. I'd just like to see how the project's going."

"Sure. Matt Carson loves a chance to show off our baby." Jack took a key from a drawer. He discarded the idea of talking about the problems around here. "Let's go take a look." He was picking Lauren up for dinner on Saturday. He couldn't help grinning.

"You like her, don't you?"

He looked up sharply at his father. "You drive me nuts with the mind reading."

"What's she like?"

"Nice. Really nice and good to look at in a different kind of way."

"Sexy?"

He shook his head at his father's faint grin. "That, too."

"Can I give a few words of, er, advice before we go?"

Jack sighed. "If I said no, would it make any difference?"

"It might. But you aren't saying no." He gripped the front of the blue plaid wool shirt he wore over a red T-shirt. "You won't forget Andy in all this, will you, son?"

Jack stood very still. "Andy? What the hell do you mean?"

"I mean Andy. He was five when Mary decided her so-called painting career was more important than her husband or son. You might make an argument for his having been too young for that to make a big impression on him. But don't bet on it.''

"I won't,'' Jack said slowly. "I don't. I put in my time thinking about it regularly. What happened isn't something I can erase and I know it's likely to be something that may cause him a few problems in the trust department in the future.''

"As long as you know that.''

"We've already had this conversation. Many times.''

"Yes. So you'll be careful, won't you?''

Jack narrowed his eyes. "Careful?''

"I know a man's interest in a woman when I see it—real interest.'' His father's mouth came together in a firm line. "What I just heard was a man who could be winding up for a shot at a major involvement.''

"You're exaggerating.'' But Jack frowned and chewed the inside of his mouth.

"Maybe. Only make sure you don't get into something that's likely to hurt that boy again.''

Jack met those wise eyes and had to look away. "I don't know what you mean.''

"Yes you do. Andy gets attached to people, maybe too attached. He's a special kid and he probably needs a woman around. But if he gets used to one and then things don't work out for you and whoever she is, Andy'll have another strike against his confidence. I don't want to see that.''

Holding his temper wasn't easy. "Neither do I, Dad. And it's not going to happen. This thing with Lauren Taylor is purely casual. Believe me.''

HUMMING, LAUREN CLATTERED down the stone steps from the third-floor studio where she took her Wednesday evening oil-painting lessons.

The old Victorian house where Mrs. Laphagia lived, taught and sold her own works stood like a dilapidated older relative between low-lying stucco buildings on the edge of the business district.

Mrs. Laphagia liked the seascape Lauren was working on. Or she said she did. The elderly lady needed her class fees to keep solvent. Lauren could never quite shake the notion that many of the compliments Mrs. Laphagia dispensed were to ensure students didn't lose heart and drop out of her class.

As she searched in her pocket for her car keys, her wooden paint case bumped against her knee. On Saturday she was having dinner with Jack Irving. The same thought had intruded dozens of times since his call yesterday. She smiled and felt nervous at the same time.

"I'd like a few words with you."

Lauren jumped and looked into Christie Taylor's blue eyes. Beside her, dressed in pink and white polka dots—shirt, jeans and even tennis shoes—Wednesday hopped up and down, her blond hair a soft curly mop.

"Hi," Lauren said when she'd recovered. "Were you looking for me?"

"This won't take long if you listen carefully," Christie said, ignoring Lauren's question.

"How did you know where to find me?"

"You keep my husband informed of your whereabouts. All I had to do was look in the back of his journal."

Lauren held back the temptation to say what she thought of snoops. "He always did that. It doesn't mean a thing, Christie. Old habits die hard, right?"

"I wouldn't know about anything old."

Lauren sighed. This type of nastiness sickened her and she wouldn't play games with a woman Susan aptly described as an airhead. That should probably be amended to vindictive, insecure airhead.

"Hello, Wednesday," Lauren said. She dropped to one knee, set down her paint case and smiled at the little girl. "You've grown since I saw you last. And you're even prettier."

The child leaned against her mother's leg and stuck a finger in her mouth. "I'm three," she mumbled.

"Yup," Lauren said. Before she could stop herself she touched the soft hair. "Getting to be a big girl. Do you like to color?"

"Uh-huh."

"Me, too. That's what I've been doing. Next time I see you I'll try to remember to bring you some new crayons."

"She's got all the crayons she needs." Christie swept the child into her arms and pressed her face into her shoulder. "Stop encouraging Dan to spend time with you. Stop giving him a shoulder to cry on. I know all about women like you."

Lauren turned first hot, then very cold. "Women like me? That's rich." If Wednesday hadn't been present she would have told Christie a few truths about her own opinions on the subject of scheming women.

"Dan's been seeing more of you," Christie said. "Telling you our private business and letting you worm your way into his confidence. It's going to stop. He told me you wanted to baby-sit Wednesday tomorrow night."

Wednesday on Thursday. Poor kid. "That wasn't my—"

"I'm going to tell him you called to say you had other plans. Understand?"

Lauren ached to lash back, but nothing would be gained. Dan had amazed her by asking if she'd baby-sit his daughter. She'd refused, and he'd begged, saying Christie didn't trust anyone they hired, but she would feel comfortable with Lauren. How little poor Dan knew about women.

"Are we finished?" she asked.

"Almost," Christie said. "If Dan asks you why you changed your mind about baby-sitting—"

"I didn't. I never said I—"

"I don't believe a word you say. You'll tell him not to come around. Got that?"

"Oh, you bet I've got it," Lauren said, wanting only to get away from this silly woman.

"If you don't get out of our lives you'll wish you had." Christie backed away, turned, and said over her shoulder, "Remember this the next time you feel like interfering in my marriage—I've got influence in this town now."

"Meaning?"

"Meaning nothing," Christie said. "Except that I'm a winner, Lauren. I get what I want—one way or another."

CHAPTER FIVE

Jack looked upward. Lauren followed his glance and saw Cara's small face drawn quickly back from her bedroom window.

"Who's that?"

"Cara Flood. She and her mother rent rooms from me."

His brows shot up. "Really?"

She laughed. "Uh-huh. It's a long story, but not very interesting." To anyone but her.

"I see," Jack said in a tone that let her know he wasn't a man to quiz. "That jumpsuit looks great. Black is definitely your thing. You look wonderful."

The warmth of pure pleasure suffused her. "Thank you. So do you," she told him and grimaced.

This time he laughed, tipped back his head to show strong teeth and deep dimples in his cheeks. "You're something. *I* look wonderful. That's a first for me."

Lauren couldn't think of a response.

She almost expected him to drive a different vehicle, but the big black pickup waited at the curb. Lauren liked him for that, for his lack of pretention. And when he helped her up the high step into the cab she was grateful she wore pants.

He walked around, his head bent over his keys. The late sun picked out those glints in his hair again. He was rangy but lithe in gray pleated pants and a white shirt, open at the neck and rolled up over his tanned, leanly muscled forearms.

"Off we go," he said, climbing in beside her and switching on the ignition.

Lauren, her stomach doing somersaults, steadily regarded the ocean. Gentle waves rolled in to curl along the state beach. No surfers were evident today. Even the usual motley assortment of mostly junker cars sporting boards on their roofs was missing.

"No surf today," Lauren said, for need of something to say.

"Do you surf?"

She shook her head. "I don't even swim," she admitted and regretted the confidence. "Not well, anyway." *Not at all* was the truth.

"I'm damned. You never learned?"

More golden hair covered his arms and the backs of his broad capable hands resting loosely on the steering wheel.

"Swimming isn't big where I grew up."

"Nevertheless you should be able to, just in case." He drove with relaxed ease. "You ought to learn."

"I'd be embarrassed."

"No you won't. I'll teach you."

She swallowed and concentrated more intently on the sea. Again there was nothing she could think of to say. Looking ahead, she was aware of his leg close to hers, his thigh flexed. This man had too strong an effect on her or maybe she was too vulnerable to any attractive male who showed interest in her.

This was just a dinner date with his son present because he felt obligated to make up for his earlier rudeness. There'd been no prior rudeness to explain his turning up at the aerobics studio, however.

"You're quiet." He inclined his head until she was forced to meet his tawny eyes. "Are you afraid of the water? I'll teach you in my pool."

"I don't have a swimsuit."

He splayed fingertips over his smile and she bowed her head.

"People always say I have a way with words," Lauren told him. "That's an example of why."

"I find you delightful. You say the first thing that comes into your head, thank God. Pretty rare in a female."

"Equally rare in a male," she said before she could stop herself.

He laughed. "See what I mean? Natural. That's marvelous. But now you think I'm a chauvinist."

Now she didn't know what to think, especially about this different, very charming, very confusing side he was showing. He was probably playing with her. Why, she had no idea.

Once beyond the main development of the town, he followed the route from Carlsbad Avenue and inland on Palomar Airport Road.

The vegetation became scrubby—a straggle of bushes and shrubs growing despite the rocky terrain. But, beyond the scattering of red-tiled roofs, a forest lined the horizon below a pale blue sky.

Minutes passed before Jack spoke again. He turned his face briefly toward her, then faced the road once more. "Do you think I'm a chauvinist?"

"I don't really know you," she reminded him.

"True."

Silence sank between them again. The low-lying buildings of Palomar Airport came into view on their left. As they drove by, a sleek white Learjet swept in for landing.

"And the great golf game goes on," Jack remarked.

Nearby La Costa, one of the nation's ritziest clubs, drew wealthy and famous players from all over the world.

"Do you play?" Lauren was increasingly aware of the awkwardness between them.

"Not if I can help it. Racquetball's my passion."

"Mine, too!" She instantly regretted her outburst.

Jack smiled at her. "You really are into fitness, aren't you?"

"It's good for the nerves as well as the body."

"And your nerves need lots of things that are good for them?" A right turn onto El Camino Real had them heading south again.

"I was only making conversation."

He thought about that. "Do I make you uncomfortable?"

"A bit."

"That's the thing about trying to know someone, isn't it? The getting past the awkward stage. Feels a bit like fencing, testing."

He was open with his thoughts himself. "I guess." Impetuously, she added, "I'm rusty at this anyway."

"Why's that?"

Lauren swallowed. "I've been busy."

"Too busy for people?"

"Too busy for men is what you're asking, isn't it?" She rested her head back. Another plane passed overhead.

"Mmm. You're right. That is what I mean."

"Dan was my first real boyfriend. First boyfriend—period. We were in grade school when we met. There were brief times when we went our separate ways, but not for long. I never really learned the dating dance.'' This man engendered frankness. ''And now I don't want to.''

''Why?'' He turned his face toward her. ''Do you like being alone that much?''

She took a deep breath that seemed to go no farther than her throat. A glance from Jack Irving had the unwelcome effect of searing the air around her. ''Maybe. Maybe I just don't like the odds against having a successful relationship.''

''What constitutes successful to you?''

This was a conversation she'd never had with anyone. With herself many times, but never aloud. ''I'm not sure. Maybe it would be a friendship where I never had to doubt that I was...wanted for myself. Maybe there isn't such a thing as a successful relationship. Knowing the other person would never change, or would always put you first would do it. Being sure that you would never wake up one morning to find the bottom had dropped out of everything you believed in.... If you knew that whatever happened, the other person would never even consider letting you down, that would be a successful relationship, wouldn't it?'' She laughed and the sound was hollow in her own ears. ''I think my interpretations belong in a fairy tale. And no one cares what I think anyway.''

''I care.''

Lauren looked at him sharply. The lines of his face had hardened and his hands were no longer relaxed on the wheel. His knuckles were white.

''Your interpretations as you call them should be written on stone—in blood—before people make promises to one another.''

''Yes.'' Her throat constricted. ''But that isn't likely to happen, so the best thing we can do if we tend to wound and not heal too quickly is to steer clear of potential disaster.''

''How right you are.''

She felt the lightness go out of the moment. He was closing up. The startling realization came that he was probably still in love with his ex-wife. What Lauren couldn't figure out was why he'd decided to hold out a tentative hand in her direction. Friendship seemed the unlikely motive. And the other possibility... Her chest expanded uncomfortably. Surely she hadn't given off vibes that suggested she'd be a willing candidate for a casual affair.

There could never be any question of that. Not for her. She made up her mind. She liked him, might be capable of really liking him, but this would be the last time she'd say yes to an invitation—not that she expected another. Obviously he'd acted on a whim.

The houses they passed became very familiar.

Lauren felt Jack's eyes on her again. "Does it bother you to come out here?"

"No," she said, and was pleased to realize she meant it. "It would have a couple of years ago, but not anymore."

But she didn't look to the right when they drove past the turn to Arenal Road.

"It's a striking house," Jack said as if seeing into her mind again. "I always admired the lines. Very clean."

He didn't mean to upset her. "Yes. We had it built," she said of the multilevel, flat-roofed white house where she and Dan had lived for ten years.

Jack turned sharply right, then left onto quiet Caleta Court. Evening jogging had often taken Lauren along this short street lined by tastefully expensive stucco ramblers with tiled roofs.

"Here we are." He drove up a sloping red brick driveway and parked before wrought-iron gates in a white stucco wall that shielded a courtyard in front of the house. "Stay put until I can help you."

She did as he asked, aware of a thudding in her chest. What was she doing here?

Jack squinted into the sinking sun. A compelling man by any woman's standards. She couldn't, must not, allow any fantasies about him. But the fitted shirt showed off a well-toned body and he moved with sure power that brought goose bumps to her arms and a tightness to her jaw.

He opened her door and smiled up at her. And the sensation that hit her now was as old as mankind, but too rare in Lauren's recent memory. She took the hand he offered and looked away, certain that if he saw her eyes he'd know what she'd felt.

When she stood beside him in the driveway, he continued to hold her hand until she turned her face up to his. He was still smiling.

"What?" She inclined her head. "Why are you smiling?"

"I don't know. Maybe I'm glad you're here." He shrugged his wide shoulders. "And maybe I'm surprised you are."

"And maybe you can't figure out why you asked me at all," she said more tartly than she'd intended. Somehow she had to get through this experience unscathed and make sure she never allowed another potentially destructive encounter with Mr. Irving.

"Dad!"

One half of the black metal gates swung inward and a boy ran out. He threw himself at Jack. Lauren would never have had any difficulty figuring out who he was. Though in the gangly stage with curly hair that was black rather than light-colored, the boy's eyes and bone structure were too similar to Jack's for him not to be the man's son.

"Hey, let up, Andy. Here's our guest."

The boy immediately separated himself from his father. A frank, assessing gaze pinned Lauren before he smiled politely. "Hi."

"Lauren Taylor." She held out a hand and immediately wondered if she'd lost her mind, but he shook hands without hesitation, his skin slightly powdery from the layer of dust she noted on his fingers. "You must be Andy."

"Yeah. Hi. We're havin' lasagna. Bernice made it up."

Lauren looked quizzically at Jack.

"Our housekeeper. She's a gem."

"She's a pain about some things," Andy retorted. "Yesterday she put Jaws—"

"That'll do," Jack said quickly, but he laughed. "Andy and Bernice get along very well most of the time. Let's go in. I expect Lauren's ready for something to drink."

The smell of the lasagna was the first impression Lauren had when she passed through the lushly planted courtyard and into Jack's cool house.

"Would you like to sit on the patio?" Jack asked.

"Um."

"We don't have to. Are you chilly? I could turn down the air conditioning. I tend to keep the house pretty cold." He moved a step behind her and she felt him at her shoulder. "Andy, did Bernice lay the table?"

He was almost chattering, Lauren thought. Her next thought surprised her. He was as nervous as she.

"Bernice did *everything*." Andy sighed audibly. "She made me tidy up my room."

"Good for Bernice," Jack said. Lauren could hear anxiety in his voice.

"I'd love to sit on the patio if you would," she said, smiling back at him.

His glance shifted fractionally, from her eyes to her mouth. "I'd like it very much." He caught his bottom lip in his teeth.

Lauren swallowed and found herself mimicking his action, pulling her own lip between her teeth. Aware of the beginning of a flush, she turned to Andy. "Lead the way to the patio, Andy. You're going to join us, aren't you?"

"What will you drink?" Jack asked.

"White wine would be lovely," she said without looking at him.

"White wine it is. Take care of her, Andy."

He touched her back before walking away across the terrazzo floors. Lauren watched him go. His fingers had left a tangible print on her shoulder. Letting out a slow breath, she smiled at Andy.

The rooms he led her through were airy. Pale shades predominated—cream and pearl gray with touches of black or brilliant blue. Not Jack's choice, she thought with certainty. Somewhere there must be a room that would be distinctively his. These austere spaces, attractive and tasteful as they were, and appealing to Lauren on some level, had to be left over from his beautiful, artistic and supposedly self-absorbed wife.

"Don't sit in the striped chair," Andy said as they emerged onto a flagstoned patio. "It falls down sometimes."

"Thanks." Lauren sat in the white chaise Andy indicated. "This is great." No austerity here. This was an area that had to belong to a lover of color.

Hanging baskets, tubs, planters on scattered low tables, flowers sprayed and sprouted everywhere. Jack had geraniums of a dozen varieties captured in small planting areas and clustered amid billowing purple lobelia in two wooden wagons.

Suddenly aware of being watched, Lauren gave Andy her attention. "Do you like flowers?"

"'Course."

Of course? Most nine-year-old boys might not be so quick with that answer. "Do you help your dad at the farm sometimes?"

"Yeah. A lot." He looked at the sky, then at his worn sneakers.

Lauren cleared her throat. Jack seemed to be taking a long time with the drinks.

"You like flowers?" Andy asked.

"Very much."

He strolled around the patio, his hands in the pockets of his jeans, scuffing at nothing in particular. "You used to live near here, Dad said."

"Yes. Just a couple of streets away. I remember you as a little boy." That wasn't entirely true. She remembered a small boy with Jack at the store, or outside in the yard when she jogged by, but he'd been more an impression than a presence.

"I don't remember you."

She almost laughed. It was too bad adults learned to play polite games. Being honest would be so much easier.

"What time do you have to get back home?"

The question jolted her. "I hadn't thought about it." She sat straighter and tightened her hold on the small purse she'd brought.

Andy circled some more. "Where'd you meet my dad?"

"Well, we first met years ago—sort of."

"Yeah. But now, I mean. He doesn't invite... He doesn't usually have people to dinner."

Lauren felt tempted to ask if Silky had come to dinner but thought better of it. "We, er, talked at a party. And I have an answering service that does work for him."

"So you work for him." He paused an instant, thinking. "Lots of people work for him. He doesn't ask them for dinner."

Glancing at the door, willing Jack to arrive, Lauren considered what was happening. "Maybe you'd better ask him about that." The beginning had seemed promising. Now a cold front was moving in and she didn't need child-psychology classes to figure out that she made the boy feel threatened.

A scratching sound distracted her. She tried to smile at Andy and leaned to look beneath the chair. The wooden box with holes in it had escaped her notice.

More scratching.

Lauren returned her attention to Andy and found him watching her intently. "That's Jaws," he said. His slender, freckled face had turned pink.

"Jaws?" She pursed her lips.

"One of my pets." Andy planted his feet wide apart. "Want to see him?"

Lauren smelled a setup but decided to play along. "Sure."

Andy approached, dropped to sit cross-legged beside her, and reached to pull a string that raised one side of the box.

The first thing Lauren saw was a long, twitching, gray-and-white nose adorned with stiffly sprouting whiskers.

Lauren's heart did a neat flip and settled back in place. Not so much a setup as a test. Well, rodents weren't high on her list of favorite things, but she'd never been squeamish.

The animal slid carefully from his hiding place and into his master's lap, where he peered sideways with a beady black eye. He endured the captivity of Andy's hands with apparent resignation.

Andy's attention was on Lauren. His narrowed eyes, the now-what-are-you-going-to-do smirk amused her.

Suppressing a rise of sickness, she fixed her own smile in place and held out her hands. "Does he go to strangers?"

"You wanna hold him?" Andy wasn't quite up to camouflaging his disbelief.

"Sure." No, she didn't, but neither was she about to be outmaneuvered by a nine-year-old.

The scratch of small pointed claws on her palms almost undid Lauren. Jaws's long sinewy body tensed in her hands but he held still, his head darting this way and that. His pink tail, like a cold, dull-skinned snake, wound about her wrist.

"He's...he's really something. Very tame." Her heart gradually stopped jumping. The creature seemed clean and he hadn't bitten her—yet.

"You like him!" Andy's grin was sincere. "Geez, you're the first girl who didn't scream. You shoulda seen Rob's mom the other night."

"Come and get your Coke, Andy."

Jack emerged through the open French doors, a wineglass in one hand, a highball glass in the other.

Andy didn't move.

"Hop to it, kiddo," Jack said, approaching. At Lauren's side he stopped and stared down. "What the—Andrew! What do you think you're doing?"

Lauren suppressed a giggle at the age-old parental reaction. "Andy said I could hold Jaws," she said. "One of the best, nope, I'd say the very best rat I ever held." The only rat she'd ever held.

"She's the only girl I ever met who likes him." Awe hung on every word. Andy turned to her and his smile was genuine. She was being silently thanked for not selling him out.

Jack's eyes met hers and she saw humor sparkle there. "Sorry I took so long. The wine was in the basement."

Lauren kept her face straight. "Don't worry. Andy's been looking after me." *And trying to scare me off.*

Jaws moved, whipping his body in a semicircle. Andy removed him, sidled past his father and across the patio. "I'll get my Coke," he said as he went into the house.

"You really are something," Jack said, giving her the glass of wine.

Lauren swallowed a large gulp and let her muscles go limp. "No big deal. Andy's proud of his pet. He wanted to show him off."

"Wanted to see if you frighten easily is more likely."

His frankness took her aback. "Why would he want to do that?" She had a perfectly good notion why but wondered if Jack, who must know the reason, would admit it.

"Just kidlike, I suppose."

No, he wasn't comfortable enough with her to say exactly what he thought.

"This is beautiful," she said when she couldn't bear the silence any longer. "Wonderful flowers."

"Thanks. Since they're my business it would be funny if I didn't have a show at home."

"Of course."

"Do you bring on your own starts?"

She stared at him blankly. "Starts?"

"For your containers?"

"Oh. No, I buy plants when I'm ready for them. I don't really have a place to keep things like that."

"Doesn't take much room. You could do it in a window."

He wouldn't relate to her dislike of clutter. Boxes of seedlings would fill needed spaces and look messy.

"Come and see the pool," he said abruptly, taking her glass and setting it on a table with his own.

Without waiting for her response, he walked on stepping stones leading from the patio, behind the planting areas to one side of the house. The pool was oval. On the far end stood a small building of stucco that matched the house and had its own tiled roof.

Jack continued around the pool with Lauren in his wake. Outside the building he stopped. "Poolhouse," he said. "There's a shower and sauna. Bar. Small lounging area. Get a suit when you can and I'll teach you to swim."

His voice was almost toneless, but why would he repeat the offer if it wasn't sincere? Lauren's stomach clenched. "Thank you. Maybe I'll take you up on that one day." The thought of entering that warm blue pool, of her body and Jack's being close, skin to skin, did amazing things to her brain...and other areas.

She was thirty-nine. A few months and she'd be forty. Jack had undoubtedly seen Silky Harvey's flawless mid-twenties body in a swimsuit—or less. Lauren turned away. She was happy as she was and intended to stay that way. Being compared to a woman fifteen years her junior wasn't something she planned on going through. There would be no swimsuit competition, or any other competition for any man.

"TIME YOU HIT the hay." Jack reached to ruffle Andy's hair. "Your grandfather's coming for you early in the morning."

"I'm not tired yet," Andy said. "Lauren, would you like to see the gym I built for Jaws?"

Jack propped his elbows on the table and regarded his son. This behavior was out of character. Usually the boy was quiet around strangers, particularly women. Not that Jack had brought more than one or two home, and never for dinner.

"You bet I would," Lauren said.

He looked from Andy to Lauren. She'd eaten well. He appreci-

ated a woman who didn't pick at her food as if she disdained anything as earthy as a good appetite.

"I think you should run along, Andy. Lauren can see the gym
another time."

Andy frowned. "I picked up the stuff in my room."

It also wasn't like Andy to persist once he'd been given an in-
struction.

Lauren got up and turned so that Andy couldn't see her face.
"You stay here with your coffee. I really want to see the gym. I
won't be long." She gave him an exaggerated wink that looked so
odd he almost laughed.

"Okay, but do make it quick, okay, son?"

Andy nodded and left the room with Lauren. She glanced back
at Jack before going through the door, then went from sight.

Jack leaned back in his chair. What had made him feel he wanted
to see Lauren at his table, and with his son?

He sat up again and drank not coffee, but brandy, taking a long
swallow from a snifter. That was it. Of course. It wasn't how she
reacted to his home, or even to him. He'd wanted to see her with
Andy.

And she was passing the test with flying colors. The brandy
burned all the way down. What test? And what was the prize for
passing? He flared his nostrils. He was certainly no prize. So far
his record for choosing the right woman was a great big zero. Mary
was supposed to have been it, the one and only. Some judge of
character he was.

Lauren was something special.

Hell, what did he know? He *thought* she was something special,
but he couldn't risk... His mouth dried out. He wanted to know
Lauren, to know her better, whatever that would mean.

Andy had reacted positively to her.

A coldness crawled into his belly. Andy must not be hurt again
by learning to care for someone who could walk away without
looking back. No, that must not happen again. A polite dinner was
all this was.

Her flat sandals made a clipping sound on the hall floor. "This
boy's got talent," she said, coming back into the room with Andy
grinning at her heels. "Jaws is one lucky rat."

Jack regarded the two of them and the coldness inside him intensified. "Some gym, huh?"

Andy's face glowed. "She likes Strangler, too."

Jack closed his eyes and shook his head. "You set that snake of yours on her, as well?"

"Strangler's got a lot of personality," Lauren said.

"For a snake," Jack muttered. Andy was taking out all the stops. Jack knew only too well that his boy judged his friends by their reactions to his creepy menagerie. "To bed with you."

"Okay, okay. I'm going." At the door Andy paused. "I play soccer."

"Oh." Lauren's smile showed interest. "Soccer's a good game."

Hers was a face he'd never get tired of, Jack decided.

"I've got a game next Saturday. Would you like to come?" Andy looked at Jack. "You'd bring her, wouldn't you, Dad?"

"Ah, yes." He'd made a horrible mistake here.

"Well, I don't know." Lauren's tone had changed, subtly, but had changed nevertheless.

Jack looked at her alertly. The smile on her face had lost its brilliance.

"It'd be fun. Wouldn't it, Dad? Rob's mom and dad always go. Lauren could talk to Rob's mom. Maybe she could tell her how Jaws isn't anything to be scared of. Then we could all go for pizza like we usually do."

"Hmm." Jack listened to Andy's rapid fire delivery, but watched Lauren. She'd laced her fingers tightly together.

"What d'ya say, Lauren?" Andy asked.

She reached behind her, found a chair and sat down. "That's so sweet of you, Andy. I'd like to come, but I'd better take a rain check this time. I...I've got something I have to do next Saturday."

"Oh." The animation fled Andy's features. He shrugged. "That's okay, then."

"I would like to." Lauren appeared to take short puffs of breath through her mouth like a woman drowning. "It just wouldn't work out next Saturday."

Jack flexed the muscles in his jaw. She'd been putting on an act, pretending to like Andy. He'd been right; Lauren didn't particularly care for children... not if they threatened to take up too much of her time.

"Night then," Andy said.

"I'll be in to say good-night shortly," Jack told him.

"Good night, Andy," Lauren said. "Thanks for showing me the gym."

Once they were alone, Jack returned his attention to his brandy glass. He was being irrational. There was no reason for him not to enjoy the company of a woman who appealed to him even if she didn't instantly fall for his son. This was a casual date, not an audition for a lifelong commitment. He'd probably never make another one anyway.

"You're quiet," Lauren said softly.

He looked up into her dark, gentle eyes and every nerve in his body leaped. "I was thinking."

"What about?"

She'd never know. "About how nice it is to sit here with a beautiful woman." It probably sounded phony, but at this moment it was true.

A blush did great things for her. "You don't have to be so nice," she said.

He studied her speculatively. "Don't you know you're beautiful?"

"You ask funny questions. You embarrass me."

"Maybe I want to. I like it when you blush."

"I don't." She drank coffee and grimaced.

"Cold? I'll make some fresh."

"No. I'll drink more wine." A laugh softened the strain that had tightened her mouth. "I'm not usually a lush, but this is very good."

There was something between them, something growing more intense with every second. She was rusty at the dating dance, she'd said. Jack swirled the liquor in his glass. Could Taylor have been the only man in her life—really in her life? Had she completely kept to herself since the divorce? He raised his eyes. Was she ready to take a lover? He shifted in his seat, felt his thigh muscles jerk.

"Perhaps it's time I went home."

He started, realizing he hadn't responded to her previous comment. "Drink the wine. And no, it's not time for you to go home. Do you play table tennis?" The instant he'd asked he felt foolish.

Her "Yes, I love it," was delivered as if the question couldn't have been more normal.

Jack searched for the next comment. "Would you like a game?" From lover to table-tennis player. None of this felt like anything he'd ever experienced.

"Now?" Lauren asked. "Where?"

"There's a game room in the basement. But you don't have to if you don't like the idea."

"I do like it." She was on her feet.

The basement was his favorite spot in the house. A big paneled room furnished with comfortable tan leather, this was where he came to listen to music and read.

Lauren walked slowly past his overflowing bookshelves, turning her head sideways to read the titles. "This is a neat room," she said and pointed at the stove. "I'd curl up by that with a book and forget the rest of the world."

"That's what I do." So, they had that much in common.

The paddles lay on the tabletop. Lauren picked one up and flipped her wrist in a way that gave Jack pause. She hadn't said whether she considered him a chauvinist. In fact, he wasn't. But he hated to lose at anything, especially to a woman.

"Warm-up?" he asked.

She nodded and started a rally. Seconds later she said, "Let's just play." Catching the ball she waited for his response. When he took up position, she served. An ace....

Jack opened his mouth to say he hadn't been ready, but changed his mind.

Lauren served again.

Another ace.

Jack couldn't bring himself to look at her. He must be out of practice or going too easy on her.

"Just a minute." Hopping, Lauren took off first one, then the other sandal. "They get in my way," she said, tossing them aside.

She could have fooled him. "More comfortable now?" He smiled inquiringly and missed her third serve.

The first game went to Lauren, twenty-one to ten.

"I didn't realize how rusty I was," Jack said. "My turn to serve?"

"Uh-huh. How long is it since you played?" She returned the ball with a vicious rolling forehand that sent the ball to Jack's backhand corner. It rose vertically, but this time he was ready.

Jack leaped, smashing the ball for a short angle shot she'd never get.

The ball hit the net and dropped back on his side of the table. Furious, he gritted his teeth. "It's been weeks. Where do you play?"

Lauren frowned. "Nowhere really. Dan and I had a table, but I don't think I've played since then."

He laughed. He had to. "And you're creaming me? I've gotta concentrate here." He pointed his paddle at her. "Not a word about this massacre to Andy."

"Not a word. Serve."

Their play evened out, but she was obviously a competitive player.

Lauren reached and ran, stooped and bounced in place. Maybe if she weren't so irresistible to watch he wouldn't keep missing shots. As it was he couldn't help mentally cataloging the magnetizing things all those moves did to her body encased in the simple black jumpsuit.

"This is fun," she said breathlessly. Her hair had become mussed, her cheeks flushed.

"Mmm." It was fun. How long had it been since he'd felt as he did tonight? "Are you thirsty?"

"Are you?"

"I asked first."

She smiled and laid down the paddle. "I'm thirsty if you are."

Her voice, the breathy quality, singed some deep part of him. "Pop, or more wine?" He went to the refrigerator behind the bar.

"Pop. Coke if you've got it."

"Sure." And she didn't say "diet."

He gave her a glass of Coke, poured one for himself and went to light the wood stove.

Lauren chose a chair and curled up on the seat with her feet beneath her. "This is so nice."

When flames flickered up the stovepipe, Jack sat on the floor. Nice it might be. Relaxed, he wasn't. "There's something I need to say."

She tilted her head. "Okay."

"I really am sorry for the way I spoke to you the other morning."

"You already apologized. I understand how edgy business problems can make you."

For some obscure reason he didn't want her to make this easier on him. "I brought the geraniums over the night before."

"I know."

He raised his face. She regarded him steadily. In her throat a pulse beat visibly. Her full breasts rose and fell as if she were still slightly out of breath. Yet again his gut reminded him sharply that he was a man in the company of a woman he found incredibly sexy.

"I was in the courtyard when Dan left your place." All week he'd told himself he wouldn't do this. No way would he broach a subject that was none of his business.

"Why didn't you…" Her lips came together in a line that trembled slightly.

Jack felt as if his insides had been ignited. "I couldn't interrupt." He curled his fingernails into his palm. "Do you and Dan still see a lot of each other?"

"More than we should." She rested her head back. Her skin was very pale, all the way down her slender neck, and all the way to the top button on the jumpsuit where a shadow hovered. "More than I want to, now. I already told you we've been friends most of our lives. When Dan's troubled, I'm the first one he turns to, the same as he always did."

"You could tell him you don't want him around."

"I more or less have."

More or less. Why did it bother him that she still spent time with her ex-husband?

Lauren jerked upright and leaned forward. "Was that why… No, of course not."

"Why what?"

"Nothing."

He breathed deeply through his nose. "When a woman says

'nothing' she always means something and it's usually something that bugs her."

"Not this time. And it was a stupid thought. I suddenly wondered if seeing Dan had anything to do with the way you spoke to me when I called the next morning." Her pale skin turned that fascinating shade of deep pink he was coming to like.

"No, nothing like that. Why should it?" He hated to lie. "Well, yes. Now that I think about it, it did bother me. You told me earlier you had a date and then you were with Dan. I immediately thought you two must still be... Well... Forget it."

"Still... You mean you think there's still something physical between Dan and me?"

"That's your business."

"He's married to someone else."

It was his turn to feel very hot. "I know. But you see how it looked, don't you?"

She took her time before answering. "Yes, I guess so. You don't know me well enough to realize that wouldn't be something I'd do." Her short fingernails ran along the side seam in her pants. "Why would it matter to you?"

"It doesn't," he lied. "I was only speculating."

The next silence was uncomfortable before he said, "You do aerobics and paint and you like to do container gardening. What else do you like?" Changing the subject had become imperative.

"Jogging. I love to jog."

"Where?"

"All over the place. The beach is good."

Jack studied her. "Who do you jog with?"

"Me." Her eyes slid away.

"You make sure you go in daylight?" Now he sounded like an anxious parent.

"Not always. It's safe down there."

"The hell it is. Why don't you jog with me?" He hated jogging, but maybe with her he'd become a convert.

"One day perhaps. Thanks."

"You said you like racquetball." A spark flew to the hearth and he deadened it with the base of his glass. "Do you have a regular partner?"

"No." Her lashes lowered, thick, casting a shadow on her rounded cheekbones. "I just play pickup games with anyone who's around."

"I like to play a couple of times a week. Play with me."

"What about your regular partner?"

"I play pickup, too." Another lie. He and Jess Parker, a local accountant, had played together for years.

When he looked at Lauren, the intensity of her gaze disconcerted him. "What is it? Am I being pushy?"

"Maybe. What is it that you want from me, Jack?"

Her directness rendered him speechless.

"Jack?"

"I...I'm not sure."

"Try and figure it out." With her nose in her glass, her dark hair fell forward to shield her face.

Jack scooted closer and touched her knee. He let his hand rest there. "I can't be that cool. I like you. Isn't that a good reason for wanting to be with someone?" Some of the other feelings he had couldn't be voiced; not now and probably never.

"If you want—" She tossed back her hair but didn't meet his eyes. "I don't have a good record with the men in my life."

He had the vague feeling that this was a landmark conversation, and that this woman was totally unlike any other he'd known. "I got the impression there hadn't been so many."

"It doesn't take many failures to get the message about what you aren't good at."

"Could we agree to give one another a chance? We could do something nonthreatening, like jog, or play racquetball, and just see what happens."

"You're hedging. I'm hearing another message, Jack. Or I think I am. And that one won't work—not for me."

"Tell me what you mean."

Footsteps on the stairs were an intrusion Jack resented. His father came into view but didn't come farther than the bottom step. "I need to talk to you, Jack," he said, his attention on Lauren.

Jack stood up. "Lauren, this is my dad. Denton Irving. Dad, Lauren Taylor."

His father nodded perfunctorily. "May I have a few words with you, Jack?"

"Now?" He checked his watch. "It's after eleven. Can't this wait till I see you in the morning?"

"If it could, I wouldn't be here."

"Couldn't we have talked on the phone?"

"I tried that. Andy was using it. I got through on call waiting."

Jack narrowed his eyes. Did his father think he was slow-witted? Sure he'd talked to Andy and Andy had said Lauren was with Jack. So Dad had hotfooted it over here to make sure Jack didn't forget the warnings about Lauren. And as long as she was in the room there was nothing he could say to set the old man straight.

"Mrs. Taylor," Dad said with more formality than Jack ever remembered hearing from him. "A little family matter has come up that Jack and I need to talk about. Would you be offended if I called a taxi for you?"

Jack swung toward his father, fury whipping along every vein. "Dad! What the hell—"

"It's all right," Lauren said from behind him. "The taxi's a good idea. That way you don't have to drive all the way back to town then out here again."

"I'll take you home," Jack said forcefully. "When you're ready to go."

She retrieved her sandals and slipped them on.

"We need to talk," Denton said, giving Jack a meaningful glare.

"Then talk. Now."

"When we're alone."

Lauren patted Jack's arm as she went to the stairs. "I'm going to call a taxi. Please don't give it another thought."

"No way." He couldn't believe his father would pull something like this.

Denton stood aside to let Lauren pass. "This is important, Jack."

"Good night, " Lauren said.

Jack started for the stairs but she held up her hand. "Relax. I'm used to doing things for myself. This is the way I prefer to go home. Really."

"Lauren—"

"I wouldn't do this if there was any other way," his dad said.

"Mrs. Taylor's obviously a sensible woman. I need your attention now, son."

"Talk to your father."

With a sense of total disbelief, Jack watched Lauren climb the stairs and go into the hall.

"You'd better have one damn good reason for this," he told his father through gritted teeth.

"The best," Denton said evenly. "Trust me."

CHAPTER SIX

Betty Flood had something on her mind, and whatever it was, she clearly had no intention of sharing it with Lauren.

"Tomorrow's Monday," Lauren said. "What about school for Cara?"

Betty, thirty, of average build and height with a pleasantly unremarkable face and light brown curly hair, stopped going through her purse and looked at Lauren. "I'll call the school first thing in the morning and tell them she won't be in."

"I see." Lauren stood near the sliding windows that opened onto the living room lanai. Outside, an uninviting gray sky pressed into a matching sea. Wind buffeted the glass. "Who did you say you were going to visit?"

Betty's bright blue eyes, the pattern for Cara's, met Lauren's. "I didn't. I said I was taking Cara away overnight." She stopped replacing items in her purse. "Look, I know I owe you openness for all you've done for me, but this is something I'm not ready to talk about."

Lauren's stomach turned. She made fists at her sides. "You don't owe me anything." But she wanted something anyway, she wanted to know what was going on and how it would affect Cara.

"Yes, I do. But you'll have to trust me this time."

Betty was planning to take Cara away. Lauren could feel it. It would be like losing Joe all over again: the empty days and nights after he left, the house silent except for the sound of her own footsteps, her own breathing.

"I'll call the school if you like," she said with forced brightness. "Then you won't have to worry. Shall I tell them she'll be back on Tuesday?"

"I'll call," Betty said gently. "And I'll tell them she'll be back on Tuesday."

Lauren let out a long breath. "Okay." She swallowed. "Do you have everything you need? Enough money?" The suitcase Betty had packed already stood in the hall.

"I don't need a thing," Betty said, bowing her head and snapping her purse shut. "You're too good to us. Lauren, I wish you'd find someone to love...." Her eyes, when she raised her face, were filled with tears.

I love Cara, Lauren wanted to shout. But Cara wasn't hers and she had no hold on the child. This oppressive Sunday should be a lesson to her, that the child was only hers on loan.

Years ago she'd been able to accept that there would be no babies of her own. She'd moved on, slowly at first, so very sad at first, but she had grown stronger with time. If sharing someone else's child was something she couldn't do without falling apart when the inevitable time to part came, then she must never share again.

The door from the kitchen opened and Cara, pushing it with her bottom, entered the room. Wisps of hair escaped her pigtails and her blue-and-white striped T-shirt was torn on one shoulder. Two brown bags filled her arms.

"Cara," Betty said, "I told you to bring the sandwiches I'd made and two cans of pop. Not everything in the refrigerator."

"I didn't. I brought my animals, just in case."

Lauren had to turn away. On that afternoon, a year ago, when the Floods had turned up on her doorstep mistakenly thinking she had rooms to rent, Cara had carried a pillow slip filled with stuffed animals. They had been the first things she'd arranged on the bed in her new room; her way of making the space her home. Something within the girl was giving her the same premonition Lauren had that she might be about to move on. Cara would never leave her animals behind.

"You don't need to take the toys," Betty said quietly. "Put them back in your room."

"But, Mom—"

"Put them back," Betty insisted. "Hurry. We've got to go."

The girl did as she was told and within minutes, after Cara had given Lauren a quick hug, the front door closed behind mother and daughter.

Someone to love.

Lauren wandered along the hall and into the small dining room with its round teak table and its pinky beige wallpaper sprigged with vertical lines of tiny blue flowers. A door on the other side of the dining room led to the kitchen. Spotless, with a center island and white appliances, the space was well utilized and convenient. A vaguely cloying sweetness perfumed the air. The hoya plant, its vines climbing from a hanging pot toward the skylight over the window, was in bloom. Clusters of flowers, pale pink, hung like waxy, upside-down umbrellas.

All empty...and silent.

A restless night, passed in a state of half sleep, half dreamlike wakefulness, had ended with this colorless morning. Lauren went to sit on a high stool near the scrubbed wooden top of the cooking island. The night had been filled with vague expectancy. She'd expected Jack to call. Now that she was alone she could admit as much. But there had been no call, no word. His father's face had told the story. Like Andy, in his first moments with Lauren, Denton Irving had seen her as a threat and, unlike Andy, he'd shown no sign of changing his mind on the subject.

This was ridiculous. Sitting here feeling sorry for herself was out of character and totally unproductive. Betty would bring Cara back tomorrow. And she'd banish Jack Irving from her mind immediately.

Coffee was needed. And a bagel with cream cheese. And maybe some ice cream. Or maybe a good hard run instead of all the above.

Jack Irving had been mildly and fleetingly interested in her and his reasons were undoubtedly all the wrong ones from her point of view. If she got involved with him she'd get involved with Andy. Then she'd start to care for the boy, and possibly even for the man.

Out of the question. She'd had a narrow escape.

So why did she feel like crying?

She'd run.

When she was halfway up the stairs, on her way to change clothes, the doorbell rang. Slowly she turned and retraced her steps.

The bell blared again. Beyond the amber glass in the door and the pattern of iron grillwork, a shadow moved. Whoever stood there was tall.

Lauren reached the door, opened it, and looked up into Jack's eyes and down at a flapping black T-shirt and black running tights slashed with winding red bands.

He spread his arms. "I was running in the area and thought I'd stop by."

"That's not very original."

"I know. What is?" He smiled and sank his teeth into his lip.

She wasn't going to attempt an answer. "I was just getting ready to go running myself."

He glanced at her jeans and sweatshirt.

Lauren shook her head. "Not like this. I was going to change."

"D'you suppose I could come with you?"

She crossed her arms and rolled onto her toes. "It's possible."

"That sounds promising. Shall I wait out here?"

"Don't be ridiculous." Moving back, she opened the door wider. "Come in. Wait anywhere you like. Kitchen, if you want. There's cold coffee and a microwave. I won't be long."

She left him and didn't look back. By the time the bedroom door closed behind her, the thudding in her chest was suffocating. This was pointless. They could have nothing together. But she couldn't stop thinking about him or wanting to see him.

The front door slammed.

Quickly she crossed to the window and peered down, half expecting to see him leaving. Outside the courtyard, Jack's black pickup stood at the curb. There was no sign of Jack. He was in her home, downstairs, waiting.

She was a mature, capable, self-supporting woman who should be able to deal with attention from an occasional male. Evidently she'd become a passing interest to the male in question today and that should make her feel good.

Rapidly she stripped to her bra and panties and donned bright yellow tights and an electric-blue tank top. Overheating while exercising had always been a problem for Lauren. With shoes and socks in hand, she went back downstairs.

She found Jack in the kitchen taking a cup of coffee out of the microwave. "You follow instructions well."

"As long as they're easy to follow," he commented and sucked a noisy mouthful from the steaming cup. "I tend to get in a lot of trouble when I misread signals." He looked at her squarely.

"I haven't given you any signals at all that I'm aware of."

"Did I say you had?"

Lauren sat on the floor and pulled on her socks. "Let's drop it."

"Fine with me."

But it wasn't fine with her. In the act of tying a shoelace, she peered up at him. "Dinner was great last night. I forgot to tell you that." She ran her tongue over her dry lips.

"You hardly had a chance. That was my fault."

His mouth held her attention. How did he kiss? Was he a man who moved slowly with a woman, thinking and feeling his way while he matched his pace to hers? Or did he proceed quickly, spurred on by his own arousal, sweeping his lover along and into his need until there was no place for thought, only a dark, obliterating heat?

"Lauren? Are you okay?"

She started. "Yes." Bending her head to hide her face, she finished tying her shoes, then bounced to her feet and pulled a rubber band from her wrist. Gathering her hair at her crown, she captured it in a thick ponytail and smoothed back strands that tried to escape.

Jack's eyes were on her breasts.

Lauren's knees felt weak. She dropped her arms and turned away. He was a man, with a man's reactions—nothing more.

"Let's go. Slam the door behind you. It'll lock." Snagging a door key from the hook by the phone, she pinned it to the waist of her tights and led the way from the house, across the road, and down to the beach.

They fell into stride, side by side, their feet scrunching on the shingle bar at the tideline.

"I wanted to call you last night."

Lauren glanced at him. He was a pace ahead and she automatically studied the movement of his back and shoulders under the thin T-shirt and the way other parts of him flexed and stretched under their spandex second skin. His body would be unlikely to go without notice from any red-blooded woman.

"Did you hear me?" he asked, raising his voice over the wind that sang in her ears.

"Yes."

His hair whipped around his head. He was younger than she, but she had no idea how much. In broad daylight, seeing her without makeup as she was today, he'd be bound to make comparisons with Silky, and whoever else had filled some of his needs. He needed someone solid, stable, unthreatening, an ear that listened without making demands. That had to be the explanation for his seeking her out.

But she still couldn't figure out why he'd chosen her for the job.

"I was afraid I'd wake the whole household if I phoned."

She wished he'd called anyway. "Don't worry about it." Sprinting, she caught up.

"Aren't you cold?" He glanced at her tank top, plastered to her body.

"No. I get hot easily and I hate that." She was acutely aware of how little the top camouflaged. Flattened to her, it rode up, baring her midriff and clinging to her breasts.

"I'm sorry about last night." Jack jogged easily, clearly holding his pace down to hers. "I don't know what got into my dad."

A wave broke and foam rushed up the beach. Lauren veered away and Jack followed.

"He obviously had something important to say. And he didn't want a stranger as an audience."

"He wanted to discuss his latest concerns about my parenting techniques. That and a few other issues. And you're not a stranger."

"Aren't I?" Light rain joined misty spray off the ocean and she blinked.

"Not to me," Jack said, keeping his gaze fastened ahead.

"We've only known each other a few days—if you can call it knowing each other."

"I can and I do. And it seems longer than a few days." He jumped over a piece of driftwood. "Gulls coming inland. A storm won't be far behind."

Lauren lifted her chin. The gulls wheeled and wailed overhead. "I love being down here when it's like this."

"I never have been before. But I think I'm addicted already." He laughed. "The company helps."

Lauren's heart thumped. "Andy's a great kid. You must be very proud of him."

"He's the center of my life. The best thing I ever did."

"And you did it right," she said impulsively.

He slid to a stop and caught her arm. "You mean that?"

"Yes, I do. He's happy, Jack. And secure. It shows and you did that for him."

"Thanks." His eyes moved beneath downcast lids. "That's about the nicest thing anyone ever said to me."

What must it be like to be a parent? Lauren took a slow, deep breath and wiped moisture from her face. No matter how hard she tried to fill every corner of her life, the empty space left by not having a child was always with her.

"Run," she said tightly. "I don't want to cool down yet."

"The rain's getting heavier." Nodding skyward, he squinted. "It's just a shower. We could sit in the lee of the wall and wait it out."

Without answering, Lauren took off in the direction he indicated. They arrived neck and neck and plunked down, cross-legged on a triangle of dry sand in a sheltered corner.

"Did you and your father get things sorted out?" She felt she had to ask.

Jack shrugged and rested his elbows on his knees. "As I said, apart from wanting to talk about Andy, I'm not sure what he came about really. We've been having some... I guess you'd say some incidents out at the farm."

"Problems, you mean?" she shivered.

"I guess you'd say that. Dumb little things that could cause total disaster. Like thermostats being changed. Sprinkler timers tampered with...whole batches of seeds mismarked. A real pain and a real potential headache for us."

"You think these things are deliberate?"

He shrugged again, glanced at her and put an arm around her shoulders. "You look cold. Hold on to me."

It was said and done so naturally that she moved closer and slipped her own arm around his waist almost without thinking until the heat of his solid body struck through the thin fabric of their shirts.

"You love your business, don't you?" she asked.

"It's the only thing I ever wanted to be involved with...as a career, I mean. My dad before me—and my mother before she died—were both totally committed to the farm and so was my grandfather before them. Back then it wasn't more than a seat-of-the-pants operation with Grandpa doing everything himself. Now Irving's is a big outfit, but I still have the feeling that family involvement is the heart of the thing.''

"That's nice." She liked what he said, and the sensation his honest enthusiasm brought. "Andy sounded as if he's going to follow right on after you."

"I hope so. But that'll be his choice."

They fell silent. Jack's rough fingers stroked her shoulder absently. Heat flashed beneath Lauren's skin...and desire. She'd identified any involvement as a potential disaster and she was allowing it to stalk her.

"How old are you?" She gritted her teeth, horrified at her bluntness.

Jack laughed. "Thirty-seven. Why?"

"I wondered."

"And I already know you're thirty-nine. Is age an issue here?"

Here? What did he mean by here? "I was only asking."

"And now you know. Any more questions?"

She felt foolish. "I guess not. Yes. Why do you want to spend time with me? Or why do you seem to want to spend time with me?"

His rhythmic stroking of her shoulder continued. "I like you. Is that good enough?"

"You didn't know me at all when you walked up to me at that party."

"We'd met before. Sort of. But that was the first time I'd had a chance to study you and I decided I'd been missing something important."

She let herself be drawn nearer. "What were you missing?"

"Getting to know a fascinating woman," he said without hesitation. "And you were missing getting to know a fascinating man, so I decided to put us both out of our misery."

She had to smile. "I guess I should thank you, huh?"

"That would be a good start."

"I like you." This conversation couldn't be taking place.

"I like you, too." Jack looked at the sky. "But I already said that. Shall I count the ways?"

"Please," she couldn't resist saying.

"An ego that likes to be stroked? Thank God you're normal. I like the way you say what's on your mind."

"The way I can be horribly rude, you mean?"

"That's it. And I like how natural you are. You aren't a primper. You just know you look terrific."

Her blush was instant and furious.

"And I like that." Jack laughed. "The way you turn red and look horrified."

"Thanks."

"And I like your appetite."

"My appetite?" She screwed up her eyes.

"Yeah. You eat well and never talk about dieting. Do you know how rare that is in a woman these days?"

"I can't say I'd considered the question." Another thought came. She glanced down at herself. "You probably think I'm overweight."

"I think you're perfect." And his appraisal, the slight sensual flare of his nostrils, swamped her with a dozen unwelcome re-- sponses.

His hand had become still on her arm, and his eyes fixed on hers.

"We should run some more." Her bones felt formless.

"Should we? Are you sure that's what you want to do?"

Lauren sighed, and scrambled to her feet. Jack held out a hand and she took it, leaned back against his weight as he pulled himself up.

"I think we should get one or two things straight," she told him in a rush. "Don't you?"

Jack frowned. "What things?"

"We're two needy people." She shook her head impatiently. "That doesn't sound right, but you know what I mean."

"I'm not sure I do. Why don't you explain?"

He gathered strands of hair that had escaped her ponytail and hitched them behind her ear. Lauren stared at him, her train of thought lost. She wetted her lips.

Jack's attention was there now, on her mouth. "What does needy mean?" he asked.

He was thinking about her mouth, as she'd thought about his earlier. He was probably also wondering about how they would kiss—if they kissed—which they never would. It was like sinking into a dream, a soft, sexy dream, and Lauren slowly pulled her hand away.

"You and I seem drawn to one another," she said, aware of the huskiness in her voice. "All I meant was that maybe it's because we both need a friend."

"Just a friend?" His golden eyes darkened.

"We've got a lot going on in our lives. I say that without really knowing if it's true of you. It is of me and I'm guessing in your case."

"It's true." He reached for, and captured, both of her hands.

"A lot of that stuff—in my case—isn't so easy to talk about. I may not be what you want even in a friend, Jack." If only she didn't long for him to tell her he wanted her to be much more than a friend.

"Why did you look so trapped when Andy asked you to go to his soccer game?"

It took an instant for her to switch gears. "I didn't realize... I don't know." She couldn't handle talking about this.

"Don't you like kids?"

Her teeth came together hard. "Why would you ask something like that? Of course I like kids."

He looked at the sand. "Of course you do. Everyone's supposed to, aren't they?"

She didn't understand his point. "I suppose so."

"Don't give it another thought. I think it was a call from Andy that brought my father rushing over last night. Andy really fell for you."

Lauren smiled, pleased. "I fell for him, too."

"Evidently he told my dad he thought you were great and that got him worrying, so he came over to make sure you weren't about to cause his favorite, only grandson any grief."

"I don't understand."

"No, of course you don't." With a hand on her neck, he turned

Lauren toward the sea and they began to walk. "It's tough on a five-year-old to have his mother walk out. My father worries that I'll introduce another woman into Andy's life who'll repeat the process."

Lauren's stomach turned over. "I don't blame him. But you wouldn't, so he should trust you."

"Yes he should."

"You would never expose Andy to anything that could hurt him, I can tell that."

Jack stopped again. "You're right. I never would do that."

Lauren looked into his eyes and read his message as clearly as if he'd spoken it. He was telling her that all he wanted from her was a casual relationship, nothing that could become important enough to eventually make his son unhappy.

"I've already told you Dan and I've been friends forever."

"Yes." His wrists came down on her shoulders. Their faces were inches apart.

Lauren breathed with difficulty. "One of the things I've learned through a failed marriage that left me with an ex-husband who's still on good terms with me is what I do best with men."

Jack regarded her intently but said nothing.

"What I'm best at is being a friend."

He continued to study her.

"So, I think that might be what I could do for you. And what you might do for me, if you want to."

"Be a friend?"

"Yes. We're both working our way through heavy stuff. If something bothers you, or doesn't go well and you need a sympathetic ear, I'm a great listener."

He tipped back his head and looked down at her. "And if I don't believe you, ask Dan, right?"

"Right. He talks to me about things all the time."

"And sometimes you wish he wouldn't. Didn't you tell me that?"

She nodded. "Yes. But with you and me it would be different. We were never—" Her skin heated. "You know what I mean."

"Oh, I do. I do, indeed." He pursed his mouth sagely. "We were never lovers is what you're trying to say?"

Lauren's knees felt wobbly. "That's exactly it. And it makes things so much simpler. It's a myth that men and women can't be friends, don't you agree?"

"You definitely seem to have this all worked out."

She took a shaky breath. "So that's what we'll do...if you ever decide you need to, that is?"

"Do?" He glanced away. "Oh, yeah. That's exactly what I'll do. In fact, regard yourself as engaged."

She stared, nonplussed.

"I'm definitely going to need your friendly services. Thank you for being so understanding. I'm engaging you as a permanent buddy."

CHAPTER SEVEN

"I'm sure you understand this is purely a business decision," the woman on the other end of the telephone line said.

Lauren wrinkled her brow, searching for an appropriate response. She felt confused and vaguely sick. "Mrs. Wakefield, are you telling me you've decided Contact is too expensive for We Serve U? If so, perhaps we should see if there's some way of negotiating terms we can both live with." Mrs. Arthur Wakefield—the woman introduced herself just that way—ran a gourmet meal delivery service.

A delicate cough preceded a short pause. "I think we should simply agree to part company," Mrs. Arthur Wakefield said. Lauren didn't miss the ice in her tone. "Maybe you'll learn something from this."

Lauren sat very straight. "Learn something?" She wiggled a pencil between her fingers, thinking rapidly. "Are you suggesting we've done something wrong? Failed to give you good service?"

"I think you know what I'm suggesting. Goodbye, Lauren."

"Mrs.—"

The line went dead. And Contact had lost the second client in two days, the second client to make veiled references to dissatisfaction with the company's service.

The buzzer sounded on the intercom and Lauren pressed the button. "Yes, Susan?"

"Just give me the word and I'll tell him to get lost."

Lauren rolled her eyes. "Is Dan trying to reach me?" Later she'd get together with Susan to try to figure out the possible cause for the recent client defections.

"He sounds irate."

"Put him through," Lauren said testily. She was in no mood for one of Dan's so-called helpful diatribes.

The line clicked, and clicked again.

"Lauren?" A diatribe was on its way. "Why didn't you just come out with it to me?"

She sucked in her cheeks. "I don't know what that means, Dan."

"Oh, yes you do. I've been through pure hell for the past week."

"I'm sorry to hear that."

He barked a short laugh. "I'll just bet you are. It took me until this morning to get Christie to tell me what happened."

Lauren leaned back in her chair. This promised to be maddening, but she'd hold her temper.

"Are you listening to me, Lauren?"

"I won't be if you continue to shout."

She heard him breathe out hard through his nose. "I thought you were above this kind of thing."

Lauren tossed the pencil on the desk. "Spit it out. I don't have time for riddles."

"You told Christie I came to see you. And you told her I cried on your shoulder about the problems we've been having."

"Did I?" How could a so-called mature male be such an ass?

"You know you did. You stopped her in the street—with Wednesday there, mind you—and told her that if she knew how to be the kind of wife I needed, I wouldn't have to come to you."

"Christie told you that?"

"Yes. She was very upset."

"Hmm." And it took a whole week for her to tell Dan this little myth. Lauren wondered why the wait. "Does she know you called me on Monday, too? And yesterday?"

"Yes. I told her. I don't believe in keeping secrets from her."

"That's commendable. Are we finished?"

"What hurt her most was the way you said you weren't interested in sitting with Wednesday for us. I'd hoped we could eventually put the past behind us and you two would be friends."

Lauren's blood began a slow boil. "I didn't tell her that, Dan." And she would choose a pit bull as a friend over Christie.

"Did you say you wanted to look after Wednesday?"

"No-o." This was all a waste of time.

"Exactly. I thought you loved kids. I thought you'd really enjoy getting to spend time with Wednesday. You can't get enough of that kid who lives at your place. And she isn't anything to you.''

"Neither is—" She shut her mouth and bowed her head. "Goodbye, Dan."

"Lauren—"

She hung up and covered her face with her hands. Irritation value was all Dan spelled these days. And his doll of a wife made her sick. Jealous, insecure, vindictive—and all because Christie knew she'd been wrong in the first place and assumed every other woman was capable of the same kind of underhanded tactics she'd used to get Dan.

The intercom buzzed again.

"Yes, Susan."

"Dan again. He says he's sorry and would you please talk to him again."

And he'd managed to sound pathetic enough to catch even Susan's hardened sympathy.

"Tell Dan I had to go out. And please don't put any calls through until I tell you it's okay."

She had two sales calls to make this afternoon. The thought of putting on a serene, confident face for strangers made her tired. But if she was going to start to lose clients for no good reason, she'd better step up her recruiting efforts.

The tap she recognized as Susan's came an instant before the door opened. "Is it safe to come in?" Susan peeked at her.

"Only if you're wearing a bulletproof vest."

"Firmly in place." Susan closed the door behind her and plopped into a chair. "Kick me out if you like, but I'd like to know what's going on with you. All week you've been snapping. When you haven't been totally silent, that is."

"I've got a lot on my mind," Lauren said shortly.

"Anything you want to share?"

She looked up sharply. "I don't know. Is there anything about your life outside this office that you'd like to share with me?"

Susan's eyes widened. "You are uptight. If I had something I needed to say, I would. I trust you. I thought you trusted me."

Guilt overtook Lauren. "Forgive me. It's more of the same and a few new twists. Dan irritates me. Christie's a bitch. We've lost two clients for reasons they say we know, when I don't have any idea what they're talking about. And I think I'm getting a case on Jack Irving." She closed her eyes. The last had definitely not been something she had planned to say.

Susan's broad grin promised to make sure Lauren regretted her indiscretion.

"You've been seeing Jack?"

"I saw him."

"When?"

"Saturday and Sunday."

"*Both* days? Wow. Fantastic." She leaned forward. "What's he like?"

Lauren looked away. "He's a nice man." And he'd "engaged" her as a buddy.

"Nice?" Susan wrinkled her nose. "He's a dish. Why haven't you seen him since Sunday?"

Because he seemed to find cozy, general telephone conversations adequate. Late at night he called to ask how she was and share a few details about his day. Then he signed off with some cheerful nothingness.

"You don't want to talk about this."

Lauren had forgotten Susan for a moment. "It doesn't matter," she said lightly. "We talk on the phone. He's got a lot on his mind these days."

"Like what?"

She told Susan something of the incidents Irving Farms had been suffering.

"That's too bad. What are they doing about it?"

"There's not much they can do, evidently. But Jack says they've got a trusted hand in each area keeping close watch on what goes on. Then, after the men go home, someone goes back to check everything again."

"What a nuisance for them." Susan spread her hands on the arms of the chair as if to get up. "Did you find out where Betty and Cara went last weekend?"

A heaviness formed in Lauren's chest. "No. I can't ask Cara. That wouldn't be right. And Betty must have told her not to say anything." She turned up the corners of her mouth. "But they seem settled back into our normal routine, so maybe it was all nothing."

"I'm sure that's right." Susan didn't look any more certain than Lauren felt. "So, you've got the hots for Jack Irving."

Lauren's blood seemed to drain to her feet. "Susan! I didn't say that."

"Don't sound so shocked." Susan stood up and plunked her fists on her hips. "There's nothing wrong with wanting to go to bed with a man—particularly if he wants to go to bed with you."

"Well, he doesn't." She was no prude, but Susan's bluntness made Lauren squirm. "Drop it, please. Any theories on why we've lost We Serve U and the beauty-supply place both in the same week?"

"Whew." Susan raised her brows. "Was that why frost was on the Wakefield?"

"Mrs. Wakefield," Lauren corrected while she mentally selected one or two much more satisfying names for the woman. "Yes. She said we might learn a lesson from losing her account."

Susan shook her head slowly. "Makes no sense. We've done good work for them. More than they've been worth, really."

"I don't suppose—" As fast as an idea formed, Lauren dismissed it.

"What?"

"Oh, you don't think one of our people might have made any comments in places where they'd have been reported to Mrs. Wakefield, do you?"

"Not a chance!" Susan's eyes flashed. "You know as well as I do that nothing we hear goes anywhere but to the person who pays for the information and has a right to it."

"Sorry." Holding up her hand, Lauren stood. "I'm puzzled, that's all. It could be a coincidence and there may be no more defections. But if there are, I'm going to have to take a hard look at things around here."

"And I'll be right behind you." Susan cleared her throat and tossed back her hair. "When do you think you'll see Jack Irving again?"

Throwing up her hands, Lauren marched to the door. "Never, as far as I can see. Forget the whole thing, will you? I shouldn't have mentioned him."

"Because you really aren't all that interested?"

"That's correct." Lauren gripped the door handle.

"Good. I like to see a woman who isn't bowled over by a guy with a to-kill-for face and a body to match. It sickens me when a woman can be turned to putty by a pair of soft brown eyes, and a mouth that looks wasted if it's not being kissed, and curly blond hair you want to run your hands through."

Lauren realized her mouth was open. "Susan—"

"Wouldn't you think a mature woman could resist a pair of broad shoulders and a muscular chest and lean hips and long, powerful legs? Disgusting weakness."

"Stop it! I thought you hadn't even seen Jack."

"Hah!" Susan gripped her waist and laughed. Tears escaped the corners of her eyes and she covered her mouth. "I—I—"

"You, what? Did you drive by his house, go to the farm, what?"

With obvious effort, Susan sobered. "No. I asked Marilyn Wood at the copy shop what he looked like. She said he had brown eyes and dark blond curly hair. And that he was tall." She snickered again. "I made the rest up. But you recognized him, didn't you?"

Lauren's mouth twitched. "Get back to work. There's nothing between Jack and me and there won't be. And don't talk about it to gossips like Marilyn Wood."

"Yes, ma'am. Anything you say."

"And no interruptions that aren't imperative. Don't forget that. I'm very busy."

Alone again, Lauren tipped back her head and closed her eyes. It would be so much easier if a woman who didn't arouse a man sexually or emotionally could feel equally ambivalent about him.

She didn't have time for this. Paying Mrs. Wakefield a personal visit might be a good idea.

The buzz of the intercom exasperated her. She leaned over the desk. "*Yes,* Susan?"

"I know the answer, but he insists I ask anyway."

"No. Tell him no, and don't even tell me the next time he calls."

"You've got it. Would it be all right if I ask him if I'll do instead?"

Lauren paused in the act of flipping off the speaker. "What?"

"If you don't want Jack Irving, is it okay if I say I'm available?"

Hot, then cold, Lauren walked around her desk and dropped into her chair. "You and I will talk later. Put him through."

Her heart broke into double time before she heard Jack say, "Hi, Lauren. Am I interrupting at a busy time?"

"Er, no. Not at all."

The muted click of Susan switching from the line made Lauren bare her teeth.

To MAKE SURE he didn't run into Jess, he'd booked the last available court time of the night. Having backed out of their regular match earlier in the evening, Jack didn't want to risk having to explain why he was available to play racquetball later as long as his partner was Lauren Taylor.

Advice from a friend was what he needed. That had been his persuasive excuse for inviting Lauren to play tonight. He underhanded a ball against the front wall, sidestepped and slapped another idle stroke before turning to watch through the glass back wall for her to come down the stairs to the lone basement court.

The only advice he needed was how to concentrate on the rest of his life when all he could think of was Lauren.

Silver striped court shoes appeared at the top of the stairs. Then came long, long shapely legs topped by very brief white shorts that curved into high cut slits at the sides. Her red-and-white striped tank top was even briefer than the one she'd worn last Sunday, and this one, tucked into the formfitting shorts, was tight over her full breasts.

Jack rolled his tongue back inside his dry mouth, smiled and held the door open for her. "Hi. I thought you'd decided to take a sauna or something."

She gave him a cool glance. "All you have to do is change. This coiffure takes time." She flipped her ponytail.

He noted her clean-scrubbed face with approval. That took a little time, too. No makeup to sweat through for this lady.

"Is something wrong?"

He'd been staring. "No." But from the moment she'd roared up to the club in her Honda—"I'll drive myself, thanks"—he'd wanted to ask what had upset her. A second question might have been, why had she come at all if she was in such a foul mood?

"Ready to warm up?"

He was already warm—and getting warmer. "Yes, ready."

"We don't have to do this, Jack. Maybe you'd rather go somewhere and talk."

Maybe he'd just rather go somewhere else—period. "I'm looking forward to this match and you're not going to wriggle out of it."

When she smiled she touched a part of him he didn't remember having. She made it impossible for him not to smile back. He relaxed a little. Her initial coolness didn't necessarily have anything to do with him.

"It's been a couple of weeks since I played," she said. "I hope you won't be bored."

He groaned and slapped a hand to his brow. "I see it all in living color. This is going to be a repeat of the famous table-tennis game. Please be kind to me."

She shrugged and pulled a red terry headband low over her brow. "I'm a lowly amateur. Almost a novice." With her racquet between her knees, she adjusted sweatbands on her wrists and pulled on a glove. "You're bigger and stronger and you'll probably wipe me out in two games, if I don't collapse first."

Sure. He swung his racquet and studied the way she went through a series of stretches. "A novice, huh?"

She ignored him and dropped to the floor to bend over her legs.

Jack leaned on the wall. Her legs were smooth, all the way up to the hint of very white lace where what there was of her shorts had hiked even higher.

"Aren't you going to stretch?"

And miss looking at her while she did? "I already have," he lied.

His father was still harping on the evils of getting involved in a relationship that could hurt him all over again—and Andy. And Jack had told him not to worry. Even if he were considering another marriage, which he wasn't, Lauren had given clear indications that marriage was the last thing she wanted from a man.

"Are you about ready?" Watching her threatened to destroy any hope he had of concentrating.

"Almost."

He shouldn't be here with her. But he'd been helpless, unable to think of not seeing her and this seemed the safest activity he could come up with.

She pulled on her toes and bent low over her knees.

Jack looked away. This wasn't working and it probably never would. He wanted her, mood swings and all. End of self-examination.

"Okay, let's go." Lauren hopped up. "You can serve."

"Ladies first."

She glanced around with mock surprise. "Yeah, well, how about men first, in the absence of ladies?"

Jack sighed and served. Jogging in place, Lauren let the ball go by without moving her racquet.

He caught the ball. "I thought you were ready."

"Just giving you a head start." She smiled grimly.

"I see. Second serve coming up."

He served again, deliberately easing up.

Lauren was a red-and-white streak he saw from the corner of his eye.

He never saw the ball until it ricocheted off a side wall for a second bounce.

Innocently checking her strings, she sauntered past him, retrieved the ball and took up position.

Ten minutes later he made a conscious decision to pull out all the stops. The lady was a vampire and he was scheduled to be her special of the night if he didn't get his act together.

He missed the next two balls.

"Game!" Her grin glittered. "This is fun."

"Glad you're having a good time," he muttered. "My serve?"

She nodded, snapping her hips from side to side.

Jack subdued a shudder. He was allowing sex to get in the way and that wasn't what this was about...was it?

He played in earnest. *The other body on this court is good old Jess. Fix the thought, Jack. That flash of red and white and skin is Jess. And you're going to blow him out of the water.*

The play took on first a furious, then what felt uncomfortably like a violent flavor. Lauren stopped meeting Jack's eyes. She was good, extremely good—he'd hand her that—but he had the uneasy sensation that each time she slammed the ball she saw something he didn't see, some enemy she punished.

Another sickening thought came. Was she punishing him? That couldn't be. She had no reason.

The pace increased even more.

After a long fight, Jack took the second game. "Want to rest?" he asked. "You look like you could use some water."

She ignored him and walked to the opposite side of the court.

"Did you hear what I said?" He narrowed his eyes and stayed where he was.

"I'm not thirsty. Serve."

"What's the matter with—"

"Serve. That's what we're here for, isn't it?"

"By all means." He did as she asked, but muffed the shot and watched her take the point, and line up for the next serve.

It was a bomb, but angry people dealt well with bombs. And he was getting angrier by the second. Skidding, ducking for a volley, he lunged to take the ball on the fly and stumbled into his opponent.

He caught her arms and stared into her black eyes. Expressionless eyes. Sweat coursed down the sides of her face and her lips were parted. Her breath came in short gasps.

Jack let his gaze linger on her mouth.

"My serve, I think." She shrugged away and the play continued, but only for one more point.

"Watch it!" Jack stretched and ran for a shot before he saw her coming at him.

Too late. They hit again, hard this time, and he couldn't stop the fall.

"Oof." Lauren gritted her teeth and grabbed for him.

They went down in a jumble of arms and legs, and red and white, and slick skin.

The face that stared up at him bore no resemblance to Jess Parker. Nor did the sleekly voluptuous body he felt all too acutely.

Breathing hard, he propped his weight on his elbows. "Are you all right?"

"Yes, damn it. I'm great."

"What's with you?" He narrowed his eyes. "What the hell's eating you?"

"Nothing." She pursed her lips and tried to squirm away. "I'm competitive. Does that hurt your ego?"

Jack pushed their racquets away and pinned her by the wrists. "My ego isn't at stake here. And you aren't even playing me. You're using that ball to beat the crap out of something that has nothing to do with me."

She rolled her head away and attempted to shift again. The motion did things she'd undoubtedly had no intention of doing. His body leaped and a dull heat inflamed his brain.

"Let me go."

"Look at me."

She struggled and he felt a violent surge of desire.

"Look at me, Lauren."

"All right." Her eyes, when they met his, brimmed with tears.

"Oh... Oh, Lauren."

He brought his mouth carefully down on her trembling lips. One wrong move and he'd lose control. Then it would all be over. Jack forced his mind into neutral and gave his all to feeling her mouth gradually soften beneath his.

Her breasts, an insistent pressure on his chest, rose and fell and dark fire pierced his belly, his groin.

Slowly, brushing, touching, tasting, he moved her face from side to side. Wrenching against his hands reminded him he still held her captive. He released her wrists and she wound her arms about his neck, sighing softly with each short breath she took.

He felt her fury ebb. Rolling sideways he brought her with him. Lauren stared into his eyes, pushed him, and sent him to his back. Straddling his hips, she took control, holding his wrists as he'd held hers, and staring down into his face.

"Lauren—"

"Don't talk." Her skin glistened. Bent over him, she studied his face, then ran a hand from his wrist, down his arm, to his chest. Resting her fingers lightly on the side of his neck, she kissed him again, parting his lips with the tip of her tongue.

Jack groaned, and shifted against his arousal. Lauren closed her eyes.

"We're on the floor of a racquetball court," he whispered in a brief second of lucidity.

Her mouth moved again, a whispering, featherlike caress that started a burning pulse.

Lauren raised her head, and used her hands on his shoulders to push herself up. He panted, watching her through slitted eyes. Moisture shone on every inch. A shining line disappeared into the cleavage between her breasts.

He had to touch her.

She bowed her head, swung from him and sat on the floor.

Jack got up slowly and knelt beside her. "Lauren." He kissed her neck and she tilted her head to give him better access. "We need to go somewhere else."

Her lips parted but she didn't say anything.

With one finger he slid a track from her jaw, over her slick skin, down to the swell of her breasts where the tank top gaped.

She shuddered and turned into his arms. "Kiss me again."

He did as she asked, pulling her to him, letting his hand slip farther inside the tank top until she shuddered again and jerked away. "No," she said quietly. "This is no good."

"You're so right."

He stood and pulled her up and they came together again in another brief, searing kiss that made him pray for privacy—now.

"We'd better go." Lauren put distance between them and held him off when he tried to catch her once more. "I'm going to shower and change."

"That wasn't enough, Lauren. Not for me."

She stroked his cheek. "Not for me, either. But I think we'd better stop this, Jack. We don't have any place to go from here."

"Why?" The anger began to return. "I want you. You want me. We're both free."

"That's not enough and you know it."

He wasn't letting her get away, not that easily. "Andy's spending the night with his grandfather. Come back with me."

"No."

"I'll behave myself."

She smiled grimly. "Why don't I quite believe you?"

"Because you don't want to?"

"Maybe."

He pressed her. "Come anyway. I won't force you into anything you don't want."

Her eyes said she was afraid she wanted what she didn't think she should have.

"Come, Lauren. There's too much between us to just walk away and pretend it doesn't matter."

"No."

"Lauren—"

"Okay!" She smoothed back escaped hair in that way that made it hard for him to keep his eyes on her face. "Okay, Jack. I'll come. But we're going to talk and that's all."

"Whatever you say." He'd take what he could get, no matter how unsatisfactory. But he knew he would pursue her one way or another.

In the locker room, he showered quickly, lathering down, rinsing with cold water which did nothing to cool his blood. From the women's locker room next door, came the muffled sound of another shower. His teeth jarred together. She'd be washing her hair, her arms raised in that posture she struck so often. And her body would be naked. He locked his knees.

Half an hour later, Lauren joined him in the balmy darkness outside the club. She wore a loose sweatshirt and jeans. Her hair had been dried and fell softly about her face. Jack rammed his hands into his pockets to keep from seizing her and kissing her again.

"We could leave your car here," he said. "I promise to get you back at a reasonable hour."

She appeared to hesitate. "Well...okay." She smiled and his heart pounded in his throat.

"I'll throw my things in my car."

As she opened the door of the Honda he was startled to hear a ring.

"What—"

"Car phone," she said matter-of-factly, reaching in to pick up the instrument. She dropped to sit on the passenger seat. "Lauren Taylor."

Noncommittal noises punctuated silences as she listened. Jack moved closer and she looked up at him, a frown drawing her brows together.

"What is it?" he mouthed.

She shook her head. "I'm sorry, Dan, but this isn't my problem."

Jack scrutinized her closely, cursing Taylor for his rotten timing.

"Look," she said. "It'll all blow over. It has before. She's young. Don't forget that."

Good grief. The guy was calling his ex-wife to complain about the current one. "Lauren!"

She covered the receiver. "This won't take long." Into the phone she said, "I really don't think it would do any good for me to talk to her. She hates me, Dan."

Jack crossed his arms.

"*You* tell her," Lauren said. "Tell her there's absolutely nothing between you and me and hasn't been..." Her chest rose sharply and something like pain passed over her features. "Dan, remind Christie that the two of you were sleeping together for months before we split up.... I'm not throwing it up at you. I'm stating facts."

He couldn't believe this. If he didn't think she'd be furious, he'd hang the phone up for her.

"Dan, you told me the reason you no longer wanted sex with me was because I couldn't make you feel alive the way Christie could. I believed you. Tell her that if she's having doubts."

Jack rubbed at his jaw. An almost uncontrollable urge to do Dan Taylor damage rocked him "Lauren."

She shook her head again, but her eyes were closed. "Yes, we did make peace," she said in a low voice. "For old times' sake. But you're asking me for too much."

Seconds of silence passed.

"She won't listen to me. If she wants to believe there's still something between you and me there's nothing I can do to change her mind." Lauren swung her legs into the car and rested her head against the seat. "Okay, yes. Please don't say anymore. I'll talk to her, Dan. But this is it. The last time."

Jack ground his hands into fists.

"Tomorrow," Lauren said and hung up. She got out of the car, evaded Jack's hand and walked around to the driver's side.

"Where are you going?" He slammed the passenger door. "Lauren, answer me."

"Home," she said. "I'm going home."

"Because of *him?*" He pointed to the car phone.

"Because of what I almost forgot." She opened her door. "I almost forgot I'm too old for this, and too tired. Take my advice, Jack. Forget me."

CHAPTER EIGHT

"Yes, I'm going to make a police report, Dad. And no, I don't want to talk about Lauren. Not to you. Not to anyone."

"Good." Jack's father settled his big, rough hands on the table. He appeared neither relaxed nor mollified.

Jack frowned. Across the restaurant he could see Barney Middleton talking to another patron. Dining out had been Dad's idea, a surprising one from a man who preferred to eat at home. The thought came to Jack that Denton Irving was a smart man who knew his son well, knew he was less likely to make a scene in a public place. Here there was a better chance that Jack would be forced to listen with apparent attention to almost anything his father decided to say.

"That night when Lauren was at my house, did you call Andy or did he call you?"

"I thought you didn't want to talk about Lauren." Dad eyed an approaching waiter.

"I don't," Jack muttered.

"That's what I was hoping to hear. You're coming to your senses."

Before Jack could respond, the waiter arrived and Barney's voice boomed across the room, "They're having the eggplant, Colin."

Jack gave Barney a wave. Barney always decided what his friends would eat. "I'll have a beer. How about you, Dad?"

They ordered and his father sat, stolidly waiting, until they'd both been served drinks. "I talked to Len Gogh and Matt Carson."

"And?"

"They're worried."

Jack slid his glass back and forth over the red-and-white checked tablecloth. "And you think I'm not?" This renewed interest his father was showing in the business would have pleased him if he didn't think it was a cover for something else, a means to oversee all of Jack's life more closely.

"I think a woman can get in the way of a man's thinking."

"Coming from you—" Jack closed his mouth and averted his face. What was getting into him? He'd almost reminded his father that his mother had mattered more to him than anyone or anything.

"Your mother wasn't like any other woman, son."

His father wouldn't get an argument on that. "I know. We were lucky."

"You've said it. And then some." Dark brows drew together. "Got any idea who's behind this nonsense at the farm?"

Saying that "nonsense" was mild for the kind of dangerous tampering they'd suffered wouldn't help. "No. Len and I can't make anything add up. It's starting to look as if the bum seed labeling was a one-time shot, but there was enough product involved to make plenty of trouble for us."

"Anything else happen? Since you found out about the seeds?"

"No. We've got a watch system going and as far as we can make out everyone's lily-white. Making the police report is just covering bases as far as I'm concerned."

His father swallowed some beer and leaned back to let the waiter put a plate in front of him. "I know I haven't spent much time around the farm in recent years. Doesn't mean I'm not interested."

Jack sampled the eggplant. "You don't have to explain. Any time you feel like—"

"I'm retired," Dad cut in. "Maybe I'd enjoy coming out a little more often. Nothing more. Andy called me."

"What?" Jack set down his fork. "When?"

"You asked if I called him or he called me. He called me. Had a lot to say about that woman."

"I see." For several minutes, Jack ate in silence. Getting angry would accomplish nothing. "That woman is Lauren, Dad. Lauren Taylor. And she's a friend of mine." He'd like her to be a great deal more. In the week since he'd seen her, a week when he'd replayed the episode at the club over and over, he'd barely managed to get her to speak to him on the phone.

"Andy talked a lot about her."

"He likes her," Jack said.

"What do you think I'm getting at here?"

Jack sighed. In bed at night he saw her...as good as felt her, damn it. He thought about her a dozen other times a day, too. And she'd made it plain she'd just as soon he went away and stayed away. Only, he wasn't giving up—not yet. Regardless of what the future held for the two of them, if anything, he knew what he felt and he wasn't finished with Lauren.

"Are you listening to me, Jack?"

"Listening, and hearing. Do you think this is any of your business?"

His father showed no sign of offence. "What happens to my grandson is my business. He's—"

"So how's the masterpiece?" Barney arrived, pulled up a chair and rested his elbows on the table. He beamed, his round face shiny. "Best Italian food in town, huh?"

Jack concentrated on his plate. "It's good, Barn." He'd like to be just about anywhere but here.

"Too long since we saw you, Denton," Barney said in a tone that spelled cheerful oblivion to the antagonism in the air.

"Got to make an appointment to see my own son these days," Jack's father said. "Figured the offer of a good meal might get to him."

"Good thinking. Good thinking." Barney chortled. "Guess the boy here's got other things on his mind, these days."

Jack looked up in time to see Barney give Dad a meaningful wink.

"What would that be?" His father's eyes were innocently lowered.

"Ah, don't give me that." Barney elbowed Denton, who dropped a forkful of food. "Sorry. Our Jack's got pretty good taste in companions, wouldn't you say?"

Jack aimed a narrow-eyed warning at Barney, who didn't notice.

"Plays a mean game of racquetball, huh?" Barney laughed and repeated the wink, this time in Jack's direction. "One of the regulars said he never saw anyone look the way Lauren does in shorts."

Jack glowered and caught his father's eye. "I wasn't aware the whole town knew Lauren and I had played a game."

"Hah! You know how this town works. We're all interested in our favorite people."

"All gossips, you mean," Jack muttered.

Barney laughed again. "Bet racquetball isn't the only game she plays well, hey, Jack?"

Jack pushed his plate aside. His father's face was cast in a mold that belonged on Mount Rushmore. "Barn, Lauren's a friend of mine. Cut the personal crap, okay?"

"Okay, okay." Barney held up his palms. "Didn't mean to step on any toes."

"Forget it." Jack felt cornered.

Barney's smile was quickly back in place. "Bit touchy about a simple friendship, aren't we?"

Sometimes, like now, it was hard not to tell Barney to get lost. "End of subject" was all Jack said.

"Maybe not." His father had been observing, his eyelids at half-mast. "What I'm going to say isn't for general consumption. Got that, Barney?"

"Got it." Barney shifted in his chair and studied his fingernails.

"I mean it. I'm only talking in front of you because I know Jack trusts your judgment. He knows the 'crap', as he puts it, is all a cover—"

"I—"

"Shut up and listen."

Jack looked sharply at his father. "Dad—"

"You, too. I may be old, but I'm not senile."

"I know that." This had definitely been a bad idea. He caught Barney's eye and saw discomfort and sympathy there—and apology.

"Some men can afford to make mistakes with women. You can't, Jack. Not when you've got a son who's obviously ready for some-one he can think of as the mother he never had."

"Dad, aren't we getting ahead of ourselves, here? Lauren and I—"

"Are just friends. Yeah, so you keep telling me. Only I know what I'm seeing in you. And it isn't anything I've ever seen before. Not even with Mary."

"Dad—"

"No. I'm pulling rank. I'm your father. You'll listen while I talk. Then, since you're no kid, if you want to forget every word, there isn't a damn thing I can do about it. Right, Barney?"

"Er, right." The normal ruddiness of Barney's face turned to puce. He picked up a glass and drank, obviously forgetting that the beer was Jack's.

"You thought you loved Mary, didn't you?"

"I *did* love her." He felt the heavy throb of the pulse at his temples.

"Do you remember how it felt when she took off to Paris to do her damn fool painting?"

"Er, Denton, maybe I should—"

"Maybe you should sit right where you are and listen, Barney. Then you won't be so likely to encourage what's wrong."

"Wrong!" The word exploded from Jack. He made fists on the table.

"Wrong," his father said calmly. "I know the signs, my boy. You're ready to take a big fall."

From the corner of his eye, Jack caught sight of Barney's miserable expression. There was nothing to be done about that. "How many times do I have to tell you you're making a big deal out of nothing?"

"That may be." His father appeared serene now. Now that the damage was on a roll. "I just want to be sure you've looked at all the angles and that you don't run blindly into the biggest mistake of your life."

"This is… I'm not talking about this anymore."

"That's good. You be quiet and I'll talk some more. I know what it's like to love someone so much the rest of the world can go to hell. And I know what it's like when you don't have that person around anymore. You've gone through it once. I saw how you hit bottom, boy. I couldn't go through that again and I don't think you can, either. And I know damn well your boy shouldn't be put through another piece of business that tells him he's replaceable."

Jack stared. "In other words, you think it would be better for me never to try for another real relationship with a woman in case it doesn't turn out?"

"In case she hurts you like you've already been hurt. Don't risk it. That's my advice."

Barney cleared his throat.

"Sit where you are," Denton snapped.

Jack felt tired. "For God's sake, Lauren's a friend, nothing more. Now, can we leave it at that?"

"Sure—" his dad picked up what was left of his beer "—once I've said one more thing. Can you tell me you don't look at that woman and think about taking her to bed?"

Blood rushed to Jack's face. "For—"

"Can you?"

"Well—"

"Exactly. I shouldn't have to tell a man of your age this, but I guess I'm just going to have to." Pulling himself very upright in his chair, his father drummed the table. "A man and a woman attracted to each other. A man and woman capable of doing what men and women do together..." He let the sentence trail.

"Dad—"

His father waved a hand. "That man and woman can't be just friends."

LAUREN PRETENDED to be engrossed in her newspaper. She was very aware of Betty moving restlessly around the kitchen.

Since the mysterious weekend trip, Lauren had tried to believe nothing had changed, but there were too many signs to the contrary.

"Business good at the service, is it?" Betty asked.

Lauren had known the other woman needed to talk but was afraid of what she wanted to say. "Generally. We've lost several customers for reasons that escape me."

"Isn't putting you in a bind, is it?" Betty was making conversation, skirting whatever was on her mind.

"Not yet. It will if it continues. I get the feeling there's something going on I'm not aware of. But it could just be that the cancellations have come in a bunch and I'm making too much of them."

"That's probably it."

Betty turned away and clattered pots in the sink. She'd be late for work if she didn't leave soon, but Lauren wasn't about to tell her so.

She rattled the paper. "How's the job going?"

"Fine!" The pots banged some more, and Betty ran water too hard into the sink. Spray splattered the window. "Darn it all anyway."

Lauren's heart thudded unpleasantly. "Leave it. I'll clean up after Cara goes to bed." The girl had been upstairs when Lauren got home and had still to put in an appearance.

"I'm on edge," Betty admitted, turning to smile sheepishly. "I've got a lot on my mind."

Lauren sensed this was supposed to be her opening to ask questions. "I know how that can be." Whatever was wrong, she had an increasingly strong hunch she didn't want to know. "Shall I call Cara down to say goodbye?"

"I'll run up before I go. She's got a bunch of homework—"

The door swung open and Cara trailed in. "Dumb math." More wisps than usual sprang into curls around her face.

"Problems?" Lauren folded her paper and put it on the table. "When your mom leaves I'll give you a hand."

Cara mumbled something about multiplication and Lauren prayed she'd be able to handle whatever new ways the school system had now found to accomplish the process.

"I suppose I'd better leave." Betty hovered.

"It is after seven." Lauren could feel Betty's indecision, feel her wanting, but not knowing how to say what was on her mind.

"You be good for Lauren," Betty said finally, sweeping the child into her arms and squeezing, "Be very good and get to bed early. And don't take up a lot of Lauren's time with your math. You can work it out yourself. You're a clever girl, thank goodness."

"Nobody else thinks so." Cara's bright eyes were cross behind her glasses. "Mrs. Beaman says I'm a dreamer."

"Oh, Cara." Betty pulled on a parka over the sweatshirt and jeans she wore for work. "You've got to learn not to spend your time gazing out the window. Your father never knew how to concentrate long enough to make something of himself."

Lauren bit her lip, holding back her irritation with Betty.

"Yes, Mom," Cara said, her small face pinched.

Be a dreamer, Lauren wanted to say. *Be who you are. You're wonderful.* And, beneath it all, seethed the longing to be able to call this child her own. That couldn't be and she had no right to the thought.

Betty gathered her purse and pulled out her car keys. "Tidy yourself up," she said to Cara. "You look messy."

Lauren felt a rush of sympathy for the woman. She was troubled and pressured and she'd had hard years since she'd been left with only rusty working skills to support a child. The previous day, Lauren had finally found the courage to broach the subject of contact lenses for Cara. Betty had looked instantly worried and cornered and Lauren decided she wouldn't mention the topic again.

"I'm off, then." Betty ran her fingers through her curly hair and smiled. "You two will be all right?"

"Of course." Cara scowled. "We're always all right. We look after each other, don't we, Lauren?"

Her stomach dropped. "We sure do."

"Yes, well—" Betty shoved the handle of her purse over her shoulder. "It's just I feel guilty sometimes."

"Guilty?" Lauren raised her brows.

"You've done so much for us."

Before Lauren could respond, Betty rushed from the house.

"Don't mind Mom," Cara said, too loudly. "She's been like that lately. Ever since..."

Lauren held her breath, waiting for the girl to say more, but Cara didn't continue. She scuffed into the living room and Lauren followed.

She was reading too much into too little, Lauren decided.

"Is school going all right?" Deliberately affecting nonchalance, she settled into the soft blue love seat that faced a matching couch. "Did your teacher like the story you wrote?"

"Yeah. And you don't have to worry about the math," Cara said. "I've got it figured out now. No sweat."

"I'm not worried about it. I like to help."

"Yeah." Cara flopped into her favorite chair, cream-colored corduroy, with a swivel base that allowed her to hook a leg over one arm while scooting herself in circles.

"Shall we watch TV?"

"If you want."

Lauren fidgeted. "Only if you want to."

"I don't want to." With one sneakered foot, Cara thumped the floor rhythmically, shoving the chair around and around.

"Is something wrong?" Lauren couldn't miss the serious set of Cara's features.

"Nah."

But there was something on the child's mind. School, home, the kids, her mother. Lauren mulled over the possibilities and felt helpless.

"Oh—" she remembered the bag beside the couch. "—I've got something for you."

The chair stopped revolving.

Lauren leaned over and retrieved the brown sack she'd substituted for the store bag. "Not much, but I thought you might like them."

Cara sat upright, her hands trapped between her knees, her shoulders hunched. Lauren could feel the girl's anticipation.

"What do you think?" She pulled out a neon green sweatshirt.

"Wow." Cara's loud breath held delight. "Awesome. That's my favorite color."

"I know."

The smile disappeared as quickly as it had come. "Mom says I'm not to let you buy me things."

"This is different," Lauren said quickly, but her heart raced. "I had some shirts made up for the service—to give out as promotional incentives." Lying didn't come easily, but this was a special occasion with extenuating circumstances.

"What does it say on the front?"

"Contact." That had been an inspiration and who knew, maybe she would get some more, for employees perhaps. "I thought it would be...well, you know...meaningful?"

Cara's blank glance said she didn't see anything meaningful; not in the way Lauren meant. "Contact. Yeah, I'll—" She frowned and pursed her lips. "It's okay."

Lauren smothered a grin. "I had two of them." She produced a second, identical shirt. "D'you suppose Jimmy would like it? I kind of thought you could add it to your club, or whatever you call yourselves. No name but Contact, maybe?"

"Yeah," Cara whispered. "Jimmy'll like it a lot. He never gets anything till his big brother's finished with it." She took the two shirts, spread them along the back of the couch and smoothed the rubberized letters Lauren had had applied. "You don't think Mom'll say we can't have 'em?"

"I know she won't." Let her try. Betty would find herself no match for Lauren at her most persuasive. "They're just leftovers, so I had to find someone to give them to."

Cara turned to Lauren. Her face was pink, her eyes glittering.

Without warning, the girl launched herself, wrapped her thin arms around Lauren's neck and buried her warm face. After an instant's hesitation, Lauren returned the hug, breathing in the scent of soap and dust and feeling silky hair on her cheek.

"I guess you really like them," she said, swallowing against the lump in her throat.

"They're totally awesome. I love you. I'll love you for always, no matter what."

Lauren's heart seemed to pause. She closed her eyes. "I love you, too." And she did. And it was worth the way she felt now for as long as she was given to enjoy it.

As abruptly as she'd thrown herself at Lauren, Cara extricated herself and gathered up her treasures. "I'll take them upstairs and put them in my bag for tomorrow."

"Great. Then a snack? Popcorn—"

The phone rang.

Cara ran, grinning, from the room while Lauren picked up the receiver and said, "Hello."

"Lauren. This is Susan. I hope I'm doing the right thing by calling, but I thought you might like to know."

Lauren's scalp tightened. "What is it? Problems?"

"Not really. At least, not the kind you mean. You probably don't want me bothering you with this."

"Susan, tell me. Now." Lauren stood very straight, every nerve on alert.

"Okay. Irving's packing plant is on fire."

A DULL RED GLOW SHIVERED in the night sky. Lauren slammed the accelerator to the floor. She'd called Jack's home and had gotten no reply. Arranging for a teenager from one of the neighboring town houses to stay with Cara had taken precious moments when all

Lauren had wanted was to rush to the farm. Now she drove much too fast, but she had to get there.

Glaring pink lights hit her rearview mirror and a siren wailed. She pulled to the side of the road to allow an engine to race by, followed by another, and a third.

Trembling, she traveled in their wake. She'd driven past the farm's huge acreage before without as much as a thought for what it represented: an old and very successful enterprise. Parked opposite the entrance with its illuminated swinging sign, Lauren peered toward the chaos she could see in the distance.

Why had she come?

The answer wasn't comfortable. Jack Irving would be there and she wanted to be here; not only as a concerned friend, but because she cared about him as a man.

In her mind she saw the way his upper lip curled away from his teeth when he smiled, the deep dimples that formed.

There was nothing she could do to help.

In the white glare of the searchlight she saw men running. Jets of water arced over flames.

She could be there, just be there—let him see her. Every day for the past week he'd called and she'd been polite but deliberately short because she was afraid, not of him, but of herself. He'd been fair enough not to mention her response to him at the club. He didn't have to. The scene replayed and replayed in her mind, in vivid color, complete with sensations.

The jury was still out in the case of Jack Irving and Lauren Taylor.

Stuffing down her doubt, Lauren got out of the car and ran across the road. Inside the farm gates a wide drive curved between the greenhouses. She ran on, toward the fire.

On her right, a shed loomed. Lights showed in windows at one end. Lauren hesitated.

"North corner, Frank," a voice boomed over a bullhorn.

Lauren shrank back. A blast of heat shivered through air laced with acrid fumes and bursts of red sparks. But the flames seemed lower...didn't they?

The men were more distinct now. Fire fighters slipped rapidly back and forth, swift in their movements as they seemed to follow hand signals and nods from each other's masked faces more than the few commands barked. Their yellow hats and suits were ludicrously cheerful splashes against the charred and crumbling outline of a disintegrating building.

A hand, closing on her arm, jarred her to the bone.

"Lauren?"

She swung around and looked into Jack's soot-streaked face. "Jack. I'm so sorry, I—"

"Get back from here." In the ghastly flicker, his eyes shone dark and angry.

"Yes. I'm sorry. I only thought you might need—"

"I do," he said. His hand moved from her arm to rest heavily on her shoulder. "The bastards. They've got what they wanted now."

"No," Lauren whispered. She cleared her throat. "Jack, come away."

"I can't."

"Then I'm staying, too."

For an instant, his stare slid to the scene behind her. "Andy's in the office. I didn't want my dad to see this so I couldn't take Andy to his place."

"Where is the office?"

Jack looked at her again and nodded over his shoulder at the shed.

"I'll wait with him," she said.

Without responding, Jack moved past her. Lauren caught his arm. "Be careful."

He nodded, studied her face for a long moment, and strode away.

Lauren watched him go, a tall, lean man in a gaping cotton shirt torn at one elbow and jeans splotched with oily black smears.

But his back was straight and he walked with purpose.

Lauren smiled, a small, tight smile. Whoever had taken on Jack Irving had started a fight that wouldn't be one-sided.

She found Andy in the shed with lighted windows. The windows were in an unpretentious office at the end of the building overlooking what, in daylight, would be flower fields.

"Hi, Andy." She approached the boy who stood, staring toward the fire.

He turned. "Hi." The corners of his mouth pulled in. "Did my dad call you?"

"No." Smiling with effort, she slid her car keys into her jeans pocket and pulled off her jacket. "I heard what was happening and came out to see if there was anything I could do."

"Boy, is my dad gonna be mad."

Lauren's smile came more easily. "You bet he will be. And I don't blame him. He's going to need you to talk to after this."

"Yeah." With a huge sigh, his chest rose and fell. "He's been...well, you know... Anyway he's gonna get even worse after this."

Lauren went to stand beside Andy at the window. "How has your dad been?"

"Grandpa would say like he had a bug...." The boy looked straight ahead but his pale face had begun to turn pink. "He's been kinda cranky for days."

So Jack had been in a bad mood for days—about a week, maybe? Just about the length of time she'd been snapping at everyone at the office and pounding the floor at the aerobics studio like a possessed woman. And it was no coincidence.

"Your dad's had a lot on his mind. I expect he's told you there have been some problems with the farm." She hoped she wasn't speaking out of turn.

"Yeah. Grandpa talked about it, too. And he's mad, too."

"Well, he spent a lot of years working here himself. He's bound to feel tied in to whatever happens to the farm."

Andy held onto the windowsill and put his nose on the glass. "I don't think it's the farm he's mad about. He seems angry with my dad about something."

Lauren felt awkward. "Fathers and sons have differences. I expect you and your dad disagree sometimes." She sighted a coffee maker and a box containing packages of hot chocolate. "Would you like something hot to drink?"

"Okay. I wish Dad would come back."

So did Lauren. "I'll heat some water."

"You like my dad, don't you?"

Startled, at a loss for words, she pushed back her hair.

"He likes you." He turned his head toward her. "Know how I know?"

"Tell me."

"He had you over for dinner and I ate with you. We've never done that before." His shrug was elaborate. "Not since my mom. That was when I was just little."

Lauren couldn't think of an answer. She swallowed. His posture was rigid, belying the unconcerned words.

"Do you like him?"

"Of course I do," she said in a rush, making much of switching on the burner under a pot of water. "I like him very much. He's a nice man. That's why I came out when I heard about the fire and he said he'd like me to come and keep you company." *A nice man.* How silly it sounded.

"You saw Dad?"

Lauren felt the child's anxiety. "Yes. Outside. I told you he asked me to come and stay with you."

"Mmm. The fire isn't so big anymore, is it?"

She glanced at the window and tore the top off a packet of hot chocolate. "Not nearly so big. They'll have it out soon. What is that building?"

"It's where they put seeds and bulbs in packages and stuff. They get shipped out from there. And plants."

"I see." She was afraid she saw too much. *They've got what they wanted now,* Jack had said. "That must be pretty important."

Andy didn't appear to hear.

Lauren emptied the chocolate powder into an old brown mug, poured hot water over it and took the drink to the boy. "Here. This'll warm you up."

His hands, when he took the mug, shook. "He wouldn't let me go with him."

"That's because he worries about you. He wants to be sure you're safe." After a moment's hesitation, she smoothed back tousled black curls. Joe's hair had been dark. Lauren dropped her hand and stared through the window. There had never been as much as a few written words since she'd said goodbye to Joe, but she thought of him often and prayed the world would be kind to him.

"I want to be sure Dad's safe," Andy said in a small voice. "I'm scared."

Lauren chewed her lip. It was happening again: the subtle pull of a child. "He'll be okay. The firemen won't let anything happen to him." Please let that be true.

"He doesn't listen to people sometimes," Andy whispered. "Not when he's mad."

Lauren looked sideways at the boy. Tears stood in his eyes. "Oh, Andy." She caught the cup the instant it would have slopped chocolate, set it down and gathered Andy into her arms.

Gradually the rigid body relaxed. He held onto her shirt and sniffed.

Minutes passed. Lauren closed her eyes and felt a trembling inside. Jack wouldn't do anything foolish, would he? She wanted to see him walk through the door.

"Do you want some of that chocolate now?" She peered down into Andy's face. "If we watch, we'll see when Jack—your dad—comes."

They stood, side by side, Lauren's arm around the child's shoulder, his around her waist, for what felt like hours. The flames steadily diminished to an occasional burst that was quickly extinguished. Shouts came to them even through windows that didn't open.

Eventually all the engines left but one. Water continued to arc over what was now a smoking hulk. The sounds of axes and falling debris joined the other noises.

"Are you two okay?"

Lauren jumped and turned. "Are you all right?" She hadn't heard Jack come in. "We've been waiting," she added lamely, searching his blackened face and clothes for signs of injury. She found none.

"I'm terrific," he said, his eyes narrowed on her and Andy. "You looked after each other, huh?"

She managed a smile. "Andy looked after me."

The boy slipped from her and went to look up at his father. Silently he walked into the man's arms and they hugged one another.

Either she had to look away or cry at the special picture they made.

She looked away. "It looks bad," she said. "Andy explained what the building was for."

"I'm glad you put it in the past tense," Jack said. He scrubbed at his eyes. "God knows what we'll be able to save. Some of the equipment may be salvageable. That'll take time."

"Does it mean—" There was so little she knew about his business. "Will it make a big difference?"

His laugh was short and bitter. "You might say that. Irving's seeds and bulbs are going to be a memory for some time. And God knows how we're going to get the cuttings ready to go out."

Lauren wound her fingers together. "You'll pick up again."

"You bet your boots I will," Jack said in a tone that made Lauren lift her chin. He was aggressively confident. She'd hate to be Jack Irving's enemy.

"It, er… Do you think it could have been something to do with faulty wiring…? Something like that?"

Jack's smile was grim. "This was no accident." He held Andy tight against his side. "The fire chief agrees but he doesn't expect to come up with a culprit. Arson gets proved all the time, but finding the creep who set the fire doesn't happen often. An attempt's being made to take us out of contention in this business. But it's not going to happen."

"You should get home," Lauren said, quietly reveling in his determination. "You're going to need all the rest you can get to deal with what's waiting for you."

"Isn't that the truth." He raised a hand and let it fall heavily to his side. For an instant Lauren saw a shadow glaze his eyes. Confusion? Frustration? Probably both and so much more.

"Is there anything I can do for you, Jack?" She knew the answer and felt so helpless.

"I've got to wash some of this filth off. You did come in your own car, didn't you?"

"Yes." Disappointment sent Lauren's stomach plummeting. He was anxious for her to go. "You will let me know if there's anything I can do to help?"

He regarded her intently. "Yes, Lauren, I'll do that. Would you mind running Andy and me home? I came with Len Gogh, my overseer. He'll be here a while longer to answer any more questions and make a report for me. I'd like to get Andy home, though.''

The pleasure his request caused was absurd. ''I'll be glad to drive you.'' She suppressed a bubble of delight that threatened to make her grin.

Jack excused himself and returned ten minutes later with damp hair and a more or less clean face.

Outside the shed, the heavy odor of burned wood drifted on the wind. Gritty particles hurt Lauren's eyes.

Jack settled one hand on the back of Andy's neck, the other at Lauren's elbow and walked purposefully toward the road without looking back.

At the car, she pulled out her keys and gave them to him. ''You drive.'' It would give him something to think about and she felt too tired to concentrate.

Jack sent her a grateful glance as if he guessed she was trying to do some small thing to help his state of mind. She climbed into the back seat and Andy sat beside his father.

They drove south until Lauren saw the dark shimmer of Batiquitos Lagoon. Jack, silent since they'd left the farm, turned the Honda left onto La Costa and headed inland.

''It was good of you to come,'' he said finally.

''No problem.''

The quiet in the car felt thick. Andy slipped sideways against the door. Jack glanced at him. ''He's tired out, poor kid.''

''He was worried about you.''

''I don't like doing that to him.''

Lauren scooted forward and rested a hand on each of Jack's shoulders. She drove her thumbs into knotted muscle. ''Calm down,'' she told him. ''Andy's fine and so will you be. This'll blow over.''

He took a hand off the wheel to cover one of hers. ''I'm not sure it will. Not without one hell of a fight. Having you with me makes it feel possible, though.''

She bowed her head, closed her eyes. ''Good.'' It would be too easy to really fall for this man, fall badly in the way that ended up leaving you with the kind of wound no one with a brain would self-inflict.

"Andy thinks you're something."

"I think he's something." And the net closed a little tighter.

"Here we are." Jack drove the little car into his driveway and Andy jerked upright. "Home, son. Get yourself inside and into bed."

Andy was slow to react. Lauren leaned forward and rubbed his back. "You okay, Andy?"

"Uh-huh." He sounded sleepy. "Are you coming in with us?"

Lauren was glad to be in the back seat, in the dark. "Not tonight. It's too late. You get to bed."

"Will you come by soon?"

She hesitated, not answering.

"I'll make sure Lauren visits us soon, son," Jack said. "Take the door key and run along. I'll be right behind you."

Lauren climbed from the car behind Andy and watched him go into the house. Jack stayed where he was. Her heart thudded slowly and hard.

Slowly she turned back. In the pale wash of a yard light, with his chin atop his crossed hands on the steering wheel, he stared at her through the windshield.

Deliberately avoiding thought, Lauren climbed into the passenger seat beside him and closed the door. "I should get home. I have to start early in the morning."

"So do I. But I'm not going to sleep anyway."

She rested her head against the back of the seat. "I doubt if I will, either. It doesn't help, Jack, but I really am so very sorry."

"I know. And it does help. We've got big trouble that could make this a losing year. But we'll get things together. This is when diversification helps and we've got that over most other operations like ours." He sighed. "Damn, this hurts. The same question keeps going around and around in my brain. I'm fair, I'm good for this town—who would want to destroy me?"

"Don't torture yourself with questions. These people are never rational." She rolled her face toward him. "I know you'll get it together."

Jack stared back at her. "I really want to kiss you, Lauren. Is that okay?" As he asked, he leaned nearer. "I think I'm going to have to even if you say no."

Every moment she spent with him spelled danger, and more danger. Without bothering to reply, Lauren shifted, slipped her hands around his neck to tangle in his hair. Breathing softly, she brought her face close to his until she felt his breath, warm and clean, on her face.

The subdued light drew a slim line of dark shadow along the firm lines of his lips, shaded his sharp, straight nose and etched the dimpled grooves beside his mouth, the cleft in his chin.

"You smell like soot," she said quietly.

"I know. Do you kiss sooty men?"

"Only one sooty man." Her eyes lowered to study his mouth, then closed as her lips brushed his.

Carefully, letting her sensitive skin, the tip of her tongue, test and taste every nuance, she gradually deepened the kiss. Jack's sigh became a groan and he urged her closer, ran his hands around her waist and over her bare back beneath her shirt. His hands, firm yet gentle, moved again, coming to rest with his thumbs stroking the sides of her aching breasts.

When they were breathless, he pulled back, looked down into her eyes, kissed them both shut and cradled her face into the hollow of his shoulder. "My timing was never brilliant."

"Seems fine to me."

He gave a short laugh. "My son's in that house. My packing plant's a pile of rubble and ash, and what I want most is to stay right here with you."

What she wanted most was to be with him somewhere much more comfortable, like in his bed, or in hers. Her body throbbed.

"I'd better get going, Jack." But she didn't want to.

"Please don't leave until you make me a promise." He pulled the keys from the ignition and pushed them into his pocket. *"Please."*

Lauren stroked his face, kissed the corner of his mouth, and made herself sit, facing squarely forward. "What's the promise?"

"That you'll see me again soon."

She looked at sticklike hala fronds silhouetted against the sky. "I don't think I can make a promise like that. I don't think I should."

"You don't have a choice."

Unable not to, she smiled at him. "Why's that?"

He patted his pocket. "I've got the keys."

Sighing, she opened the door, got out and walked around the hood. By the time she reached his side he was out of the car and towering over her.

"Give me the keys, Jack."

"Will you see me again?"

"I don't know."

Gently he used his hips to push her against the car. "We'll have to work on that." With a finger and thumb he tilted up her chin and smiled into her eyes. The look flickered to her mouth and he lowered his lips slowly until they barely touched hers. Grazing back and forth, so lightly Lauren's legs weakened and tingled, he teased her mouth open with his tongue.

The kiss was tantalizing. Holding her with his fingers and his lips, Jack balanced her nerves on the edge of wildness before he raised his head again.

"Jack, I—"

This time he pulled her close, so abruptly she let out a small cry. "I'm not taking no for an answer." His next kiss was so thorough she was left panting. "Do you believe me now?" he said when he finally raised his head.

"We'll talk about it when we aren't both exhausted and over-emotional."

"No. I mean it, Lauren. This time you aren't getting away without telling me when I can be with you again."

"Why do you want to?" she asked and suffered a moment's shame at her own need to hear him tell her over and over. that he desired her.

"Today's Wednesday," he said. "That means you'll have two days to get ready."

She leaned back to see his face. "Get ready?"

"Buy a swimsuit."

"I don't know what you're talking about."

"Of course you do. You and I have a date on Saturday. Between now and then we'll both concentrate on the very serious pressures of our businesses. But on Saturday, I'm yours...and you're mine."

A chill worked up her spine. "I may be missing something, but I don't see what a swimsuit has to do with any of this."

Jack locked his hands around her waist, held his hips to hers and swung her gently back and forth. "I'll pick you up in the middle of the day. Say noon?"

"To go swimming? I don't swim, remember?"

"Exactly." His body, where it touched hers, was unyielding. "I'm going to teach you. Do *you* remember that? Only first we're going to lay around and do nothing. I've decided that what appeals to me most is being with you in the water when it's very, very dark."

She tingled all the way to her toes. "Jack—"

"Shush," he said against her lips. "Maybe we'll both learn something."

CHAPTER NINE

Candace Lane presided over her boutique with an air that suggested she'd consider it a deathblow to discover she didn't have what a potential customer desired.

"*Why* would you want to cover it up?" She rolled her eyes and tweaked the plunging neckline of the one piece coral-colored swimsuit Lauren wore even lower. "Most women would give their eye-teeth for a fraction of what you've got."

Lauren tried not to notice how much of her breasts were revealed between and on the sides of the stretched contours of the suit's top. "I wish I only had a fraction of it," she muttered grimly. "This won't do it, Candy. I'm not comfortable."

Candace puffed, sending her long blond bangs flying. Gracefully slim herself, she favored animal prints and sparkle but always managed to appear like a *Vogue* model. "Are you going to swim at the club, or what?"

"I don't know yet." The more tight-lipped she remained, the better in this town.

"If you're going to try for a tan," Candace rolled her eyes again, "though how you'd do that around here at the end of a May like we're having, I don't know. But if you are, why not go for a bikini? I've got a terrific little black number that has your name on it, darling."

"No way." Lauren shook her head emphatically, longing to get out of the coral suit.

Candace splayed long, pale peach-colored fingernails over her full mouth and appeared deep in thought. She hummed, running her eyes over Lauren. "Stay right where you are. Get that off and I've got something coming right up."

Lauren went into the dressing room, stripped, donned the robe hanging there and waited.

The door flew open and Candace triumphantly brandished a handful of what looked like black lace. "This is you. I don't know why I didn't think of it before. When I took it I thought, 'there isn't a body in this town to wear it.' I must have known you were coming in and then forgotten."

"Candy—"

"No. I won't listen to arguments. Put it on now."

The door slammed shut and Lauren held up the wisp of black stuff. If it didn't stretch a whole lot it was probably intended to be worn as panties with suspenders and a shirt underneath.

Grumbling, she tossed aside the robe and slipped into the suit. It did stretch and grow thinner and thinner until it covered, or almost covered, the essential parts like a black net body stocking. Clusters of polka dots, artfully placed, were scattered on gossamer thin Lycra that showed much too much skin beneath.

"I'm waiting," Candace sang out. "You've had plenty of time."

Wincing, Lauren stuck her head around the door. When she was sure she was still the boutique's only customer, she sidled out and stood, arms crossed, her weight on one leg.

"Oh my God." Candace dropped into a chair and stretched out her leopard-clad legs. "There's no justice in this world. I'd sell my soul—even my Porsche—to look like that."

"No way," Lauren said. "I'm not auditioning as a tabletop dancer."

"In that suit you could audition for anything you wanted and get it. It's yours and I'm not taking any arguments."

"Candy!"

"Have I ever steered you wrong?"

"Well." In fact, Candace had always sold her clothes that Lauren ended up enjoying. "I guess not."

"Exactly." With a satisfied grin, Candace got up and pulled Lauren's arms to her sides. Then she tweaked and molded the suit, pulling it higher at the hip, farther apart where the top angled down from thread thin straps. "Jack Irving, eat your heart out."

"Candy! What did you say?"

But the woman sauntered away, a knowing smile on her lovely face. "I'll just ring that up for you."

Lauren returned to the sidewalk, a small, shiny pink *Candace* box in hand and feeling slightly stunned. This whole town knew she'd been seeing Jack Irving.

She hurried across the street, checking her watch and silently berating herself for what she'd agreed to do next. After several attempts, she'd made contact with Christie Taylor and they were meeting for lunch at Garcias on State Street.

Lauren drove through town, dread mushrooming with every block she passed. The silver Mercedes she recognized as Christie's was already parked outside the restaurant.

She could drive on and pretend she'd forgotten the date. No, she couldn't. She'd promised Dan this one last favor and she'd do it to make sure he had no more excuses to badger her with. And anyway, it had begun to suit her to think of him as well settled in his marriage, hadn't it? Lauren wasn't sure she wanted to examine the question too closely.

Inside the cool, stucco building with its exposed beams and bright splashes of color, a pretty waitress in a peasant blouse and full skirt smiled and ushered Lauren across exposed wood floors. "Mrs. Taylor's waiting for you," the girl said and Lauren registered then quickly discarded the thought that Mrs. Taylor was waiting for another Mrs. Taylor. She'd once thought of changing her name back to Erickson, her maiden name, but never got around to the paperwork that entailed.

She slipped into a chair opposite Christie who leveled a hostile and slightly unfocused stare in her direction. The large margarita in front of her was almost drained and Lauren came to the uncomfortable conclusion that it might not have been Christie's first.

"How are you?" Lauren asked politely.

Christie lifted her chin. "Short of time."

"Oh." Lauren declined a drink from the cocktail waitress and asked for coffee. "We could order lunch if you're ready."

"I won't be eating. Let's get this over with. I'm only here to please Dan."

Which made two of them. Odd how one not-very-honorable man could command so much obedience. Lauren reminded herself that she was doing this for old times' sake, nothing more.

"How does it feel to be the one who lost out?" Christie's voice was slurred.

Lauren sighed. She bowed her head. "You and Dan have been married three years. My marriage to him is old, worn-out and not very interesting history."

"But you haven't forgotten, have you?" Christie tossed back her blond hair. "You'd still like to find a way to come between us if you could."

"No," Lauren said, striving for patience she didn't feel. "I've gotten to the point of thinking of Dan as someone I've known for a very long time—nothing more." Just when had that point come? Years ago? Maybe even before he'd said he was leaving?

Christie pouted. "And you think you can hold that over me. All the years you two have known each other. You use that to keep him running to you every time he decides he needs a shoulder to cry on."

"According to Dan, you made that suggestion before—to him. And you told him I was the one who let you know he'd been talking to me. It isn't true and you made up a lie because you're insecure. And now I think I'll go."

"You're jealous," Christie said. She tipped back her head and drained her glass. "You know Jack Irving's only after what he can get out of you and then he won't want you any more than Dan did. So you want to try to get Dan back again."

Lauren's cheeks burned. "What a horrible thing to say." And how was it that everyone in this town, a town where she hardly socialized at all, knew about the attention Jack had shown her?

"It may be horrible, but the truth hurts, doesn't it?" Christie gave a smug smile.

"Okay." Lauren took her wallet from her purse. "Dan asked me to tell you there's nothing between us. So I'm telling you, there's nothing between Dan and me. I'm not interested in him anymore. I wouldn't be here if I didn't believe he's basically a nice guy who gave in to an overdose of mid-life crisis—with a lot of help from you."

"You bitch."

"Be quiet. The people in my life don't talk like that." Lauren stood up and tossed down enough money to cover the price of coffee. "My advice to you is to examine what it is that makes you so insecure. Then see if you can't make something worthwhile of your marriage—for your child's sake if not for your own.''

''What do you mean, for *my* child's sake? Wednesday's Dan's, too.''

Lauren sighed. ''Yes, so you make a point of telling me whenever you get the chance. And I meant that, as well. Excuse me, but I've got a business to run.''

''Really? Still?''

''Yes.'' Lauren stopped and frowned. ''What did you mean by that?''

''Nothing.'' Christie signaled the waitress who was already approaching with Lauren's coffee. When the girl had put down the cup, frowned at Lauren and taken Christie's order for another margarita, Christie added, ''I meant that for someone with a business to run you seem to have a lot of free time to meddle in other people's lives.''

''Goodbye.''

''Stay away from Dan. Don't even talk to him. If you do, I'll make things even worse for you.''

Lauren hesitated. There was something that began to niggle here. ''How would you do that?''

''Isn't there somewhere else you'd rather live? You don't have anything to keep you in Carlsbad really, do you?''

Setting her mouth in a firm line, Lauren walked out and got into her car. She was barely aware of driving through sunlit streets and her heart didn't settle back into a normal rhythm until she was safely inside her office.

Predictably, Susan gave her only a few minutes to settle in before presenting herself on the other side of the desk, a stack of memos in hand.

''Don't tell me,'' Lauren said wearily. ''Someone else wants to quit.''

Susan sat down. ''As a matter of fact, two of them. Small Talk, the kids' clothing shop, and Sabina's. That's the tanning salon on—''

''I know where it is.'' Lauren sank back in her chair, deep in thought.

"Well," Susan said when the silence grew long, "what are you thinking?"

"That there's a certain pattern in all this. Put it out of your mind. I think I can deal with the problem as soon as I can decide on the right line of approach."

"If you say so." Clearly, Susan ached to ask what Lauren meant but sensed the timing was very wrong. "Would it be okay if I left a few minutes early today?"

Lauren looked up. "Hot date?"

"Well—" Susan visibly battled with her natural reticence over her private life "—as a matter of fact, yes." Her ivory skin turned bright pink.

Lauren grinned. "This has to be serious. I've never seen you look like an excited kid over anyone before."

"I don't now," Susan said crossly, getting up.

"Okay, okay. Have it your way."

There was a tap on the door and Yolande, one of Lauren's newest operators, poked her head into the office. "A gentleman to see you, Lauren. Mr. Irving. Shall I show him in?"

Susan made owl eyes and went toward the door.

"Er, yes." Lauren's stomach made a complete revolution. She ran her fingers through her hair, moistened her lips and gripped the edge of her desk.

"Thanks for seeing me. This won't take long." Denton Irving came in and closed the door firmly behind him.

When Lauren recovered from her surprise, she stood up. "Hello, Mr. Irving. How nice to see you."

"Hmph."

"Sit down, please."

"That won't be necessary. I understand you were out at the farm the other night. When that damn fire was going."

"Yes," Lauren said. "It was awful. I'm so sorry it happened."

Denton Irving straightened his shoulders inside a blue plaid shirt. "So am I. My son's had enough hard knocks in the past few years. He didn't need that."

"Of course not. No one needs that kind of thing."

"I'm not interested in anyone but my son. And my grandson." The man's dark brows were a startling contrast to his thick head of wavy white hair. His brown eyes bored into her. "I'm sure you have some idea why I'm here."

She didn't. "Is there anything you think I can do to help?"

"Four years ago my son's wife left him. She left him with a five-year-old boy to bring up. Did you know that?"

"I knew some of it. Not any details, though." Crossing her arms, Lauren willed her heart not to skitter.

"The details aren't something you need to know. Jack's very private about that part of his life and he wouldn't appreciate my telling you things he hasn't told you himself."

"Of course." So why was Irving here at all?

"Jack's a good man. He's also a vulnerable man—although he doesn't think so. He thinks he's immune to being swept away by... You know what I mean."

Lauren cleared her throat. Her answers weren't something she thought Denton Irving wanted. She was supposed to listen and agree.

"It would be too bad if Jack got involved with someone who didn't share his values." Those piercing brown eyes impaled her.

"What exactly are you trying to say?" Lauren said when she couldn't wait any longer. "Are you suggesting I'm pursuing Jack and that I'm bad for him?"

Irving half turned toward the door. "I'm suggesting whatever you want to think I'm suggesting. And by the way, Jack and I are very close. He wouldn't take kindly to you trying to put me down."

"I wouldn't do that," Lauren said heatedly. Her temper was wearing thin. "Get to the point, please."

Irving looked at his big, work-worn hands and cleared his throat. "It was good of you to go out to the plant the other night."

"I wanted to." His change in tactics bemused her.

"Awful lot of women stay away from the first hint of trouble."

She sucked in her bottom lip. He was trying, as best he could, to say something nice.

Producing a large and wrinkled red handkerchief, he mopped his brow. "Andy said you were kind to him."

"Andy's easy to be kind to."

"I think so." He glared at her again. "Spunky little kid. Deserves the best. So does his father."

"It's nice to see someone who really likes the members of his own family," she said softly. "You'd take on any fight for them, wouldn't you?"

"That's neither here nor there," Irving said gruffly. "Thank you for being there for my son and my grandson. I appreciate it."

"You're very welcome." Lauren turned up the corners of her mouth. "I hope this is going to be the last of their bad luck."

"Yes, well, look, young woman, I've got to say the rest of what's on my mind."

Lauren took a deep breath. She wouldn't be able to stop him if she wanted to.

"Even if Jack can take care of himself, which I'm pretty sure he can, Andy can't. He's got some buried scars that I want left that way—buried. Are you getting my drift?"

"No, I'm not." But perhaps she was. He was suggesting she had the power to hurt Andy.

"Then I'll make it clearer. Playing with a man for your own ends might be all right if there wasn't someone else who stood to suffer. When there is, it isn't all right. Think about it. That's all I ask."

Something near pain stole around Lauren's heart. Denton Irving thought she'd encourage Jack for nothing more than sexual reasons and not care if Andy got hurt in the process. "I resent the suggestions you're making, Mr. Irving. I'm not a woman on the hunt for a man I can use and then throw away when I feel like it."

"Maybe," Irving said. "But I had to say my piece just the same."

"No you didn't." Lauren walked to the door, opened it and stood back. "What you've implied is an insult. Thanks for the tip of the hat for what little I was able to do the other night. Now I'd appreciate it if you'd leave."

"Gladly." But when he drew level he stopped. "You will think about what I've said?"

"Oh, I doubt if I'll be able to avoid it." She turned away and repeated in a whisper, "I doubt if I'll be able to avoid it."

CHAPTER TEN

Jack regarded the outside of the aerobics studio with distaste. In the sports bag he carried were a pair of shorts, a T-shirt and the closest thing he could find to the appropriate shoes the woman on the phone had insisted he should have.

There was no point in waiting.

Tipping his Stetson lower over his eyes, he pushed open the door and walked in behind the rows of gyrating bodies. He was going to hate this but he couldn't think of another way to show her he wasn't accepting her brush-off—no matter what the effort cost him.

He found his way to the locker rooms, quickly changed and returned to the studio. What a lousy way to spend a Friday evening.

"Are we having fun yet?" a woman in a shiny yellow bodysuit yelled from her position facing the group.

"Yes!" came the roar over a pounding beat from the music sound system.

Jack sidled to the back, jogged in place and began searching for Lauren. There she was, in the second row, dressed in red tonight: red leotard and tights and a red sweatband around her brow and beneath a bobbing ponytail.

He studied the man in front of him and tried to copy his movements. If the things his muscles started to do meant anything , the instructor's warning to get here for the warm-up had been valid. But that might have given Lauren a chance to leave before he could talk to her.

Every time the steps changed he fell behind. Like a damned overseas telephone call, he thought. An echo.

"One and two and one and two," the instructor called. "Swing those elbows, saw and saw and lift those knees, to the left, to the right."

He began to get the hang of it as long as he didn't think of anything else.

Between Jack and Lauren were three rows of bodies in violent motion. Sidling, trying to concentrate on the moves, he worked his way to the end of the back row. A step took him one line forward, another step a second, and then he was behind and a short space to the left of Lauren.

The woman to his right turned.

He didn't.

"Ouch." She hissed the word as she continued moving.

"Sorry," he responded, trying to catch up.

"You're going the wrong way," the woman said, glaring.

Jack smiled weakly, turned, and took the opportunity to slip more or less between Lauren and a man beside her.

"Circles in the air and strut your stuff!"

Facing forward, Jack attempted the hand moves demonstrated while trying, not very successfully, a hip-clicking walk the woman made look so easy.

The man he'd crowded muttered something Jack was sure he didn't want to hear anyway and made more room.

And Lauren turned her head to look directly up into his eyes.

"Hi." He smiled.

Her mouth opened but she didn't say a word.

"You left a message with my secretary."

"Yes." She seemed to throw more energy into the routine.

"You canceled our date for tomorrow."

"That's right."

"Then you wouldn't speak to me."

She turned to the right and he followed suit.

"Why wouldn't you speak to me?"

"What are you doing here?" The words jarred out as she broke into a knee-lifting trot.

Jack shuffled his feet and started trotting just in time for everyone else to shift to a different exercise. "I tracked you down."

"I'd never have guessed," she said through barely parted lips. "I thought you came here all the time and being next to you was a coincidence."

"Sarcasm doesn't suit you."

"I told you I'd decided it would be best if we didn't see each other again."

"Bounce and kick and bounce and kick!" the instructor yelled.

Jack groaned. He might not survive this. "You decided, Lauren. I didn't. I want to talk about it."

"Who told you I'd be here?"

"I never betray confidences." When he'd tried to reach her this afternoon, for the third time, her secretary had taken pity on him and told him where to find her in the evening. "Your phone was off the hook when I tried you at home after work."

"Was it?"

"How much longer does this go on?"

"Hours."

"Oh God." He'd begun to sweat. "Let's get out of here."

"I'm enjoying myself."

He groaned. "I'm not."

"Then leave. No one's keeping—" She paused, looking past him.

Jack glanced over his shoulder, into the smiling, interested eyes of the man whose place he'd usurped. He smiled back. "We're just having an intimate chat," he told the man.

Lauren, when he checked her face, had turned almost as red as her suit. He became aware, as she obviously had, that an oasis of silent, listening concentration had formed around them. The only sounds were the music, the thud of feet and the instructor's voice.

Abruptly, Lauren broke from the line and hurried to the changing rooms. Jack did the same. He pulled on his jean jacket, grabbed his gear and made a dash for the door to the street.

He made it with about a minute to spare before Lauren charged out and collided with him.

"You made a fool of me in there," she said. She wore a white sweat suit over the leotard and tights.

"I wanted to get your attention. It worked." He held her arm although she showed no sign of trying to get away. "You promised me you'd come out to the house tomorrow."

"And I changed my mind, Jack." She sounded so miserable he longed to take her in his arms and quiet her. "I've given it a lot of thought and I've decided there's no point in us spending time together."

He pulled up her chin until she had to meet his eyes. "Do you really believe that?"

"I...I think so." Her lower lip trembled and he felt a slight shift in power here.

"Let's go somewhere and talk about it."

"I need to go home for a shower."

"You can shower at my place. And then you'll be ready for that swim."

"No."

"Why? Didn't you buy a suit yet? We could go shopping and—"

"I already bought a suit." Immediately she bit her lip and averted her face.

Jack saw victory in sight. "Ah. Good. The pool will relax us. We'll talk better there."

"It's going to be dark soon."

"I'll follow you home to get your suit."

Lauren sighed deeply and he felt her giving in. "It's in my car."

"Better yet. We'll get it and leave your car where it is."

"Jack. Please don't push. I told you I've decided this is no good."

He smoothed damp hair away from her face. "But you bought a swimsuit to use at my house. Sounds to me like there's still hope for me."

"You can do much better."

"Oh, but you are so wrong," he said softly, drawing closer, feeling the pull of her sweet, full lips. "So wrong."

"All right." She stepped back. "I'll come and wade in your pool. But only if you promise to bring me back when we've done that and I'm ready to go. Promise?"

He grinned. "I promise. When you're ready to leave, I'll bring you back." But he'd make sure she wasn't ready to go for a long, long time.

Carrying her bag as well as his, he followed Lauren to her car where she retrieved a little, shiny pink box from the back seat. He eyed it curiously and she caught his look.

"The swimsuit," she said, her mouth pursed.

On the drive to his house they spoke about the fire. His idea, not hers. "The fire chief says it was definitely arson. But, like I told you on Wednesday, there's about a zero chance of catching whoever did it." By drawing her into the most painful subject in his life at the moment, he was deliberately trying for a more intimate bond.

"I've lived here a long time," she told him. "What I know about the flower business is sketchy at best, but I always thought everyone got along pretty well. Do you think this has something to do with a rival farm?"

"That seems the most obvious, doesn't it? But there hasn't been another grower who hasn't shown up in person to offer help. And every one of them is angry on my behalf, and maybe a little scared on their own."

She rested her head back. "I would be, too, if I were them. They must wonder who'll be next. But who do you think would have a reason to attack your business if it isn't someone in competition with you?"

Just being with her made him feel better—good even. She had a lucid mind in addition to all the other things that drew him to her.

"I don't have the answers, Lauren. Let's make a pact. This is Friday evening and we won't talk about my rotten business problems."

"I'll try. You might have a harder time."

He turned the truck onto the street in front of his house. "Then it's up to you to stop me if I get onto the subject again. There's nothing I can do tonight. Is that a deal?"

"A deal."

Once they'd parked, he helped her down from the cab and let them into the house.

He switched on lights and Lauren peered around. "Where's Andy?"

Not meeting her eyes, he said, "Dad wanted him for the night. The two of them are great buddies."

"I gathered."

He frowned, puzzled at the response, but didn't comment. "You must be starving. I am."

"Sort of." She followed him into the kitchen and dropped her bag.

When he looked at her, at the clean glow on her face, the way the white sweats touched every curve, his appetite fled. He smiled valiantly. "I'm glad you're only sort of hungry. We should swim before we eat."

Lauren held the pink box to her chest. It looked about the right size to contain half a dozen handkerchiefs. And Lauren looked mutinous.

"Why don't you go out to the poolhouse and change? The lights are on in the yard. There are towels and a couple of robes out there."

Balk was written all over her face. She stood her ground. "I've changed my mind. I'm very hungry. Why don't I make us something?"

"It isn't a good idea to swim on a full stomach."

"Maybe we should skip the swim and just eat."

She could be genuinely afraid of going into the water. "Look, you can stand in the shallow end where the water's only up to your middle. And I'll make sure you don't get frightened."

"I'm thirty-nine. I haven't learned to swim yet. Why bother at this stage? I know I'm not going to like it."

Inspiration hit. "You're probably right." He nodded sagely. "Absolutely right, in fact. They say it's not a good idea to force new ideas on people who don't like taking risks. You stay here and see what you can find for us to eat. I'll take a dip for half an hour or so. Then we'll eat outside. We may need jackets, but it's a nice night."

He left the kitchen via the French doors and sauntered away. Of course, he might have misjudged her personality and her pride, but he'd take that chance. The worst that could happen was that she'd make his dinner, something he usually had to do for himself and Andy on Friday and Saturday nights.

Ten minutes later, when he was already in the water, he pretended not to see Lauren walking determinedly to the poolhouse. She looked neither right nor left and her pointed chin was set at a determined angle. Jack dove, smiling to himself. He'd been right. Challenge was Lauren Taylor's middle name. She'd call his bluff at any personal cost.

When he was certain she'd gone into the little white building, he turned on his back and floated and tried to quell the jumpy excitement in his belly. He wasn't a sex fiend, he reminded himself, just an average...just a man with an active mind and body and sex drive.

The door to the poolhouse opened and a figure swathed in a large, white terry robe, slowly approached.

Jack righted himself to wave. "Hi, don't push yourself to do this. There's no shame in not being able to manage something everyone else can do. Not if you come from Laramie, Wyoming." He flipped up his toes and floated again. Nonchalance, as much as an impression of indifference, was the key here. Indifference and a few sharp digs at her clearly competitive spirit.

"Is this the shallow end?"

"Yes." Turning on his side, he stroked lazily. "Sit on the steps in the corner and get your feet wet. I had that put there for Andy to paddle. He used to wear water wings and wait for me to tow him. Hey!" With a kick, he stood on the bottom and bobbed. "I should have thought of that. Would you like water wings? I'm sure I didn't throw 'em out. Might make you feel safer."

"I don't need water wings. I'm going to get the hang of this very quickly. I would have before if I'd wanted to, but the occasion never presented itself."

"Of course." Using a slow crawl, he swam the length of the pool and rested his elbows on the wall. The outdoor lights cast a subdued glow, turning the water to transparent, iridescent turquoise.

Lauren walked to the edge and carefully bent one knee while she tested the water with a toe. Then she turned her back.

Jack started a leisurely swim back in her direction.

She undid the belt on the robe, paused, and slipped the white thing off.

His last breath might be just that—his last. Air trying to go in warred with air he'd planned to breathe out.

Lauren didn't spend time in the sun, but her skin was smooth and olive toned. What he could see of the black swimsuit, cut to a low V at the back, covered very little of that skin.

She turned. "How deep is it right here?"

Jack swallowed and managed to expand his lungs. "About three feet. Wait, I'll give you a hand."

Ignoring the hand he proffered, she sat on the edge and kicked her feet gently to and fro. He stroked close and stood up, slicking his hair back.

"Doesn't feel so warm to me."

"It will be when you get in." Looking at her, as she was now, would warm him in a freezer compartment.

The suit was something else. She was something else. Some sort of black stretchy, lacy stuff, held up over incredible breasts by a string that tied behind her neck, clung to the softly sleek and rounded curves of her body. And, where there weren't little groups of dots, the fabric was so thin her skin showed through.

"Come on." He offered her his hands. After a moment's hesitation, she slipped her fingers into his and let him help her down.

Hissing through her teeth, she looked shocked and made a grab for a more substantial hold. She found his shoulders and her fingernails dug in. Jack kept a smile on his face. He'd better also keep his eyes on *her* face. If he didn't, he was in danger of losing his mind.

"Now what?" She clung to him, the water lapping beneath her breasts.

He took a deep breath and willed the rest of him to calm down. "Do you think you could put your face in the water?"

"No." She shook her head emphatically. "I can't even do that in the shower."

In the shower. He was a cerebral man, a man more interested in minds than bodies. The hell he was, at least not right here and now.

"Floating's easy. Want to try?"

She looked dubious and moved closer. "How do you stay up?" The tips of her breasts, in the rough lacy fabric, brushed his chest.

Think, don't feel. "I'm going to turn you around. Relax and do as I tell you."

Obediently, but with every muscle rigid, she allowed him to revolve her. "Feel my hands on your back?"

"Yes." Her voice was tiny and shaky.

"Trust me. I won't let you go. Lean on my hands and let your feet come off the bottom. They'll float up and you'll be on top of the water."

"I can't do that."

"Yes you can. Try. And try to relax."

Very slowly, she put her weight into his hands. "My feet are off. Don't drop me!"

"I wouldn't drop you, Lauren." He'd like to hold her for the rest of the night, here or anywhere else. "There you go. Feel the water keeping you up?"

"Don't let go!"

"Never. Not till you tell me to."

"I'm not going to tell you to."

Gradually her body leveled. "You're doing it," he cried. "Let your muscles go floppy and get your bottom higher."

She laughed shakily. "I can't."

"You can." Sliding his hands farther beneath her, he moved smoothly until he was at her side. "Lift here." Firm pressure under the appropriate part brought her hips up.

He felt her relax. A smile softened her features. "This feels good. I never knew it would feel like this."

"You never tried before?"

"No."

"Isn't there a pool at—" He shut his mouth, furious for almost mentioning the house she'd shared with Dan.

"Dan's had one put in now. There wasn't before." She didn't appear perturbed at the reference.

"Stretch out your arms."

When she made no attempt to do as he asked, Jack took first one and then her other arm and arranged them, palms up.

He felt her beginning to trust the water. Her eyes closed.

For minutes he supported her, watched the smile on her lips. With one finger, he smoothed away a strand of hair that trailed across her cheek. She opened her eyes again and looked directly up at him.

"Feel good?" he asked quietly.

"Mmm. Do I have to do more things now?"

"Not now. Floating's enough for the first time."

Her eyes fluttered shut again and he towed her a little deeper.

Very carefully, Jack eased his hand away and he watched her bob.

Suddenly Lauren flailed and grabbed. "You let go!"

He laughed and caught her around the waist. "You were doing it all by yourself until you panicked. You can do it all by yourself."

Nothing in her eyes, or in the death grip of her fingers into his sides, suggested she believed him.

"Hold me!"

"I am holding you." He was also standing on the bottom. "Put your feet down. Go on, do it."

Her face tight, she stared at him until she made contact with cement. "I thought it was too deep." She laughed, put a hand over her mouth. She looked, Jack thought, very young.

"You look lovely when you laugh," he told her.

"Thank you." She sobered.

"I like looking at you." Slowly, his hands about her waist, he circled, swinging her with him. "Shorts suit you, and tank tops, and sweatbands and leotards. Everything."

"Stetsons suit you. You look sexy in a Stetson." She hunched her shoulders and covered her mouth again. And this time she turned pink.

"I sure like it when you blush." He smoothed her cheek. "I'm going to wear a Stetson all the time. Wait right here and I'll get one."

When he made as if to leave, she laughed.

Jack glanced upward at the dark sky. "Stars. Millions of them. See?"

She followed his pointed finger. "Mmm. Millions."

"Are you warm now?"

"Very warm."

He swung her, swung her again. And she laughed softly, tilting her head.

They stopped. He didn't know whether he'd been the one to stand still, or she had, but they stood very still.

Her mouth, when he brought his lips to hers, was damp, and her face, her ear, her neck. Bending over her neck, he raised her to her toes and crushed her to him.

"You...smell...wonderful." Between each nipping kiss he heard her sigh.

She stretched up, wrapped her arms around his shoulders and kissed him fully, at first opening his mouth wide to admit her tongue, then concentrating on nibbling his lower lip.

A trembling surge burst through him, hit low in his belly, his groin.

"I don't understand," she said against his jaw.

"What don't you understand?"

"Why me? Why now?" The touch of her suit was an erotic massage. Everywhere it rubbed him he felt first the silken texture of her skin and then the rough stimulus of fabric that had to be intended for that purpose. And only that scrap of black kept him from seeing and holding all of her.

"You're not answering me."

His fingers were on the bow at the back of her neck. "The only answer I can give you is that it's right and it's what I want. Isn't that enough?" Instinctively he ground his thigh between hers. Lauren gritted her teeth and dropped back her head.

Jack recognized his own feeling as triumph. He thrust his leg harder against her and pulled the string undone.

Her eyes flew open. "Jack?"

"I think you want this, too."

"I think..." Her full lips parted and she held the tip of her tongue between her teeth.

The suit top stayed in place until he slowly peeled it down. Taking in short breaths, he supported the weight of her breasts. Wedged astride his thigh, she held his shoulders. Jack watched her flesh grow turgid beneath his touch. At the pressure of his thumbs her nipples sprang hard.

She turned her face away and muttered something.

Unable to resist, he bent to suck—and tongue. Kissing, working his way up, he asked, "What, Lauren?"

"They're too big," she said. "Too much."

He caught her chin between finger and thumb and made her look at him. "Who says so?"

She shook her head and he knew a moment's wild jealousy. He wouldn't ask the same question again.

"They're perfect. You're perfect."

"So are you." She touched him, slipped her hand inside his suit beneath the water.

His mind went wild. Struggling, he worked her suit down, took a breath and dove beneath the surface, dragged his face the length of her to pull the black wisp from beneath her feet.

Lauren's fingers in his hair, tugging him up, brought him, gasping, face-to-face with her again.

"I never wanted anyone like this," he told her, hearing the ragged pitch of his own voice. "Let me carry you?"

Her face was flushed, but she pulled away a little, frowning. "Carry?"

Grinning, he kicked onto his back, pulling her over him. "Wrap your legs around me."

She did as she was told and he was aware, as she must be, that he nudged the opening to her body. A fraction of an inch and they would be joined. But still they held back, prolonging ecstatic torment.

Grasping her waist, he urged her higher until he could take her breast into his mouth. He heard her cry out, felt the contraction of complex muscles on his belly.

"I want to take you to bed," he said, suddenly convinced that, when they'd make love, he'd want to lie with her, then make love again and finally, sleep with her in his arms.

Lauren said nothing as he towed her to the side and lifted her to sit on the wall. "I'll be back."

In moments he returned with their suits. He allowed himself an instant of desperate longing while he stared at her voluptuous body in the night's brush of white light and soft shadow.

With a single movement, he pulled himself up beside her. "Ready, Lauren?"

"Ready?"

"To come with me."

She stood up abruptly and picked up the robe she'd used. Puzzled, he watched her pull it on and belt it tightly. "I guess I'm ready."

"Are you all right?"

"Of course." She held out a hand and hauled him up.

His stomach sank. The passion, the wildness, had subtly ebbed away. Testing his will, sensing he mustn't do anything fast now, he gathered her close and rested his chin atop her head. "You never told me why you'd decided not to keep our date tomorrow.'' They couldn't lose what had started in the pool. *He* couldn't lose it.

"I thought maybe I would be simplifying your life.''

He leaned away to see her face. "I don't understand.''

"Forget it. I shouldn't have said anything. Let's go inside.''

"No. Tell me.''

"I...I wouldn't want to do anything to hurt Andy.''

Her words took seconds to register. "Why would... How could you do that?''

"According to your father—'' With a small strangled sound she wrenched away.

Jack frowned. "What's my father got to do with this?'' He was afraid he might know.

"Nothing.... Well, he, er... We ran into each other and...he thanked me for coming out to the farm after the fire.'' He saw her swallow. "Oh, he loves you and Andy so much, Jack. He worries. He—he mentioned how he hoped I wouldn't be a... He doesn't want Andy hurt again, like he was when his mother left.''

When he tried to make her face him, she moved farther away.

"My father doesn't always think far enough before interfering in my life. But he means well. He's very important to me.''

"Of course he is.'' She gathered the sodden suit and a towel. Half turning, she raised a hand in a resigned gesture. "It's wonderful to see a family as close as you and Andy are with your dad.''

"Thank you.'' He could *feel* it happening, the cooling between them.

"Jack. Forgive me, but I think I'd like to change and go home.''

Frustrated, he searched for the right thing to say. "Don't go,'' was the best he could muster.

"I—I really must. It's getting late.''

"But, I thought—''

"I know what you thought. So did I. Sometimes the physical gets in the way of common sense, don't you think?'' She paused and faced him. "Maybe this is going to seem like an odd time to ask. But would you be comfortable telling me what happened with you and your wife?''

Closing his eyes, he bowed his head. "I don't like to go into this. It's so simple, it's crazy.''

"I'd still like to know."

"All right. Mary and I met and married in college. As long as she was the center of my life we had a great marriage. Then Andy came along and she moved farther and farther away from both of us." The old tightness formed in his throat. He didn't love Mary anymore, but he loved what he'd thought she stood for. And he hated what he'd lost.

"So that was it. She changed and you decided to part?"

"I didn't decide anything. She felt she'd missed her opportunities by not pursuing her art. One day I came home and found Andy with a baby-sitter. Mary had moved out. Within two months we were divorced and she'd gone to live in Paris and paint. She's still there."

Lauren took a step closer. "She just left the two of you, to go and paint?"

"Yeah. That's why I got bent out of shape that night I met you at the aerobic studio and we went out to eat. You said you liked to paint and the dash of déjà vu sent me into a tailspin."

"I'm not Mary." She wrapped the robe more tightly around her.

"No. But I'm me and I'm only human. Warts and all."

"I'm sorry."

He didn't want pity. "Will you come into the house with me?"

"Did you send Andy away tonight hoping I'd come back with you?"

Lying wasn't his thing. "I guess it was in the back of my mind."

"How do you feel about Mary now?"

"Sad. But I don't love her." He'd taken awhile to come this far and that, at least, felt right.

"Did you know your father worries about another woman becoming important enough in your life to be able to hurt you—and Andy when the thing falls apart? And he seems convinced it would fall apart eventually."

Jack wrapped a towel around his waist. His skin had cooled. His ardor hadn't. "I know what my father thinks. He doesn't have to worry."

"Can you be so sure?"

"The only way I'd be putting Andy at risk would be by bringing in someone into our family who wasn't likely to be permanent while he's still at an impressionable age.''

He reached for her, but she eluded him. ''He's nine. Have you worked out some theory as to what *isn't* an impressionable age?''

Shrugging, he looked at the sky. ''Who knows? Fifteen. Eighteen. I don't think about it because it isn't going to happen.''

''I see,'' she said quietly. ''Very sensible.''

''I'm not a dumb kid anymore. I think things through.''

''Yes.'' She picked up a spare towel. ''I wonder what time it is.''

''Why?''

''I just remembered. I promised the woman who rents rooms from me that I'd look after her daughter tonight.''

He narrowed his eyes. ''Don't leave now.''

He heard the long sigh of her breath. ''Yes, Jack, I must. Remember what you promised earlier, when I agreed to come?''

''No!'' How had he allowed this to happen?

''You promised to take me back to my car when I was ready to go—''

''Lauren, in the pool—''

''Please try to forget the pool. Put it down to the stars and the water. Blame it on a frustrated divorcée, if you like.''

''Lauren—''

''No.'' She walked toward the poolhouse. ''I won't be long. I'm ready to go home.''

''If it were Dan asking you to say, you would, wouldn't you?'' He hated the question as soon as it was uttered.

Lauren stood still but didn't look at him. ''What did you say?''

He took a deep breath. ''You'd do anything for him.'' Why couldn't he stop himself from saying these things? ''Hell, I'm sorry. I shouldn't have said that.''

''I don't blame you.''

''Why *do* you let him push you around?''

''I don't.'' She faced him. ''It may look that way, but I don't. But since we're on this subject. Are you still in love with your exwife?''

He stiffened. ''I told you I wasn't.''

''Did you? It seems we don't really believe one another when it comes to the important stuff." Her black eyes were shadows he couldn't read. "Distrust is no basis for...for anything between a man and a woman."

"What are you really afraid of, Lauren?"

"Nothing, I—"

"No." He caught her hand and she didn't pull away. "Don't sidestep this. There's something going on, something you're not telling me."

"Okay." With one long finger she traced the tendons on the back of his hand. "I'm afraid of myself. I'm afraid I'm not tough enough to take a chance on getting hurt again."

"Why would you decide you're going to get hurt?" He looked away, searching for the right words. "Why can't you just let go and enjoy what we could have together?"

"Because I want it too much. And if we became lovers but never anything more, how would I feel when you eventually moved on?"

"You're getting ahead of things. Way ahead."

She laughed. The sound jarred him. "As the old saying goes, 'Once bitten...' and so on. You asked the questions and I gave you the answers."

"Could we talk some more about this...over a drink?"

Lauren brought her lips together and they trembled. "For my sake I'm going to say no. I like you, Jack. I really like you. But I want to leave now. Please stop trying to make me change my mind."

"Maybe you're right." He felt tired, beaten. "Take your time. I'll meet you in the truck."

JACK HAD NO INTENTION of risking Andy's happiness. Lauren tossed and turned in her bed. He'd ignited feelings she remembered well, but had chosen to eliminate from her life, and the reawakening of them wasn't comfortable.

Moonlight through venetian blinds drew silvery stripes across her quilt. She pushed herself to sit up and traced a pallid line.

There was no risk to Andy because Jack wouldn't get into a deep involvement as long as the boy was at a vulnerable age.

Having made his own decision, he should have asked her what decision she'd made about future relationships. Yes, she was overwhelmingly attracted to him. Lauren closed her eyes and hugged her middle, remembering the sensation of his skin on hers, his muscular limbs entrapping her willing body. But she'd made a pact for the future, too. Her independence. One marriage had taught her the perfect attitude for her to adopt with a man: never go beyond friendship.

With Jack, friendship would be impossible to maintain. The sexual attraction was too strong.

What had he been saying when he spoke of waiting until Andy was safe from hurt? That then would be the time to take a woman totally into his life, to marry her, maybe?

Lauren closed her eyes. They'd parted with no plans to meet again, but she knew they probably wouldn't be able to stay apart. When she'd told him some of her fears, Jack had responded that she was thinking too far ahead. Well, he might only be concerned with immediate gratification; Lauren already knew the price she'd eventually pay if she allowed herself that luxury.

Somewhere in the house something creaked, and creaked again like careful footsteps on the stairs.

Lauren sat very still and listened.

A door closed softly.

In one bound, Lauren was out of bed and wrenching open her door. She rushed along the hallway and stopped outside Cara's room. A line of light showed beneath the door.

Lauren tapped.

There was a rustling before Cara called out a wobbly, "Come in."

Lauren opened the door and went to the girl's bed. She sat against her pillows, her streaked, puffy face evidence of copious tears.

"What is it?" Lauren dropped to kneel beside her and reached for her hand.

Cara put small, cold fingers into hers and tried for a smile. "Hi."

"Hi. Can't you sleep?"

"Oh, yes. Um. Yes. I'm going to sleep now."

Lauren spied a suspicious bump in the bed, beside Cara's legs. "You went downstairs, didn't you?"

"Um." A huge swallow sounded painful. "Um, I was thirsty."

"Ah." Lauren eyed the lump. "What's in your bed?"

Without glasses, Cara's blue eyes were huge. "Nothing."

Lauren bit her lip. "Cara, I know it's something. And I can see you're upset. We're buddies, aren't we? Tell me what's wrong."

Cara gulped and her mouth quivered. "I didn't want you to see. I didn't want you to feel bad."

Lauren's stomach turned over.

With her gaze on Lauren's face, Cara reached into her bed and extracted the two bright green sweatshirts she'd been given.

Lauren wrinkled her brow. "What... Did something happen to them? It doesn't matter. We can get... I've got some more."

"It's...not..." Cara hiccuped. "Jimmy got in trouble and it's my fault."

"Oh, Cara, no." Lauren pulled the girl close and hugged her. "Why did Jimmy get in trouble?"

"Because I gave him the shirt. His mom got real mad and said he's not to talk about his family to anyone...about them being poor."

"I see." She didn't.

"Jimmy's mom says proud people don't like charity."

Lauren held Cara away and smiled at her. "She's right. But sometimes people mix up charity with simple kindness. Don't worry, it'll all work out."

With a little help, most things could be worked out. Lauren hunched her shoulders. She was a long way from completely giving up on Jack Irving; a very long way.

CHAPTER ELEVEN

"Why'd you come for me tonight, Dad?"

Jack sat beside Andy on his bed and stretched out his legs. "I missed you. Is that okay?"

"I guess. Grandpa didn't look too pleased."

"Grandpa understands." He'd have to. "I'm pretty good about sharing you with him."

"He misses Grandma."

Jack looked down on Andy's tousled, dark hair. "He talked to you about that?"

"Yeah. He always does."

Jack narrowed his eyes, considering. "What does he say?"

Andy leaned against him and peeked into his cupped hands where part of Strangler's two-foot length was coiled. "He says she could do anything he could do—only better."

Jack laughed. "Boy, I bet she'd have liked to hear him say that. He's right, though. She was something. Do you remember her?"

"'Course." Andy snorted. "What d'ya think? She only got real sick... I was six. I remember everything that ever happened. Grandpa and I talk about all that sometimes."

"*All* that?" Jack eased away to see the side of his son's face. "What kind of stuff is that?"

Andy shrugged and wound Strangler around his wrist. With a forefinger, he stroked the California King's head and stared into flat, beady eyes.

Stopping on the way back from dropping Lauren off to bring Andy home had been self-indulgent. But thinking about her was an activity to be avoided. And being alone until he could put more distance between what had to be and what had seemed possible while she was with him, was also to be avoided. Tonight he needed Andy as a tangible reminder of what was most important in life.

What he also needed tonight was a way to stop dwelling on the financial disaster the figures were starting to indicate at the farm.

"What stuff do you and Grandpa talk about?" Jack prodded.

"All kinds of stuff." Strangler worked his creamy-colored body up Andy's arm.

Jack put a tentative finger on the black stripe that ran the length of the reptile's back. "I thought I told you not to bring Strangler into bed."

"Snakes are clean," Andy said thoughtfully. "We just kind of hang out for a bit before I go to sleep."

"Don't ever forget to lock him up before you do go to sleep. Not unless you want to wake up and find hamster bones on the rug. Or Jaw's whiskers."

Andy let out an exasperated puff. "Jaws is too big. And Strangler wouldn't do that kinda thing 'cause I got him when he was a baby. He's trained."

"Want to bet?" Jack eyed the sleek body. "Wait till you bring your first girlfriend home and that thing decides to do what's natural." The King was capable of vibrating its tail like a rattler. Despite the fact that the species wasn't poisonous, the effect of the rattle, particularly if accompanied by the foul-smelling fluid it could eject, might put off the hardiest of souls.

"I'm never going to have a girlfriend." Andy scowled. "Girls are dumb screamers. Anyway, Strangler gets all he needs to eat and I always put him away."

Jack hadn't missed Andy's eagerness to drop the subject of his conversation with his grandfather. "Do you and Grandpa talk about your mother?"

After a short silence, Andy slipped from bed and put his snake into the old fish aquarium where he lived on a bed of pine needles and mulch beneath a roof made of perforated metal.

"Andy?" Jack patted the bed beside him. "Do you?"

"Some," Andy said, slipping back beneath his covers.

"Your mother's a nice woman." Muscles flicked in his jaw. No kid should be brought up to believe he was the product of someone worthless, not if he was going to think he was worth something himself.

"That's not what Grandpa says," Andy muttered.

Jack rested his head against the wall. He'd been afraid of that. "Your mother calls, y'know."

"Yeah."

"She asks how you are. That's why she calls."

"She doesn't want to talk to me."

Jack locked his hands behind his neck. This conversation was overdue. "Mary... Your mother's afraid of upsetting you. Maybe, when you're older, you'll be able to get to know her."

"Nah. I don't want to. Grandpa says if she wasn't selfish she'd have stayed with us. He says she loves me, but she loves her painting thing best. He says you gotta be careful not to let people get...powerful?" Andy craned his neck to see Jack's face. "Yeah, powerful. Grandpa says a guy's gotta learn to be his own person. I think that means it's dumb to care a lot about anyone."

If Jack could put his hands on his father right now he might forget the "honor thy father" bit. He settled his features in an expressionless mold. "Do you care a lot about Grandpa?"

"'Course!"

"How about me?"

"'Course I do!"

Jack smiled down. "And I care a lot about you, so it can't always be dumb, can it?"

Andy thought about that. "No, I guess not. Grandpa says you'll never let anyone else do what Mom did to us."

"He said—" Tilting up his chin, Jack managed, with difficulty, to order his thoughts. "I know where my dad's coming from and he's right. But I don't want you worrying about these things. Did you talk about the fire?"

"Yeah. We did the other day, too. He says you'll come out of everything okay because you're so diver—diver—"

"Diversified." For now he intended keeping the lid on the truth: they were far from okay. "He's right and that's something he and my mother get all the credit for. What I inherited was the product of their foresight, and Dad's father before them."

Andy snuggled closer. "I'm gonna do what you do one day, aren't I?"

"If you want to." Pleasure swept through Jack. "College first, then come and work with me if you want to. But keep your options open, Andy. You may decide there's something else you want to do.''

The boy shook his head. "No way. Len says I gotta take flori-culture.''

Jack laughed. "That's a helluva big word for a nine-year-old.''

"Matt told me about the new poinsettia. The bud mutation stuff and everything. He says it's gonna be sold for the first time this year.''

"Yup. It's going to knock the socks off every buyer who sees it.'' If he could figure out a way to ship the damn thing. "It's the most spectacular sport we've ever developed. I expect Matt told you sport's the word for mutant. That baby's got to help tide us over until we come back from some of the damage our pyromaniac caused.'' Just thinking about the new sport's debut excited him.

"Did Lauren see Lava Pearl yet?''

Jack brought his teeth together. "No. And we don't talk about it to anyone but Len and Matt and Grandpa, okay?''

"Yeah.'' Andy didn't sound convinced.

"I mean it, Andy. Only people really close to us can be trusted.''

"Lauren can be trusted. She's kinda close, isn't she? Even Grandpa said she was nice to come around after the fire.''

His father had said something positive to Andy about Lauren? There might be hope in every quarter if only she'd loosen up and give them a chance.

"Dad?'' Andy elbowed him. "Lauren's our friend.''

Care was still essential. "Lauren's a nice person.''

"She's neat.'' Wriggling, Andy turned to sit, cross-legged, facing Jack. "She likes my pets and she doesn't treat me like a little kid.''

Lauren, Lauren. Yet again she'd left him with the comment that she hoped they could enjoy each other as friends. Whatever had happened by the pool was probably a lesson he had to learn. She'd let him know that she was a passionate woman—God, she was passionate—but she wasn't interested in any sort of binding attach-ment. Clearly, sex wasn't in the cards for Lauren if the partner wasn't someone she thought she could...love? He definitely wanted sex with her. But the rest of what he felt was still hazy except that he knew he liked and respected her.

"Dad, when's Lauren coming over again?''

Jack started. "Uh, I don't know." He couldn't bring himself to say it was possible she never would.

"When the packing plant was on fire she stayed with me."

"I know. We just talked about that, remember?"

"She was nice and she was worried about you, just like I was."

"Was she?" He looked away. Andy wasn't telling him anything he didn't know, but he couldn't sort out what it all meant.

"Are we going surfing tomorrow?"

"I don't know." He felt hollow and he had a hunch there would be only one way to fill that void, which meant he would keep right on feeling hollow.

"You promised." A sleepy drawl let Jack know Andy would be asleep soon.

"Sure I did. After I spend a couple of hours at the farm, we'll go surfing. You can help me work so I can get through faster." He always found things for Andy to do that made him feel useful while they also taught him more about the business.

"Can Lauren come with us?"

Jack turned cold. "I don't think so, son. I expect she's busy."

"We could ask. Maybe we could take a picnic. Rob's folks do that. His mom makes all kinds of stuff. I've been with them."

"I know." And he knew that he was hearing how badly Andy wished he had a mom.

"I bet if I asked Lauren, she'd help us make sandwiches and things."

Jack eased his hands from behind his neck and swung his legs from the bed. "Lauren doesn't swim. I don't think she'd like it at the beach with us."

"She'd be fine." Andy looked wide-awake again. "We could teach her."

The pool by moonlight flashed before Jack's eyes and a picture of Lauren, both with and without the black swimsuit. He averted his eyes. "We'll go by ourselves this time, okay?"

"If you say so. But I bet she'd like it. Then we could come home and have dinner. She said she'd paint a picture of trees to stick on the back of Strangler's aquarium. Maybe she's done it by now."

His father had been right, damn it. Andy was ripe to attach himself to another mother figure. "Lauren told me she's busy all day tomorrow." A necessary lie.

"Oh." Andy wrinkled his nose. "So when's she coming over again?"

"I'm not sure."

"You like her, don't you? I do. And she likes you?"

Jack had the sensation that a noose was tightening around his neck. "I like Lauren very much. She's a good friend. When she's got some spare time I'll invite her over."

"Good." Scooting, Andy pushed inside his bed, turned to punch his pillow, and settled down.

Seconds later, as Jack held very still, he heard the boy's regular breathing.

Whatever was in the cards for him and Lauren, if anything, Jack had better make sure it didn't give Andy ideas about a substitute mother to bake apple pies and join the PTA. Not only was Lauren not applying for that type of position, she'd laugh at the idea.

For once Dad had been right; Andy was vulnerable, and it was his, Jack's, job to put his boy first.

Carefully he left the bed, put off the light and slipped into the hall.

Without deciding what to do next, he wandered out to the pool. He was a lucky man to have a son who wanted little more than to be loved by his dad and grandfather and possibly by a mother figure who was a distant memory now.

Jack rolled up the legs of his jeans, sat on the edge of the pool, and put his bare feet into the water.

He couldn't forget Lauren...not ever.

CHAPTER TWELVE

The artist's case standing in the corner of her office served as one more irritation in an already totally irritating and confusing day. The third day of its kind in a row. If she weren't so disturbed, she'd go to the painting class tonight as planned. But she was disturbed.

Lauren got up from her desk and spared the case another glance as she went into the outer office where the accountant was packing papers away.

"Is it going to be all right now?" she asked the bespectacled man who'd been dealing with the books for Contact even before Lauren purchased the firm.

"Looks to be." Sandy-haired, pleasant looking in a nondescript way, Sam Brill was, as he always reminded her, around to keep her out of jail. As far as she knew, the comment was the only joke in his repertoire and since he was a nice man she contrived to laugh each time he used it.

"So we won't need another extension from the IRS? I really don't want to miss the June date they gave us."

"That shouldn't be necessary." Sam never made completely positive or negative remarks. "I'll probably be by for your signature in a few days."

Once he'd left, Lauren surveyed her domain and took some satisfaction from the fact that all terminal operators were hard at work...except Susan.

Lauren frowned at the empty chair. Probably in the ladies' room. She went there herself and found no sign of Susan.

Rather than return directly to her office, she went out to the sidewalk to breathe some of the soft warm air of a beautiful afternoon.

Sitting on the edge of a concrete planter ablaze with purple and yellow pansies, she closed her eyes to concentrate on the breeze in her hair. What a perfectly crummy weekend she'd had, followed by an equally crummy Monday.

"Lauren? What are you doing?"

At the sound of Susan's voice, Lauren's eyes snapped open. She blinked. "Hi. Taking a breather, like you. Great out here, huh?" A movement caught her eye, a man leaning to pull shut the passenger door on some sort of low, silver-gray sports car parked at the curb. Dark hair, dark glasses, a lean face. He glanced in their direction and Susan raised a hand in a brief wave.

Lauren crossed her arms and grinned. "Do I sense a lovers' tryst?"

"Hardly a tryst." But Susan sent a longing gaze after the departing car and its driver. "He had a few spare minutes so I came out to talk to him. You don't mind, do you?"

"No, I don't. As I'm always telling you, you put in your time and more. He looks interesting, by the way."

She waited, but Susan didn't volunteer any information.

"Sam Brill's finished. Looks as if the glitch in the return is finally worked out. One more nitty-gritty nuisance over with for a while."

"Good." Susan perched beside her. "Why are you unhappy?"

So it showed. Why she should imagine it might not, Lauren had no idea. She'd never been able to hide her feelings. "The usual," she said.

"Man trouble. Otherwise known as Dan Taylor."

"Dan's not the problem. I can cope with him."

Susan cocked her head. "Jack Irving, then. Did you see him on Friday?"

The innocent expression didn't fool Lauren. "Thanks to you, he found me at the studio."

"He told you I said where you were?" Susan looked outraged.

"No." Lauren smiled. "He said he never betrays a confidence. But it wasn't hard for me to figure out you were the culprit."

"I'm not confessing anything."

"You don't have to. You're a soft touch for a persuasive man, that's all."

"Well, he sounded so..." With an embarrassed laugh, Susan lifted her hair off her neck. "Caught. I'm sorry things didn't go well."

"They did," Lauren said. "At first. Let's drop the subject." Not that she'd been able to stop thinking about it for more than minutes at a time.

"What happened?"

"Nothing…. Oh, darn it, anyway. I've tried to call him half a dozen times today but his secretary keeps putting me off. Obviously he doesn't want to talk to me so I might as well forget him."

Susan turned and tilted her head to look Lauren in the eye. "Do I hear something more than casual interest here?"

"Are you more than casually interested in tall, dark and handsome with the spiffy car?" Lauren responded belligerently.

"Possibly. And I'm not unhappy. You are."

She had a point. "We got along beautifully for a while." An understatement for an interlude that would stay with her forever. "Then we got into discussing deeper stuff and everything blew up in my face."

"He turned off?"

"Yes…. No, I did."

"Ah. Why are you trying to reach him?"

Was she completely sure why? Lauren picked a pansy and shredded its stem. "I think I should tell him I was out of line reacting the way I did and that I'd like… I like him and I don't want it to be all over between us. Maybe I want to tell him I think we should give it another chance."

"Then do it." Susan crossed her arms as if a simple dilemma had been solved.

It wasn't simple. "We're going to start feeling the effect of the clients we've lost before long."

Susan wound a strand of hair between her fingers. "I know. But that's not a great way of changing the subject, Lauren."

"This week I'm going to visit all the people who've terminated and ask some very direct questions. It makes no sense that every one of them refuses to give a reason for taking their business away."

"I agree. And I think that's the best thing you can do. What are you going to do about Jack?"

The woman was like a bird dog after a kill. "Forget him."

"Will that make you happy?"

"No." She'd never win prizes for caution.

"Then go after him. Do it today. Tonight."

"I already told you he won't talk to me."

Susan got up and pulled Lauren to her feet. "We've got work to do. Then you've got a mission."

Lauren sighed. "What am I supposed to do? Accost the man?"

"Exactly. And I know the perfect safe topic for the pair of you. Discuss business reversals. You've had some problems. So has he."

"I don't see—"

"I do. Interested doesn't begin to cover that man's attitude toward you. Go tell him you need a shoulder to cry on and order him to cry on yours. There's nothing like shared trouble to bring two people together."

WHY HAD SHE ALLOWED herself to be talked into this? The sound of the doorbell echoed through Jack's house. If his truck weren't parked in the driveway she'd have been able to hope he wasn't at home.

There was still time to hop back in her car and flee.

"Lauren!"

The door had opened and she looked down into Andy's clear brown eyes. "Hi." Hitching the package she'd brought higher under her arm, she smiled. "Is your dad in?"

"Yeah. Out back reading bank stuff."

"Well...I won't disturb him. I just thought I'd stop by." Stop by an area that was miles from her home and office where she had no reason to go if it weren't for coming to this house. She handed Andy the package and a rolled-up piece of canvas in a rubber band. "These are for you."

He held up the roll. "It's the picture for Strangler?"

"Yes. I promised, remember?"

"Yeah." He fidgeted with the rubber band. "My mom's an artist. In Paris."

Unsure how to react, Lauren caught her tongue between her teeth. "I think I knew that."

Andy rubbed a hand down his jeans. "I got a letter from her."

"That's nice."

"I haven't seen her since I was a little kid."

Lauren cleared her throat. "She must think about you a lot."
Ridiculously, she felt tears prickle.

"Nah. I don't think so. But she says she's gonna come and see
me." His color had heightened and Lauren saw his chest expand.
He was confused, uncertain how he was supposed to feel.

Searching for inspiration, Lauren shifted from foot to foot. "Your
mother wouldn't be coming all the way from Paris if she didn't
really miss you." Did she also miss Jack? Did he miss her? The
sinking sensation was unwelcome.

"Maybe. Dad says—"

"Who's there, Andy?" Jack's voice preceded his arrival at the
door behind his son. "Oh."

"Look at this, Dad." Andy quickly unrolled the canvas on which
she'd painted a miniature scene composed of rocks and greenery.
"This is for Strangler. Isn't it neat?"

"Neat," Jack said, looking not at the painting but at Lauren.
"That was nice of you. Andy said you'd told him you'd do it."

"It isn't great. But Strangler's probably not an expert on technique. I used canvas and oils because I thought it would hold up
better than anything else. Anyway, I won't keep you."

"Hey, this is something." Andy had ripped the paper off the
package. "A book on reptiles. Geez, look at the pictures. Thanks,
Lauren. Are you coming for dinner? I found this new spider. My
book says it's an okay one to have."

"Lauren's coming in, aren't you?" Jack said. In an open-necked,
black polo shirt and dark gray pleated pants, he looked casually
appealing.

She jiggled her car keys. "I guess so."

"Of course you are." He put a hand on Andy's shoulder. "Go
look at your book. I'll call you when it's time to eat."

Once inside the house and alone with Jack, Lauren straightened
her back and reminded herself of her plan. Andy's announcement
about his mother's visit had caught her off guard, but it didn't have
to change anything tonight.

Jack touched her shoulder. His arms, in the short-sleeved shirt,
were tanned and muscular. "Can I offer—"

"No you can't." She interrupted tersely. "I've tried to reach you
several times today and you wouldn't speak to me."

"Really. Well, now I guess you know how I felt on Friday."

"Paying me back makes you look small. I thought better of you."
He could have been preoccupied at the prospect of seeing his wife
after so long...his ex-wife....

"You thought better of me." Jack mimicked her tone in a way
that made her squirm. "You sound like a school marm."

"Too bad. You and I have a lot in common. Besides that, we
like each other, or I think we do. So we're going to get past the
other night's fiasco." Her own boldness surprised her.

"Fiasco?" His face was calm, his eyes questioning. "Funny, I
might have called it a lot of things. Fiasco wouldn't have been one
of them. I thought it was mostly wonderful."

Her cheeks flamed. "I've come to take you to dinner. Andy, too,
if he'd like to come."

"Interesting." He leaned against the wall in the entrance to the
living room she found so cool and uninviting. "What is this? A
guilt offering?"

Lauren took in a gulp of air. "Guilt? Why should I feel any
guiltier than you? We both overreacted."

He seemed to consider what she said. "Maybe you're right. How
did you feel afterward?"

"Awful."

"Me too. What do you think we can do about it, if anything?"

"Let me take you to dinner," she said, lifting her chin. "You're
having some hard times and so am I. We could help each other
without having to end up in bed—" Her face heated again and she
glanced around. There was no sign of Andy.

Jack looked at his feet, but not before she caught his smile. "We
could help each other. I agree with that much. Sure I'll have dinner
with you. We're having meat loaf."

"I'd like to take you out. If we're going to try doing things as
equals you should be able to allow me to do that."

"I—" He seemed to think better of whatever he'd been about to
say. "Fine. There's a girl across the street who's usually available
to sit with Andy at short notice. I'll call her."

"I said he should come, too," she said, suddenly panicky at the
thought of being alone with Jack again.

"It's a school night. And he'd rather stick around here, anyway."

WHEN HE REALIZED they were going to Barney Middleton's place, Jack mentally cursed the coincidence but made no comment. With a little good fortune, tonight would be one of Barney's nights off. Otherwise he could imagine the gibes he'd have to endure the next time they met, or, if he was really unlucky, in front of Lauren.

"You do like Italian food?" she asked as they walked beneath the green-and-white striped awning over the door of Grazie. "I haven't been here since... The last time I was here was with Dan, but the food was very good."

He admired her evident determination to be open, regardless of how difficult that might be. "I love Italian food."

Barney was at the reception desk.

Grimacing behind Lauren's back, Jack drew a finger across his throat and prayed Barney would understand and curb the wise-cracks.

"Hello," Lauren said. "Do you have a table for two?"

Barney did better than curb the wisecracks. In his best phony Italian accent—a travesty that sounded like a man from the Bronx with terminal allergies—he said, "For you, beautiful lady, the best table in the house." He glanced at Jack as if he'd never seen him before in his life and ushered Lauren ahead.

With a flourish, Barney seated her, presented a menu and whipped the napkin across her lap. "May I get the so-lovely lady something to drink?" Dropping a menu in front of Jack, he continued to ignore him.

"White wine," Lauren said, smiling warmly. "A Chardonnay. How about you, Jack?"

"He'll have Chianti," Barney said as he sailed away.

Jack waited for Lauren to comment on their reception but she'd apparently noticed nothing unusual. Across the room with its sparse Monday-night crowd, he saw Joannie Middleton and knew a moment's anxiety. Joannie made no secret of her conviction that "man was not meant to live alone." Barney went to his diminutive blond wife's side and bent to whisper something. Joannie's eyes met Jack's and she smiled. Then the smile disappeared and she turned her back.

"Not baby-sitting for the renter's child tonight?" He felt awk-ward, an unusual sensation.

"I did what you did for Andy—arranged for a neighbor to come in."

He looked at her over the menu. "Isn't that her mother's job?"

Her head jerked up. "I...I meant her mother arranged for a baby-sitter."

"Andy really likes you," he said without intending to.

"I really like him, too. He's very natural."

"Melon with prosciutto." The waiter Jack recognized as Colin put a large plate in the middle of the table.

While Colin spoke, Barney poured white wine for Lauren and placed the bottle on ice. He circled Jack, clicked his fingers, and took the Chianti basket Joannie bustled to put in his hand.

Lauren had finally sensed something different. She sat back, her lips slightly parted, and Barney removed the menu from her fingers.

"Did you order this?" She sounded bemused.

Jack cleared his throat. "Er, yes."

Apparently satisfied, she set to work, eating with the gusto he was coming to appreciate.

Jack ate a little melon and leaned on his elbows to watch her over the rim of his wineglass. Her hair shone like black satin. The silk dress she wore was jade green, vivid enough to wash out the complexion of a less vibrant woman. Tailored lines did nothing to detract from a curvaceous body he was having a hard time not visualizing naked.

"I had a tough time not calling you over the weekend," he said suddenly and closed his mouth firmly. This was strange. He'd never been a man to speak without thinking first.

Lauren's beautiful, shy smile wiped out the sensation of having made a fool of himself.

"I'm sorry you didn't give in." Her breasts rose and fell with her deep breath. "I kept hoping the phone would ring and it'd be you."

He speared a slice of melon, cut it mechanically into pieces, and pushed them around his plate. "I'm sorry I avoided you today." This was taking humble pie too far. Later he was bound to regret his rashness.

"I don't blame you. I was a pain on Friday night."

The air felt thinner. "You were beautiful on Friday night. Some things shouldn't be rushed and I was rushing them."

Colin's smooth approach was a relief. "Antipasto," Colin said sonorously. "We have salami and pepperoni, mixed cheeses, olives, artichoke hearts, carrots, cauliflower. The marinade is *Signor* Barney's own secret recipe." He refilled the wineglasses. "Enjoy!"

Jack hardly dared meet Lauren's eyes. He did meet Barney's fatuous grin before he swept into the kitchen.

"This looks great." Lauren rested her wrists to look over the elegant platter. "But there's so much. I don't understand how you told them what we wanted."

He made an airy gesture. At least she hadn't dressed him down for assuming she'd like what he liked. Which he hadn't. Not that she had any way of knowing...

"I don't remember them having set meals here. Is that what you do? Order by number or something? Like a Chinese restaurant?"

Jack cleared his throat and attacked the salami. Around a mouthful he made a more or less affirmative noise.

"Very unusual," Lauren said. "But a good choice."

He made a mental note to let Barney know what he thought of this effort. "You said you were having some difficulties with your business."

"Yes." She drank wine slowly, as if deep in thought. "We've lost more clients than makes any sense. Considering we give good service."

He certainly had no complaints. "Are you stepping up efforts to get new accounts?"

"Yes. That's my domain. I don't always like making sales calls, but with an operation that's still fairly small it makes sense to keep the staffing overheads down as much as possible. And I don't do such a bad job. I always seem to get an interview at least."

"I just bet you do."

"Excuse me?"

Keeping his eyes averted, he drank some of his own wine. "I said I'm sure you get interviews. You're very professional." And if she did cold calls in person, she'd only have to encounter a male to be assured of a hearing.

Joannie Middleton approached. "How is everything?" She rested a hand on Lauren's shoulder and smiled down.

"Wonderful."

"What a beautiful dress. Only someone with your marvelous coloring could wear such a strong color. I envy you."

"Thank you." Lauren smiled as Joannie walked away, then glanced at Jack with a puzzled frown. "Nice woman," she said.

"Yes." The easiest thing would be to explain his long-standing connection with the Middletons, only he'd delayed too long. "Do you have any solid theories on why you're losing business?"

"Uh-huh. I think so." Again she drank, her expression shuttered. "I wish I had a few answers."

Lauren sat forward. "Ah, yes. More problems?"

"No, thank God. We've got enough to deal with. I've got cleanup going around the clock. That plant has to be rebuilt in record time. But I do keep expecting more trouble. I can't seem to help myself."

Colin glided toward them, holding aloft what resembled a huge, circular, yellow dish. Barney popped from behind him to clear away the existing plates.

The "dish" was a hollowed-out wheel of cheese. "The specialty of the house," Barney said with something close to a giggle. "The giant Gouda shell, filled with the finest pasta." He kissed his fingers.

Shaking his head, Jack crossed his arms. Colin retreated, to be replaced by Joannie with fresh dinner plates. She stood beside Barney as he drew himself up very straight. Hitching back a jacket cuff, he pointed and stated, "*Penne,* with a light cheese sauce, and linguine with clam sauce, naturally. And here we have the fettuccini with marinara, cannelloni stuffed with a spicy beef, *mostaccioli*...ah—" he kissed his fingers again "—with pesto, of course. And vermicelli. A feast."

"For two special people," Joannie said with quiet reverence. "Enjoy."

They withdrew together.

"Weird," Lauren said.

Jack laughed explosively, brought a fist to his mouth but gave up trying to camouflage his mirth. "I should have said something before we came in here. Barney and Joannie are old friends of mine."

"They are?" Lauren looked completely bemused. "You didn't even say hi to one another."

"Well—" he shook his head "—I'm sorry. Eat. Before all this gets cold. The Middletons would never forgive me."

Evidently Lauren decided against further questioning in favor of making a valiant attempt to attack the mountain of food.

"Wow," she said after a few minutes of silent eating. "This is really something. Is it even *on* the menu?"

"Nope. Nothing I eat here ever is. They always decide what I need and they're usually right."

"Nice," she said, wrinkling her nose. "Everyone needs to feel special and they do that for you."

He put down his fork. "You're nice. You say the damn nicest things."

Lauren shrugged, smiling at him. "So do you."

He never remembered feeling with another woman what she made him feel. He realized they were staring at each other but he made no attempt to look away.

Lauren did. "The fire was awful. But surely you won't have any more trouble now."

"Maybe. But I can't quite make myself believe it. I walk around feeling someone's watching me. It's as if there's a way for who-ever's done these things to know my intentions almost before I know them myself. I've stopped writing things down at the office. I'm keeping records at home and dealing with transactions directly over the phone. But if there's any delay getting the poinsettia cut-tings out, we might as well kiss this year off and look at the worst setback in our history."

Lauren laced her fingers together on the table. "I'm going to believe all the bad times are over for you," she said firmly. "And I'm going to believe you must have had the most unbelievable run of accidents. You've got to do that, too, Jack, or you'll drive your-self mad."

"Exactly what I've told him."

Jack started and turned to find Barney at his shoulder.

"Joannie and I have told Jack that all this trouble is because his stars are in the wrong place," Barney continued seriously. "Only now they've moved and everything's gonna be peachy again. Isn't that right, Jack? Isn't that what we've told you?''

Jack sighed. "Sometimes I don't think you're real, Barn. Why don't you just pull up a chair instead of hovering around, *overhearing?*''

"No, no. Wouldn't dream of it, would we, Joannie?''

"Wouldn't dream of it.''

Jack swiveled in the other direction to find Joannie at his left shoulder. He faced Lauren and raised his brows in apology.

"Eat more,'' Joannie said. "You're too thin, Jack.''

"I'm not too thin.'' Maybe what Barney said about his wife loving him for his body was no joke. "And I can't eat another bite.''

"It was so good,'' Lauren said, straight-faced but with laughter in her eyes.

"Jack's like family to Joannie and me,'' Barney said. "We go back a long way, right, Jack?''

"Right. I've eaten a lot of pasta.''

Barney punched his arm. "You and me got more between us than pasta. I get involved in these so-called civic projects and you help me figure out how to pull 'em off. *After* you tell me I shouldn't be involved.''

All true.

"This is a great guy,'' Barney said to Lauren. "One of the best. They don't make 'em any better than Jack Irving.''

Jack closed his eyes. "Are you staying or leaving, Barn?''

"We're leaving,'' Joannie said. "And we're glad to see two such deserving people together, aren't we, Barn?''

"Deserving?'' The echo was out before Jack could stop it.

"Well.'' Barney made an expansive gesture. "Lauren…you don't mind if I call you Lauren? We met once when you were with that louse of… We met some years ago and I feel I know you.''

Chewing her bottom lip, Lauren inclined her head.

"Yes,'' Barney said, turning red. "Anyway, as Joannie and I have said, you're not only beautiful, you're hardworking and…and *deserving*. Just like Jack.''

"Absolutely right.'' Joannie nodded her blond head vigorously. "You two don't have any idea how many times Barney and I have said what a good couple you'd make. Both special, good-looking, kind and…'' She gestured, searching for more compliments.

"Deserving?" Lauren offered.

Holding back laughter, Jack buried his nose in his wineglass and immediately realized his mistake. He began to choke.

A sharp thud in the middle of his back, delivered by Barney, left him gasping for air. "Thanks," he sputtered. "This has been some meal. I hate to suggest it, but maybe it's time I got you home, Lauren.''

"You haven't had dessert," Joannie said. "Or coffee. There's ricotta cake, or maybe a little spumoni—"

"No, thank you." Lauren put her napkin on the table. "Jack's right. I do have to go.''

"Of course…." Barney spread his hands. "You two young people have other things to do with a beautiful night.''

Jack wanted out—now. "Could I have the bill?" He sent a little frown to Lauren who showed signs of saying she was paying.

"This special dinner is on us," Barney said. "And don't argue. We'd be offended, wouldn't we, Joannie?''

"Oh, absolutely. Offended.''

"And we wouldn't want that. Good night to both of you.''

Lauren got up. "Thank you very much.''

Smiling with ice in his eyes, Jack sent Barney a silent warning of discussions to come, and shepherded Lauren from the restaurant.

"Could we walk for a while?" he asked when they set off along the secluded alley that housed Grazie. He felt her shaking beneath the hand he'd rested at her waist. "Are you okay? I'm really sorry about… Lauren?''

"Oh, it was great. Hilarious." Chuckling, she threaded her arm through his. "If I hadn't decided where we'd go I'd think you set me up. They genuinely think the world of you.''

"You noticed?''

"I'd always heard Italian people were friendly and wanted the best for everyone, but I never experienced anything like that before.''

"I hope you never will again. Incidentally, they're not even Italian.''

She looked up at him, the breeze lifting her hair. "No? Well, they do think a lot of you, anyway. They think you're really... *deserving!*''

"Aargh!" He settled his hand on the back of her neck and pulled her against him. "Don't say that again, or else."

Lauren spun away, catching his hand, and broke into as rapid a jog as her high-heeled shoes allowed. "Or else what?"

"I'll think of something." He kept up easily. "To the water?"

"How did you guess?"

The alley opened onto Carlsbad Avenue at Walnut. A short distance took them across the wide road fronting the ocean. "I'm crazy about this place at night." Lauren took her hand from his and went to lean on a railing above the beach.

Standing behind her, he watched her hair blow, and the silky dress flatten to her body. "You make anything fun."

She turned her head abruptly and moonlight glistened in her eyes. Just as quickly, she looked out to sea again. Surf sighed over coarse sand and the salt air smelled fresh.

"Does it bother you that I'm saying how much I enjoy being with you?"

"I don't know how to read you, Jack."

The light that touched her hair cast a satiny streak over the water.

"I'm not very complicated." Moving close, he rested his hand on her back. Gently, he rubbed his fingers up and down her spine and felt her shudder. "I want to be with you."

"We are together."

Exerting the slightest pressure, he urged her toward him. "Someone said men and women can't be friends." Stroking her cheek, he studied her mouth.

"What does that mean? You and I are friends."

It meant he was crazy about her, body, mind, the whole package. "But it doesn't work, does it? Not that way? Is it wrong for me to want you so badly?"

She rested her face in his palm. "Why do you?"

"Why? I wish there was a simple answer. I'm human would be one way of putting it. But there's so much more." He touched his lips to her brow. "There is for you, too. I'm right, aren't I, Lauren?"

"Yes."

"What are we going to do about it? We keep edging closer and ending up with a bigger gap than ever between us. Physically, anyway. Whenever I'm not with you, I want to be. I can't seem to concentrate on much else."

She hugged him so fiercely he steadied her. "I wish I could explain what I feel. It's too soon. That means it's too soon for a lot of things."

"Try explaining." It wasn't too soon for him to feel he'd break apart if he couldn't be with her completely, and soon.

"Okay." Almost roughly, she pushed away. "Yes, I feel there could be something strong—*is* something strong between us. And, yes, not sleeping alone tonight appeals to me. But filling lonely hours, even if you're with someone you like isn't a good enough reason for having sex. Not for me."

He whistled. "You don't pull punches, lady."

"No. And in case that didn't sum it up, Andy's waiting at home for you and I'll be going back to a little girl and a baby-sitter."

Her message was clear: Lauren wasn't interested in a casual anything. "I enjoy honest people." Why couldn't he say exactly what it would take to make things good and right between them? "Lauren, I...I care about you. Will you see me again?"

"I hope so." Her hair whipped across her face and she raked it back. "Probably."

Saying he was happy would be a lie. His body wasn't letting him forget he was a man. "We'd better walk to your car. I wish I'd driven so you didn't have to go so far."

"You didn't invite me out. I invited you." She walked back the way they'd come and he followed.

"How long have the little girl and her mother rented from you?" Making conversation had become very important. The thought of letting her go again made his every step an effort.

"Over a year. It was an accident. But that's a long story. Her name's Cara. She's nine." Lauren raised an animated face. "She's lovely, Jack. Bright, and wise the way some children who haven't had enough time to just be young are wise. She always thinks of the other person first. Most adults have forgotten how to be that way...if they ever knew."

First impressions could be wrong, even second, or third impressions, and from what he was hearing he'd swear Lauren really cared about this child.

"She turned up on my doorstep—" she clasped her hands behind her back "—with Betty, her mother. They thought I had rooms to rent and... Anyway, with Joe gone, I had two empty rooms. The rest's history as they say."

He almost checked his stride. "Joe?"

At the curb, she paused until he was beside her, then turned away, toward a shack that rented surfing gear. "More dull history. Joe was my foster son for six months."

He swallowed. "You never mentioned him." He had to hold the prize for misjudgment.

"There wasn't any reason. I only had him for...for a little while. As soon as his dad could manage, he took him back. Nice kid. He'll do fine, I think, I *hope*." She gave a short laugh.

Jack looked past Lauren. In some ways she was an enigma... actually, in many ways. She seemed lost in thought.

The story went that Lauren hadn't had children with Dan Taylor because she didn't want them. The fact that Dan Taylor and his second wife immediately chose to have a child was supposed proof. Without much thought, Jack stored the gossip away. Now he'd lay bets this lady had always wanted children very badly. He thought over the comments she'd made, searching for hints. With or without anything direct, he was suddenly convinced that for some reason she'd been unable to have a baby. But if she didn't feel like sharing that with him, he certainly couldn't raise the subject.

Lauren still wasn't talking.

In the window of the surfing shack, blown up larger than she was in real life, Silky Harvey posed for posterity in a pouting, bosom-thrusting ad for a wet suit that was unzipped to the waist.

Silky was a good kid. He gazed until the smiling face and blond hair blurred. Kid was the operative. Nice in a fluffy way and with nothing more stimulating between her ears than an overdeveloped certainty that she was sexy. So different from Lauren. Beautiful Lauren who seemed oblivious to being a knockout capable of paralyzing a man's brain.

He realized she'd said something. "I'm sorry, Lauren. What did you say?"

Her face was tilted up to his. For an instant she looked toward the window, then back. "I said we should go." She stepped around him. "It's late."

"Not too late. We could walk a little more, couldn't we? I'd like to know more about Joe."

She evaded his hand. "No."

Puzzled by the sudden change in her manner, he caught her elbow. "Did I say something wrong?"

"No." Her eyes slid away from his to a point behind him.

He twisted around but saw nothing but the shack. "You make a habit of this, don't you? Switching on and switching off?" The despair he felt shook him.

"You should give up on me. I don't even seem to know my own mind."

"Try explaining it to me." His own frustration was a mirror of what he saw in Lauren's eyes.

"I can't. Do you think you could let it go? Could you be patient with me for a while? Again?"

He picked up a strand of her hair and let it slip through his fingers. "I don't seem to be able to do anything else."

CHAPTER THIRTEEN

Leaving the office for a short break in the middle of the morning had been Susan's idea. "Thank you for thinking of this," Lauren told her, appreciatively sniffing her espresso. "I didn't realize how badly I needed to get away until I was outside." They sat at one of a group of white wrought-iron tables in front of a café a few doors away from Contact.

Susan squinted into the sun and reached into her bag for sunglasses. "I'm looking for ways to leave Yolande in charge for short periods. She's still tentative about being alone in the office. Anyway, don't pin any badges on me. I've been dying to find out how things went last night."

"You're so good to listen to my woes all the time. But you don't have to today. Just sitting with a blank mind is enough for now."

"Oh, no you don't. I said I'm not up for awards. I'm curious, Lauren. Nosy, if you like. *What happened?* You said you saw him."

"His wife's coming home for a visit."

"He's divorced."

"His ex-wife."

Susan stirred her coffee slowly. "And he made a deal of telling you that?"

"No. Andy mentioned it. Jack never did. Which probably means he thought it would put me off and he'd only think that if he wants to have his cake and eat it, too. In other words, he wants someone as a safe stopgap while he's hoping for a reconciliation when his wife—ex-wife—comes home."

Susan snorted. "You've got quite an imagination. You don't know any of that for sure."

"No. But it's possible." She couldn't bring herself to tell Susan about the way Jack had stared at Silky Harvey's picture last night, like a thirsty man longing for a fresh drink. He'd made her feel every one of her thirty-nine years. She had to stop thinking about him and putting herself in line for another shot at the role of castoff when someone younger and more exciting came along.

"Lauren, don't second-guess the man."

"I'm not. It's obvious, isn't it? I'm not going to make any demands because I'm not looking for anything permanent. That makes me perfect for him." *Was* she second-guessing him?

"What does that make *him?* And are you sure you aren't interested in something permanent, as you put it?"

Lauren stared, then shook her head. "Of course not. Let's change the subject." She wasn't pining for a commitment from Jack, was she? Even the idea frightened her.

"Did you cry on each other's shoulders like I told you to?" Susan continued blithely. "I told you shared trouble is a sure way to form a bond."

"Yes. Evidently nothing else has happened. And, as he said, there's been enough trouble already. From what he said when we were driving—we went out for dinner—they've got every move they intend to make at the farm choreographed. He's dealing directly over the phone with clients and playing his cards close to his chest. And they've got watches posted, and double watches, so there should be no chance for anyone to pull anything." On the trip back to his place the choice had been between silence and safe conversation. They'd chosen the latter.

"I'd love to meet him. He sounds like a smart cookie."

Smart and with an irritating ability to crawl into her every unoccupied waking moment. "Jack's an interesting man. He thinks of every eventuality. I guess he's going to wait for the last moment to announce whatever he's doing from here on. Whatever that means. He says that'll make it impossible for certain kinds of sabotage."

"Being prepared's probably smart, but I don't think there'll be any more incidents, do you? After a major fire that got all that attention, it would be crazy."

As usual, what Susan said made sense. "You're probably right. And I hope you are, for Jack's sake." Not that she expected to be seeing much of him after the cool way they'd parted last night.

A jumping, waving figure caught Lauren's attention. "Is that Yolande now?"

Susan swiveled around. "Certainly is. I was afraid our reprieve wouldn't be very long. She's good in her way, industrious, but her initiative is zero."

"I've noticed," Lauren agreed grimly, already on her feet.

As she drew close to Yolande the woman said, "You didn't have to rush back."

Lauren heard Susan groan but put her hand on Yolande's shoulder. "What is it?"

"Someone named Betty called. She said she's going out for a while, so she'll call again later and you're not to worry."

"Thanks." As far as Lauren could remember, Betty had never called the office and she should be sleeping now.

By the time she reached her desk Susan was closing the door behind them. "I know what you're thinking and don't."

Lauren rounded on her. "You don't know what I'm thinking."

"Yes I do. And you're chewing skin off your mouth. Stop it. Just because Betty calls, it doesn't mean she's going to tell you… Well, it doesn't mean a thing."

She made up her mind. "If anything happens that I absolutely have to deal with, call. I'll either be on my way home or already there. I'll check in myself as soon as I can."

"You're overreacting."

"Maybe. Thanks for being here for me."

All the way home she alternated between feeling guilty for leaving her responsibilities in someone else's hands at a crucial time, and nerve-fraying fear of what she'd find at the town house.

The moment she opened the front door she remembered what should have been her first thought. Cara was out of school for the day.

"Hello," Lauren called. When she listened, instead of a response, she heard the sound of running water.

Relief made her weak. Taking deep breaths, she strode into the kitchen.

Cara, soapsuds swelling around the short sleeves of her blouse, stood on tiptoe at the sink. Absorbed in some task, she hadn't heard Lauren.

"Hi, sweetie," Lauren said, trying not to shock the girl.

Cara jumped and spun around, sloshing water over the floor. Billowing in the soapy water was something green.

"What are you doing?"

"Washing." She rubbed her cheek against a shoulder.

Lauren moved closer. "Aren't those the sweatshirts I gave you?"

"Yes." Cara swallowed convulsively. "I'm not doing anything wrong."

"Of course not," Lauren said gently. "But why?"

"People are proud y'know. Don't blame Jimmy's mom for being mad at him. She's had a tough time. Jimmy's told me all about it."

Lauren pulled out a chair and sat down heavily. "Should I call Mrs. Sutter and tell her it's okay for Jimmy to have the shirt?"

"No!" Cara looked horrified. "She wouldn't like it. It's better not to make her think about it. You can't fix everything."

Sometimes Cara made Lauren feel like the child. "I made things hard for you with those darn shirts."

"Nah. We love 'em. We...we put 'em on at school sometimes. It's just that you gotta do what makes things easy. Some kids say me and Jimmy are goin' together 'cause of the shirts."

"And that bothers you?" Why hadn't she left the damn things in the shop, or just bought one for Cara?

"No. Jimmy and me know we're only friends. Who wants to go with someone? That's dumb."

Dumb, except when one friend or the other wanted more than companionship, or when both of them wanted more, but one, namely Lauren, knew that the moment she gave in to her instincts she'd be on the road to being alone again.

"Don't worry about Jimmy and me." Cara had come quietly to rest a damp hand on Lauren's neck. "When we grow up we're gonna remember each other and we'll feel good about it."

Lauren hugged the thin little body, buried her face against a fragile shoulder. "You bet you will." She closed her eyes against smarting.

"Lauren! I tried to reach you at the office. I was going to call again."

She kept an arm around Cara and turned to see Betty bustling into the kitchen, more dressed up than Lauren had ever seen her.

"Cara—" Betty frowned at her daughter "—I told you to get ready."

Cara moved away from Lauren. "I was doing something. It won't take me long."

"Not now. You'll have to go as you are. It's a good job I packed your bag." Betty tutted and turned to Lauren. "I was going to let you know we'll be away overnight, if that's all right."

That Betty felt she even had to pretend to owe her an explanation pained Lauren. "Of course. Have a wonderful time."

"We will. Come on, Cara. We'll be late."

"But I've got to—"

"I'll finish up for you," Lauren said, smiling. "Run along."

Within minutes they were gone with no explanation.

Lauren felt drained. Cara was slipping away from her; she could feel it. At the sink, she finished squeezing out the sweatshirts and then took them to the dryer in the laundry room. Wise little Cara. She belonged to Betty, not to Lauren. But these trips didn't have to mean anything momentous. Why was Betty so secretive about them?

Dragging, Lauren gathered her purse and headed for the front door. She made it as far as the foot of the stairs. Just for once she'd give herself permission to be human. Let Susan cope for a few hours.

RINGING CAME TO HER dully through the quilt she must have pulled over her head. Pushing her hair out of her eyes, Lauren fumbled for the phone.

Dial tone. But the ringing was still there.

She sat up, shivering in her satin gown.

The doorbell.

Shoving at the covers, she swung her feet from the bed, grabbed the robe that matched the gown and pulled it on as she ran for the stairs.

How long had she slept? She'd decided to go to bed at around three after Susan had assured her everything was under control. The house was gloomy now.

"Coming," she called, wrapping the robe around her and tying the belt. Could Betty have changed her mind about staying away overnight?

Fumbling, she drew off the chain and threw open the door.

Jack Irving, his hands in the pockets of worn jeans, looked at her from beneath the brim of a black Stetson. Grim summed up his countenance accurately.

"May I come in?"

Before she could respond, he crossed the threshold, swinging his shoulders to pass her. "Is anyone home with you?"

"No."

"Did you check through the peephole before you opened the door?"

"N-no."

He looked her over thoroughly. "I could have been anyone. This isn't Disneyland."

She raised her head. "Really? And I thought you were Mickey Mouse."

"Don't be smart. Women alone in their homes get attacked all the time. And most of them don't come close to looking the way you do right now."

Her skin flashed hot. "You have one hell of a way of delivering a compliment. If that's what it was."

"Take it any way you want to. Do you happen to have anything to drink?"

Lauren closed the door and leaned against it. "What's the matter with you?"

He took off his hat and raked at his hair. "This has been a hell of a day. I wanted to see you," he said quietly. "I need to be with you."

Lauren felt her blood drain to her feet. Jack was in trouble. Real trouble. "Come in." She grabbed his hand and pulled him behind her into the kitchen. "Sit there," she ordered, indicating the table.

Settling his hat back on his head and tilting it low over his eyes, he spun a chair on one leg and sat astride the seat, his arms draped along the back.

She couldn't even see his eyes and, as sexy a picture as he might make, there were limits to the potency of any kind of charm. "Take your hat off."

"Huh?" He lifted his chin and squinted out at her. "Oh, sorry. Forgot." The Stetson whizzed across the table to rest in a corner.

Quelling the urge to demand that he tell her what was on his mind, all of it, immediately, Lauren surreptitiously checked to make sure the slippery robe was well in place over her skimpy gown.

"Looks great." Jack hadn't missed a move. "Something to drink would really be nice, Lauren."

Keeping one hand firmly beneath her breasts, she scuffed, pulling a step stool with her, to the cupboard over the microwave. Carefully she climbed up and opened a door. "Yuck. All this stuff must be years old."

"That usually means it's good.

She eyed the selection skeptically. "I do have some jug wine in the refrigerator."

"This isn't a jug-wine situation."

"Okay. Cherry-chocolate liqueur, separated and with what looks like pink syrup floating on top. Galliano with rust around the cap. Ah, crème de menthe. I don't suppose the little brown things floating in it mean anything."

Jack groaned. "Keep going."

"Believe me. It only gets worse." She scrabbled far back and found a cardboard cylinder she didn't remember buying, or receiving as a gift. The top came off easily and she extracted a bottle. "Full. Must be really awful. Glenfid...Glenfiddy-something."

"Glenfiddich. Thank God. Gimme."

Descending as gracefully as possible, she gave him the bottle. "What is it?"

"Single malt. First-class stuff."

"Ah." She tried to sound intelligent. Alcohol wasn't anything she knew much about. "I'll get you a glass."

"Get two. I don't like drinking alone."

"I wasn't aware you liked drinking at all."

"I don't usually." He shunned ice and half filled each of the two highball glasses she gave him. "Sit there where I can see you." He indicated the chair he pulled beside his and she sat down, so close she could see dark flecks in eyes that were the same color as his single malt.

Jack took a long swallow, coughed, wiped his mouth with the

back of his hand and closed his eyes. "Medicinal purposes," he muttered. "Have some."

Lauren drank and gasped. A rasping noise came from her throat. She couldn't speak. The liquor burned all the way down, while she struggled to take a breath.

Her eyes were squeezed shut when she became dimly aware of the glass being removed from her relaxing fingers. A thud in the center of her back made her cough—and breathe again.

"You okay?"

Through teary eyes, she saw Jack's wavering face and nodded.

"Don't drink any more. You aren't up to it."

She shook her head.

"It won't be wasted." Still peering at her, he added the contents of her glass to his and sat down again. "You sure you're okay?"

"Yes," she croaked. "Fine."

Jack rested his chin on the chair back and closed his eyes. "Lauren, you ought to kick me out. I'm using you."

Her head cleared. "No you're not." She offered a hand and he grasped it. "Tell me what's happened."

He drank again. "I've been so careful. Whoever did it... Damn it. Someone found out what I thought no one knew, but the truck drivers and me. Oh, honey, I'm not sure I can pull it out anymore."

She waited patiently, stroking his fingers.

"Three Irving trucks of cut flowers arrived at the wholesalers this afternoon," he said. "Those drivers have been working for my family for years. They're absolutely clean. But when the trucks were opened there wasn't a box inside that wasn't full of mutilated blooms. Ruined, Lauren. The whole damn shipment ruined."

Appalled, Lauren got up, pushed the chair aside and knelt in front of him. She took his face in her hands, smoothed his hair. There seemed nothing to say that could come close to telling him how helpless and angry she felt.

Jack rubbed her cheek distractedly with the backs of his fingers. "Someone knew what was supposed to be completely secret—the time those trucks were due to leave. I'd swear they went from the farm in good condition. I'd also swear they left with someone in the back of each truck, working like crazy to demolish the cargo, then waiting for an opportunity to get away.''

"No one saw anything?''

"Nothing. Not a damn thing. The police are on to it, but I don't expect any results.''

"Oh, I hate them!'' She jumped up and paced. "I wish I knew who it was.''

"So do I, sweetheart,'' Jack said.

He sounded different. Lauren quieted, looked at him. He'd called her sweetheart. "It'll be all right,'' she told him, knowing she was trying to convince herself as much as Jack.

"When you say that I almost believe it. But it's bad, Lauren, really bad. I'm down to pinning everything on Irving's Lava Pearl.''

She tilted her head inquiringly.

Jack laughed shortly. "A poinsettia. It's a sport—that's a mutant—out of a chance seedling called Flame Pepper. This will be the first year we offer it for sale. It's beautiful. Red-orange bracts with pearly-cream veins. Short and lush. And it's a state secret as far as I'm concerned, Lauren.''

"I wouldn't say anything.''

"I know you wouldn't,'' he said quietly. "You know, all afternoon while I was going through hell, I kept thinking about you. I promised myself I was going to come looking for you as soon as I could. I'm glad I did. So glad.''

Her heart skittered, and thumped. "I'm glad, too.'' She wouldn't burden him with her worries about Cara—not that he was likely to understand.

"Being with you is special,'' he said, getting up and setting down his glass. "Come here.''

Lauren went, slowly, and leaned on the edge of the table where she could see his face. "We all need someone to trust,'' she said. "If I can be that for you, I'm very glad, Jack.''

"You can. You are. From the first time we talked, I felt—I don't know—something different, I guess. Now I think I know what it is.''

She thought so, too. He felt the way she did. And she felt... Her stomach dropped and she bowed her head to hide a grimace. Was it possible that Jack could be feeling what she did at this moment?

Susan had asked the question: was she sure she didn't want anything permanent with Jack? And she, Lauren, had denied it. *Wrong*. Fear of abandonment aside, she wanted Jack because she loved him, loved him more than she'd ever loved anyone.

Overwhelmed, she turned away, only to have him ease her back, and wedge her between his lean body and the hard rim of the tabletop that pressed into the backs of her thighs.

"Was it okay for me to come?"

Lauren tilted her head, rested a hand on his chest. "It was very okay, Jack. I... There's no one else I want to be with."

He raised her fingers to his lips and kissed them, keeping his eyes on hers. "No one else tonight? Or does that mean there might be other times when I'd be the preferred candidate?"

She smiled, wrinkled her nose. "I guess this is 'fess up time, huh? Well, I'll take a chance. There don't seem to be any times left when you wouldn't be the preferred candidate."

Any vestige of a smile deserted Jack's face. "Those are the sweetest words I ever heard."

Lauren couldn't speak.

"When will your little Cara and her mother be back?" Jack said, his voice husky. He rubbed his hands up and down her arms on top of the smooth satin.

She shook her head.

"Does that mean you don't know?"

"They aren't coming back tonight."

He let out a long breath. "If you want me to go, I will. But if you'd let me, I'd give my soul to stay with you all night. Just to hold you and watch you sleep. You make me believe there's still sanity in this world."

"Doesn't Andy do that?" She'd had to say it.

"Yes, sweetheart. Yes, of course." He used a thumb to tilt up her chin. "See why you're so right for me? You keep me on track. Andy's my anchor, but he's also just a little boy. You're a woman, Lauren, alive, incredibly sensitive and sexy and... Say you understand."

"I understand." She understood that waves of desire shivered over and into her and she was incapable of stopping what was happening.

"We can be so much for one another." His breath whispered across her mouth and he kissed her softly, took her bottom lip gently in his teeth, slipped his tongue along the sensitive skin just inside. "I've been waiting a long time for you."

Her body flamed. Jack found her desirable. He wanted to be with her when he was troubled. Surely that could be enough for as long as it lasted.

Jack spanned her waist and lifted her to sit on the table. She kept her knees tightly together, but he leaned his thigh against them, watching her eyes, smiling slightly, until she relaxed and he moved in close, smoothing away the robe and gown to run his hands up to her hips. Still smiling, he slipped his long fingers beneath the lace at the legs of her tap pants and massaged her bottom.

"Jack—"

"Ssh. You are so smooth. So soft."

She wrapped her arms convulsively around his neck and buried her face in the shoulder of his denim shirt.

"Hey," he said, nuzzling the top of her head. "Something wrong?"

"Nothing." Nothing and everything.

"Look at me."

Cautiously she raised her head but kept her eyes lowered. "It's..." She inclined her face and fiddled with the shirt buttons. One came undone, and another, and another, until she could pull the tails free and bare his chest. Thick hair, dark, as she remembered from the pool, spread wide. She stroked, kissed, stroked and bent to kiss the ridges over his ribs and the flat plane of his belly and his navel.

She felt him tremble and the tightening of his fingers on her arms.

"Lauren." His voice was thick. "Is it all right?"

For a moment she didn't understand. Then she nodded. "Yes. Nothing will happen." She knew a moment's sadness that what he couldn't know meant that she was unable to get pregnant.

He worked the panties down, lifted her and slipped them away. Places deep inside her throbbed with need, but still she felt a shyness.

Jack framed her face and kissed her fully, deeply. "Relax, my love. It's right. Let go."

He must be able to feel her tension. "It's been..." Embarrassment thickened her tongue. "It's been a long time," she said in a rush. "Years, Jack."

"Do you know how good that makes me feel?" He gazed into her eyes while he slid the robe from her shoulders. The gown followed, brushed aside under hands that found and supported her breasts. Jack bent to kiss her urgent flesh, murmuring incoherent endearments and nipping, teasing, while she arched toward him in a mute plea for more and more of him.

"I'm glad there hasn't been anyone else since..." A shadow passed over his features. "I'm glad, Lauren. Forget everything, sweetheart, everything but us." Gently, he pulled her arms from the gown and it fell about her waist.

Lauren felt the last vestige of control snap. With fingers that were suddenly sure, she unsnapped and unzipped his jeans. But it was Jack who finished undressing while she touched whatever she could reach of him.

Then he was facing her, lifting her, hooking her legs around his lean hips. For an instant she tried to pull back, but he held her fast against him, used his thumbs to part the tender, engorged folds that awaited him.

Their joining was swift, a wild thrusting. Lauren cried out against the first dull ache of protest at his stretching.

Jack stopped, panting. "I'm sorry. Lauren, I'm sorry. I'm hurting you."

"No." She tried to move against him, to make him move.

He held her still. "Slower, love. It'll be okay, but it's got to be slower at first. Okay." He kissed her neck, her shoulder. "Okay, my love."

She let go, let him take her weight and do the work. And the discomfort ebbed, replaced by exquisite, mounting pain. She didn't have to tell him she was ready. As if his body read hers, he took it all and made it his own.

In the stillness of the kitchen with its commonplace trappings, Lauren found perfect passion and felt a peace that she'd never known.

Jack rested her on the table, his arms a vise around her body, the satin a pool at his feet. "You are beautiful," he said. With long, slow sweeps he stroked her back. "I'm never going to get enough of you, Lauren."

HE WATCHED HER through slitted eyes. She lay on her back, staring at the ceiling through moon-silvered darkness.

If he spoke, she might respond and say what he didn't want to hear, that she didn't feel what he'd finally figured out he felt himself. He could love this woman for the rest of his life, if she'd let him. She hadn't given any hint that she knew that's what he'd been suggesting from the minute he turned up on her doorstep, however many hours ago that had been.

Lauren turned toward him and he closed his eyes. Her touch, feather-light, settled on his neck. With the back of her finger, she skimmed the side of his face, his jaw, and brought her palm to rest against his chest.

He heard a small sound and looked at her. "You awake?" he whispered.

"Yes." She sounded...choked.

"Okay?"

"Mmm. I like having you here with me." She pressed herself to him, wrapped her arms tightly around his neck and buried her face under his chin. "I don't want to think about anything but right now."

Jack stroked her back. "I'm not going to." He didn't want to face the future, but not because he didn't want to think about the two of them. "This is corny. But I feel as if I've come home. This isn't going to be enough, Lauren. I'm going to keep on wanting to be with you." How far did he dare go? How much could he say, suggest, without some definite sign that she felt for him what he felt for her?

She pushed him to his back, rested on an elbow on each side of his head, and kissed him deeply. Her breasts were an insistent, soft pressure on his chest, and where her thighs parted over one of his, he felt her growing moist. He closed his eyes. Caution told him to let her take the lead, but she was ready for him again, and he was ready for her.

Abruptly she arched her back, supported herself on outstretched arms while she looked down at him.

Jack shifted his attention to her breasts. Gently he covered them, then raised his head to kiss first one, then the other. She cried out softly and let her hair fall over his face.

He dropped back, ready to receive her, but she rolled away and lay beside him again, staring at the ceiling. "It's... Jack, I'm afraid."

"Afraid of what?"

She stopped him from trying to take her into his arms. "Of myself. Lying here, feeling wonderful and wanted, I got frightened. You know why?"

"Tell me, sweetheart."

"Because there were things I didn't really admit about myself until tonight. I've come close to looking at the truth about the past, but I've always avoided it at the last minute. I—" She sighed and brought his hand to her lips. "I'm not as nice as I've told myself. I used to be able to totally convince myself that I was devastated by my divorce. And I thought it was because I was generous that I was able to keep on being there for Dan when he had problems he wanted to share with me."

He laughed. "You were. And you are. Too generous."

"No, Jack." Her eyes glittered. "I'd started falling out of love with Dan a long time before he walked out on me. Oh, I don't mean I would have ever ended my marriage, but in some ways it was a relief, and by being kind to Dan I'm paying him back for the guilt I feel because I stopped loving him." She rested the back of her hand on her mouth. "That's awful. What must have hurt me most when he finally said he was leaving was feeling I'd been...let go? Told that I was second-best?"

Jack stroked her hair, kissed her shoulder. "You're something. You think everything through so honestly."

Her small laugh was bitter. "Sure. Given enough time."

"But Dan had been drawing away from you. I heard you tell him that on the phone in your car outside the club. He'd been sleeping with Christie. A woman has to sense a thing like that. No wonder you stopped loving him."

"I'm not sure it hadn't happened even before Christie. It was almost as if we were a habit. We *were* a habit."

"With someone capable of giving you all of himself the story would be different."

"Would it? I'm not sure I believe that's possible. Dan once explained to me his theory on monogamy. He doesn't think it works for men."

Jack held himself tightly in check. She wasn't getting his message. "He's entitled to his opinions. He can't speak for everyone."

"I guess not."

He had to break the tension. "Andy keeps asking me to invite you to do things."

"Does he?" She moved her head to see him.

"Yes. He wanted to take you surfing. I told him you don't like the water much, but he said you could make the sandwiches and come and watch."

She giggled. "Already a small version of a grown male with all the role components worked out."

"He just wanted you with us. If I ever get another spare day away from the farm, will you do something with Andy and me?" She was fond of children. He was sure of that now. He'd offer her everything he had to offer and the next move was up to her.

Lauren didn't answer.

Jack frowned. "Lauren?"

"Oh, Jack. Yes. Yes, I'd love to do something with you and Andy. He's the nicest kid." Her eyes crinkled with her smile. "I'll never forget the way he set me up with Jaws."

"Neither will he." Jack laughed and touched the tip of her nose. "He still talks about you being the only girl who isn't afraid of his pets. He talks about you a lot, in fact."

Lauren grabbed his finger and held it gently between her teeth. He leaned to kiss her temple.

"Who's Andy with now?"

"My father. He often spends the night there."

The phone rang.

Jack didn't move. Lauren scooted up to sit against the headboard and turned on the light. Pulling the sheet over her breasts, she picked up the receiver. He felt as much as saw her become very still.

Silently, she handed the receiver to him. By the time he put it to his ear she'd slipped from the bed and gone into the bathroom.

"Hello."

Static and popping preceded the faint voice that said, "This is Mary."

He fell back on the pillows and checked the clock beside the bed. Nine o'clock. "Hello, Mary." He wasn't even sure what time it was in Paris. "How did you find me?"

"Denton suggested I should try this number. I had to talk to you."

He waited. Dressed in a white terry robe, Lauren came from the bathroom and sat in front of a small dressing table. She switched on a lamp and picked up a hairbrush.

"Did Andy get my letter?"

"Yes."

With slow, deliberate strokes, Lauren brushed her hair. In the mirror, her eyes held his.

"Is he excited?"

"Excited?"

"About my coming to see him? I wondered... I'm not sure I should."

He rested the back of his wrist over his eyes. "I'm sure you should."

"Why?"

"Because you said you would, that's why. You don't make contact after so long and get people's hopes up, only to turn around and say you've changed your mind." He felt murderous. The violence of his reaction stunned him.

"I wrote because I was a bit low. Things weren't going so well and suddenly it seemed appealing to come there for a while."

Nothing had changed with her. She was still first, second and always in her own mind. Use the people who love you if it suits you, then shove them away when you don't need them. "Doesn't it still sound appealing to come?" He couldn't bear to have Andy undermined again.

"Well...I'm going to have a show, Jack. Finally, it's happening and I'm so excited. Maurice... Jack, tell Andy something came up, will you?"

"No." Not this time. He was out of excuses. "Look, this isn't the best time to talk. I'll call you later—tomorrow. Bye."

He shoved the receiver into its cradle and threw back the covers. In two strides he was behind Lauren, pushing his hands beneath the robe to knead her shoulders.

She wouldn't meet his gaze.

"That was Mary...my ex-wife."

"I gathered. You asked her how she knew you were here."

"My father gave her your number as a possibility." And later he'd have more to say about that.

"I see." She set down the brush and sat immobile.

"Come back to bed." He bent to kiss her neck.

"I don't think so."

The robe fell open under his hands. Watching her in the mirror, he pulled her back against him, covering her breasts, moving his hips slightly at her back. "Come with me, Lauren."

"You were telling her you wanted her to come."

He turned cold. "Only for Andy's sake."

Lauren stood, ignored the robe that slid to the floor, and faced him. Tears were in her eyes.

"Please don't look like that. Mary has nothing to do with us." His desire for her was something neither of them could miss. "We're what matters. Doesn't that mean something to you?"

She sighed. "It means more than I can explain."

"Same here. But you don't trust me, do you?"

Pink washed her cheeks. "Men haven't given me a whole lot to trust."

"Men?" He raised a brow. "You already admitted the one man in your life who let you down had probably fallen from favor before he dropped the bomb. Does one man who didn't know what he had, or what he was losing, mean the rest of us are no good?"

"No," she said, shaking her head. "But I saw the look on your face when you were talking to her. You were persuading her to come."

He raised his hands to hold her, thought better of it and turned away. "For *Andy*. I can't force you to believe me, but that's the only reason, Lauren."

She rubbed her shoulders.

His attempt at a laugh failed. "Can you believe us? Two people who just made wonderful love, but who don't trust each other?"

"I don't want to feel this way."

"Then don't." He faced her again. "I could say that I wonder if you're the type of woman who'll grow bored with any man after a while. After all, you got bored with Dan."

"It wasn't the way you make it sound."

"Maybe. But I've only got your word for it." If he had to shock her to make her see reason, he would.

"It's true."

He picked up the robe and held it while she slipped it on. "Do you really think I want my ex-wife to visit?" While he spoke, he picked up his jeans and pulled them on.

"I don't want to, but I know what I heard."

"Yeah. Okay. Well, I guess you're going to have to decide what you believe, all by yourself." He was too wound up to think straight.

Lauren laced her fingers together. "It wasn't my ex-spouse who called while we were in bed. It was yours."

"I've spent more than my share of time listening to you and your ex-husband. You're still joined at the hip."

"That's not fair!"

"No," he said quietly and put on his shirt. "None of this is. It's damned stupid. But you don't get it about me, do you? You don't get any of what I've been trying to say to you for hours, or why I'm upset right now."

"Jack—"

"It's okay. It's fine. Just the way it should be. Two people helping one another through some lonely hours. You don't have to be able to really know me, or read my mind. But there's unfinished business between us. Remember that."

She made no attempt to argue, or to stop him from leaving.

CHAPTER FOURTEEN

Lauren slammed her car door with enough force to jar her arm to the shoulder. The whole world was so damn high-handed, so ready to be drawn into mean little intrigues.

She needed a few more minutes to calm down before going into the office. Leaning on the hood of the Honda, she took deep breaths. Damn Christie Taylor, anyway. Jealous, treacherous, but without the smarts to carry off her tricks and not get caught.

Another car rolled into sight, sun scintillating off its silver hood. It stopped a few yards from Contact's premises. Within seconds, Susan appeared and ran to the driver's side of the sports car. The tinted window rolled smoothly down and the man Lauren remembered from before smiled up at Susan, who bent to kiss him.

Lauren smiled, folded her arms and looked at her feet. She didn't want to spy.

There was no way to get to the office without being seen. She went to the back of her car and opened the trunk. Within seconds the sleek silver beast slipped past.

"Lauren?"

She winced and shut the trunk, grateful to have found a pile of folders to fill her hands. "Oh, hi, Susan." Looking both ways, she trotted across the street. "Wait till you hear what I just did."

They went into the building together and were soon closeted in Lauren's domain. "You're in a better mood today," Susan said.

Throughout yesterday, Lauren had found it impossible to think of anything but Jack and the previous night when they'd been together. "I'm busy today. And I've got what I want."

Susan settled into a chair. "What would that be? A way to work things out with Jack?"

Lauren already regretted having confided in Susan the day before, but she'd needed someone and Susan had been her only choice. "I just came from seeing Mrs. Arthur Wakefield and I was right."

"Right?" Susan looked blank.

"Mrs. Wakefield had been told by a little bird that Contact wasn't to be trusted, that we tend to be careless with privileged information."

Susan shot to her feet. "What the hell does she mean?"

"Calm down, calm down. It's all right. All I had to do was figure out the common denominator between our defectors and I was home free."

"I'm not following you."

"Catering services, beauty supply firms, a beauty salon, a tanning salon, one of the best children's clothing shops in town and on and on. Ring any bells?"

Susan thought. "No."

"Christie Taylor!" Lauren swung around to stare through the window. "It was the clothing store that gave me the idea. Then I took a chance. I managed to confirm that Christie uses We Serve U. And that Mrs. Wakefield socializes with Christie. Then I followed up and it was easy to find out Christie's connections with the other businesses."

"What did you do then?" Susan sounded incredulous.

"I went to Mrs. Arthur Wakefield and told her I know Christie had suggested she no longer use us."

"Good grief. What if you'd been wrong?"

"She'd already quit us. How much more egg could I have on my face? Dan wouldn't have allowed Christie to take things any farther. But Mrs. Wakefield folded like a house of cards. Christie told her we run around chatting about our clients' business to anyone who'll listen."

"But what difference is it going to make?" Susan still didn't sound enthusiastic.

Lauren spun to face her. "I reminded Mrs. Wakefield that her husband has his sights set on public office in this town and that it wouldn't do for his wife to be linked to malicious gossip. She couldn't agree with me more. The lady is very sorry and is going to make sure everything possible is done to put right the terrible wrong that's been done us. She's going to speak to the other clients personally," Lauren finished triumphantly.

Susan shook her head. "Sick," she muttered. "I'll never figure out why Dan married the little toad."

The door opened and Lauren jumped. Dan marched into the room, glaring at Susan who planted her hands on her hips and showed no sign of leaving.

"I want to talk to you," he told Lauren. "Alone."

"I'll stay," Susan said belligerently.

Lauren looked at the ceiling. "I don't want to talk to you, Dan. And if you say one thing out of line, you're gone. I can handle things, Susan. Thanks for the support."

"I don't think I should leave—"

"Go ahead," Lauren said quickly, raising a brow significantly. "I expect you'll be getting some interesting calls."

A smile spread slowly over Susan's face. "Yes." She eyed Dan. "I'm looking forward to them."

As soon as the door closed behind Susan, Dan advanced on Lauren. "You're not going to like what I intend to say."

She smiled tightly, oddly sorry for him. Evidently, news traveled even faster than she'd thought in this town. Someone must already have told him about Christie's vendetta.

"Why don't we sit down, Dan? Would you like some coffee?"

He frowned. "No. You know I don't drink coffee."

Lauren sighed and went to the coffee maker to pour herself a much-needed cup. "I seem to have forgotten a lot of things about you. There isn't any need for me to remember, is there?"

"There's no need to be nasty. I'm not staying. I just want to warn you about Jack Irving."

She turned, almost spilling from her mug. "What do you mean?" Jack was a subject burned permanently into her brain, she thought of little else, but Dan was the last person she intended to discuss him with.

"You two have been getting pretty tight."

Lauren realized her mouth was open and she closed it firmly.

"He's not right for you," Dan said. "I'm only telling you this because I care—"

"What happens to me?" Lauren finished for him. "How dare you? Get out!"

"Now, Lauren. Calm down. If there's one thing I can't stand, it's a hysterical woman." His chin came up and he looked down at her with those familiar, striking blue eyes—eyes that showed he considered himself superior in intellect and that the possibility of being wrong never occurred to him.

A deep breath, intended to calm her, only served to stop her from shouting. "I wonder how many women, at this very moment, are being told they're hysterical by insecure men who want to control them. Off you go, Dan. The end. Finish."

"Don't be ridiculous. When I asked if you were seeing Irving you didn't deny it."

"I would have if I'd known you were going to make the subject your business."

"You told me how bad business has been for him."

Lauren leaned on her desk. "No, I didn't. You told me you'd heard a lot of rumors about Jack having difficulties. I didn't disagree." And in the future she wasn't going to be having any personal conversations with Dan. "I've got work to do."

"It is true that he lost a whole shipment, isn't it?"

"This discussion's over."

"You said so. I know it's true. And I know he needs money. Has he talked about money with you?"

"Talking about other people's business runs in your family, doesn't it?" Lauren said, crossing her arms. The statute of limitations on being nice had run out.

Dan, immaculate in a light gray suit, appeared to turn over her comment. "Answer my question about Irving and I'll let that pass."

"But I won't." In a few succinct sentences, she told him about Christie's meddling. "For old times' sake I don't intend to take any legal action," she concluded.

For the first time in her memory, Dan appeared at a loss for words. He pulled a pack of cigarettes from his inside pocket and sat down in front of her desk.

"I prefer people not to smoke in here."

"I'm not just people." But he put the pack away.

The prick of pity Lauren felt quickly died. "It's time you were, to me—long past time. Goodbye, Dan."

"Lauren—"

"No. There's not going to be any changing my mind this time."

He gripped the arms of the chair, searching her face for any sign of weakening. "You really mean it." Pushing himself upright, he straightened his jacket. "So be it. But don't say I didn't warn you about Irving."

Disgusted, Lauren went to sit behind her desk. Shading her eyes with a hand, she bent over her papers and, after an interval, heard the door open. From the outer office came the muted patter of keyboards and the sound of her operators' voices. Dan hadn't even said he felt badly about what his wife had tried to do.

The door closed.

Letting out a sigh, Lauren fell back in the chair and threw her pencil down—and looked up at Jack Irving.

"Been having another cozy chat with ex-hubby?"

She couldn't think of a thing to say. Dressed in worn jeans and a light denim shirt open at the neck and with the sleeves rolled up past his elbows, he looked as if he'd come from helping clear charred debris at the packing plant.

"Commiserating with him, were you? He must have broken his neck getting here after I kicked him off my land."

"I don't know what you're talking about."

"Sure. You didn't tell Dan baby I'm in so much trouble I don't know where next week's grocery money's coming from. You didn't tell him how badly devastated we've been by the fire."

"Hey, wait a minute." She got up and walked around to stand in front of him. "Just a minute. I don't know what brought this on, but there isn't any one in town, or a lot of other places, who doesn't know about the fire."

He came a step closer. "And the flower shipments? Does everyone in town know about something I told you yesterday? You didn't mention that to Dan?"

Her blush was instant.

Jack's laugh was unpleasant. "What did you do? Wait just long enough for me to be out of your bedroom and call the guy? Did you tell him I was ripe to make a cheap sale on a bundle of land that's been in my family for generations?''

"I admit I mentioned the shipments when he called this morning about—about nothing in particular. And I'm sorry. I should have been more careful, but it never struck me..." Maybe she deserved criticism for being too trusting, but not for maliciousness. "Do you mean Dan came and tried to buy property from you?"

Jack scowled and averted his face. "As if you didn't know. That wasn't the guy's ghost I just passed. Don't tell me he wasn't giving you a progress report. He *told* me, Lauren." He shoved his hands in his pockets and stared at her. "He told me he knew from you how bad things were and so, as a gesture to a friend of yours, he was offering to take some property off my hands."

"Jack—"

"*Let* me finish. Of course, what he could offer wouldn't be top dollar because he'd be making a long-term investment 'at best,' taking a flyer for a *friend* and hoping he could come up with a way to turn a *small* profit in the future. But at least I'd get some of the operating capital I obviously need right now. I almost puked."

"I knew absolutely nothing about this." And she didn't know what she felt more strongly—amazement at Dan's underhanded tactics, or fury with Jack for believing she was involved.

"You can't let him go, can you?"

Lauren flinched, stepped back, and came up against the desk. "That's not fair. I told you...I was honest with you about Dan."

"And I trusted you with things I haven't told another soul." He regarded her steadily. "Do you still love him?"

Lauren made fists at her sides. She felt the sting of tears. "How can you ask that?"

"I *am* asking. You shared things with him that I thought were between the two of us."

"They were.... They are. I... Jack, I..." Why couldn't she tell him she loved him?

"When it comes right down to it, you don't have any defense, do you?" Jack made a disgusted sound. "I'm out of here."

He strode from the room, closing the door firmly behind him.

"Jack!" But it was too late. Just as it had been too late last night when she'd finally run downstairs only to find he was already driving away.

MIRRORS DIDN'T LIE? Lauren twisted from the mirror on her dressing table. She wasn't young anymore. But neither was she old. There were lines where once the skin had been smooth, but her face would be described as good, even interesting. And although she didn't like everything about her body, it, too, was good, fit.

But Jack Irving was younger, eligible, possibly still in love with his ex-wife and, if not, would undoubtedly find it easy to find someone younger and more exciting than Lauren Taylor.

The house was silent. She'd come home to a note from Betty saying she had the night off and had taken Cara out for a few hours.

Dressed in sweats, Lauren left her bedroom and started downstairs, in time to meet Betty and Cara coming in. Betty carried a brown paper sack, Cara, a huge bouquet of flowers.

Lauren frowned. "What's going on?"

"These are for you." Cara dumped the cellophane-covered blooms in Lauren's arms. "And Mom's got champagne."

Lauren looked questioningly at Betty, who ducked her head and hurried into the kitchen. Cara's hand, slipped into hers, made Lauren jump.

The girl smiled up at her, a whimsical smile with her lips pulled in. "Come on."

Lauren allowed herself to be led into the kitchen. Betty had set two wineglasses on the table and was struggling with the champagne cork. "We're going to drink a toast." For a woman with something she thought should be celebrated, Betty sounded miserable.

"Come on," Cara whispered, urging Lauren to a chair. She took the flowers back, half filled the sink and dumped them, cellophane and all, into the water. "We gotta find a vase."

The cork finally popped, shooting across the room. Cara hunched her shoulders, never taking her gaze from Lauren's face.

Very carefully, Betty filled the two wineglasses and then poured a small amount of champagne into a juice glass. This she gave to Cara.

Lauren's heart beat so hard she felt sick. "What are we celebrating?"

Betty stood up very straight, her face flushed. "The flowers are because you've done so much for Cara and me. And the champagne's because I wanted you to be glad for me and for Cara. I'm getting married again."

AT THE TAP on her door, Lauren rolled away, toward the window. There was nothing else to be said, nothing she could say without crying and, so far, she'd managed not to do that in front of Betty and Cara.

The tap came again, and, at the same time, the door slid open, then closed again.

She felt the covers at her back lift, and a small, bony person slipped in behind her. "I listened outside," Cara said. "I've been crying, too."

Lauren squeezed her eyes tightly shut. Evidently Betty's romance with a policeman she'd met through her job had been blossoming for months. Now he'd accepted a job as a sheriff in a small Wisconsin town and wanted nothing more than to live a quieter life there with Betty and Cara as his family.

Cara shook her shoulder. "Jimmy and me are gonna write. You and me can write, too."

"Sure." And she should be too glad for the child to be sorry for herself. "It's wonderful, Cara. You and your mom, and Bill, you're going to be a family and that's what you need most."

"He's nice," Cara said. "He took us to see Gram. His mom lives in San Diego and we went there. She likes me."

"Of course she likes you."

"Mom helped me clean my room this afternoon."

Lauren couldn't speak.

"She knows you're gonna feel sad so everything's gonna be gone before you come home tomorrow." Cara gulped. "Is it all right if I leave Sam?"

Lauren reached to turn on the bedside light and sat up. It no longer mattered that Cara would see the tears.

Cara sat up, too, and leaned against Lauren. In her arms was the most decrepit, the most loved of her stuffed animals—a bear worn shiny and hairless by years of cuddling.

"Oh, you can't leave Sam behind." Lauren laid a finger on one of the bear's mismatched blue-button eyes. "Before you knew it, you'd be missing him so much I'd have to send him to you."

Cara raised her pointed face. "No. Things get lost in the mail. You look after him and then I'll have to come back and visit him one day."

CHAPTER FIFTEEN

"It's true, then?" Matt Carson asked.

Jack glanced at Len Gogh and back at Matt. The younger man had never been someone who'd shown signs of wanting to know people. Jack certainly didn't know him—and Len, in his noncommunitive way, had made similar comments about his second-in-command's social skills.

"Matt—" Jack struggled to keep calm. "Look, the fact is our backs are against the wall and we're going to have to come out of this any way we can. Irving's isn't going to be written off as history."

Matt, tall, slim, dark-haired and with an angularly good-looking face, shoved round, wire-rimmed glasses up his nose and settled expressionless hazel eyes on Jack. The baggy jeans and loose brown shirt he wore blended into the background with the greenhouse from which he'd just emerged.

Silently Len handed over several photographs of poinsettia.

"Son of a bitch," Matt said. He peered closely, then thrust the photos at Jack. "These are shots of Lava Pearl."

"Wrong," Len said tightly. "That's what we're telling you. They're shots of what look like Lava Pearl. Flame Talon is what Edgerton's are calling this one."

Matt let out a long, tuneless whistle. "And they've beaten us to it. Right? They've got it on the market first?"

"Yeah." Jack shuffled the photos. "I can't believe it. Damn, it's going to be hard to come back from this one."

"That's it." Matt threw up his hands. "Count me out. I'm gone."

"Just like that?" Jack shook his head. "You're needed here."

Matt pulled a floppy canvas hat from his back pocket, rammed it on his head and pulled the brim down around his ears and eyes. "Three years' work down the tubes is all the prodding I need. I'm sorry for you, Jack, but I can't help. I'll be clearing out of Carlsbad now."

"And going where?" Len asked. His neutral voice didn't fool Jack. Len thought Matt was escaping a difficult situation and Len wasn't a man who'd be likely to approve of quitters.

"Home for a start," Matt said, walking away. "Back to Montana as fast as I can make it. I've already been approached for a professorship in floriculture. I guess I'll take it."

Standing with Len, Jack watched Matt walk away. "I never understood the guy," he muttered. "But he's good at what he does."

"Yeah." Len pulled a stick of gum from his pocket, unwrapped it and stuffed the wad into his mouth. "Look on the bright side. We're going to need every penny we can save and he was expensive."

Jack only half heard what Len said. A familiar red Honda wound its way up the track. He should feel frustrated at the sight of that car, furious at the prospect of having to deal with the biggest dilemma in his life—even bigger than the disaster that had smashed down around his ears this morning—but what he felt was a lifting of the blackness simply at the thought of seeing Lauren.

"My wife and I live very simply."

"Hmm?" Jack realized Len was talking to him.

"Cecelia sells every piece she makes. Somehow or other her pottery's become some sort of status symbol in the art world."

"I'm glad," Jack said politely. Lauren got out of her car and, amazingly, Andy appeared from the passenger side and pointed in Jack's and Len's direction.

"Anyway," Len continued, "with no kids and no expenses to speak of, I can afford to work without pay for as long as it takes."

Jack turned to him, momentarily speechless. "That's not necessary."

Len sniffed and hitched at his overalls. "It may be. We'll pitch in, Jack. We'll pull it off."

If he hadn't been unsure how the other man would react, Jack would have embraced him. "Let's take it a day at a time. Thanks, Len."

"Gotta go." Evidently Len wasn't as concerned as Jack about

the effect of his actions on others. He thumped Jack on the back and ambled away.

Lauren and Andy had moved from sight behind the open trunk of her car. Andy was supposed to be at his grandfather's house where he often spent Saturday mornings. Jack started walking, but moved out of the way as Matt Carson drove by in his ramshackle green truck with sagging wooden railing rigged atop the bed.

The truck drew to a stop in front of the Honda. Lauren appeared, waved apologetically, and moved her car to the side of the track to allow Matt to pass.

Jack reached the Honda as Lauren got out again. She glanced over her shoulder. "Who was that?"

"Matt Carson. He's my…until this morning he was our poinsettia guru. Why?"

"No reason." She faced him and the uncertainty in her eyes made him want to grab her and just hold on. "I just wondered."

"He was rude," Andy said, carrying what appeared to be a picnic basket. "He told Lauren to move her… He said to move her car fast," he finished, coloring slightly.

"Figures," Jack said. "He's in a hurry to get back to Montana— today by the sound of it."

"Andy," Lauren said, "would you take the basket into your dad's office?"

"Well… Yeah, sure." He caught his father's eye. "I was walking over here from Grandpa's and Lauren saw me. She gave me a ride."

"I hope that was all right," Lauren said, resting a hand on the back of Andy's neck. "I told him I didn't think I qualified as a stranger."

"You don't," Jack said, unable to stop staring at her. "We'll be right in, Andy."

Once the boy was gone, Lauren stood in front of Jack. She pushed back hair that was blowing in her eyes. "What I'm doing is out of character," she said simply. "I decided maybe it's time I tried something a little daring."

In tennis shoes, red walking shorts and a baggy white cotton shirt, with her legs bare, she looked young and vulnerable.

"Daring how?"

"Forcing a confrontation. I've never been good at that."

Jack screwed up his eyes against a sudden squall that whipped fine rain into his face. "Your timing couldn't be worse." Even if he did wish he could take her into his arms and pretend the world was a wonderful, safe place.

"I'm sorry." Lauren pulled in the corners of her mouth. "I called your place and your housekeeper said she was there to drop off dry-cleaning or something."

That sounded like Bernice, always ready to spill her own and his business to anyone.

"She told me you were working today. So-o, I decided to bring a picnic lunch. Bernice said you don't eat properly out here."

"Bernice says too much." But maybe he should thank his house-keeper, grab the woman in front of him, and kiss her until he forgot he might be on the verge of bankruptcy.

"I could just go away again," Lauren said. "But you do have to eat. And now, since Andy's here, he does, too. And then, if you're interested, I think the least we owe each other is a chance to say our piece. We've got unfinished business, Jack. I don't like that."

"Neither do I." And he admired her guts. The effort this was costing showed clearly in every tense line of her body. "Let's get inside out of the rain."

They ate in his office and he found he took second place to Lauren in Andy's attention. Lauren didn't appear to notice that all Andy's remarks were aimed at her. The two talked about Andy's menagerie, and soccer, and Mr. Baggs, Andy's hated math teacher.

"Do you know Cara Flood?" Lauren asked suddenly.

Jack noticed the tone of her voice changed, lowered, and she distractedly wrapped the remainder of her sandwich in her napkin.

Andy's brow puckered, then cleared. "Yeah. She's a whiz. Even Baggsy leaves her alone."

Lauren nodded. "Cara's going to do well." She fell quiet.

"Jimmy Sutter's her friend. He's okay, too."

"Cara's moved away," Lauren said and Jack saw the corners of her mouth twitch.

"Yeah?" Andy's mouth was full of cake.

Jack frowned. "Why don't you take a piece of that out to Len? He's probably in Sixteen." Much as he'd like to just sit and observe these two, he was going to have to figure out what direction to take in the months to come.

Within seconds, Andy had left with a sandwich and a huge piece of cake for Len.

Lauren began repacking the basket. "I've obviously chosen a bad time for this," she said. "But maybe there wouldn't be a good one."

He hated the flat, empty feeling the thought of her leaving brought. "Thank you for coming," he said. "We'll talk. We do owe each other that much. But—" He covered his mouth. There was no reason not to tell her what had happened, but he didn't want to hear the saga aloud again.

Lauren looked at him sharply. She straightened slowly, a crease forming between her brows. "Something else has happened," she said, gripping the arms of her chair. "You said my timing was bad. Why?"

"Because, metaphorically speaking, I got kicked in the teeth this morning. It's going to take years for me to climb out again, if I ever manage to do it at all."

"What—"

"Don't ask." He opened the top drawer of his desk, took out two sheets of paper and pushed them toward her. "These tell the story. They came in overnight. Then these arrived by courier this morning." He fished the crumpled photos from his pocket and threw them down.

Lauren began to read. "Flame Talon?" She glanced up at him and back at the first sheet. "Edgerton's in Florida producing sport. Flame Talon," she read aloud. "Photos to follow. We've already advertised product. Name change won't be problem. Can't risk unreliable delivery. Cancel Lava Pearl. Will advise on other orders."

Jack waited for her to raise her face again. "Final straw," he said. "That's the first of a rash of cancellations we're probably going to get. I'm going to be building from scratch, or trying to."

"I don't get it." Lauren stood up. "Why should this Flame Talon affect you?"

He snorted and pushed a photo into her hand. "That's Flame Talon. Describe it to me."

She stared down. "Orangy red," she said very softly. "With

cream veins. Oh, Jack, how can this be? This is the same as Lava Pearl, isn't it?''

"Sure looks that way. And I can't tell you how it happened, except that it seems like I've gathered a lifetime's bad luck in a couple of months. Unfortunately, customers have been alerted to the sport. When I warned them we could be a bit patchy with delivery, they were naturally disappointed, but we could have been up to full production by next year. Only along comes this Florida outfit with something that looks like a duplicate and they're ready to step right into our shoes. Uncanny. And I can't do a thing but retreat and regroup.''

"It won't affect the other varieties you produce, will it?''

She was bound to see all the possible ramifications. "You see what that customer says? Will advise on other orders. We're in limbo. Edgerton's could push their advantage. They must think they've died and gone to heaven.''

"Or gotten very lucky,'' Lauren murmured. She looked at the second piece of paper. "They came in under your price, too? It's so close. How could that happen?''

"Damned if I know.'' He felt cold, and tired. But having Lauren here was more comfort than he'd hoped for. "The response came in on the service. It was waiting for me this morning. I guess that means Edgerton's got their prices out yesterday and they just happened to be barely lower than ours. Add that to the other factors and we don't look good at all—even with customers we've had for more years than I've been alive.''

Lauren dropped the memos and the photo back on his desk and sat back, staring into space. "Service? You mean my service?''

"Uh-huh. Of course. With the time differences across the country I often get messages overnight. The customer likes that option.''

"Of course.'' She chewed a knuckle.

Jack sat forward. "What are you thinking?'' As he waited, she appeared to become paler. "Lauren, what is it?''

"I've got to go.''

He stopped her before she reached the door. "What the hell is wrong with you? Tell me.''

"Please.'' She breathed rapidly through her mouth. "You tell me one thing, then just let me go.''

"Lauren—"

"I'll be back. I promise." She clutched his arms now. "It wouldn't be possible to... How would you deliberately copy someone else's special poinsettia? Are they hybrids or whatever you call them? Do you keep records about them?"

"They aren't hybrids." His stomach knotted. "It's what they call bud mutation. And it's complicated, Lauren. Sure there are records, but I guess the only way you'd get an exact copy would be by getting hold... That's not possible. No one could have taken cuttings without Matt noticing. He watched over everything as if they were his kids. No, this is just one of those crazy things that can happen."

"And the fact that it happened after you had so many other things go wrong has made it perfect for these other people, because you don't have the resources to fight back right now?"

He nodded.

"And Edgerton's timing their pricing quotes and probably other things just right, tied the whole package up for them?"

Suddenly incredibly weary, Jack nodded slowly. "It sure did. Are you making some other point?"

Lauren opened the door. "I hope to God I'm not. I'll get back to you."

PEOPLE COULD BE PULLED into situations over which they had no control. Then it could become difficult, or impossible to get out. That had to be the explanation. Or she could be completely wrong and her whole theory was a myth.

She'd only been to Susan's apartment in Oceanside once. When Lauren left Vista Freeway, she drove slowly north, feeling her way. In the misty rain, the landscape appeared sodden brown.

Via Clara. "Darn it." The street sign caught her eye as she drove by and she found a place to turn around.

What if she was wrong? She took long, slow, calming breaths. Discovering she was wrong was exactly what she should hope for.

Susan lived on the upper floor of a house owned by an elderly woman. A separate entrance had been made via an outside stairway.

Lauren parked beside Susan's decrepit brown Dodge and turned off the Honda's engine. Jack's face was what she had to keep before her, the way he'd looked when she left him: dully angry, disappointed, resigned. If she could change that, she would, even if it signaled the falling of the curtain on any hopes she still had for the two of them.

If she *was* right, no more time could be wasted.

Susan opened her door before Lauren could ring the bell. "Lauren?" She looked surprised and pleased. "Hey, what a surprise. Come on in."

The apartment was small and threadbare, but very clean. Lauren stood in the middle of the sitting room where a Paganini violin concerto played softly from a tape deck. The choice of music surprised her. But then, there was very little she really knew about Susan Bailey.

"Coffee?" Susan asked. "Or a drink? I have wine or—"

"Nothing, thanks."

Susan bit her lip. "I'm sorry about Cara, Lauren."

"You already told me that. So am I."

"You're lonely, aren't you?"

"Yes." She was wrong. She had to be. "I'm trying to keep too busy to think about it."

Susan smiled and straightened the cushion on a green velvet chair. "Sit down. What were you doing? Just driving around? I'm glad you came here."

Lauren turned away. Yes, she missed Cara—so much it hurt— but what was happening here could eclipse even that. "How's Matt Carson?"

"He's..."

In the silence that followed, Lauren pressed a fist to her mouth. She could scarcely breathe. The man in the green truck had seemed so familiar; the way he'd stuck his head out the window. Sitting in Jack's office, she'd mentally replaced the round-framed wire glasses with dark lenses, removed his floppy hat, and then she'd been almost sure. Now there was no doubt.

Susan walked around her, a puzzled smile on her lovely mouth. "I don't remember telling you his name."

"You didn't. Oh, Susan, how could you do it? How could you take privileged information and give it away? That's what you did, isn't it? You copied messages meant for Jack and gave them to Matt Carson."

"I—" Susan backed away. "—No. Matt's good. He's done all the work out there and he deserves to get more for that than a pat on the back while Irving's takes all the credit."

"Oh my God." Lauren sat down abruptly. "You encouraged me to keep on seeing Jack. Then you asked questions and I answered them. I thought you were my friend."

Susan spread her hands. "I didn't know you'd meet him. That was chance. And I already knew most of what you told—" Her hand went to her mouth.

"You knew about the awful things that happened before I did," Lauren said quietly. "But I was the one who warned you that Jack would be sending messages himself at night."

"He always did that!" The panting noise Lauren heard turned to jerky little sobs. "Matt says Jack's going to be okay again in a year or so. This is Matt's one chance, that's all."

"And where do you come into this? How is Matt's one chance going to affect you?"

"We're getting married." She began to cry. "Does Jack Irving know?"

"Not yet. He will."

"Don't," Susan begged. "I'll tell Matt he's got to stop now. He left for Los Angeles last night. When I talk to him, I'll make him stop and we'll go away. He'll be back in a few days."

"What exactly is he supposed to stop?"

Susan sank to the edge of the couch. "All he wants is to start his own farm outside L.A. He's already got the land. He used the facilities at Irving's to do some research for what he's going to raise. He won't be in competition with Jack...not really."

Lauren gritted her teeth, trying to sort through what she was hearing and how it might connect to what she'd seen earlier. "Matt left last night?"

"Yes. I gave him..."

"You gave him copies of some messages that came through Contact."

"Yes." Susan's voice was barely audible.

"Do you know what they meant?"

"No. But Matt said it was time for him to leave for a while."

"And what about you?"

"When he comes back, he'll settle things here and we'll go away together."

Lauren struggled to stay calm. "Do you have his address in L.A.?"

"No." Susan laced her fingers tightly together on her knees. "Matt said it was best that I didn't."

"Susan, how could you want to be with a man who would set fire to part of another man's livelihood? What if someone had been killed in that plant?"

"Matt didn't have anything to do with that!" Susan jumped up. "He was as upset as anyone. He told me."

Lauren stared, incredulous. "And he didn't have anything to do with any of the other bad things that happened to Jack?"

"No! All he did was raise some sort of plants. Starters, he called them." She paced. "He was upset about all those things."

"Because they weakened Jack's business?"

"Yes. Exactly. Matt said Jack wouldn't have much to fight with for a year or so. But all I did was give Matt copies of messages so he could time some of the things he was going to need to do to get going himself."

"And you didn't think that was wrong?" Lauren was aware of how urgent it was for her to get to a phone, but not without all the facts. She had to ask one more question. "How often did you give messages that referred to prices?"

"I don't know. Sometimes."

"Like last night?"

Susan rocked rapidly. "Yes. There was something like that last night."

"And then Matt left for L.A.?"

"Yes."

She rushed to the door and outside.

"Lauren!" Susan was on her heels, running down the steps. "What are you going to do?"

Lauren opened her car door and paused. "I'm going to find a phone. What you do is your business...for now. Matt Carson didn't leave town last night, Susan. I saw him less than two hours ago. He'd just told Jack he'd be leaving today. For Montana."

CHAPTER SIXTEEN

Lauren put a mug of coffee in front of Susan and returned to the swivel chair that had been Cara's favorite.

"Thanks," Susan said. She picked up the mug and scrunched into a corner of the couch. "I wanted to see you, but I didn't know if you'd even talk to me."

"Staying angry was never something I was good at," Lauren said. "If I had been it wouldn't have taken me three years to tell my ex-husband to stay out of my life." Even now, while she despised what Susan had helped cause, she couldn't help feeling sorry for the woman. But she hadn't expected Susan to turn up on her doorstep at seven in the evening, without a coat, and damp from the drizzle that had seemed perpetual for three days.

"The police came to see me a couple of hours after you left. I thought they'd arrest me or something, but they just asked lots of questions and said I shouldn't try to leave the area. Then they came back again yesterday and asked more questions about Matt."

Lauren used a foot to rock herself back and forth. "Did they tell you anything that's happened?"

"No. I hoped you would, though. What does Jack think they're going to do about Matt?"

"I don't know." She lowered her eyes. Since her telephone conversation with Jack on Saturday afternoon, two days ago now, she'd heard nothing from him. "The police talked to me, too. They came to the office this morning."

"Did they say anything about Matt?" Desperation loaded Susan's voice. "Have they talked to him?"

"I don't know about that, either. Have you talked to him?"

"No."

"I didn't think so." And she couldn't condemn someone else for loving too much for their own good. Her own future felt like a mine field to be crossed, but she knew that whatever happened she'd keep right on loving Jack.

"You don't think Matt's going to come back for me, do you?" Susan whispered.

"From Los Angeles? Or from Montana?" Lauren asked and felt ashamed of herself. "I'm sorry. No, I don't think Matt's going to come back because I think he did a lot of illegal things here and knew it was time to get out. He never expected anyone to find out about him, of course. After all, when he didn't show up again the way he promised you he would, what could you do? Where would you start looking? You certainly wouldn't tell anyone what he'd been doing at Irving's because you had a part in that."

Susan seemed oddly smaller. Lauren knew it was an optical illusion, but the other woman appeared to diminish in her corner, becoming like an aged child with too much hair that was too red and luminous green eyes too big for her face.

"You'll be all right," Lauren said, with absolutely no conviction. "You'll come through this. There'll be someone else for you one day." How could she be saying those words? Did she hope, at some level, that the empty message she spread, like a Band-Aid, over Susan, would somehow become true for herself?

"Do you think Matt did all those awful things to Jack? The fire, the damage to the flowers, the seeds mismarked?"

"I'm sure he did. Those things and more."

"He couldn't have been in three trucks at one time."

"No. Obviously he had help. But that doesn't make him less guilty."

Susan put down her mug with a clatter. "I think he did them, too," she said in a low voice. "I don't want to, but I do. He should have called me by now. Why did he lie to me? Why didn't he want me to go and be with him?"

"He couldn't ask you to go to his farm, Susan, because he doesn't have one. Or that's what I think. I think he sent cuttings to another farm somewhere else so they could pretend they raised a special plant themselves and made a lot of money that should have been Jack's."

"Why did he hate Jack?"

Lauren closed her eyes. "That's what's so awful. He didn't hate

Jack. He didn't care one way or the other about Jack. Matt was just doing a job for money and the job entailed hurting Jack. That's all of it.'' And her own supposedly innocent little business had helped Carson time everything beautifully.

"I'd have gone with him, anyway."

Lauren started and opened her eyes. "What?"

"I love him. You think I'm bad for that, don't you?"

She settled her hands on the chair arms. Tears welled and she blinked. "I think you're a good woman who did something bad. And I think Matt Carson is crazy that he didn't see what he had in you and that he couldn't forget whatever money he was going to make by ruining another man."

Susan got up. "I'd better go. At least you and Jack have each other now."

Lauren saw Susan out, knowing she'd try to help her if she could.

The phone rang and she hurried into the sitting room.

No. The calls that came in every hour or so were only from Contact. Susan had been the one who fielded after-hours queries. Until Lauren could find a replacement lead, she'd have to deal with the questions herself. This one could wait. She had to get out of this house and run, run so hard she wouldn't be able to think.

Already dressed in sweats, she pinned on her door key. The phone stopped ringing, then started again.

Slamming the front door behind her, Lauren set off for the beach without bothering to stretch. *At least she and Jack had each other now?* Did they? She intended to keep on praying that they would one day.

No more feeling sorry for herself. She'd get on with her life, even if it eventually had to be somewhere other than in Carlsbad.

"LAUREN!"

Wind off the ocean, laden with moisture, muffled his voice and threw the name back at him.

That wind was good, clean. He felt as if he'd been holed up in smoky offices for weeks instead of only since Saturday afternoon.

Where the hell was she? He leaned over the railing above the beach and tried to make out the shape of anything that might be moving.

Nothing.

The night was black and filled with noises. Her car was parked in its usual spot and there were lights on at her place, but there'd been no response to his telephone calls earlier, or to his ring at her door minutes ago.

She could be inside and just not answering. He should have tried to reach her before tonight, but things had proceeded so quickly and the police had either been with him, or coming or going.

And, if he were honest, he'd admit he'd needed a little time to think about what he was going to do about Lauren Taylor.

Lauren liked the wind and rain. When they'd run together on the beach he'd been the one to want to quit.

A light farther down the promenade sent an illuminated stripe across the sand. A shadow slipped across that stripe.

Jack vaulted the railing to a ramp and broke into a run. His jeans, damp now, and his jacket hampered him. He ran on, grateful he wore sneakers rather than boots.

"Lauren! Wait!" He still couldn't see her, but he could feel her now. Wet sand gave beneath his feet and he pushed harder with each stride.

He reached the pale line of light on the beach and paused. The wind quieted momentarily and he glanced around. She couldn't have gone too far.

A sound came to him and he turned to his left. "Lauren? Are you there?"

"Yes. By the wall." He heard her clearly this time.

His eyes had grown accustomed to the darkness. Something pale waved. He smiled and broke into a jog, stopping when he stood over her. "Hiding?"

"Not really. Sheltering. This is where we came before, remember?"

Jack dropped to his haunches beside her. "I remember everything I want to remember." He touched the back of her hand with his forefinger. "I want to remember everything about you."

"Am I needed for something?"

Her face was indistinct and he leaned nearer. "Oh, yes."

She sighed. "The police again? Do I have to go to them this time?"

"I'm the one who needs you." Carefully, he moved to sit beside her on the triangle of more or less dry sand in the lee of the wall. Just looking at her, feeling her near him, made his throat ache with longing.

"You know I'll help you if I can," Lauren said. "I'm sorry, Jack. I guess I'm not much of a judge of character in the employee department."

"Because of Susan Bailey?"

"Who else?"

"I employed her boyfriend."

She was silent for a moment. "That was different."

"Really? One day when we've got nothing better to do, you'll have to explain the theory behind that."

"I don't blame you for wanting to stay away from me."

"If I wanted to stay away from you, why am I here now?" He was going to have to make sure they shared the work needed for whatever relationship they were to have. The reward would be worth anything it took to get it.

"Jack—" Her voice broke.

He scooted close and pulled her against him. "What? I'm sorry it took so long for me to be with you. It's been mad. Lauren, you're not going to believe what I've got to tell you."

A cold hand found his neck and slipped inside his collar. He drew in a breath and held it.

"Tell me," she said.

"Matt Carson didn't go to L.A."

"We knew that."

"We didn't know anything, sweetheart. He didn't go to Montana, or anywhere else."

Lauren craned around, her face close to his. "He's still here? Why? Did they catch him before he left?"

"Nope. On all counts. It was Martin Edgerton they caught, at the Palomar Airport where he was about to take off in his own plane for Florida."

"Edgerton? The name of the people in Florida with the poinsettia," she whispered. "Do you mean...?"

"Exactly. There never was a Matt Carson. The guy who supposedly worked for me is heir apparent to the Edgerton operation. He does have a degree in floriculture. He really knows his stuff or he couldn't have pulled off what he did in the three years he was here, but the credentials he showed me, everything he presented to me was phony."

"Why did... I don't understand how they chose you, or knew what you were doing here."

"We were successful. They were successful, but less so. Evidently they decided to send Matt—or whatever his name is—up here to see if he could figure out a way to get what we had. And he eventually did it."

"With help from me."

He shook her gently. "Sometimes I can really tell why the male is the superior sex."

"What!" Lauren grabbed the lapels of his jacket.

Jack chuckled. "You females don't always think too clearly. You lead with the heart or something equally unreliable. If it hadn't been for you, my dear, the guy would have gotten away with the whole thing. Thanks to you, the police got to the house he rented in the middle of nowhere near the airport in time to see him leaving in the Alpha Romeo you described.

"They followed him to the airport where they let him board his plane, the plane they were told Martin Edgerton flew back and forth to Florida regularly."

Lauren tugged on his coat. "It doesn't sound real."

"Fact is invariably stranger than fiction. Isn't that what they say? Anyway, our strong, silent saboteur didn't do so well under interrogation. He spilled the lot and cried for Dad to come and bail him out, which he tried to do. Daddy also folded and filled in a few other details. Sonny boy flew my rooted cuttings down to Florida in his little plane—tidy as you like. Lauren—" he raised her chin to look into her eyes "—I'm serious. If you hadn't come along, they'd have gotten away with it."

"Then I'm glad I did," she told him softly.

He heard his own nervous laugh. "So am I. But this isn't all about flowers, is it, sweetheart?"

"Isn't it?"

"No. Two people who irritate one another as much as we do have to have a hell of a lot going for them."

She didn't laugh.

"It's cold out here, Lauren. And damp."

Without a word, she nestled her face against his shoulder.

"Hey," he said, stroking her damp hair. "Aren't you going to talk to me? Do you want me to leave you to think, or something?" She smelled of fresh air and salt. If he kissed her, she'd taste of salt.

"No!" Her head shot up. "I just don't know where you're coming from. Or where I want you to be coming from, for that matter. Or where I'm coming from. Or—" She caressed the side of his face. "Or maybe I know what I want and I'm scared to death you don't want it, too."

"Shh." He rested a finger on her mouth. "I don't think it's very complicated. Can we go some place warm to talk?"

"I don't want to go home."

Her vehemence tightened his jaw. Maybe things were slightly more complicated than he wanted to admit. "Would that be because the little girl isn't there anymore?"

She nodded. "Partly. Jack, I really miss her. I can't pretend about that."

"I thought so. I was going to suggest my place anyway."

"You must be tired. If you need to go home I'll understand, Jack. We'll talk tomorrow, or whenever."

"Uh-uh." He stood up and pulled her to her feet. "Nothing doing. You just said you didn't want to go to your place."

She gave a shaky laugh. "I'm glad you said that. I lied when I said I'd understand if you left me. I need you. And I really don't want to go home."

"Even if you did, you couldn't. I've got to take you to my place."

"You've *got* to?"

He held her arm and started to walk. Lauren didn't move fast enough and did a rapid sidestep to keep her balance.

"Hold it!"

Jack kept going. Bulldozer technique was required.

"Jack! You're pulling me off my feet!"

"I'd rather you said *sweeping,* but I'll take what I can get. Come on. We're late."

"Late for what?"

"My father's waiting for us."

Now she dug a heel in the sand and tried to wrench away. Jack swept her easily into his arms and gritted his teeth at the effort it took to make headway on the sand with the added weight.

"Why is your father waiting for us? He doesn't like me."

If he bent his face a few inches, he could kiss her. Jack looked straight ahead. Self-control could be learned in small increments. "You only *think* my father doesn't like you. Andy's waiting, too."

"Why?" She shrieked the question.

"Because they sent me to find you."

KIDNAPPING IMPLIED being taken away against one's will. Leaning against the window in Jack's pickup, Lauren admitted to herself that kidnapping didn't apply in this situation.

He drove too fast.

"What's going to happen about the poinsettia?" she asked timidly.

"Edgerton's is closed down at this point. The rest—what happens with our supply this year—remains to be seen. Things aren't going to be miraculously cured because the truth's been exposed, but at least I think we're going to get a fighting chance."

Too soon, he swept into the driveway at his house, leaped from the cab and came around to open her door. He half lifted her, sliding her down his length until they stood, toe-to-toe. Lauren took a jerky little breath, and another. Jack bent slowly over her until she felt the warmth of his mouth a whisper away from hers.

Lauren closed her eyes.

"Hey, Dad! Lauren!"

Jack groaned and rested his forehead on hers.

"We've been waiting for you!"

By the time Andy reached them, Jack stood beside Lauren, his hands in his pockets, his weight resting on one leg. "Hi, sport. Sorry we took a while."

"Yeah, well. Grandpa's getting…well, you know how he gets."

"I know." Jack sounded grim. He rested one hand on Andy's neck, the other at Lauren's waist and walked into the house.

Denton Irving sat in an ivory satin chair in the living room, looking out of place in his red plaid shirt and baggy navy blue corduroy pants.

He stood up and cleared his throat. "All sorted out, is it?"

Lauren glanced at Jack whose face showed no expression.

"Not quite, Dad," he said.

She longed to ask what it was that was supposed to have been dealt with, and by whom.

Denton made a disapproving, snuffling noise, jutted his chin and thrust a hand in Lauren's direction.

She only hesitated an instant before accepting a bone-crushing shake.

"Thank you for what you did," he said, sounding ferocious. "Good head on your shoulders. Always admired that in a woman. Jack's mother was that way. You ask him."

"I will," Lauren said, taken aback.

"Get your coat," Denton ordered Andy. To Jack he said, "I put what we talked about beside your bed."

Lauren looked at Jack just in time to see him turn an interesting shade of red.

"Going to be all right, is it?" Denton almost shouted.

Jack finally moved. "We hope so, Dad. These things take time."

Denton snorted and aimed a dark stare in Lauren's direction. "Young people never think their elders know anything. You think an old man doesn't remember. You ready, Andy?"

The boy zipped his windbreaker. "Yes, Grandpa."

"That's all right then." He ambled from the room, shooing Andy before him. "Never mind what I think," Lauren heard him say, "go ahead. Throw it all away. But don't come to me with a long face afterward."

"What was all that about?" Lauren asked when she and Jack were alone. "And where on earth is he taking Andy at this time of night?"

Jack shuffled his feet. "I don't know what it was about. Dad often takes Andy. You know that."

"I think nine-year-old boys belong in bed at almost ten on a school night."

"Nag," Jack said, not quite under his breath.

"I'm not a nag," Lauren said, incensed. "I believe in responsible parenting is all."

He seemed about to speak, then changed his mind.

"What? Say what you're thinking, Jack."

"When I first started to get to know you, I thought you didn't care much for kids."

Her sweats were damp. She concentrated on how uncomfortable she felt.

"Lauren? You do like them, don't you?"

She sighed deeply. "Yes, Jack. I love them. Do I get to go home now that I've seen Denton and Andy?"

"No," he said simply. "You don't have a car."

"You do."

"You said you didn't want to go home."

"I don't like fencing matches. I'm not much of a game player."

"Hah!" He shrugged out of his jacket and tossed it on one of the pale chairs. "You could have fooled me. You knock the socks off me every time we play any kind of game."

She tried not to appear smug. "Your coat's wet. It'll ruin the chair."

"Good. I hate that chair. It's time we redecorated the place."

She forebore mentioning that the time to redecorate wasn't while you were trying to dig yourself out of potential financial ruin.

"You're wet," he told her.

"I'm all right."

"No you're not." Taking her hand, he led her into the hall. "We'll find you something dry to wear."

She thought, and immediately discarded the notion of his coming up with something belonging to his ex-wife. Her next thought was that he was undoubtedly leading her to his bedroom.

Heat sped into every part of her.

He did take her into his bedroom. Big, untidy—and with a platform bed that showed signs of having been hastily made. The black-and-white striped quilt hung slightly askew and matching pillows were piled carelessly on top. Books, heaped higgledy-piggledy on a lacquered table, pushed two black-and-gold Chinese vases perilously close to one side.

Lauren looked around curiously. Here she felt Jack. There was strength and style and a masculinity that was more comfortable than overwhelming. She turned to find him looking at her.

He smiled, his gaze lingering on her, before he went to pull shut the wooden louvers at a recessed floor-to-ceiling window.

"Now," he said, all business. "Take everything off and I'll see what I can find."

She sucked her bottom lip between her teeth to stop a laugh. But she didn't move.

"You can put on my robe if I can find it." He strode into the bathroom and checked behind the door, then, grumbling, disappeared into a closet to emerge with a dark green terry robe. "You should be warm enough in this." He tossed it to her.

"Thanks." Suddenly tired, she eyed the bed longingly, but bypassed it to go into the bathroom. "Jack, are you going to put my things in the dryer, or what?"

"Probably not," he called.

Trying not to look at herself in the mirrored walls of his black-and-white bathroom, she stripped to her bra and panties and donned the robe. He was probably in some sort of shock after all that had happened and didn't even know his behavior was bizarre.

Lauren did look at herself then: damp hair hanging around her face, almost no lipstick, and dark smudges from the remnants of mascara. The latter did a great job of making sure no one would miss the little lines at the corners of her eyes. Quickly she washed her face and scrubbed it dry with one of Jack's black towels. Clean and shiny was preferable to sallow and grubby. Since all she had with her was her door key, there was nothing more to be done.

She emerged to find Jack wearing only very skimpy red briefs. "Red!" She grinned, then made the mistake of laughing.

There was no hope of evading his flying tackle. They landed together in the middle of his comfortable bed and Lauren made no attempt to move beneath his weight.

The gentling in his eyes, the softening around his mouth knocked out any humor the moment had held. He stroked back her hair and tilted his head sideways to study her. "We promised each other that we'd have a chance to say our piece. Isn't that what we said on Saturday before the balloon went up?"

"Yes, Jack."

"I was an idiot about Dan and the real estate thing. You didn't know anything about it."

"No, I didn't. I tried to tell you, but—"

"I know. But the man's an ass. I can't imagine what you ever saw in him. And I hate the way you let him stroll in and out of your life like—"

"I don't anymore. When you came roaring in, I'd just told him a few truths he won't forget in a hurry—or forgive."

He rested a thumb on her bottom lip. "You know what all my bluster was about, don't you?"

"Tell me."

"I'm jealous of him."

"You don't have to be. Not anymore."

Jack propped his head. "No. You may have to remind me of that, though, I warn you. I love you, Lauren. That's kind of blunt. Not too flowery. But I do love you so very much."

"I—" She closed her eyes and felt a tear squeeze free and course down her temple. "Great. Now I'm crying."

"Women are strange. I've always thought so."

"I love you. I love you. I love you." Lauren sniffed and laughed. "More than I can tell you."

"Oh, sweetheart." His lips brushed hers lightly. "We're going to have good times together. Lots of good times."

She took a deep breath, rubbed the tears from her eyes and looked at him. "My turn to be blunt. I've never talked about my not being able to have babies."

"You don't have to now. I guessed as much a long time ago."

He always seemed to make things easier for her. "Jack, I would have said something, but it seemed weird to talk about an issue that didn't matter if we had no future together."

"It still doesn't matter, darling." Carefully he lifted her head and cradled it against his neck.

She became very still, very quiet inside. "I'm thirty-nine. That's past a sensible age for having babies, anyway."

"Yes it is. All that matters to me is you." He rocked her slowly.

"I could never get pregnant." Her skin felt icy. "The reasons can be parroted off, but they don't mean much, even to me except that I'm infertile."

Jack rested her back on the pillow and sank his teeth into his bottom lip.

There was nothing he could say, she knew that—nothing she wanted him to say. But she didn't want him to view her as less than she was: a complete woman.

"I mean it when I said I already figured this out, you know," he said finally. "It still troubles you, doesn't it? That's why you tend to draw back when children start to get close to you. It's why you've only gone so far with Andy."

She laughed before she could stop herself. "Half right, half wrong. Not such a bad attempt at analysis. No, not being able to conceive doesn't bother me anymore. I think I adjusted well to that. But I am afraid of coming to love children only to lose them again. It's happened twice—with Joe and Cara. And I'm afraid of loving Andy, then having to move away from him." Only it was already too late; she'd begun to care for the boy.

"How about his father?"

She wriggled to see him more clearly. "Am I afraid of loving you? I already do. I told you." And he'd told her. His words still rang in her brain.

"I'm cold." Scooping her to sit on one side of the bed, Jack threw back the quilt and blankets. Settling himself against the pillows, he extended an arm. "Lie with me."

Lauren swallowed almost painfully. Never removing her eyes from his, she took off the robe, tossed it aside and joined him beneath the covers. "What did you mean just now?"

As if he hadn't heard her, Jack bent his head and kissed Lauren, a gentle but infinitely demanding kiss. Gentle now, was the message she received, but that it was only the beginning.

He raised his head again and looked at the lips he'd left parted and waiting. A lamp, behind Jack on a bedside table, cast deflected light over his powerful shoulder and threw graded shadows over his strongly muscled chest.

"I wondered," he murmured, "if you might be afraid of your love...of loving Andy's father for some reason."

Her breathing became shallower. "I was. But I don't think we always have a choice about these things."

"You thought I still cared for Mary. I don't, you know. I only felt that it might be bad for Andy if his mother didn't come to see him when she'd said she would. He knows he's less important to her than her painting."

"I understand."

"It doesn't matter. She's not coming anyway. But I guess I tend to worry too much about Andy sometimes because he doesn't seem to care." This time he kissed her throat. "He seems a whole lot more interested in making sure you keep coming around."

"Does he?"

"Mmm." His attention centered on her shoulder while he carefully moved aside her bra strap. "Smart. Like his dad. Same taste exactly, evidently. You said you don't think we have much choice in these things. In who we love, you mean?"

"I've got to say it again, Jack. I love you so much." And her eyes chose this moment to fill with tears again. And her throat felt so closed, it ached. "I can't help it," she managed to whisper.

For what felt like forever, he looked at her. "Do you know," he said, "I actually worried about losing you because you might decide something else was more important than I could ever be to you? I invented every reason not to let myself love you."

"But it didn't work."

He smiled then, tipped back his head and grinned down at her. "No, it didn't work. Wow, am I glad it didn't work."

She wanted to laugh and leap about but more than that, she wanted to make wild love with him. "We take the prize for insecurity. Who do you see when you look in the mirror?"

Jack shrugged, and frowned. "A man. An ordinary man, I guess."

She did laugh at that. "Ordinary? You're spectacular."

"Okay." He framed her face. "Who do you see in the mirror?"

"A slightly overblown woman approaching middle age."

He flopped onto his back and shouted, "That's hysterical. My toes curl just at the sight of you. And that's the mild part. Come here, you.''

The phone rang.

"Oh, go away.'' Jack moaned and pulled her into his arms. "We're not answering that.''

"It might be an emergency.''

"I don't care.'' He tried to kiss her.

"Maybe something's wrong with Andy.''

Jack drew back his head, reached across her and snatched up the receiver. "Yes.''

Lauren watched his face. He sank to the pillows and closed his eyes. "Yes,'' he repeated. "Just a minute. Hold the line.''

Promptly, Jack thrust the phone under the pillow and crawled from the bed to kneel on the floor. He took her hand and laced their fingers together. "I want to spend the rest of my life with you.''

"What is it?'' Lauren whispered hoarsely. "What's wrong?''

"Forget everything but what I'm saying to you.'' Propping himself on his elbows, he kissed her lingeringly. Slipping his hands around her neck, he pulled her into his arms. "How did I get so lucky?''

"Thank you.'' She smiled and shook her head. "Everything I try to tell you comes out wrong.''

Reaching behind him, Jack scuffled among the books on the table until he produced a tiny brown leather bag. "Will you marry me?''

"I beg your pardon?''

"I'd like you to be my wife...please. And—'' he wrestled the bag open and pulled out an old fashioned ring set with a square-cut emerald and diamonds in a starburst ''—this was my mother's. It would mean a great deal to my father if you would agree to marry me and accept this ring, to seal the pact? Good grief. That sounded asinine. Please, my darling, *will* you marry me?''

"Yes.'' Lauren eyed the phone cord leading to the pillow. "Is this being recorded or something?''

Jack ignored the question, took her finger and put on the ring before retrieving the phone. He hesitated. "Thank you, Lauren. You've made me very happy.''

"Me, too."

Into the phone he said, "Sorry to keep you waiting. Yes, Lauren loves the ring, Dad." He closed his eyes once more. "Yes, you can tell Andy it's okay. We'll see him tomorrow. Good night."

Lauren took the receiver from him and hung up. "You came looking for me tonight knowing you intended to ask me to marry you and expecting me to agree?"

"Knowing you'd agree," Jack said. "Occasionally your logic is almost flawless."

He switched off the light.

LOVER, STRANGER
Amanda Stevens

CHAPTER ONE

His lungs were bursting as he thrashed his way through the jungle, trying to elude his predators. Over the lacy treetops, the moon rose full and majestic, illuminating the path of broken limbs and trampled grass he left in his wake. It was only a matter of time before they picked up his trail.

The sky was clear and inky black, like a giant, obsidian bowl that had been turned upside down and painted with thousands of tiny, white stars. Pausing to catch his breath, he searched for the brightest star among them, Polaris, the north star that would guide him toward the village. There he would hopefully find a phone, or at least transportation to take him out of this godforsaken place. If he could somehow make it to the border…

Off to the west, he heard the rumble of an engine, distant at first, but drawing steadily near. A beam of light from a high-powered searchlight arced over the terrain just missing him, and then moments later, he heard shouts. Laughter. His trail had been discovered. The killers were closing in, and they were enjoying the hunt.

Heart pounding, he plunged through the lush foliage. Low-hanging branches slapped at his face and arms while man-sized roots tangled with his feet. Amber eyes, ruby eyes, emerald eyes glowed from the trees and from the darkness all around him. Every step was a new danger, a new terror. God, how he hated the jungle!

Finally stumbling into a clearing, he found himself on the edge of a jagged precipice. Mist rose from the raging river that sliced its way through the limestone cliffs a hundred feet below him. Ahead, the ravine sprawled into a yawning gap of nothingness. Behind him, the shouts of his pursuers rose in excitement as they spotted him in the moonlight.

There was nothing to do but head back into the jungle for cover. But before he could run, gunfire echoed through the stone canyon.

The noise was so muted by the mist, the scene so surreal, that for a moment, he hovered at the edge of the precipice, unsure what to do. Then he felt the sharp blast of pain in his side, looked down and saw the blood and realized he'd been hit. Realized he wasn't going to make it to the village, much less to the border.

As if in slow motion, he fell backward into nothing but vapor and air...

"DR. HUNTER? Can you hear me?"

He opened his eyes and saw a woman's face leaning over him. Dressed all in white, she looked radiant. Other-worldly. An angel, he thought. So he hadn't made it after all.

"Dr. Hunter?"

He blinked as the angel spoke again. Was she talking to him? She was gazing down into his eyes, smiling, but that name she kept calling—who was Dr. Hunter?

"He's coming around, Dr. Kendall," she said over her shoulder.

A man appeared beside her. He wore the same look of concern on his face as she did, but he wasn't smiling and his eyes were dark with something that might have been suspicion.

"Well, well," he said. "Glad to see you've decided to rejoin the land of the living, Ethan. You certainly gave us all a scare tonight."

Ethan? Who was Ethan?

He closed his eyes for a moment, trying to clear his head. Obviously he was in a hospital somewhere. These people seemed to know him, but he'd never seen them before in his life. Nor had he ever heard of anyone named Ethan Hunter. It had to be a case of mistaken identity, but—

A tiny bubble of panic floated to the surface of his consciousness. If he wasn't Ethan Hunter, who the hell was he?

He searched his mind and found no answers.

"How are you feeling, buddy?" Dr. Kendall peered down into his face.

Buddy? Did that mean the two of them were friends?

But Kendall didn't look particularly friendly. In spite of his easy bedside manner, there was something about his eyes, a glimmer of hostility that was faintly unnerving.

The man they called Ethan stared up at him, frowning. "I feel sort of...out of it.'' The sound of his own voice shocked him. It was raspy and coarse, and the effort to speak hurt his throat. He put a hand to his neck and winced at the pain. The skin was bruised and tender.

Dr. Kendall must have glimpsed the fear in Ethan's eyes for he said, ''Take it easy. Your vocal cords and larynx have been stressed. Don't try to talk any more than is necessary.''

Ethan tried to swallow past the pain and the panic. ''What happened?''

''We're hoping you can tell us.''

He thought for a moment. ''I had this strange dream about running through a jungle... Someone was trying to kill me.''

Kendall's shrug was dismissive. ''I'm not surprised. You've sustained a concussion. You look like hell, but you're damned lucky to be alive.''

You look like hell...

The realization hit him suddenly that he had no idea what he looked like. He put his hands to his face. The skin was bruised there as well, and a thick bandage wrapped around his skull.

Scanning his surroundings, he searched for a mirror but didn't see one. Which was probably just as well. If the pain in his face was any indication, he wasn't at all sure he was ready to see his reflection.

''What were you doing at the clinic tonight, anyway?'' Kendall asked suddenly, his tone edgy.

''I'm...not sure.'' Ethan squeezed his eyes closed, trying to remember what had happened to him, but nothing came to him. He tried to fight back the suffocating panic that threatened to engulf him. *Who the hell am I?*

Stay calm, a little voice warned him. *You have to figure this thing out. Your life could depend on it.*

He drew a long breath. Okay. He just needed a few minutes to get his bearings. There was no cause for alarm. He had a concussion. Short-term memory loss was common enough with head injuries, wasn't it? Maybe they could even give him something—

But wait a minute. If he was a doctor—Dr. Ethan Hunter—he would know that, wouldn't he? He would know how to treat a concussion and temporary amnesia. He would know how to cure himself.

But he didn't. He didn't know anything at the moment, and his panic came rushing back.

Dr. Kendall touched his arm, and Ethan flinched. Why didn't he like this man? And more importantly, why didn't he trust him enough to confess his amnesia to him?

As if reading his thoughts, Dr. Kendall's eyes narrowed. "The police are outside, Ethan. We've stalled them as long as we can, but there's a detective who's been champing at the bit ever since you were brought in. Are you up to talking with him?"

About what? Ethan wanted to know. But he remained silent. For some reason he didn't understand, it seemed imperative that he not give himself away. That he remain calm and as much in control as he could be under the circumstances.

But just what the hell *were* the circumstances? Why couldn't he remember who he was?

The door of his hospital room opened, and a man wearing an ugly green suit walked in. He was in his early fifties, stoop-shouldered, with salt-and-pepper hair slicked straight back and plastered with hair cream. His face was deeply creviced, his eyes shadowed with years of hard service and even harder drinking.

He walked over to Ethan's bed, pulled up a stool and sat down. Removing a yellow number-two pencil and a black notebook from his inside jacket pocket, he licked the lead of the pencil, then scribbled a hasty note. Without looking up he said, "So you're Dr. Hunter."

Ethan said nothing.

"I'm Sergeant Pope, HPD."

HPD. Ethan searched his mind. Honolulu Police Department? Harrisburg? Hartford? Houston? Where was he?

Wait. There was an unmistakable twang in the detective's easy drawl. Okay, so they were probably in Houston, but why? Did he live here?

He glanced up, and as his gaze met Pope's for the first time, Ethan sensed a keen intuition and intellect that belied the faint air of ennui that settled like an old blanket over the aging detective.

Watch yourself, Ethan thought, though why he should fear the police he had no idea. Was it because in his dream, the Mexican authorities had been chasing him through the jungle? Was that why an almost innate sense of wariness had surfaced the moment the detective had walked into the room?

"I've heard a lot about you," Pope was saying. "My wife showed me an article about you in the paper a couple of months ago. Had a real nice shot of you in your downtown office, but I can't say you look much like that now."

Ethan thought about the thick bandage wrapping his skull, the raw bruises on his face and neck. "No, I guess not."

Pope thumped the pencil eraser against his notebook. The sound was barely audible, but for some reason it grated on Ethan's nerves. "The article told all about that free clinic you built in the Mexican jungle, and how you spend several weeks a year down there, operating on underprivileged kids. They gave you quite a write-up. The wife was real impressed." The thumping stopped suddenly. "Hey, I'll have to tell her I met you tonight."

"Sure, why not?" Ethan said, because he didn't know what else to say. His throat still hurt. He reached for the glass of water on the stand beside his bed. The nurse—Nurse Angel, he now thought of her—was instantly at his side, helping him to drink. Her hand wrapped around his on the glass. Her touch was soft, caressing. Intimate.

When Ethan lay back against the pillows, he saw that Pope was watching him. The detective had seen the encounter. Ethan was sure of it.

Pope said, "She was thinking about calling you. My wife, that is." He put a finger to his nose and pressed it to one side. "She has a deviated septum like you wouldn't believe. She's been wanting a nose job for years."

So...he was a plastic surgeon? Somehow Ethan would never have guessed that.

Almost inadvertently his gaze dropped to his hands, resting on top of the sheet. There was dried blood caked beneath his nails and a wedding band on the third finger of his left hand.

His heart raced when he saw the ring. If he was married, where was his wife? Had she been contacted? Shouldn't she be at his bedside at a time like this?

As if on cue, Nurse Angel moved back into his line of vision and gave him a knowing wink.

Pope, momentarily distracted by the nurse's dazzling smile, said, "Listen, will y'all excuse us? I'd like to speak to Dr. Hunter alone."

Dr. Kendall nodded tightly, then turned to Ethan. "Dr. Mancetti said she'd be back tonight to check on you. In the meantime, if you need anything, I'll be around for a while."

"Great," Ethan said, though he didn't have the faintest idea who Dr. Mancetti was, nor did he have any intention of calling on Dr. Kendall's services.

Nurse Angel bent over Ethan's bed, fluffing his pillow and patting his arm. "I'm pulling a double shift tonight," she confided in a throaty whisper. "If you need anything, Dr. Hunter, *anything at all,* you just call me."

"Thanks," he murmured, his gaze lingering on the sway of her hips beneath her snug uniform as she turned and walked out of the room.

Sergeant Pope seemed mesmerized by the movement, too. For a moment, neither man spoke, then the detective mentally shook himself. "The staff here seem pretty concerned about your welfare, doctor. You must be a popular guy." There was a mocking glint in his eyes as his gaze dropped to the wedding ring on Ethan's finger.

Ethan resisted the urge to hide his hands, caked blood and all, beneath the sheet.

For a moment, Pope busied himself with his notes. Then, his voice edged with a weariness Ethan didn't trust, he said, "We may as well get this over with. I'd like to file my report and get home before midnight, and you look like you could do with some rest." He paused. "Can you tell me what happened tonight?"

Ethan shrugged. "I'm afraid the details are still a little sketchy." He made a vague gesture toward his head. "The concussion..."

Pope nodded. "I spoke with your doctor a little while ago. She said it might be a few hours, or even a few days before you could fill in all the blanks. But let's just go over what you do know."

Which is nothing, Ethan thought. *Nada.*

The only thing he could remember was the dream. Running through the jungle. Being pursued by men who wanted to kill him. And falling...falling...

Then, like a bolt of lightning, another memory shot through him.
He was in a room that contained an examination table, metal cabinets and a sink. He felt groggy, out of it, but he could smell an-
tiseptic. Knew, dimly, that he was in a place he didn't want to be.

Someone was in the room with him. Someone with a gun...

"I remember being in a doctor's office," he said, almost to himself. "In an examination room, I think."

"You were found at your clinic here in town," Pope supplied.

Ethan put a hand to his head, touching the bandage. "Someone
was with me. A man. I think we fought. I heard a woman scream...
then gunfire...then..." He trailed off as his head exploded in pain.
He clutched his temples with his hands. "I was hit with something
hard...something metal..."

"We think it was a flashlight," Pope said. "We found one with
blood on it at the crime scene, but we won't know if it's your DNA
until we get it back from the lab."

Ethan closed his eyes, trying to remember the rest, but his recollection was hazy at best. In some ways, the jungle dream was
much clearer to him. But was it more than a dream? Was the jungle
scene somehow connected to what had happened to him earlier in
that office?

Why couldn't he remember? Why didn't he know who he was?

He groaned, whether from actual pain or memory, he wasn't sure.

"Did you recognize the man in your office?" Pope asked.

It had been dark inside the examination room, but the blind at
the window was open and moonlight flooded in. The man was wearing a ski mask, but Ethan could tell that he was staring down at
him in the pale light, grinning as he aimed the gun at Ethan's face.
"Got to make this look good, pretty boy," the gunman said, as he
turned to the drug cabinet behind him and rifled through the med-
ication, choosing and discarding with an expertise that was chilling.

By contrast, Ethan's movements were slow and lethargic. Almost
dreamlike. It was as if he were caught in an invisible web he
couldn't break free of.

Then, unexpectedly, the door to the examination room opened
and a woman screamed. As the gunman whirled toward the sound,
Ethan, acting on pure instinct and adrenaline, lunged toward him.
The gun went off as Ethan crashed into the man, dragging him

downward. From the doorway, where the woman had screamed, the only sound was a thud, a soft moan, then silence.

The gun came free as the man hit the floor. Both he and Ethan scrambled toward it, but the weapon slid out of reach beneath a steel cabinet. As the two of them fought, Ethan became aware of a siren in the distance. Someone had heard the gunshot and called the police. The man must have heard the siren, too, for his struggles became even more desperate. More deadly. He got his hands around Ethan's throat and squeezed, squeezed, until stars exploded inside Ethan's head.

From somewhere deep inside Ethan, a primal urge, some killing instinct rose to the surface, and he reached upward, his thumbs finding the man's eyes. The man screamed and released him, but before Ethan could use his advantage, the gunman found a new weapon. He grabbed something metal from the floor and struck Ethan's head a vicious blow.

Dazed, Ethan fell back. Before he could regain his strength, his equilibrium, the man was on him. He hit Ethan's head...his face...again and again until blackness mercifully swallowed the pain.

Ethan glanced at Detective Pope. "That's all I remember." But at least now he knew how he'd gotten the bruises and the concussion, how his vocal cords had gotten stressed. What he didn't know was why. "I don't know what happened to the gunman after I lost consciousness, or why he didn't kill me."

Pope's gaze flickered over Ethan. "My guess is, he panicked. He heard the sirens and ran. Not likely we'll find any prints on the flashlight or anywhere else. I suspect he went to that clinic prepared. He knew exactly what he was looking for."

"Which was?"

"Drugs, more than likely."

Ethan touched a bruise on his cheek, remembering the blows, wondering if his face resembled a slab of raw meat, because that was the way it felt.

Got to make this look good, pretty boy.

He hadn't related that part of the memory to Sergeant Pope. Nor did Ethan say what he was now certain of—that the gunman hadn't gone to the clinic looking for drugs. He'd gone there to kill Ethan.

Then why not tell the police? that voice inside him demanded.

Because his instincts told him not to. Because Ethan was very much afraid when the truth came out, when he finally remembered everything, there might be a chance a cop would be the last person he could turn to for help.

He realized Pope was watching him again, and Ethan tried to shutter his expression, tried to hide his fear and dread.

"Can the rest of this wait until morning?" he asked suddenly, wanting to be rid of the detective. Ethan knew instinctively that he had to watch his step as he had never had to watch it before. Someone wanted to kill him. It was like a drumbeat inside his head. Someone wanted to kill him, and he had no idea who. He didn't even know who he could trust. For all he knew, Sergeant Pope was the enemy.

Was it Ethan's imagination, or had the detective's expression suddenly turned suspicious?

"I'll try to make it quick. Just a few more questions," Pope said, paging backward in his notes. "Let's see…oh, yeah, here we are." He paused, reading, then glanced up. "Dr. Kendall told me you'd been in Mexico for the last couple of months or so. He said you were due back three weeks ago, but you'd had some emergency surgery down there. An appendectomy, I think he said. You weren't supposed to travel for several more days, but then you decided to come back tonight. Why the sudden change of plans?"

The jungle dream came rushing back to Ethan. He could smell the dank scent of rotting vegetation, could see the Hummer's lights bouncing over the uneven terrain, could actually feel the throb in his side from the bullet.

Or was the pain from the appendectomy incision? Was the dream nothing more than a drug-induced vision while he'd been under the knife?

He said vaguely, "I had something I needed to take care of."

One of Pope's brows rose in surprise. "Must have been pretty important if you were willing to risk your health."

Ethan hesitated, not knowing how to respond. *You're a doctor, so think like one. Why would you come back from the jungle before you were supposed to?*

Aside from the fact that the Mexican authorities were trying to kill you....

But Ethan didn't think he wanted Pope to know that. So he said instead, "There's a patient I have to see."

"Is that why you went by the office tonight before going home?"

"How did you know I didn't go home first?"

"Your luggage was still at the clinic. So was your wallet and briefcase. We'll get everything back to you as soon as we're finished with it."

"Thanks," Ethan mumbled, his mind racing. A wallet would contain a driver's license, credit card, money. A home address.

Sergeant Pope said, "From your story, I gather the gunman was already inside the clinic when you arrived."

"I'm pretty sure he was," Ethan said, though he wasn't at all sure of anything. His first memory was of staring up into the gunman's masked face. Ethan had no recollection of getting off a plane, arriving at the office, or of anything else.

Except fleeing through the jungle...

He remembered that all too clearly.

"Did you call your assistant and ask her to meet you at the clinic?" Pope asked.

"My assistant?"

"The woman who walked in on you and the gunman. Amy Cole."

Dammit, be careful. "Oh, yes. Amy." Ethan wondered if he'd answered a little too quickly because Pope's gaze narrowed on him. "How is she, sergeant? She wasn't seriously hurt, was she? She saved my life tonight."

Something flickered in the detective's eyes. "Dr. Kendall didn't tell you?"

"Tell me what?"

"Amy Cole's dead. Shot right through the heart. Poor kid never knew what hit her." Pope shook his head. "Damn shame, a beautiful woman like that."

Ethan felt the air leave his lungs in a painful rush. He had no recollection of the woman, didn't even remember what she'd looked like, but he could still hear her scream. Could still see, in his mind's eye, the gunman whirl toward the door and fire.

And now Ethan was more certain than ever that the gunman had come to the clinic to kill him. Amy Cole, whoever she was, had taken a bullet that was meant for him.

Whoever *he* was...

CHAPTER TWO

"This is suicide, Dr. Hunter. I won't allow you to do it." A middle-aged, stoutly built commando in a nurse's uniform planted her hands on her hips and blocked Ethan from the door to his room. The lines in her weathered face were deeply etched and as unyielding as the starch in her pristine uniform.

Ethan had hoped to slip out of his room unnoticed and make his exit before anyone missed him, but this woman—he glanced at her name plate—Roberta Bloodworth had caught him in the act. What a name for a nurse!

"Don't worry," he lied as he finished buttoning his blood-stained shirt. "I'm feeling much better. All I need is a good night's sleep in my own bed."

Actually, he felt like hell. His head throbbed, his face hurt, his whole body ached as if he'd been hit by a bulldozer. But the pain was the least of his worries. At the moment, he didn't even know where his own bed was, or who he should be sharing it with.

All he knew was that he had to get out of here. He had to find some answers. Somehow he had to figure out who was trying to kill him, and why.

"Just look at you," the nurse scolded. "I hardly even recognize you, and the way you sound, like some horror movie ghoul." She wagged her finger in his face. "And I shouldn't have to remind you how dangerous a head injury can be. You shouldn't be alone to-night."

"I won't be alone." He slipped on his suit jacket. "My wife will take care of me."

"Your...wife?"

Too late, Ethan realized his mistake. He'd made assumptions about the ring on his finger that obviously he shouldn't have made. Were he and his wife separated? Divorced?

Damn. Was he widowed?

He gave her a wink. "Well, let's just say, I won't be alone, okay?"

"Same old Dr. Hunter," she grumbled, but there was a spice of mischief in her close-set eyes as she continued to challenge him.

Ethan sensed that beneath her gruff exterior, she held a genuine affection for him. It made him feel a little better. Maybe everyone wasn't his enemy after all.

But...could he trust her enough to tell her about the amnesia? Would she be able to help him?

Or would she insist on calling the police? Or worse, Dr. Kendall?

Ethan still couldn't shake the notion that Kendall held a deep malice toward him. What had happened between them in the past?

For a moment, he considered asking the nurse about Kendall, but something warned him not to. Something told him not to press his luck with Roberta Bloodworth because she, of all people, might see right through him.

He tried to smile disarmingly. "Anyway, you know what they say about doctors. We make the worst patients. You should consider yourself lucky to be rid of me."

She threw up her hands in exasperation. "All right, it's your funeral. Why should I care?" But as she turned toward the door, he heard her murmur, "Take care, Ethan."

After she left, Ethan checked the pockets of his jacket. A stick of gum, a parking stub, a Post-it note with a phone number he didn't recognize. As if they were precious gemstones, he carefully returned the items to his pocket. Opening the door, he quickly surveyed the corridor, then stepped out, searching for the nearest exit. He spotted the elevators and headed toward them as the bell pinged on one of the cars and the door slid open.

A woman emerged, looking windblown and slightly breathless. Their shoulders touched as they brushed by each other, and for a moment, their gazes locked.

Ethan's immediate impression was that, for the most part, the woman's features were neither beautiful nor plain, but fell somewhere in the category of interesting. Her eyes, however, were extraordinary, so light a blue they almost appeared translucent.

She wore a tailored navy pant suit, and her dark red hair was cut short and tucked behind her ears, in a style that was deceptively simple. She looked professional, no-nonsense, a woman with a definite purpose.

All this Ethan saw in a heartbeat, a man noticing and acknowledging an attractive woman. With a mumbled, "Excuse me," he entered the elevator, giving her hardly more than a second thought. But just before the doors slid closed between them, he saw her turn and stare after him, in a manner that filled him with unease.

Did he know her?

He started to press the open button to confront her, but what would he say? How could he be sure she was a friend and not an enemy? Maybe she'd come to the hospital to finish the job someone else had botched earlier.

Not a pleasant thought, but one he couldn't ignore. Truth was, he couldn't afford to trust anyone.

As he left the elevator and headed through the hospital lobby toward the street entrance, he tried to take stock of what he had learned about himself. His name was Ethan Hunter. He was a plastic surgeon. He was married…or at least, had been married. He had just returned from Mexico, where he'd undergone an emergency appendectomy, and he'd been badly beaten tonight by a man who had wanted to kill him.

The wound in his side tingled as he pushed open the glass door and stepped outside. A blast of hot air greeted him, and he realized it must be summer in Houston. Even though it was late, after ten, the cloying heat was almost suffocating.

He could see the city's impressive skyline in the distance and wavered for a moment, unsure what to do, where to go. Maybe it hadn't been such a great idea to leave the hospital. He should have at least figured out where he was going first. Maybe he should have somehow gotten his wife's number and called her to come and get him.

Somehow that didn't seem to be an option he wanted to explore. Neither was waiting around in a hospital room for his would-be killer to come and find him.

Ethan couldn't explain it, but he hadn't had a choice in leaving the hospital. He'd been compelled to flee. He knew he had to run. Knew he couldn't afford to stay in one spot too long.

Headlights arced across his face, and he threw up a hand to shield his eyes. For a moment, he thought he was back in the jungle. He could see the searchlights scouring the mountainside. Hear the rush of water below him. Feel the sharp punch of the bullet as it entered his side. Then he was falling...falling...

Someone grabbed his arm, and Ethan whirled, reaching blindly for his enemy, pulling the body tightly against him as he pressed his arm into a soft, pliant throat.

GRACE DONOVAN SAW her entire life flash before her eyes. The arm that pressed against her windpipe was like an iron vise. The more she struggled, the harder he squeezed. Forcing herself to go limp, she waited for the infinitesimal relaxation of her assailant's muscles, then she chopped upward, using both hands as she'd been taught.

His hold loosened without breaking, but at least she could breathe. She gulped air into her lungs, then stumbled away when he finally released her.

"Are you crazy?" she managed to gasp.

He was looking at her as if she were a ghost. He stared at his hands, then back at her. Then stared at his hands again. "I could have killed you." His skin looked deathly white in the sodium-vapor streetlight.

"No sh—kidding." Grace massaged her throat, glaring at him. Headlights swept across his face, causing the bruises to stand out starkly against his pallor. "Why did you attack me like that?"

He was still staring at his hands. "I don't know."

Grace kept her own hand at her throat, suddenly feeling very vulnerable and not liking it. "Look, you don't have to worry," she said dryly. "I don't think there's any permanent damage."

He glanced up, his brown eyes shadowed with an emotion Grace couldn't define. "You're okay then?"

She frowned. "I'll be fine, but I wasn't talking about myself. I meant you...your hands. You're a surgeon, right?"

He didn't answer, just stood staring at her in the gloom. Grace shivered even though it was June and the heat rising from the concrete was thick enough to cut with a scalpel. She could feel her hair curl at the back of her neck, but wasn't sure whether it was because of the humidity or the man standing before her...the way he was looking at her.

She cleared her throat. "You are Dr. Hunter, aren't you? Dr. Ethan Hunter?"

"Do I know you?"

He took a step toward her, and Grace fought the urge to retreat. It wasn't like her to be so easily spooked, but the bruises and bandage gave him an almost maniacal look as he stared down at her. There was something about his eyes...a darkness that was chilling. She wondered, fleetingly, what she was getting herself into.

"We've never met. But I saw you briefly upstairs."

"At the elevator," he said, as if it had just occurred to him.

She nodded. "I came here to see you. The nurse told me you'd checked yourself out. Do you think that's a good idea? If you don't mind my saying so, you don't look so good."

"I'm fine." As Grace watched, he lifted his fingertips to probe his battered face. The action reminded her of a blind man, trying to "see" with his hands.

"Why were you looking for me?" he asked suddenly.

She released a long breath, not realizing until that moment she'd been holding it. "I want to talk to you about what happened tonight. I've spoken with the police. They told me about the shooting. I've just come from the morgue."

She had his full attention now. His brown gaze scoured her face. "The morgue?"

Grace wrapped her arms around her middle, shivering suddenly as if she were still in the cold-holding room where Amy's body had been taken. This was the important part. It was crucial that she convince him. "I want to talk to you about Amy Cole."

Something flashed in his eyes. Regret? Guilt? Or was it merely a trick of the light? "You knew Amy?"

"She was my sister."

He looked stunned. "I'm sorry. I don't know what else to say." He spread his hands in supplication, glancing away, then back at Grace. "She saved my life tonight."

Despite the hoarseness, his voice was deeply compelling. Dusky and sensual, it called forth emotions from inside Grace she had no wish to unveil. Not now. Not when so much was at stake. Not when her sister's death was on the brink of being avenged. Nothing else could be allowed to matter. Certainly not a man with a battered face and a voice as seductive and deadly as a storm-swept sea.

She tried to conjure up an image of her sister, but the memories had faded.

Ethan touched her arm, and Grace jumped as if she'd been burned. "Are you all right?" he asked.

She swallowed over the sudden fear in her throat. "I'm fine. But unfortunately, my sister isn't. That's what I want to talk to you about. I want to know why Amy's dead, Dr. Hunter. I want to know what you had to do with it."

The shadows in his eyes deepened. "What do you mean?"

"I think you know exactly what I mean." Grace forced herself to remember the past. To use her emotions. She unfolded her arms, letting one hand grip her purse strap. The other hand balled into a fist at her side. "I know all about you and Amy. Your *affair*." She all but spat the word at him and saw him wince as if she had physically struck him.

When he didn't try to defend himself, Grace said coldly, "She told me all about it. She also told me that you'd gotten her involved in something dangerous. Something she said might end up getting you both killed, and it looks like she was right."

This time, he didn't flinch at her words. He stared at her with eyes as cold and dark as a moonless winter night. "I don't know what you're talking about."

"Oh, I think you do." She lifted her chin. "Amy's dead, Dr. Hunter, and I think you know more about her murder than you're saying. I came here to get some answers, and I'm not leaving without them."

"Then you may be waiting a long damn time." He turned to walk away from her, then stopped suddenly, looking around at the street and passing cars.

Grace walked over to him and caught his arm. The muscles beneath her hand flexed defensively, like tempered steel. Her hand dropped to her side. "You can't just walk away from this. You owe me the truth. You owe it to Amy. She was in love with you, dammit!"

His fingertips brushed against the bandage. He suddenly looked very lost. "I didn't know."

Grace glared at him, telling herself not to react to his emotions, to the look of desperation lurking in the depths of his eyes. He was a dangerous man, and she couldn't afford to forget it.

"What do you mean, you didn't know? Amy never told you how she felt? You must have guessed. She was never very good at hiding her feelings."

He glanced down at Grace, as if on the verge of confession. Then he shrugged and turned away. "I'm sorry about your sister. Deeply sorry. But I can't help you. There's nothing I can tell you. I don't have the answers you're looking for."

"Then you leave me no choice." Grace opened her purse and took out a stack of envelopes tied with a blue ribbon. "Amy wrote to me regularly in the past few months. These are her letters. They're all about you, Dr. Hunter. About the promises you made to her. The favors you asked of her. I'm sure the police would be interested in seeing them."

He turned at that, his expression stark in the streetlight. Whatever flash of vulnerability Grace might have glimpsed earlier had vanished. His gaze narrowed on her. "Is that threat supposed to frighten me? Why should I assume the police would have any interest in your sister's letters? What did she accuse me of?"

Grace hesitated, meeting his gaze. Then she glanced away. "All right, I admit, she never mentioned anything specific. But she said enough to arouse my suspicions, and I think her letters might make the police more than a little curious as well."

"Then why haven't you already handed them over?"

"Because I wanted to talk to you first."

"Why?"

"I have my reasons."

He studied her for a moment. "Is it because you're afraid your sister may not be an innocent bystander in..." he made a vague gesture with his hand. "...all this? Is it because if you go to the police, they may start to probe a little too deeply?"

His perception surprised Grace. "That's part of it," she admitted reluctantly. "But it's more than that. I don't exactly trust the police."

That seemed to interest him. He lifted a dark brow. "Why not?"

"Because Amy is just a statistic to them. Another case. One of a dozen homicides that take place in this city every week." She paused, biting her lip. "But she was my sister, Dr. Hunter, and I'll do anything to bring her killer to justice. Right now, you're the only one who can help me do that."

His brow rose again, but when he remained silent, Grace pressed her point. "I don't want to go to the police, but if that's the only way I can gain your cooperation—"

He moved swiftly, grasping her forearms and hauling her toward him. Grace started to struggle away, but something in his eyes, a terrible look of desperation, made her momentarily yielding.

"Don't you understand?" He gazed down at her, his eyes darker than Grace could ever have imagined. "I *can't* help you. I don't know anything."

"Then why are you so afraid of the police?" she asked, unable to tear her gaze from his. Her breath caught in her throat. She wondered, suddenly, if she had pushed him too far.

For a moment, he seemed to undergo some intense inner struggle. A myriad of emotions flickered across his features, then he let his hands drop from her arms and backed away from her. "I don't know anything about your sister. About those letters. About our... relationship. I don't remember her. I don't even remember my own name or what I look like. I don't remember anything. Is that clear enough for you?"

Grace stared at him in shock, watching the shadows flicker across his features. Where he stood, one side of his face was in light, the other in darkness. It was a strange illusion, almost as if she were talking to two distinctly different men. Unnerved, she said, "Are you telling me you have amnesia?"

He didn't answer, just stood there staring down at her. He was dressed in a suit, dark gray and beautifully tailored. The jacket was open, and Grace could see the dark droplets of blood on the front of his white shirt.

That, more than anything, reminded her of why she was here. Her heart jolted uncomfortably. "My God," she said. "You don't remember *anything?*"

"Not much," he muttered. His expression became shuttered again, as if he were already regretting his confession.

But had it really been a confession? Was he telling her the truth, or trying to cover his tracks?

Damn, Grace thought. *Amnesia could change everything.*

She tried to assess this new situation while wondering if she should proceed as planned. She stared at him for a long moment, watching for the telltale flicker of desperation she'd glimpsed earlier, searching for a flash of fear, anything, that might give him away.

But she saw nothing. It was as if a mask had descended over his features. In some ways, this masquerade of control frightened her more than anything else, because it showed her how easily he could deceive her if he chose to.

"What did the doctor say about your condition?" she finally asked.

He shrugged. "I understand it may take days, or even weeks, to fill in the blanks."

"From what you just said, it sounds like we're talking about more than a few blanks."

He shrugged again.

Grace glanced around, realizing how vulnerable they were standing out in the open. In spite of the intense heat, she shivered. "Look, maybe it isn't such a great idea for you to be on the street like this."

"I'm fine," he said, almost angrily. "Don't worry about me."

"You're not fine," she countered. "You were almost killed tonight. Hasn't it occurred to you that whoever did this to you…to Amy…could come back?"

"That's not your problem." But she knew he had thought of it. She could see it in his eyes. She wondered if that's why he'd left the hospital.

"Well, I'm sorry, but I've made it my problem," she said, backing her shoulders. Staring him down. "I want to find my sister's killer, and at the moment, you're my only clue. I'm not letting you out of my sight."

He scanned the night sky, as if looking for guidance. Searching for the way home. His expression looked bleak in the moonlight.

"What was it you said earlier? Amy told you I'd gotten her involved in something dangerous? Something that might end up getting us both killed? Wasn't that it?" His gaze met Grace's and she shuddered. "If I were you, I wouldn't want to be standing between me and the next bullet."

SHE FOLDED HER arms over her breasts, in a manner that was unmistakably determined. He saw that same stubbornness in the set of her jaw and chin. In the way her gaze met his without wavering. "I told you. I'm not going anywhere until I get some answers."

"And I told you, I don't have those answers."

"Yes, you do. You just don't remember them. That is, if you really do have amnesia."

"You don't believe me?"

Her blue eyes flickered, but she said nothing.

Ethan told himself her opinion of him didn't matter, but for some reason, anger shot through him. She didn't even know him. She was basing her judgment solely on what she'd heard from her sister. And if he and Amy Cole had been having an affair...if the relationship had gone bad...

The wedding ring on his finger was suddenly a dead weight. He resisted the urge to remove it. For all he knew, he might still be deeply in love with his wife...ex-wife?...estranged wife?

Then why would he have had an affair with Amy Cole?

Ethan shook his head, trying to clear the fog, but the haze only deepened. So many things he didn't know. Couldn't remember. What had happened to him in Mexico? What had he been involved in that had gotten Amy killed tonight?

He stared down at her sister. His initial impression of her remained. She was a woman with a definite purpose, but there was something in her eyes that belied her tough exterior. The pain of her sister's murder?

Guilt stabbed through him. Amy Cole may have died because of him. He wouldn't be responsible for another woman's death. "Look," he said. "I don't care whether you believe me or not. I'm getting the hell out of here. And if you're smart, you won't follow me."

She took a warning step toward him. "You're not getting away from me that easily."

"Don't be stupid," he said in exasperation. "I don't want you to end up like your sister."

Something flashed in her eyes. A momentary look of uncertainty. "I won't. I'm not Amy. I can take care of myself."

He shook his head in regret. "You don't know what you're getting yourself into. *I* don't even know."

"I know that I won't rest until I find my sister's killer," she said softly. Her eyes glowed with an emotion so deep, so fierce that Ethan felt unsettled just watching her. "Can you really afford to send me away? Where will you go? Do you even know where you live? At least let me get you off the street. Let me take you someplace where you'll be safe."

He stared at her for a long moment, trying to resist the temptation she placed before him. "I don't want to get you involved in this."

"Don't be stupid," she said, flinging his words back at him. "What choice do you have?"

"Actually, there is choice," he said slowly. "I could still decide to go to the police for help."

She gave him a sidelong glance. "I don't think so."

Meaning he *couldn't* go to the police. Meaning whatever he had been involved in was not something he would want the cops to know about.

Like it or not, she had him exactly where she wanted him.

"All right," he said. "I guess we're stuck with each other. For the time being, at least."

Her expression was anything but triumphant. "Looks that way. Come on. My car's over here."

As Ethan followed her to the parking lot, he had a feeling that he was walking blindly into something every bit as dangerous, every bit as deadly as the jungle.

CHAPTER THREE

They headed west on Memorial Drive. Ethan knew this because he studied the road signs, hoping to recall a memory. Though they were in the middle of the city, the street became progressively more wooded. The streetlights along the dark green colonnade illuminated high walls and gated drives. Ethan glimpsed large houses beyond the walls, with curving driveways and lush vegetation skillfully showcased by landscaping lights that gave everything a soft, green glow.

Ethan searched for something familiar, a landmark that would strike a chord, but the street remained as unfamiliar to him as his own name. As his own face.

He touched the bruises and grimaced. It was time to evaluate the damage. "Do you have a mirror in here?"

She threw him a surprised glance. "On the visor, but—"

"What?"

"Be prepared," was all she said.

He pulled down the visor and slid back the cover on the lighted mirror. It was so narrow, he could only see a portion of his face at a time. He adjusted the visor, staring first at the thick bandage on his forehead, then at his eyes—both of which were blackened and one almost completely swollen shut—then at the ugly, raw bruises on his cheeks, and finally his lips, cut and also swollen. Kendall had been right. He looked like hell.

He looked like a stranger.

Adjusting the mirror again, Ethan returned to his eyes. Dark brown, what he could see of them. Black lashes. Thick eyebrows. He ripped the bandage from his head and heard her gasp.

"You probably shouldn't have done that," she muttered.

Black hair, matted with blood, tumbled over his forehead, covering the long crescent of stitches over his left brow.

Got to make this look good, pretty boy.

Ethan didn't say anything for a long moment. Couldn't say anything.

She braked for a light, and he could feel her watching him. But he couldn't tear his gaze away from his reflection.

"It's all superficial," she said softly. "The cuts and bruises are only skin deep. They'll heal. In a few days, you'll look like a new man."

He studied his eyes, searching for the windows to his soul. A new man? What had the old one been like? A doctor who operated on poor children in Mexico? A husband who cheated on his wife? A man who had gotten a woman killed tonight?

He could still feel her watching him, and he turned suddenly, capturing her gaze. She looked momentarily startled, as if she'd just seen him for the very first time. Or as if she'd glimpsed something in his battered features she hadn't expected.

Was there a redeeming quality hidden among that mass of bruised flesh?

He wanted to think so. He fervently wanted to believe it.

"You're a very good-looking man," she said suddenly.

He almost laughed. "In a Frankenstein sort of way."

"No, I'm serious." She glanced in the rearview mirror. Then glanced again. The light changed, and the car accelerated. "Trust me, you're very handsome."

"I thought you said we'd never met."

He saw a brief frown flicker across her features. "We haven't, but I've seen pictures of you. Amy showed me."

Amy. He tried to conjure an image of the dead woman, a memory of his feelings for her, but he felt nothing. Saw nothing.

He studied the woman beside him. Her profile was shadowed in the subdued light from the dash, and she kept glancing in the rearview mirror, as if she expected them to be followed. He wished he knew what she was thinking, and why he couldn't bring himself to fully trust her.

There was something about her...

Something about the pain in her eyes...

He had no doubt that she'd experienced grief. That her sister's death had affected her deeply, but the pain seemed muted somehow, not sharp and fresh as one would expect. Amy had only been dead a few hours.

This woman seemed too in control. Too determined.

Her gaze left the road for a moment to meet his. He felt an odd stirring somewhere inside him. Suspicion? Desire? Funny how those two emotions weren't mutually exclusive of each other. Far from it.

"Do you look like her?" he asked.

She turned back to the road. "You mean Amy? Not really. She was fair like me, but blonde. And she didn't have freckles. She was thinner than me. Taller. Very beautiful."

Was that a trace of envy in her voice? Ethan said, "I don't even know your name, or where you're taking me. I don't even know why I should trust you."

"Which question should I answer first?"

He paused. "The last one, I guess, because depending on your answer, the other two might not matter anyway."

Her blue gaze touched his again. Again he felt the jolt. "Have you ever heard the expression Honor Among Thieves? That sort of fits us, I guess. You can't go to the police without possibly incriminating yourself, and for reasons of my own, I don't want to involve the authorities, either. The only way you can protect yourself is to find Amy's killer before he finds you. And as it happens, that's the same thing I want. It makes sense that we help each other."

"Even if we don't exactly trust one another?"

She shrugged. Ethan thought her answer couldn't have been more eloquent.

After a moment, he said, "And if we do find Amy's killer. What happens then?"

She didn't hesitate. "I bring him to justice. After that, I don't give a damn what happens to you."

"That's cold."

"It's honest."

She braked for another light, but this time, she didn't look at him. She stared straight ahead, her hands gripping the steering wheel.

"So," she said, "do you still want to know the answers to the first two questions?"

He almost smiled. "Surprisingly enough, yes."

She did glance at him then. Her eyes seemed like starlight. Soft and clear. Very mysterious. "My name is Grace Donovan. And I'm taking you home."

He lifted a brow, felt the faint pulling at his stitches. "Your home?"

"No, yours."

The light changed and the car started forward.

"How do you know where I live?"

"Amy showed me once."

He paused. "Has it occurred to you that we may not be able to get in? I don't have keys."

"Did you check your pockets?"

"Of course. The police have my wallet and briefcase, along with whatever luggage I brought back from Mexico."

"Let's hope they don't find anything incriminating," she said. "At least not until we see it first."

She was blunt to the point of brutal. Ethan had to admire her guts. "What makes you think my house will be safe?"

"Wait till you see the place. It's like a fortress."

Ethan tried to picture his home. Tried to imagine himself living in a house that could be described as a fortress, but the only thing he could conjure was the smell of the jungle, the roar of the river, the adrenaline rush of danger. Somehow those things seemed more familiar to him than the estatelike homes they were passing on Memorial.

After a moment, he said, "Your last name is Donovan, not Cole. Are you married?"

"Actually, no. Amy was, briefly. Right out of high school. It lasted about a year. The guy was pretty much a lowlife. She always did have lousy taste in men." Their gazes clashed—hers defiant, his oddly defensive.

He said, "Can I ask you something? You say you want to find your sister's killer, but—"

"But what?" she asked sharply.

"You don't seem exactly...torn up about her death."

He saw her knuckles whiten on the steering wheel. "Because I'm not crying? Not falling apart? Because I want to see her killer brought to justice? There are different ways of expressing grief, Dr. Hunter. Believe me, I know.''

"I'm sure that's true. But you seem so—'' Again he floundered for the right words, and she turned to stare at him in challenge. "In control,'' he finally said.

"I don't consider that a bad thing. Do you?''

"Amy's only been dead a few hours.''

"No one's more aware of that than I am.'' She shot a glance in the rearview mirror.

"What about your parents? Have you called them?''

"Everyone's been notified who needs to be,'' she said. "You don't need to concern yourself with my family. Or with my emotions, for that matter.''

"But I feel responsible for Amy's death, even if I didn't pull the trigger. I need to know about her,'' he said urgently. "I need to know what kind of person she was. Why she became involved with me—other than the fact that she had lousy taste in men.''

"I'm sorry. That was a cheap shot,'' she allowed almost grudgingly. "Look, I may as well tell you. Amy and I weren't very close. In fact, until a few weeks ago, we hadn't spoken in years.''

Surprised, he studied her profile in the dash lights. "Why?''

She shrugged. "We had a falling out. It was stupid, but we just never made up. Resentment and jealousy have a tendency to run a little too deeply, you know?''

He heard the pain and regret in her voice and said instinctively, "Was it over a man?''

She grimaced. "How very perceptive of you. That man she married right out of high school? He was my fiancé.''

Ethan didn't know what to say to that. In the silence, she laughed, a brittle little sound that didn't quite ring true. "Guess I have lousy taste in men, too.'' She paused again, drawing a breath. "Maybe now you understand why my emotions may not be what you think they should be. But I am grieving for my sister, in my own way. And I'll have to live with all these regrets. That's why it's so important for me to find Amy's killer. To focus on getting her justice. Because if I don't...if I let this guilt eat away at me...'' Her eyes closed briefly. Her hands trembled on the steering wheel. "This is the last thing I can do for her, Dr. Hunter. Do you understand?''

"I think so." Ethan was more affected by her words than he wanted to admit. He turned to stare out the window.

Beside him, Grace murmured, "She was only twenty-four. Just a baby. Did you know that?"

The scenery blurred past Ethan. "Do you know how old I am?"

"Thirty-seven, according to Amy."

"Am I still married?"

When Grace didn't answer right away, he turned to stare at her. She shrugged. "As far as I know, a divorce was never anything but a promise."

"Then my wife—"

She shrugged again. "May be at home waiting for you. We'll soon find out."

She turned into a long, circular drive, coming to stop in front of a house that could only be described the way she had earlier—as a fortress. Nestled in a forest of ancient oaks trees and towering pines, the house was white and bleak, a modern, four-story structure with walled courtyards, security cameras and a windowless bottom floor.

The wall of glass blocks on the second floor reflected soft light from within, as if someone were indeed home waiting for him. Ethan stared up at the stark lines of the house and wondered what he might find inside. His past? A wronged wife?

Neither prospect buoyed him.

"How do you propose we get in?" he asked doubtfully. "I already told you, I don't have keys, and even if I did, I wouldn't be able to turn off the alarm system."

"Why don't we just go ring the bell?" Before he could protest, Grace got out of the car and strode toward the courtyard gate.

Dread hanging like a dark cloak over his shoulders, Ethan opened the door and followed her.

When he stood next to her, Grace pressed the button on the intercom, and after a few moments, a voice sputtered over the speaker. "Yes?"

Grace opened her hands, palms up, as if to say, "You're on," and Ethan cleared his throat. "It's me. Ethan. I forgot my key."

A surprised silence ensued, then a woman with a Spanish accent said, "Dr. Hunter? I'm so glad you're finally home. *Un momento, por favor.*"

Almost immediately the lock on the gate was disengaged from inside the house, and the gate swung open. They walked through the lush courtyard toward the front door. Somewhere on the grounds, Ethan heard a sprinkler, and a dog barked in the distance. He glanced up at the winking light on the security camera mounted inside the gate, and thought again of the jungle. Of eyes watching him in the darkness.

The door was drawn back, and a tiny woman wearing a gray-and-white uniform appeared in the light. She took one look at Ethan and gasped, her hand flying to her mouth.

"Dr. Hunter, are you all right?"

"I will be," he assured her.

"Dios Mio." Quickly she crossed herself, then took his arm, murmuring in Spanish while she gently ushered him inside. "What happened?"

"It's a long story."

As she fussed over him, Ethan tried to study his surroundings without giving himself away, but it was hard to contain his reaction. The inside of the house was even more overwhelming than the outside. The jungle theme of the courtyard had been carried through to the foyer, and—he discovered moments later when they climbed a circular staircase—to the second-floor living room.

Giant palms and tree ferns stretched toward a vast ceiling of skylights, while dozens of potted orchids with magnificent purple, yellow and white blooms added to the exotic atmosphere. From his perch across the room, a huge blue-and-yellow parrot tracked them with beady, knowing eyes.

It was like being back in that jungle. Ethan suddenly felt claustrophobic. He allowed the maid to lead him to a deep leather chair, and wearily he sank into it.

She drew up an ottoman for his feet, still muttering and clucking like a mother hen. "What happened, Dr. Hunter?" she asked again when she finally had him settled to her satisfaction. "Was there an *accidente?"*

"He was mugged," Grace said.

The maid whirled, as if she'd only now discovered Grace's presence. She turned back to Ethan, her dark eyes wide and frightened. "Should I call the *policía?"*

Her English was almost flawless when she chose it to be. Ethan had the impression her lapses into Spanish were more by design, a reminder, to herself perhaps, of the heritage she'd long ago left behind.

"I've already spoken with the police," he told her.

She wrung her hands. "I knew something was wrong. I expected you home hours ago. When you called from the airport in *Méjico,* you said your flight was on time. Then you didn't come..." She broke off, her gaze easing back to Grace.

Ethan said, "This is Grace Donovan. She gave me a ride home from the hospital."

Grace walked over beside Ethan, and the maid's gaze followed her, narrowing.

"How do you do?" Grace held out her hand. The maid took it tentatively. Grace said, "I'm sorry. I don't believe I caught your name."

"Rosa."

Nicely done, Ethan thought, although why he felt the need to hide his amnesia from his housekeeper he had no idea. He hadn't told Dr. Kendall or Sergeant Pope of his memory loss, either. He hadn't confided in anyone but Grace, and again, he didn't know why, except that she was Amy's sister, and he'd felt he owed her something. Some sort of explanation.

She was only twenty-four years old. A baby.

He fingered the bruises on his throat, in some perverse way welcoming the pain.

Rosa said anxiously, "Can I get you something? *¿Agua? Té?*"

"No, thank you." For the first time, Ethan noticed a shopping bag and purse on the white leather sofa beside the chair where he sat. He glanced at Rosa. "Were you on your way out?"

She looked faintly uncomfortable. "*Sí.* I was going to stay with my daughter tonight. She has a new *bebé,* remember? Her husband is out of town, and tomorrow is my day off. We talked about this on the phone earlier, but with everything that's happened—" She broke off, staring down at him, shaking her head. *"Tu linda cara...tu pobre linda cara..."*

Ethan automatically put a hand to his face. "Don't worry. It looks a lot worse than it is. You go on. Go be with your daughter. I'm fine.''

She looked doubtful, but Grace said, "Yes, don't worry about Dr. Hunter, Rosa. I'll look after him."

Rosa's gaze darkened disapprovingly. "What about Señora Hunter?"

"What about her?" Ethan asked, tensing.

Rosa hesitated. "She called earlier. She said Dr. Kendall told her you were coming back tonight. If she comes here and finds you—" Her gaze shot to Grace. "Last time...the acid...your car..."

Ethan exchanged a glance with Grace. To Rosa, he said, "Look, don't worry. I can handle Señora Hunter. You go be with your daughter and *nieto*. I insist."

She glanced at Grace, shaking her head and muttering, "Trouble," as she turned and collected her purse and shopping bag from the sofa. "*Mucho* trouble."

GRACE WANDERED AROUND the magnificent living room while Ethan followed Rosa downstairs. She could hear them murmuring in low tones, but couldn't tell what they were saying. After a few moments, their voices faded, and Grace assumed they'd walked to the back of the house, where a rear entrance probably led to the garage.

After a few minutes, Ethan came back into the room from a different entrance, and Grace turned to him expectantly. "Everything okay?"

He nodded. "I told Rosa the concussion was playing tricks with my short-term memory. I asked her to help me with the alarm code."

"Did she?"

"Everything's set. We're armed and dangerous."

"I like the sound of that," Grace murmured. She felt the weight of her gun in her purse and almost smiled. Thank goodness it hadn't been necessary to use force to convince him to cooperate with her. Not yet at least.

"Did you get that part about your wife? 'The acid...your car.' I wonder what happened."

Ethan's mouth thinned. "I'm not sure I want to know. Sounds like we have a real loving relationship."

Grace sensed that Rosa's words bothered him more than he let on. She said reluctantly, "Do you think she found out about your affair with Amy? Maybe it was a sort of *Fatal Attraction* in reverse."

He turned away. "I really don't want to speculate on the state of my marriage."

"But we have to," Grace said. "That's the only way we'll find answers."

He turned to stare at her. "Do you really think my wife had something to do with Amy's murder?"

Grace shrugged. "It wouldn't be the first time jealousy got out of hand."

His gaze, if possible, darkened. "Is that what Amy intimated in her letters? Was she afraid of my wife?"

"She mentioned her a few times. She called her Pilar. I think there'd been some trouble. But I think the danger Amy referred to came from a different source. Something to do with your clinic in Mexico. If you're up to it, I thought we might go over her letters together. Something might jog your memory."

He ran a weary hand through his hair and walked away.

"Of course, we don't have to do it right now," Grace murmured.

He didn't seem to hear her. He wandered around the room, touching a table here, a chair there, as if he could somehow absorb the essence of the room, of who he had been, into his consciousness.

After a few moments, the almost preternatural silence got to Grace. She walked over to stand beside him. "This is quite a place."

He traced the curved stem of some exotic potted flower, then clipped a red bloom with his thumb nail, as if the delicate blossoms were no more rare or precious than a dandelion. The scarlet petals fell like drops of blood to the surface of the glass table. "It feels more like a prison than a home," he finally said.

"A prison?" Grace glanced around the spacious room. The dense foliage gave the illusion of nature at her most primal, and the enormous skylights afforded a magnificent view of the night sky. She made a sweeping gesture with her arm. "It seems more like a jungle to me. Wild. Primitive. Look, you can even see the moon."

Ethan glanced up, and Grace could have sworn she saw him shudder. He turned away, heading toward a door at one end of the long room. He opened it and switched on a light.

Grace came up behind him. "What's in there?"

"Looks like an office or a study."

"That should be a good place to start searching for clues, right?"

She sensed him tense. He seemed reluctant to enter the room.

Grace said, "Want me to go first?"

"No," he said over his shoulder. "I'll just have a quick look for now."

Grace frowned. Obviously he didn't want her following him into the study, but why? What was he afraid she might find?

She turned and walked back to the middle of the room. A movement to her right startled her, and she whirled, automatically grabbing for the gun in her purse. But then she saw the huge parrot preening himself, and realized she'd forgotten all about him. He'd been quiet and still since they arrived, but now all of a sudden, he'd grown restless.

Grace tentatively approached his perch. His movements weren't restricted in any way. She supposed he could fly around the room if he chose to, but all he did was take a couple of nervous, sideways steps on the perch.

A cage with an open door sat on a pedestal near the perch, and Grace guessed that was where he took his meals and got his water. Maybe he was even trained to go potty there as well, she thought, because the room was immaculate.

She stood a couple of feet back from the perch and watched him for a moment. His beady little gaze held hers. "Hey," she said softly, trying not to alarm him. "What's your name?"

He cocked his head and continued to stare at her.

"What's the matter?" Grace asked. "Cat got your tongue?"

All of a sudden, he let out a piercing squawk and flapped his wings so vigorously that Grace screeched, too, and covered her head. When he made no move to attack, she let out a breath of relief and relaxed.

"Sorry," she told him. "It was just a figure of speech." She could have sworn the bird looked sullen and put out. Grace decided she'd better make peace. Moving toward him, she made a kissing sound with her lips and crooned, "Polly want a cracker?"

"Look at the size of those headlights!" the parrot screeched.

Grace jumped at the unexpectedness of his speech. At the crudeness of his words. She gaped at him in shock. "What did you say?"

The bird repeated the line.

"That's what I thought you said."

The parrot fluffed his wings. "I don't think they're real," he said importantly.

"How would you know, you little buzzard!"

Grace's tone seemed to excite him. He raced sideways along the perch, squawking in a loud voice, "They're not real! They're not real! I should know, goddammit!"

"Why you—" Grace made a menacing move toward the parrot, but he put up such a fuss, she instantly retreated.

Behind her, Ethan said, "What's going on? I thought I heard voices."

Grace quickly took several more steps away from the bird. "Your little friend here and I were just having a rap session."

"That thing can talk?" Ethan walked toward the parrot.

"I wouldn't get too close," Grace warned. "He's a little... unpredictable."

But the enormous bird was on his best behavior for Ethan. They stared at each other for a long moment, then Ethan said, "What's your name, fella?"

"What's your name, fella?" the bird said in perfect imitation.

Ethan laughed, a sound that sent a shiver sliding up Grace's spine. "All right, I'll go first. My name's Ethan. At least...I think it is."

The parrot blinked. "My name's Ethan," he mimicked.

Ethan glanced at Grace. "This is getting us nowhere fast. You try."

Grace shook her head. "I don't think so. I don't care for birds." Not this particular bird, anyway.

Ethan turned back to the parrot. "Her name's Grace."

"Look at the size of those headlights!"

Startled, Ethan jumped, then his gaze flew to Grace. A spark of amusement—or was that curiosity?—flared in his brown eyes, and

Grace's face flamed as his gaze dropped almost imperceptibly to her chest.

He turned back to the parrot. "What else can you say?"

"I don't think they're real." The bird looked straight at Grace. Then he strutted and preened on his perch.

"Proud of yourself, aren't you?" she muttered. She pointed at Ethan. "How about picking on him for a change?"

As if he understood her every word, the bird cocked his head and stared at Ethan. "Hey, pretty boy."

Grace threw up her hands. "That does it—" She broke off when she saw the look on Ethan's face. He had grown very still, his expression grim as he turned away from the parrot.

"What is it? Did you remember something?"

Behind them, the parrot gave a long, shrill wolf whistle. "Hey, pretty boy. Hey, pretty boy," he sang.

Ethan flinched. "No, it's not that." His gaze didn't quite meet hers. "I'm just tired. I think I'd like to get some rest now."

Grace got his meaning loud and clear. He wanted her to leave. He wasn't about to invite her to spend the night here.

But she was reluctant to let him out of her sight. He'd sustained a concussion, among other injuries, and probably shouldn't be alone. And, contrary to what he'd said, she was almost certain the parrot had triggered a memory for him. Why wouldn't he admit it? Why wouldn't he tell her?

"I'm a little worried about you," she said. "I don't think it's a good idea for you to be alone tonight."

He shrugged. "You said yourself, this place is like a fortress. Now that I know how to arm the alarm system, I should be safe enough."

Grace bit her lip. "Maybe. But I'm not just talking about that. You've got some pretty serious injuries. A head trauma. That's nothing to take lightly."

He looked at her then, his expression ironic. "You don't have to worry about me. I'm a doctor, remember?"

His words did nothing to reassure her. But there was very little Grace could do, short of forcing him at gunpoint to let her stay. She fingered her purse strap, considering.

"If you're sure..."

"We can talk more tomorrow." His tone was final.

"Well...I guess I'll see you in the morning then," Grace said reluctantly.

They started down the stairs together, and he put his hand on her elbow to guide her. Grace was surprised that she didn't pull away, and even more surprised that she didn't *want* to pull away. The touch of his hand sent a shiver of awareness down her backbone. It should have frightened her, but instead, it reminded her that she was still alive. Still a woman. And it had been a very long time—too damned long—since any man had done that for her.

They paused in the foyer while Ethan turned off the alarm system. Then he opened the door, and pressing another series of buttons, disengaged the lock on the courtyard gate. He followed her outside, and they stood in the driveway to say their goodbyes.

It was nearing midnight. The air had finally cooled, and a lazy breeze drifted through the ancient trees, sounding like rain. The moon was still up, almost full. The freshly watered lawn glistened like diamonds in the milky light, and on a trellis outside the courtyard, a moon flower opened to her lunar mistress.

The night was beautiful, clear and starry, but Grace knew the darkness could be deceptive. She peered into Ethan's eyes, wondering what secrets were hidden deep within those fathomless depths.

Moonlight softened his bruised and battered face, and for a split second, Grace had a glimpse of what he really looked like. She caught her breath, remembering what she'd told him earlier. He was a good-looking man, but she thought his allure had little to do with his physical appearance, and everything to do with the man beneath. The mysteries he had unwittingly buried.

She had the sudden and unexpected urge to kiss him, to see if it would stir his emotions enough to uncover those secrets.

As if sensing her scrutiny, he turned and captured her gaze. Grace wondered fleetingly if he could tell what she was thinking. If he knew what she wanted at that moment.

She was almost certain that he did.

"I'd better be going," she murmured, realizing too late just how dangerous her situation had suddenly become.

But when she would have walked away, he caught her arm, turning her back to face him. Their gazes met again, his deep and mystical; hers, she feared, open and far too revealing.

"Thank you for bringing me home tonight," he said. His voice, deep and raspy, had an unnerving affect on Grace.

"You don't have to thank me," she said. "I had my own reasons for doing so."

"Still—" He broke off, his gaze moving away from her. "I'm sorry about Amy. I hope you believe that."

At the mention of Amy, an image of Grace's sister came rushing back to her, reminding her of exactly why she was here. What she had to do.

"If you really mean that," she said softly, almost regretfully, "then I shouldn't have to convince you to help me find her killer."

"I don't think we'll have to find him," Ethan said, his gaze suddenly alert as he searched the darkness around them. "I think he'll find us. I wouldn't be surprised if he's out there right now, watching us."

Grace's gaze shot over her shoulder at his words. She shivered as her hand tightened on her purse, the urge to remove her weapon almost overpowering. "Do you really think so?"

He shrugged in response.

Grace released a long breath. "Look, you've really spooked me. Are you sure you'll be all right here alone?"

"He won't make another move tonight. It's too soon."

She frowned. "How do you know that?"

Ethan gazed down at her, bewilderment flashing across his features. "I don't know," he said hoarsely. "I don't know how I know that."

ETHAN WATCHED AS Grace eased her car around the circular drive, then pulled onto the main street. Within moments, the taillights disappeared from his sight, and only then did he walk back into the house, locking the courtyard gate and resetting the alarm behind him. He climbed the staircase again, and for several seconds, stood at the edge of the junglelike room, reluctant to enter.

A deep uneasiness came over him, but he tried to tell himself it was only natural. He had amnesia. He'd almost been killed tonight, and the sister of the woman he'd been having an affair with had all but implicated him in her murder. Why wouldn't he feel uneasy?

But it was more than that. Something other than that. He wondered if his discomfort had more to do with Grace herself than with her accusations, or even the bizarre situation in which he found himself.

She wasn't telling him everything. He knew instinctively that there was more to Grace Donovan than she'd let on, but Ethan had no idea why he felt this way. He'd seen the grief in her eyes, the pain in her expression when she talked about her sister. He was sure her emotions were genuine, and yet his earlier doubts about her came rushing back. Her reaction was not that of a woman who had just learned of her sister's murder. The guilt, the anger, the obsession to find a loved one's killer were emotions that would come much later.

So what was going on here? Why did Ethan have the feeling that he was a pawn in some very dangerous game?

Was Grace a player, or was she, too, a pawn?

She had explained her relationship with Amy. They hadn't been close. A man had come between them, and they hadn't spoken in years until recently. Until Amy had contacted Grace and told her of the affair with Ethan.

He foraged his mind for a memory of Amy Cole, some remnant of his feelings for her. But there was nothing, and for some reason he couldn't explain, he was almost certain that she'd never meant anything to him.

So was that the kind of person he was? The kind of man who would use a woman for whatever he wanted or needed from her and then discard her without a second thought? Had he done that with his wife?

The cloying scent of the orchids made his head hurt. Ethan hurried out of the room, seeking the shelter of the study he'd found earlier. He didn't want to think about his wife or Amy Cole, and since he didn't remember either of them, it was easy enough to put them out of his mind.

Grace Donovan, however, was a different matter.

At the thought of her, Ethan's uneasiness returned full force, and suddenly he realized where his discomfort was coming from, at least in part. He was attracted to her. He had been from the first.

She wasn't beautiful by any stretch of the imagination, but she was attractive in her own way, and definitely intriguing. And those eyes...

Those eyes could melt a man's soul. He was sure of it.

Her figure wasn't tall and thin, but lush and womanly, and when he'd grabbed her earlier in the hospital parking lot, he'd felt the hardness of her muscles, the toned grace of her body.

If push came to shove, he knew she could hold her own, and that made her all the more alluring. She didn't need taking care of. She didn't need protecting, and that should have rubbed Ethan's male ego the wrong way, but instead it piqued his interest. Made him wonder things he had no business wondering. He was still a married man, even if he couldn't remember his own wife.

He'd left the light on in the office earlier, and now as he entered the room, he tried to put Grace out of his mind and concentrate on his surroundings. There had to be something in here that would trigger a memory for him. Something that would give him a clue as to what he'd been involved in. What had gotten Amy Cole killed.

Slowly, he walked around the room, studying the framed diplomas and certificates that he'd only taken the time to glance at earlier. He'd been educated at Harvard and Johns Hopkins. He was a board-certified plastic surgeon. He'd received dozens of awards and citations, and had corresponded with dignitaries all over the world.

Among the framed letters on the wall was one from the president of the United States, commending him on his work with underprivileged children born with disfigurements.

Ethan studied his hands. Did he really have the ability to wield a scalpel, the power to change people's lives? Children's lives?

Could that ability and power, all that training and instinct, be subdued by amnesia?

According to the letters and articles, Dr. Ethan Hunter was not only a brilliant surgeon, but a renowned humanitarian. But if he was such a great guy, why the hell was someone trying to kill him?

One whole side of the office contained dozens of framed newspaper articles written about him, but only one carried a photograph. For some reason he couldn't define, Ethan had been reluctant to do more than glance at the picture earlier. He knew it was a photo of him. In spite of the battered condition of his face now, he'd recognized the features. The brown eyes, the dark hair, the angular jaw and chin were the same ones he'd seen in the mirror in Grace's car.

And yet...

The man in the picture was him and it wasn't.

He couldn't explain it any better than that. He didn't feel connected in any way with the image in the photo, and the moment he'd seen it earlier, a dark haze had descended over him. Try as he might, he hadn't been able to compel himself to take that picture from the wall and study it more closely.

He removed it now and carried it with him to the desk, snapping on a brass lamp as he sat down. Placing the picture before him, he fought off a wave of dizziness as he forced himself to look down at his likeness, to study and absorb his own features.

In the photograph, he was standing in front of a white, one-story building with a lush, tropical backdrop. An older, shorter man with a thin, black mustache was in the picture, too, and Ethan's arm was draped over the man's shoulder. They both wore khaki pants and white shirts, both were smiling for the camera, but there was something about Ethan's expression...

Something about the other man's eyes...

He was frightened, Ethan thought suddenly. In spite of the smile and the reassuring arm Ethan had thrown over his shoulder, the mustached man looked scared half to death.

Shaken, Ethan forced himself to read the accompanying article concerning the reopening of the clinic in the Mexican jungle after a half dozen or so *banditos* had destroyed the place once they'd raided it for drugs. The other man in the picture was a Dr. Javier Salizar, a pediatrician who worked full-time at the clinic and who had been on duty the night the *banditos* attacked.

Fortunately, there had been no overnight patients at the hospital. Dr. Salizar had been all alone, and he'd been forced to flee into the jungle and hide until the terrorists had gathered what they wanted and left, burning the clinic to the ground in their wake.

According to the article, Ethan had provided his own personal funds to restore the clinic, and had used his own hands to help rebuild it. He'd spent months of his time getting the clinic operational once again, and the people in the surrounding villages revered him almost like a god.

Ethan didn't understand why, but the article deeply disturbed him. He sensed something bad had happened at that clinic. Something had made him flee, like Dr. Salizar, into the jungle, but not because he had been pursued by *banditos*.

In his dream, Ethan hadn't seen the men chasing him, but he had known just the same that they wore uniforms. They carried guns. He had almost been killed by the Mexican authorities, but Ethan had no idea why.

All he knew was that in some dark and dangerous way, he was tied to that clinic. To that jungle. And the killers that had pursued him in Mexico had followed him here to Houston. To his home.

Hands trembling, Ethan put the picture away and rifled through the paperwork on top of the desk. He turned on the laptop computer and perused the directories, but the files meant nothing. The case studies, medical notations, and patient consultations may as well have been written in a foreign language. Nothing clicked for him. Nothing at all.

Why didn't anything in this office trigger a memory? Why couldn't he remember being a doctor?

Almost frantically, Ethan searched through the desk. At the bottom of a drawer, a gold frame caught his eye. It had been stuffed face-down under a stack of folders. He pulled it out and stared down at a picture of a woman.

This was no snapshot or newspaper clipping, but an elegant studio shot with lighting that complimented the woman's ebony eyes and her full, ruby lips. Thick, glossy black hair had been pulled back to reveal a face as beautiful as it was flawless.

Movie-star glamorous, the woman stood in front of a grand piano, wearing a strapless black evening gown and opera-length, black gloves. Her body was thin, but incredibly shapely. The word that came instantly to mind was statuesque.

She wasn't smiling for the camera, but her lips were parted seductively and her eyes were heavy-lidded and sensual. At the bottom of the picture, scrawled in red ink, were the words: *To my husband, with much love and gratitude, Pilar.*

So this was Ethan's wife. He knew instinctively she'd had the picture made especially for him, and he'd put it away in a drawer face-down.

...the acid...your car...

Ethan stared at the photograph for a very long time, wondering how long they'd been married and what had gone wrong between them. She was an exquisite woman on the surface, but somehow her utter perfection left him cold.

Did I do this to you? he wondered. *Did I make you into this... work of art?*

A work of art without a soul, something told him.

He thought of Grace suddenly, of the unevenness of her features, the short, red hair, the lips that were neither lush nor thin, but in his mind, just right. Her light blue eyes held more life, more mystery, than this woman's ever could.

Disturbed by his thoughts, Ethan put the picture away and closed the drawer. It wasn't fair to give a woman he didn't remember unfavorable attributes in order to justify his attraction to Grace. And that was exactly what he'd been doing.

Had he also tried to justify his affair with Amy Cole? Had there been other women in his marriage?

What kind of husband would treat his wife in such a manner?

What kind of doctor would be pursued through the Mexican jungle by the *policía?*

Ethan wondered if he really wanted to know the answer to any of those questions.

GRACE CLOSED AND locked the door of her hotel room, then slung her jacket toward a chair. Flopping down on the bed, she kicked off her shoes, leaned back against the headboard, then removed her cell phone from her purse and punched in a number she knew by heart.

In spite of the late hour, a woman with a throaty voice answered on the first ring. "Hello?"

"It's Grace."

There was a brief pause before the woman asked, "Are you all right?"

"Amy's dead, Myra."

"Yes, I know."

"What the hell happened tonight?" Grace exploded. "What went wrong?"

"Everything. God, it's all a mess. Hunter wasn't supposed to come back to Houston for at least another two weeks. We would have had plenty of time to set up a sting, but now..." Myra Temple trailed off while she lit up a cigarette. Grace heard her exhale angrily. "As it is, we've rushed the whole operation. We're down here without proper backup or support, and we screwed up. It happens."

"Yes, but this particular screwup cost a woman her life," Grace said angrily. Myra seemed more concerned about the potential damage to the operation than about Amy's death, but that should have come as no surprise. The woman was coldly and consummately professional. Nothing got in her way, and until tonight, Grace had thought she was becoming exactly like her mentor. She'd thought she had the guts to do whatever had to be done to bring a killer to justice.

But after tonight...

"Amy should have been under surveillance. Why wasn't she?"

"She was," Myra snapped. "But somehow she managed to slip through. My guess is that after speaking with us yesterday, she panicked. She had second thoughts about what she'd done, and so she got in touch with Dr. Hunter, probably by cell phone, and warned him that the Feds would be waiting for him when he landed here in Houston. Then she devised a way to get out of her apartment without us knowing."

"How?" Grace demanded.

"Maybe she donned a wig and borrowed her neighbor's car. How the hell should I know? It doesn't help matters that these idiots in the field office down here don't know their butts from a hole in the ground. We can't count on much help in that regard. In any case, Amy appears to have been a lot smarter than I gave her credit for." Myra's tone was a mixture of disgust and admiration.

"So how did Eth—Dr. Hunter manage to get away from us? You were watching the airport yourself."

A loud silence. "He didn't land at Bush Intercontinental Airport," Myra finally said testily, clearly annoyed by Grace's veiled criticism. "I guarantee you, I would have recognized him if he had.

We're checking all the private airfields in the area now, but he undoubtedly chartered a plane. Sometime during the flight, he contacted Amy again, and they made plans to meet at the clinic."

Something in her tone made Grace's heart thud against her chest. "Myra, you don't think—"

"What?"

Grace tensed. Her hand clutched the tiny cell phone. "You don't think *he* killed Amy, do you? Because he found out she talked to us?"

Another pause. "It's possible, but I don't think so. I think he was followed, probably all the way from Mexico, and ambushed at the clinic. I think you and I both know who killed Amy Cole, Grace."

Grace closed her eyes, dredging up a name from the past. A face from her nightmares. Trevor Reardon. A man who had changed Grace's life forever.

"By the way," Myra said softly. "That was a brilliant stroke on your part—pretending to be Amy's sister."

More like an act of desperation, Grace thought. Aloud she said, "Actually, it was Amy's idea. She introduced me to one of her neighbors as her sister. Then she later told me she didn't have any family, but no one in Houston knew that about her because she didn't like to talk about her past."

When Grace had arrived at the clinic earlier to learn that Amy was dead and Ethan Hunter had been severely beaten, she knew she had to come up with a reason that would put her in close contact with him. And if everything Amy had told her about him was true, Grace was fairly certain Ethan would be wary of the authorities. She couldn't tell him the truth because he would never trust her, never agree to cooperate with her, and so she'd impulsively devised the cover of being Amy's grieving sister. A woman who wanted to find the killer just as badly as Ethan did.

Grace wondered if the ruse had worked, or if like her, he had suspicions.

She ran her fingers through her bangs. "Look, there's another contingency we hadn't counted on. Dr. Hunter now claims he has amnesia."

"Yes, I know," Myra said. "According to his chart, he's suffering some short-term memory loss due to a rather mild concussion."

Grace should have known Myra would have done her homework thoroughly. She'd probably been over Ethan's hospital room with a vacuum.

"I'm afraid it's a little more severe than that," Grace said. "He claims he doesn't remember Amy. Or even his own name, for that matter."

She heard Myra suck in her breath sharply. "You mean he doesn't remember *anything?*"

"That's what he says."

Grace could almost hear the wheels turning in Myra's brain. After a few moments, she said, "Do you think he's faking?"

Grace thought about the darkness and confusion in Ethan's eyes earlier, the desperation that had flashed across his features. Had that been a reaction to what had happened to him in the clinic? Or because he genuinely couldn't remember?

Grace found herself wanting to believe him and that scared her. It was imperative she remain objective. Dispassionate. A consummate professional.

She wondered suddenly what Myra would think if she knew how attracted Grace was to Dr. Ethan Hunter. Would she pull her off the case?

"Well, so what do you think?" Myra's impatient tone brought Grace out of her reverie, and she realized she'd lapsed into silence for a few seconds too long.

She took a deep breath, willing her tone to remain even. "I thought he might be faking at first. I mean, it seemed a little too coincidental, if Amy did tip him off that we'd be waiting for him. But after spending some time with him tonight, I'm inclined to believe him. He seems genuinely distressed."

Myra's tone was pensive. "So maybe this doesn't have to change anything. Let's think about it for a minute. Whether he's faking or not, your cover should hold up. If Amy told you the truth and she really had no family, there won't be anyone coming out of the woodwork to dispute your claim. And if he *does* have amnesia, it could even work to our advantage. Make him easier to control."

An image of Ethan's bruised and battered face materialized in Grace's mind, and something fluttered in her stomach. Was it pity? Guilt?

Maybe it was just plain old fear, she thought, although for her, that could be the most dangerous emotion of all.

"You aren't having second thoughts about using him, are you?" Myra asked casually, but Grace was immediately on her guard. Was she being tested?

She gripped the phone with grim determination. "Not at all. Ethan Hunter is a means to an end, nothing more."

"Good," Myra said, satisfied. "Because we're getting close, Grace. Can you feel it?"

Grace's stomach knotted with excitement. Or was it dread? "Yes."

"This amnesia thing could be a blessing in disguise, exactly what we need to gain Hunter's cooperation. But we still have to be careful," Myra warned. "Don't do or say anything that will tip him off. I don't have to remind you that one false move and this whole thing could still blow up in our faces."

"Don't worry." Cradling the phone against her shoulder, Grace removed the SIG-Sauer from her purse and released the magazine, pulling back the slide to make sure the gun was unloaded. Then methodically she reloaded the weapon and looked through the sights, relieved to see that her hand was steady, her nerves steeled. "I've waited a long time for this."

"I know you have," Myra said. "But just remember, this can't become a personal vendetta. Once you allow your emotions to get in the way, you become a walking dead woman."

"I understand. You don't have to worry about me. You taught me well."

"I hope so," Myra said softly. "I hope so..."

After they ended the call, Grace poured herself a whiskey over ice and walked out to the tiny balcony of her room. It was still hot. At Ethan's house, the lush tropical foliage, both inside and out, had at least given the illusion of coolness, but here, the heat clung to the concrete and mortar like a desperate lover.

Grace lifted the glass to the back of her neck, letting the cool condensation slide against her skin as the events of the night and remnants of her former life played themselves out in her mind. Funny how one tragic moment, one careless decision could change a person's life forever, could mold you into someone you didn't even recognize anymore.

But tonight she'd glimpsed a bit of the old Grace. Tonight she'd remembered what it was like to be attracted to a man. She'd *felt* something, standing outside with Ethan.

Downing half the contents of her glass, Grace shuddered as the liquid caught fire in her throat and stomach. Myra's warning seemed to reach out from the darkness and taunt her.

Once you allow your emotions to get in the way, you become a walking dead woman.

CHAPTER FOUR

The sun streaming in through the tall windows in the third-story master suite awakened Ethan the next morning. He'd tossed and turned for hours the night before, sleeping sporadically, dreaming about running through the jungle and then falling. As in most nightmares, he never remembered hitting the ground but instead would awaken abruptly in a cold sweat, his heart pounding, adrenaline still rushing through his veins.

He sat up now and looked around, slowly letting the events of last evening filter back in. He'd hoped that by morning his memory would have returned, but his mind was still pretty much a blank. He still had no idea who Ethan Hunter really was, what he might have done, or why someone wanted to kill him. All he knew for sure was that he had to somehow keep it together. He had to remain sharp until he could find out what the hell was going on.

His body aching, he pulled himself out of bed and headed for the shower. Like the bedroom, the master bath was huge and luxurious, with lush, green carpeting, intricate tile mosaics, a step-up marble bathtub, and a shower stall that could easily accommodate two.

Turning on the water in the shower, Ethan stood staring at his reflection in the mirror over the double vanity. The bruises on his face were still prominent, but the swelling had gone down, and the pain wasn't quite so severe. He almost looked human this morning, although his face was still one he didn't recognize.

Stripping away the last of his clothing, he examined the appendectomy scar on his lower right side. The wound was surprisingly large, about four inches long, and still tender to the touch. Ethan stared at the scar, trying to remember the surgery, but nothing came to him. Nothing but the fleeting memory of being pursued through the jungle. The echoing sound of gunfire. The lingering unease that

Dr. Ethan Hunter was a man he wasn't sure he wanted to get to know.

Ignoring the twinges of pain from the cuts and bruises, he stepped under the hot water, washing briskly, trying to elude the questions whirling inside his head by concentrating on the mundane. Showering. Getting dressed. Finding something to eat.

Back in the bedroom, he gazed at the clothing hanging in the massive walk-in closet. The expensive suits and custom-made shirts were as unfamiliar to him as the face he'd studied in the bathroom mirror.

Finally, randomly, he grabbed something casual, a pair of charcoal pants and a cotton knit pullover. The pants were loose in the waist, and he wondered if he'd lost weight after his surgery. The shirt fit fine, but the shoes he pulled from the closet were a little snug. He started to find another pair, but then froze when he heard a noise. Somewhere downstairs a door opened and closed.

It occurred to Ethan that Rosa might have come back, but she'd said last night that today was her day off. She planned to spend the time with her daughter. So who was downstairs then?

Ethan scanned the room for a weapon. His eyes lit on the nightstand next to the bed, and he crossed the floor to search through the drawers. If he kept a gun in the house, he reasoned that would be the logical place for it, but his search was fruitless.

Removing the shade from the heavy brass lamp on the night stand, Ethan jerked the plug from the wall and picked up the base. As a weapon, it was cumbersome at best, but he didn't have time to look for anything else. Whoever was in the house might even now be slipping up the stairs to ambush him.

Heart thumping, his senses on full alert, Ethan left the bedroom, making his way toward the stairs. He paused on the landing, peering over the railing into the jungle-like living room below him. Nothing moved. No sound came to him.

In sock feet, he slipped silently down the stairs, his gaze searching every nook and corner of the room. There were any number of places an intruder could hide, but the most obvious place seemed to be the study. The door was ajar, and Ethan was almost certain he'd closed it last night before going to bed.

He crossed the room and flattened himself against the wall outside the study, listening. From inside, he could detect shuffling sounds, as if someone was going through his papers.

Nerves pumped, Ethan glanced inside. And tensed.

A woman stood before an open safe, busily removing what looked to be bundles of cash. He recognized her immediately from the picture he'd found in the desk last night. The intruder was his wife.

She didn't see him at first. Ethan watched her for several seconds as she stood at the safe. The red suit she wore was so short and so tight that she didn't appear to be armed, but the thought crossed Ethan's mind that she was probably extremely dangerous anyway. A woman scorned could be deadly.

He set the brass lamp on the floor, then stepped into the room. Her head jerked toward the door, her hand flying to her heart when she saw him. She blinked once, then twice before she finally managed to get her shock under control. "Ethan!" Her voice was lyrical and very feminine, traced with a Spanish accent. "I didn't know you were home."

Ethan glanced at the bundles of cash. "I can see that."

She made no move to close the safe door, nor to hide the money she'd stacked on top of his desk. Instead she took one of the bundles and brazenly thumbed through the bills. "I heard you were in the hospital." Glancing up, her gaze flicked over his bruised features. Something flashed in her eyes, an emotion Ethan couldn't define. "You look and sound terrible," she said.

"Thanks." He returned her perusal, taking a long moment to study her features, and decided that the photograph in his desk, as spectacular as it was, didn't do her justice. She was even more beautiful in person. The deep V-neck of her jacket revealed a magnificent cleavage while the impossibly short skirt highlighted impossibly long legs.

But what drew Ethan's attention more than her grace and sultry beauty was the fact that she appeared to be stealing him blind.

As if reading his mind, she glanced down at the money and shrugged. "It's not like you don't owe me."

When he didn't protest, she gave him an odd glance, then turned back to the safe. Her hair cascaded down her back, almost to her waist, gleaming like ebony when she tossed it over her shoulder.

"What are you doing here anyway?" she asked, her voice muf-fled as she reached inside the safe. "Bob said you'd been beaten up pretty badly. He thought you'd be in the hospital for several more days." She withdrew another packet of bills, then turned to face him, her dark eyes challenging.

"Bob who?" Ethan asked, without thinking.

She arched a perfect black brow. "Bob Kendall. Your ex-partner, remember? Who else would I be talking about?"

Ethan was immediately on his guard. Kendall was his ex-partner? If the hostility in the man's eyes last night had been any indication, the arrangement had ended badly. Ethan wondered what had gone wrong, in his business and in his marriage.

He stared at his wife, trying to dredge up a memory, some left-over emotion, but nothing came to him. Nothing but a faint uneas-iness as he watched her.

"When did you talk to Bob?" he asked.

Something that might have been guilt flashed over her features. She began stuffing the money into a large black tote bag. "He called me last night. He was at the hospital when you were brought in, and he thought I'd want to know what happened."

Ethan remembered what Rosa had told him last evening, that Pilar had called here at the house because Kendall had told her Ethan was returning. Why? he wondered. There had been none of her clothing in the closet upstairs, no makeup or feminine toiletries in the bathroom. It was obvious she no longed lived here, so why had she called Rosa to find out when he was returning?

And why wait until he got back to rob his safe? Unless, of course, things hadn't gone according to plan—

Had Pilar and Kendall been behind Ethan's attack last night? Had they somehow arranged for him to go to the clinic before coming home? Had they wanted to kill him?

Ethan studied his wife and wondered why that notion didn't seem preposterous to him. Was it because Pilar Hunter struck him as a woman who would get what she wanted no matter who she had to hurt in the process?

But she was also a woman Ethan had married, must have once loved. He wondered how he could feel nothing, not even anger, toward her now.

Her task completed, she closed the bag and slung the straps over her shoulder. She walked around the desk and started by him, then paused. "Bob told me about Amy. I guess I should say I'm sorry."

Ethan said nothing.

For the first time, he sensed an uncertainty about his wife, as if she didn't know whether to say more or end it here and now. Then she smiled. "I never believed you loved her, you know. Not like you once loved me." Gazing up at him, she lifted a hand to his face.

Ethan resisted the urge to step back from her. Instead he held his ground, letting her place a cool palm against his bruised skin. For one long moment, he stared down at her perfect features, her incredible beauty, and wondered again why he felt nothing.

And she knew. Like a lightning bolt, anger whipped across her features. "*Cabrón,*" she muttered as she turned and brushed by him. Outside the doorway, she glanced back. "You do look terrible, you know. Besides the bruises, I mean. You've lost weight. Your eyes..." she trailed off, studying him.

"What about my eyes?" he asked sharply.

"They're cold. Even colder than I remembered." She shuddered. "You are not the man I married, Ethan. You haven't been for a very long time."

WHEN GRACE ARRIVED at the house a little while later, she was amazed to see how much better Ethan looked. Even though the bruises hadn't faded, the swelling in his face had gone down so that his features were no longer distorted. She could tell more clearly what he looked like, and when he'd first opened the door, she'd caught her breath in surprise.

"I...hope I didn't get you up," she said, her gaze slipping over him. He was dressed, but his hair was mussed and he wasn't wearing any shoes. His casualness made her feel stuffy in her beige pantsuit, silk shell and brown flats.

"I've been up for a while," he said, his voice still hoarse. He stood back so she could enter. Grace stepped past him into the foyer, then waited while he closed the door and reactivated the alarm.

"Have you remembered anything?" she asked anxiously.

He gave her a look. "You don't waste any time, do you?"

Grace shrugged. "Why should I? Someone out there killed my sister last night, and he may come back to finish you off. Who has time for formalities?"

"I get your point," he said dryly. "And the answer to your question is, no. I haven't remembered anything."

"Nothing at all?"

"Nothing that makes any sense."

Grace glanced up at him, trying to read his expression. "Well, if it's any consolation, you look much better today. Almost like a different man."

"So I've already been told." He turned and started for the stairs.

"By whom?" Grace asked quickly. "Has someone been here this morning?"

He paused on the bottom step, turning to glance over his shoulder. "My wife was here earlier. I caught her taking money out of the safe in the study."

Grace frowned. "What do you mean, you *caught* her?"

"Just that. Apparently she no longer lives here. But I guess she decided to come back and help herself to whatever cash I might have left lying around."

Grace took a moment to assess this new information. So Ethan had met Pilar Hunter face to face. Grace couldn't help wondering how the meeting had gone, or what he'd thought of the woman. What he'd felt for her. From the pictures Grace had seen, Pilar was an incredibly beautiful woman.

Absently, Grace ran a hand down her pantsuit, smoothing invisible wrinkles. "So what was it like seeing her?" she tried to ask casually. "Did she give you any clues about your relationship? About what might have happened between the two of you?"

Ethan paused. "I don't have any idea what happened between us, but I'll tell you one thing. She struck me as a woman perfectly capable of throwing acid on my car. Or in my face, for that matter."

The bluntness of his words threw Grace for a moment. "Do you think she may have had something to do with Amy's death?"

"I wouldn't rule out the possibility," he said grimly. He turned and started up the stairs. "Come on up. We can talk about this later. I've located the kitchen, and I'm cooking breakfast."

Grace followed him up the stairs and through the living room.

The parrot, fully awake and preening on his perch, let out a loud squawk when he saw her.

"Don't even start," she muttered.

"What?" Ethan said over his shoulder.

"I said that's a good start. Learning your way around the house, I mean."

He gave her a quizzical look, then led her through a dining room with a high ceiling and a magnificent stained glass window, into the kitchen, with its stainless steel appliances, satillo tile floor, and wall of atrium doors that gave a broad view of a backyard pool and waterfall.

Ethan walked over to the range and dished up a plate of bacon and eggs, then added a pile of buttered toast. "Have you eaten? There's plenty for both of us."

Grace eyed the food longingly. She'd started the day with her usual meal, one half of a grapefruit and a cup of coffee. If she ate bacon and eggs, she'd have to add at least half an hour to her daily workout in the gym, not to mention an extra mile or two to her run. For a moment, she considered that it might be worth it. She hadn't had a piece of bacon in ages.

Willpower, she reminded herself. She had to remain sharp both physically and mentally. "Just a glass of orange juice for me."

He poured them both a glass of juice from a pitcher he removed from the refrigerator, then carried his food to the breakfast table. Grace followed him. He took the seat facing the atrium doors and outside, while Grace sat across from him, with a clear view of the kitchen door. She kept her purse on her lap.

For a few moments, neither of them said anything. Ethan ate ravenously, as if he hadn't had a solid meal in days. Grace tried not to stare at him, but his looks had changed so dramatically overnight, she couldn't help studying his features.

When he caught her watching him, she said, "I can't get over the changes in your appearance. It's amazing."

He shrugged. "There was a lot of room for improvement. I looked pretty horrible last night."

"I didn't mean it like that," Grace said. "You must be a really fast healer, that's all."

"Maybe." A shadow flickered over his features, and Grace wondered what he was thinking. If he was remembering something. She couldn't help wondering what he'd been like before all this happened. Would he have been the kind of man she would have wanted to spend time with? Doubtful, if everything Amy had told her was true.

"Were you able to get some sleep last night?" she asked him.

He grimaced. "Some. I'm still not used to this place. It…doesn't feel like home to me, but I guess that's to be expected, considering."

Grace nodded. "It'll take time. I gather you've done some exploring this morning."

"I've been over this place from top to bottom. Nothing triggered a memory. But at least I did find the kitchen. And a gym downstairs. I want to start working out as soon as possible. Build back my strength."

Grace's gaze dropped to his broad shoulders and chest, the muscular arms bulging beneath the short sleeves of his shirt. She remembered the strength in those arms last night when he'd grabbed her, the hardness of his chest when he'd held her against him. If he was out of shape, she could only imagine what he would be like at his peak. "You don't want to rush it," she said. "Amy said you'd had surgery recently. An appendectomy, I believe."

"That's what I've been told, but I don't remember the surgery, either. Although I do have a scar on my side." Again his features momentarily darkened, as if he'd suddenly remembered something he had no intention of sharing. Grace wondered what he was keeping from her.

"Tell me more about your meeting with Pilar," she said.

The cloud over his features changed, but didn't fade. "Not much to tell. Like I said, I found her in the study taking money out of the safe."

"Did she say why she was doing that?"

Ethan pushed aside his plate as if his appetite had suddenly deserted him. He glanced up. "She seemed to think I owed her."

"Because of Amy?"

He shrugged.

"I've seen pictures of Pilar." Grace paused. "She's a very beautiful woman."

"Yes, she certainly is."

"Did you, you know, *feel* anything when you saw her?"

One dark brow rose at the question. "You mean attraction?"

"I'm just trying to figure out what your relationship with her is," Grace said, almost defensively.

"Like I said earlier, apparently we're separated. She wasn't here long enough for me to find out much of anything, but she did mention Amy. She knew about the shooting."

Grace glanced at him in surprise. "What did she say?"

He shrugged. "Let me put it this way. I don't think Amy's death came exactly as a blow."

Something that might have been sympathy crossed his features, and Grace lowered her eyes. Even though her deception was necessary, it didn't make it any easier. "How did she find out about Amy's death?"

"Do you remember Rosa mentioning a man named Kendall? She said that Pilar had called to find out what time I would be home, because Dr. Kendall had told her I was arriving last night. Kendall was at the hospital when I was brought in. He was in my room when I came to. Evidently he called Pilar and told her what happened."

Grace thought about that for a moment. "Do you know anything about this Kendall?"

"Only that he's my ex-partner."

Grace paused. "Do you think Pilar and Dr. Kendall might have something going on?"

Ethan's expression didn't waver. "I wondered about that. I've also wondered why Pilar waited until I got back to come here and take money from the safe. According to the police detective I spoke with last night, I was in Mexico for weeks, recovering from the surgery. She could have come over here at any time and taken that money. Why wait until I got back?"

Grace frowned. "What are you getting at?"

"Well, just think about it for a minute." He toyed with the juice glass. "Why would she wait until now to take that money out of the safe?"

"Maybe she didn't need it until now."

"Exactly," Ethan said. "Because maybe all along she thought

there would be a lot more where that came from." His gaze went past Grace to focus on the backyard. She didn't turn, but she could hear the faint tinkling of the waterfall cascading into the pool, and she wondered if he was thinking about the jungle. Why did he seem to have such an aversion to it?

"After Pilar left this morning, I went through the safe myself," Ethan finally said. "I found a life insurance policy for five million dollars that named her as the beneficiary. I'd be willing to bet that's a lot more than she took out of the safe."

"So what exactly are you saying, Ethan? That Pilar was behind what happened to you last night? You think she tried to have you killed?"

His gaze met Grace's. "I don't know why that surprises you. You said yourself last night this whole thing may be a *Fatal Attraction* in reverse. Don't you think a woman is capable of murder?"

Grace thought about the killer she wanted to bring to justice, felt the weight of her own gun in her purse. "Yes," she said grimly. "I know there are women who are very capable of killing. Who might even take pleasure from it. But as I also told you last night, from the things Amy told me, I don't think Pilar is the one who wants you dead. Or at least, I don't think she's the one who tried to have you killed."

Her distinction was not lost on Ethan. His gaze on her cooled. "You were pretty clear in that regard. You think I did something to set last night's events in motion. You think someone is trying to kill me because of something I did in Mexico. Something illegal."

His voice was hard, unyielding, but Grace sensed an undercurrent of anguish. A hint of desperation in his tone. She shrugged. "Look, I'm just going by Amy's letters—"

"Amy's *letters*," he said, shoving back his chair and standing. "Amy *said*." He strode to the atrium doors and stood staring out into the sunlit garden. "I know she was your sister, and I'm sorry she's dead, but I don't remember her, and from what you told me last night, you didn't know her that well, either. What if everything she told you about me was a lie? What if she was setting me up somehow?"

Grace turned in her chair to stare at him. "You don't really believe that."

"Why is it so hard to believe?" His jaw hardened as he turned to face her. "Why is it so easy for you to believe that I was involved in something that got her killed? You don't know me. What do you really know about me?"

Before Grace could answer, he walked back over to the table and stood staring down at her. The look in his eyes made her shiver. "And it suddenly occurs to me," he said slowly, "that I don't know anything about you, either."

"Of course, you do," Grace said, ignoring the tiny spark of panic that flared inside her. She stood, trying to take away his advantage, trying to regain control of the situation as she met his gaze and they squared off.

His eyes narrowed on her. "What do I know about you? Your name? That you're Amy's sister? I know those things because *you* told me."

Grace moistened her lips. "What are you driving at?"

"Maybe I've been a little too trusting. Maybe I should have asked a few more questions last night."

"Ask them now," Grace said, her voice growing cold. "I'll tell you anything you want to know."

The silence in the kitchen was deafening. When he spoke, his voice was almost too calm. "Who do you work for?"

Grace's heart thumped against her chest. She fingered the gold clasp of her purse. "Don't you mean *where* do I work? I work for a legal firm."

"You're a lawyer?"

She shook her head. "I went to law school, but I never took the bar exam. I'm more of a...researcher."

"What does that mean?"

"It means I spend a lot of time behind a computer and doing legwork for my superiors. There's a lot of grunt work involved in what I do."

He paused again. "You don't have an accent," he accused. "How long have you lived in Houston?"

She answered without hesitation. "Not long. I transferred down here from Washington, D.C."

"What did you do there?"

"Same thing."

"Why did you move to Houston?"

"To be near my sister." That was the first outright lie she'd told him all morning, but Grace knew there would be plenty of others. She'd say and do whatever she had to in order to gain his trust. That was the way she'd been trained. The way she lived her life. She couldn't afford to get an attack of conscience now simply because a man with a battered face and a hidden past was awakening feelings inside her she had thought were long dead.

"What about your family?" he asked. "Where are they?"

"My parents have been dead for years." Without warning, the old memory came storming back. Grace thought she had buried it, along with her emotions, someplace safe, someplace impenetrable, but all of a sudden it was back, the explosion in her mind as shattering as the one that night had been.

In the beat of a heart, she was a teenager again, running down the street toward the sirens. Seeing the fire licking red-orange against the night sky. Hearing the screams of the people trapped inside the white frame house. Her mother and father. And at an upstairs window, beating against the panes, her hair in flames, Grace's sister. Her beautiful, beautiful sister...

"Everyone is gone," she whispered. Ethan touched her hand, and Grace jumped, forgetting for a moment where she was. Who she was supposed to be. She stared up at him, fighting back the scream that tore at her throat. The horror that had made her who and what she was.

"I'm sorry," he said. His eyes, cold and suspicious before, were now clouded with guilt. It was hard for Grace to witness that guilt, knowing what she knew.

He's not innocent, she told herself. *Don't be fooled.*

She opened her purse and withdrew her wallet, showing him her driver's license, her social security card, and then fishing out a business card that contained the name and address of a downtown law firm. The business cards had been printed overnight. The address and phone number had been supplied by the field office here in Houston.

"You can call them if you like," she said, handing the card to

Ethan. The call would be forwarded to either Myra or a support operative who would bear out Grace's story. If Ethan actually went by the office, the receptionist would refer him to one of the partners who had been briefed and would know how to field the inquiry. "But I am who I say I am. My name is Grace Donovan, and I am looking for my sister's killer."

He nodded, as if he'd seen something in her face that had convinced him. He sat down at the table, looking as if the remainder of his strength had suddenly drained away. "Did you bring Amy's letters with you today?"

Grace sat down beside him. She could smell the faint scent of soap and shampoo, and wondered if, like her, he'd spent a long time in the shower that morning, trying to scrub away the past. Or what he feared might be there.

"No, but I brought this." She pulled a newspaper clipping from her purse, and placed it face up before him. The article was accompanied by a picture of a blond man who looked to be in his early thirties.

Grace stared long and hard at that picture, then turned away, shuddering. "I found that clipping in Amy's apartment one day. When I asked her, she denied knowing anything about it, but I could tell she was upset. Frightened. She'd cut this picture out of the paper for a reason, but she wouldn't tell me why."

Ethan picked up the clipping and scanned the article. "Trevor Reardon," he read, then glanced up. "It says he's on the FBI's Ten Most Wanted List."

Grace nodded. "He was convicted on three counts of first-degree murder and sentenced to life in prison without parole. He escaped several months ago and has been underground ever since."

"So what does this have to do with me?" Ethan asked.

"You don't recognize him? Look closely." As he examined the picture of Trevor Reardon, Grace studied Ethan's features, looking for a flicker, any telltale sign of recognition.

After several seconds, he handed the clipping back to her. "I don't recognize him. Am I supposed to?"

"Are you sure?" Grace asked anxiously.

"As far as I know, I've never seen this man before." Ethan's voice was edged with impatience. "And I don't think I like what you're implying."

"I'm not implying anything—"

"The hell you're not. What connection do you think I have to a convicted murderer? Just what kind of man do you think I am?"

"I don't know," she said softly, her gaze meeting his in defiance. "Isn't that what we're both trying to find out?"

For a long moment, his gaze held hers, then he glanced away. Running both hands through his hair, he stared at the ceiling. "What connection do you think I have to this Trevor Reardon?" he asked again.

Grace paused. "I think you may have given him a new face."

CHAPTER FIVE

Ethan stared at her as if she'd taken leave of her senses. Then, as the full meaning of her words sank in, he stared at her in horror. "Why would I do that?" He was a doctor, for God's sake. A humanitarian, according to the articles and awards in his office. Why would he knowingly give a murderer a new face, a new life?

Something that almost looked like sympathy flashed across Grace's face before she could subdue it. In the blink of an eye, however, the mask was back in place. She stared at him dispassionately. "It's possible you were somehow coerced."

"But that's not what you think, is it?"

She hesitated, her gaze resting briefly on the picture of Trevor Reardon's face, then lifting to Ethan's. Any trace of sympathy she might have felt earlier had vanished. "No. I think you did it for money," she said bluntly.

"But why would I?" he demanded. "Look at this place. These clothes. It's obvious I already have money."

When Grace said nothing, he grabbed her hand and stood, drawing her to her feet. "Come with me."

"What? Where?" Her voice sounded almost panicky. She grabbed her purse and slung the strap over her shoulder.

Without another word, Ethan pulled her out of the kitchen, through the dining room and living room toward the study. The parrot gave a weak little squawk as they hurried passed him, but Ethan ignored him.

Inside the study, he walked to the middle of the room and gestured to all the framed awards and citations on the walls. "Look at all this stuff." He walked over and took one of the framed letters down, then held it out to Grace. "Do you know what this is? It's a letter from the president of the United States commending me on my work in Mexico. This one is from a senator, this one from our ambassador to Mexico." He went on and on, until he'd taken a half dozen or so frames from the wall and piled them in Grace's arms.

Apparently unimpressed, she stacked them on his desk.

Ethan knew his movements were almost frantic as he removed another frame from the wall, but he couldn't help himself. He had to convince her, and himself, that what she was thinking was ludicrous. "Why would somebody who has done all this work for underprivileged children, received all these accolades, risk losing everything by changing a murderer's face?"

"Because all that philanthropy takes a great deal of money, and you also have very expensive tastes." Grace made a sweeping gesture with her hand. "You can't buy all this with citations and awards and letters from the president. Plus, you have the perfect cover. Your clinic in Mexico is remote, practically inaccessible, from what Amy said, and perfectly legitimate."

"Except for the fact that, according to you, I operate on criminals on the side," he said bitterly. "I give them new faces so they're free to go out into the world to rape, murder, and steal at will."

Grace's gaze didn't quite meet his. "Reardon probably found out about you from someone in prison. When he escaped, he made his way across the border and somehow found your clinic in the jungle. I think he gave you a great deal of money, probably millions, to give him a new face."

"*Millions?*" Ethan frowned. "The article said he'd been in prison for over six years. Where would he get that kind of money?"

"At the time he was caught, it was estimated that he'd amassed a fortune worth well over thirty million dollars. It was never found."

Ethan stared at her in surprise. "So who is this guy anyway?"

Grace paused. "He's an ex-Navy SEAL and an explosives expert who sold his services to the highest bidder. He became a mercenary, an assassin, sometimes a terrorist. It didn't much matter to him what the job entailed so long as the price was right. He enjoyed killing and he was good at it. It was all a game to him, one he made a lot of money from. The first time he escaped prison, he went after the FBI agent who had captured him. Reardon firebombed the agent's house and wired all the doors to explode when the people trapped inside or the rescuers on the outside tried to open them. There was no way in or out. The agent, his wife and a daughter all died in the fire.''

Her expression remained coldly dispassionate, but Ethan sensed she wasn't quite as calm as she appeared. There were lights inside her eyes. Tiny flares of rage when she spoke. Was she thinking of her sister?

''After that, he remained free for several years,'' Grace said. ''He was a master of disguises, always staying one step ahead of the authorities. He may even have gone out of the country for a while. But then he made one very serious mistake. The only one in the agent's family who hadn't been killed in the fire was a teenage girl who'd sneaked out of the house that night. Reardon came back to get her.''

''Why?'' Ethan asked. ''How could the girl hurt him?''

''Because she could identify him, for one thing. And because she was a loose end. From everything I've learned about Reardon, he doesn't like loose ends. He's almost obsessive about it.''

''So what happened when he came back for the girl?''

''There was another agent, a woman. She was the murdered agent's partner. She'd made it her life's work to track down Reardon and send him back to prison. She knew he'd eventually come after the girl, and when he did, she got him.''

Ethan didn't much like the sound of that. ''You mean she used the girl as bait?''

Grace shrugged. ''That's one way of putting it. But she also saved the girl's life. To her, the end justified the means.'' Grace picked up one of the framed citations and studied it closely.

Ethan used the opportunity to study her. She seemed as focused as ever this morning, her voice steady, her expression still as determined as he remembered it.

But what he hadn't remembered was how the blue of her eyes lightened or darkened depending on her emotions, or how the tint of her lip gloss reminded him of lush, ripe strawberries. What he hadn't remembered was the scent of her perfume, so subtle it seemed hardly more than imagination, or the way her modestly cut jacket only hinted at the womanly curves beneath. Ethan hadn't remembered any of those things—or was it that he had just been working very hard to forget them?

"How do you know so much about this Reardon?" he asked her.

They both glanced up at the same time, their gazes locking. Ethan's gaze was drawn to her lips when she spoke. "A lot of the information is in the article I showed you, plus, after I found that clipping in Amy's apartment, I did some research. I wanted to know why Reardon's picture seemed to frighten her so much."

"You think Amy knew what was going on in the Mexican clinic?"

"I think she at least suspected, and that's why she was so afraid." Grace set aside the frame she'd been holding. "Amy had been to the clinic with you on at least one occasion. She even alluded to the fact that she'd seen a man down there, a patient, whose face was covered in bandages. She didn't know who he was, but she found his presence at the clinic strange because most of your patients down there are children. I think she came back here and somehow started putting two and two together."

Ethan walked over and stared at the picture of him and Dr. Salizar in front of the Mexican Clinic. If everything Grace said was true, no wonder Salizar looked so frightened. Ethan wondered if the clinic had really been burned to the ground by *banditos,* or if one of his former patients had come back looking for him.

He turned to Grace. "So you think Reardon killed Amy because she was on to him?"

"No. I think Amy was a bonus. I think you were the target because you may be the only person in the world who has seen Trevor Reardon's new face."

In spite of himself, Ethan felt chilled by her words. "And now I can't identify him because I don't remember him."

"That's the ironic part," Grace said. "He could be anyone. Your next-door neighbor. The mailman. Anyone. If Trevor Reardon wants you dead, the only way you can survive is to somehow find him first."

"You mean use myself as bait," Ethan said, marveling at her coolness. "Like the FBI agent used the girl."

Grace shrugged. "It makes sense. You're a loose end. Sooner or later, Reardon will come after you."

"And when he does?"

She shrugged again. "When he does, we have to be ready for him."

He looked at her and just shook his head. "Has it ever once occurred to you that you and I are hardly trained to capture a murderer, let alone an ex-Navy SEAL who has a penchant for explosives?" For a moment, Ethan thought she was actually going to smile at his words. She almost seemed to be enjoying herself, and he said angrily, "For God's sake, this isn't a game, Grace. I'm a plastic surgeon without a memory, and you're a—what did you call it—a researcher for a law firm? What in the hell makes you think we can pull this off?"

"Have you got a better plan?" she demanded. "You certainly can't go to the police."

Ethan closed his eyes briefly, remembering the jungle, the fear, the certainty that the men who pursued him *were* the police. Had the Mexican authorities been on to him? Was that why he'd been running?

If what Grace suspected was true, if Ethan had in fact aided and abetted criminals by selling them new faces, then he would more than likely be looking at a stiff sentence of his own if he were to go to the police. And maybe, if he had done all the things Grace thought he had, prison was exactly where he should be.

But there was still some doubt in Ethan's mind, still some lingering suspicion that Grace Donovan hadn't told him everything. That she had left out something very important, and until he could figure out the whole story, he wasn't about to throw himself on the mercy of the court.

"Maybe I can't go to the police," he said. "But I still don't understand what's stopping you."

"I thought I explained myself last night."

"But it still doesn't make sense. I don't want to seem cruel, but you can't help your sister by getting yourself killed. If I'm Trevor Reardon's target, then I don't want you anywhere near me."

"Don't be ridiculous," Grace said, frowning. "You can't do this alone. You need me. I can watch your back. We can watch each other's back for that matter, because I'm not giving up on this. Reardon killed my sister, and I'm going to make damned sure he pays. If you won't help me, I'll go after him on my own."

And she would do it, Ethan thought. He could see the determination in her eyes, in the defiant way she held her chin and jaw. She would go after Reardon alone, and then Ethan would have *her* death on his conscience.

The thought of her getting hurt or killed made him almost physically sick. "You don't know what you're getting yourself into," he said.

She lifted her chin. "Yes, I do. I'm not helpless. Believe me, I can take care of myself."

"Against an assassin-turned-terrorist?"

Her gaze flickered but didn't waver. "He's a man. He has weaknesses. We know two things about him. He's dangerous and he's compulsive. He won't be able to resist coming back to finish what he started. All we have to do is be ready for him."

She made it sound so easy, but somehow Ethan knew she wasn't being naive. She really believed what she was saying, and her confidence was almost enough to convince him. Almost.

"So what's our first move?" he asked.

Sunlight from the window fired the red highlights in her hair as she tucked a strand behind her ear. "I guess the best way to flush him out is to go about your normal business. If Reardon is after you, then he's probably made a point of knowing your routine."

"I hope you're not suggesting I see patients today," Ethan said dryly. "I don't think I'm up for that. And I don't think they would be, either."

"No, of course not," Grace said. "But you can always check in with your office, maybe even go by there. After that, we'll play it by ear."

He said suddenly, "Do you have a key to Amy's apartment?"

"No, why?"

"Because you found one clue there already. Maybe there are others."

"You don't think the police will have cordoned off her apartment?"

Ethan shook his head. "Not likely. From what the detective told me last night, they're inclined to believe someone broke into the office looking for drugs, and Amy was shot when she surprised him. The police will be canvassing the neighborhood this morning, look-

ing for witnesses and evidence dropped or stashed by the suspect.
They may never feel the need to search Amy's apartment."

Grace mulled that over. "You're probably right. Like I said, I
don't have a key, but I can get us in."

That confidence again. Ethan stared at her admiringly. "All right.
You can make yourself at home down here while I go up and finish
dressing. Then we can get out of here."

UPSTAIRS, ETHAN HURRIED over to the nightstand by the bed and
opened the top drawer, removing the stack of bills he'd found in
the safe that Pilar had somehow missed. Then he picked up the
pistol he'd found in the safe. The gun was small, a high-caliber,
custom-made job that almost fit inside Ethan's hand.

He tested the weight of the gun as a strong sense of déjà vu
slipped over him. He'd had that same feeling the moment his hand
had closed over the weapon in the safe. It was the first thing he'd
come across that had seemed familiar to him since waking up in
the hospital last evening.

Ethan knew how to use the gun. Not just a gun, but this particular
gun. He knew the sights would be accurate, the trigger pull crisp
and the recoil minimal. He couldn't even remember his own mother,
and yet he knew how to field strip this weapon and reassemble it
in a matter of seconds.

Trying not to think about what that might mean, he slammed
back the slide to put one bullet in the chamber, flipped on the safety
with his thumb, then slipped the pistol into the back waistband of
his pants. Next he peeled away several bills from the wad of money
and stuffed them in his pocket. The rest he returned to the drawer.

The shoes he'd been wearing the night before were beside the
bed where he'd kicked them off. He slid them on, thinking briefly
how much better they fit than the ones he'd tried on earlier that
morning. His final preparation was to grab a jacket from the closet.
It would be hot outside, but he needed something to conceal his
gun. No use revealing *all* his secrets to Grace. Not yet at least.

As he walked down the stairs to join her, Ethan couldn't help
reflecting on how much better he felt with money in his pocket and
a high-powered weapon within his reach.

Just what the hell kind of doctor was he anyway?

THEY DROVE SOUTH on Gessner Road, a long street that was beautiful in some areas and cluttered with shopping centers, convenience stores and apartment buildings in others. The section near Ethan's house was particularly lovely, with its tree-shaded sidewalks and flower-strewn median.

The abundance of towering oaks and loblolly pines was one of the things that had surprised Grace most about Houston. She had expected a dry, sprawling metropolis dotted with oil wells and ugly refineries, but the city was very wooded with houses and glass office buildings almost hidden beneath thick canopies of green.

Out of the corner of her eye, she saw Ethan staring out the window, watching the road signs, trying to familiarize himself with the city. For a moment, she tried to put herself in his place, but it was impossible to imagine what he was going through. To have no recall of who you were, what kind of person you'd been, but to have every reason to suspect the worst. To have been told everything he'd been told that morning—

Grace nudged away the guilt prodding at her conscience. Everything she'd done was necessary. Every lie and deception essential. She wouldn't spend time regretting what couldn't be helped.

Crossing Westheimer, one of the main thoroughfares in Houston, she turned right on Richmond, then pulled into an apartment group called The Pines.

The complex was like a number of others they'd passed along the way—two-story buildings that housed between four and eight "garden" apartments per unit. The grounds were immaculately groomed, with huge pink and white oleander bushes hugging the sides of the buildings while tall pine trees, circled by beds of impatiens and monkey grass, shaded the common grounds between the units.

Grace parked in front of the leasing office, shut off the engine, and turned to Ethan. In spite of the trees, the intense heat and sultry humidity invaded the car. She lowered the windows, but without a breeze, it didn't help much.

"Maybe you'd better let me go in alone," she said. "I don't want to make anyone suspicious."

She saw from his expression that he understood her meaning. Though improved, his bruised appearance was still enough to raise eyebrows. He nodded and watched her open the car door. Grace felt his eyes on her until she disappeared inside the office.

As always, the air conditioning hit her full blast. That was something else Grace had yet to get used to—going from a furnace to a freezer in a matter of seconds. Houstonians seemed to think they could compensate for the soaring temperatures outside by turning their AC to frigid. Even wearing a jacket, Grace found herself shivering.

A woman with frosted blonde hair sat reading a book behind a large desk near the doorway. The red-and-blue rhinestones on her T-shirt sparkled in the overhead lighting as she reached up and removed her glasses. "May I help you?"

Grace walked over and stood in front of the desk. "I hope so. My name is Grace Donovan. One of your tenants is…was…my sister." She broke off and glanced down at her hands. After a split second, she said, "Her name was Amy Cole. She lived in 4C."

The woman's gaze grew anxious. "You said, was."

Grace bit her lip. "She was killed last night."

The woman gasped. Her manicured fingers flew to her fuchsia-stained lips. "I'm so sorry. H-how did it happen?"

Grace released a long, shaky breath. "I can't really go into the details right now. It's…still so fresh. I'm sure you understand."

"Of course." The woman was at a loss. She stared helplessly at Grace. "Is there anything I can do?"

"As a matter of fact, yes. I need to get into Amy's apartment."

A frown flitted across the woman's features. "Did Amy have you listed as the next of kin on her leasing application?"

"I'm not sure," Grace admitted. "I've only lived here in Houston a few weeks." She paused. "You see, the problem is, I have to choose something for them to…for Amy to…wear."

Understanding dawned in the woman's face. Pity deepened in her eyes. She reached inside her drawer and withdrew a key. "This is a master. I'll have to let you in myself. I can't just give you the key."

"I understand," Grace said. "And that's fine. I appreciate your help."

The woman got up and they started for the door. "I can't tell you how sorry I am. Amy was a good tenant. Always on time with her rent. Except for that one incident, there was never any trouble with her.''

Grace paused with her hand on the door knob. "What incident are you talking about?''

The woman bit her lip, as if worrying about how much to tell the dead woman's sister. "There was a man, Amy's boyfriend, I guess. I gather he was…married.'' Her gaze flashed to Grace's face. Seeing no signs of resentment, she continued. "He was at her apartment one night when his wife showed up. I live here in the complex, you know. Right across the parking lot from Amy's apartment. Anyway, the woman created such a disturbance I finally had to call the police.''

"What did she do?''

Another pause. The woman's frown deepened. "She had a gun. She shot out the tires on her husband's Porsche, and then threatened to use the gun on Amy.''

AMY'S APARTMENT WAS decorated in soothing pastels—green, peach and cream. The colors reminded Grace of warm breezes and flower-scented afternoons. Of youth and innocence and everything she'd lost one cold Saturday night.

The apartments Grace had occupied since that night fourteen years ago, when she'd lost her whole family, were places where she slept and sometimes ate. They were never home. Not like this.

For the first time since she'd heard about Amy's death, Grace let herself feel the impact of the loss. She hadn't known Amy well. They'd spoken on only two occasions, once here in Amy's apartment. But Grace had sensed something about the young woman, a loneliness that had touched a chord deep within Grace's own darkness.

The door to Amy's apartment opened, and Grace turned. Ethan stepped tentatively inside. "All right if I come in now?''

Nodding, she motioned him in.

Ethan walked into the room, looking around. "Nice place,'' he murmured.

"Do you recognize it?''

He glanced at her. "Why? Have I been here before?''

Grace started to tell him the story the manager had related to her, but then decided he'd had enough blows for one day. "I thought you might have, considering."

He walked over to a pine bookshelf and picked up a picture, studying it intently.

Grace knew the picture. Amy had told her about it the night they'd first met, when Grace had come here to talk about Ethan. The photograph was of Amy and a boyfriend who had long since gone his own way, but Amy had told Grace that she liked the way the two of them looked together so she'd kept the picture on display. Grace could see why. Blond and fair, dressed all in white, Amy looked radiant, almost ethereal against a snowy Rocky Mountain backdrop.

Grace walked over and stood beside Ethan. "That's Amy," she said softly. Her eyes were drawn to the picture, and for the first time, she detected a similarity between Amy and Pilar Hunter. The resemblance was not so much in their faces but in the perfection of their features.

"Evidently you have a thing for beautiful women," she said.

Ethan glanced up, his eyes locking with hers. "Evidently, I do."

His gaze dropped almost imperceptibly, touching the curves of Grace's body only briefly before lifting to her face. Something dark flickered in his eyes. Something that made Grace's heart pound in awareness.

For a long moment, neither of them said anything, but the attraction between them was electric.

This can't be happening, Grace thought. *Not here. Not now. And especially not with this man.*

She had a job to do. A killer to find. Nothing could get in her way.

And yet, something *was* getting in her way. Clouding her judgment. Threatening her whole way of life.

She knew that he was going to kiss her, but Grace was powerless to stop it. Powerless to fight it. Powerless to do anything more than close her eyes briefly before his lips touched hers.

And it was only a touch. Nothing more than a faint skimming of their lips, but Grace's heart pounded an erratic rhythm inside her breast. When she made no move to resist, he deepened the kiss, almost urgently, and finally Grace heard the warnings that were screaming inside her head. *You can't do this! You're risking everything!*

Besides which, he was a married man.

Immediately, Grace stepped back, glaring at him angrily, trying to convince herself she'd had no part in the kiss. Trying to reassure herself it would never, ever happen again.

She waited for the platitudes and the apologies. The *I'm sorry. It was a mistake. I don't know what came over me* excuse.

Instead he stared down at her, his dark eyes openly defiant, as if he were daring her to deny the blatant sexual chemistry between them.

Without a word, Grace turned and walked out of the room.

CHAPTER SIX

Inside Amy's bedroom, Grace stood leaning against the wall, eyes closed, while she tried to get her heartbeat, her emotions, under control.

What would Myra say if she could see her protégée now—pulse pounding, hands trembling, stomach fluttering like a schoolgirl's? This was so unlike Grace. She never lost control.

She opened her eyes and took several long breaths. All right, so the kiss had been a mistake. No question about that, but there was nothing to be done but put it behind her. Stop thinking about it and get back to work.

Grace knew all about using work to forget. There had been times when her job was all that had kept her going. After all she'd been through, a kiss seemed so inconsequential.

And yet…

It hadn't been just a kiss. That was the problem. It had been an acknowledgment of the attraction—the dangerous kind—that existed between her and Ethan Hunter. The kind of attraction that made people forget who and what they were, and why they shouldn't be together.

But that can't happen, Grace told herself firmly. *It won't happen.* After all the years of indifference—of *celibacy,* for God's sake—it would take more than a man without a memory, a man with a dangerous past, to awaken her sleeping libido.

Grace would make sure of it.

She drew another long breath and glanced around. She knew it was pointless to search Amy's bedroom. Anything helpful or incriminating would have already been removed. So instead, she opened the closet and glanced through Amy's beautiful clothing, selecting a simple black knit dress and a pair of black heels. Opening the jewelry box on Amy's dresser, Grace removed a string of pearls and a pair of matching earrings.

Just as she closed the jewelry box lid, she heard voices from the other room. Grace thought at first Ethan had turned on the stereo or TV, but when she walked to the bedroom door, she saw a man in a powder-blue suit talking with Ethan.

Grace had never met the man, but she knew who he was. As she entered the room, both pairs of males eyes turned on her, and a shiver of apprehension slipped up her spine.

Ethan introduced her to Sergeant Pope with the Houston Police Department, and the detective lifted his grizzled eyebrows as he took her in. "You were at the crime scene last night. I didn't meet you myself, but Webber told me about you. He said you were pretty distraught. Only natural, I guess, considering."

"Yes, Sergeant Webber was very courteous under the circumstances," Grace said. "I appreciated that."

"Refresh my memory," Pope said. "I don't seem to remember what you were doing at the clinic last night."

Grace glanced at Ethan. He was staring at her curiously. Maybe even a little suspiciously, and no wonder. She'd failed to mention to him that she'd been at the crime scene just minutes after he and Amy had been taken away. Any hint of the passion she'd glimpsed in his eyes earlier had vanished.

She turned back to Pope. "Amy and I were supposed to have dinner. She called and said she might be running a little late because she was going by the clinic first. I went to the restaurant and waited for her, but after a while, I got worried. The clinic isn't in the safest area of town, you know, so I decided to go by and check on her." Grace paused, her gaze dropping to the black dress draped across her arm and the pearls and shoes clutched in her hands. "The police were already there when I arrived." Her gaze lifted to Ethan's. "Dr. Hunter and Amy had already been taken away."

"That's what you meant last night when you said the police had talked to you?" Ethan asked.

She nodded. "They told me what had happened, and then Sergeant Webber asked me to go down to the morgue with him and identify Amy's body." Grace shuddered, remembering the coldness of the room, the steel vaults. The dead bodies. She would never get used to that. Never.

The detective glanced at first Grace, then Ethan. "How did the two of you hook up?"

Before Ethan had a chance to answer, Grace said, "I went by the hospital to see how he was doing. When I learned he was checking himself out, I volunteered to drive him home. And then knowing how difficult it would be, he offered to come over here with me today. I thought it was...very considerate."

The suspicion in Ethan's eyes turned to puzzlement. *Who are you?* his expression seemed to be saying. *What the hell do you think you're doing?*

"I hope we haven't done anything wrong, Sergeant." Grace widened her eyes innocently. "Letting ourselves in here, I mean. There wasn't any crime scene tape on the door, or anything."

Pope's gaze narrowed on her. "How *did* you get in? You have a key?"

"The apartment manager let us in. I explained that I needed to get some of Amy's clothes for her to be...buried in. The funeral is tomorrow."

The detective looked surprised. "Tomorrow? That's rushing it a little, isn't it?"

"Not really." Grace shrugged. "Amy and I don't have any family, no out-of-town relatives to wait for. I just want to get it over with as soon as possible. There won't be a problem...getting her body released, will there?"

Again Grace felt Ethan's gaze on her, but this time she kept her attention on Pope. His awful blue suit, greased hair and world-weary expression didn't fool her one bit. He was sharp. As soon as he got back to the station, he would check out her story. Grace had no doubt about that.

"Shouldn't be a problem," he said. "The coroner has already filed his report. Didn't take long to figure out the cause of death." When Grace winced, he said, "Sorry. Sometimes you forget."

He took a few steps into the room, gazing around. With his back still turned to them, he said, "So why did you check yourself out of the hospital, Dr. Hunter? You were in pretty bad shape when I left you last night."

Ethan exchanged a glance with Grace, one that said, *We're going to talk about all this later. Trust me.*

"I wanted to get home, rest in my own bed. I don't like hospitals."

Pope turned at that. "Worrisome hang-up for a doctor, wouldn't you say?"

"Not at all," Ethan said smoothly. "I think you'll find most of my colleagues have that same 'hang-up.' You've heard the expression Doctors Make The Worst Patients. I'm afraid it's true."

He was good, Grace thought. Quick on his feet. Almost frighteningly so. She stared at him with new admiration.

"I came by to see you this morning," Pope said. He withdrew a wallet and a passport from the inside pocket of his suit coat. He handed the items to Ethan. "I wanted to give you these. I'll have someone deliver the luggage and your briefcase to your house later today."

Ethan gazed at the wallet and passport for several seconds before putting them away in his own jacket pocket. Grace could only guess what he was thinking. A wallet meant information. A passport could mean freedom.

The detective finished his perusal of the room and turned back to them. He nodded to the clothing in Grace's arms. "Looks like you got what you came for. The mortuary you select will take care of the arrangements with the morgue."

"Thank you." Grace turned to Ethan. "I guess we should be going then. I still have other arrangements to make."

"Right."

They headed for the door, but Pope made no move to follow them. "I'll lock up when I leave," he said pointedly.

They left him standing in the center of the room, studying Amy's apartment with a keenness, an intensity that Grace found particularly unnerving. She hoped to hell he didn't stumble across something one of Myra's operatives might have missed.

OUTSIDE, ETHAN TOOK her arm when she started down the sidewalk toward the parking lot. "Not so fast," he said. "I want to know what was going on back there."

Grace glanced up at him. "What do you mean?"

"For starters, I'd like to know why you didn't tell me about your being at the clinic last night. You led me to believe the police had called you to tell you about Amy."

"No, I didn't," Grace argued. "All I said was that I'd talked to the police. And I did. What difference does it make if I was at the clinic or at home?"

"What were you doing at the clinic?" Ethan's hand was still on her arm. His grip wasn't tight, but Grace knew that if she tried to walk away, he would hold her. He had too many questions right now to let her go.

"Just what I said. Amy and I were supposed to meet. When she didn't show up, I got worried so I went to the clinic looking for her." Grace knew her words were convincing, but she wasn't as certain about her expression. She slipped on her sunglasses, not wanting to reveal too much.

After a moment, he said, "Why didn't you tell me about Amy's funeral?"

"You didn't ask." When he started to protest, she interrupted coolly, "You didn't ask, so I figured you didn't care. Amy didn't mean anything to you."

His gaze darkened as he stared down at her. "How do you know that?"

"Because you wouldn't have kissed me if she had." There, Grace thought. She'd brought up the kiss deliberately so they could get it out in the open, so that she could make her feelings for him very, very clear. She glanced down at his hand on her arm, arched a brow over her sunglasses, and he released her.

"Then you must not have cared about her either," he said.

"How dare you say that to me? She was my sister."

Ethan's gaze darkened. "Are you denying that you kissed me back?"

"I didn't." Grace was surprised to find that her outrage was more instinctive than studied. She wasn't sure she quite understood it.

"We kissed," he said, glaring down at her. "It was a mutual action. And just because I'm not denying it doesn't mean I'm exactly proud of what's happening between us."

Grace hadn't expected that. She stared at him uncertainly. "What do you mean?"

"I'm a married man, Grace."

It was like a slap in the face. Not that Grace had forgotten his marital status. Far from it. But in truth, that was only one of many reasons why she couldn't allow herself to become involved with Ethan Hunter. She supposed she should be glad that he'd suddenly developed scruples.

"All right," she said calmly. "We both agree that it was a mistake. It won't happen again. There's no reason why it should have to affect our working relationship. We're both adults."

Something glinted in his eyes. "You think it'll be that easy?"

"Yes," she said simply. "Because it has to be."

After a moment, he said, "All right. We'll forget about the kiss. We'll pretend it never happened. We'll promise ourselves it won't happen again, but there's something else we need to get straight."

"What?"

His gaze held hers. "I may not have my memory, but I'm not as stupid or as helpless as you seem to think. I don't know why you won't go to the police with what you know, but I'm pretty sure it has nothing to do with Amy."

Grace was glad her eyes were hidden behind the dark glasses. "I don't know what you're talking about. I already explained why I don't want to involve the police."

"Because you don't want to ruin Amy's good name. Because to the police she's just another statistic. It doesn't wash, Grace."

Her heart started to pound, whether from his accusations or from the way he said her name, Grace wasn't sure.

He didn't touch her again, but she couldn't have moved if her life depended on it.

His eyes narrowed suspiciously. "You're talking about catching a cold-blooded murderer. An assassin, you said. It takes a little more than guts to do that."

"I know that," she said almost angrily. "I'm not as stupid or as helpless as *you* seem to think."

"Oh, I don't think you're stupid or helpless." His gaze deepened on her. "Far from it. I think you're very, very clever."

"Don't give me too much credit," she muttered. Because this conversation certainly wasn't going the way she'd anticipated.

"You're not telling me everything," he accused. "Don't think I don't know it."

"I would never make the mistake of underestimating you," Grace said truthfully. Especially not now. "But I've told you everything I know. I've tried to make you understand why this is so important to me. Don't you see? If I had shown up at the clinic a few minutes earlier last night, Amy would still be alive. If I hadn't turned my back on her years ago, she never would have moved to Houston in the first place. She never would have gotten involved with...you. I've always let her down, and now she's dead because of me." Grace paused, feeling the old horror rise up inside her as the memories came swarming back. It had taken her a long time to beat back the monsters, to subdue the night terrors that had once threatened her sanity. Amy's death, and the man who had killed her, had brought it all back.

"How can I live with myself if I let her killer go free?" Grace whispered.

Ethan couldn't see her eyes, and Grace thought fleetingly that perhaps she should remove her sunglasses and let him witness the anguish, the sudden tears that were almost as foreign to her as the attraction she felt for him. She wasn't opposed to using her emotions to get what she needed, but this was too much. Too...intense.

"I can tell you've been hurt," Ethan said softly. "When you drift off like that, I can tell you're experiencing grief. But I'm not sure the grief is for Amy."

When Grace said nothing, he took a step toward her, towering over her like a menacing embodiment of her conscience. "I don't know what's going on here," he said. "I don't know what part I played in Amy's death, or why you seem so willing to work with a man you have every reason to despise. But I do know this." He removed her dark glasses, then put a gentle finger beneath her chin and tilted her head back so that he could stare down into her eyes. "Attraction or not, God help you if you're lying to me."

GRACE LET HERSELF into her room that night and reached for the light switch. Her hand froze before she made the connection. Something was different about the room. She could detect a subtle scent that didn't belong there.

Standing motionless, Grace listened to the dark. Then very quietly, she slipped her hand inside her purse and withdrew her gun, releasing the safety as her gaze searched the darkness. A breeze touched her face, and she realized suddenly that the sliding glass door was open. She started across the room toward it just as a voice said from the balcony, "It's only me, Grace. Put away your gun."

Grace let the weapon drop to her side, but she didn't put it away as she stepped out on the balcony to join Myra Temple. The woman sat in darkness, the only substance to her shadowy form the arcing glow of her cigarette as she lifted it to her mouth. In the silence that followed, Grace could hear the tiny crackle as the flames ate away at the paper holding the tobacco.

"How did it go today?" Myra asked. Her voice, husky from years of smoking, was one men dreamed of.

Grace replaced the gun in her purse before answering. "I think he'll cooperate."

"How much did you tell him?"

"Almost everything. The truth is almost always more convincing than lies. I've heard you say that dozens of times."

The cigarette lifted again. "He still thinks you're Amy's sister, though. You didn't tell him the truth about that."

"No." Because a man who had managed to stay one step ahead of the law wasn't likely to throw in his lot with an FBI agent. Not a man as resourceful and wealthy as Ethan Hunter.

She thought about their last conversation, the threat he'd given her, and in spite of the heat, Grace shivered. "You have someone watching the house tonight?" she asked.

"Huddleston and Smith have the first watch, but they'll be relieved after midnight, just like last night."

Grace nodded, satisfied. She wondered suddenly what Ethan was doing all alone in that house. Or was he alone? Had Pilar decided to pay him another visit?

Against her will, Grace conjured up an image of Ethan's wife— the lithe body, the glossy hair, the incredible face. What a handsome couple they would make. In her mind's eye, Grace could see the two of them together, in each other's arms. Naked. Kissing. Making love.

She thought about the way Ethan had looked at her today in

Amy's apartment, the brief kiss they had shared, and the image changed. She could see herself in his arms. Naked. Kissing. Making love.

I'm a married man, Grace.

"So what are you doing sitting out here in the dark?" she asked Myra, trying to dispel the forbidden image in her mind.

She sensed rather than saw Myra's shrug. "Strangely enough, I've been thinking about the past."

"Don't tell me you're getting maudlin." Grace sank into the green plastic lawn chair next to Myra's. "You always told me the past is a dangerous pitfall, one that should be avoided at all costs."

Grace heard the tinkle of ice against glass as Myra lifted a drink to her lips. "I know, but lately it's become harder and harder for me to avoid that particular pitfall. I find myself reflecting at the oddest times. I guess it comes with age."

"No way," Grace said. "You're still a young woman." Still vibrant and beautiful, though there'd been times when Grace could have sworn her mentor ate nails for breakfast. Grace wasn't the only one in the Bureau who had thought so. Myra Temple was almost legendary.

Myra sighed, an uncharacteristic sound for her. "I may not be old in the real world, but forty-three can be ancient in our world, Grace."

She had a point. Grace fell silent for a moment, contemplating her own life. In twelve years, she would be Myra's age. Would she then *want* to look back, to reflect as Myra had put it? Somehow Grace couldn't imagine it.

Myra picked up a tiny whiskey bottle—the kind stocked in the room bar—from beside her chair and set it on the plastic table between them. The seal on the bottle was broken, but Grace knew Myra's own drink contained no alcohol. She was very disciplined in that regard. The empty bottle was to make a point.

"All right, so I had one drink last night," Grace admitted, wishing she didn't sound so defensive. Wishing she didn't have a reason to be. "But that's all. It won't happen again. You can take the bar key with you if it makes you feel any better."

Myra tossed her cigarette butt over the balcony to the asphalt parking lot below them. Tiny sparks rained down in the darkness.

"That won't be necessary. I know you remember how bad it was for you back then. But you're strong now, Grace. Stronger than me in a lot of ways."

Grace didn't think that was possible. Myra was unparalleled. She would never consider drinking alone in the middle of the night, much less making love to a man whose secrets just might be even darker than her own.

"Do you remember the first time we met?" Myra asked suddenly. "You were only seventeen, but I sensed that resilience in you even then. I hated the fact that your father always seemed hell-bent on breaking you."

Don't, Grace thought. *Don't take me back there.*

She closed her eyes, letting the hot breeze blow across her face, willing away the melancholy that seemed to have gripped both her and Myra.

Beside her, Myra shifted restlessly in her chair. "You came by the office to see your father that day. He'd just learned I was to be his new partner. He wasn't too pleased to discover I was a woman."

"Some things never change," Grace said. "The Bureau is still a man's world."

"True enough," Myra said. "But you're becoming a damned fine agent, Grace. You've earned a lot of respect."

"So have you. You paved the way for women like me. I'll always be grateful." For that and so much more, but Grace left the words unspoken. Over the years, she and Myra had developed an internal method of communicating. They'd been through a lot together, but Grace couldn't help wondering if this was to be their final assignment. When Trevor Reardon was no longer their nemesis, who or what would then become their raison d'être?

Myra stood and stretched. "By the way, we lifted some fresh prints from Hunter's clinic last night after the police left. I'll let you know as soon as I hear back from the lab."

Grace got up and walked her to the door. In the light from the corridor, Myra suddenly looked much older than her years. It made Grace uneasy, watching her.

Grace remained at the door until the agent disappeared around a corner. After a moment, Grace heard the ping of the elevator and the sound of the doors sliding open and then shut again. Only then did she close and lock her door. But she didn't turn on the light. She stood in the darkness as the memories came flooding back.

Putting her hands to her ears, she tried to shut them out, but Myra's pensiveness tonight had inadvertently opened a Pandora's box. In her mind, Grace saw the house where she'd grown up bursting into flames. She heard her mother's terrified cries, her father's anguished shouts, and her sister's tormented screams.

Grace closed her eyes, trembling. It had taken her years to get those images out of her head. Years of therapy and cold indifference before she no longer saw her sister, her hair in flames, at every window. Years of single-minded devotion to her career to block out the argument she and Jessica had had just hours before her sister's death.

Like a roller-coaster out of control, Grace's mind whipped around the perilous corners of her past, plunged downward into the murky depths of her memory. Faces flew past her. Scenes blurred by her. She wished she could stop them—she would do anything to stop them—but it was too late for that. Too late to do anything but huddle in the darkness and remember.

There had been a man. Grace had sensed from the first that he was different, someone special, but she hadn't learned until later just how extraordinary he was. When she'd first met him at the library during the Christmas break of her senior year in high school, all she'd known was that he was a dashing older man, probably at least thirty, and more sophisticated and worldly than she could ever have imagined.

She'd also thought that he was the most handsome man she'd ever seen. When he looked up from the book he was reading and smiled at her, Grace knew instantly he was the one. The two of them had a connection, some special bond that had drawn her to him. His eyes were blue, his hair golden brown, and even in the dead of winter, he was suntanned, as if he'd just come from the slopes of some exotic ski resort.

Grace grew so nervous, just watching him, that she dropped the book she was holding. His smile broadened, as if he knew he was the source of her anxiety and was pleased by the knowledge. Grace turned and all but ran from the room.

The next day, she saw him again at the library. This time, her nerves in check, she took a seat two tables away from his, facing him. Every time she looked up from her book, she found his gaze on her, and Grace's insides quivered in delicious anticipation.

On the third day, he approached her. He stood over her table, hands planted on the surface as he bent down to whisper in her ear. Grace could smell the intoxicating scent of his cologne, could see the faint shadow of his beard, and her heart went wild. This was no boy, but a *man*.

"Do you want to get out of here?" he whispered, his voice deep and knowing.

Grace could only nod. He removed the book from her hands, then pulled her to her feet. Clasping her hand in his, he led her outside to the parking area, to an expensive sports car that made Grace catch her breath.

"This is your car?"

He dangled the keys before her. "Would you like to drive it?"

Grace had her license but her father rarely let her behind the wheel of the family sedan. His career in the FBI had made him overly protective of his family, and Grace's nature had made her openly rebellious. The two of them often clashed. She wondered fleetingly what her father would think if he could see her now.

In spite of her defiant nature, the image subdued Grace a little. This man was a total stranger after all. She shook her head. "I'd better not."

"Oh, come on," he said in that dark and silky voice. "You know you want to. For once in your life, live dangerously."

The challenge was irresistible. Grace took the keys from his fingers, and he opened the door for her. So gallant and so unlike the boys she'd dated. She slid behind the wheel and waited until he climbed into the passenger side before starting the car.

The engine roared to life, the sound thrumming through Grace's veins like a shot of pure adrenaline. So this was power, she thought.

The man put his hand over hers on the stick shift, helping her find the right gear. His touch made her shiver. Grace glanced at him warily. "Where are we going?"

"Anywhere you want to go, Grace."

That stopped her for a minute. Her excitement cooled. "How do you know my name?"

He smiled, pulling a card from his pocket and holding it up to her. It was her library card. "You dropped it that first day," he said, "When you were running away from me."

"I wasn't running away from you," Grace protested, not wanting him to think of her as a child.

"Maybe you should have." His smile turned mysterious. "I'm a dangerous man, Grace."

"I know."

Their gazes met and held for the longest moment, then he reached over and grasped the back of her neck, pulling her toward him. His mouth found hers and almost instantly, Grace felt his tongue plunge inside.

She knew she should pull away. This man was way too old and way too experienced for her, and he was a stranger. A stranger who kissed her like no boy had ever kissed her. Who made her feel the way no one had ever made her feel. Who whispered to her things no one had ever told her.

"You're very beautiful," he murmured. "You have no idea how special you are to me, Grace."

Something warm unfurled inside her, some womanly need that made her cling to him, that made her groan against his mouth, that made her want him in ways she'd hardly dared dream about.

She drove them to his apartment a few blocks from where she lived, and they talked a little, trying to get to know one another, trying to ease the almost unbearable tension between them. But all the while they both knew the inevitable would happen—*had* to happen—before she left him that night.

They met again the next night, and the next. Grace was barely allowed to date boys her own age, so she knew bringing him home to meet her parents, especially her father, was out of the question. She started sneaking out of her room at night, begging her younger sister, Jessie, to cover for her.

Unlike Grace, Jessie had never been rebellious. She had always worked very hard to please their father, and lying to him went against her nature. Grace understood that, but her sister's conscience didn't matter enough to Grace to make her want to stop seeing *him.*

On the night of the fire, Jessie had been especially troubled by Grace's deception. She even threatened to tell their parents and take her own punishment for the duplicity if Grace left the house again without their permission.

Grace lashed out at her, calling her a Goody Two-shoes. "Why don't you mind your own business for once," she snapped before climbing out the window and slipping away into the darkness to meet her lover.

That night, he seemed different. Before, he'd always been dark and intense, even moody at times, but Grace had found those qualities deeply compelling. Tonight, however, he was almost ebullient, laughing and smiling, whispering to her that he had a secret.

It was only…afterward that Grace learned what his secret was.

"Would you like to know my real name?" he asked, drawing her fingers to his lips and kissing each one of them.

Grace gazed up at him in confusion. "Your name is Jonathan Price."

He laughed out loud. "Jonathan Price is a fictional character, you little idiot. I got it from a novel."

Grace didn't much care for the insult. She pulled away from him.

He didn't even seem to notice. "I go by many names, but the one you may have heard of is Trevor Reardon."

He laughed again when he saw the horror dawn on her face.

"That isn't funny," she said, shaken. Nothing about him was the least bit amusing. In fact, he was beginning to scare her. Grace jumped up, pulling on her clothes while he lay on the bed, smiling that taunting little smile. "Trevor Reardon is in prison," she said.

"So you have heard of me." He propped himself on his elbow. "I didn't think your old man could resist bragging about the coup he pulled off when he captured me. But didn't he also tell you that I'd escaped from prison a few weeks ago? Didn't he warn you I might come back for revenge?"

Her father *had* been acting strangely lately, even more protective than usual, making the whole family promise to be home by dark every day. Maybe that's why Jessie had been so frightened when Grace had started sneaking out of the house at night. Maybe she'd known something Grace hadn't.

Dressed by this time, Grace started backing toward the door. She didn't believe him, *couldn't* believe him, and yet…

What if he was telling her the truth?

What if he was Trevor Reardon?

She put a hand to her mouth, trying to swallow back a rising tide of nausea. "Who are you?" she whispered. "Why are you doing this to me?"

"It's all been a game," he said. "And you've been so much fun." He got out of bed and stood naked before her. "But playtime's over, Grace. It's time to get to work."

Her hand on the door knob, she said weakly, "If I scream someone will hear me. The police will come."

"Oh, I wouldn't wait for the police if I were you. Your family may need you, even as we speak."

She saw the truth in his eyes. Knew that he had done something unspeakable to her family while she lay in his arms.

Grace turned and fled the apartment. He didn't try to follow her, but she could hear his laughter echoing in the darkness all around her.

Five blocks away from her house, she heard the sirens. Two blocks away, she saw the flames. When she reached the driveway, she heard the screams.

Oh, God, oh, God, oh, God, was all she could think as she rushed toward the burning house. Someone grabbed her and held her back. She struggled to free herself, and it was then that she looked up and saw Jessie at their bedroom window. Sweet little Jessie pounding at the double panes, screaming in terror and agony as her clothing and hair caught fire.

And somewhere in the darkness, Grace could hear Trevor Reardon, still laughing....

As the memories all but consumed her, Grace slumped against the wall of her hotel room, weak and dizzy. Even after all these years, the thought of his mouth on her, his hands touching her sent her flying to the bathroom. She lay spent and trembling on the floor moments later, the memories still closing in on her like a crushing weight. She willed them away, but they resisted. They weren't through with her yet. There was still more to be endured, other horrors to relive.

Groaning, Grace rolled to her side, feeling the cool tile against her cheek.

After that night, the guilt and grief over her family's deaths had almost killed her, but Trevor Reardon hadn't been finished with her. Dressed as one of the cops standing guard at the church, he attended the funeral service for her family three days later. Grace knew this because he called her afterward and described in detail the clothing she'd had on, right down to the tiny pearls she'd worn in her ears.

The knowledge that he had been that close to her again very nearly drove Grace over the edge. If it hadn't been for Myra Temple, Grace wasn't sure she would have survived.

But Myra helped her through the worst of those days. She forced Grace from the pit of despair she'd crawled into. Made her stop drinking. Made her realize that Reardon would win again if Grace let him.

So with Myra's help, Grace went on to college and eventually graduated from law school. After a while, she could even pretend she led a normal life. At times, she even managed to forget that a killer was out there somewhere, still waiting for her.

But Myra never forgot.

On the night Grace graduated from law school, Reardon was waiting for her in her apartment. He grabbed her, threw her on her bed, and, knife to her throat, told her exactly what he was going to do to her.

But then Myra came bursting into Grace's bedroom, and the agents with her had quickly subdued Reardon. Myra calmly walked over to him, and with a hand that was completely steady, put a gun to his head. For a moment, Grace thought she would pull the trigger. Wanted her to pull the trigger.

But then Myra lowered the weapon, Reardon was taken away, and Grace collapsed in the agent's arms. Grace promised herself that the tears she shed that night would be her last. That she would never again allow herself to be vulnerable. To be a target.

Within a month, she made the life-altering decision to follow in her father's footsteps at the FBI. When she was accepted so quickly, she suspected that Myra had pulled some strings, but Grace didn't care. She was completely focused. She knew exactly what she wanted from life. While Trevor Reardon was confined to a maximum security prison some seven hundred miles away, Grace began and completed the rigorous training at Quantico, Virginia.

She became an agent as dedicated and single-minded as any who had served before her. If she was lonely at night, she tried not to think about it. If she had difficulty making friends, she told herself she didn't have time for relationships anyway. If she shied away from serious involvements, she knew that was the way it had to be. There was no room in her life for anything but justice.

For Grace, her emotional isolation had become a normal way of life.

But then three months ago, news had come to her of Trevor Reardon's second escape. She hadn't been surprised. Or frightened. In fact, there had been a certain sense of inevitability about it all. She'd always known he would come back for her. She was the one loose end that would torment him.

But it would be different now, Grace thought, lying in the bright glare of the bathroom light. This time, she would be ready for him. This time, she was the hunter.

And when they met again face to face, she and Reardon, this time, only one of them would walk away.

CHAPTER SEVEN

The aroma of frying chorizo awakened Ethan the next morning. He sat up in bed, wondering at his ability to identify the scent of the spicy Mexican sausage when he still had no recall of his past life.

The enticing smell drew a rumble from his stomach, reminding him that he'd skipped dinner the previous evening. He got up from bed and hurriedly showered and shaved. Staring at himself in the mirror, he noticed that the bruises were fading, the swelling had gone away, and the cut was starting to heal.

He studied his features dispassionately. Ethan supposed his appearance would be considered above average by most standards, but to him, there was still something disturbing about his face. Something that wasn't quite right.

Not wanting to dwell on the possibilities, he left the bathroom and hurriedly dressed, letting the spicy aroma lead him downstairs and into the kitchen.

Rosa stood at the range, stirring the cooked chorizo into a batch of fluffy scrambled eggs. She turned when she heard Ethan enter the room.

"*Buenos días,* Dr. Hunter." She gave him a critical once-over. "You're looking much better this morning."

"Thanks. I feel better." He walked over to the breakfast table and sat down at the place she had set for him.

"I made your favorite today. Chorizo and eggs."

"Smells great." Ethan watched as she dished up a plate of the sausage and eggs, then brought it to him. She waited while he sampled a bite, then beamed when he almost choked on the peppery food.

"A little extra Tabasco sauce this morning," she explained. "It'll get your blood flowing, speed up your recovery."

Ethan's blood was flowing all right. He felt as if it were about to explode out the top of his head. "Do you think I could have a glass of orange juice?" he managed to gasp.

Rosa stood with her hands on her hips, watching him. "Since when do you like orange juice?"

"Since I found a pitcher in the refrigerator yesterday."

"That was for me," Rosa said accusingly. "You don't like orange juice, not even fresh squeezed. You drink *jugo de tomate.*"

Tomato juice didn't sound the least bit appealing to Ethan, but if it would put out the flames dancing on his tongue, he was willing to give it a shot.

"All right, tomato juice then."

Rosa still hesitated. "That cut on your head, Dr. Hunter. It still makes you strange, no?"

"Strange is a good word for it," he muttered.

Rosa turned and hurried over to the refrigerator. She brought him back a tall glass of chilled tomato juice. Ethan took a quick drink, then another. It wasn't half bad.

He set down the glass and glanced up at Rosa. "You were right. *Jugo de tomate* hits the spot."

She nodded in satisfaction, then circled the air with her finger near her ear. "*Extraño.*" She started to turn away, then stopped. She stared down at him, her dark eyes clouding. "I read in the paper about Amy Cole. Dr. Hunter, why didn't you tell me what had happened to you the other night?"

"I didn't want to worry you, Rosa."

She bit her lip, twisting her hands in her white apron. "That poor child. I only met her once, when she came here to the house looking for you, but she was very nice to me."

Ethan nodded, not wanting to encourage a line of conversation to which he had nothing to contribute. He didn't remember Amy. He didn't remember anything about her, only the sound of her scream before she'd died.

He glanced down at his plate, willing away the image.

Rosa must have mistaken his silence for grief. She murmured something comforting in Spanish, then turned and went back to her work.

Ethan took a few more bites of his food, then shoved his plate away. At the thought of Amy, his appetite had deserted him. After several minutes of strained silence, he said, "By the way, how's your daughter and her baby?"

Rosa turned at that, her look one of astonishment.

"What's the matter?" Ethan asked in alarm. "Did I say something wrong?"

Rosa's amazement turned to discomfort. Her dark brows knitted into a frown. "No. It's just that…why do you want to know about my daughter, Dr. Hunter? It's been a long time since you ask about her."

"It…has?"

Rosa hesitated. "We don't talk about our personal lives to each other. That was the agreement we had when I first came to work for you. You said it would be better that way."

"Better for whom?"

Her shrug seemed ominous somehow. She came back over to the table and stood staring down at him. "Dr. Hunter, are you sure you're okay? Maybe you should go back to the hospital." She pronounced it "ohs-pee-tahl."

"Don't worry about me." Ethan tried to shrug away her concern. "I told you it might take several days for the effects of the concussion to wear off."

"I know, but it's not just that." Rosa paused again. "You don't act the same. You don't talk the same. You don't even look the same…" She trailed off, one hand creeping to her chest as if she had the sudden urge to cross herself.

Ethan frowned. "I still have a lot of bruising on my face, and my voice is still a bit hoarse." He wondered why his tone suddenly sounded so defensive.

"Maybe," Rosa agreed, but she didn't look convinced. "I still think you should go back to the hospital."

Ethan tried to smile reassuringly. "Just give me a few more days. I'll be back up to speed in no time."

Rosa muttered something he couldn't understand as she turned back to the stove.

Ethan got up and carried his plate and glass to the sink. "Do we have a phone book around here somewhere?"

"In the cabinet next to the door," she said, watching him. Ethan thought she was probably dying to ask him who he wanted to call.

In spite of the agreement about their private lives, he could see the curiosity—or was that suspicion?—simmering in the black depths of her eyes.

 He retrieved the Yellow Pages directory from the shelf, and carried the two heavy volumes back to his place at the table. Thumbing through the A-L volume, he located the page he wanted, then quickly scanned the entries underneath Guns. He memorized the name and address of a store on the Katy Freeway that looked promising, but he had no idea how to find it. All he knew was that his house was somewhere off Memorial Drive.

Checking the map at the front of the book, he discovered that the Katy Freeway was the name of the feeder road that ran alongside Interstate 10, and that the gun shop was not far from where he lived. He was fairly certain he could find it.

Closing the book, he put both volumes back in their places and turned to Rosa. Her expression was still dubious.

If you only knew the whole story, Ethan thought. Aloud, he said, "Do you happen to know where my car keys are?"

"No. But I know where you keep your spares." She opened a drawer, pulled out a key, and tossed it to him. Ethan decided the Porsche emblem on the key ring was a good omen.

He pocketed the key. "By the way, I think it would be a good idea to get the alarm code changed. I'd like for you to contact the security company as soon as possible."

Following the covered walkway to the garage, Ethan opened the side door and pressed the lighted button on the wall to activate the automatic garage door opener. The heavy door slowly lifted, letting in sunlight, and Ethan, getting his first look at the Porsche, whistled softly.

Black and sleek, with a mirrorlike finish that was almost blinding, the sports car looked ready and able for action. But almost equally impressive was the vintage candy apple–red Corvette that sat alongside the Porsche, and the white 1964 T-Bird that was parked next to the Vette.

Ethan took a moment to admire all three cars before climbing into the Porsche and backing it out of the garage. Shifting into gear, he gave the car gas, then heard the satisfactory burn of rubber as he headed down the driveway.

A Porsche, a Corvette, and a Thunderbird, he thought admiringly. For the first time since he'd awakened in the hospital, he considered the possibilities—and the privileges—that came with being Dr. Ethan Hunter. Maybe there were certain aspects of his personality that he could admire after all. He apparently had fantastic taste in cars.

And in women.

If the picture he'd seen of Amy Cole yesterday was any indication, she'd been as beautiful as his wife, Pilar, but for some reason Ethan couldn't explain, neither woman seemed real to him. They were almost too perfect, as if he had chosen them—or created them—to be admired rather than loved. In spite of their great beauty, both women left him cold.

Ethan supposed he could attribute his lack of an emotional response to his amnesia, but how would that explain the exact opposite reaction he had to Grace? Her imperfections—the cleft in her chin, the freckles across her nose, the tiny mole beneath her right eyebrow—were infinitely more appealing and more seductive than flawless features could ever be.

She was a real woman and she would know real passion. Ethan was sure of it. He'd glimpsed that passion in her eyes yesterday, before he'd kissed her. Before she'd fled Amy's living room in a vain attempt to run away from their attraction.

But the chemistry had still been there when she'd come back. Still there when he'd gazed into her eyes outside the apartment, and later, when she'd dropped him off at his house that evening.

It had still been there when he'd fallen asleep last night, thinking about her...

In the space of two short days, Grace Donovan had gotten under his skin in a way he knew no other woman had before her. But a relationship with her was impossible, for any number of reasons. He had no memory. He had no idea what he might have done in his past. And the one thing that did seem certain was that he was a married man. He may have had an affair with Amy Cole, but he wouldn't do that to Grace.

What about Pilar? a little voice taunted him. *Aren't you the least bit concerned about your wife's feelings?*

Ethan tried, he really tried to feel something for his estranged wife, but nothing came to him. Nothing but an uneasy feeling that Pilar might have been behind his attack two nights ago, that she might have been the one who had wanted Amy dead.

He glanced in the rearview mirror. The streets weren't crowded this time of day, and Ethan had noticed a white sedan pull out of the neighborhood behind him and trail several car lengths away. But just when Ethan began to think he was being followed, the sedan signalled and turned into the parking area of a large office building.

Just to be on the safe side, Ethan circled the block. When he came back around, the car was still in the parking lot and no one was inside.

A few moments later, Ethan pulled into the shopping center off the Katy Freeway. The gun shop was located between a dry cleaners and a sporting goods store. He parked at the far end of the lot, near the sporting goods store, then removed the unloaded gun from the front seat of the car and slipped it into his jacket pocket.

At this time of morning—a few minutes after ten—stores had just opened. There was no one inside the gun shop except for a clerk who stood behind the counter, polishing the glass. He buzzed Ethan in, and when he entered the store, he could hear another worker in the back, moving inventory.

"Mornin'," the clerk at the counter greeted. He was a tall, lanky man of about fifty, dressed in a white western shirt with pearl buttons and Wrangler jeans that rode low on lean hips. "What can I do you for?"

The store was filled with weapons of varying makes and caliber. Ethan wondered why he didn't feel the least bit intimidated by all that firepower. The thought crossed his mind again that he was no ordinary doctor. Far from it, if what Grace had told him was true.

He stepped up to the counter and pulled the gun from his pocket, laying it carefully on the glass counter. The clerk whistled softly, much as Ethan had done when he'd first seen the Porsche.

"Ain't that a little beauty? What's your askin' price?"

"I'm not here to sell it. I wondered if you could tell me something about it. My father-in-law left it to me when he died," Ethan improvised. "I think it's custom-made."

"Oh, it's custom all right." The clerk picked up the weapon and studied it almost reverently. "It's a 1911 Colt revolver that's been specially modified. See these night sights? Those set your father-in-law back a pretty penny."

Ethan watched the clerk handle the weapon with an expertise that seemed oddly familiar. "Do you have any idea where he might have gotten these modifications?"

The clerk sighted an invisible target, squinting one eye as he took aim. "There's a gun shop over in Arkansas that does this kind of work. They modify weapons of this caliber—guns that can easily be concealed—for police SWAT teams, the FBI Hostage Rescue Units, and even for some of the elite units of the military."

That caught Ethan's attention. "Elite units of the military? You mean like the Navy SEALs?"

The clerk palmed the weapon and tested its weight. "Was your father-in-law a military man?"

"Not in recent years."

"You mean that you know about." The clerk gave him a conspiratorial wink. "Some of those guys are mighty secretive, you know. They don't talk about their work."

Ethan paused. "This gun shop in Arkansas would probably keep records of their custom orders, right?"

The clerk scratched his head. "More than likely. But if it was ordered through a police department or the military, they wouldn't have a record of the individual the gun was issued to. They might be able to track down the particular law enforcement body or branch of the service that owned the weapon, but I doubt they'd be able to give you that information. And even if they did, it wouldn't do you any good."

"Why's that?"

"See this?" With his index finger, the clerk traced along the side of the gun barrel. "The identification number has been filed away."

Ethan took the gun from the clerk's hand, holding the weapon to the light. He could barely detect the faint imperfection in the barrel where the number had been removed. Someone had gone to a great deal of trouble to conceal his handiwork. The metal had been polished until the scratches in the finish were all but invisible.

The clerk's eyes narrowed with what might have been suspicion.

"Looks like your father-in-law—or someone—wanted to make sure this piece couldn't be traced back to him."

"Well, thanks for your help." Ethan gathered up the weapon, said his goodbye, then hurried out of the shop. He was glad he'd had the foresight to park away from the store. He'd seen the suspicion in the clerk's eyes, and wondered if the man might even now be calling the police. But if he was, he'd have to come outside to get the license plate number from Ethan's car.

Sliding behind the wheel, Ethan quickly started the Porsche and backed out of the space. No one had come out of the gun shop, and he couldn't see anyone at the window. Still, he headed down the street in the wrong direction just to avoid driving by the store.

And all the while, the gun was almost a living, breathing entity in the seat beside him.

He's an ex-Navy SEAL and an explosives expert who sold his services to the highest bidder. He became a mercenary, an assassin, sometimes a terrorist.

Was it possible he had somehow come into possession of Trevor Reardon's weapon? Had Ethan brought it back to the States with him, put it in his safe for—what? Protection? Because he knew Reardon might someday come after him?

Ethan lifted a hand to wipe the sudden beads of sweat from his brow. That had to be it. That had to be the reason he was in possession of such a weapon.

Because the other explanation that came to mind was almost too terrifying to contemplate.

"HE'S NOT HOME?" Grace repeated. "Where did he go?"

The housekeeper shrugged, giving Grace a cool appraisal. "He had errands."

"He didn't give you any indication where he was going?" Damn, Grace thought. Why would he just leave like that? He'd known she was coming over this morning. Why hadn't he waited for her?

And why the hell hadn't someone called her to warn her that he was roaming around out there somewhere, making a target of himself?

Rosa eyed her with open disapproval. "I don't ask where he goes. It's none of my business," she said pointedly.

Grace could tell Rosa didn't like her, and therefore, didn't trust her. Grace had run up against the problem before. She sometimes came across as too abrupt, too impatient, too hard. Women didn't like that. Neither did some men, for that matter.

She forced a softness in her tone. "Look, I don't mean to be such a nuisance, but I need to tell Dr. Hunter about the funeral this afternoon."

"Funeral?"

Grace bit her lip and nodded. "You heard about Amy Cole? Dr. Hunter's assistant?"

Rosa crossed herself. "Yes. Such a shame. So young and so *bella.*"

Grace nodded. "Amy was my sister, Rosa. I came to tell Dr. Hunter about the memorial service this afternoon."

Rosa's expression changed dramatically. The wariness and suspicion vanished, leaving her features set in gentle lines of compassion. *"Lo siento."* She reached for Grace's hand and pulled her inside. "Please. Come in out of the heat."

She led Grace upstairs, saying over her shoulder, "I'll fix you something cool to drink. Then you can tell me about your sister."

Her soothing tone made Grace want to do exactly that. For the first time in years, she found herself wanting to tell someone about Jessie, about her goodness and purity, and about her unfailing conscience. Jessie had been one of those people who had truly been a blessing to this world, while Grace—

The parrot's harsh squawk brought her abruptly back to the present. She glanced across the room, where the magnificent yellow-and-blue bird strutted with supreme confidence on his perch.

When he saw Grace watching him, he flapped his wings and screeched, "They're not real! They're not real! They're not real!"

"Shut up, Simon, you stupid bird!" Rosa scolded. To Grace she said apologetically, "He's a terrible creature. He picks up everything he hears on the *televisión.*"

Grace wondered which programs he'd been watching. Jerry Springer? Howard Stern, maybe?

She followed Rosa into the kitchen and watched while the housekeeper prepared two glasses of iced tea. They both sat down at the breakfast table—Rosa obviously having dispensed with any formalities—and sipped their drinks.

After a moment, she said, "You came to tell Dr. Hunter about the funeral?"

Grace nodded. "It's at four o'clock this afternoon at the Chapel Hill Funeral Home. I...thought he might like to be there."

Rosa looked as if she wanted to comment but kept silent.

Grace took another sip of her tea. "How long have you worked for Dr. Hunter?"

Rosa shrugged. "A long time."

"You must know him pretty well." Grace studied the older woman's face.

"Dr. Hunter is not an easy man to know. He's very..." Rosa struggled for the right word. "*Complicado.* Complex. There are some who consider him a saint."

"Are you one of them?"

A slight hesitation. "He's no saint. He has his faults, quite a few of them. But he is, in many ways, a very good man."

"You're referring to the work he does at his clinics here and in Mexico."

Rosa nodded. "Especially the one in *Méjico.* The children who come there would break your heart. Many of them have been horribly disfigured since birth. They've become outcasts in their own villages. They've never known anything but ridicule."

Grace wondered how he could possibly be the same man who changed criminals faces for money. Was Ethan some sort of Dr. Jekyll and Mr. Hyde, a man with two very distinct personalities? The notion made her shiver. "How did you meet Dr. Hunter?"

Rosa shrugged, but her expression suddenly became very sad. "It was a long time ago, in Mexico City. When my daughter was young, I worked in a *barra* in a very bad part of town. Marta and I had a little one-room *apartamento* on the second floor, little better than a hovel, but it was all I could afford. Sometimes when I worked late, Marta would get lonely. She would sneak downstairs to be near me. I didn't want her to. She was already starting to look like a woman, and she was so beautiful that men were already starting to notice her. One night a fight broke out, a drunken brawl. In the confusion, a man grabbed Marta and pulled her outside. He tried to—'' Rosa's eyes closed briefly, as if the memory had become too painful to relive. Grace understood that feeling all too well.

''What happened?'' she asked gently.

Rosa shuddered. ''Marta fought him off as best she could and started screaming. He pulled a knife and cut her. The whole side of her face was…mutilated.''

''I'm sorry.''

Rosa shrugged away Grace's pity. ''She was horribly scarred. People would stare at her on the streets, and children would run away from her. Marta withdrew completely into herself. She was very…ashamed of her face. Years passed, and then one day I heard about Dr. Hunter. That was before he had his clinic in the jungle. He use to come to Mexico City twice a year and work in one of the hospitals. People there spoke of him as a god. It was said the handsome young doctor could perform miracles, that he could transform the most hideous monster into an angel. Marta was no monster. She was a badly scarred and frightened child. But Dr. Hunter was my only hope.''

''Was he able to help her?'' Grace asked, caught up in the story in spite of herself.

''Eventually. Marta was frightened of him at first—frightened of every man who came near her—but Dr. Hunter spoke to her so gently that she soon forgot her fears. He told her it might take several operations, but when he was finished, she would be beautiful again. And she was.'' A tear trickled down Rosa's cheek, and she quickly brushed it away.

Grace was more affected by the story than she wanted to admit. It was hard enough to do what had to be done, but when she thought of Rosa's daughter and of all the children Ethan had helped, Grace couldn't help asking herself if ridding the world of a man like Trevor Reardon was an equal exchange for depriving it of a doctor as talented as Ethan.

Not daring to ponder the question, Grace rose. ''I'd better be going. I still have a million things to do.''

Rosa nodded sympathetically and stood, too. Just as she started for the kitchen door to show Grace out, the phone rang.

Grace held up her hand. ''Go ahead and get that. I can let myself out.''

In the living room, she couldn't resist stopping by the parrot's cage. The two of them had formed some kind of strange bond, Grace decided. A sort of mutual disrespect for one another. Besides which, she needed something to take her mind off Rosa's story and the doubts it had created for her.

"So your name is Simon, huh? As in Simon Says?"

The bird cocked his head and stared at her.

Grace cocked her head and stared back. "Well, why don't you say it, Simon? I know you're dying to."

Simon blinked, but remained silent.

After a moment, Grace crooned, "They're not real, they're not real, they're not real. Come on, what do you say, Simon?"

The bird fluffed his wings importantly and squawked, "I say we get rid of the bastard once and for all."

SINCE AMY COLE had no family, Grace, in keeping with her cover, had taken care of all the funeral arrangements. She'd kept the service simple, ordering an elegant spray of white roses to rest atop the mahogany casket while a framed picture of Amy, the one from her apartment, was displayed on a nearby pedestal.

The small chapel was surprisingly crowded. Grace glanced around the room, trying to sort out who was who. Several people clustered around the apartment manager from Amy's complex, and Grace decided that most of them were probably Amy's neighbors. Some of the others were undoubtedly from work. But aside from the manager, Grace didn't recognize any of the mourners.

She glanced at her watch, wondering what was keeping Ethan. He'd been incommunicado with her all day, and although he'd been under surveillance for most of that time, Grace had yet to be given a report on his movements.

When ten more minutes had gone by and he still hadn't shown, she began to worry. Could something have happened? Had Reardon somehow managed to slip through the trap they'd set for him?

A sour taste rose in Grace's mouth at the thought. She wanted Reardon, but at what price? Two days ago, she would have said any price, but that was before she'd met Ethan. Before she'd allowed him to get to her.

Now she wasn't sure what she would do if the choice came down to Reardon or Ethan.

You're a fool, a little voice whispered inside her. *You don't know this man. You don't owe him anything.*

True, but in the last two days, he'd awakened something inside Grace she had thought forever dead. Feelings. Attraction.

Need.

She closed her eyes briefly as a wave of doubt rolled over her. She didn't want to need anyone. She couldn't afford to. Need was synonymous with vulnerability. Weakness. And Grace had to remain strong. She had to remain focused. If she didn't, she might not be able to save herself or Ethan.

But what if Reardon does manage to penetrate the screen? that same voice taunted her.

Grace told herself it was impossible. The plan would work.

But would it? Hadn't this operation already been full of surprises? Amy Cole was never supposed to die. In fact, she shouldn't have been anywhere near the clinic that night. Her cooperation with the FBI had been critical in formulating the plan to capture Trevor Reardon, but because Grace hadn't been honest, Amy had gotten scared. If Myra's hunch was right, Amy had gone to the clinic to warn Ethan that the Feds were on to him. And she'd gotten herself killed in the process.

Grace blamed herself for that. Though she wasn't a mind reader, she should have interpreted the signs. Amy was crazy in love with Ethan. When she suddenly realized what her cooperation with the authorities would mean for him—and for herself—she'd panicked. Grace should have seen it coming, but she'd never been the best judge of what love could do to you. What it could *make* you do.

In fact, she had been the very worst judge.

Not wanting to start an avalanche of memories, she turned her attention back to the crowd. A man had come in and gone straight to Amy's picture. He stood staring at it for a long moment, then walked over to the casket, running his fingers along the smooth surface of the lid. He began to sob quietly.

Uneasy, Grace watched him. Who was he? How had he known Amy? She'd told Grace she had no family or close friends, other than Ethan, but this man had obviously been deeply affected by her death.

Someone touched Grace's arm and she whirled. The chaplain, Bible clutched to his chest, stood at her side. He looked to be in his mid-forties, tall and thin with arrow-straight posture. His cheekbones were classically high, giving what would have been an otherwise plain face an almost regal look. His lips were thin, his nose a bit broad and his dark brown hair was streaked with gray. Grace thought he had the kindest eyes she'd ever seen, but even as that notion flitted through her mind, trepidation swept over her. Had she met him before?

He held out his hand to her, and Grace reluctantly took it. His handshake was warm and firm, not in the least offensive, but a shiver racked her just the same. As soon as she deemed it appropriate, she withdrew her hand from his.

The chaplain smiled. "You're Amy's sister, I understand."

Grace hesitated. Lying in the service of her country was one thing, but deliberately deceiving a man of God something else. "We weren't close," she said carefully.

"That often happens in families. A rift occurs, time passes, and before anyone can imagine, it's too late. But take comfort in the knowledge that it never is really too late. You will see your sister again."

Grace's gaze fastened on the man's clerical collar. She realized suddenly why he seemed so familiar to her, why he made her so uneasy. She had not been around a clergyman since her family's funeral, but now she had a vivid recall of that day, of the minister from their church holding her hand, offering her comfort in the knowledge that she and her family would someday be reunited in the hereafter.

It was only later that Grace had decided her only comfort would come here on earth, when she put Trevor Reardon away forever.

The man at the coffin was still crying. The chaplain smiled sadly. "If you'll excuse me…"

Grace watched him approach the casket and put a gentle hand on the man's shoulder. The chaplain spoke to the weeping man softly, and after a bit, his sobs subsided. He turned and walked away from the casket, his gaze brushing Grace's before he seated himself at the back of the chapel.

It was nearing on four o'clock. Rosa came in and nodded to Grace before finding a seat near the front. The group of people from Amy's apartment complex settled near the middle. Others scattered about the remaining pews. Just as the chaplain took the podium, two last-minute arrivals started everyone whispering among themselves.

Grace recognized the woman at once. Pilar Hunter had looked exquisitely beautiful in the pictures Grace had seen of her, but in person, the woman was breathtaking.

Unlike almost everyone else in the chapel, she'd refused to wear black, choosing instead a sleeveless dress in dusky blue linen that did incredible things to her dark hair and eyes. The hemline was short, her heels high, and her bare legs went on forever. Grace couldn't help glancing down at her own attire—a simple silk jersey dress that she had once thought flattering. For the first time that afternoon, she was almost glad Ethan hadn't shown up.

The man with Pilar took her elbow and guided her toward a pew. They settled directly behind Grace, and she caught a strong whiff of Pilar's perfume—a heavy, exotic scent that seemed to capture the essence of the woman herself.

As the chaplain started the service, Grace became increasingly aware of Pilar's presence, as if the woman was staring at the back of Grace's head. She remembered what Ethan had said about his wife, that she seemed like a woman capable of throwing acid on his car or in his face. Grace understood what he meant. In the brief glimpse she'd had of Pilar, Grace had sensed an undercurrent of suppressed violence that was almost as tangible as her perfume.

I say we just kill the bastard and be done with it.

Could she and Myra have been wrong? Grace wondered suddenly. What if Trevor Reardon hadn't been behind the attack in Ethan's clinic? What if someone else wanted him dead?

Grace tried to put the notion out of her head. She couldn't afford to get sidetracked or to let down her guard. That was exactly what Reardon would want. For all she knew, he might be in this very room now, watching her from a distance and laughing. Laughing…

Grace looked up and her gaze met the chaplain's. He smiled at her and nodded almost imperceptibly before he bowed his head to pray for Amy Cole's immortal soul.

CHAPTER EIGHT

Ethan stared at the pile of shoes on his bedroom floor as a headache beat a painful staccato inside his brain.

What the hell was going on here?

Why didn't any of these shoes fit him?

His movements almost frantic, Ethan tried on another pair, and then another. Every shoe in his closet was too small for him. The only pair that fit him were the ones he'd been wearing the night he woke up in the hospital, the ones he'd been wearing ever since.

The loafers had been fine with casual clothes, but today, getting dressed for Amy's funeral, he'd found a black suit, white shirt, and somber tie in the closet. When he'd brought out the appropriate shoes, he'd discovered they were too small for him, as was every other pair of shoes in the closet.

He didn't understand why. Granted, the clothes he'd been wearing were loose, but that could be explained by weight loss following surgery. And he knew he'd had the appendectomy because he had the scar to prove it. The dreams of being shot, of falling off a cliff were just that—drug induced visions. The memory loss was due to the blow to his head. His wariness of the authorities—well, Grace had explained that to him as well.

Clearly, everything that had happened to him had a logical, if disturbing, explanation.

Except for the fact that none of his shoes fit.

Ethan picked up the black dress shoe and studied it. Why would he—why would *anyone*—buy dozens of pairs of expensive shoes in the wrong size? It made no sense—

Without warning, the pain in his head became razor-sharp, blinding. Dropping the shoe, Ethan put his hands to his head, pressing tightly as he squeezed his eyes closed.

An image shot through him. He could see someone running for

his life through a jungle. He could smell the dank scent of the vegetation, feel the cloying heat, hear the sounds of pursuit behind him. He *knew* the man's fear. But the man's face was not the one Ethan stared at in the mirror.

And yet...

The man in the vision was him and it wasn't.

Unlike the picture that Ethan had seen of himself downstairs in the study, he felt connected to the man running through the jungle. He knew him in a way he did not know the stranger staring back at him from the mirror.

But...why?

Why was he having another man's visions?

Why did none of the shoes in his closet fit him?

Why was he in possession of a gun that may well have been issued to someone in one of the special forces of the military? Someone like an elite Navy SEAL? Someone like Trevor Reardon?

Why did a plastic surgeon know how to use a weapon like that?

An explanation came with another blinding flash of light.

Pain exploded inside Ethan's head, and for a moment, he thought he was going to be sick.

WHEN THE SERVICE was over, Grace looked up to find Ethan standing in the doorway of the chapel. As his gaze met hers, she felt a physical jolt. It was almost as if a bolt of pure adrenaline had ping-ponged between them.

He looked pale, Grace thought with sudden anxiety. Shaken. What had happened to him?

She got up and started toward him, but was waylaid several times by well-wishers—first by the apartment manager, then by a neighbor, and then by Rosa, whose initial frost toward Grace had thawed. The housekeeper squeezed Grace's hand comfortingly, then, her glance moving over Grace's shoulder, she pursed her lips in stern disapproval.

Grace followed her gaze to find Pilar and her escort on a collision course with Ethan. Wondering if an unpleasant scene was about to erupt, Grace glanced around the room. Most of the mourners had filed out of the chapel by this time. The grieving man remained seated, his head bowed in silent prayer, while the chaplain stood at his podium, waiting for everyone to leave. The late afternoon sun shining through the stained glass window behind the clergyman gave him an almost angelic appearance. The image should have been comforting, but for some reason it was not.

Hoping to abort a possible spectacle, Grace walked over to stand beside Ethan. Their gazes met again, but neither of them said anything.

Pilar stared at her coolly. Even this close, Grace couldn't find a single imperfection in the woman's complexion.

"So you're Amy Cole's sister." Her voice, light and musical, was as attractive as the rest of her, and the Spanish accent gave her a hint of mystery. "I'm Pilar. Ethan's wife." The slight emphasis on the last word made Grace wonder again about Ethan and Pilar's relationship.

"How do you do?" Grace extended her hand, but the woman's fingertips barely brushed against her palm.

Pilar stared at her critically. "You don't look anything like her, you know."

Grace assumed the comment was meant to cut. "My sister was very beautiful," she said.

Pilar raised her narrow shoulders in an elegant shrug. "In a trampish sort of way."

For the first time, Ethan stirred to life beside Grace. "For God's sake, she's dead. Can't you show a little respect?"

Pilar's dark brows rose in mild outrage. "The same respect she showed for our marriage vows?"

"Why did you come here?" Ethan demanded. He turned to the man standing next to Pilar. "Why did you let her come?"

The man laughed softly. "You don't 'let' Pilar do anything. You should know that better than anyone." He turned to Grace and put out his hand. "By the way, I'm Bob Kendall. I'm very sorry about your sister."

So this was Ethan's ex-partner. Unlike Pilar's, his handshake was firm, and his fingers lingered against Grace's for just a moment too long.

She instantly disliked him. He was too smooth, and his gray eyes were too insincere.

He said to Ethan, "Are you feeling all right, buddy? You look a little pale."

"I'm fine," Ethan said tersely.

"Still, it might not hurt to give Mancetti a call. I don't imagine she was too happy to learn you'd checked yourself out of the hospital."

Ethan didn't answer. Instead he turned to Grace, muttering, "When can we get out of here?"

She shrugged, feeling Pilar's dark eyes scouring her. "Now. I've made arrangements for a private burial."

Ethan nodded. His eyes were shadowed. Haunted. Was it Amy's funeral that had gotten to him? Had he finally remembered her? Remembered that…he cared for her?

Ethan turned toward the door, but Pilar caught his arm. "You can't just walk off like this. We're not through, Ethan."

He stared down at her for a long moment, then very deliberately removed her hand from his arm. "You could have fooled me."

OUTSIDE, THE SUNLIGHT, even at five o'clock, was still brutal. Ethan pulled a pair of dark glasses from the inside of his suit coat and slipped them on. He hadn't been able to rid himself of the headache. A handful of aspirin had dulled the pain, but the confusion whirling inside him was still as strong as ever.

Beside him, Grace tried to match her steps to his, but he had a good eight inches on her. He slowed, then stopped altogether in the shade of a huge water oak. The lower limbs were so heavy, they'd been braced to keep from snapping. Spanish moss dripped silvery green from the gnarled branches, giving the tree a forlorn, almost ghostly appearance. In the distance, the cars in the parking lot wavered in the rising heat from the pavement. Their inconsistency seemed surreal and out of place, but the eeriness matched Ethan's mood.

Grace said a little breathlessly, "What happened to you? I was beginning to worry."

He gazed down at her. "Were you?"

"Of course. You know as well as I do the danger you're in."

"Do I?"

A brief frown flitted across her features. "What happened, Ethan? Why were you so late getting to the service?"

The way she said his name, in a voice that was just the tiniest bit husky, made him want more than ever to discount his earlier thoughts. But the question was like a mantra inside his head.

Who am I? Who the hell am I?

He studied Grace's features, thinking how lovely she looked today, and how very calm she seemed for having just come from her sister's funeral. Her mood was somber, as was the black dress she wore, but there was something about her eyes—an alertness, an intensity—that mystified him and made him believe he wasn't the only one who had secrets.

He took her arm and drew her deeper into the shadow of the oak tree. "What if I told you, I'm not the man you think I am?"

Her eyes instantly deepened. "What do you mean?"

He paused, wondering what to say, how to tell her his suspicions. *I may not be Dr. Ethan Hunter. In fact, I may be...*

He couldn't even finish the thought. His heart began to beat wildly against his chest. Ethan was sure he'd never felt so alone, so out of control, so lost as he did at that moment.

And Grace. God help him, he was still drawn to her. Still attracted to her. Still *wanted* her. In some perverse way, more than ever because he knew if what he feared was true, he could never have her.

In fact, it might even come down to the basic choice of his life...or hers.

She was still staring up at him, her incredible blue eyes deep and intense. He wondered what she was thinking, if she had even an inkling of what he was feeling.

She touched his arm. The action made Ethan almost groan out loud.

"Have you remembered something?"

"No. But what if I told you—" He wanted to tell her about the shoes, and possibly the gun, but a movement at the entrance of the chapel drew his attention. A man came out of the building and paused, looking around. Ethan dimly recognized him from the funeral service. He'd been seated at the back, weeping quietly, when Ethan had arrived.

Ethan glanced at him, then turned his gaze back to Grace. But out of the corner of his eye, he saw the man start toward them.

"Do you know who that man is?" he asked Grace suddenly.

She turned, following his gaze, and Ethan saw her tense. "No. I saw him inside, though. He was pretty torn up."

Ethan watched as the man approached them. He had the kind of face that made it hard to judge his age, but something about the way he walked, the way he dressed—casually in khaki pants and a button-down collar shirt—gave Ethan the impression that he was fairly young, no more than late thirties. The receding hairline was probably premature, as were the lines around his eyes and mouth.

As he neared them, Ethan heard Grace catch her breath. He thought that her gasp was not because she suddenly recognized the man, but because of the look of unadulterated fury on his face. Ethan saw Grace's hand slip inside her purse, but before he could wonder about her intentions, the man stepped up to him. He was shorter than Ethan by only an inch or so, but their builds were similar. They stood almost chest to chest.

"Dr. Ethan Hunter?"

"Yes?"

Without warning, the man hauled off and punched Ethan square in the face. Pain flashed white-hot over his already bruised flesh, and as Ethan staggered back a step, red-hot anger shot through him. Almost instinctively, he lunged at the man, but Grace jumped between them.

"Stop it!" she ordered, putting a hand on each of their chests with surprising strength and authority. She turned to the stranger. "Why did you do that?" she demanded.

The man's gaze was still furious. "He had it coming!"

Ethan said coldly, "The hell I did. I don't even know who you are."

The man glared at him. "Of course, you wouldn't remember me. Why should you? I was nobody important, just the man Amy was going to marry, that's all. Until you came along."

Grace must have sensed the anger welling inside him again, for she gave him a shove. "Calm down," she said. "This is not the place for violence."

The man looked immediately contrite. His blue eyes flooded with tears. "No, you're right. Amy wouldn't have wanted that."

He took a few steps away from Grace and Ethan, as if struggling to gather his composure. But he continued to glare at Ethan. "We did meet once. I guess you don't remember. I came to Amy's apartment to beg her to come back to me, but...it was too late. You'd already seduced her away from me."

The raw pain in the man's eyes made Ethan's stomach knot. He didn't know whether he was really Dr. Ethan Hunter or not, but at that moment, the one thing he was certain of was that he didn't much care for Dr. Hunter or the way he treated people.

Grace said softly, "I didn't know Amy was ever engaged. She never mentioned it."

"That's odd," the man said, wiping at his eyes. "Because she never mentioned having a sister, either."

GRACE COULD FEEL Ethan's gaze on her, but she kept her eyes trained on the man before her. Something about him seemed very pitiful to her. He was not unattractive, but the way he dressed, the receding hairline, the ordinary features must have made him feel like a moth to Amy's butterfly. No wonder he harbored such animosity toward Ethan. He was the epitome of everything this man was not.

Grace said carefully, "Amy and I were estranged for several years. We hadn't spoken with each other until very recently."

"I guess that explains why she never wanted to talk about her family." The man stuck out his hand. "My name's Danny Medford."

"Grace Donovan. You already know Dr. Hunter," she said with irony.

He shot Ethan a killing glance before turning back to Grace. "I don't suppose it would be possible—" He broke off, looking ill at ease.

"What?" Grace prompted.

Danny looked at her hopefully. "Do you think we could get together sometime? You know, to talk about Amy?"

He seemed a nice enough guy, but Grace had no wish to perpetuate the deception, to contribute in any way to the man's pain.

However, with Ethan looking on, she had little choice but to keep up the farce. "I'd like that. Maybe in a few weeks when it isn't so painful to talk about her."

He nodded, smiling wistfully as he fished a card from his shirt pocket and handed it to her. "That's my work number. I'm there at all hours. Feel free to call anytime."

Medford Engineering, the card read. Grace slipped it in her purse and smiled. "It's been nice meeting you, Danny."

"Likewise." He turned to Ethan. "I wouldn't be surprised if you and I meet again someday."

There was no mistaking the threat in the man's words, but Ethan merely shrugged. "I'll be ready next time."

After the man had disappeared into the parking lot, Ethan fished a handkerchief from his pocket and wiped away the trickle of blood at the corner of his mouth.

"Yet another of Dr. Hunter's enemies," he said enigmatically, watching the man's battered Toyota sedan pull out of the parking lot. "They seem to be coming out of the woodwork."

"He seems harmless enough."

Ethan lifted a brow as he daubed at his lip. "Easy for you to say."

Grace almost smiled. "I meant comparatively speaking. The enemy we really have to worry about is Trevor Reardon."

"I wonder." Ethan's eyes grew dark and distant, as if he'd gone someplace in his mind that Grace had no wish to follow. Or had he gone to a place she'd already been to?

There was still blood on his lip. She took the handkerchief from his hand. "Here, let me."

She blotted the droplet of blood as gently as she could, but Ethan winced at her touch. He took her hand and pulled it away. For a moment they stood that way, her hand in his, eyes locked, until Grace's stomach began to flutter wildly.

She was accustomed to butterflies. She got them the first day of every new assignment, every time she had to draw her weapon, or when she faced danger. But this was different, because the greater threat was coming, not from Ethan, but from within herself.

She shivered, watching him. So much about him she didn't know, but the one thing that was all too real was her attraction to him.

Her feelings for him. She couldn't explain them. They made no sense. But the emotions raging inside her were so real and so intense, that if he were to kiss her at that moment, Grace knew she would have no willpower to resist.

What few relationships she'd had over the years had been with men who had no expectations of a future with her. There could be no future with Ethan, either, and yet Grace found herself yearning for something she'd never wanted before. The hollowness inside her heart made her feel lost and lonely in a way she hadn't felt in a long, long time.

She almost hated Ethan for that. Hated him for making her lose confidence in her ability to do what needed to be done. For making her want him.

Grace closed her eyes, letting the heat of the day wash over her. The humidity curled the fine hairs at the back of her neck, and she could feel the silk of her dress clinging to her body. She had a sudden image of cool water lapping at her toes. Of a fragrant breeze rippling through her hair. Of a man lying naked beside her, whispering in her ear...

When she opened her eyes, Ethan was staring down at her so intently, Grace thought he must have read her mind. She caught her breath.

"What are we going to do about this, Grace?"

She didn't try to misconstrue his meaning. The sparks between them were all too obvious. "There's nothing to be done. We just have to...ignore it, I guess."

"You think that's possible?" His eyes darkened, so much so that Grace had to glance away. She had to find a way to subdue the power he had over her.

"It has to be, because as you pointed out yesterday, you're a married man. Just because you can't remember your wife doesn't mean you don't still have feelings for her. You might even still love her."

He almost laughed. "Do you really believe that?"

Grace remembered the coldness in Pilar's expression, the emptiness in her eyes, and she shuddered. "I don't think you still love her. Maybe you never did, but it doesn't change the fact that you are still married to her. I don't take that lightly, Ethan."

"I wish I could say the same." Grace didn't think he was trying to be facetious. His eyes were too haunted for that.

"And that brings us back to Amy," she said quietly. "I don't want to be another one of your conquests. I won't be."

"I don't even remember Amy," he said. "Everything you've told me about her…it doesn't even seem real. It's like…someone else had the affair with her. Someone else married Pilar. It wasn't me. I'm not that man."

Grace wished she knew what to say to him, but she didn't. She wished suddenly that what he was telling her was true—that he wasn't Dr. Ethan Hunter, but someone entirely different. Someone free and honorable. Someone with whom she just might have a second shot at life.

But reality and fantasy were two different concepts, and no one knew that better than Grace.

"Ethan—"

"I'm *not* that man, Grace."

He could almost convince her when he looked at her that way. When he skimmed his knuckles along the side of her cheek, brushed back the hair from her face with a touch so gentle, Grace could have wept. She closed her eyes briefly, wanting him to kiss her with every fiber of her being, and knowing all the while that if he did, there would be no chance for her then. Everything in her world would be lost.

She took a step back from him. "Losing memories doesn't change who you are. What you've done."

"What I've done." The shadow in his eyes deepened. He raked his fingers through his hair, turning away from her. "There's nothing that will ever change that."

"No, but there is such a thing as redemption. Restitution."

His gaze came back to meet hers. "And how do you propose I pay for my sins?" he asked grimly.

Grace shrugged. "Helping me bring a man like Trevor Reardon to justice is a good place to start."

Ethan's expression hardened. Something that Grace couldn't quite define flashed in his eyes. "That sounds so naive, but somehow you don't strike me as the Pollyanna type. I may not remember who I am or what I've done, but I don't think I'm the only one here with secrets.''

Grace's heartbeat quickened. "What do you mean?''

He gazed down at her, studying her. "I don't know who you are any more than I know who I am. We're strangers, and yet...we seem to have some kind of...connection. Even you can't deny that.''

"Maybe our connection is Amy,'' Grace tried to say calmly.

He shook his head. "I don't think so. I can't help but wonder if you're holding something back from me.''

"Like what?''

He hesitated. His gaze grew even more pensive. "Did we know each other before?''

"No.'' Grace's heart pounded like a piston. He was getting too close. His suspicions were mounting by the minute, and she didn't know what to do to stop them. If he found out who she was...how she was using him...

God help you if you're lying to me.

"I told you before,'' she said. "We'd never met until that night outside the hospital.''

"Then what is this connection we have?'' he asked almost urgently.

Grace shrugged. "Attraction. Chemistry. Call it what you like, but that's all it is.''

"Why do I feel as if it's something more?'' Ethan grabbed her forearms and pulled her toward him. "Why do I feel as if I know you better than I could ever know the woman who claims to be my wife? Why do I know how your lips would taste if I kissed you right now? How your body would feel beneath mine if we—''

"Please don't,'' Grace said breathlessly. She put her hands to his chest, but it was a meaningless gesture. She wasn't going to push him away. It took every ounce of her strength not to pull him closer.

"You feel it, too. I can see it your eyes.''

"Please—''

He drew her so close, their lips were only a heartbeat apart. "You want me to kiss you,'' he said almost accusingly. "Almost as much as I want to.''

"Ethan—''

The space between them evaporated. "Tell me to stop," he murmured against her mouth.

Grace said nothing. Instead she closed her eyes and waited for the inevitable to happen. Waited for her life to come tumbling down around her. When it didn't, her relief—or was it disappointment?—was so intense, her head spun dizzily. She opened her eyes and gazed up at him.

Something glimmered in his eyes, something that looked almost like triumph. He dropped his hands from her shoulders and backed away. "I told you it wouldn't be easy," he said, in a tone that sounded more like a threat than a warning.

GRACE LAY IN bed that night, wide awake and listening to the street noises outside her hotel. The room was dimly illuminated by streetlights and neon signs that caused shadows to leap and cavort across the walls and ceiling, like demons celebrating some dark victory.

Earlier, she'd opened the curtains so that she could see the balcony outside the sliding glass doors. Airplane lights twinkled in the night sky, and between the slats of the balcony railing, she could see the faint movement of pine boughs stirring in the breeze. She would have liked to open the doors, letting in the breeze and the scent of evergreen, but she never slept with the windows open. Her doors and windows were always closed and always locked.

Grace stared out into the darkness and thought about Ethan, wondering what he was doing tonight. His house was under surveillance and secured by a state-of-the-art alarm system that even an FBI agent couldn't find fault with. There was no reason for Grace to worry, and yet she *was* worried. She couldn't shake the uneasiness that had invaded her thoughts since she'd left Ethan at the chapel this afternoon.

I'm not that man, Grace.

What had he meant by that? What had he meant when he'd said, *What if I told you I'm not the man you think I am?*

Was it wishful thinking on his part? The denial of a man with no memory learning things about himself that were more than just unpleasant?

No wonder he was so confused. The man who altered criminals' faces for money was a direct contradiction to the man Rosa had told Grace about earlier. A man who could transform hideous monsters into angels. A man who changed children's lives forever.

Was Ethan Hunter a saint with a badly tarnished halo, or a Dr. Jekyll and Mr. Hyde—a man with two entirely different sides to his personality?

Grace shivered in the gloom, considering all the possibilities but trying not to dwell on the one thing Ethan had said that perhaps troubled her the most.

Why do I feel as if I know you better than I could ever know the woman who claims to be my wife? Why do I know how your lips would taste if I kissed you right now? How your body would feel beneath mine if we—

Grace sucked in a long breath, trying to remember her objectives, but the situation had taken a turn she couldn't have anticipated. It had seemed so easy when she and Myra had first devised the plan. Come to Houston. Set up surveillance and a cover for Grace. Wait for Dr. Ethan Hunter to arrive from Mexico and then approach him. Convince him to cooperate so that Trevor Reardon could be drawn out into the open.

But then everything had gone wrong. It had all happened too quickly. Ethan had come back from Mexico weeks earlier than planned, before complete backup and support were in place. And then Amy Cole had died. The entire operation had had to be hastily revised, and now everything hinged on Grace's ability to perpetuate her deception. To remain close to Ethan.

But what happened when it was all over? Originally, Grace hadn't stopped to consider what would happen to Ethan once Reardon was safely behind bars again. Or dead.

But Ethan had his own sins to answer for, and leniency would depend on the extent of his cooperation. Grace hadn't thought to be involved in anything beyond Reardon's capture, but now she realized how difficult it would be to walk away, to never look back, to betray a man she was deeply attracted to.

For a moment, she considered calling Myra and asking for advice, but somehow Grace thought this was beyond the older agent's field of expertise. She didn't think Myra had ever been torn like this. Grace couldn't even imagine Myra Temple falling in love.

She couldn't imagine herself falling in love, either. Though it was true she was attracted to Ethan, that they shared a connection she couldn't begin to explain, it certainly wasn't love. It couldn't be love because Grace was immune to that emotion. She'd promised herself a long time ago that she would never again be vulnerable, and love made you vulnerable. It made you weak. It made you forget who you were and what you had to do.

Grace knew exactly who she was. She was a federal agent on the trail of a ruthless killer. And she knew what she was. A woman who would do anything to bring down the man who had nearly destroyed her.

Ethan Hunter could not be allowed to get in her way. She would use him and she would betray him. And in the end, she would walk away from him.

SOMETIME AFTER TWO in the morning, Grace managed to doze off. But her dreams were filled with distorted images from her past and her present. She saw Trevor Reardon smiling down at her, but before she had time to draw her weapon, his face turned into Ethan's. And he was still smiling. Still taunting her.

Grace hovered in that nether realm of dream and reality. She knew she was still sleeping, but she was powerless to control the images playing themselves out in her mind.

In her dream, the phone was ringing. As if watching a movie, she saw herself pick up the receiver and lift it to her ear. "Hello?"

There was no response, but she could tell someone was on the other end. She caught her breath, waiting, while a fine sense of dread seeped over her. "Who's there?"

Silence.

Then a deep, seductive voice said in her ear, "I liked what you were wearing at the funeral today, Grace. Black becomes you."

They were almost the exact words Trevor Reardon had spoken to her fourteen years ago, after her family's funeral. Fear exploded inside Grace, and she gasped in horror.

Wake up! It's only a dream! she tried to warn herself.

Some part of her knew that it was a nightmare, but Grace was powerless to break free of it. She tried to fight her way to consciousness, but it was as if invisible hands were holding her down, pulling her more deeply into sleep.

It all seemed so frighteningly real. Grace heard herself say, "Where are you?"

And that sensuous voice replying, "Closer than you think."

"How close?"

Another pause, then, "You still favor pearls, I see."

There was something about his voice, something that triggered a flash of insight. Grace struggled through the layers of sleep, trying to cling to that elusive revelation that had come to her in the dream. Something about his voice...

Yes! That was it! She'd heard that same voice recently, only...somehow it had been different, distorted. She hadn't recognized it because he'd disguised it.

As the cobwebs of sleep began to clear, Grace lay beneath the covers, trembling. The dream lingered. The fear it generated made her head swim, and she couldn't think straight. For a moment, Grace considered fixing herself a drink to steady her nerves, but that wouldn't help. It never had before.

She glanced at the nightstand beside the bed, wondering what time it was. In the glow of the clock face, she saw the tiny pearl studs she'd worn to Amy's funeral yesterday.

Forcing herself to get up, Grace crossed the room to the window and stared out into the gloom. Dawn was breaking over the city, and she could see a fleet of low-lying clouds moving in from the coast. The castoff glow of the sun, still hidden below the horizon, tinted the edges with a golden pink that gradually deepened to violet.

It was that strange time of morning, before the sun came up, when the shadows outside deepened and the night terrors had yet to flee.

Grace's first instinct was to run. To pack her bags and leave the city as fast as she could. And that impulse surprised her. She'd thought about this operation long and hard, even before she'd learned Reardon had escaped from prison a second time. She used to daydream about meeting him face to face. She used to picture his features on the targets she destroyed with her pistol at Quantico and wonder what it would be like to look him in the eye the exact moment she put a bullet through his heart.

Reardon's face would be different now, but somehow Grace had thought she would know him anywhere. She'd wanted to believe that the evil inside his soul would radiate from his body like an oily, black aura, but no one she'd met recently had aroused that kind of suspicion in her. She'd even considered the possibility that Reardon was hundreds, perhaps thousands of miles away, and that whoever had killed Amy and had tried to kill Ethan was someone else. Pilar or Kendall or even, as the police thought, a stranger looking for drugs.

But Grace had no more doubts. She was sure now that she'd heard Reardon's voice recently, but she couldn't think where. At Amy's funeral? She'd talked to a lot of people there she hadn't known, men and women who claimed to be friends and acquaintances of Amy's. Had one of them been Trevor Reardon? Had she been that close to him? Had he...touched her?

Grace shuddered in revulsion. Obviously, Reardon had managed to disguise his voice well enough to fool her for a while, but there was a quality about it that couldn't be altered. In her sleep, Grace had remembered that quality.

Was he out there somewhere? Was he watching her even now? Was he finding her in the crosshairs of a high-powered weapon, laughing all the while at her foolishness? Her weakness?

Grace's insides quivered with fear and dread, but she forced herself to remain at the window. She was safe for the time being. Reardon wouldn't shoot her here. Not from a distance. He enjoyed killing too much. For him, death was a personal experience. An intimate one. He would want to enjoy it to its fullest potential.

When he came for her this time, Grace knew it would be more for pleasure than revenge.

CHAPTER NINE

"Buenos días," Rosa greeted the next morning. She stood back so Grace could enter.

"Good morning, Rosa. Is Ethan in?"

"He's upstairs in his study."

She led Grace up the stairway and through the living room, then tapping on the study door, she opened it a crack and announced Grace's arrival.

Ethan was sitting behind his desk, studying a legal document that was several pages thick. When Grace entered the room, he looked up. "Morning. Or is it still morning?"

"Barely." Grace glanced at her watch. "It's just after eleven."

Ethan's eyes looked a bit unfocused, and his lower face was shadowed with beard. Grace wondered if he'd been to bed at all last night, or if like her, his sleep had been plagued with nightmares. Self-doubts.

He glanced at Rosa still hovering in the doorway. "You can leave whenever you need to. Don't worry about me. I'll manage just fine."

Rosa's dark eyes darted from Ethan to Grace, but this morning she didn't appear to be as disapproving. Grace wondered if she'd managed to win the housekeeper over, but if she had, it was a hollow victory because it had been won by deception.

Rosa shrugged. *"Adiós* then. I'll see you in a few days."

After she'd gone, Grace turned back to Ethan. "Where's she going?"

"Her grandson is sick, and her daughter needs help so I gave her some time off. Under the circumstances, I thought it a good idea to get her out of the house for a few days." His ominous words reminded Grace all too clearly of the dream she'd had last night.

"As a matter of fact," Ethan said, "I've been thinking about your safety as well. I want to talk to you about something."

He seemed different this morning, and Grace's first thought was that he'd gotten his memory back. "What about?"

"I realized this morning that I've never even been to your apartment. I don't even know where you live."

Grace frowned. "So?"

"So...how safe is it? Do you have a security system? A gated entry? A guard who patrols the grounds?" Ethan sat forward suddenly, his dark eyes intense. "If Reardon is watching my every move as you seem to think, then he knows you and I are working together. He knows you're Amy's sister. He may even know where you live."

There was no doubt in Grace's mind that Trevor Reardon knew where she was. Not after last night. "We can't do anything about that," she said, evading Ethan's questions. "But believe me, I take every precaution. You don't have to worry about me."

"But I do worry." His eyes deepened, and Grace could have sworn his gaze dropped to her mouth. She couldn't help remembering the way his lips had felt against hers. "What precautions do you take? Do you own a gun?"

She forced herself to hold his gaze. If she looked away, she would be admitting her discomfort. "Why do you ask?"

He shrugged. "It's a logical question. How are you going to catch Reardon if you don't have a weapon?"

Grace hesitated. "All right, yes, I have a gun. And before you ask, yes, I do know how to use it."

"Why does that not surprise me?" he muttered.

"I've also taken some self-defense courses." She wasn't sure why she added that except perhaps to let him know that if push came to shove, she could more than hold her own—against Reardon or anyone else.

"Somehow I think it may take more than a karate chop to bring down an assassin turned terrorist," he said dryly.

Grace almost allowed herself a smile. "That's what the gun is for."

Their gazes met. Something that might have been admiration glimmered in his eyes. "Still, I think you'd be safer, maybe we'd both be safer, if you moved in here with me. The security system is first rate, and besides—what was it you said the other day? You watch my back and I'll watch yours? It would be easier to do that if we were both in the same location."

She wasn't sure why his words surprised her so much. Maybe because when she'd hinted the same thing that first night, he'd made it all too clear that he had no intention of inviting her to stay in his home. Now, he was acting as if the idea was his and that it made all the sense in the world.

Grace knew she should leap at the chance to move in with him. Her main function in this whole operation was to get as close—and stay as close—as she could to Ethan so that when Reardon came after him, she would be ready. But now she had to wonder if proximity to Ethan would be such a good idea. Would she be able to remain alert and focused, or would her attraction to him make her careless? Reckless?

A shiver of awareness slipped over her.

"What's wrong?" he asked. "You know as well as I do it makes sense for us to stick together."

"Yes, I know, but—"

"But what?" His gaze became even more penetrating. "Are you afraid to move in here? Are you afraid of me?"

"No. Of course not," she said almost too quickly. "I'm not afraid of you."

"Then who are you afraid of? Reardon? Yourself, maybe?"

Grace felt a prickle of anger at his assumption. "Contrary to what you seem to think, I'm not the least bit worried that I won't be able to constrain myself in your presence."

Amusement flashed in his eyes. "Then what's the problem?"

"A little thing called appearances," she said. "What will your neighbors think if I move in here with you? You're still married, Ethan."

"Not anymore." He picked up the blue-backed legal document from his desk and handed it to her.

"What is this?" she asked doubtfully.

"A courier delivered it this morning. It's a final divorce decree." Something very subtle changed in his voice. "As of today, I'm a free man, Grace."

She took the document and skimmed the front page. "I don't know whether to offer my congratulations or my condolences," she tried to say lightly.

One dark brow arched. "You've met Pilar."

When Grace said nothing, he sat back in his chair and his eyes grew pensive. "It's strange to have proof of the ending of a marriage I don't even remember. But I guess this explains why Pilar was so eager to clean out the cash from the safe. A little something extra added to the settlement."

Grace handed the document back to him. "Have you heard from her?"

"No, and I don't expect to. Unless I see her tonight."

"Tonight?"

He paused. "A woman called me this morning. She said her name was Alina Torres. She talked for five minutes straight before I finally figured out she's Hun...my secretary."

"What did she want?" Grace asked.

"She reminded me that I have an invitation to some sort of charity benefit tonight at the Huntington Hotel. The proceeds will go directly into a building fund for a new children's wing at St. Mary's Hospital. According to Alina, I'd previously sent my regrets because I hadn't planned to be in town, but now that I'm back, she thought it would be a good idea for me to go. It seems I'm being presented with some sort of citation."

Grace's frown deepened. "Do you want to go?"

"Not particularly. But I've been thinking about what you said the other day. That the best way to draw out Reardon, or whoever wants to kill me, is to go about my normal business. The event tonight is written up in the paper today. If Reardon is keeping tabs on my activities, then he's bound to see it."

Ethan handed Grace a folded newspaper, and she read the headline.

Gala to Honor Dr. Ethan Hunter's Work with Underprivileged Children

He was right, she thought. A public event like this was just the sort of thing that would appeal to Reardon's macabre sense of humor. Still, she felt compelled to warn Ethan. "It could be dangerous. It would be very easy for Reardon to slip in with the crowd unnoticed. Especially since we don't even know what he looks like anymore."

"Isn't that the idea?" Ethan scowled. "I'm supposed to be a target, right?"

Yes. And the end justifies the means, Grace tried to tell herself. But even so, her first inclination was to try and talk him out of going. To somehow convince him to stay here, inside his fortress, where the locks and alarms just might keep him safe.

Out there, he *would* be a target. Bait for Reardon. And there was no guarantee Grace would be able to protect him. She wasn't even sure she could protect herself against Reardon.

She drew a long breath. "Is there any way you can get me an invitation?"

"I'm way ahead of you," he said. "Alina is sending over a ticket today, but you won't be seated on the dais with me."

"That's fine. It's better if I'm in the back, so I can keep an eye on the entire room."

He studied her for a moment, then his gaze dropped to the purse in her lap. "You'll be armed, I take it?"

She nodded. "Under the circumstances, I wouldn't leave home without it."

Their gazes held for what seemed an eternity, but in reality was hardly more than a second or two. But in the space of a heartbeat, Grace saw something in Ethan's eyes that she knew was mirrored in her own. Excitement. Anticipation. The thrill of the hunt.

They were suddenly two kindred spirits embarking on a perilous journey together. A journey that would be fraught with danger, intrigue and, because of the danger, passion.

Passion heightened by the knowledge that for them, tomorrow and regret might never come.

HE LIKED WHAT she was wearing. Her gown was midnight-blue, shot through with silver threads that shimmered in the light. She'd fastened a glittering clip in her hair that helped to glamorize the simple style, and her lips were tinted a dark, enticing red.

Ethan and Grace stood in the regal ballroom of the Huntington

Hotel, their images reflected by the dozens of gilt-framed mirrors lining the walls. Overhead, twinkling chandeliers cast a rich ambience over the hall, while the tinkle of champagne glasses and the sound of muted laughter further enhanced the mood.

Ivory candles flickered on round tables covered with fine linen and set with gold-rimmed china, sparkling crystal and silverware polished to a gleaming finish.

Ethan, gazing at Grace, thought that she had been created for candlelight. The soft, dancing light brought out the drama of her features, deepening the blue of her eyes and igniting the red highlights in her hair.

She met his gaze briefly, then turned away, but not before he'd seen the desire in her eyes, in the tantalizing way she parted her deep red lips. Ever since she'd met him earlier at his house before coming here, the sparks had been flying between them.

Ethan's gaze slipped over her, moving from those lips to the pale skin of her throat, and then lower, to the lush curves outlined by the silky fabric of her gown.

Impulsively, he leaned toward her and whispered against her ear, "If you're carrying a concealed weapon in that dress, you're incredibly creative. And I mean that as a compliment."

He saw her smile, and realized, with something of a shock, that he'd never seen her do so before. She was always so serious, so...intense. Was she that way in every facet of her life?

Grace held up a glittering evening bag. "Don't worry. I told you I'd come prepared."

"And you were so right." His gaze moved over her again, and he wondered if he'd ever been as aware of a woman's allure as he was Grace's tonight.

Don't, a little voice warned him. *Don't get involved in something you can't finish. You don't even know who the hell you are.*

The tuxedo he'd pulled from the closet earlier fit him well enough, but like all the other clothing he'd worn, it wasn't a perfect fit. Nothing in Ethan Hunter's life was a perfect fit, except maybe for the way he felt about Grace.

He'd known from the first there was something special about her, something...intriguing about her, but her appeal was far more than just the physical attraction he felt for her. He'd meant what he said yesterday. They were connected to each other. He just didn't know how or why.

He touched her arm and felt her tense. "Would you like some champagne?"

Grace's gaze focused on the tray of sparkling wine as a waiter hovered nearby. "Maybe later. I want to keep a clear head tonight." All around them, people were starting to find their seats. Grace nodded toward the dais at the front of the room. "I think they're waiting for you."

"Wish me luck."

For a split second, he considered leaning down and kissing her, but then thought better of it. But when he would have turned away, she caught his arm at the last moment. Her blue eyes deepened on him. "You don't have to do this. We can find another way to get Reardon."

He stared down at her. "I thought this is what you wanted, Grace." To catch Reardon at any price. And after that—what was it she'd told him that first night? She didn't give a damn what happened to Ethan.

Her eyes were very blue and very mysterious in the candlelight. Ethan couldn't quite define the emotion he saw simmering just beneath the surface, but the possibilities tightened the nerves in his stomach.

"Just be careful," she murmured. Then she turned and walked away.

GRACE SAT AT a table near the back of the mirrored ballroom with a group of doctors and hospital administrators. She absently listened to the conversation around her as she scanned the crowded hall, looking, not just for Reardon, but for the agents she knew Myra would have in place tonight.

As for Myra, Grace had spotted her earlier, looking wonderful in a black sequined gown that would probably cause Vince Connelly, their section chief back in Washington, to have a heart attack when he got her expense account.

Grace didn't know where Myra was seated, but as her gaze continued to scour the room, someone else caught her attention. Pilar, on Bob Kendall's arm, made an entrance that could only be called spectacular. Dressed in a strapless red evening gown, Ethan's ex-wife had every male head in the room turning to stare at her admiringly.

The man beside Grace muttered something she couldn't understand. He'd introduced himself earlier as an administrator at a local hospital, and Grace had told him that she was a "friend of a friend" who had wangled an invitation for the event.

She turned to him now and asked, "I'm sorry. What did you say?"

He shrugged and lifted his champagne glass to his lips. "Pilar Hunter and Robert Kendall are the last two people I'd expect to see at an event honoring Ethan Hunter."

"Do you know them?" Grace tried to act no more than mildly curious.

"Only by reputation," the man said. "And rumor."

"Rumor?"

"Bob Kendall used to be Ethan's business partner. The two of them started a practice right after completing their residency. After a while, Ethan became somewhat of a celebrity. He started believing his own press and decided he no longer needed a partner. Most of the assets were in his name, and he had the hot reputation. Kendall had been content to work in the background and let Ethan have all the glory, but when Kendall was forced to go it alone, he discovered that most of his patients weren't willing to follow him. He was all but ruined. It's taken him a long time to even come close to where he was before."

Grace listened to the story with interest. "So what is Dr. Kendall's connection with Pilar?"

The man beside her smiled knowingly. "I suspect she's become his consolation prize. And not a bad one at that, I must say."

FROM HIS PLACE on the dais, Ethan examined the crowd, wondering how many of his enemies had bothered to show up tonight. Or should he say, Ethan Hunter's enemies?

What would the people in the audience say if he stood up suddenly and proclaimed that he wasn't who they thought he was? That he, in fact, had no idea who he was.

But even if he really *was* Ethan Hunter, he was still a fraud. A doctor who used the cover of his good deeds in order to take blood money from criminals. A man willing to risk everything for the sake of greed.

Ethan let his gaze move to Grace. She sat near the back of the room, but he could see her face in the candlelight. She was talking with the man seated to her right, and for a moment, Ethan felt a terrible envy well up inside him. He wanted to be the man near her. He wanted to be the one draping his arm across the back of her chair so that he could lean toward her and talk to her in low tones that no one else could hear.

He wanted to whisper things to her that he'd never told anyone else.

But how could he be sure he hadn't? How could he know how many women had come before her? How many he'd claimed to love?

Ethan stared at her, letting a dozen different emotions wash over him. He told himself he had no right to feel that way about her, because if he was Ethan Hunter, he didn't want to drag her down with him. And if he was someone else…someone who had been pursued through the jungle by the Mexican authorities…

He stopped himself, not wanting to dwell on the mysteries hidden somewhere in his mind. Not wanting to consider how, if he wasn't Ethan Hunter, he had come to have the man's face.

But whoever the hell he was, Grace Donovan should remain off limits, he thought gloomily, even though he knew she was no innocent in all this. Earlier, when he'd left her to take his place on the dais, he'd turned to see her talking to a woman in a black evening gown. The conversation had been brief and by all appearances casual, two women bumping into each other and then lingering for a moment to make small talk, to perhaps compliment one another on their gowns.

But Ethan had sensed something else was going on. An uneasiness had come over him as he stood watching them. Then the older one had looked up and caught his eye. She'd smiled briefly, as if acknowledging his interest, before saying something to Grace. The two women parted, and Grace hadn't looked back as she'd walked across the room to find her table. But Ethan was almost certain the dark-haired woman had said something to Grace about him, and that she'd known he was watching her.

Now, as she sat talking to the man beside her, she seemed just as determined to avoid Ethan's stare. He watched her for a long time, all through dinner and afterward, until, with something of a start, he heard his name being called. He looked up to find that a man had taken the podium. He introduced himself as Dr. Frank Melburne, then proceeded to introduce to the audience everyone else on the dais.

The names were a jumble to Ethan. He didn't bother to memorize them as he surveyed the crowded room, searching for the face of a killer.

Melburne spoke for several minutes, elaborating on the need for a new children's wing at St. Mary's, and how Ethan's work with underprivileged children, both here and in Mexico, should be an inspiration to all of them. He held up the framed citation that was being presented to Ethan, then concluded by saying, "And now I'd like to present the man of the hour, Dr. Ethan Hunter. Ethan?"

Ethan got up and walked to the microphone. He had anticipated being asked to say something tonight, but he hadn't prepared a speech. What the hell was he supposed to say? He didn't remember any of his deeds, good or bad. He didn't even know who he was— only that he was a man hunted by a killer.

Ethan stood at the podium, gazing out at the audience. Here I am, Reardon, he thought. *Where the hell are you?*

"I'm very honored to be here tonight," he finally said, his gaze lingering for one split second on Grace. "But what if I were to tell all of you that I'm not the man you think I am?"

WHAT IS HE DOING? Grace wondered uneasily. She watched Ethan from a distance, realizing that if Reardon were going to make a move tonight, it would be now. Ethan was an open target, and Reardon would relish an audience. She tensed, her gaze darting around the room as she fingered the gold clasp of her evening bag.

From the podium, Ethan said, "I'm not the man you think I am because I don't deserve this award. I'm sure there are any number of my colleagues here tonight who are much more deserving than I."

"What a surprise," the man beside Grace muttered. "Humility is not something one expects from Ethan Hunter."

Grace ignored the comment, focusing her attention on the room instead, watching for any sudden move, for anyone who looked the least bit suspect. A rustle near the center of the room drew her attention, but for a moment, she couldn't tell what was going on. Then Pilar, her red dress glowing like a beacon, stood and lifted her champagne glass toward the dais.

"False modesty doesn't become you, Ethan." Her clear, lyrical voice rang out over the ballroom. "Why don't you say what you really think about all these people? What you've told me dozens of times in the past? There's not a man or woman in this room—" she swung her glass around, sloshing champagne over the rim "—who can touch your skill as a surgeon. What do you call all of them? Oh, yes. Meat cutters. But you...you're different, aren't you, Ethan? A genius who can change a mortal woman into a goddess. I'm proof of that, aren't I?"

She stood in the center of the room, spreading her arms as if inviting the whole world to look upon her beauty, to worship it. She didn't appear to be carrying a weapon, but Grace slipped open her purse, her hand closing around the SIG-Sauer pistol.

Pilar slowly lowered her arms. "But what do you do once you've created perfection? What is left then but to...destroy it?"

The room grew almost unbearably silent as everyone stared at Pilar. Grace found she couldn't tear her own gaze away. Something about the woman seemed almost...pathetic.

Out of the corner of Grace's eye, she could see Ethan still at the podium. He made no move to leave the dais or to silence his ex-wife. Like everyone else, his attention seemed to be riveted on her.

A man wearing a dark suit and an ear piece that immediately identified him as one of Myra's agents moved in toward Pilar. Before he could reached her, Bob Kendall jumped up and grabbed her arm. For a moment, the two of them almost scuffled, and then he said something to her that no one else could hear. Pilar resisted, then seemed to melt into Kendall. He put his arm around her and led her from the room.

Grace remained standing, adrenaline pumping through her veins. She combed the room, and saw Myra at the back near one of the colonnaded entrances, talking to Joe Huddleston, an agent Grace had known since Quantico. Huddleston turned and followed Pilar and Kendall out of the room. The agent who had been heading toward Pilar quietly faded into the background.

The room erupted into a cacophony of coughs and excited murmurs. Ethan remained at the podium. After a moment, he said, "Now that my fan club has left, we can get back to the business at hand."

Everyone remained stunned. Then there was a smattering of nervous laughter that took a few seconds to build. When everyone grew quiet again, the tension seemed to be somewhat relieved, and Ethan said with a shrug, "No matter what I say now, it's going to be anticlimactic, so let me just conclude by telling you how grateful—and how unworthy—I am to be receiving this honor."

Dr. Melburne, who had been standing behind Ethan on the dais, took his cue. He stepped forward, handing the citation to Ethan and shaking his hand before quickly retreating into the background, as if not wanting to diminish the honoree's glory.

Ethan turned to say something to Melburne, then bent to retrieve a paper he'd knocked from the podium. For an instant, Melburne stood framed in the spotlight, his expression one of shock as his hand went to his chest.

When he brought his hand away, Grace could see his fingers were dripping with blood. A crimson bloom spread across the front of his shirt as he fell backward onto the stage.

CHAPTER TEN

When he saw Dr. Melburne fall, Ethan automatically went into a crouch as he whipped the gun from underneath his jacket. As the ballroom exploded in pandemonium, Ethan's gaze probed the room, trying to locate Grace, but it was impossible. People were screaming and mauling each other to get to the exits.

Gun still drawn, Ethan knelt beside Melburne and spread open the man's jacket. The entire front of his shirt was red, and blood gurgled from his mouth. Ethan glanced up at the row of stunned doctors on the dais. They seemed incapable of moving.

"Someone help this man," Ethan shouted. "Hurry!"

The command spurred them into action. Two of the doctors crawled along the dais to where Melburne lay and began working on him. Ethan saw one of the others barking orders into a cell phone, presumably calling 911.

Taking one last look at the fallen man, Ethan jumped from the dais into the mob scene on the main floor of the ballroom. He still couldn't see Grace, but he knew he had to find her before Reardon did. She could be in every bit as much danger as Ethan.

THE MOMENT GRACE saw the blood on Melburne's fingers, she drew her weapon. A woman at the table screamed while the man who sat next to Grace gazed at her in shock. "What the hell—"

"I'm a federal agent," Grace said. "All of you get down and stay down."

Whether they believed her or not, they didn't hesitate to follow her orders. They all hit the floor, scrambling for a position beneath the table.

Grace glanced around. The room was in chaos as men and women either tried to flee or were scuttling beneath the tables. She couldn't locate Myra, Huddleston or any of the other agents. Turning back to the dais, she saw Ethan leap to the floor and then plunge into the terrified throng.

What the hell was he doing? He should be trying to find cover. That bullet had been meant for him. If he hadn't bent to retrieve the paper—

Grace shuddered. Weapon at her side, she started through the crowd toward the dais. The majority of the exodus was taking place at the back, where the colonnaded exits were located. Grace made her way to one side, hugging the wall as she tried to catch another glimpse of Ethan. If he'd been hit… If she had let him get hit…

To Grace's right, a closed door was skillfully hidden between two of the mirrors. Until she was almost upon it, the door looked like one of the intricately carved wall panels. Cautiously, Grace opened the panel and glanced down a long corridor. It appeared to be some sort of service hall with swinging doors that led to the kitchen and work areas.

Near one end of the corridor, a man in a white waiter's uniform cowered in a corner, his hands still clutching a circular tray of dirty dishes.

Grace started toward him. "I'm a federal agent," she said. "Don't move."

The man's expression was one of shock. He muttered something she couldn't understand. As Grace neared him, she saw that he was a middle-aged Hispanic with a swarthy complexion and dark, piercing eyes. A thin, black mustache traced the line of his upper lip, and a tiny gold hoop glinted from his left earlobe.

His eyes were wide with fright, and his hands trembled so badly, the crystal and cutlery made a jingling sound on the tray.

"Don't shoot, *por favor.*" His tone was pleading, his voice heavily accented as he stared at the gun in Grace's hand.

She took another step toward him. "Just stay calm," she advised. "*¿Habla usted inglés?*"

"*Sí. Un poquito.*"

"Are you alone here? Have you seen anyone else in this hallway?"

His dark eyes lifted to hers. He nodded.

"Where? *¿Dónde?*"

He pointed down the hallway behind her. Grace glanced over her shoulder.

She sensed more than saw the man move toward her. She whirled back around, but as she did so, he slammed the tray into her stomach as hard as he could. The breath flew from her lungs, and Grace stumbled backward, falling against the wall and sliding to the floor. The man took off running toward the end of the hallway. He looked back only once before disappearing around a corner, but in that split second, Grace could have sworn she saw recognition flash across his features.

"Stop!" she commanded, but her gun had slipped out of her hand when she fell. She scrambled toward it, but the man was gone.

Fighting for breath, Grace pulled herself up from the floor and started after him. The adrenaline rushing through her veins was almost like a drug high. Her head spun dizzily, but she didn't hesitate.

Why had he run from her?

The most logical explanation was that he was an illegal alien who didn't want to be deported, but as Grace rounded the corner where she had last seen him, another thought came to her.

If he was nothing more than an illegal alien, why had she glimpsed a look of recognition on his face?

By THIS TIME, hotel security had descended on the uproar in the ballroom. HPD would be close behind, and Ethan decided it probably wasn't a good idea to be seen with a loaded gun. He slipped the weapon beneath his jacket, into the waistband of his pants, as he hunted through the crowd. Where the hell was Grace?

Out of the corner of his eye, he caught a flash of midnight-blue, but when he turned, all he saw was his own reflection in one of the mirrors lining the side wall of the ballroom. Then one of the panels in the wall moved, and he realized it was a door that someone had just gone through. Ethan started across the room.

It seemed to take forever to tear his way through the hysterical crowd, but Ethan finally reached the side of the ballroom and located the door. He opened it and peered cautiously inside. Broken crystal and china lay strewn on the floor where a tray had been dropped.

Ethan started to back out of the hall, but then he noticed something else on the floor. An earring sparkling among the shards of broken glass. Grace's earring.

Drawing his gun, Ethan listened for a moment, then started down the corridor toward the sound of a closing door.

GRACE SHOVED OPEN a swinging door, and stepped into a damp, humid room with dim lighting.

The area was cavernous and eerie in its silence. Laundry bags hung from an overhead conveyor, and she stood motionless, searching for movement, the telltale swing of one of the bags as someone brushed by it.

Nothing moved. There wasn't so much as a whisper of sound.

As silently as she could, Grace reached down and removed her high heels. Then in stocking feet, she moved along the rows of laundry bags, searching for Reardon.

As she neared the end of one of the long aisles, the hair on the back of her neck rose. A breath of air touched her skin, as if someone had moved behind her.

Heart racing, Grace spun.

FOR A LONG moment, they stood staring at each other. Neither of them lowered their weapons as they faced off. Grace's gaze went to the gun in his hand, and one brow lifted ever so slightly. Then she raised a finger to her lips, warning Ethan to be silent. She motioned for him to take the right side of the room while she turned to search the left.

He hesitated. Something told him he wasn't used to following orders, that he was the one who was usually in control of a situation like this. But under the circumstances, he couldn't find fault with Grace's logic. Split up. Circle the room. Force Reardon, or whomever she had cornered, out into the open.

Ethan made his way through the mountain of laundry bags stacked in bins along the side of the room. There were any number of hiding places, and flushing out their quarry might not be so easy. But just as the thought occurred to him, Ethan caught sight of something in one of the bins. A flash of black among all the white linen.

He eased forward, until he was directly in front of the bin. The black he'd seen was the arm of someone's tuxedo jacket, but he didn't think it belonged to Reardon. Someone was still wearing the jacket, and a crimson stain was spreading slowly over the soiled laundry hiding the body.

Silently, Ethan unearthed the victim. He didn't recognize the man, but he knew the ear piece the man still wore indicated a cop of some kind. Obviously, he and Grace weren't the only ones on Reardon's trail.

He wondered who the victim was, but he didn't take time to search for his ID. The bullet hole through the man's neck was enough for Ethan.

He had to find Grace.

THE ECHO OF her heartbeat sounded deafening to Grace. She wondered if Reardon could hear it. Wondered if he was taking pleasure from it.

The damp humidity in the laundry room was almost stifling. Grace found she had a hard time breathing. Sweat trickled down the side of her face, but she didn't waste a motion on swiping it away. She couldn't let down her guard for even a second.

At the far end of the room, away from the entrance where she'd come in, a sound finally came to Grace. At first, she wondered if it might be Ethan, but then as she stood listening, she identified the creak and rumble of an elevator car sliding down the cable.

Grace whirled and took off toward the sound. She didn't bother now to try and conceal her movements. If Reardon made it inside the elevator before she could get to him—

She fought her way out of the suspended laundry bags just in time to see the heavy metal doors sliding closed. Grace lunged toward the elevator, jamming the button with the heel of her hand so hard, pain ripped all the way up to her elbow. Ignoring the pain, she tried to pry open the doors, but it was no use. The car began to ascend.

ETHAN EMERGED from the forest of laundry in time to see Grace pound the elevator door in frustration. When she heard him approach, she looked around, wild-eyed and desperate.

"The stairs," she said hoarsely. "Come on. We have to find him."

She didn't wait to see if Ethan followed her, but turned and raced through the door, retracing their steps down the corridor to a door marked Stairs.

He wondered why he didn't try to reason with her, why he didn't try to stop her from pursuing a cold-blooded killer. She was in danger, but it never occurred to Ethan to grab Grace and hold her back. She was too competent. Too coldly determined, and besides. She had a gun. If he tried to stop her now, she might just use it on him.

Ethan caught her on the stairs and overtook her. She wouldn't care for that, he thought fleetingly, but he was still a man, still had enough of the protective instinct to want to go first and blaze the trail. If he couldn't take out Trevor Reardon, Ethan could at least do enough damage so that Grace would have a chance.

They burst through the stairwell door on the second level. Two uniformed maids stood in the hallway chatting beside their carts. They looked up in surprise and then in terror when they saw the weapons.

"The service elevator," Ethan said. "Where is it?"

Neither of them said anything, but one of them pointed to the far end of the corridor. Grace darted past Ethan, and he swore, wishing she'd stay behind him.

They were only halfway down the hall when they heard the elevator doors swish open. Grace gasped in dismay and lunged forward, throwing herself at the elevator and managing just barely to get her fingers between the doors.

Ethan put his hands above hers, and as the doors yielded to their pressure, both Grace and Ethan jumped back and raised their weapons.

The doors slid open, but the car was empty except for a white, blood-stained waiter's coat lying on the floor.

GRACE SPUN, HER gaze frantically searching the hall. But she knew Reardon hadn't gotten off on this floor because he'd never been in the elevator to begin with. She'd let herself fall for the oldest trick in the book.

She whirled back to the elevator and started to step inside, but Ethan caught her arm. She flung off his hand. "What are you doing? He's still in the laundry. We have to get back down there."

Ethan put away his gun. "He's gone, Grace."

"You don't know that," she said angrily. "He may still be down there. You don't have to come with me, but I'm going back. I'll search every inch of that place, look in every laundry bag down there if I have to, but I'll find him. He won't get away. I won't let him—" She stopped herself as she realized how she must sound to Ethan. How she must look. Like a woman completely out of control.

And that's exactly how she felt. Reardon had thwarted her again. Made her act without thinking.

Grace forced herself to step out of the elevator, to take a long, deep breath. Ethan was still staring down at her, and the look on his face was not one Grace thought she could easily forget. His eyes were dark and narrowed, his mouth set in a grim, forbidding line. She found herself shivering and wondering about the outcome when and if Ethan Hunter and Trevor Reardon ever came face to face.

Ethan wasn't like any doctor she'd ever known before, that was for damn sure.

She said almost calmly, "Where did you get the gun?"

He shrugged, but his gaze darkened. "I found it in the safe at the house. I thought it might be useful tonight."

Grace was tempted to give him the old lecture about weapons in the hands of amateurs, but she was suddenly too weary. And besides, she had a feeling Ethan Hunter could handle a gun as effectively as he could wield a scalpel. She was the last person to underestimate him.

She slipped her own gun back inside her purse. "I guess you're right. Reardon's probably long gone by now."

"He left a calling card in the laundry," Ethan said. "Or at least someone did. There's a man with a bullet through his neck down there. I think he's a cop."

"My God," Grace whispered. Was he one of Myra's agents? Someone Grace knew?

She turned back to the elevator. "We'd better get back down there. Maybe you can help him."

Ethan caught her arm. "Nobody can help him, Grace. He's dead."

She hesitated. "We still have to call someone. We can't just leave him down there."

"I know exactly what we have to do."

Grace glanced up at him. Something in his voice alarmed her. "What do you mean?"

Ethan's expression turned grim. "We were fools to think we could do this alone. Reardon is a killer. A master criminal who has escaped from prison twice. And now at least three people are dead because he's after me. First Amy, then Melburne, and now the man downstairs. How many more people have to die because of me?"

The guilt in his eyes was not an easy thing to witness. Grace said urgently, "This isn't your fault. You didn't kill those people."

"That's not what you said the first night I met you." His voice hardened with disgust. "You said I had a part in Amy's death. And if everything you suspect is true, you were right."

Grace stared helplessly at Ethan. She didn't know what to say to him.

He put his hands on her shoulders, gazing down into her eyes. For the longest moment, they stayed that way as a myriad of emotions flashed across his face. Then he said, "I can't risk your life to save my own skin, Grace. I won't. I'm calling Pope and telling him everything. I'm going to end this tonight. I don't care what happens to me, but we have to get the police involved. Now."

His words blew Grace away. She couldn't believe he was willing to subject himself to a police investigation, to face a prison sentence in order to keep her safe from Reardon.

How long had it been since someone had cared about her that much? Since she had allowed anyone to care about her?

Until that moment, Grace hadn't realized just how lonely she'd been all these years. How empty her life had become.

Now that knowledge was almost like a physical ache inside her.

She closed her eyes briefly, making a decision that she knew might cost her everything. When she spoke, she heard her voice quiver with emotion. "You don't have to call anyone," she told Ethan. "I am the police."

CHAPTER ELEVEN

Back at Ethan's house, Grace stood at the second-story window, staring out. From her vantage, she could see over the brick wall surrounding the grounds to the street beyond where an unmarked car was parked at the curb. The neighborhood sparkled with lights, but the dark sedan blended into the shadows cast by the water oaks lining the sidewalk.

In the opposite direction, where two streets intersected and formed a tiny parklike area in the median, a man stood smoking in the dark. Grace could see the glowing tip of his cigarette lift and fall.

Though from this distance, she couldn't see his radio or his weapon, she knew he would have both, and that he would remain in constant communication with Myra and with the man in the car. After tonight, the operation had suddenly become personal to every agent and support personnel working the case. Joe Huddleston, a well-liked and respected agent assigned to the field office here in Houston, had been killed. Murdered in cold blood, his body stuffed down a laundry chute at the hotel like so much dirty linen.

Grace had known Joe for years. They'd gone through training together at Quantico. He was one of the few agents in the FBI who knew her entire story. And now he was dead. Because of Reardon.

For a moment, Grace's hatred threatened to consume her, but she forced herself to stand back, take a breath, look at everything logically. There would be time enough later to mourn Joe's death. For now, she had to remain focused.

Could she be absolutely sure that Reardon was responsible for Joe's death? Was Reardon the man she'd seen in the corridor of the hotel? If so, his disguise—whether temporary or permanent—had been nothing short of miraculous.

Grace's mind went back over the events of the evening. The last time she'd seen Huddleston was when he'd followed Pilar and Kendall out of the ballroom. Was it possible that Pilar's little scene had been a diversion? Was she or Kendall—or perhaps both of them—responsible for the shot that had been meant for Ethan tonight? Had they killed Joe Huddleston?

Grace knew that Myra had someone working on that angle even now, but the older agent was still concentrating most of her efforts on Reardon.

When Grace had contacted her earlier, before leaving the hotel, and told her what she planned to do, Myra had been against it. "You can't tell him the truth, Grace. What if he runs?"

"I don't think he will," Grace had argued. "And besides, I don't have a choice. If I don't tell him the truth, he's going to the police. The last thing we need is to get HPD involved any more than they already are."

She'd finally managed to placate Myra, but Grace knew Ethan wouldn't be quite as easy to appease. She wouldn't soon forget the look on his face when she'd told him she was the police. A federal agent, she'd barely managed to get out before the hotel security and several HPD officers had descended upon them in the corridor.

Grace wasn't sure why, but Ethan hadn't said anything to the authorities about what she'd told him. Instead, he'd let her take the lead, and when it had come time for him to give a statement, he hadn't said or done anything to give her away. That action, as much as anything else, made Grace realize how much he had come to trust her. How much she owed him.

And now it was time to pay the piper, she thought, turning away from the window. Ethan, who had gone straight to the kitchen to mix himself a drink when they'd gotten home, would want an explanation, and she had better be convincing. For more reasons than one.

Across the room, Simon moved restlessly on his perch. Grace drifted over to him and stood staring at him for a moment.

"What did you mean yesterday when you said, 'I say we just the kill the bastard and be done with it'?" she asked him.

The bird tilted his head and squawked, "They're not real."

"Forget about that," Grace said impatiently. "We're way beyond that now."

The bird strutted along his perch. "Book him, Dano!"

For God's sake, Grace thought. The bird was a walking, talking advertisement for daytime TV.

"Who do you think I am, Jack Lord?" she muttered.

"That's a good question," Ethan said. She turned to find him standing behind her, a drink in each hand. "Who are you, Grace?"

She moistened her lips. "I told you earlier. I'm a federal agent."

"FBI."

She nodded. "That's right."

"Is your name really Grace Donovan?"

"Yes."

"And I'm supposed to believe this new story? Accept your word for everything?"

"I can show you my ID and my badge if you like."

"Don't bother. I'm sure they can be faked just like business cards. And sisters." He offered her one of the drinks. When Grace declined, he said bitterly, "Oh, that's right. You're still on the job, aren't you?"

"Look." She ran her fingers through her bangs, wondering how she could possibly explain her motives in a way that would make him understand. Make him forgive her. "I'm sorry I didn't tell you the truth from the start. But I couldn't. It wasn't my call to make."

His gaze narrowed on her. "So you were just following orders?"

She hesitated. It would be easy to blame everything on her superiors, but the truth was, the deception had been her idea. Hers and hers alone.

She drew a long breath and released it. "Maybe I should start from the first."

"Maybe you should," he agreed. He downed one of the drinks and set the empty glass aside before turning back to her. "I'm listening."

Grace turned and walked back to the windows that looked out upon the street. The surveillance was still in place, but she wondered why that knowledge didn't alleviate the uneasiness growing inside her. After she told Ethan the truth, would he allow her to stay? Would he accept her protection?

"Three days before Amy Cole was murdered, she walked into the Federal Building here in Houston and asked to speak to an FBI agent. She said it was urgent. The man she eventually talked to was Joe Huddleston.''

She sensed rather than saw Ethan's surprise. ''The agent who was killed tonight?''

Grace nodded. ''Joe and I went through training at Quantico together. We'd kept in touch over the years. He knew that my superior in Washington was coordinating efforts to locate Trevor Reardon. After he talked to Amy, he got in touch with us immediately.''

''What did Amy tell him?'' Ethan came to stand beside her at the window.

''She said that her employer, Dr. Ethan Hunter, the renowned plastic surgeon, was using his clinic in Mexico to operate on criminals' faces for money.''

''What proof did she offer?''

Grace paused. ''None. All she had were suspicions.''

He made a sudden, angry movement that startled Grace. ''Are you telling me you have no proof that anything illegal went down? This whole thing has been based on one woman's suspicions?''

''I know how that must make you feel, but—''

''Oh, I don't think you do,'' he said coldly. ''I don't think you have any idea how I feel at this moment.''

''You have every right to be angry,'' Grace said, wishing his eyes didn't look quite so dark and quite so deadly. ''But let me finish before you start jumping to conclusions yourself.''

He let that one pass. He turned back and stared out the window with a brooding frown.

''Amy showed Joe Huddleston a picture she'd clipped from the newspaper of Trevor Reardon. It was the same one I showed you. She said that she was almost certain she'd seen Reardon talking with Dr. Hunter...with you...a few months ago at the Mexican clinic.''

Ethan glanced at her, his gaze still hard. ''Go on.''

''Like I said before, Joe knew my superior, Myra Temple, was coordinating the Bureau's efforts to track down Reardon. After Amy left, he called me and told me what had happened. When I briefed Myra, she agreed that we needed to come down here and talk to Amy ourselves, see if her story held water. We didn't discount the possibility that she could have been delusional, or that she was a

rejected mistress out for revenge. We wanted to consider every possibility.

"And after talking with her, both Myra and I believed her. We
both thought she was on to something. Myra and I started working
with the field office here in Houston to set up a surveillance and
possibly a sting if it was necessary to get your cooperation."

He spared her a brief glance. "Just what were you willing to do
to *get* my cooperation?"

Grace shrugged. "Whatever it took."

A look she couldn't define flashed across his face. "I accused
you once of being cold, remember?"

"Yes. And you were right." She forced herself to shrug. "I am
cold. Ruthless. I'll do whatever it takes to catch Trevor Reardon."

Ethan's gaze hardened on her. "Why does it mean so much to
you?"

Grace tried to suppress a shudder. She wanted to be honest with
Ethan, but there were some things she'd never told anyone. Some
things she still couldn't talk about. "He's a killer. A cold-blooded
murderer. I don't want anyone else to die because of him."

"And that's all it is?" Ethan's voice had a strange quality that
Grace had never heard before.

She shivered again. "Isn't that enough?"

He fell silent for a moment, contemplating everything she'd told
him. Then he said, "What went wrong? Why is Amy Cole dead?"

Grace released a long breath. "After talking with her, we didn't
expect you back in the country for at least two weeks. We thought
we had plenty of time to set everything up, get everyone in place
so that no one would get hurt. But evidently Amy got cold feet.
She may even have found out about your impending divorce and
then had second thoughts about what she'd done to you.

"When she found out you were coming back early, I think she
got in touch with you and warned you that the Feds would be
waiting for you. We had the airport staked out, along with your
house and Amy's apartment. We thought we had it all covered, at
least as best we could with such short notice, but then you chartered
a plane and flew into a private airfield. We think you somehow
contacted Amy, either by cell phone or through a neighbor, and the
two of you made plans to meet at the clinic, possibly to get rid of

incriminating evidence. Amy somehow managed to slip through our surveillance, and then hours later, she turned up dead.''

Grace glanced up and saw Ethan's reflection in the window. He was staring at her, and the look on his face...the expression in his eyes unnerved her.

"That still doesn't tell me what happened to her," he said slowly. "Unless you're implying that I killed her.''

Grace spun toward him. "No, that's not what I think. That's not what any of us think. Trevor Reardon followed you, probably all the way from Mexico. He ambushed you at the clinic and made it look like you'd stumbled upon a robbery, an addict looking for drugs. I never thought you killed Amy," Grace repeated. Somehow she had to make him believe that. She had to at least give him that.

"How did you know to go to the clinic?" he asked.

Grace shrugged. "That was purely a hunch. What I told you before was true—I was supposed to meet Amy that night. When she didn't show and I found out she'd slipped out of her apartment unseen, I knew I had to find her. I knew she could be in danger. So I went to the clinic, almost as a last measure. When I found out what had happened, I knew I couldn't tell the police who I really was. The homicide was their jurisdiction, and if they found out Amy had been working with the FBI, we would have had to bring them in on the case. It would have tipped off Reardon that we were on to him, and so I told them I was Amy's sister."

Ethan cocked a dark brow, staring down at her. "You didn't think she might have a real sister who would come forward and dispute you?''

"I knew she didn't. She'd already told me she had no one, and that she didn't like to talk about her past. I felt the cover would be reasonably secure.''

"And so then you decided to approach me." Ethan turned back to the window. "I still don't understand why you didn't tell me the truth. Wouldn't that have been simpler?''

"Maybe," Grace agreed. "But I couldn't take that chance. I had no reason to believe you'd be willing to cooperate. Why would you?''

"I don't know," he said flippantly. "To save my life, maybe? Because it would have been the decent thing to do?''

Grace said nothing.

After a moment, Ethan said, "I guess my amnesia was a bonus for you then."

She didn't bother to deny it. "It made you vulnerable. You couldn't go to the police without incriminating yourself. And without a memory, without knowing who wanted you dead, you couldn't protect yourself, either. I made sure you had to turn to me."

He winced at that. "Tell me something, Grace. How far were you willing to go to get my cooperation?"

"I already told you. Whatever was necessary."

"Did that include this?" He turned suddenly and grabbed her shoulders, forcing her to face him. His eyes were dark and turbulent, his expression like an icy mask. When he kissed her, Grace's first instinct was to push him away, to somehow try and regain control of the situation.

But a split second later, she felt the ice inside him begin to melt. She knew, instinctively, what he wanted at that moment. What he needed.

She kissed him back with every ounce of her strength. With every fiber of her being. With every emotion that raged through her mind and body and soul.

When he finally pulled away, they both stood shaken by the experience. Grace's knees trembled weakly, but she forced herself to remain steady, to stare up at him as openly and honestly as she dared.

"That was never a lie," she finally whispered. "The way I feel about you is something I never counted on."

His hands were still on her shoulders. He stared down at her for a long time, his breathing ragged. "How do you feel?"

Grace's heart pounded against her chest. It had been a long time since she'd had a conversation like this. Since she had felt this exposed. "It's like you said once. We're connected somehow. I don't understand it, but…it's more than just attraction. It's as if…"

"We're meant for each other," he said.

Grace closed her eyes. "But I *can't* feel that way. I can't let my emotions get in my way. I can't forget who I am or what I have to do. And I can't forget who you are, either."

"Who I am." His hands dropped from her shoulders and he turned and walked away from her.

Grace hesitated, unsure whether or not to follow him. But he didn't go far. He walked to the center of the room and stood looking around, as if he suddenly realized he didn't belong there.

For a long moment, neither of them said anything, then he turned to her. His gaze was shadowed with an emotion that made Grace's breath quicken. "I'm not the man you think I am."

"You've said that before." She moved across the room toward him. "And I think I understand why you feel that way. It's like there're two sides of you. One man operates on criminals' faces for money, while the other can change monsters into angels. That man can give children without hope a whole new life. That's the man you really are, Ethan. That's the man you remember. The other one doesn't seem real to you because you don't want to be him."

Uncertainty flickered in his eyes. Then his gaze darkened again. "That's a rather whimsical explanation for an FBI agent, Grace. I don't think you buy it any more than I do."

"You're wrong. I do believe it." On impulse, Grace put a hand on his sleeve, felt him tense at her touch. "I know there's something fine and decent about you. I know there's goodness in you, just like there's darkness." She paused, searching for the right words. "Who knows what brings that darkness to the surface, but I think we all have the capacity for it. I think there's darkness in all of us."

His brow lifted at that. "Even you?"

She gave a bitter little laugh. "Maybe even especially me. I'm not sure I'm in any position to judge you, no matter what you've done."

He didn't seem to hear her. He'd turned away and walked back over to the window to stare out. After a bit, he said, "It's been a long day and I'm beat. We can talk about this in the morning, decide what to do then."

Grace had brought a bag over earlier before they'd gone to the Huntington, but after her confession, she wasn't sure he'd let her stay. But it appeared now that he'd accepted her presence, and for the time being at least, wasn't going to ask her to leave. Grace was glad. She would hate to have to force the issue now.

"That's probably a good idea," she agreed. "We could both use some rest. I'll see you in the morning."

She waited for him to turn and acknowledge her leaving, but he remained at the window, his back to her. He didn't even say goodnight, and after a moment, Grace turned and left the room.

A FEDERAL AGENT. A cop.

Ethan should have known. And maybe a part of him had known. He couldn't say her revelation had come as that much of a shock. He'd always known there was something Grace wasn't telling him. That there was more to her than a grieving sister.

No wonder she had seemed so confident in her ability to deal with Trevor Reardon. She was trained to deal with the likes of him.

Ethan thought about that for a moment. How did that make him feel? he wondered. Knowing that Grace was an agent who had not only been sent here to find Reardon, but to also protect Ethan in the process. How did he feel about his life being put in a woman's hands? In Grace's hands?

He tried to muster up the requisite resentment, but it wasn't in him. There were too many other things about the situation that troubled him more. The fact that she had lied to him, deceived him into believing she was Amy's sister. The fact that those lies had seemed so easy for Grace.

He'd been a means to an end for her. It was as simple as that.

Oh, he knew she was attracted to him. She couldn't hide it and she hadn't bothered to deny it. But her desire to find Trevor Reardon far exceeded her desire for Ethan, and that fact bothered him the most. She was a consummate professional before she was a woman, and Ethan knew that situation wasn't likely to change any time soon. At least not for him.

He remembered the way her eyes had burned with an inner fire when she'd first told him about Reardon, and an uneasiness Ethan couldn't explain swept over him.

What was it about Reardon that made Grace so passionate in her hatred of him, that made her almost careless in her pursuit of him?

What had made this assignment so personal for her?

Ethan knew the answer even before the question had completely formed in his mind, and a sick feeling rose in his throat as he stood staring out into the darkness.

GRACE STOOD WRAPPED in a towel at the bathroom mirror as she blow-dried her short hair. Afterward, she gazed at her reflection for a long time, wondering if she had done the right thing by telling Ethan as much as she had. But she hadn't really had a choice. Once he'd decided to go to the police with the story, she'd had to tell him the truth, and trust that he would continue to cooperate with her.

But why should he? She'd lied to him, deceived him at every possible turn. Why would he want anything more to do with her?

The end may have justified the means, but right now, Grace was having a hard time dealing with her conscience. She had deliberately put Ethan's life on the line in order to capture Reardon, and she hadn't even had the decency to tell him why. At least not completely.

Her past was something Grace had never told anyone. She couldn't even talk about it with Myra. What Trevor Reardon had done to her and her family was too personal, and Grace had never gotten over the guilt, let alone the shame.

She hadn't told Ethan because she hadn't wanted to see the disgust in his eyes over what she had done.

Grace didn't want to see it in her own eyes, either. She turned away from the mirror and walked into the guest bedroom where she'd left her suitcase earlier. Digging through the contents, she pulled out a pair of white silk pajamas and put them on. As she was turning down the bed, the door behind her opened.

Grace grabbed her gun from the top of the nightstand, going instantly into a crouch while, with a two-handed grip, she swung the weapon toward the door.

Ethan stood just inside the room, his gaze going first to the gun in her hand, then to her face. He wore jeans, no shirt, and his dark hair glinted with moisture, as if he'd just come from the shower. Grace's hand trembled on the weapon as she stared at him, her awareness of him surging over her in a crest of heat.

As he walked into the room, she hesitated, then slowly lowered the weapon. She placed it on the nightstand behind her.

Ethan came over and stood in front of her. He didn't touch her, but his nearness made Grace's breath quicken. The look on his face made her heart pound inside her. She was tempted to put her hands on his bare chest, to feel the hardness beneath her fingers.

"You're her, aren't you?"

Grace stared up at him as a shock wave rolled over her. "What are you talking about?"

"The FBI agent's daughter you told me about. The only one in his family who didn't get killed in the fire. The one Trevor Reardon came back for. You're her."

She turned away, but he put his hands on her arms, forcing her to face him. She didn't want to. She didn't want to see the look in his eyes.

"Why didn't you tell me?" he demanded.

"I couldn't. After all these years, it's still too…painful." And she still couldn't look at him.

He put one hand under her chin, tilting her head up so that she had no choice but to meet his gaze. What she saw in his eyes wasn't disgust. It was another emotion that took Grace's breath away.

"What happened that night?" he asked softly.

"Please." Her eyes closed briefly. "I can't talk about it. I've never talked about it."

"Don't you think it's time you did?"

"It's too personal." She put trembling fingertips to her lips. "I don't think I *can* tell you. I don't think I want you to know."

"You said earlier that you weren't in any position to judge me. That goes both ways, Grace."

When she looked up at him, his eyes were so dark and so haunted, she thought for a moment she was staring at her own reflection. She took a step back from him, and he let her go.

He walked to the window to stare out into the darkness. "I think I may be exactly the person you need to talk to." There was something about his voice that was different.

Grace shivered, staring as his profile. After a moment, she said, "My father was the agent who arrested Reardon. The FBI had been after him for a long time, years. After he left the military, he became a killer for hire, an assassin at first, taking out government officials in foreign countries and certain high-powered businessmen for money. Then he fell in with some zealots in the Middle East and discovered they were willing to pay big bucks to someone with his expertise to carry out their dirty work. The notoriety appealed to Reardon, as did the money. And the killings.''

She paused, trying to get her thoughts in order. Trying to dispel the tormented images twisting and turning in her mind. "My father tracked him for over two years and was finally able to arrest him. But before Reardon could stand trial, he escaped. I'd heard my father mention his name at the time of the arrest, but he never told us about Reardon's escape. I guess he didn't want to worry us, and I don't think he really believed Reardon would come after him. He thought Reardon would flee the country, but my father underestimated Reardon's obsession with order, with tying up loose ends."

Ethan glanced at her then, but he still said nothing.

Grace took a long breath and continued. "He got into our house one day when everyone was gone and planted a bomb. He rigged all the doors and windows with explosive devices that were wired in to the main timer. When he detonated the bomb, the other devices were then triggered to explode if anyone tried to open the doors or windows from the inside or the out. It was an unbelievably intricate design and one he'd used before, on an Italian businessman's home several years before that. When the bomb exploded, the whole house erupted into flames. My mother and father were on the ground level, but my sister was trapped upstairs. I saw her at the window. Her hair and clothes were on fire—''

Grace broke off abruptly as the images bombarded her. Ethan had turned to face her, but he didn't move toward her. "I can't imagine what that must have been like for you.''

Grace shrugged. "No one can. I arrived right after the first bomb exploded, but the fire spread so fast, they didn't have a chance. The booby-trapped doors and windows were almost overkill.''

"Where were you?'' Ethan finally asked. It was the question Grace had been dreading.

She squeezed her eyes shut as if she could somehow stop the screams inside her head. "I was with him. I was with Trevor Reardon.'' She put her hands to her face and turned her back to Ethan.

The room was so quiet, Grace could hear the blood pounding in

her ears. She sensed Ethan's shock, the deep revulsion he must feel
for what she'd just told him.

After a moment of stunned silence, she felt his hands on her
wrists, pulling her hands away from her face. "Tell me the rest,"
he commanded softly.

Grace shuddered. "I'd met him a few days before the fire. I
realized afterward that he'd sought me out. It was all part of his
game, the ultimate way to get back at my father, and I was so
gullible. So *stupid*. I fell for everything he told me because I wanted
to believe an older, sophisticated man could find me special and
desirable. He seduced me," she said, trying to swallow past the
nausea that rose in her throat. "But I let him. I *wanted* it."

When she would have turned away, Ethan clung to her hands.
"How old were you?"

"Old enough to know better."

"How old?"

She drew a long breath. "Seventeen."

"You were a kid, Grace. You were no match for Reardon."

"But I should have known," she said in anguish. "I should have
known who he was, what he planned to do. I should have been able
to stop him."

A tear slid down her face, the drop of moisture as foreign to her
as the look of compassion in Ethan's eyes. Releasing one of her
hands, he wiped the tear away with his fingertip, the gesture so
gentle and so caring that Grace felt more tears, deeper tears rising
inside her. With sheer force of will, she blinked them back.

"You've carried this guilt inside you all these years," Ethan said,
staring down at her. "Don't you think it's time to let it go? Don't
you think it's time to forgive yourself for having once been young
and naive?"

"I didn't just go out and skip school," she said almost angrily.
"I didn't stay out past my curfew. My whole family was killed
while I—"

"There was nothing you could have done to stop Reardon. Deep
down inside, you have to know that. He would have done what he
did whether you had been with him or not. The only difference was,
you stayed alive. And I think that's what you haven't been able to
forgive yourself for."

Grace bowed her head, overcome with emotion. She couldn't say a word, couldn't deny or acknowledge what he was saying. All she could do was let him reach for her gently and draw her into the warm circle of his arms.

A part of her wanted to resist, because she knew she was vulnerable tonight in a way she hadn't been in years. She needed Ethan's arms around her more desperately than she would ever have thought possible. And that scared her. Terrified her.

Neither of them said anything for a very long time. They stood motionless, Ethan's arms around her while Grace battled the demons inside her that had threatened to destroy her for years.

After a while, the demons didn't seem quite so powerful. The images inside her mind weren't quite so strong. Grace lifted her face to Ethan's. "I've never told anyone what happened back then. There are those in the Bureau who know. Myra Temple, the woman who saved my life when Reardon came back for me, and Joe Huddleston. A few others who knew because they were around when it happened. But I've never been able to tell anyone else. I've never trusted anyone enough."

Something flashed in Ethan's eyes, an emotion so dark, Grace shivered. "I hope you've done the right thing telling me."

She pulled back a little to stare up at him. "I don't understand."

He hesitated. "I hope I'm worthy of your trust."

Grace knew instantly what he meant. He was no longer thinking about what she'd told him, but about his own past. About the things he'd done. The demons he now had to battle.

She reached up and touched his face with her fingertips. "I meant what I said earlier. I know there's goodness in you. And now you know about the darkness in me. Does it change the way you feel?"

He almost smiled at that. "If anything, it only strengthens the bond between us. It makes me want you even more."

The fire in his eyes was suddenly an emotion Grace did recognize. Passion. The powerful kind. The reckless kind. The kind that matched the slow heat building inside her.

With a sense of inevitability that was almost stunning, Grace watched as he lowered his head toward hers. Their gazes clung for a long, scorching moment before his lips touched hers. Grace's eyes drifted closed as a shudder ripped through her. Ethan's kiss was powerful, electric, breathtaking. An explosion of desire that made her knees grow weak and her heartbeat thunder.

This was not attraction, she thought weakly. This was not chemistry. This was…destiny. This was a moment that had to be, no matter what the consequences.

She wrapped her arms around his neck and threaded her fingers through his hair. Ethan's own hands splayed against her back, holding her closely for a moment before starting to move over her in slow, deliberate strokes. Her back, her hips, her breasts, and then upward to cup her face. He broke the kiss to whisper against her mouth, ''God, Grace…''

She couldn't have put it more eloquently herself. She pulled him to her, kissing him with an urgency that left them both gasping for breath. He pushed her back on the bed and moved over her, his fingers ripping loose the buttons on her pajamas so they could lay skin to skin. Heartbeat to heartbeat.

Grace shivered as his body molded to hers, as his mouth ground into hers. She accepted the assault, welcomed it. Wanted more of it.

They rolled over, and Grace was suddenly on top, staring down at him. His eyes were heavy-lidded and seductive, his mouth a sensuous invitation. She kissed the scar above his brow, his temple, then skimmed along the side of his face to tease his earlobe with her tongue.

He groaned and shuddered as she pressed her body into his and moved against him. After a few moments, he rolled them again, and now he was back on top, back in charge, and Grace was pliant beneath him. And then he did to her exactly what she had done to him.

The teasing became almost unbearable. The buildup almost the release. Grace's fingers moved to the buttons at the front of his jeans, but to her surprise, his hand closed over hers, stopping her.

His lips hovered over hers, a breathless heartbeat away. Then he lifted himself, so that for a moment they were staring into each other's eyes. His gaze was still clouded with passion, intense with longing, but another emotion simmered just beneath the surface. An emotion that made Grace almost gasp when she saw it.

Regret. Maybe even guilt.

She lay staring up at him, helpless with her own desire.

"I can't do this," he said.

A rush of humiliation swept over her. "What?"

He lifted himself off her and sat on the edge of the bed, his back to her. He put his hands to his face and scrubbed. "I can't do this to you."

Grace sat up, too, wrapping her pajama top around her and drawing her knees up to her chest. She rested her cheek on her knees, saying nothing. Embarrassment heated her skin, but it was a remorse that wasn't pure because even in the face of rejection, she still wanted him. Her body still quivered with need.

"I told you before that I'm not the man you think I am." He turned his head slightly, so that she could see a little of his profile. "I deliberately let you misunderstand what I meant. You think there're two sides to my personality—a good one and a dark one. And now that I've lost my memory, the good one is winning out. But you're wrong, Grace. Dead wrong."

He turned on the bed to face her, and Grace lifted her head to stare at him. "What do you mean?"

"I'm not Ethan Hunter."

Grace sat up, forgetting about the torn-away buttons on her top. The silk parted, and for just an instant, she saw Ethan's gaze waver. Then he glanced away, running a hand through his dark hair. "I'm not Dr. Ethan Hunter," he repeated.

Grace said breathlessly, "If you're not Ethan Hunter, then who are you?"

He shrugged. "I don't know. I don't even know *what* I am. What I may have done. When I woke up in the hospital a few days ago, the only thing I could remember at first was running through the jungle, being pursued by men with guns. Those men were the Mexican police, and they shot me. Here." He touched a spot on his side hidden by his jeans. "I fell from a cliff. When I came to in the hospital and found out who I was—or who I thought I was—I convinced myself that the whole episode was just a dream. The scar on my side was from the appendectomy I'd supposedly had recently. And everything else started to fall into place. I remembered then that I'd been in a clinic, that a man wearing a ski mask had been standing over me with a gun. I remembered Amy walking in, and then the fight I had with the gunman. He knocked me unconscious, and I assumed that's how I got the amnesia.''

Grace stared at him in shock, not knowing where he was going with his story, but sensing it might be a place she didn't want to follow. ''That's what everyone assumed. I don't understand, Ethan. Why do you think you're not Dr. Hunter?''

''Because I don't think the skills of a surgeon, especially one as talented as I'm supposed to be, would be something I would forget.''

Grace frowned. ''You can't know that for sure.''

''Then how do you explain the other things that I didn't forget. Like how to use a weapon.'' To demonstrate his point, he picked up Grace's gun from the nightstand, ejected the clip, pulled back the slide to remove the bullet from the chamber, and then slammed home the magazine once again. He stared at the weapon for a moment, then laid it aside with a visible shudder.

''A lot of people know how to use a gun.''

He stared at her. ''So you're saying you don't think it's strange that I remember how to do what I just did with your gun, but I wouldn't have the faintest idea what to do with a scalpel if you handed me one right now.''

Grace shrugged. ''Amnesia is a tricky thing. I'm just saying that from what you've told me so far—''

''There's more,'' he said darkly. He got up and started to pace the room. ''The man I dream about in the jungle—I know his fear. I know he's me. But his face isn't the one I see when I look in the mirror.''

A cold chill slipped over Grace. ''But maybe it is just a dream.''

''Maybe. But how do you explain the fact that there are dozens of pairs of shoes in my closet, and not a single one fits me. They're all too small by at least half a size.''

Grace couldn't explain that. The chill inside her deepened. ''Are you sure? You tried them all on?''

''Every last one of them. The clothes aren't a perfect fit, either, but I attributed that to a weight loss following surgery. But I can't explain the shoes. Can you?''

Grace wrapped her pajama top more tightly around her. ''There has to be a logical explanation.''

"And then there's the gun," Ethan said, as if he hadn't heard her. "I found the pistol you saw earlier in the safe downstairs. I knew the moment I saw it that the gun belonged to me. I knew exactly what it would feel like to shoot it, the accuracy of the aim, the pull of the trigger. Everything. I took it to a gun shop here in town and found out that it was probably customized by a place in Arkansas that does special orders for police SWAT teams, the FBI, and some of the elite forces of the military. Like the Navy SEALs, for instance."

"The Navy SEALs—" Grace broke off, gasping. She stared at Ethan in open shock. "My God. What are you saying?"

He stopped pacing and turned to watch her for a long moment before moving toward the bed. Grace had to fight the urge to retreat.

He placed his hands on the bed and leaned toward her, his eyes those of a stranger. "I'm saying that I don't know who I am. I don't know how to explain everything that's happened to me, the dreams I have, the shoes that don't fit, the gun that was custom-made for me. Even the connection you and I seem to have."

He paused, his gaze intensifying on her until Grace's breath became suspended somewhere in her throat. "What I'm saying is that for all I know, I could be the man you're looking for. I could be Trevor Reardon."

CHAPTER TWELVE

Grace put a hand to her mouth to hold back the scream that tore at her throat. She stared at the space where Ethan had stood only moments before, and nausea rose in her stomach like a tidal wave.

He wasn't Trevor Reardon. She knew it couldn't be true, and yet the moment Ethan had said the words, the doubts had begun to mount inside her. She hadn't been able to hold back her horrified gasp, and when Ethan had seen her face, he'd turned and strode from the room, slamming the door behind him.

The sound still echoed in the silent room. His words still rang in her ears. Grace shook her head, trying to dispel the almost hypnotic effect his words had had on her. She couldn't move, couldn't think, couldn't reason.

Weakly she reached for her purse on the nightstand. Taking out her cell phone, she dialed Myra's number. The throaty voice answered on the second ring.

Without preamble, Grace said, "Did you hear back from the fingerprints you sent to the lab?"

If Myra had been sleeping, she gave no indication of it. She sounded wide awake and fully alert. "The ones we lifted from Dr. Hunter's clinic?" Grace heard Myra's lighter click open as she lit up a cigarette. "Strange that you should be calling about that."

Grace was instantly alarmed. "Why?"

Myra hesitated. "Actually, we lifted several sets of prints from Dr. Hunter's office, some from around the desk area that we were pretty certain were his. But just as a control, we also took some from the water glass in his hospital room." She paused to take a long drag on her cigarette. Grace wanted to scream in frustration. "When we ran all the prints through the computer, we found that the ones from the glass were flagged."

Grace sat on the edge of the bed, frowning. "Flagged? By whom?"

"I don't know yet."

"Wait a minute," Grace said. "Are you saying the prints from the glass didn't match any of the prints in Dr. Hunter's office?"

"No, they did. Only, the prints that were a match didn't belong to Dr. Hunter."

Grace gripped the phone until her knuckles hurt. "Myra, are you saying the man in this house with me isn't Ethan Hunter?"

There was another long pause. Then Myra said slowly, "It's possible."

Grace's breath rushed from her lungs in a long, painful swish. "Just when the hell were you going to tell me?"

"As soon as I had all the facts. Listen, Grace, I just got this information myself a little while ago. I didn't know what to make of it. I've been trying to find out what I could from the Information Division, but they haven't been exactly forthcoming. It's all hush-hush. I don't understand what it all means yet, but Connelly said the lab is suddenly crawling with agents."

"FBI?"

"He doesn't think so."

"Then who?"

"We don't know, but if that man isn't Ethan Hunter, then someone else is looking for him. And not only that, they want to make damned sure they know when and if someone else finds him. That's why the prints were flagged, and now Connelly is catching hell."

"What has he told them?"

"Nothing yet, and he won't until he finds out just exactly who and what we're up against." Myra paused again. "It may be time to pull you out, Grace."

Grace's heart was thumping so hard against her chest she thought her ribcage might explode. But she had never been one to walk away from an assignment until it was finished. And this one was far from over.

She drew a long breath, trying to calm her racing pulse. "If we pull out now, the whole operation craters. We may never find Reardon. I don't want to run that risk. Until we find out what's going on, I think I should stay put."

"This could get very sticky," Myra warned.

"I'm aware of that."

After a moment, Myra said, "Maybe you're right. Whoever he is, he had us fooled. He may be able to fool Trevor Reardon as well."

Grace's mind was a whirlwind of chaotic thoughts. After hanging up the phone, she paced the room nervously. Never had she been so unsure of a situation before, so out of control of an operation as she was at that moment.

Who was he? her mind screamed. Who the hell was he?

Spinning toward the nightstand, Grace grabbed her gun and gripped it in one hand while crossing the floor to lock her bedroom door. And all the while she kept telling herself that what she was thinking, what Ethan had suggested was crazy. He couldn't be Trevor Reardon. She would have known, for God's sake. He couldn't have fooled her again. Not so completely.

Her legs shaking with nerves, Grace sat down in a chair facing the bedroom door. She propped her feet on the edge of the bed and put the gun in her lap. There would be no sleep for her tonight, but just to be on the safe side, she wouldn't lie down. She would remain in this chair, awake and vigilant, until morning came and with it, hopefully answers.

YOU'RE SO BEAUTIFUL. *Do you have an idea how special you are to me, Grace?*

Trevor Reardon's voice awakened Grace with a start. She gasped and grabbed her gun, aiming at first one spot in the room and then the next.

It took her a long, terrified moment to realize she was alone in the room and she'd been dreaming.

Reardon's voice, whispering in her ear, came back to her and a shiver of dread tore up Grace's spine. The dream had seemed so real. She had heard his voice so clearly, that indefinable quality that had haunted her for years.

Grace thought she'd only dozed off for a few seconds, but when she glanced at the clock on the bedside table, she realized she'd been asleep for almost an hour. It was nearly three o'clock in the morning and the moon was up. The sterling light danced along the fringes of the room, deepening the shadows in the corners.

The moon glow was what alerted Grace first. Earlier, she'd turned on the lamp on the nightstand, but now it was off. And the faintest scent of men's cologne lingered in the air.

Grace's heart boomeranged against her chest. Ethan hadn't been wearing cologne earlier. He'd come straight to her room from the shower, his hair still damp and smelling of shampoo, his skin scented only with soap.

But the smell of cologne on the air was unmistakable.

Slowly, Grace got up from the chair, her weapon drawn. The first thing she did was search the bathroom, then she crossed the bedroom to the door. It was still locked, and for a moment, she told herself she was imagining things.

But that whisper came back to her. *You're so beautiful. Do you have any idea how special you are to me, Grace?*

And she knew without a doubt it had been no dream. Reardon—or someone—had been in this room with her. He'd managed to pick the lock on her bedroom door, but that was no surprise. The flimsy bolt wouldn't keep out a determined ten-year-old, let alone a criminal mastermind.

No, the surprising part was how easily he'd been able to slip through the surveillance surrounding the house, and then disable the alarm without detection. Unless, of course, he'd been in the house all along.

Grace closed her eyes, terror stealing over her. She gripped the pistol, forcing herself to open the bedroom door and move out into the hallway. But with every step she took, she heard Ethan's warning. *I'm saying that I don't know who I am, Grace. I don't know how to explain everything that's happened to me, the dreams I have, the shoes that don't fit, the gun that was custom-made for me. Even the connection you and I seem to have.*

Grace was on the stairs now, moving stealthily downward. The living room below was silent. Eerie. The shadows ghostly in the moonlight.

She came to the bottom of the stairs and moved into the living room.

What I'm saying is that for all I know, I could be the man you're looking for.

Slowly, Grace crossed the living room toward the study. A thin line of light glowed at the bottom of the closed door. Someone was inside.

I could be Trevor Reardon.

Grace paused outside the door, catching her breath and steeling her nerves. Then she reached out and swung the door inward.

Ethan sat behind the desk, his face dimly illuminated by a lamp that had been angled away from him. He looked up when Grace entered, seemingly unconcerned by the gun she had pointed at him, and smiled. A smile that was as charming as it was inherently evil.

CHAPTER THIRTEEN

The man seated behind the desk was Ethan, and he wasn't.

Grace couldn't quite believe her eyes. She blinked once, then again, but the face before her didn't change.

She saw almost immediately that the faces weren't identical, but there was a very strong resemblance. This man, Dr. Hunter she presumed, was a little smoother around the edges. Polished to a high gloss of sophistication, while the Ethan she knew was tougher, more dangerous looking.

However, as Dr. Hunter rose and came around the desk to stand in front of her, Grace thought her initial assessment of him might have been wrong. The glint of greed and deadly determination in his eyes was unmistakable.

"Where's Ethan?" She kept the gun leveled on him.

Dr. Hunter cocked a dark brow, very reminiscent of the man she knew as Ethan. "You mean my look-alike? Don't worry, he's safe. For the time being, at least."

Grace wondered what that meant. Her hand trembled slightly on the gun, but she used all of her resolve to steady it. "Where is he?" Her tone hardened with threat. "I want to see him."

"You will," Dr. Hunter said. "But I've a few things here I have to take care of first."

"I don't think you're in any position to bargain," Grace said coldly. "In case you hadn't noticed, I'm the one with the gun here."

"Oh, I couldn't help but notice," Hunter said smoothly. Then his voice hardened. "But in case you hadn't noticed, we aren't exactly alone."

And with that, a man stepped through the door behind Grace and put a gun barrel to her head. "Drop the gun, *por favor*," he said with a heavy Spanish accent.

When Grace hesitated, Dr. Hunter said, "Better do as he says.

For all his gentle appearance, Javier can be quite vicious. Besides which, you can't possibly take us both out.''

He was right about that. When Grace lowered her weapon, the man behind her reached down and took it from her hand. Then he tossed it to Dr. Hunter.

The man called Javier walked slowly around Grace, still keeping the weapon drawn on her. When he was in front of her, she stared at him, recognizing the dark hair, the coal eyes, the thin, black mustache. He was the man she'd seen in the corridor outside the ballroom of the Huntington Hotel, the man she had pursued into the laundry room, and possibly the man who had murdered Special Agent Huddleston.

''You already know who I am,'' Dr. Hunter was saying. ''This is a colleague of mine, Dr. Javier Salizar. He runs the clinic in Mexico when I'm not around. It's been a mutually advantageous arrangement over the years, but now that I'm bowing out, he'll be free to use the clinic to continue the small but very powerful drug cartel he's building.''

Salizar made an abrupt movement with his gun, one that had Grace's heart pounding in alarm.

Dr. Hunter put up a hand, as if to restrain his colleague. He said something in rapid Spanish, then to Grace he said, ''But I still don't know your name.''

She saw no reason not to tell him. ''Grace Donovan.''

''FBI, I presume?''

She shrugged.

''Well, at least you're not denying it,'' he said. ''Not that it matters. Now that you've seen me, I'm sure you realize I can't let you go.''

''Is that why you killed Huddleston?'' When Hunter glanced at her blankly, she said, ''The agent at the Huntington Hotel.''

''Ah.'' Hunter steepled his fingers beneath his chin. ''He saw me at the hotel while he was shadowing Pilar and Bob. I couldn't let him go after that.''

Grace glanced at the gun in Salizar's hand, then at Dr. Hunter, assessing her situation. Unfortunately, she didn't see a way out. Not yet at least. ''How did you get in here?''

"Past your surveillance, you mean? It was pathetically easy. We were back here before you arrived from the Huntington."

"But Ethan told me he changed the alarm code."

"So he did, but I almost always have a backup plan. Once when I came back from Mexico, my loving wife had changed the code so that I couldn't get into my own house. After that, I had the security company program in an override code that only I knew. Pilar never pulled that stunt again."

The smile vanished from his face, leaving in its place a cruel sneer that made Grace shiver. If she had underestimated Dr. Hunter's capabilities before, she would not do so now.

"Why did you give him your face?" she asked suddenly.

The charming smile was back in place. He shrugged nonchalantly. "Because I knew Reardon would come after me. And if not him, then some other criminal whose face I've changed. They're all extremely grateful at first, but then they get to thinking. Paranoia sets in. Their plastic surgeon is the only one who can identify them. Sooner or later, one of them was bound to come after me."

Grace frowned. "So you created yourself a double? How did you think you could pull that off? Eventually someone would catch on."

"Not if the double was dead," Dr. Hunter said with another shrug. "I had it all planned out very carefully. Or so I thought," he added ironically. "I brought him back to Houston, dumped him in my clinic, and then one of Dr. Salizar's American associates was to shoot him in the face before he came to and make the whole thing look like robbery. Only, your friend decided to wake up before he was supposed to, and he managed to save himself. Imagine my surprise when I found out what had happened, that my look-alike was still alive and poking around in my life, digging up secrets I didn't want exposed."

"An autopsy would have revealed he wasn't you," Grace said. "You couldn't change blood types, fingerprints, DNA."

"There was no reason to," Dr. Hunter said almost impatiently. "With both Amy and him dead in the clinic, there would have been no reason to suspect he wasn't me. Especially since I'd made sure my passport and ID were on him, along with my wedding ring. There would have been no need for anything other than the most rudimentary autopsy, and I'd taken care of the blood type by changing my medical records at the hospital before I went out of the country. I thought of everything.''

Not everything, Grace thought. She wondered if she should tell him about the fingerprints, about the fact that the FBI were on to him. But if cornered, he might become even more desperate, and Grace wasn't willing to admit yet that she couldn't somehow find a way out of this.

"Who is he?'' she tried to ask without emotion. "Where did you find him?''

Dr. Hunter smiled. ''That's the beauty of it. He's no one anybody would ever come looking for, except maybe for the police. He was affiliated with one of Dr. Salizar's rival drug cartels, and the Mexican authorities shot him while he was trying to escape capture.''

Affiliated with a drug cartel? A sour taste rose to Grace's mouth. *He's no one anybody would come looking for, except maybe the police.*

Not Trevor Reardon, she thought weakly, but someone perhaps just as dark.

''Apparently, he fell off a cliff, and some of the locals found him and brought him to me,'' Dr. Hunter said. ''I'll spare you the details, but suffice to say, his face was badly damaged, and he had a severe head trauma which resulted in acute amnesia. When he woke up, he didn't remember who he was or how he'd gotten to the clinic. He remained heavily sedated at the clinic while I came back here. He couldn't remember his past before he arrived at the clinic, and the drugs ensured he wouldn't remember his time there. We were spared a lot of questions that way. I even brought his gun back here with me so there would be no way to identify him. Once his wounds had healed sufficiently, I went back to Mexico and began the reconstruction on his face. He didn't remember anything about his former life, so I gave him a new one.''

She lifted her chin, staring Hunter straight in the eyes. ''I'm a federal agent,'' she said. ''This house in under surveillance. The minute you fire one of those guns, the place will be crawling with FBI.''

''You mean the three men watching the house? Javier's American *amigo* has taken care of them for us.''

The sick feeling inside Grace deepened. Three more agents dead? God—

Dr. Hunter turned to Salizar and spoke rapidly in Spanish, something about the American Salizar had apparently hired for the job. As best Grace could tell, there'd been a last minute change in plans, and in spite of Hunter's cool demeanor, he was worried about the new man.

When Hunter turned back to Grace, she said, "What are you going to do with me?"

He shrugged. "Oh, I have plans for you. Lofty plans, you might say."

Dr. Salizar had moved behind her, and now Grace saw Dr. Hunter nod to him over her shoulder. She whirled, automatically putting up a hand to defend herself, but she was too late. The butt of the gun caught her square in the back of the head.

With a blinding flash of pain, Grace pitched face forward to the floor.

WHEN SHE AWAKENED, the pain was a dull roar in her head. She lay facedown in what she first thought must be a van or a truck, but the rumble of engines below her and the sway and dip as they hit air pockets told her they were airborne.

She struggled to rise, but her head swam sickeningly, and when she tried to move, she realized her hands were bound behind her. With an effort, she rolled to her side, then managed to sit up, gazing around.

Ethan was directly in front of her, leaning against the wall of the plane, his hands behind him and his eyes closed. One side of his face was covered in blood, and Grace's heart lurched in terror. For one heart-stopping moment, she was positive he was dead. He was so still and his face was deathly pale.

But then very slowly he opened his eyes and focused on her. A look of intense relief flooded over his features, and Grace realized he must have been conscious for some time now, and wondering the same thing about her.

"Are you all right?" he whispered, throwing a glance toward the front of the plane.

Grace nodded, unsure of her voice. "Are you?"

"I will be, as soon as I get these ropes loose."

His brow wrinkled in concentration as he strained at the bindings. Grace glanced around, assessing their situation. They were in the rear of the plane. Luggage and crates of supplies were stacked near the back, and directly opposite, a door opened to the front. Grace could see two or three rows of seat backs, and beyond that, a curtain that closed off the cockpit.

The cargo door was on the wall nearest her, but without parachutes, the exit wouldn't do them much good.

She glanced back at Ethan. "What happened?" she whispered.

"They were waiting for me when I came back downstairs. They were in the house when we got back from the hotel."

"Yes, I know. The agents watching the house are dead."

Ethan's eyes flickered briefly as he struggled with the ropes.

"Where are they taking us?" Grace asked, working at her own bindings. Her wrists grew raw from the effort.

"I heard them mention Mexico. Hunter still thinks he can pull this off."

Grace glanced up. "You've seen him then?"

Ethan's gaze met hers, and something dark flashed in his eyes. "I've seen him."

Grace wondered what he was thinking, what it must have felt like to come face to face with his reflection. She tried to temper the rush of emotion she felt for him by reminding herself of what Hunter had told her—that the man she knew as Ethan had been involved with a drug cartel in Mexico.

But looking at him now, Grace couldn't bring herself to believe it. Didn't want to believe it. If he never got his memory back, would that side of him disappear forever?

Could he live with that? And could she?

Maybe it was all a moot point anyway if they couldn't find a way out of their current predicament.

As if reading her mind, Ethan said, "He still thinks he can get rid of me and have everyone believe he's dead."

"It's been him all along," Grace said. "Not Reardon. Hunter hired someone to kill both you and Amy so that everyone would think he was dead."

"Not a bad plan," Ethan said dryly.

"Except for the fact that the FBI knows you and he are not one and the same man."

Ethan's movements ceased. He looked up at her. "What?"

"We lifted some prints from the water glass in your hospital room and ran them through the national database. My superior knows that you're not Dr. Hunter."

"Who am I?" A look Grace couldn't identify crossed over his features. Fear. Dread. Hope. Uncertainty.

What could she tell him that would alleviate his worry? "You aren't Trevor Reardon," she said.

"Then who am I?"

"I...don't know yet."

His gaze on her hardened. "How long have you known this? From the first?"

Grace shook her head. "No. No. I just found out tonight. I didn't have a chance to tell you—"

Before she could finish, a shadowed blackened the doorway to the front of the plane, and Grace looked up to find Dr. Hunter staring down at her. It was still so uncanny to see how much he looked like Ethan.

Grace glanced at Ethan. His gaze was riveted to Dr. Hunter. She couldn't imagine what this must be like for him. For the first time that night, she wondered what he'd looked like before the surgery.

"You're both awake, I see." Dr. Hunter moved into the cargo area, and Dr. Salizar followed him. Salizar carried a gun in his hand, and another gun—Grace's—was stuck in the front waistband of his khaki trousers.

Hunter walked over to one of the crates, opened it, and extracted three parachutes. He handed one of the chutes to Salizar, then buckled himself into the other.

"Go tell your amigo it's time to set the automatic pilot," he told Salizar. "I hope to God you're right about him, Javier. I hope he can be trusted."

Salizar handed Hunter one of the guns. "Don't worry. Julio vouched for him."

"That makes me feel so much better," Hunter muttered.

A fine dread slipped over Grace as she realized his intent. He,

Salizar, and the pilot would parachute from the plane, leaving Ethan and Grace tied up inside.

She glanced at Ethan, but his gaze was still on Hunter. "Who am I?" he asked suddenly.

Hunter arched a brow at Grace. "You didn't tell him?"

Grace felt Ethan's gaze on her and she turned to him quickly. "He didn't tell me who you are. I swear it."

Hunter laughed. "I didn't give you a name, but I did give you a few details. But don't worry," he said to Ethan. "You two will have an hour, maybe two before the fuel runs out. Or before you crash into a mountain."

Grace said almost desperately, "You'll never get away with this. The FBI knows Ethan isn't you. They have his fingerprints."

That stopped Hunter for a moment. He stood gazing down at Grace, a frown playing between his brows. "Well, that is unfortunate, but it can't be helped. I guess instead of playing dead, I'll just have to disappear somewhere and live out the rest of my life on my Swiss and Cayman Island bank accounts. Which is exactly what I intended to do anyway."

"But now you'll be a hunted man," Grace said. "You're a murderer. The FBI will track you to the ends of the earth, not to mention Trevor Reardon."

A man came through the door behind Hunter. He wore a red baseball cap pulled down low over his features. In one hand, he carried a parachute; in the other, one of Salizar's guns.

Hunter said over his shoulder, "Where's Javier?"

"He'll be along in a minute." The man kept his head bowed, as if studying the parachute in his hand.

"Is everything all set in the cockpit?" Hunter asked him.

The man nodded, then walked over to the cargo door, threw back the catch, and slid the door open.

A rush of wind streamed inside, the fury catching Grace off guard. For a moment, she was afraid the force might pull her through the opening. She worked even harder at the ropes around her wrist. When she glanced at Ethan, she could tell he was doing the same thing. His gaze on her seemed to say, "Hang in there. We'll get out of this somehow."

Grace desperately wanted to believe him, but even if they got free of the ropes, Hunter, Salizar, and the pilot were all armed.

Hunter finished buckling his parachute and turned back to Grace. "You can stop worrying about Reardon," he shouted over the roar of wind through the opening. "His cleverness has been greatly overrated. I've managed to stay one step ahead of him so far, and where I'm going now, he'll never find me."

"Is that so?" The man wearing the red cap looked up, and for a moment, Grace stared at him in puzzlement. Then, as if in slow motion, he lifted his hand and removed the cap from his head, revealing a receding hairline.

Dr. Hunter swung around, reaching for his weapon. But Danny Medford had a gun leveled at Hunter's chest, and Grace saw horror and recognition dawn on the doctor's face.

"Reardon!"

It didn't register with Grace what Medford's sudden appearance meant at first, but then, as the realization hit her, she turned to stare at him, terror spiraling through.

"You're—" She couldn't even say his name. Before she could hardly catch her breath, he fired the gun, and a stunned look crossed over Dr. Hunter's features. Then he slumped to the floor.

Reardon bent down and with a knife, cut away the straps of Hunter's parachute. Then he tossed the blade aside, and rolled the body out the open cargo door.

Grace's heart pounded inside her. She turned to stare at Ethan. She could tell from his expression he was as shocked as she was. And he was still working to free himself from his ropes.

Reardon walked over to Grace and stood grinning down at her. For the first time, Grace saw behind his new face and the contacts he wore, to the evil that couldn't be masked. "What's the matter, Grace? Don't you recognize me?"

Fourteen years ago, he had been the handsomest man Grace had ever seen. Now his features were almost plain, his good looks sacrificed for his freedom.

He knelt, caressing her face with the barrel of his gun—her gun, she recognized. Obviously, he'd killed Dr. Salizar and taken the gun from him.

Reardon put his hand around Grace's neck, and her skin crawled at his touch. Her stomach rolled sickeningly. When she would have jerked away, he said, "You're so beautiful. Do you have any idea how special you are to me?"

Grace felt the bile rising in her throat. On the other side of the plane, she could see Ethan openly struggling at his ropes. Reardon noticed him, too, and nodded in Ethan's direction. "I see the clone wants to come to your rescue."

Ethan looked up, his gaze meeting Reardon's. The look on Ethan's face chilled Grace to the bone. He was a match for Reardon. She had no doubt of it.

Reardon must have sensed it, too, for he stood abruptly and disappeared through the door to the front of the plane. When he came back moments later, he had Salizar's chute. He tossed it out the door. Grace saw the wind whip it away in a blur.

The only parachute left on board was Reardon's. He came back to stand over Grace, and for a moment, she thought the end had come. He was going to finish her off.

Ethan said, "You touch her, and I'll kill you."

Reardon cocked his head, staring at Ethan. "Do you know who I am?"

Ethan almost smiled. "Yes. And that's going to make killing you all the more pleasurable."

A look that might have been admiration flashed in Reardon's eyes. Or was it fear?

Then he laughed, a sound that took Grace straight back to that night fourteen years ago. She closed her eyes as the horror swept over her.

"I admire your nerve, my friend, but you are hardly in any position to make threats." He turned to Grace. "And you. Imagine my surprise when I followed Hunter to the clinic that night and saw you there. After all these years, we finally meet again, Grace. I believe it's destiny, don't you?"

When Grace didn't answer, he said, "You've made everything very convenient for me. I can take care of you and Dr. Hunter in one fell swoop, and you—" He turned back to Ethan. "You've seen my new face, so I'm afraid it's *adiós* for you as well. The only thing left for me to do," he said, walking over to the open door and preparing to strap on his parachute, "is to look up my old friend, Myra."

Grace strained at her ropes. She couldn't let Reardon get away. She couldn't let him get to Myra. As she struggled furiously with the bindings, something caught her eye. A flash of metal. The knife Reardon had tossed aside.

"Oh, and one last thing," he said, turning back to Grace. "That last night you and I spent together. I called your father when you'd gone into the bathroom. You didn't know that, did you? The last thing on his mind before he died was the knowledge that his precious daughter was with me. I wanted you to know that before you die."

Fury swept over Grace in a blinding flash. She lunged at Reardon, but before she could reach him, before he even had time to sense her intention, Ethan was on him. Somehow he'd gotten loose from his ropes, and now the force of his attack almost sent both him and Reardon plunging out the open door. Reardon dropped the parachute, and Grace saw it slip over the side of the door.

Both men fell to the floor of the plane, the gun in Reardon's hand whipping upward before Ethan could grab his wrist. Then he slammed Reardon's hand against the floor of the plane, and the gun went flying.

The fight was ugly. The men were evenly matched, one as deadly and cold-blooded as the other.

Grace scooted sideways, turning so she could get one hand around the knife. Twisting it awkwardly, she began to saw at the ropes around her wrist.

Her heart almost stopping, Grace saw Reardon roll toward the open doorway, pulling Ethan with him. With a vicious kick, Reardon sent Ethan half over the edge. Ethan clung to the metal frame around the opening, but the wind force almost ripped him away. Grace could see the strain on his face, the sheer force of his willpower as he began to pull himself inside.

Reardon stood poised in the open doorway, clinging to an overhead support to brace himself against the rush of wind as he stared down at Ethan.

Desperately, Grace hacked at the ropes around her wrist, felt the sting of pain as the blade found skin. Then she was free. In one fluid movement, she rolled on the floor and grabbed the gun just as Reardon lifted his foot to kick Ethan loose from the door.

Grace screamed Reardon's name over the rush of wind and when he turned to her, she saw his eyes widen in surprise at the gun in her hand. Without hesitation, Grace pulled the trigger. The force of the bullet, combined with the wind velocity, knocked Reardon from the plane. Grace heard him scream and saw the scarlet bloom on his chest before he disappeared into the darkness.

In a flash, she was on her knees in front of the doorway. She grabbed Ethan's arms and helped pull him inside. They lay panting on the floor of the plane for a long moment before Grace scrambled back to the opening, peering out into the darkness.

"He's dead, Grace. You got him," Ethan said.

Grace turned back, her gaze uncertain. "I hope you're right. God, I hope you're right."

They stared at each other, letting the adrenaline rush carry the emotions through their bloodstream. Then Grace said, "I don't suppose you knew how to fly a plane before your amnesia?"

Ethan's gaze darkened for a moment, and then he said, almost grimly, "I think I might have."

CHAPTER FOURTEEN

They were on the ground at an airfield just across the border from Brownsville, Texas. Grace was in the police magistrate's office, talking with Myra on the telephone and filling her in on all the details.

Myra listened, and then when Grace was finished, said, "After all these years, you finally got him. How does it feel?"

Grace hadn't had time to deal with her emotions. She supposed what she felt most strongly at that moment was uncertainty, about her future and about Ethan's. She said almost urgently, "What's happening on your end? Have you found out anything else about the fingerprints?"

A long hesitation, then Myra said, "Turns out, the agency who flagged his prints is the DEA, Grace. Evidently they've been looking for him for a long time, and now they're demanding that we turn him over to them."

Grace sucked in a long breath. "Are you sure? There could have been a mistake. A computer glitch."

"There's no mistake. You've got to bring him in, Grace. You don't have a choice."

ETHAN COULD TELL from the look on Grace's face that the call hadn't gone well. "You talked to your superior?"

She nodded. She started to say something else, then turned to stare across the street at a seedy-looking bar that blasted tejano music.

"Let's take a walk," she suggested. "It's a little noisy around here."

They strolled along the cobblestone sidewalk until they reached the edge of town. The night seemed darker over the desert, with only a few stars and the moon to soften the gloom. In a few hours, it would be dawn, but right now, daylight still seemed a long way off.

Without looking at her, Ethan said, "I'm going back to the jungle, Grace. Back to that clinic. I have to find out who I am. I have to know...what I've done."

"Ethan—"

He took her arms, turning her to face him. He stared down into her eyes, feeling the connection with her as he had never felt it before. Maybe because he was about to sever it.

"That call you just made. What you found out wasn't good, was it?"

He saw the denial flicker over her features, then she closed her eyes briefly. "It doesn't matter."

"Yes, it does." His grip tightened on her arms. "You're a cop, Grace. An FBI agent sworn to uphold the law. How can you say who I am and what I've done doesn't matter?"

She gazed up at him. "Going back to the jungle may be the most dangerous place for you. If you come back with me—"

"You'll see that they go easy on me?" He shook his head. "I'm not above the law, Grace. If I've done something wrong, something...bad, then I'll take my punishment for it. But not until I find out the truth for myself. Not until I know the whole story. Can you understand that?"

What he was asking of her went against everything she stood for, everything she believed in. A wave of guilt rolled over Ethan for what he was about to do, but there was no other way.

He took a step back from her, and he saw her bewilderment in the moonlight. Then her disbelief.

He took another step away from her, backing into the desert as he leveled the gun on her.

"It's the only way, Grace. I can't ask you to give up everything for me. I won't. So don't try to follow me." It was more of a plea than a warning, but for one split second, he sensed her resistance.

"This isn't goodbye," he promised.

"Then why do I feel like it is?" she said, before turning and walking away.

GRACE SAT IN the cubicle Myra had confiscated at the Houston office and tried to ignore the tension that fairly sizzled in the room.

Two huge men wearing black suits and identical scowls stood on either side of Grace while Myra sat across a metal desk from her. When Grace had first entered the office, less than twenty-four hours after her flight back from the border, Myra had introduced the two men as her counterparts at the DEA. Which meant they had considerable clout.

Myra folded her arms on the top of the desk and said, "Please tell Agents Mackelroy and Delaney what you told me, Grace."

Grace glanced up at first one man, and then the other. She shrugged. "He got away."

Mackelroy, the larger of the two men, came around to perch on the edge of Myra's desk. "How?"

"He pulled a gun on me."

She could see the disbelief in the man's eyes before he flashed a glance at his partner. Mackelroy said, "Tell us exactly what happened."

Grace complied, leaving out only the part she deemed too personal for them to hear. Some of what had gone down between her and Ethan was none of their damned business.

Mackelroy leaned toward Grace, his gaze intense. "Do you have any idea where he is now? It's imperative that we find him."

Grace met his gaze. "Why do you want him so badly? Who is he?"

The two men exchanged another glance. Then Mackelroy said almost urgently, "His name is Tony Stark. He's one of our agents. For the last two years, he's been under deep cover, infiltrating one of the drug cartels down in Mexico."

For a moment, Grace thought she hadn't heard him correctly. She stared at him, stunned. Then she said slowly, "He's a DEA agent?"

Mackelroy nodded. "The last we heard, he'd been arrested by some local authorities who were working for a rival cartel. Somehow he managed to escape, and then he just disappeared. We assumed he was dead, but then his fingerprints turned up in the computer. The rest you know."

Grace felt as if she had just been sucker punched. She couldn't breathe, much less talk.

Myra said throatily, "Of course, we'd like to cooperate as much as we can, but Grace has told you everything. Stark is down in Mexico somewhere, wandering around without a memory. If he were one of my agents, I wouldn't waste time in getting down there to find him.''

BY THE END of the week, Grace was back home in Washington. She'd filed the last of her reports and attended one final debriefing before leaving the J. Edgar Hoover Building in a downpour.

She stood at the window of her apartment, and stared out at the city. It was Friday, past eight o'clock, and the city was coming alive. The streets were still clogged with government workers and officials wending their way southward, to the suburbs in Maryland and Virginia. The ones who lived in the city were finding little pockets of shelter in the hundreds of bars and bistros scattered throughout Washington.

The rain had stopped a little while ago, and a breeze drifted in from the Potomac River. The heat of the day gave way to a crisp coolness of evening, and the sky deepened to violet.

Grace had never felt more at loose ends after wrapping up a case, because this had been no ordinary case. Trevor Reardon was dead, and for the first time in fourteen years, she felt the weight of her guilt begin to ease. She knew she could let go of the past now, say goodbye to a family she would never stop missing.

But in some strange way, the emptiness inside her had deepened. The lonely years of her life stretched before her, and Grace suddenly realized how much she'd given up to her dedication. A home. A family. A man she could love.

A future that made her want to get up in the mornings.

Ethan had done this to her, Grace thought without bitterness. Ethan had made her realize what she was missing, what her sacrifices had cost her. He had reminded her that she had once been capable of love. Might still be.

She closed her eyes briefly, resting her forehead against the cool glass. She wondered where he was now, if he was safe, if he had been found by the DEA and told who he was. What he was.

She had known all along there was goodness in him.

Grace turned when the doorbell sounded and reluctantly left her place at the window to answer it, figuring it was Myra trying to talk her out of the resignation Grace had tendered after her last debriefing. But it was time for a change. Time to try her hand at being a lawyer, which was what she'd always wanted to be.

She pulled back the door. "I'm not changing my mind, Myra—"

Ethan stood on the other side, dressed in jeans and a dark cotton shirt, a raincoat slung over his shoulder. His dark hair glistened with moisture as he gazed down at her uncertainly.

"I wasn't sure this was the right place," he finally said.

Grace stepped back to let him enter. "How did you find me?"

"Some of my friends at the DEA office in Houston helped track you down."

Grace's heart quickened. "Then you know?"

"A couple of agents were waiting for me at Hunter's clinic down in Mexico. I guess they somehow figured out I'd be going there to find some answers." He gave Grace a pointed look, and she quickly turned away.

"It would seem a logical place to start searching for you," she said, leading him into the living room. She glanced around at the dismal atmosphere of her home. Come Monday morning, she was going to start redecorating, Grace decided. A new career, a new apartment, a whole new life.

Where would Ethan fit into her plans? she wondered. Or would he want to?

She motioned toward the sofa, but they both remained standing. "I've been wondering about you, you know. Where you were. How you were doing. There're a lot of things we've left unsaid, Ethan."

He smiled, and Grace caught her breath. He looked different all of a sudden. Like a new man. "My name is Tony."

She smiled, too, her heart pounding inside her. "I know, but that'll take some getting used to."

He watched her move toward the window. She stood with her back to the glow of city lights, and the way she looked almost took his breath away.

He walked over to stand beside her, and they both turned to stare out at the glistening night. "I don't have my memory back," he finally said. "Not all of it, but bits and pieces are starting to come back. And I've been told quite a lot." He turned to her. "I've seen pictures of myself, the way I looked before. Unless I agree to more surgery, I guess I'm stuck with this face.''

"It's a nice face," Grace said softly.

"You don't think of...*him* when you look at me? You don't feel revulsion?''

She reached up and touched his cheek very briefly with her fingertips. "I see you. No one else. It doesn't matter what you look like. Appearances are only skin deep. It's who you are that counts.''

He gazed down at her, resisting the urge to touch the fiery strands of her hair, to let the softness sift through his fingers.

She turned back to the window, but he could see that she was watching his reflection. After a moment, she said, "It must seem so strange, finding out about yourself like that. You must have had a million questions.''

His gaze met hers in the window. "There was one question in particular I was anxious to find the answer to.''

She faced him. Her eyes were very clear and very blue. He thought she had never looked more beautiful. "What question was that?''

He did touch her then, lifting his hand to smooth back her hair, letting his fingers slip through the silkiness. He saw her eyes close briefly. "Can't you guess?''

She took a breath. "Are you married?''

He grinned. "That's the one.''

"And?" she asked impatiently, folding her arms across her breasts. She put up a good front, but Tony was gratified to see the flash of uncertainty in her eyes.

"I'm not married," he said softly. "Never have been.''

"And never will be?" she challenged, the doubt in her eyes changing to a teasing glint.

"I wouldn't say that." He raised his other hand and threaded his fingers through her hair, then kissed her. Her lips quivered beneath his, and Tony thought in wonder what an incredible woman she was. A woman who could face a cold-blooded killer without showing fear, but one who trembled at his kiss.

He pulled back, staring into her eyes. "The connection is still there, Grace. Do you feel it?''

"Yes." She smiled. "Oh, yes.''

"The question now is, what are we going to do about it?"

She looked up at him slyly. "You could kiss me again." After he complied, she said, "We have some unfinished business, you and I."

Her boldness thrilled him. "We've got all night. There's nowhere in the world I have to be."

She slipped her arms around his neck. "As a matter of fact, I find myself in the same situation. I'm not an FBI agent anymore," she told him. "I resigned today."

He lifted his brows at that, but instead of asking her why, he said, "I'm not a DEA agent anymore, either. I wouldn't be much good in the field without a memory."

Grace sighed deeply, but it wasn't an unhappy sound. More one of relief. "So what are we going to do?"

He wrapped his arms around her, pulling her close. "I don't know, but we have the rest of our lives to figure it out. I do know one thing. I want to get to know you, Grace. I want to know everything about you. The last few days don't seem real somehow. I want to spend time with you without looking over my shoulder. Without wondering if this moment will be our last."

"Wow," Grace breathed. "You want all that? And here I thought we were just going to spend the night together."

"That's a start," he said seriously. "Believe me, that'll be one hell of a start."

More fabulous reading from
the Queen of Sizzle!

LORI
FOSTER

with

Forever and Always

Back by popular demand are the scintillating stories of
Gabe and Jordan Buckhorn. They're gorgeous, sexy
and single...at least for now!

Available wherever books are sold—September 2002.

And look for Lori's **brand-new** single title,
CASEY in early 2003

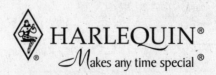

Harlequin invites you to experience the
charm and delight of

A brand-new continuity
starting in August 2002

HIS BROTHER'S BRIDE
by *USA Today* bestselling author
Tara Taylor Quinn

Check-in: TV reporter Laurel London and noted travel
writer William Byrd are guests at the new Twin Oaks
Bed and Breakfast in Cooper's Corner.

Checkout: William Byrd suddenly vanishes and while
investigating, Laurel finds herself face-to-face with
policeman Scott Hunter. Scott and Laurel face a painful past.
Can cop and reporter mend their heartbreak and get to the
bottom of William's mysterious disappearance?

HARLEQUIN®
*M*akes any time special®

HARLEQUIN®
INTRIGUE®

**brings you a new miniseries from
award-winning author**

AIMÉE THURLO

**Modern-day Navajo warriors, powerful,
gorgeous and deadly when necessary—these
secret agents are identified only by the...**

Sign of the Gray Wolf

In the Four Corners area of New Mexico, the elite investigators of the Gray Wolf Pack took cases the local police couldn't—or wouldn't—accept. Two Navajo loners, known by the code names Lightning and Silentman, were among the best of the best. Now their skills will be tested as never before when they face the toughest assignments of their careers. Read their stories this fall in a special two-book companion series.

WHEN LIGHTNING STRIKES
September 2002

NAVAJO JUSTICE
October 2002

Available at your favorite retail outlet.

HARLEQUIN®
Makes any time special ®

HIWLS-TR